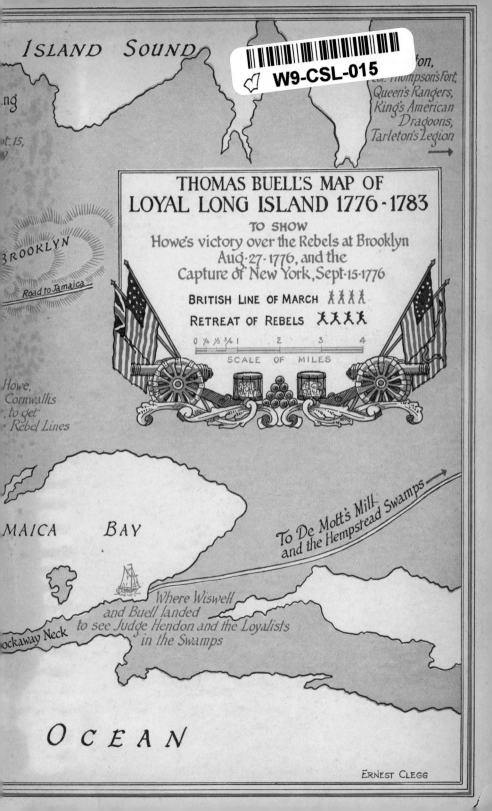

In 1821 Chief Justice John Jay said to his nephew William Heathcote DeLancey: "Let me tell you, William: the *true* history of the American Revolution can *never* be written." Jay declined to give his reasons, saying, "You must be content to know that the fact is as I have said, and that a great many people in those days were not at all what they seemed, nor what they are generally believed to have been."

—EDWARD FLOYD DeLANCEY's introduction to Jones's *History of New York,* lii.

Oliver Wiswell

BIBLIOGRAPHICAL NOTE

First published ....Nov. 22, 1940
Reprinted twice before publication
Reprinted ....Dec. 12, 1940

Oliver Wiswell

KENNETH ROBERTS

NEW YORK

Doubleday, Doran & Company, Inc.

1940

PRINTED AT THE *Country Life Press*, GARDEN CITY, N. Y., U. S. A.

To

BOOTH TARKINGTON

A COMPLETE BIBLIOGRAPHY of source material consulted during the writing of *Oliver Wiswell* is published in the limited edition of this novel. For all practical purposes, the following books admirably present the Loyalist side: Henry Belcher, *First American Civil War*, Macmillan, London, 1911; Moses Coit Tyler, *Literary History of the American Revolution*, Putnam, 1897; Lorenzo Sabine, *Loyalists of the American Revolution*, Boston, 1864; Egerton Ryerson, *Loyalists of America*, Toronto, 1880; James H. Stark, *Loyalists of Massachusetts*, Boston, 1910; Sidney George Fisher, *True History of the American Revolution*, Lippincott, 1902, and *Struggle for American Independence*, Lippincott, 1908; Alexander Flick, *Loyalism in New York*, Columbia University Press, 1901; *Journal and Letters of Samuel Curwen*, Boston, 1864; Arthur Johnston, *Myths and Facts of the American Revolution*, Toronto, 1908; Lewis Einstein, *Divided Loyalties,* Houghton Mifflin, 1933; *Journal of Nicholas Cresswell,* New York, 1928; Claude H. Van Tyne, *Loyalists in the American Revolution,* New York, 1929; Charles Francis Adams, *Studies Military and Diplomatic,* Macmillan, 1911; Thomas Anburey, *Travels Through the Interior Parts of America, 1776–1781,* Houghton Mifflin, 1923; Edward McCrady, *History of South Carolina,* Vol. 3, Macmillan, 1902.

The author gratefully acknowledges the generous assistance of

Booth Tarkington, *Kennebunkport, Maine*
Major A. Hamilton Gibbs, *Middleboro, Mass.*
Ben Ames Williams, *Chestnut Hill, Mass.*
Clara Claasen, *New York City*
Thomas B. Costain, *Bethayres, Pa.*
Marjorie Mosser, *Kennebunkport, Maine*
R. W. G. Vail, Director, *New York State Library, Albany, N.Y.*
Dorothy C. Barck, *New York Historical Society, New York City*
Ray Palmer Baker, *Rensselaer Polytechnic Institute, Troy, N.Y.*
Stanley Pargellis, Yale University, *New Haven, Conn.*
C. S. Brigham, Director, *American Antiquarian Society*
Loring McMillen, *Staten Island Historical Society, Richmond, S.I.*
Nelson Doubleday, *Oyster Bay, N.Y.*
John Spargo, *Old Bennington, Vt.*
Mary G. Nye, *Vermont Historical Society, Montpelier, Vt.*
Malcolm Johnson, *New York City*
Colonel Lawrence Martin, *Library of Congress*
Victor Hugo Paltsits, *New York Public Library*
Wilmer R. Leech, *New York Public Library*
Gerald D. McDonald, *New York Public Library*
Charles Knowles Bolton, *Shirley, Mass.*
Gustav Lanctot, *Public Archives of Canada, Ottawa*
Rupert Hughes, *Los Angeles, California*
Clifford K. Shipton, Librarian, *American Antiquarian Society*
Helen McIntyre, *Boston, Mass.*
Lillian F. Robins, *Freeport, N.Y.*
Randolph G. Adams, *William L. Clements Library, Ann Arbor*
David C. Mearns, *Library of Congress*
John S. Taylor, *Greenville, S.C.*
R. L. Meriwether, *University of South Carolina, Columbia*
Elizabeth Hyde, *Charleston, S.C., Free Library*
Harold G. Rugg & Paul Allen, *Baker Library, Hanover, N.H.*
Dorothy M. Vaughan, *Portsmouth, N.H., Public Library*

Contents

BOOK I

☆

Boston

CHAPTER I

My FATHER, Seaton Wiswell of Milton and Boston, was an attorney. Daniel Dulaney, greatest of American lawyers, once wrote that he was as richly endowed with foresight as were the majority of his generation with hindsight.

He was one of the foremost men of his time, a colleague and intimate of those great Americans, Daniel Dulaney, Governor Hutchinson and Samuel Seabury, all of whom had to hear themselves reviled as traitors by lesser Americans.

To my father's foresight I owe the most satisfying thing I have had in life—the desire to write history truthfully. Not only did he persuade our great and good neighbor, Thomas Hutchinson, historian and governor, to take an interest in me; but when, in 1772, John Trumbull of Yale attacked his own and other American colleges for deriding polite literature and English grammar, my father at once sent me to Yale to study under Trumbull.

It was while I was at Yale in April, 1775, that I received word of my father's illness; and in spite of all that happened as a result, I shall always be thankful that I instantly set out for Milton to be with him.

That was how I came to be in the shadow of Great Blue Hill between Dedham and Milton in the dusk of April 17th, 1775, and how I happened to encounter a Boston mob in action.

Except for that I never would have seen the destruction of Henry Wade's barn or the mutilation of his cattle, nor would I have rescued Thomas Buell.

Lacking that warning of the lengths to which a Boston mob would go, my days on this earth might have been considerably shorter, and

3

in all likelihood I would have escaped a deal of trouble; but almost any sort of trouble, I have found, is preferable to a suddenly abbreviated life.

One of the beauties of the country about Milton is the rolling nature of the land. On all sides are small patches of level ground, but nowhere is there a plain. Gentle elevations sink to undulating green meadows and rise again to higher hills that flow from the base of those five smoothly rounded blue knobs that seem, to residents of Milton, to stand like a sheltering rampart between them and the turmoil of the outer world.

I was skirting one of the shoulders of Great Blue Hill, expecting each moment to see spread before me the distant twinkling lights on Brush Hill and Milton Hill, and beyond them the rising triple wave of golden pin points that meant Boston, when my mare threw up her head and shied; and in the same moment I saw, at the foot of the slope before me, a sliver of orange flame licking at the corner of a barn.

When I raked the mare's belly with my spurs and went down the hill on the run, trusting to luck that she wouldn't step on a rolling stone, the sliver of flame opened out at the top into a billowing cloud of glowing smoke, and above the rattle of the mare's hoofs I heard a singular wailing chorus like the clamor of far-off sea gulls.

The blazing barn was set far back from the road, at the end of a long double row of sugar maples; and as I galloped between the trees, their bare branches, in the light of the flame toward which I rode, became a skeleton funnel—a giant spider's web of a funnel. Queerly, I had that thought, and without reason—so far as I knew then—the feeling that I was like a fly caught in that web: caught, and not to escape. Presciences like these do come to us sometimes, even when we're lighthearted boys on the way home from school, and though most of them don't come true, now and then one of them does—as this did.

The wailing chorus, as I neared it, turned into a malignant clamor that swirled into my ears like an icy breeze and raised goose flesh between my shoulders.

At the end of the alley of sugar maples I found myself before a two-storied house whose white front, in the dusk, was rosy in the light from the blazing barn; and silhouetted upon that warm-colored background were shadows of men who ran from the open front door, dropped burdens and returned again within the house. All the while, as they hurried in and out, they maintained a kind of howling: threatening, exultant, wolfish.

Whether the mare stopped of her own accord, or whether I pulled her to her haunches at the sight of all those yammering, scurrying figures, I cannot say. I only know she ceased suddenly to go forward, backed into the shadows of the maples and stood twitching and trembling beneath me; while I, who had vaguely thought to be of help in the quenching of a fire, sat open-mouthed and staring.

There was no doubt in my mind as to who these men were. Ten years before, when I was a child of twelve, a Boston mob, in a frenzy over the Stamp Tax, had made an assault upon the house of my father's dearest friend, Thomas Hutchinson, chief justice and governor of Massachusetts, enraged against him for no reason except that he held office under the Crown. Like my father and every other man of sense in the Colonies, Hutchinson had done everything in his power to prevent the Stamp Tax. He was a native of Boston, a lover of his country, an able historian, a man of taste and penetration—but the mob, idiotically conceiving him to be an enemy, destroyed his furniture and all his belongings, hacked his pictures to shreds, burned his precious manuscripts, notes and books; then broke into his cellar and drank itself into insensibility.

Selfishly I might have been grateful to that mob, because Hutchinson, after installing himself in his summer home on Milton Hill, had told my father that later, when I was older and a better scholar, I should have employment in collecting historical material to replace that which had been burned—a prospect warmly to my liking.

I hadn't myself seen the mob that destroyed the governor's house; but from his own lips I knew what a raging mob was like, and I knew I was seeing such a one now by the light of the flaming barn. I knew, too, I was seeing something ferocious and dangerous, something crazier than any wild beast.

The eyes of the men who made up this mob were insane; their yelling mouths contorted to senseless shapes. These creatures, all in violent action and gesture, were unkempt; pale and dirty they had come out of cellars and out of the gutter, but now in the rosy light they were pink and ragged grotesques, wholly unrestrained and apparently incapable of ever becoming human again.

My impulse was to back the mare deeper into the obscurity of the maples, wheel her about and set off for Milton Hill as fast as she could gallop; but I didn't. Instead I sat fascinated. As for the mare, she seemed in like case and stood trembling, pricking her ears at those scuttling creatures as they flurried in and out of the house, bringing forth pictures, furniture, silver, bed linen, mirrors, garments of every description from the doorway and tossing them helter-skelter upon the muddy lawn.

There's something about a rioting mob that seems to paralyze at least a part of the brain of the spectator. I only half realized what was happening when four dark figures dragged a black mare from the other side of the blazing barn and howled to draw the attention of those who were in the house. Behind the black mare ran a gangling, week-old colt.

At a shouted order from one of those that held the mare, two of the mob leaped at the awkward, long-legged colt and threw it to the ground. When its mother kicked and plunged, one of the four dark figures struck her behind the eye. Another kicked her in the belly with the sound a flail makes when it strikes a padded threshing floor. Black demons, shouting, wrenched the mare's head until she fell to the ground beside the colt. Others caught her legs. One of those who had thrown her down whipped a knife from his pocket. Another pried open her jaws; and the man with the knife seized her tongue and cut it off.

From the tongueless mouth came that dreadful and unbearable sound—a horse's scream.

The man with the knife capered triumphantly, threw the bleeding tongue on the ground, and went for the colt.

For a moment there was such confusion of dark figures that I couldn't see what was happening, but from somewhere within the tumultuous cluster that seemed to center upon the colt I heard an enraged bellowing.

Then I saw the colt running away, and upon the spot where it had lain there stood a terrible figure. It was like a strange enormous bird —a gigantic pallid-feathered bird that had shed a part of its feathers to reveal here and there a skin of repulsively shining black. Except for its feathers, this black-lacquered figure was as naked as an antique statue; and, like a statue, it stood poised, its hands hooked like talons, vainly threatening that tumultuous mob.

Never before had I seen a man who had been tarred and feathered; but I didn't need to be told that I was looking at one now. There may be sights that make a spectator feel more degraded for belong-

CHAPTER II

I KNEW Milton Hill as well as I knew my own bedroom, so I brought the mare to our back door through byways and across fields without questioning or hindrance from any of the self-appointed committees at that time pestering every traveler upon the road.

"You're safe now," I told the tarred and feathered man. I'd put my greatcoat about him as we rode; and now, having dismounted and helped him down as gently as I could, I picked the garment up from the ground where it had fallen and wrapped it about him again.

He leaned against the fence that separated our property from the fields of Anthony Gulliver, and, breathing heavily, gave me as acknowledgment no more than a grunt, for which I couldn't blame him.

I tied the mare to a post, went to the back door of our house and tried the latch. The door was locked. When I rapped upon it, I heard faint movements but got no answer. I rapped again more loudly, and this time the voice of Andrew Carter, my father's English servant, asked who was there.

"It's Oliver," I said. "Open up."

I heard bolts shot back. The door opened three inches and was held there by a chain, and in the lighted entryway I saw Andrew with a fowling piece in his hand.

"For God's sake," I said, "what are you looking for? Indians?"

Andrew put down the gun and unhooked the chain. As the door swung open, his faded blue eyes moved downward from my face to stare at the front of my coat. When I looked down myself I saw that the gray cloth was daubed with tar and dappled with bits of feathers.

9

Andrew couldn't take his eyes from the smears and feathers. He just stood there staring, and I saw his hand shake.

"How's my father?" I asked.

He put out his hand and with trembling fingers touched a feather. I caught his wrist. "How's my father?"

"Pretty good, Mr. Oliver," Andrew said. "Doctor Miller's in there now. Where—where'd that tar and those feathers get on you?"

"If Father's better, why's the doctor here?" I asked.

"It wasn't anything much, Mr. Oliver. Just a sort of shock. I hope nobody's done nothing to you, Mr. Oliver!"

"Of course nobody's touched me," I said. "I've got a sick man out here. Help me get him in; then put the mare in the stable and see she's well fed."

When I brought the tarred and feathered man into the brightly lighted kitchen, I clearly saw for the first time what he looked like.

Not only was his whole body covered with tar, but gouts of it filled his ears, clung to his nostrils, weighted his eyelids. His hair was a black crust; lumps were caked beneath his arms, between his fingers and toes.

The tar alone was bad enough, but the feathers embedded in it gave the man a look of indescribable foulness. His legs were bloodstained from the wounds made by the rail on which he had been ridden. It seemed terrible that he was alive; he was more dreadful to see than if he'd been a mangled dead man.

"Call Doctor Miller," I told Andrew. "Tell him you want him to taste something you're making for Father. Tell him anything, but get him out here. Don't let my father know, and stay with him till the doctor comes back."

Andrew seemed to shy, white-eyed, from the figure lying upon my greatcoat on the kitchen floor; and in the shying he left us. Not for an instant could I drag my own gaze from the blackened body and the grotesque head that moved ceaselessly from side to side in its silent expression of suffering.

Far away, beyond the door, I heard Andrew's formal English voice going on and on, haltingly explaining to my father and Doctor Miller, until I longed to wring his neck.

When Doctor Miller came at last into the kitchen, he was smiling skeptically; but his smile quickly vanished when he saw the tar-daubed man at my feet.

Pale instantly, Miller went down on one knee, whispering, "Yes, yes! Yes, yes"; and his face was mottled with red spots when he looked up.

"How long ago did this happen?" he asked. "Why was it done?" His voice trailed off in angry mutterings.

The man on the floor opened his eyes. They were so bloodshot that they looked as red as a wood duck's. "This was just practice," he said. "Them that did it was experimenting with a new kind of feathers— sea-gull feathers. There ain't enough chicken feathers to let 'em tar and feather all that don't agree with 'em." He made a straining sound and closed his eyes again.

Doctor Miller looked baffled. "Sea-gull feathers! Where could they catch enough sea gulls for such purposes?"

The man on the floor breathed hard. "I forgot to ask," he said. "I was busy trying to get my printing press out of Wade's barn when they burned it."

"They burned Wade's barn?" Doctor Miller asked. "What Wade?"

"He lived in Dedham," I told him.

"Then it must have been Henry Wade!" the doctor said. "What in God's name would they want to attack Henry Wade for? He must have helped half the people in town with money or advice. What did they do to him?"

"He got away," the man on the floor said. "He and his daughters got into the woods."

The doctor stared blankly at him; then got to his feet and turned to me. "I want lard—lots of it; scissors; towels. Go see your father and send Andrew out here. Don't say anything to your father about this. He's all right, but he shouldn't be upset."

I rid myself of my tar-daubed coat and left the kitchen, glad enough to stop looking at the man upon the floor. I found that our best parlor, off the sitting room, had been turned into a bedroom. In the bed was my father, smiling the same wry smile with which he questioned reluctant witnesses; and from Andrew's hangdog look, I knew he was suffering acute discomfort. Except for a drooping right eyelid, my father seemed as well as ever.

"I'm glad to see you, Oliver," he said. "I thought I recognized your voice in the kitchen. When Andrew called the doctor I feared for a moment you'd been brought home with a broken neck." He gave me a piercing glance. "Somebody must have told Andrew not to talk; and since that somebody could only have been you, I'd be glad for an explanation of all this secrecy."

"Secrecy?" I said. "I don't know what you mean by secrecy. Andrew, step into the kitchen and give the doctor a taste of that broth."

"Broth?" my father asked. "I thought Andrew was making hot punch."

"I meant punch," I said. "Go to the kitchen as I told you, Andrew."

My father hooked a forefinger over his lips as Andrew hurriedly left the room. I knew the gesture of old. It meant he was about to demolish my attempt to mislead him.

"Now let's see, my son: You arrive considerably later than you usually figure on reaching home. Then you come to the back door, which isn't customary; you spend ten minutes in the kitchen looking at a punch that you absent-mindedly speak of as a broth; and then you send Andrew in here for the doctor, and give Andrew orders not to answer my questions. As I see it, my boy, there are two explanations: either you brought a young woman home with you, or there's a sick man out there that's badly in need of attention—so badly in need of it that you may have had to loan him your coat and great-coat. Whichever it is, I don't propose to be kept in the dark about it. Doctor Miller wants me to think I'm a sick man myself, Oliver, and the worst thing in the world for a sick man—or a well one, for that matter—is uncertainty."

His smile took on the satirical quality that sometimes made even judges uncomfortable. I recognized it as one of my father's stage properties; nevertheless, it inclined me to be careful.

"Well," I said, "I *did* bring a sick man with me, but he's not badly off. Doctor Miller'll have him up in no time."

"What's the matter with him?"

"Not much of anything," I said. "He fell from a tree and suffered a few contusions."

"Indeed," my father said. "Where did this happen?"

"Out near Great Blue Hill," I said. "I mean, in that general direction."

"I see," my father said. "He suffered a few contusions five or six miles from here, so instead of leaving him at the nearest house, you bring him all this distance, and take the trouble to come in by the back way, which means you traveled circuitously. To me this indicates that you didn't wish him to be seen. The usual reason for such con-

cealment nowadays is the need to escape a rebellious mob. Your
friend was hiding from a mob, wasn't he? In fact, since he needs
Doctor Miller, he'd actually been mobbed, hadn't he?"

"Yes," I admitted, "he had. I got him away. They'd burned Henry
Wade's barn and tarred and feathered this man. He'd been keeping a
printing press at Wade's."

As the words left my lips, I realized for the first time that by bringing this unfortunate fugitive to our home, I might be exposing my
own father to the same fate that had overtaken Henry Wade.

"My God," I said, "I never thought—I'll move him—I'll—I'll have
Andrew carry him——"

"I'm afraid not," my father said. "Where would you send him? I
can tell you plenty of men in Milton who'd be willing to take him
in, but what'll happen if they're found out? There isn't a lawyer or a
doctor—not a man of position or property in this neighborhood—
who wouldn't do just what you've done; but if it got to be known,
there'd be only one answer. No, no, Oliver, your friend'll have to stay
right here in this house. Bring him in, my boy. Let's find out where
we stand."

"He looks pretty bad," I said. "Let Doctor Miller work on him a-
while, and tomorrow——"

"Bring him in," my father said again. "I've seen Boston mobs, and
I've seen the things they do. I've seen men split up to the middle
from being ridden on rails by those lovers of Liberty." He laughed,
and added, "Those lovers of Liberty who won't allow anyone else the
liberty of disagreeing with 'em! Bring him in, Oliver! If he's worth
saving, the kitchen's no place for him."

There was nothing more for me to say, and I went to the kitchen.
Already the mob's victim looked a little less horrible; for around his
middle he wore a bandage of toweling, his matted tar-filled hair had
been clipped close with a pair of buttonhole scissors; and thanks to
Andrew's activity with a lard-soaked rag, the black coating had so
far vanished from our guest's forehead, eyes and lips that he stared
up at me like a sick, half-painted clown.

"Doctor," I said, "maybe you can handle my father, but I can't. He
wants this man brought into his room, where he can talk to him
while you do your doctoring."

"Land alive, Oliver," the doctor protested. "Do you want to kill
your father? I forbid it!"

"That's all very well," I said, "but I've got my orders. They're to bring him in. After we get him there, you can explain to my father that you've forbidden his presence, and maybe you'll be allowed to take him back here again."

Doctor Miller looked disgusted. "That father of yours! I've never been able to do anything with him, and neither has anybody else! If we don't do as he says, God help us!" Then he took his patient by the arm. "Oliver, pick up those towels! Andrew, bring more lard. We've got a lot of work ahead of us if we want this man to look half human by morning."

My father, propped up in bed, watched us inscrutably as we rubbed and larded and larded and rubbed the tarred and feathered man until we began to have a fair idea of what he was like.

His eyelids were heavy and his eyes, a large part of the time, directed downward and veiled behind those drooping lids, so that he gave the impression of being a contemplative, ineffectual dreamer —a bucolic innocent. When, however, the lids lifted, his glance darted out from beneath them with such intensity and rapidity as to make the beholder wonder whether he had seen correctly. That sudden upward flash of his eyes carried with it profound skepticism, piercing inquisitiveness, unquenchable hopefulness, amused impatience; it showed beyond a doubt that whatever he might be, he emphatically wasn't helpless, innocent or ineffectual.

His name, he told us, was Thomas Buell, and by trade he was a printer; but so amply did he qualify that statement in a deceptively flat, expressionless voice that printing seemed the least of his callings. He was also, we gathered, a repairer of military arms; a maker of fashionable ornaments for military caps and cartridge boxes; a painter and gilder of escutcheons; an engraver of seals, dies, punches and copper plates; a marker of silver plate with elegant ciphers and arms; a cutter of blocks and ornaments for printers; a maker of models for canal locks, paint-grinding mills; machines for cutting and polishing crystals and precious stones, and last of all an inventor of anything that needed inventing.

I thought, as I listened to his deceptive voice recounting his accomplishments, that every small American town seemed to breed at least one Thomas Buell, who could do almost everything under the sun, and did so many things passably well that he never shone particularly in anything.

Buell was, he went on to tell us, a native of Newport, Rhode Island, where he had early imbibed the broad-mindedness peculiar to that refuge for Jewish, Catholic and Quaker outcasts from Puritan Massachusetts. He considered Newport the gem of all the towns within the American colonies, and he said he never would have left it except for an unfortunate physical handicap. He had a delicate stomach, and from boyhood the food in Newport had disagreed with him.

When, therefore, he heard that the use, by Connecticut housewives, of wooden nutmegs made it possible for Connecticutters to eat anything, he had moved to Norwich, Connecticut.

"That's interesting," my father said. "So it's the wooden nutmegs that are responsible for what Connecticutters eat! I always wondered how they could do it!"

Buell gave my father a guileless glance. "Well," he said, "Connecticut's a funny place. I'd say the nutmegs and the food were due to the same thing, instead of the food being due to the nutmegs."

"I don't follow you," my father said.

"Look, Mr. Wiswell," Buell said. "There was a doctor in Norwich— Doctor Elisha Perkins: fine man: tall: handsome: educated—partly— at Yale. He invented something he called Perkins' Metallic Tractors, and I made some of 'em for him. Ever hear of 'em?"

We shook our heads.

"You will," Buell said. "This country won't be able to get along without 'em, the way it's headed now. They were two little pointed pieces of metal, three inches long, round at one end and sharp at the other, like a horseshoe nail. One was made out of copper, zinc and gold; the other of iron, silver and platinum; and if you had rheumatism, erysipelas, headaches not due to drinking, gout, venereal pains, toothache or other ailments, you only had to draw the tractors over the affected part to obtain immediate relief. When not being used medically, they were mighty handy for picking the meat out of walnuts."

My father eyed Buell satirically. "Did you, by any chance, ever attempt to use these Metallic Tractors yourself?"

"Oh my!" Buell said. "I used 'em all the time! The first thing I'm going to do, when I get to a forge, is make me another pair of Metallic Tractors."

"My dear young man," my father protested. "Such instruments as you describe can't help but be wholly worthless."

"That's where you're wrong, Mr. Wiswell," Buell said. "You let me show a pair of those Metallic Tractors to any man, and describe their properties, and inside of two minutes I can tell for certain whether he's a rebel or a sensible citizen. There ain't a rebel in America that wouldn't beggar himself to buy a pair, and there ain't a sensible man that would give a shilling for 'em—and a shilling is what they cost to make, though Perkins always charged five guineas a pair for 'em."

My father looked at Buell with growing respect. "I'm surprised you ever left Norwich."

"My stomach wouldn't stand Connecticut," he said, "and I had a little trouble with Perkins when I made a few tractors out of iron and brass and sold 'em for three guineas a pair. Perkins didn't like it, so he spread the word that I had a machine for making wooden nutmegs cheaper than anyone else. Well, I thought I'd try Philadelphia after that, on account of hearing that there was nothing like Philadelphia scrapple for a delicate stomach."

When scrapple had proved a disappointment, he told us, he had gone on to Baltimore in the belief that his weak stomach might be cured by terrapin. He found terrapin no better than scrapple; so when a brother printer spoke highly of the clam chowder peculiar to New York, he went there and obtained work in the printing establishment of James Rivington, whose political sympathies were similar to his own.

To his distress, he found New York's clam chowder downright poisonous—perhaps because it was made without milk; so he was more than ready to believe a rumor that no food in America could equal that south of Boston, in the section influenced by the Wayside Inn.

A little later he heard of an opportunity to take a small printing press to that very neighborhood and print the pamphlets of those opposed to the disloyal and violent activities of Boston demagogues and mobs; and the chance seemed almost like a direct answer to prayer. That was how he had happened to be located in the shadow of Great Blue Hill.

"And I have no doubt," my father said, "that you found the cooking of the Blue Hill Lands exactly what you needed."

Buell shook his head. "I thought for a while that pumpkin pie for breakfast kind of helped me, but in the end I had to give it up. For the last three months I ain't scarcely been able to touch food—a little meat or sausage for breakfast, maybe, with a little ale and sour-milk cheese. That's all. It's the same, no matter where I go. Whatever I eat, I get a feeling as if I had a twelve-pound shot in my stomach, and if I try to wash it down with liquor it changes to an eighteen-pounder." He looked more hopeful. "I saw a printer last week who'd been in South Carolina. They got a dish down there—corn bread with a kind of a juice on it—that cured him of all sorts of troubles. I can't remember what the juice was, but I been thinking if I could get some of it——"

"Perhaps it was potlicker," my father said. "I believe they're addicted to it in South Carolina."

"Potlicker!" Buell exclaimed. "That's just what it was!" He thrust out his underlip and gazed down at it as if in hopes of finding marked upon it the route to the far-off home of potlicker.

"So you printed pamphlets!" my father said. "Were they pamphlets that might be familiar to us?"

"They might," Buell said. "Massachusettensis wrote 'em."

"Indeed!" my father said. "Do you happen to know who Massachusettensis really is?"

Both Doctor Miller and Andrew, on their knees just then, ceased to ply their lard-soaked rags and looked quickly at Buell's face, and so did I.

"I wouldn't know," Buell said vaguely. "I just set the stuff and struck it off. I guess maybe Wade got the blame—though God only knows how anybody ever traced the pamphlets to him."

Every American who loved his country and wanted to see it saved from mob rule and civil war knew the writing of Massachusettensis —knew, too, that if his identity should ever be discovered by the so-called Sons of Liberty who were turning all our colonies into mad-houses, he'd be torn limb from limb in an hour. We all wanted to know who he was, and yet we didn't, because he might be close to any of us. For all I knew, he might be my own father; and for all my father knew, perhaps, he might be I.

"Well," my father said, "I'm glad to hear that's a secret Sam Adams hasn't learned." He looked fixedly at Buell. "I suppose you hold no hard feelings toward those that destroyed your press and tarred and feathered you?"

Buell's eyes, which had been fastened on his outthrust underlip, lifted to my father's. "Hard feelings? Well, those wouldn't be quite the words for what I hold, Mr. Wiswell! There ain't much of *anything* I wouldn't do to the men that had me tonight. I've been around with some pretty hard characters in my day; but I never saw anybody to equal those that pulled Wade's house to pieces. If I knew who they were and where they lived, I figure I'd be doing this country a service if I dug 'em out of their holes and blew their heads off. What's the use of killing crows and porcupines, and letting people like that stay alive?"

My father and Doctor Miller exchanged a quick glance; then my father turned to me. "How do they feel at Yale, Oliver?"

"It's hard to say," I said. "President Stiles is a narrow-minded man who's almost forgotten that he's an educator, and wants to jam his political opinions down the throats of his students. He thinks it's splendid for Committees of Inspection, Committees of Vigilance, to spy into the principles, actions and private affairs of every member of the community, but a lot of us don't think so. He believes every man, without regard to his station, profession or character, should be forced to believe as Stiles believes, but a surprising number don't like to be bullied by Stiles or anybody else. Scores among the faculty and students want to be allowed to live and work in peace, so they're silent, hoping Stiles won't bedevil 'em. Generally speaking, we're all of us against what England's doing over here, and there's nobody that doesn't think she needs a lesson in how to run colonies. A lot of us feel the way you do: that she ought to be taught by constitutional means; but there's some who say she can't be taught without a fight."

"I don't believe it," Doctor Miller said brusquely. "That'd be civil war, and you can't make me believe Sam Adams and Hancock would push this country into a civil war just to further their own crazy ideas."

My father smiled. "I'm afraid you don't know what a demagogue's capable of, Josiah. That's what Sam Adams is: a demagogue—a rabble-rouser."

Buell leaned forward to poke Doctor Miller on the shoulder with a tarry forefinger. "Don't think I ain't grateful to you, Doctor, and to everybody in this house; but you ought to wake up—you and all the others in this province who don't believe Sam Adams' rabble mean to fight."

He shook a black fist at the rest of us. "Why do all your New England almanacs have a page in 'em telling people how to make gunpowder? What does all this arming and drilling mean? Why should mobs go out and steal King's stores and King's cannon? What are they collecting military supplies in Concord and Worcester for?

Why do you think Sam Adams has spies watching us—watching every man that he suspects of wanting to settle our differences with England in a peaceful way? Hell, Concord's full of molasses, salt fish, oatmeal and flour for the use of an army! It's full of cartridge paper, bombs, flints, musket balls, powder, fuses, billhooks, spades, camp kettles and wooden mess bowls! What do you think they're going to use 'em for? To play squat tag? Don't be a fool! Those things are to fight with, and when you get enough things to fight with, you fight! Anybody that ain't weak-minded ought to know that!"

"I don't believe it," Doctor Miller said again. "John Hancock wouldn't——"

Buell made a convulsive movement, as if to leap to his feet. "He's the worst of the lot! He's a convicted smuggler who'll cut his own country's throat, just to save himself from jail! If this country keeps on being a colony of England, John Hancock'll have to pay a hundred thousand pounds to England for the smuggling he's done. One hundred thousand pounds! Wasn't he found guilty and fined? Ask Mr. Wiswell! He's a lawyer, and he knows it's so!"

"That's true, Josiah," my father said.

"You bet it's true," Buell cried. "Sam Adams wants us to fight England and turn this country into a slaughterhouse, just because he hates kings and noblemen. Hancock wants us to fight England, and be damned to what the rest of us want, just to keep from paying a fine he can't afford to pay; and by God, I'll bet Adams and Hancock have their way! That's how you'd bet, too, if you'd ever had a Boston mob after you! Why, these people that've been listening to Sam Adams aren't human any more! They're crazy! They can't think: they can't reason! They believe any damned lie Sam Adams tells 'em! All they want to do is destroy everyone and everything who dares to get in their way—who dares to think different!"

With his forefinger he violently freed a lump of tar from his ear. "For God's sake, wake up! If you don't, Adams'll send his madmen to hang you and hack you! They'll burn your houses, strip your wives, split you apart on fence rails! There won't be a decent doctor or lawyer or man of property left in all America, and the country'll be governed by riffraff out of gutters!"

His agitation had grown upon him; again he spread out his arms, displayed himself pathetically. "Look at me if you want to know what they'll do! I'd be dead, Mr. Wiswell, if your son hadn't taken me across his saddle and risked being tarred and feathered himself!

Look at me now, half skinned! My God, can anybody see me and doubt what they'll do!"

He sat back in his chair, shaking. Andrew and I renewed our work upon him with our smeared towels.

"You'll feel better in the morning," Doctor Miller said tranquilly. "You've been through a pretty hard experience."

Buell was silent. So, too, was my father; but when I looked at his closed eyes and his set lips, I saw that he knew all too well that Buell had spoken the truth.

CHAPTER III

THE UGLY portents of the night before seemed a dream when I came downstairs the following morning and looked out across the slope of Milton Hill to the shimmering expanse of marsh and river, harbor and bay, stretching off toward Boston and the open sea.

Surely those villages and spires, those darkly rounded patches of forest, those gems of islands floating so serenely on the blue waters to the north, could never hold lovely part in the lives of men willing to plunge all this peace, all this beauty, into the frenzy and destruction of a civil war!

No; Buell must have been wrong. Not even such a demagogue as Sam Adams, waking to the gleaming blue and gold of a New England April, could steer a course that would bring death and ruin to thousands of his countrymen.

Civil war, on such a shining April morning, was the least of my troubles. Two other problems loomed larger by far. For one thing, I wanted to get Thomas Buell out of the house before his presence became known and brought enmity upon my father; and I wondered how soon, in all decency, I could set him on his way to the corn bread and potlicker of South Carolina.

An even more pressing problem, to my way of thinking, was how soon I could cross the fields of Milton Hill to Sally Leighton's.

Sally Leighton's father, Vose Leighton, was a neighbor of ours and the proprietor of a general store in the town of Milton; and he owned two brigs, of which his seven sons took turns being captain, and on which every member of the Leighton family had at one time or another sailed to foreign parts, sometimes accompanied by friends.

In the beginning my closest friend in the Leighton family had been Soame, at whose side I had fought bitter snowball fights against boys from Dorchester, caught smelt and eels in the winding backwaters of the Neponset River, and killed many a rattlesnake on the sun-warmed ledges of Great Blue Hill.

What I had liked most about Soame Leighton, I think, was his irrepressible gaiety. He found the whole world amusing; and I, perhaps because of living alone with my father, and being of a sober turn of mind, took the keenest pleasure in the droll comments Soame was forever making. There were times, in my early days, when my stomach ached from laughing at Soame's efforts to escape his sister Sally, who was as determined to stay near Soame as he was to avoid her.

We were fifteen; she was a gangling girl of twelve; and Soame, lying with me behind a hedge and watching her tireless efforts to track us down, made dark comments upon her manner of running, which he found awkward; upon the size of her eyes, which seemed to him like saucers; upon the length and thickness of her hair, which put him in mind of the nest of a giant oriole; upon the girlish quality of her voice—though for the life of me I couldn't see what other sort of voice he expected a girl to have.

That same year Soame persuaded his father to let me go on a voyage to Havana on one of the Leighton brigs. Albion, oldest of the Leighton boys, was captain; Steven and Jeremiah, the ten-year-old Leighton twins, were cabin boys; Soame, Sally and I were passengers.

For the first time, on that trip, I found myself unmoved by Soame's drolleries at Sally's expense. I can see her now, staring at Soame with a hurt half-smile when he said girls had no business on a ship because they couldn't do the things men did. When she was hurt, or when she felt deeply, those eyes of hers looked black—a soft and melting black with something shy and pleading about them, extremely moving. That was how she looked at Soame, and a little at me, too; then she took a red bandanna from around her hair, fastened it to her belt in back, whipped it between her knees and knotted it to her belt in front.

"It's not so!" she cried. She put her hands on her hips, stamped her foot upon the deck, and seemed to grow even slenderer and straighter. "It's not so!" she said again, and her eyes, that seemed black, but weren't, seemed addedly to snap and sparkle. "There isn't a place you can go that I can't!" She turned, ran to the bulwarks, swung herself into the main chains and went up the ratlins like a squirrel.

Soame just laughed; but when she went over the futtock shrouds instead of through the lubber hole, he stopped laughing; and as for me, my heart, as they say, was in my mouth. When she started up the topmast ratlins, Soame shouted to his brother Albion; and even as he did so, Albion bawled at her to come down. Perhaps she didn't hear, for she went up past the topmast cap and, spiderlike to us who stood open-mouthed below, seemed to glide effortlessly toward the royal truck. She clung there, both arms hooked over the distant wooden block, legs clasped tailorwise around the slender mast. Swinging in slow arcs against the blue West Indian sky, she called down to us words I couldn't hear, either because of her distance from me, or because of the deafening thudding of my own heart.

From that moment I saw Sally Leighton as above the criticism of dull clods like Soame and me. Who were we, indeed, to speak lightly of one who was always graceful, always gentle, always beautiful? She had a way of standing on the bulwarks and balancing herself there, as light as any bird, by holding to a shroud. In that position, she was curved like a bow against the uneasy motion of the brig; and it was Soame's pleasure, one morning, to speak drolly of her outthrust stomach. I saw nothing droll about it, and we had our first words—words that culminated in the third mate throwing a bucket of salt water over the two of us.

Never, since that voyage, could I be separated from Sally Leighton without acute discomfort, without being assailed by a score of fears —that she might fall in love with another; that she might die of a fever; that she might be thrown from her horse, or be wrecked in the little sloop on which the two of us had spent so many happy summer days, fishing in the lee of Dorchester Heights, or cruising a serpentine course among the islands of the western channel, from Spectacle Island around Long Island to Nicks Mate, Gallops Island and Nantasket Roads.

If ever I lost Sally, I told myself each day, the rest of my life would be a barren desert, and I doomed to wander alone within it.

Thus the second of my problems, as any young man can understand, was the first one on which I acted. I'd have gone to see Sally in the morning if I'd dared; for while it was morning I seemed to need her more in the morning than at any other time.

Of course I felt the same way in the afternoon, and at sunset and all evening.

I'd found, however, that Sally's mother, while amiable enough about my visits in the afternoon or evening, looked at me with some jaundice in her eye if I came in the morning. She seemed to feel, even in my tenderer years, that it was a boy's duty to be doing something disagreeable at home in the morning—or else she feared that if I came in the morning, I'd stay all day, and that was more than she felt herself able to bear, even for Sally. So it wasn't till afternoon that I stopped near the syringa bushes that screened the Leightons' side door and whistled a private whistle—the four dropping notes of a yellowleg.

Almost before the last note had left my lips, a window flew open, and I saw Sally smiling down at me. "Don't move," she cried. "I won't be a minute."

She vanished, and I stood there grinning foolishly at the open window, thinking how fortunate I was to be in love with a girl who didn't simper or pretend; who listened gravely when I told her how I felt about her, instead of saying "La!" and feigning indifference. She was as sweet, too, as she was kind; and she had brains, which struck me then—and still does—as unusual.

Like my father and myself, she had been an admirer of Governor Hutchinson; and when the governor assured my father that if I was sent to Yale, I could be of service to him, her interest had been genuine. She was possessed, as the years went by, to know what I was reading; and she was forever at me to bring her my books so that she could read them herself.

If I were as accurate as a historian is supposed to be but never is, I'd say that Sally's hair was brown; but I always think of it as black; and her face, which should have been swarthy from long summer months of sailing, had a sort of pearly gleam to it. She was as wiry as a whiplash from hauling up the anchor and pushing at the tiller of her little sloop, and from lifting her mare, seemingly by main strength, over all the stone walls within a ten-mile radius of Brush Hill; but she didn't look it. Her father, who was corpulent from sampling the foods and liquors he imported, thought her sadly deficient in substance. She looked, he said, as though a sou'west squall would blow her all the way to Chelsea: as though she'd been pulled through a knothole; but to me she seemed not so deficient. Mr. Leighton, who weighed less than a full-grown steer, yet not much less, wished to see his weight reflected in his daughter's. Being slighter of figure than he, I liked her as she was.

When she came out—in less than a minute, as she had promised—and stood looking up at me, the top of her head, when I lifted her an inch and held her to me, was level with my chin.

She caught my wrist and let her fingers lie along my palm—a way she had that made my heart thump like a drum. "You never told me, Oliver! Why didn't you tell me you were coming home? Think if I'd been away! Is it your father, Oliver?"

"Yes: he had a stroke—a little stroke," I said, "but I think he'll be all right if he isn't unduly excited. The doctor says that if he can have rest and quiet, he'll probably live for years."

"Oh," she cried, "he must, Oliver! How can he die when everybody loves him! We'll make him live for years and years!"

We walked toward the long avenue of poplars that Governor Hutchinson had planted on the hillslope near his house when we were children. As a boy I had jumped in and out of the holes his workmen had dug for those very trees; and the governor himself, tall, slender, pale-faced, smiling, had stood looking down at me and warning me not to be planted by mistake for a poplar. Those poplars were thicker than my body now, and so tall that the orioles' nests among their upper branches were hard to see.

We sat in their lee, as we had sat on countless afternoons and evenings, looking across to the narrow ribbon of Boston Neck that joined our Blue Hill Lands to the triple hills of Boston. To our right was the expanse of green and blue and gold that had always seemed to me the fairest prospect in the world—those rounded green jewels tipped by the sun with gold and set in a sheet of azure: Dorchester Heights, Bird Island, Governor's Island, Castle Island crowned with the gray fortress of Castle William, Thompson's Island, the twin breasts of Spectacle Island, the curved green dragon of Long Island, and its three offspring, Nicks Mate, Gallops Island and Rainsford Island, that guard Nantasket Roads.

"We'll be going sailing in another month, Oliver," Sally said. "We ought to paint the boat. Will you be home long enough to help do it?"

"I don't know," I said. "I'll wait a few days and see how my father feels. I don't believe I'd better plan on going far away till I'm sure he won't be disturbed by my going."

She nodded, opened her lips as if to say something about my

father; then closed them again. I had the sudden thought that she was concealing something from me.

"Sally," I said, "something's happened in these parts since I went away the last time. Things are different here than they are around New Haven. I felt it ten or fifteen miles south of Worcester, almost as soon as I left Connecticut. Men kept stopping me on the road, asking who I was and where I was going—miserable-looking men: the worst sort of ignorant yokels."

"I know very little about politics," Sally said hurriedly.

"Since when?" I asked. "You were interested enough when your father and my father worked together against the Stamp Tax."

"Things have changed since then," Sally said.

Quick pictures leaped into my brain to plague me: of the mob at Wade's house, of the blazing barn, of a screaming mare, blood gushing from her mutilated mouth, of the shifty-eyed rascals who had howled with delight at Buell's maltreatment; who had split him open with a fence rail.

"By God," I said, "I hope they don't change much more! All the human dregs of the country are rising to the top."

I described to her, as well as I could, what had happened to Buell, and how I'd brought him to Milton.

Sally jumped to her feet. "You shouldn't have told me," she whispered. "Don't speak of it—not to a soul!"

"Oh, I know, I know," I said. "It might bring enmity on my father from the riffraff. But wasn't it a horrible thing, Sally! It made me ashamed of being a human being!"

"Please, Oliver, be careful," Sally cried. "You mustn't say such things openly! Oliver, I—I don't want anything to happen to you." She moved a step away from me. "Oliver, you mustn't talk about it!"

"Not talk about it? Not even among friends?"

"No—not to anybody!"

"But I can't help it, Sally! I can't keep wholly silent about such a thing as that, can I?"

"Yes, you must, Oliver! Wholly!"

"But to you——" I began.

Her eyes didn't meet mine, and her look puzzled me, almost dismayed me.

"To you, Sally, I can——"

"No, not even to me."

"What!"

"Yes," she said. "I—I mean it." For a moment she seemed distressed, gave me a troubled side glance that seemed to carry a pleading. "I mustn't talk politics."

I was astonished. "But this is beyond politics. It's a question of humanity—I mean of inhumanity—horrible inhumanity——"

"Oliver! Don't, please!"

"Sally! I don't understand! I'm telling you——"

She caught my arm and shook me to silence; then pressed her palm against my lips. "You're not to tell me! I don't want you to tell me! I won't know how you feel—I won't! If anybody asks me, I want to say I don't know."

I tried to move my lips from beneath the fierce pressure of her palm.

"No!" she cried. "No! I can't tell you—I can't explain—— Oh, Oliver, I can't bear to have such things come between us!" Abruptly she turned, swung away from me and set off for home.

I stood for a moment, astounded, completely at a loss; then strode after her, caught up with her. She almost ran, and I had ado to keep beside her. We said nothing more until we reached her side door. On the step she turned and faced me, her head level with mine, her eyes troubled and her cheeks flushed. "I was afraid this would happen, Oliver."

"Afraid I'd tell you I've been helping a persecuted man, Sally?"

"No; afraid you'd want to talk politics with me. I won't do it!" She spoke now with an intensity that gave me a breathless understanding of her meaning, and with a stricken heart I comprehended a little that an abyss might open between us if I'd let it. I made up my mind not to let it.

"Sally dear," I said, "we won't talk politics. We'll talk about the boat. I'll paint her with you, Sally. This is the eighteenth of April? When shall we start?"

The side door opened and Sally's mother looked out at us. "Oliver!" she exclaimed. "I didn't know you were home! Come in; come in!"

She turned to Sally. "I couldn't imagine where you'd got to. Didn't you remember this was the eighteenth, and that we're to have supper early?"

"Oliver's father isn't well," Sally said hurriedly. "I'm afraid he ought to be at home. I don't think he'd better come in."

"Of course he'll come in," Mrs. Leighton said heartily. "Come right in, Oliver."

In spite of the earliness of the hour, Sally's father and every last one of her seven brothers were in the dining room. As I followed Mrs. Leighton, her hearty voice seemed to fill the house. "Home to see your father, I suppose, Oliver. I declare, it seems a pity Providence had to go and strike him down when there's so many useless people in this world!"

Soame jumped up to greet me, and his voice was sympathetic. "We heard about your father, Oliver! I was thinking today it was too bad you weren't here, so to persuade him to move to Boston. Sit down, Oliver, sit down! You've got time for a bite with us before we have to run."

I looked around the table at Mr. Leighton and Soame's six brothers. Not one of them looked up at me or said a word; they just went on cutting at the cold corned beef upon their plates. Their knife blades made little cold clinking sounds that somehow made me flinch. All of them, Soame included, wore rough clothes, as if for a hunting expedition.

I was puzzled by Soame's words; puzzled by this strange conclave of Leightons, this uncivilized supper hour, this frosty reception from neighbors with whom I'd been on close terms all my life.

"Take my father into Boston?" I asked. "Why should I take my father into Boston? What's the matter with Milton?"

"Nothing," Soame said hastily. "Not if your father likes it." I felt, rather than saw, him shoot a quick glance at his father. "I thought I heard somewhere that he didn't care much for Milton any more."

"That's not so," I said. "I've often heard him say he'd rather live in Milton than any place in the world. What gave you the idea he doesn't like it?"

Mr. Leighton boomed heartily at me from the head of the table. "Don't pay any attention to Soame, Oliver. He's just talking to hear himself talk. What's the news in New Haven?"

I glanced at Soame, and it seemed to me his eyes had a message for me—a message of apology or warning or entreaty: one that, to my vague discomfort, I couldn't understand.

"New Haven?" I asked slowly. "New Haven?" But my mind wasn't on Mr. Leighton's question. Why were all the Leightons dressed in rough clothes? Why were all of them, from Albion down to Jeremiah and Steven, hastily eating a cold supper while the sun was still high? Why should my friend Soame, for the first time during our long friendship, be trying to give me a message he didn't dare to speak outright? On what sort of mysterious mission could they be going, if all of them were needed, and yet none of them would so much as hint to me that I should go too?

Mr. Leighton's voice was impatient. "Yes, New Haven," he repeated. "You've just come from New Haven, haven't you, Oliver?"

Soame glanced up at me with that drolly serious look of his. "Father wants to know whether Connecticut people ever discuss England, or whether Connecticut's getting too elegant to be a part of this world."

"I see," I said. "Well, Connecticut's a sensible province. You hear great arguments about England, but most of the arguments end in agreements."

"Agreements," Soame said. "No wonder Father thinks there's something wrong with Connecticut! What do they agree on?"

"They agree that the best thing the colonies can do is follow the Galloway Plan."

The Galloway Plan had been a wise and noble-minded measure for a practicable and permanent union between the American colonies and England, introduced in the Continental Congress by Joseph Galloway, a distinguished Philadelphian, speaker of the Pennsylvania Assembly. He had called it The Plan of a Proposed Union between Great Britain and the Colonies, and it had been strongly supported in Congress by some of the wisest statesmen in that body, among them John Jay, James Duane and Edward Rutledge.

"The Galloway Plan was defeated." Mr. Leighton's tone was dry. "You don't hear about it any more."

"That's only because Congress suppressed all mention of it in their minutes," I reminded him. "Congress doesn't want it talked about, and yet it was defeated by only one vote."

"Only one vote?" Soame asked politely. "That's like missing a deer by only one mile, isn't it?"

"Perhaps it is," I said, "and perhaps it isn't. That particular miss wasn't by a mile, and I doubt if it should be called a good miss, at that. I don't see the goodness myself. Five colonies voted for the Galloway Plan and six against it. Edward Rutledge called the plan 'almost perfect', but those that defeated it are doing everything in their power to keep it from the knowledge of the people. That's the basis of the arguments in New Haven. There's a lot of feeling down there that if a plan's almost perfect, and meets the approval of some of the wisest men we've got, it shouldn't be suppressed or permanently rejected at a time when mobs are destroying free speech and upholding lawlessness."

Mr. Leighton made a contemptuous sound. "Mobs! You mustn't believe all you hear about mobs, Oliver! Every time more than two men in Massachusetts raise their voices against the outrages that England's inflicting on us, the English in Boston want the world to believe they've been threatened by a mob that'll stop at nothing. That's all nonsense, my boy! It's the British who're keeping us from the rights and privileges of Englishmen. They're the lawbreakers: not we! They've stolen our liberty from us, and we'll never get it back by means of the Galloway Plan or any of the other plans proposed by enemies of liberty."

"There's no argument in New Haven about some of the things you say, Mr. Leighton," I said. "We're all agreed that England'll have to govern these colonies differently; but there's considerable difference of opinion about our loss of liberty. I haven't lost any liberty yet under English rule, but I've lost plenty of it under the rule of Americans. Congress has done its best to hide the Galloway Plan from me, so I won't think contrary to what Congress wants me to think. And from what I know about the Sons of Liberty, there's no part of these colonies where freedom of speech hasn't been suppressed, the liberty of the press destroyed, and the voice of truth silenced—not by legal means, but by the orders of self-appointed and ignorant committeemen and by little mobs of lawless and equally ignorant men."

Albion Leighton drew a chronometer from his pocket, stared earnestly at it, rose from his chair and went from the room without a word or a glance for me.

I heard Sally whisper, "Oliver! Oliver!"

I knew what she meant, but my blood was up. "You mean I'm not to speak what I feel? Your father asked what they're saying in New Haven, and I'm trying to tell him, but he seems to insist that these stories of mobs are British lies. I've been collecting information about what's been happening in these provinces, Sally, and trying to sift the true from the false. Suppose I denied that a mob had deprived men of their natural rights within five miles of where we're sitting now? Suppose I said such things didn't happen? What would you think of me as a gatherer of information?"

"What would I think?" she repeated. "Why, I'd think you were telling the truth. What else could I think? There's never been a mob in this town."

"Never!" Mr. Leighton echoed. "This town had the greatest sympathy for Governor Hutchinson when the Boston mob destroyed his house. Didn't he live peacefully here?"

"He's not living here now," I said. "He had to go to England to live, didn't he? And what happened to the men who wished him well when he went? Weren't they made to eat their words? And what would have happened to those men if they hadn't eaten their words as ordered?"

"You're begging the question," Mr. Leighton said. "You're talking like a constitutional lawyer. When I say Milton's a law-abiding town, you talk loosely about mobs and lawlessness. You'll never hear of a mob in the town of Milton."

I was already in a state of irritation, but Mr. Leighton's reference to constitutional lawyers set my inwards aboil. My father was a constitutional lawyer; so was Daniel Dulaney; so was Governor Hutchinson; so was John Jay; so were many of the most distinguished and patriotic men in the American colonies. I knew that if I said what was in my mind to say, I might set the whole Leighton family against me, but something within me refused to be held in check.

"If you don't hear of a mob in Milton, sir," I said, "it's because people are afraid to speak. If they *are* afraid to speak, that means liberty of speech is gone—and not because of any fault of England's! I saw a mob last night, and I hope I'll never see another! They burned Henry Wade's house, five miles from here; and what they did to Henry Wade and his family, God only knows. They found a poor devil of a printer in Wade's barn, and they tarred him and feathered him and rode him on a rail, and I trust that's something that'll never happen to any friend of yours! Why, they even tortured helpless animals—put out their eyes and cut out their tongues, Mr. Leighton—and for nothing except that those animals happened to have the misfortune to belong to a man the mob hated."

The Leighton twins, Steven and Jeremiah, rose and, saying nothing, giving me not a glance, clumped from the room.

Mr. Leighton looked at me coldly. "Where'd you hear all this poppycock?"

"I saw it! I saw Wade's house gutted! I saw a mare's tongue cut out! I saw Buell ridden on a rail and torn wide apart!"

Mr. Leighton looked at me sharply. "Buell? Who's Buell?"

My heart sank, and I affected a calmness I didn't feel. "That's what I heard the mob call him. 'Buell the printer', they called him."

I felt Soame and the three remaining Leighton boys, John, Richard and Timothy, staring at me; but when I turned to face them, their eyes were on their empty plates. Almost immediately, with one accord, John, Richard and Timothy noisily pushed back their chairs and trooped into the kitchen, leaving Soame sitting silently beside me.

Murmuring words I couldn't distinguish, Mrs. Leighton rose and bustled after her six sons. In the same moment a thought seemed to strike Mr. Leighton. "Soame," he said, getting to his feet, "I want a word with you in private."

Soame rose to his feet and stood uncertainly behind my chair.

"Soame!" Mr. Leighton said sharply.

Soame put his hand on my shoulder. "Well, Oliver, I hope I'll see you soon."

"Of course you will," I said. "Why shouldn't you? What ails you, Soame?"

He turned from me and went quickly to the door, which Mr. Leighton was holding open. Mr. Leighton walked out after him and slammed the door hard.

I sat there with Sally in a strange, uncomfortable silence. "Well, Sally," I said at length, "I don't know what's happening, but I hope it won't make any difference—that is, I hope you and I won't——"

She got up. "Of course not," she said. "I——"

I felt frightened. "Sally, can't we talk together, just for a little while? Won't you come outdoors again with me, where we won't be interrupted? I've been away from you so long, and now something's coming between us. We shouldn't let it, Sally! I'm getting a queer feeling, as if the whole world might drop to pieces beneath me! Please, Sally——"

She wouldn't look at me. "I have to speak to my brothers before they go," she said hurriedly. "I'm sorry, Oliver. I——" She made a helpless gesture, turned, ran to the door that led to the kitchen, and was gone without a backward look.

I sat down and waited. After a while I heard a step overhead that I knew for hers, and understood she'd gone upstairs by the kitchen stairway. Then I heard Mrs. Leighton's voice; it came from overhead too. I was sure she was talking to Sally—though I didn't hear any response. After that I heard no sounds at all in the house; still I waited. The pale gold of an April sunset lay across the dining table, and the shadows of the salts and peppers, the tall sugar shaker, the silver fruit basket, lay long and blue across the white cloth and the soiled dishes. I stayed until the shadows were gone and the objects on the table undistinguishable in the twilight. Then I went home.

CHAPTER IV

W<small>HEN</small> I tried to tell my father what had happened at the Leightons', my words came haltingly. No one had spoken to me roughly in that house; yet it seemed to me that hatred had breathed upon me there. For years I'd been on the best of terms with all the Leightons. Of course I'd had differences of opinion with one or another of Sally's brothers at times, but never once an argument or dispute that ended in ill feeling. But tonight every one of them, barring Soame, had refused to meet my eye; had given me no words at all, civil or uncivil.

I told my father I didn't understand.

"I think I do," he said. "What you found there is something you'll have to expect if you insist on keeping your independence of thought. You and I and most of our close friends want to avoid war. More than that, we want to avoid the bitterest of wars—civil war. Your friends the Leightons don't think the way we think, and so I'm afraid they've actually begun to hate us. You feel that change; it's happened lately. You'll never again find the Leightons agreeable, Oliver, unless you tell them you're against settling our differences with England by peaceful means." He stared hard at me.

"I couldn't do that," I said. "It wouldn't be true. I can't say I want a civil war, can I, when I don't?"

"Probably not," my father said. "For my part, I'm more interested in what I feel to be the truth than I am in what the Leightons think. You might possibly be more interested in the Leightons than in the welfare of your country."

"No," I said, "I'm not; but I don't want Sally to begin to hate me as her father and brothers apparently do. It's strange. I don't see why the Leightons feel they have to hate me personally."

34

My father raised his eyebrows. "You've been reading history without applying what you've read to your own circumstances. Don't tell me you're going to be like everybody else, and refuse to see what's before your eyes—refuse to admit the truth about these liberty-loving people of Massachusetts."

"I know we've always been more jealous of our liberties than others," I said, "but that doesn't explain——"

My father's smile was a wry one. "Jealous! That's not the word, my boy! The Pilgrim Fathers who came here in 1620 were true friends of liberty. They exercised full liberty of worship for themselves, and permitted others to worship as they pleased.

"But the Puritan Fathers, who settled Massachusetts Bay eight years later, were another breed of cats. They established a colony so cruel and so bigoted that it's without precedent or parallel in any Protestant country. The Puritan Fathers abandoned the church and the form of worship which they professed in England, and on arrival here set up a new church—the Congregational Church. Under that new rule, nobody could vote in this liberty-loving colony, nobody was eligible to public office, unless he was a member of that church! Those who wouldn't conform to Puritan beliefs—those who tried to worship as Presbyterians or Episcopalians or Quakers—were persecuted by whipping, banishment or death.

"The persecution that drove Puritans out of England was nothing by comparison with the persecution practised here by those same Puritans. They couldn't endure chastisement with rods in England, yet they scourged their fellow refugees in America with scorpions. In their eyes, tolerance was despicable and intolerable. They felt an actual physical loathing for opposition; and from the day they reached America, they alone among the colonists hated England and seized upon every possible occasion for agitation and dispute.

"There, Oliver, is the sum and substance of the differences between us and the Leightons. The Leightons hate the oppressive measures inflicted by England on these colonies, and so do we; but they also hate England, and we don't. We think the British Constitution is a good constitution—one under which this country of ours will eventually be happier and more prosperous than under any other; but they don't think so, because their hatred of England makes them see everything English as wrong. That same hatred of England makes them hate us the moment we admit to seeing anything good in anything English. What's more, Oliver, the Leightons are Congregationalists and we're Episcopalians, and the old religious intolerance is coming to the surface again after all these years. Until we conform to all their beliefs, my boy, they'll scourge us with scorpions."

"Well, sir," I said, "I know you're right about the Puritans; but I hope you're wrong about the rest of it. It doesn't seem possible that the mistakes of a hundred years ago can be repeated today—and at our expense."

My father sighed. "There's something you want to bear in mind, Oliver. All of us know history repeats itself, but mighty few of us recognize the repetition until too late."

I knew my father was right; but how right he was I didn't even begin to suspect until late on the following day—which, for a time, I was sure was the saddest day I would ever know.

The early morning was bad enough; for even while I sat in my father's room, watching him eat breakfast, Andrew brought him a letter from Vose Leighton—a letter delivered at our back door by an unknown man, who had refused to wait for an answer. The letter was unsealed, which was unusual.

I sat all asweat while my father read it to himself, for I had a foreboding that there was something in it about me—something I wouldn't like. As my father read, his lips twisted into a smile in which there was no amusement.

"Well," I said, and I'm afraid my voice was unsteady, "I suppose he says Sally's too young for me to be calling on, or some such piece of hypocrisy."

My father looked at me soberly. "No, Oliver. Vose doesn't dodge —not about you and Sally. His letter doesn't make pleasant reading, but you'd better read it. If you continue to feel as you do, you'll probably hear worse things about yourself—especially if you continue to live near Boston. Just remember, my boy, that these people here are in a kind of frenzy: they're not responsible for most of the things they think and say. Buell wasn't far wrong when he insisted that rebels were bound to believe in Perkins' Metallic Tractors."

I took the letter from him, and while I read it he stared through the window at the far-off marsh and blue water, that seemed to quiver a little in the warmth of the April sun.

"To Seaton Wiswell, Esqre," [the letter said] *"I had hoped there would be no necessity of mentioning such matters to a neighbor, but*

my family is as one in wishing to avoid further relations with all those who are not hearty in the cause of liberty. I plainly saw yesterday afternoon that your son is disaffected. He spoke against the Congress, and intimated that lovers of Liberty have no right to protect themselves against the outrages of Ministers who are assassins and lost to all honor. Such beliefs, sir, are repugnant to me and to all honest and patriotic men. While your son holds such views, there can be no common meeting ground between my family and your own. I trust my words are plain. Not only does this letter require no answer, but I will ask you to remind your son that any attempt on his part to communicate with my daughter, either in person or in writing, might easily bring her, too, under suspicion as an enemy to Liberty and her country.

"I am, sir,

"Yr. obdt. humble serv't,

"Vose Leighton."

The letter made me feel as I had felt years ago, when I smoked half of one of my father's cigars. My mouth was coppery; my body drenched with cold perspiration; my stomach all atremble.

I got up, weak and dizzy, unable to say anything to my father even if I'd wanted to, and somehow got myself out of the house to stumble blindly across the fields to the north of Milton Hill. When I came back, I think I might have gone on pitying myself if I hadn't found Andrew in a state of agitation and apprehension. In listening to his story, I forgot my personal troubles.

All the morning, Andrew said, he had been conscious of something unusual. He had seen men hurrying singly along the roads with muskets over their shoulders and haversacks on their hips; and once he had seen as many as thirty or forty setting off toward Boston in a group. He had gone to the village to learn the reason for this unusual activity, but those he questioned only shook their heads and said they'd noticed nothing out of the ordinary.

On his way home he had questioned the servants at the Chases, Cranes, Claflins, Hutchinsons—people of the highest standing, and all close friends of my father—but none of them had any information.

He was certain, he said, that our own villagers knew more than they were willing to admit, but that they were suspicious of him and wouldn't tell him what was going on. Consequently, he said, he knew it was something we wouldn't like.

"According to some," he said, "those men with muskets were going to the marshes to shoot ducks."

"Ducks, Andrew! Since when have duck hunters taken to going out thirty and forty at a time?"

"That's what I told 'em," Andrew said, "and they just looked at me—looked at me hard, till I got to feeling shaky inside. I never had such feelings before, Mr. Oliver, and they don't rest well in me."

Andrew's report was disturbing. I was worried about my father, worried about Buell, worried about Sally; but there seemed to be nothing I could do. Without quite knowing why, I prowled aimlessly about the house, inside and out, filled the water hogshead in the cellar, hid some provisions in the potato bins under the kitchen, and had Andrew give the horses a double allowance of hay. At dusk I took a lighted candle into the little room off the kitchen where Buell lay grumbling at his bandages and longing for the day when he should find perfect food.

"It stands to reason," he said to me argumentatively, "that somewhere there's exactly the kind of eating that'd agree with me. More'n half the people you ever knew have had stomach misery, and got over it through certain nourishments they recommend to other people because it agreed with themselves, but turns out not to agree with these other people. Isn't that so? You know it is!

"Well, if *they* found what don't revolt their stomachs, why shouldn't I? It's waiting for me somewhere, and all I got to do is find it. Sometimes I've had a feeling it was just around the next corner—but up to now it never was. If I had just exactly the right food in me, I wouldn't have to wear these bandages. I'd heal right up! My stomach knows when it isn't getting the right treatment, and it always tells me so. It's telling me so right now."

"What seems to be disagreeing with you?" I asked.

"Everything I've eaten. That's what my stomach's telling me as clearly as if it used the very words."

"I'm sorry," I told him. "I'll try to see you have a better diet while you're here, if you'll tell me what's agreed with you at some time in the past."

"I can't," he said. "Nothing ever did. My stomach's gifted with a strong voice, but it can't tell me what will. It can only tell me what don't. I've tried liquor on it, because I've always longed to know how it'd feel to be right good and drunk; so many people seem to prize it. Always had to stop before I got the way I wanted to be, though, because my insides would speak right up. I'd start hiccuping and couldn't stop till something startled me.

"Sometimes I've thought fine French wines might help, and I'd have gone over there and tried 'em long ago, but the trouble is I knew I couldn't get work over there because they won't use an English printer on a French printing press. Prejudiced! Just because he doesn't know their language! I tried liquor that was too sour and put sugar in it, and tried liquor that was too sweet and put pickles in it; but no! I'd get almost a scream from my inner parts and——"

The autobiography was interrupted by a sharp rap at the kitchen door. I heard Andrew move across the floor; and from the silence that followed, I knew he was standing in the entryway, listening.

"Who is it?" I heard him ask. "Who's there?"

There was a guarded soft answer that brought me into the entryway before Andrew had finished drawing the bolt. I loosened the chain and threw open the door. Sally stood upon the step outside, her hands at her breast, her head turned from me as though she listened for pursuit.

"Sally!" I caught her wrist and drew her in, but when I'd have held her close, she pushed me off, silently latched the door behind her, and stood with her back against it.

"Sally," I said, "your father's letter—thank God you're not letting it stop our——"

"Hark!" she whispered breathlessly. "They know Buell's here! Get him out of the house. Soame says maybe they won't do anything to you if they find he's not here."

"Do anything to *me?*" I said. "They won't——"

"I mean your father," she interrupted. *"Maybe* they won't; you can't tell! Be careful how you speak to them! Be careful! They're excited—terribly! I think they hardly know what they're doing."

"They, Sally? Who is 'they'? Sally, what——"

She put her hand to her throat and spoke rapidly. "You don't know what happened! There's been fighting. The British went out to seize the stores at Concord and Lexington, and the whole country has risen against them. Our people killed more than a hundred of them—British regulars! Our people fought them all day, driving them back into Boston! Make Buell understand he'll be safe if he can get into Boston!

"Other—other people are being harried into Boston, too, Oliver: all who sympathize with the British; yes, all who don't speak out on our side. That's the only place they're safe. Buell will be safe if he can get into Boston."

I stared at her. "A hundred *regulars!*" I said. "Who brought you such a tale, Sally! Do you think these farmers could kill a hundred British regulars? Why, there's nobody——"

Sally's cheeks were white, but her eyes were brilliant in the light of the candle Andrew held. "I had seven brothers there," she said. "Soame's come back on his little bay pacer. Did you ever know Soame to lie, Oliver? He told me to tell you to get Buell away—if there's time!"

If there was time! Then the mob was already on its way! What if that mob saw Sally come out of our house! What if it suspected that she had come to warn us! . . . My blood ran cold at the memory of Henry Wade's wife and daughters struggling and stumbling through the briers and alder thickets of Dedham. . . .

I caught her by the shoulders. "Wait, Sally! I'll tell Buell. I can't let you go back alone!"

I swung about and ran to the door of the little room off the kitchen. It was bolted.

"Let me in, Buell," I cried. "You've got to get up! I've got to get you out of here!"

The door opened, and there stood Buell, already dressed in a suit of my old hunting clothes.

"That knock scared me," he explained, working at buckles and buttons. "Then I heard some of what she said, and I knew I had to stand clothes on me, and I guess I can. You got guns in the house, ain't you? Pistols too, maybe? I'd like to borrow a pair. There'll never be another mob get me!"

I ran back into the kitchen.

It was empty, except for Andrew, who stood staring at the closed door. It was empty and silent—so silent that the ticking of the painted clock on the shelf beside the stove was like metallic rapping on my eardrums.

"My God, Andrew!" I cried. "You didn't let her go!"

Andrew groaned. "She just slipped out like a ghost, Mr. Oliver. I couldn't stop her. I never had the chance!" He caught my arm.

"You can't go after her, Mr. Oliver! Your father, sir! He needs you more than she does!"

My father—— Yes, he needed me: so did Buell. . . . I could only hope with all my heart that Sally would be safe.

In the closet off the front hall, where by lantern light I loaded the pistols for Buell, there was a little window, and fingernails tapped urgently upon the glass from outside. I opened the window, and Buell spoke in a low voice from the darkness, "Give the second one all the powder she'll stand, Oliver! Fill her up to the muzzle with buckshot—if you've got any. I wish to God I had a couple of Perkins' Metallic Tractors to put in!" By no means as an afterthought he added quickly, "Don't waste time, Oliver! I can hear 'em coming up the hill!"

I rammed in the last wad, passed the pistols out to him with a powder flask, a bag of bullets, some spare flints and a full water bottle. Buell swooped upon them like a pickerel.

"If it hurts you to walk," I said, "there's a drainage ditch a hundred yards to the eastward. You could lie in it."

"Don't worry about me." Buell's voice, low, already came from a little distance. "Hurry and load up your own pistols. I'll see you in Boston."

There was the faintest sound of his moving furtively among the bushes; then a silence that wasn't complete, for the night seemed heavily murmurous.

In the distance there was a conglomerate sound that defined itself too soon as far-off grumbling voices and the irregular clatter of many boots upon a rocky hill road.

I felt empty inside as I listened; I can't otherwise describe the sensation of a man who hears such sounds and well knows that he and his are what they come seeking.

Andrew and I didn't look at each other's faces, but I saw his hands were shaking—and so too were mine—as he helped me load a pair of heavy pistols and our two big duck guns. Then I tightened my belt and went in to warn my father.

I blurted it out. "Father, it looks to me as though we might have trouble. I mean we might have it within the next few minutes. It's because of my thoughtlessness."

My father's face, against the pillow, looked serene. "I've been expecting it," he said, "but it's not what you call your thoughtlessness

that's made me look for it. Whatever happens, I'd like to have you
bear in mind, always, that you've never done anything I wouldn't
want a son of mine to do."

That didn't make me feel happier. "If I hadn't tried to help
Buell——"

"You regret it?" my father asked.

"No," I said, "I don't regret it for myself, but if it makes trouble
for you——"

"If you don't regret it, Oliver, nobody regrets it. I wouldn't have
had you do anything different. Buell's nothing but a symbol of the
times; and if we have trouble, it's the times that'll trouble us: not a
helpless human atom like Buell. What is it you're afraid of, son?"

"Well, sir," I said, "I don't believe the doctor'd want me to tell
you——"

"No, I suppose not," my father said. "Doctor Miller, like most of
the members of his distinguished profession, thinks all humans re-
spond the same way to given circumstances; but I know better. I'm
not as ill as Miller thinks I am, and I'm prepared for almost anything
you can tell me, my boy, so go ahead."

"Well, sir," I said, "the Sons of Liberty tackled the British regulars
this morning, unless Sally's mistaken, and killed about a hundred of
'em. Soame Leighton was with the rebels, and he sent word by
Sally, which he wouldn't have done unless it was serious. He wanted
to warn us that the mobs are out again—that they know I brought
Buell here—that they know we're against mobs, and may take this
opportunity to—to——"

My father sighed. "So they tackled the regulars, did they? That's
bad, Oliver! That's what we've been fearing!"

I saw I needed to say no more, and he seemed to have nothing
more to say; so we waited silently, and I felt only relief when Andrew
came softly through the doorway with the pistols under his arm and
a duck gun in each hand. When he looked at me with raised eyebrows, and rolled inquiring eyes toward my father, I nodded.

He gave me one of the duck guns. "Already there's some of 'em
outside the back door, Mr. Oliver, and more coming. They ain't
knocking nor saying anything. They're just standing around, waiting."

He took the pistols from beneath his arm and placed them on the
table beside the bed. "You better keep these, Mr. Wiswell."

"I don't believe I want them, Andrew," my father said. "I wouldn't care to shoot my own townsmen over a difference of opinion about politics. Keep 'em yourself if you think you need 'em; but I suggest you'll be better off to put 'em away where you can't get at 'em. The trouble with a pistol is that if you show it, you've got to use it, and once you use it you've committed yourself."

My father eyed Andrew over the top of his glasses with the same satirical smile with which he defied an opposing lawyer to answer an unanswerable argument.

For the first time in my life I couldn't smile with him. I could only stare at him and think of the duck guns we'd loaded. Even as I stared, the whole house echoed to a thumping on the front door—a thumping that might have been made by a club or the butt of a pistol.

Well, here it is, I thought, and I went into the front hall.

"Who's there?" I called through the closed door. "I'm Oliver Wiswell. What's wanted?"

There was a moment's silence. Then a hoarse voice said abruptly, "Open the door and we'll tell you."

"I can't," I said. "My father's sick. We can't have a lot of people in the house. Go round to the back door and I'll talk to you."

I heard mutterings from the other side of the door; then the same voice said, "All right."

When I started toward the kitchen, Andrew came to the door of my father's bedroom. "I'd better go with you, Mr. Oliver, hadn't I?"

"No," I said. "Stay with my father. He might need something." I went to the back entryway, unbolted the door and opened it, but only an inch or so, leaving the chain fastened. Dark figures were grouped around the steps.

"I'm obliged to you for your courtesy," I said. "What can I do for you?"

A shrill voice mocked me in affected ladylike accents—"Obliged to you for your courtesy! Oh dearie me!" Harsh laughter raised hackles on my spine.

One of the crowd came up close to the opening. He wore no neckcloth, and lank hair hung from beneath his cap.

"Buell's here," he said. "We want him. Bring him out or we'll come in and get him!"

"There's nobody in this house except my father, his servant Andrew, and myself," I said. "That's the truth, and I'll swear it on the Bible."

"We'll be judges of that," the man said. "We know Buell's been in this house, and Buell's an enemy to this country. He's a supporter of assassins—a friend to those who'd destroy our homes and liberties."

"There's no one named Buell here," I repeated. "There's no enemy to this country in this house. There's nobody here but my father, who's always lived in this town, and Andrew, who's never had any other home, and myself. Everybody in this town knows my father. No better American ever lived. We're enemies to no one. We don't want to destroy anyone's home or liberty! You can't make these accusations against me! Why, I was born here. I know the Blue Hills and Neponset marshes as well as any one of you, I don't care who he is."

"You brought Buell into this house," the man persisted. "You stopped at Henry Wade's farm night before last and helped a man get away, didn't you?"

"I've told you twice there's no such person in this house. You're barking up the wrong tree."

"Break down the door," somebody shouted.

Scattering voices repeated the words; others called loudly for order.

"Look here," I said, when I could make myself heard. "You tell me you want Buell; and though I've sworn he's not here, you insist he is. I tell you again, he isn't! If all but two of you will move back from this door, I'll let those two in and they can scour the house from cellar to attic."

At that there was a bedlam of shouting, and fists and clubs threatened me. There may have been cool heads in the lot, but not enough to be reassuring. The few who called for order seemed to be trying to push the others back; but the uncomfortable fact was that they were all surging closer and closer to the door.

I picked up the duck gun from the corner where I'd left it.

"Now look here," I said, "I gave you my word that I'm alone in this house with my father and Andrew. I offered to let two of you come in and search. I'm being fair, and you aren't, so it appears to me you're not telling the truth. I don't believe you're after Buell at all. It looks to me as though you want to get in here and kill a sick man—kill my father! Is that what you want, by any chance?"

"We want Buell," the leader said doggedly. "We don't aim to hurt you or your father or anybody else that rightfully belongs in this house; but I've got to tell you this, Wiswell: you've given aid and comfort to enemies of this country, and that's something we won't have. You've got to leave this town—you and your father too!"

"Leave it?" I said. "Leave this town? We can't do that! Why, it's our home! This land is ours! My father built this house more than thirty years ago. We've no other place to go! Besides, my father's sick. He's had a shock and shouldn't be moved. Doctor Miller said any disturbance would probably be fatal to him. That's why I asked you gentlemen to move from the front door. He needs rest, nursing, Doctor Miller's attention. He'd——"

"He won't get Doctor Miller's attention in this town," the leader said brusquely. "Doctor Miller doesn't live here. He moved to Boston in a hurry this afternoon. So did every other doctor and lawyer that thinks the way Miller and your father think. Not a soul that's left in Milton would raise a hand to help your father. You might as well recognize it. We don't want either of you around here. You've got to go, both of you. What's more, you've got to go tonight!"

"Tonight?" I echoed. "You know that would be murder, don't you?"

"We had people murdered today, out at Concord and Lexington," the leader said. "They were murdered by friends of yours in red coats."

"Oh, for God's sake," I protested. "Why don't you tell the truth! They're no friends of ours! My father's against misrule just as much as you are, and so am I!"

Upon this, from all about the steps there arose a great booing, and through the crack in the door the leader wagged a finger close to my face. "That ain't so! You've been heard to say the Sons of Liberty are suppressing freedom of speech, silencing the voice of truth, and establishing lawlessness throughout the Colonies!"

He spoke shoutingly and was rewarded by an angry howl from dozens of voices.

His finger stabbed at me through the crack. "Didn't you say that? I dare you to deny it!"

I just stared at him. His information must, I knew, have come from one of the Leightons, and there was nothing I could say.

"That's what you said," he cried. "That means you're against us, so you must be friends of the British! Well, we'll run no risks from the likes of you! Go join your friends in Boston! You can't stay here to spy on us and stab us in the back! If you're not out of this house in half an hour, we'll set fire to it! We'll get Buell when he comes out. You and your father can either go, or stay and burn here and in hell, too, afterwards."

Voices angrier than his yelled from behind him. "Hell, burn the house now! We'll burn it anyway, whether they go or not! Let's have a fire quick! Burn it! Burn it!"

"I'll take your half-hour," I said desperately to the leader. "We'll go!"

CHAPTER V

In twenty minutes Andrew and I were harnessing our little mare, while the crowd stood peering in at my father where he lay in the entryway. We put a heavy dressing gown over his night gear, with shoes and thick stockings upon his feet, and we placed thick quilts under him and blankets over him. His eyes were still calm, as was his spirit.

"Bring your mother's portrait with us," he said to me. "Perhaps they'll let you take our clothes and the family silver, too. You might want your children to have the silver. I think we'll never again set eyes upon what we leave behind. Perhaps they'll let you have a few of our books. Books are a comfort when you're discouraged."

As I helped Andrew harness the mare and back her between the shafts of our carryall, I was in an icy rage at the witless cruelty of these misguided dolts who were thus torturing a man who had proved himself as indomitable and resourceful a defender of the rights of America as any man living. Into my mind came the words of the great Samuel Seabury when he urged Americans to ignore one of the recent insane and useless measures passed by our first Congress, and to resist the mobs that went by the name of committees.

"Will you," he demanded, "submit to committees chosen by the weak, foolish, turbulent part of the country people; by half a dozen fools in your neighborhood? Will you open your doors to them? Let them examine your tea canisters and molasses jugs, and your wives' and daughters' petticoats? Will you bow and cringe and tremble and quake—fall down and worship our Sovereign Lord, the Mob? By Heaven, I will not! Before I submit, I will die!"

The trouble with Seabury was, he'd never seen a mob, and I had.

47

Worse, I'd not only seen a mob; I was now in the midst of one; so was my sick father; and dying wouldn't advantage us.

The moment Andrew and I picked up my father and put him in the carryall, those near the back door began to push into the house through the entryway; but a dozen or more hung back to watch us surlily. When he had settled himself in the seat, I put my arms about my father to save him so far as I could from being jolted, Andrew tightened the reins, clucked to the mare and started her down the hill.

"Walk your horse," one of the men about us said to Andrew. "We're seeing that you go into Boston and nowhere else! We're going with you!"

Never, at night, had I seen so many people on the road to Boston. We passed little groups resting beside bundles; and men with muskets—sentinels of a sort, they seemed to be—appeared at intervals to stare appraisingly at us. Those with bundles, I realized, were in the same straits that we were: they had aroused the suspicion or the ire of the mobs; were guilty, probably, of nothing but speaking their mind, and were therefore undergoing banishment from their home.

I thought for a time that the whole of that dark journey would be made in silence; for our attendants said nothing, and the sentinels, apparently recognizing them, asked us no questions. Then, far ahead, I heard the sound of drunken singing, and liked it even less than I liked the silence.

As we drew closer to the maudlin howling, I loosened the pistols in my belt, and devoutly hoped I'd have no cause to use them; but after what I'd seen done to Buell, I knew that anything might happen.

The singing, we presently found, came from a man who staggered in the road, swinging a tin lantern whose dim rays made speckles of yellow light on his knees and feet but on little else; and his drunken outcries had to do with his experiences at Concord and Lexington that very day. I didn't like the words of his song—

> "Shot the Red Coats in the road;
> Scalped 'em neat and handy!
> Going back to scalp some more!
> Yankee Doodle Dandy!"

He wavered to the side of the road as we neared him, hiccuped shockingly and raised his lantern to look inside our carryall.

"Tories," he bawled thickly. "Two more Tories to be scalped! Come out 'n' be scalped, Tories!"

It was Tom Buell. His face was blackened, as if by biting the ends from cartridges, and across his left eye he wore a dirty bandage. So convincing was his acting that he almost frightened me. One of our guards remonstrated, but not severely.

"Stand back there," he said. "You got no call to interfere with these people!"

Again Buell hiccuped. "I ain't, hey? Like hell I ain't! I got as much call as anyone has! You wasn't at Lexington and Concord, and I *was!* Where was you when I was preserving the liberties of the Colonies? Maybe you was in bed, thinking up speeches to make to people who were interfering with those you don't want interfered with! Well, brother, don't waste your eloquence on me, because I got a call to interfere with anyone I want to, 'specially Tories. I interfered with plenty of 'em today—one of 'em a general with brass buttons! What's two more to me—especially if they ain't got on brass buttons! I knocked 'em down as if they was weeds!"

"Well, keep away from these people," our guard said. "We're giving 'em safe-conduct to Boston."

"Boston?" Buell asked thickly. "Is that so? Tha's just where I want to go! Been trying to find Boston for hours 'n' hours! Got to be sure all the damned Tories are inside it, where they belong."

With that he began to march lurchingly beside the carryall. When our attendants were brusque with him, he damned them for lily-livered insects who had frowsted under rocks while he had torn redcoats to pieces with bare hands. He even poked into the back of the carryall, prodding among the few belongings we'd been allowed to bring away with us. His disgust at what he found seemed as genuine as it was noisy.

"Good Godfrey," he cried, waving his lantern recklessly, "look at that painting! I could do better on a barn door with a mop! And what's this stuff? I s'pose they call it silver! Feels like tin to me, but I guess it's too heavy! Mostly lead, that's what it is, and not enough to make bullets out of!" Another hiccup racked him.

"And books!" he shouted. "Books nobody would read, even if he'd be damn fool enough to like reading! Books! Books smelling of fish glue so strong a baby'd get sick if you put 'em in a chair to sit him up to the table on! To hell with Tories! Nine tenths of 'em like reading, and it rots their minds! Not one of 'em's any good, and not one of 'em's *got* anything that's any good! All they got's fish glue and tin silver and pictures of starchy old ladies!"

He burst into his ribald rendition of "Yankee Doodle" once more, and, steering a zigzag course beside us, seemed too good a patriot for the stomachs of the Sons of Liberty who accompanied us. One of them begged him repeatedly to stop his singing, and they walked aloof from him.

When we came at last to the beginning of Boston Neck, I had for the first time a true sense of the turmoil that had descended upon our country. The rebels had erected barricades to keep the troops from coming out of Boston—barricades of logs, baskets filled with sand, rocks piled between planks, bags of earth. Behind the barricades was an assemblage of people who, in appearance and behavior, were such a crowd as might gather upon the outskirts of a burning town.

On both sides of the road were men, women and children huddled in groups and packed in carryalls, chaises, carts, farm wagons, hay-ricks. They had heaps of belongings with them—furniture, bedding, portraits, silver, and all sorts of bales and bundles—as though they were fleeing from an overwhelming disaster. Like ourselves, they were refugees from mobs in towns around Boston, and they were frightened.

The children were like cowed animals backed into corners; some whimpering; others hiding their faces against their mothers' skirts, or cowering close to bundles or beneath wagon seats. The women's faces were pale; their hair was disarranged; their clothing dusty and draggled. The men with them were silent and watchful, as if they expected to have to fight their way through to safety.

I saw a score of familiar faces among those near us—Charles Flood, the Medford merchant; Edwin Purcell of Roxbury, noted for his charities; Miles Graham, the Cambridge lawyer; the Rev. Ebenezer Patten of Cambridge; Dr. Ellery King of Dorchester; Jeremiah Stapleton, the Dorchester shipowner; Francis Pray, one of Dedham's largest landowners.

A thin trickle of people moved through the barricade toward Boston; but most of them, because of the stupidity and self-importance of the militia officers guarding the gates, seemed condemned to stay where they were for the rest of the night—and we, I suspected, would stay with them.

The militia officers were questioning all those who sought to pass: writing names in little books, comparing lists, and interrupting their futile labors to shout senseless orders that seemed forgotten as soon as given.

As far as we could see in the darkness, on either side were little fires around which crouched a motley throng of armed men who might have been vagrants. Never before had I seen in one place so many ignorant-looking, poverty-stricken fellows. Like the mob at the burning of Henry Wade's house, they were pock-marked, furtive-eyed, slack-lipped, shambling, hoarse-voiced. Their laughter, when they laughed, was abrupt and flat, or like the crackling of thorns beneath a pot.

Many were old, old men; almost as many were boys. There were Negroes among them, and a few Indians with paint-daubed shirts hanging down outside their breeches, according to the peculiar custom of so-called Christian Indians.

A cow had been butchered near us, and men with bloody arms were tossing slabs of meat to a clamoring group whose voices were like the squalling of gulls above a school of herring.

The crowd of refugees in which my father and Andrew and I found ourselves was surrounded by a ring of these strange warriors, and thus, being close to them, I took note of how many were without stockings or shoes; how many, too, seemed misshapen; how many went in actual rags. They stared back at us curiously and contemptuously.

There was something about the long lines of fires, the odor of roasting meat, the smell of wood smoke, the shouting and running of the militia officers, the staring and the hoarse cries of the encircling mob, that gave me the feeling of being out of America and in another land—a different world from that in which I had hitherto spent my life.

In a chaise near us sat a man and a woman with bundles piled high around their feet, and when one of the militia officers thrust a tin lantern close to their faces and demanded their names, he was answered by a voice as sweet as it was gentle.

"Please be kind to us," it said. I saw the lady's clasped hands, and then her pretty profile against the yellow lantern light.

"You'll get the treatment we give everybody," the officer said. "What's your name?"

"Loring," the lady said. "Mrs. Joshua Loring of Dorchester. Oh, sir, you have a wife yourself! You have children! We must go through the gates! We must!"

My father smiled a little. "Elizabeth Loring," he whispered. "If I were a betting man, Oliver, I'd bet all I had that she'll have no trouble getting through."

Everybody who lived in our part of the world knew Loring and his pretty wife. They went, as the saying goes, everywhere; and if ever more than two people gathered at a gaming table at any house where Elizabeth Loring was a guest, Elizabeth Loring was among them.

The militia officer seemed unimpressed by her sweet voice and her pretty face. "My wife and children ain't got anything to do with this," he said. "You'll go through when it's your turn. What's in those bundles?"

"But you don't understand," Mrs. Loring pleaded. "The time's so short and it would be so horrible if anything happened here! Oh, sir——" She caught her breath, and I heard the sound of a smothered sob.

In the dappled light from the lantern, the face of the militia officer was stolid.

"There ain't nothing going to happen to you," he said, "but I got to write down what's in those bundles."

Mrs. Loring gasped and I saw her clutch her side. "Joshua!" she murmured weakly. "I must have a doctor!" She gasped again. "Oh, I feared this! Oh, the shame of it!"

"What's the matter?" the militia officer said.

Mrs. Loring's voice abruptly became shrill. "Matter! You call yourself a man! Nothing going to happen to me, indeed! You good for-nothing hulk! Can't you see what's the matter without being told every last thing? Are you as ignorant as you are blind!" She gasped again, a gasp that was a stifled shadow of a scream. "My poor baby!"

The jaw of the militia officer dropped. "Baby! You ain't——"

"I am, I am! Oh, how can men be such cruel monsters! Haven't you a spark of humanity? What have I done that I should be kept waiting here at such a time as this!" Her sobs were heartbreaking.

The militia officer ran to the gate in the barricades. I heard him shouting. A moment later he hurried back, seized the Lorings' horse by the bridle and dragged it toward the gate.

As the chaise moved forward, Buell darted out from the crowd, seized the bridle of our own mare and jerked us after the Lorings.

Militiamen and refugees alike cursed us; women and children scuttled screaming from almost beneath our wheels; our hubs scraped and thumped against those of other vehicles; but when the Lorings reached the gates, we were close behind. They went safely through, toward Boston; but scores of angry faces gathered around us, and a guard reached over Buell's shoulder to place a rude hand upon our little mare's bridle.

"Let go that rein!" Buell shouted.

"What for?" the guard said. "You got *men* in that carryall! They ain't having babies too, are they?"

Buell seized him by the slack of his coat, and his voice was menacing. "I'll baby you! I've come all the way from Milton with these people tonight, just to take 'em into Boston, and that's what I'm going to do: take 'em into Boston! Earlier today I was out to a place called Lexington, that you fellers probably ain't never been to! Still earlier I was in Concord. Before that I was in Malden. I been marching all day and killing people all day, and I'm tired enough to kill a few more if they bother me. What's more, my feet hurt me, and I've lost all the sleep I'm going to lose over these Tories! I'm going into Boston right now, so I can lay down and get me some sleep. I'd as soon be dead as try to stay awake any longer, and if anybody thinks he's going to keep me standing here, he's damned badly mistaken!"

From his belt he took a pistol, rapped it sharply against his heel to knock powder into the pan, applied his eye to the muzzle to make sure it was loaded; then slapped our mare resoundingly upon the rump.

As we lurched forward, I set my muscles in anticipation of a fusillade of shots from those scarecrow soldiers behind the barricades; but after we had passed the gate and clattered onto the narrow strip of Boston Neck, I heard nothing save the thump of Buell's feet beside us and the clop-clopping of the Lorings' horse just ahead.

When we reached the British fortifications on the Boston end of the Neck, the Lorings' chaise was surrounded by a group of laughing young officers.

"You'd better see if you can help her, Oliver," my father said. "Those officers appear not to understand the situation."

I jumped from the carryall and ran to the Lorings. In the light of the officers' lanterns, Mrs. Loring's smiling face was beautiful. "La!" I heard her cry, "I blushed and blushed at the things I had to say; but I declare I'd have told 'em I was going to have twins—yes, and would have *had* them too, if that were needed to get me into Boston!"

I returned to our carryall and climbed in. "I think that's a lady we needn't worry about," I told my father.

The Lorings' chaise rolled on, and the next moment we took its place with the group of officers about us. When they learned our names, they motioned to us to go on into the city. "Register at headquarters tomorrow," one of them told me. "You've been fortunate. Some of those who came through tonight have had pretty hard treatment."

He turned suddenly on Buell, who was moving wearily beside us toward the open gate just beyond.

"Here, you," he shouted, "get back to those barricades where you belong!"

Buell stopped, passed a hand clumsily over his face, looked surprised at feeling the bandage across his eye, and abruptly pulled it off, disclosing his shining shaved head.

"Me?" he asked. "Me get back to those barricades? Oh no! Those fellers tarred and feathered me two days ago. It's God's wonder they ain't cooking me over their campfires along with their sour salt pork. You give me eight or ten fellers to go back with, and I'll chase the whole rebel army all the way to South Carolina; but if you think I'm going back there alone, you ain't been taught how to do the right kind of thinking!"

CHAPTER VI

Wʜᴀᴛ we'd have done in Boston without Tom Buell, I don't know.

Many of my friends considered him a stormy petrel, a trouble-breeder, a sort of daily herald of disaster, and it's true he'd been the direct cause of our exile from home; yet I've never doubted that my father and I would have been driven from Milton almost as promptly, even though we'd never heard of Buell.

As time went on, I often seemed to be in trouble because of Buell; but in all likelihood I'd have encountered the same troubles if I'd never laid eyes on him again after we passed the British bastions and set off up Orange Street toward the Common and Tremont Street, where our friends lived.

The fact remains that Buell collected the money which so-called patriots of Boston owed my father for his legal services but refused to pay; Buell found food for us when those who had been our friends seemed determined that we should starve; Buell brought me the information that I subsequently used in the second volume of *Civil War in America;* Buell got us a vessel when to have stayed on land meant misery or death, and to have sailed in any other would have resulted in grinding poverty for all of us and a vastly different life for me.

George Leonard was a shipowner who lived near the corner of Queen and Tremont streets; and since my father was his attorney as well as his friend, George Leonard's house was the first one to which we went. We didn't get there till after midnight; but Leonard was still up, and opened the door to me when I banged down the knocker.

He was a red-faced man of about thirty-five, with watery blue eyes and a seaman's clumsy hands; and he lumbered a little in his walk, as though his ankles hurt him. Like everybody else in Boston at that time, he had a chain the size of an anchor cable on his door, so that it opened only a few inches; and when he peered out at me through the crack, I saw he held a pistol in his hand.

Through the narrow opening I told him who I was, and asked whether he would give my father shelter until we found a place to live. Instantly he unfastened the chain, handed me the pistol, ran out to the carryall and lifted my father as though he were no heavier than a child.

"By God, Seaton," he told my father, as he carried him up the steps and into the house, "it looks to me as though everybody in the world was crazy—everybody but us! You don't have to tell me what happened! I know without being told! You've got brains, so they threw you out of your home! Well, that's what they'll do to all of us if they get the chance!"

He stopped at the partly opened door of his sitting room and kicked it open. About a table sat seven men, some in pea jackets; the others in the wrinkled blue coats affected by mariners since time immemorial.

"Here you are, gentlemen," Mr. Leonard cried. "Here's another of 'em: Seaton Wiswell—best lawyer in Massachusetts! Those that aim to govern this country have no use for such men. Always bear that in mind, gentlemen! They'd rather have a Sam Adams, who never did anything successfully except make trouble. Help yourself to the port, gentlemen; I'll be back as soon as I get Mr. Wiswell to bed."

He turned toward the stairs; then went back to the front door, still carrying my father.

"Take your horse and carryall around to the stable," he shouted to Andrew. "You'll find my black man in the kitchen when you've finished. Who's that other man out there?"

Buell rose from the curb, where he'd been sitting, and started off down Queen Street.

"Look out for him," Leonard warned Andrew. "He's probably one of Sam Adams' damned spies!"

Buell stopped abruptly, as if he'd run into a stone wall, and turned to face Leonard. "I ain't had the pleasure of your acquaintance," he said, "but I don't mind saying you look old and fat. If you wasn't, and didn't have a sick man in your arms to boot, I'd pull a leg off you for saying that."

Leonard turned an astonished face toward me.

"That's Tom Buell, a friend of ours," I explained.

"You should 'a' said so," Leonard told me. "We might 'a' had words!" To Buell he added testily, "Well, come in! Come in! Don't stand out there all night!"

Buell gave him a cold answer. "I'll just be moving along."

"Nonsense," Leonard cried. "I like people that don't mind pulling legs off those that accuse 'em of being rebels. Step right in and I'll show you some legs to pull off."

George Leonard carried my father to the third floor, and put him gently on the four-poster that loomed up in that high-ceilinged room almost like a house within a house. Buell, who had followed him all the way, dropped to the floor at the foot of the bed, and seemed instantly to slumber.

Leonard pulled the coverlet over my father. "There you are, Seaton. Your boy'll put you to sleep as snug as a bug in a rug, and this room's yours as long as you want it."

"Thank you, George." The heartiness of my father's voice astounded me—not because of his gratitude to Mr. Leonard, but because of the strong full tone in which he spoke. I'd been all along in an anguish of spirit for fear of what this night journey might do to him; but there was color in his cheeks, his eye was bright, and strangely indeed our wretched adventure seemed to have done him good. Plainly he was better than he had been at any time since my return from New Haven.

My thought had been to find Doctor Miller if I could, but looking at my father, it seemed to me I could postpone that until morning. I had the medicines in my pocket, and set them on a table beside the bed. He glanced at them, looked at me and smiled. "Next dose isn't due till after breakfast," he said. "Perhaps by then I'll have decided to begin sitting up. I told you I was better than Miller thought, didn't I?"

Leonard beamed upon him. "Consider this house your own, Seaton, and don't have hard thoughts of me because I run away from you. You've had a hard day, and I've a deal of business to transact before this night's over."

My father smiled wryly. "I won't impose on your hospitality long, George. I want you to trade me a year's rent of one of your houses in payment for my accumulated fees. We Bostonians like our independence, you know."

Leonard moved back from the bed as though a bee had stung him. "Independence!" he exclaimed. "That's a word you'll wish you'd never heard before the year's out!"

He seemed to forget the business that might occupy him the rest of the night. "Seaton," he whispered, seating himself on the edge of the bed, and wagging a thick forefinger at my father, "we're in for it! Sam Adams and the rest of 'em have been moving up on us for years, all mealy-mouthed, telling how much they loved the King; talking about their fundamental loyalty to the mother country; but they came out in the open today at Concord and Lexington! The truth is, they're loyal to nothing but their own selfish interests; and unless we fight them for our rights, they'll take every last one of those rights away from us. They'll take away our government, our laws, our property, and freedom of thought and speech."

He turned on me. "You're ready to fight 'em, aren't you?"

"Well, sir," I said, "I'd rather not—not till all other methods fail. The British are fair-minded, and if we give 'em time, they'll relieve us of unfair laws. Then Adams and Hancock will agree to a peaceful settlement of everything."

Leonard looked as though he might explode. "'If we give 'em time'! Heavens above, my boy! There's no time left! Before Concord and Lexington there was time for Adams and Hancock to agree to a peaceful settlement; but they've never wanted to, and now they won't! No matter what's offered to Sam Adams now, he'll never be satisfied! He's a perpetual malcontent! He was at the bottom of his class at Harvard because his father was poor; and because of that he hates everyone with property. He can't make money or keep it, so he argues that everyone who can must be dishonest. He was made tax collector of Boston, and lost his position because he ran £10,000 behind in his accounts; so now he hates the government that ousted him! Since he can't save anything, he believes no one should be allowed to save, but that all earnings should be distributed among those who can't earn. Sam Adams is powerful in this province because he tells the malcontents, the incompetents, the lazy, the idle, that they're the only honest people: that they're held down by the wealthy English, the wealthy merchants, the wealthy shipowners. He makes 'em want to kill every Englishman, every shipowner, every merchant, so that they can be wealthy shipowners and merchants themselves!"

He jumped up from the bed and stood beside it, his big hands clenched. "Yes, and look at John Hancock, echoing every word that Adams says! Your father knows what he is—a miserable little over-dressed incompetent. He threw away his father's fortune! He's been treasurer of Harvard College, but he can't account for £15,000 of Harvard's money! He's £100,000 in debt to the government for smug-gling! If he can't overthrow this government and its laws, he'll be ruined! He'll have to pay that £100,000! He'll have to make good his shortage to Harvard! He'll never let this thing be settled peacefully —unless we force him to! Don't tell me you won't help us!"

"Well, sir," I said, "I'd rather not take sides—not just yet, anyway. I've spent the last four years learning how to write history, and if I can write what's going on under my nose, and write it truthfully, I think I ought to do it."

"Good grief!" Leonard cried. "Writing'll do you no good! You've had your house and land taken from you already, haven't you? You'll never get them back without fighting! You saw those seven men downstairs. They're sea captains. You know what I'm doing with the money I've made these past fifteen years? I'm putting every cent into all the ships I can buy—seven armed ships! I've hired those seven captains to sail 'em, and I'll fill 'em with guns that can shoot and men that know how to lay 'em, and then I'll send 'em out to try to keep Sam Adams and his friends from starving us to death—which is what they'll do if they can! If all of us should sit in a corner, mak-ing hen tracks with a pen, what do you think will happen to our country and to us?"

My father rose on his elbow, and for the first time since I came home there was an eager light in his face, and on his lips the smile that all the justices in Massachusetts knew so well. "Every man's entitled to his opinion, George. I'll be against the Sons of Liberty to my dying day because they say we're not entitled to our opinions; and so, I hope, will Oliver. But I'll never take a leaf out of their book, and I trust Oliver won't. I'll never use force to try to make my enemies think the way I think, George—partly because I don't be-lieve in it, and partly because it's useless. You can't destroy ideas by force, and you can't hide 'em by silence."

Leonard spoke contemptuously. "You're dodging the issue!"

"Let me finish," my father said. "Oliver doesn't want to resort to arms, and he has a reason for it. He wants to tell the truth about what's happening; and as I see it, such an occupation will be of more benefit to humanity than a red-faced general who sends a thousand men up the wrong side of a hill with no results except to rob a few hundred women of husbands. Don't be too hard on him, George. Don't behave like a Son of Liberty!"

"If any child of mine refused to fight," Leonard growled, "I'd——"

Buell groaned, rose to his knees and clung to the footboard of the bed, staring at us with bleary eyes. "For God's sake," he said, "can't a feller get a little sleep?"

He rubbed his shaved head, stared in surprise at his hand, then got to his feet and faced George Leonard. "Oliver Wiswell saved me from a mob two nights ago," he said, "and that ought to entitle him to do what he wants to for a little while. I don't aim to write anything, and seeing as how Oliver helped me a good deal, I'm willing to do a little something for him. I'll do my own fighting, and when I'm through, I'll do some for Oliver, and glad to do it. You might say that'll be better than having the two of us fight, because I'll only take up half the room that two men'll take up, and since I'll be working for both of us, I'll naturally fight twice as hard as I ordinarily would if I was alone."

Mr. Leonard looked baffled. "How's that?"

Buell coughed dryly. "What I'm getting at is that the three of us, one a good friend of yours, made a long trip from Milton just because a lot of your enemies took a dislike to us; and now *you're* taking a dislike to us too. In fact, it looks to me as if you planned to throw us out on the street. Mr. Wiswell's too sick for that, Mr. Leonard, and if you want to know what I think——"

Leonard's voice was bitter. "I don't! A man that won't fight against the riffraff that's put an end to government and business in this country doesn't belong under this roof!"

He turned back to my father. "Seaton, I don't believe that you and your son know what they've done to friends of ours! Do you know they've mobbed clergymen like Henry Caner of King's Chapel, William McGilchrist of St. Peter's in Salem, Joshua Wingate Weeks of Marblehead? Do you know they've mobbed almost every Harvard man who's been admitted to the Massachusetts Bar—Jonathan Bliss, Andrew Cazneau, Ward Chipman, William Brown of the Superior Court, Samuel Fitch of the Advocate Court, Jonathan Sewall the attorney general, Timothy Ruggles, Speaker of the House, Daniel

Leonard, Martin Howard, the chief justice of North Carolina, Judge William Brattle, Sampson Blowers who defended Captain Preston, Daniel Bliss, Robert Auchmuty, and fifty others I could name?"

My father stared at him sadly. "You tell me they're driving out every good man they've got?"

Leonard slapped the coverlet angrily. "Every last one! They've even turned on every physician and surgeon of prominence—Dr. James Lloyd and Dr. Nathaniel Perkins; Dr. Samuel Stearns and Dr. William Paine; Dr. John Jeffries and Dr. William Lee Perkins; Dr. John Calef, Dr. Thomas Bolton, Dr. Joseph Adams, Dr. Samuel Danforth, Dr. John Joy, Dr. Michael Goldthwait, Dr. Miles Whitworth, Dr. Benjamin Loring. Every damned one of 'em's in Boston, Seaton, property seized, goods destroyed, families insulted! Why, my God, Seaton, I could go on all night naming merchants, soldiers, printers, ship captains, country gentlemen, officers of the Crown that have been chivied out of Salem, Marblehead, Dedham, Worcester—why, John Chandler and his whole family, all the sons—all the Chandlers— were treated like dogs by the Worcester mobs! Yes, sir: the finest men we've got have been thrown out of every town in this state, and most of 'em are right in Boston tonight, half of 'em dependent on charity already, and they're not the hundredth part of the people who've suffered for thinking the way we think!"

"Not the hundredth part?" my father asked, and something in the tone of his voice made me look at him quickly. His lips were twisted a little, and at the corner of his mouth was the merest faint beginning of a wry smile. "Why isn't this known, George? Why haven't we heard of all these outrages?"

"Why?" Leonard said. "Why? Because the Sons of Liberty won't let the news be published! Because they make themselves heard, and we don't! Because we're silent from inclination as well as from necessity, hoping to be allowed to live in peace—hoping the storm'll blow over. And all the time Sam Adams is out on the street corners, behind that soup-stained weskit of his, yowling about the boys who want liberty or death! To hear him talk, anybody'd think there isn't a soul on the American continent who doesn't think just the way he thinks. But he's a liar, Seaton! For every two of Sam Adams' Liberty Boys there's three of us, only we're such idiots that we keep our mouths shut while Sam Adams stuffs the people with lies that gag an honest man."

"I see," my father said slowly. "We aren't getting the truth. Well,

George, if ever a situation needed a man able to recognize the truth and trained to write it, this one does." Upon this I understood the subtle wry smile that had been for a moment at the corner of my father's mouth.

Leonard groaned. "You never said a truer word, Seaton! Why——" He stopped abruptly, made a grumbling noise, stared angrily at my father, scratched his jaw and looked absent-mindedly at the ceiling.

Buell yawned. "What happened to all those judges and doctors?" he asked. "I'd certainly like to know what was done to 'em. Yes, and there's two or three other things I'd like Oliver to write about at the same time. You take this taxation without representation that the Liberty Boys are always hollering about: something ought to be said about that. Oliver, when you're telling the truth about what's done to those of us who believe in law instead of liberty, tell those lunatics what'll happen to 'em if they get a good war tied to their necks. You saw the fellers out at the barricades tonight, and you could tell the kind of men they were just as well as I could. They'd steal the pennies off a dead man's eyes! Well, if you use fellers like that to fight a war, you'll have to pay 'em all the money in the world to get 'em to fight, won't you? And to get that money, you'll have to tax everybody that's got a penny, won't you? And those that get elected to Congress won't have any, will they? They will not! So the fellers who're taxed to pay for the war, they'll be taxed without being represented, won't they? Just remind 'em of a few of those things, Oliver. They won't believe you, but it's the truth, so you'll have to remind 'em just the same. Why, those fellers don't know *nothing* about taxation without representation—not yet they don't; but they'll know plenty when they begin to pay for a war!"

He yawned again. "I'm kind of afraid Mr. Leonard won't finish that business of his downstairs unless we stop talking and let him do what he's got to do."

He spoke more gratefully. "Sometimes, Mr. Leonard, I get to thinking there ain't anybody in the world who isn't a scoundrel and a murderer, and then somebody turns around and behaves so kind to me that I'm ashamed of myself for having hard thoughts for anyone. Here's Oliver Wiswell took me in when it was as much as his life was worth to do it; and now here's Mr. George Leonard giving me a place to stay in a city I always thought was pretty hardhearted."

George Leonard, embarrassed, made inarticulate and contemptuous sounds. To my father he said, "Well, Seaton, make yourself at home and we'll see you have what you want as soon as you get your strength back."

He glared at me, nodded brusquely, half swallowed the words "Good night, my boy," and stumped noisily down the stairs.

CHAPTER VII

THE house to which George Leonard took us, when my father was able to be about again, was on the high land of Sudbury Street, and from its front steps we looked across the Mill Pond and the blue waters of the Charles River to the near-by hills of Charlestown—hills so close that I could see the color of the cows that fed upon those grassy slopes.

Leonard had been uncommunicative about the house until we were in his carriage and on our way to it. "Strictly speaking, Seaton," Leonard said, "I suppose it isn't what you want; but there's no doubt in my mind that if you can give satisfaction, it's what you ought to have."

"Give satisfaction!" my father exclaimed. "Give satisfaction to whom!" Then he smiled. "I suspect, George, that you're undertaking to plan the rest of my life for me. Don't people go wrong when they plan somebody else's whole future?"

Leonard's voice was scornful. "You wouldn't say that if you knew my aunt Ora."

"So that's it!" my father said. "You're taking us to your aunt Ora's house! I've never had the pleasure of meeting your aunt Ora, but from your terse mention of her it's clear that she'll take a deal of pleasing. Do you think, George, that if I should live under the same roof with your aunt Ora, I'd be free to speak as I wish? Remember, George, the Sons of Liberty have already robbed me of so much freedom that I can't risk losing more."

Leonard looked disturbed. "Seaton, I'm doing the best I can. Wait till you see Aunt Ora. She can be right nice to anyone she happens to take to—indeed she can! You see, damn it, Seaton, living quarters aren't easy to find in this city. Think of the crowd that's been driven in! Why, these past two months there's been more'n a hundred people would have taken up quarters in this house if Aunt Ora hadn't been in it!"

"I see, George. You mean more than a hundred drew the line at Aunt Ora?"

"Yes, but only because she didn't seem to take to 'em, Seaton. When she doesn't take to you, she's got kind of a way of antagonizing you, I admit; but look how it was! She got chased out of Cambridge herself, and being she's my own mother's sister, I naturally put her in the best house I own. I wouldn't have dared not to. Once I'd done that, the house was hers, and I wouldn't consider putting anyone in with her that she didn't take to—and neither would she."

"I see," my father said. "You didn't feel it would be for the best to take her into your own house, George?"

Leonard was aghast. "Into my own house? No, Seaton! I didn't feel it would be for the best at all! Aunt Ora married a Byles—Professor Belcher Byles of Harvard—but she was a Barrell: a Salem Barrell. You know as well as I do the Salem Barrells were shipowners, like me, and look at all the ship captains that come traipsing into my house every day! I can't have trouble with my ship captains, Seaton! Why, there never was even a mere child of a Salem Barrell that couldn't ask more questions about ships in a day than a Jamaica nigger mate could think up in a week! And do ship captains like all those questions being asked of 'em, either by a nigger or by a woman? I got to keep peace with my captains, Seaton! You ought to be able to see for yourself I couldn't put Aunt Ora in there! An owner's got to have *some* regard for the men he employs."

My father looked up at the pleasant sky. "Of course, George. Could you lend us this coach and your horses and driver an hour longer than you expected to? A whim's come over me. I've just got the notion I'd like to take lodgings on the opposite side of town. I'm sure we could find——"

Leonard protested loudly. "I won't hear of it! This house of mine I'm taking you to is as nice a place as there is in the whole of Boston, and Aunt Ora doesn't use any of it except the lower floor. The truth is, Seaton, she's only a woman, and needs protection. If all the rest of the house stays empty, General Gage is likely to billet British soldiers all over the upper part of it, and if that happened, I doubt if Aunt Ora'd stay there. If she had soldiers billeted on her, you can't tell where she might take a notion to come; it might prove mighty interfering. Besides, I want you to have the best I've got."

My father continued to look at the sky, and his expression seemed to worry Leonard, who became more earnestly persuasive.

"Your son tells me you're better, but you aren't a well man yet," he urged. "You need a woman near you; but if you got not to liking it, why of course she'd be all the way downstairs, and it's a well-built house. When you're upstairs you can't hear anything that goes on down below. You'll be mighty comfortable on the upper floor of this house of mine, Seaton.

"If these rebels aren't put in their place mighty soon, things won't be comfortable in Boston or anywhere else. If such things are going to happen, you owe it to yourself and to your son to be as comfortable as you can; and you'd be mighty comfortable with Aunt Ora."

I doubted that my father was persuaded of approaching great comfortableness, but he made no further protest when the carriage stopped before the house on Sudbury Street and Leonard, motioning to me to bring my father, stamped up the steps and banged down the knocker.

We were admitted by a wisp of a female servant whom Leonard addressed familiarly as Maggie; and while we waited in the front parlor, Maggie trotted up and down the hallway carrying glowing coals on a shovel and dropping pinches of powdered cloves on them, so that the house was filled with a spicy fragrance.

The room was a pleasant one, furnished with stiff-looking chairs that surprisingly were comfortable, and a wealth of small tables on which were displayed miniatures, snuffboxes, patch boxes, paper weights, perfume bottles, fans and seals.

Above the mantel was a portrait of a sharp-eyed man whose expression was disapproving, while his nose and cheeks hinted that one more bottle of wine before he sat for his picture would have brought them to the same hue as his plum-colored coat.

Leonard jerked his thumb at the painting, and his lips formed the word: "Belcher."

"What?" said my father.

"Belcher Byles." Leonard explained. "That she's the widow of. Mr. Copley took this picture of him. It's the spit 'n' image of Belcher! Never could teach his pupils at Harvard right unless he had three bottles of port in him. She's proud of the portrait. Mention it to her if you get a chance. Kind of softens her up."

From the hall came a slow and measured tapping; and at the sound George Leonard, shipowner and employer of seven sea captains, sat guiltily erect in his chair, his eyes downcast, and upon his face a look of virtue.

The tapping stopped and the door into the hallway opened. The lady who stood there was small in stature; yet she seemed to project herself enormously into the room, as though some inner force surged ahead of her insignificant body. Her cheeks were round and pink, her brown eyes sharp; and small lines at the corners of her straight lips seemed to indicate inflexible resignation. I thought of her as old when I first saw her; but beneath the lacy cap upon her head her hair was a glossy brown; and I soon suspected that the melonlike protuberance of her stomach was due less to her too, too solid flesh than too many petticoats. Her dress was gray satin; on her plump arms and hands were black lace mitts; her stick, with which she rapped sharply upon the floor when she greeted George Leonard, was of ebony tipped with ivory.

"Aunt Ora," Leonard said, rising, "I've brought Mr. Seaton Wiswell and his son to see you and your nice house. Excuse Mr. Wiswell for not getting up. He's been sick. They drove him away from his home in Milton." He coughed. "They like Uncle Belcher's picture, Aunt Ora."

Mrs. Byles nodded at us grimly, tapped the floor sharply with her stick. "George," she said, "this may be a nice house, but these fireplaces eat wood as if it was paper. Every room but the kitchen is colder than Greenland, and if you don't get us some wood immediately, we won't even be able to cook. Even if you *do* get it, we'll probably freeze."

She turned a defiant stare on my father. "What's everybody coming to Boston for? Why all of 'em should rush to live in Boston is more than I can understand! East wind, dust, rebels, no heat, east wind, all the human riffraff west of Greenwich, and more east wind! I haven't been warm since Belcher died!"

My father cleared his throat. "As Mr. Leonard says, my son and I have been admiring Mr. Copley's portrait of your learned husband— one of his very best, I should say. Intellect in a sitter seemed to add magic colors to his palette."

Mrs. Byles looked up at the painting. "I never noticed that purple look about Belcher's nose until Copley painted it. Belcher was a very busy man, and we went a great deal, socially. I hardly saw

Belcher in the flesh till we were in bed together, and then it was too dark to see the color of his nose, of course. When Copley finished Belcher, he wanted to do me, too; but I wouldn't run the risk—not after that purple nose."

My father glanced at the portrait through half-closed eyes. "It's really not purple," he said. "The flesh tones, of course, are rich. You'll see the same thing in the portraits of many of the English noble families."

He picked up a fan from the table beside him. "Would this by any chance be a Carlo Van Loo?"

Mrs. Byles looked discontented. "I don't know. My mother brought it back from France after one of her voyages. She was a Barrell."

"Indeed," my father said. "Salem is indebted to your family, Mrs. Byles. I think a great deal of Salem's excellent taste in art and architecture was due to your family and one or two others."

Mrs. Byles looked haughtily at George Leonard; but he was staring at the ceiling, seemingly wrapped in thought. "Salem has its advantages," she told my father, "even in the winter. It's warmer than Boston, and I'd have gone to Salem after my trouble in Cambridge, but chose Boston because my nephew lives here. People ought to go where they have relatives."

She fixed my father with a speculative eye. "I suppose you're looking for a place to live."

"Yes," my father admitted. "I hoped to find a house to myself, but George thinks that's not easy, so perhaps I'd best throw myself on the mercy of Ward Chipman or some other brother lawyer. Lawyers can sometimes get on together, whereas separately they may be difficult for other people to endure—perhaps the most difficult."

Mrs. Byles' eyes strayed to the portrait of her husband. "Do you think so indeed! I'd say all men are hard to get along with. I doubt that lawyers are worse than soldiers or painters or college professors —and of course they can't help but be better than drapers or other tradesmen."

My father shook his head sadly. "No, Mrs. Byles; it's a lawyer's nature to quibble. We like arguments. We lean toward the letter of the law. There's no doubt about it: lawyers ought to live by themselves."

Mrs. Byles examined the ivory head of her stick. "Probably you're right. There's nothing I dislike as much as arguments. I make it a rule never to argue: never! I say what I think, and there's an end of it; and so I'll say this, Mr. Wiswell: If you go out and get one or two rooms in one of the only neighborhoods where there are any left, you'll never have a moment's peace! You'll hear nothing but mobs careering through the streets; drunken soldiers bellowing at each other; carts banging over the cobbles, and Sam Adams' helpers hurroaring and hurrooing about the rights of man—rights they're bound nobody but themselves shall have!"

"It's not a pleasant prospect," my father admitted, "but I'm afraid there's nothing else to be done."

"Mr. Wiswell," Mrs. Byles said earnestly, "you'll be far more comfortable on high land in this city than in the lowlands. The hills are healthier. Now, you take this house here: We're high up, overlooking the harbor and the river. It's cool in summer, and not as cold in winter as it might be. I never saw an easier house to heat, and it's even quieter than Cambridge, which is almost the same as saying it's quiet as a vacuum."

My father looked baffled. "I was under the impression you said the fireplaces burned a vast deal of wood."

Mrs. Byles tossed her head. "And why not? Did you ever know a fireplace that didn't? To tell you the truth, Mr. Wiswell, I slept badly last night. I often do, without a man in the house. I may have spoken hastily about those fireplaces, but the truth is that our fireplaces in Cambridge burned three times as much wood as these do. If you wanted to live here, you could have the whole of the upper floor. You could——"

"But Mrs. Byles," my father said, "you know very little about my son and me."

Mrs. Byles thumped her stick upon the floor and rose quickly. "No, I don't want to take the chance any longer that soldiers may be intruded upon me here. There's fish chowder and chocolate custards for supper, and you and your son shall share 'em with me."

CHAPTER VIII

THAT was how we began to make our home with Mrs Belcher Byles.

Our greatest concern, for a time, was how to obtain enough food to feed all of us. The town was crowded not only with refugees, but with British soldiers. Fourteen foot-regiments as well as several companies of artillery—a matter of five thousand men jammed in among a population of ten thousand—were housed in barracks, warehouses and tents on every part of the little peninsula on which Boston was built.

The streets were crowded with British officers; there were so many of them that at times it seemed to me a sizable army could have been recruited from officers alone—an army large enough to defeat any military force that could have been raised by the rebels in the surrounding country.

In view of the dark looks and vituperative remarks directed toward officers and men alike by the rag, tag, and bobtail of the city, I'm bound to say that these Britishers behaved as well as any men could; but they made living difficult for the rest of us, because they bought up so much provisions that the prices of everything were beyond the reach of those who had no British gold.

The uncomfortable fact was that my father and I, not to speak of Andrew and poor Buell (we brought him in too upon Mrs. Byles), had no money at all; for there had been little enough in our house when we had been forced to leave it, and it just happened that my father's illness found him with the bulk of his accounts uncollected, and most of his savings invested in ventures to Spain and the Sugar Islands. A large part of his clients were Milton men; and many of these, unfortunately, had been treated like ourselves—had fled from their homes to Boston for shelter, and had as little as we. A few of his best accounts, it is true, were in Boston; and to one of the gentlemen who thus owed him, I went as soon as we were settled on Sudbury Street.

His name was Ezra Jeffers and he was an owner of warehouses and tenements in the poorer parts of Boston. In spite of his wealth, he wasn't a citizen of whom Boston could be proud; but he had relatives who were even worse than he, and my father had protected him when those relatives had tried to break a will in which an uncle had left him a large estate.

I found him in the counting room of his biggest warehouse at the foot of Hammett's Wharf. Two young clerks sat at high desks opposite the door, and Mr. Jeffers lurked behind them in a low chair, like a spider peering out between two captive flies. His eyes were cavernous under bushy gray brows; and his lips, pursed by nature, took on an acidulous pucker when I stated my errand.

"These are hard times, Mr. Wiswell," he said, "and this request of yours is mighty sudden: mighty sudden! Seems strange your father never presented a bill in all these months, and now wants the whole of it in a minute!"

"Well, sir," I said, "he had to present it sometime, of course, and today seems as good to him as any other."

"Hm," Mr. Jeffers said. "I suppose you got some kind of document authorizing you to collect this account?"

Fortunately my father, knowing Jeffers, had foreseen the possibility of some such demand, and had given me a letter making me his agent. When I silently handed it to Mr. Jeffers, he adjusted a pair of eight-sided spectacles, and read it with a face that grew sourer and sourer.

"This here's dated from Sudbury Street," he said, handing the letter back to me. "That's something new, ain't it? Always lived in Milton, haven't you?"

"Yes," I said, "we lived in Milton—until recently."

"When did you move into Boston?" Jeffers asked.

"About a week ago."

"Have some trouble out in Milton?"

"Well, in a way," I admitted, "but it was a mistake. There's not a more patriotic man in this country than my father; yet the men that made trouble for us called themselves patriots. I'm putting it mildly, Mr. Jeffers, when I say they behaved shamefully."

Jeffers grinned. "No doubt, no doubt! Now I'll tell you, Mr. Wiswell: money's mighty scarce these days: mighty scarce! I can't spare a penny just now; but when things get better, I'll let your father have as much as I can afford."

"Mr. Jeffers," I said, and my gorge rose at having to beg for something that by rights belonged to us, "Mr. Jeffers, my father's in need. He needs food, and he needs medicines."

"I'm sorry to hear it," Jeffers said. "I certainly am sorry to hear it. Seems as though a man like your father'd have plenty of friends he could borrow from. Seems like most of the money in this town belongs to them that sympathize with the British."

"Well, sir," I said, "I didn't come here to have a political discussion, so I'll only say that my father doesn't sympathize with the British any more than with anyone else; but he sympathizes with government as against anarchy; with the Constitution as against mob rule."

"Ain't that being a Tory?" Jeffers, almost openly looking cunning, spoke sharply. "That's Toryism, ain't it?"

"Not according to any definition I ever heard," I said. "Toryism isn't preserving a government and resisting rebellion; but that's neither here nor there, Mr. Jeffers. My father made it possible for you to obtain your uncle's estate intact. His bill's a small one, considering what he saved you; and he'd take it mighty kind, Mr. Jeffers, if you could just let him have a little on account."

Jeffers shook his head. "I ain't obliged to pay a debt to a Tory, and there ain't any legal way he can make me." He glanced at my face, went hastily to the high desk of one of his clerks and picked up a heavy ruler.

Arguments, I saw, were useless; recriminations a waste of time. I put on my hat and left that miserable place, wretched to have failed, and ashamed of myself for having descended to a kind of wheedling.

At Mrs. Byles' I climbed dejectedly to my room, determined to find a better way of approaching the rest of my father's debtors; and while I sat at my desk, wondering how to state my case so that I wouldn't be suspected of Tory leanings, I heard Buell's footstep upon the stair and called to him to come in.

"Tom," I said, "this town has some horrid people in it."

"Only horrid, Oliver? I guess it has worse than that. I guess it's got more worse-than-horrid people in it, man for man, than almost any place there is, except maybe Newport and perhaps New York and Norwich, Connecticut. They're the only other places I really know. More indigestible food, too; I mean indigestible by me. As for the people, I've been watching 'em on the streets the last few days, cursing and spitting at everybody that's got on decent clothes, and I'm pretty near ready to get one or two of 'em off alone somewhere and make a few pointed remarks. What particular one did you see today that you think's horrid, and is probably worse than you think?"

While I told him about Jeffers, he thrust out his underlip and stared at it so fixedly that I feared his eyes might remain permanently crossed.

When I had finished, he seemed wholly unmoved.

"That Jeffers don't sound like anybody to worry over," he said. "Why, he's got a little property, most likely! The ones I don't like are them that don't have nothing. You just can't do anything with them at all."

He didn't even want to discuss Jeffers, and seemed more interested in telling me about the Loyalist regiments which were being formed to patrol the streets of Boston and defend citizens and soldiers alike from the insults and attacks of mobs.

"There's four regiments of 'em," he said—"The Loyal Americans, the Loyal Legion, the Loyal Fencibles and the Loyal Something-or-other. Colonel Timothy Ruggles, that fought in the Old French Wars, is going to have charge of 'em. I thought maybe I might enlist in one of 'em, if only I could be free of interfering officers and army rules. If you're connected with an army, as near as I can make out, you can't shoot at anybody without you get orders to, and I ain't so sure right now I'm willing to wait that long.

"Now you take these Boston mobs: they ain't tied down by rules and regulations; nobody's responsible for anything they do; and they ain't answerable to officers. They don't have to stand up in a line and be shot at, and they don't have to wait for an official war or a regular battle if they want to kill somebody. They just go and shoot him any time they feel like it; and then some important feller like Sam Adams, who got 'em started shooting in the first place, says Oh my! Oh my! He ain't sure they should 'a' done it! Right in spite of his regret the feller that was shot stays shot, which was what was intended of him to do.

"No, Oliver: the more I think of having to do what somebody else wants me to do, and whenever he happens to want me to do it, the less I like it. Then again, these officers around here don't excite me any. I don't believe they're much good, and it strikes me as nonsense to run the risk of letting someone who ain't much good tell you what to do—not if you get killed because he's been kind of mistaken. How's that for reasoning?"

"I think it's sound," I said. "Military men aren't much different from men in other walks of life. There aren't many really able lawyers or writers or tailors or King's ministers or cooks or college tutors in this world—as we had occasion to know in Yale—and soldiers certainly aren't an exception to the rule."

Buell looked relieved. "That's just what I think! You take these British officers: they're nice-looking young fellers, but you ought to hear some of the things they're saying about that Lexington fight. They're saying that the rebels who attacked 'em shot at 'em from behind trees and stone walls instead of coming out in the open and getting killed like good soldiers would, and got a right to. It appears to me those officers are arguing that the main duty of a soldier in action is to get killed, instead of to kill, and that argument kind of deters me from struggling to become a soldier. This young Lord Percy, I heard that he says the rebels were pretty smart to keep out of sight the way they did, but it seems he's the only one who holds to that theory. He's a real nice feller, young Lord Percy is; but the rest of 'em look to me as if they didn't know sour grapes! They're old soldiers, too, who've been in the business ever since their fathers bought 'em commissions to keep 'em from getting arrested; and if they're that thick-witted about soldiering, how much are all these new soldiers, that're just beginning to learn soldiering, going to know?"

He scratched his head. "Then there's the matter of food to be considered. If I got into any kind of a regiment, I'd have to eat whatever food the rest of the regiment was eating, and that'd probably be worse for me than getting shot. These commissaries that sell food to the army have to get the worst meat they can find, and charge the army high prices for it, or else they wouldn't be getting rich, like a commissary has to. Bad food makes me low in my mind; and if I got indigestion enough, I might get so unhappy I'd shoot somebody, orders or no orders, and it'd be just as likely as not to be the wrong person and get me hanged. I'm just weighing the pros and cons, Oliver. The pros look awful weak."

He rose to his feet and yawned. "Speaking of food, it looks to me as if your father isn't getting the sort of vittles he ought to have. Codfish is all right in its way, but we had it sixteen different ways last week. We had it broiled, baked, stewed, fried, creamed, mashed with potatoes, and cold. We've had cods' cheeks, tongues-and-sounds, and fish-head chowder. That's sixteen, ain't it? Anyhow, we've had it every way except raw, and used every part of it except the eyes, liver and scales; but the way I felt last night, I was suspicious they'd been in too, in that codfish hash she gave us. Felt to me like eyes coming up. It appears to me an invalid like your father ought to have something more tasty and nourishing than codfish! Andrew ought to get your father a nice leg of lamb or a good fat turkey."

As an afterthought he added, "A man was telling me that down in Virginia they smoke turkeys like ham, and that they're real good for weak stomachs. I bet if I could have some smoked turkey, I'd feel like a new man."

"Turkey!" I exclaimed. "Leg of lamb! Do you know what leg of lamb is quoted at today? You have to pay a whole guinea for a leg of lamb! Twenty-one shillings!"

Buell looked thoughtful. "That's a lot of money for anything smaller than a cow; but if your father needs it, I should think you'd be willing to pay even that much."

"I would," I said, "and gladly; but the truth is we're pretty near the end of our rope. I hoped to be able to get twenty-five pounds from Jeffers today, but I didn't; and what's more, I'm beginning to be afraid I'm not going to be able to collect from any of my father's creditors. We can't hide the fact from 'em that we've been driven out of Milton, and that means we have no standing in the law courts, even if the mobs had left us any law courts to appeal to. What's worse, Sam Adams keeps reminding people like Jeffers that if they'll make this country independent of England, they'll never have to pay their debts to Englishmen or to anybody they can claim is on the English side."

Buell coughed with singular dryness—a habit of his, I'd learned, when he was contemplating something outrageous or incubating an idea that meant serious trouble for somebody. "Just let me look at that list of people that owe your father money. I'm busy today, on account of having to make me a few pairs of Perkins' Metallic Tractors; but if I ain't busy tomorrow, I'll try to get around and call on one or two of 'em."

"I don't believe it'll do us any good, Tom."

"Well, it won't do any harm to try," he said. "Where's the list?"

Buell was missing all the next day, and the following night as well, but on the morning of the second day Andrew came to me to say he'd just found him asleep in the stable.

I went to see, and found Buell with his head pillowed on a sack, bulky with what it contained. His mouth was wide open, and from it came snores that sounded like a stick drawn rapidly along the palings of a fence. His chin, cheeks, and upper lip were dark with soot, so that in a dim light he seemed to have a two-weeks' growth of beard. From under his hat hung the lank hair of an ancient and uncombed wig, and he wore a coat I had never seen before—a dark greatcoat vastly too large for him, beneath which his body looked strangely swollen. To wake him I put my hand on his protruding stomach, which felt knobby and hard as a rock but still had sensation, for he choked in the middle of a snore.

"Don't shoot," he said heavily, sat up partly, then lay back and let his head rest peacefully upon his sack again.

"Are you sick, Tom?" I asked. "Are you hurt? Has somebody been shooting at you?"

He opened his eyes. "Not to speak of," he said. "Last night I felt kind of bad because I didn't have a horse and carryall when Jeffers' place was torn down; but I feel all right now."

"Jeffers' place torn down?" I asked. "Who tore it down?"

Buell unbuttoned his greatcoat and exhibited four dead chickens like a feathered cuirass upon his chest. "Why," he said, "it seems Jeffers wrote a letter to General Gage, offering to sell him some supplies for the army—foolish thing to do in times like this. Somebody dropped the letter and it got picked up by one of the Sons of Liberty, so the Sons went down to Jeffers' warehouse last night and broke in. I happened to be passing just as they busted the door off the hinges, and I picked up a few things for fear they might be destroyed by the wrong people. Then there was a butcher shop next door, and somehow I seemed to find myself in there by mistake. Anyway, I was all confused, and after I left I seemed to have these chickens on me."

He looked depressed. "I couldn't find a turkey, but I picked up this sack in Jeffers' place to keep it from getting all stepped on; and when I wandered away from the butcher shop, I was surprised to find a leg of lamb and a few other odds and ends in it."

From his pocket he took the list I had given him two days before. "Here," he said, "you might as well keep this. Nothing's happened yet to the other people on it, but I took the liberty of crossing out Jeffers' name. I heard somewhere he owned the building the butcher shop was in, and the butcher owed him for rent; so as Jeffers owed your father, whatever I did in my wanderings here and there, it makes a case of complete justice."

Toward the middle of May all of us who hoped to see a peaceful settlement of our differences with England were heartened by the arrival of three great soldiers—General William Howe, General Sir Henry Clinton and General John Burgoyne. General Howe had led men up the steep cliffs of the St. Lawrence to the Plains of Abraham and helped capture Quebec for Wolfe; and it was his brother, young Lord Howe, who had been the idol of provincials and regulars alike in the Old French War, and had been killed during Abercrombie's blundering attempt to capture Ticonderoga.

With such men to lead the British troops, every law-abiding Bostonian agreed, it would be a simple matter to disperse the noisy, slovenly, argumentative militiamen who had surrounded Boston, and whose laughable bickerings and unruly departures from camp were common knowledge.

The stories of the insubordination and independence of those citizen soldiers were almost beyond belief. All the men in the ranks, we heard, considered themselves—probably rightly—the equal of their officers. At any rate, it was true that they argued endlessly against any commands of which they disapproved. Numbers of them were continually picking up their scanty belongings and marching off to their homes, sometimes with their officers and sometimes without them; and when ordered to proceed to a certain spot, they more likely than not straggled off somewhere in the opposite direction.

With distinguished officers, veterans of many hard-fought campaigns, to lead the well-trained British troops, it was a certainty that those hobbledehoy battalions could be dispersed whenever General Howe decided it ought to be done.

I hoped it would be soon; for Boston, after the peaceful beauty of Milton, was, for me, a sort of purgatory; and I longed to escape from it as a man longs to escape from behind prison bars. How I longed to escape from it, no one can understand, unless he be, by chance, a young man wholly in love with the girl from whom he has been parted suddenly and strangely. To make my feelings worse, I dared not write her for fear an intercepted letter from me might, as Vose Leighton had sent word to my father, bring her under suspicion of sympathizing with the hated ones who dared oppose the mobs. My craving to hear from her was at times a gnawing pain, and I wondered unhappily whether the strength of the barricades was the reason that no word from her came through those barriers to me.

Again and again, mobs were in the streets all night long, daring the British to stop them. In broad daylight tumults were forever breaking out between the lawless ones and those who strove to keep order. At one moment a street might be as peaceful as a graveyard; then without warning a hatless man would burst from a doorway— or out of an alley, or even crash bloodily out through a window —with half a dozen other ruffians in full cry after him, and go pelting off out of sight, leaving nobody the wiser as to what had happened, or what might become of the poor wretch who was being pursued.

The streets were hot and dusty; the horses, lacking proper fodder now that the rebels had forbidden the bringing of it into the town, were scrawny and unkempt. Children had a sickly, greenish look, which may have been due to the long winter through which they had lately passed, or the result of not enough food and that bad.

Every day people whose sympathies lay with the rebels left the town for fear of what might happen to them when the British finally sallied out across the Neck and put those scarecrow troops to rout; and every day more and more of those who refused to be dictated to by mobs, ignorant committees and rabble-rousers came pouring across the Neck and up Orange Street.

I spent half my time in the South End, watching those poor people come in—whole families of them: people of education, refinement and substance; their goods piled in carryalls or farm wagons or even wheelbarrows; women in silks, helping servants drag the family linen, silver and portraits to a place of safety; men of standing, looked up to for decades as the wisest and most reliable in their communities, but now scuttling like harried animals to the shelter of the King's guns.

I took down the names and experiences of scores of these refugees; and the more cases I accumulated the more I boiled within at
the inhumanity of fanatics who could wrench fellow men by brute
force from their homes and drive them into strange surroundings
to starve and die.

There was something shocking about the change that came upon
those people as soon as they found themselves safe and sound on
the Boston side of the barricades; their unutterable relief was so
visible. You could see color come back into their faces; you could hear
gaspings as they dared to breathe again. Usually they were silent
until they'd left the barricades some distance behind them; then as
they found themselves in Boston streets they became loudly gar-
rulous.

The women chattered and laughed shrilly; and the men were gaily
talkative, as men are when they find themselves still alive and well
after some narrow escape. The loss of their houses and belongings
hadn't had time to be realized, and so didn't yet distress them. In
these first moments of safety they took it lightly that they were coming almost penniless into a town where lodgings were scarce and
food was precious. Weight was off them; they were haggardly joy-
ous in their relish of the freedom to think once more as they wished
and to speak as they thought.

Yes, I hoped that General Howe would strike soon. I hated the
town, its noises, its smells; hated the ever-present feeling of hidden
hostile men lurking all around us. I wanted to get my father out
of this place where we might actually starve if anything happened
to Thomas Buell. Even more than that, I had a yearning for home
and for those blue hills and green meadows and woods that had always been as much a part of my life as my father himself had been.

Another way of saying this might be for me to say again that I was
sore with homesickness—that I was constantly homesick for Sally.
My need of her was like a continuing physical pain, sharper than
hunger.

Almost inextricably mingled with the quick pictures of her that
moved forever through my brain were memories of the swelling
bulk of Great Blue Hill; the winding ribbon of the Neponset River;
the emerald gems of islands floating on the surface of the harbor;
the freshness of an east wind bringing faint odors of the sea and the
sweet breath of the marshes to cool the slopes of Milton Hill on a
sultry summer evening; the flashing of a million fireflies on an August

night; the faint sweet smell that comes from the earth when it slowly takes to its bosom the last of winter's snow; the most poignant of all perfumes: that which rises from a meadow on a July night, when fallen hay lies upon it in windrows.

I felt starved and sick without all these and without Sally. I thought if I couldn't have Sally and them, there was nothing else on this earth that I wanted.

Sometimes my thoughts about Sally brought upon me a shivering apprehension of things I couldn't bring myself to face. She'd taken risks to help me and my father; she hadn't in so many words declared that she held me to be of the enemy—but there was that day when she left me to wait and wait for her downstairs, and didn't come. She'd said she wouldn't talk politics, and she hadn't spoken her mind clearly to me; but above all she was a Leighton, and there had been seven Leightons at Concord and Lexington.

Sally Leighton! Ah, what was she thinking of me now? I didn't doubt she thought of me: I knew she did; but thought can become hostile, and lovers knew long ages past that love can become hate.

I couldn't learn what Sally thought of me unless the ragged army of rebels could be driven back to their homes; unless Sam Adams could be persuaded to stop setting poor men against rich men; unless all of us could have the liberty the rebels prated of and had taken from us—the liberty to live in our own homes unmolested.

May, I thought, would never pass; and June, because of its balmy nights and long warm afternoons, threatened to be even longer— for there is something about June, as almost every poet has cried, that sharpens a lover's longings; makes love in absence unbearable.

How hard—nay, how tragic!—that June would be, I couldn't have foreseen.

CHAPTER IX

THE thing came upon us as suddenly and violently as a thunderstorm bursts upon a mountain valley.

The scene at which I looked from my bedroom window on the sixteenth of June might have been a peaceful twilight canvas by Ruysdael: a strip of glassy blue water—the Charles River—and reflected in it the three velvety green hills of Charlestown Neck, with the squat white houses and churches of Charlestown snuggled at the foot of the largest hill.

The upper windows of the houses at the top of the rise of Sudbury Street, where we lodged, looked down upon the roofs of the houses across the street, and upon the lower rows of roofs of the houses on the lower streets that descend to the docks and wharves along the harbor and the river.

Thus from my window at Mrs. Byles' I had a clear view well above the opposite roofs and descending rows of housetops, and in the early evening was staring yearningly at those three swelling hillslopes thrust between the cool waters of the Charles River and Boston Harbor. The yearning with which they filled me was not a romantic one: I was wishing that I could once more see cows upon them, this wish of mine being inspired by a craving to eat meat and to get good milk for my father, even if I had to go by night and steal. Two months before there had always been herds of cattle browsing on the slopes of the Charlestown peninsula—sturdy black-and-white ones; fawn-colored cows so fat that their backs were concave and their bellies half hidden in the lush grass through which they slowly moved.

There was none there now. Those meadowed hills, all treeless

81

grazing ground, showed not a sign of human or animal life upon them that sundown of the sixteenth of June. They were the epitome of peace. Never, since we'd left the quiet of the country, had the evening light fallen more softly and gently.

At daybreak the next morning those same hills had become the thunderous fountainhead of rebellion, hatred, destruction. In the earliest misty dawn the walls, floors and windows at Mrs. Byles' shivered and resounded to the crash of cannon shots. I jumped out of bed and went to the window. The hills across the vaporous river were no longer peaceful. In the dawnlight they were swarthy and dismal; and the top of the middle hill was disfigured by earthworks that had been thrown up during the night. They were roughly in the form of a square, and all around the irregular low walls of earth, within and without, hundreds of men moved restlessly, so that the whole hill was astir. From where I was, the swarming intruders upon the peace of that hill looked like sheep, seen from a distant height, crowding along the fence that encloses them, or huddling in corners.

From the river, halfway between our house and the middle hilltop, two frigates, shrouded in white smoke, had begun an incessant slow banging. So close were hills and ships that I could see the cannon balls moving in rapid arcs against the pale lower sky, and flicking spurts of earth from the green pastures around the new earthworks.

Below me, on Sudbury Street, men ran and shouted; and as if by magic the housetops between ours and the river bristled with humans, as if the whole town were sprouting in the moist warmth of a June morning.

I was hastily pulling on my clothes when Buell came in, fully dressed, crossed to the window, spat enormously from it, and leaned far out to follow the course of his expectoration. When he drew back his head, he looked pleased. "Well, Oliver," he said, "you better get your father up to this window. Unless I miss my guess, those fellers over on that hill have bit off more than they can chew."

For the first time since I had met him he seemed completely happy, and as he went to the door he gave my shoulder a friendly squeeze. "This'll be a great day for us, Oliver," he said; "a great day! Get your father up here as soon as you can, and I'll be back in an hour or two with all the news. We better get ourselves ready to drink a few toasts and do a little singing, because this ought to be the end of all our troubles." He bolted from the room and down the stairs.

"Here," I shouted after him, "you'll miss it yourself, won't you?"

"Not me!" he bawled from below. "It takes time to get soldiers across that river, and there's a mess of things we ought to have if we're going to make a day of it."

The street door slammed behind him, and I went to my father's room. His wig, freshly powdered, lay on the pillow beside him; and his best watered-silk coat and breeches were being examined by Andrew for spots.

I looked doubtfully at my father. "Are you sure you're equal to this?" I asked. "If you're coming to my room to watch, I can move my bed right over beside the windows, and you can lie there and see everything."

My father looked noncommittal. "Andrew says the rebels fortified Breed's Hill, and aren't to be allowed to stay there. As a rule, battles are decided by luck, my boy; so I think I'd feel a little better if I were dressed."

What he said mystified me, because I was sure battles were decided by generalship: not luck. However, I made no comment, and since he seemed bent upon dressing, I helped Andrew get clothes upon him as quickly as we could.

By the time his wig was adjusted and the powder brushed from his coat, the cannonading had slackened to a slow and weary booming, and I feared we might have missed the crisis of what was taking place across the river; but when we got my father into my room and to the window, nothing had changed upon that middle Charlestown hill. The same sheeplike little men still moved within the square entrenchments that might have been the foundation for a warehouse. Beyond the middle hill was another, higher hill, and over the shoulder of the farther one trickled an irregular stream of antlike figures, all moving toward the newly made entrenchments.

The guns of the frigates on either side of the peninsula were silent now, as if fatigued by the increasing warmth. It was one of those sultry, airless mornings, peculiar to Boston, when grass droops in the moist heat, and the waters of the harbor and the Charles are pallid and a little greasy.

Not a man, so far as I could see, had left the tops of the houses that led down like huge steps from Sudbury Street to the flat wharves along the northern rim of Boston; but the clumps of house-top watchers were now speckled with white and bits of light blue and pink; for most of the men had taken off their coats, and among the watchers were hundreds of women and children in summer gear.

White was upon the faces of these people, too; I felt that I was pale myself, and the thinning smoke drifting up from the river was pallid. So was the river, and so seemed the very light of day itself.

My father, settled in an easy chair, stared and stared at the trenched and fortified hill, and at the steadily growing herd of seeming sheep within the rude fortifications upon it. We could make out that the sheep were still furiously at work.

"Have they brought up guns?" my father asked.

"I can't see any," I told him. "They're just digging."

My father moved uneasily in his chair. "If Gage doesn't stop 'em before they put cannon on that hilltop, this won't be a pleasant town for anyone. Run up on the roof, Oliver. See if you hear drums. Surely it's not possible that Gage and Howe don't know what's happening."

When I stepped from the attic bulkhead, I felt as though I'd come into a sort of uncovered, overheated theater; for the roofs on either side, as well as the higher ones behind, were thick with people staring open-mouthed at the amphitheater spread before us. All the faces were a little distorted, as are faces at a play; some frowning; some smiling foolishly; some slack-lipped.

While I strained my ears for the sound of drums, the booming from the river rose to such a crescendo that it puffed sultry air against my face in gusts and pressed my eardrums like the push of thick hot fingers. This time the booming came not only from the ships, but from a battery on Copp's Hill—the little fortified elevation on the Boston waterfront commanding the waterways on both sides of Charlestown Neck. With this thunderous renewal of the firing, a thin babbling like the far-off calling of sea gulls arose from all the crowded housetops.

When I descended to my own room, Andrew had brought coffee. Doctor Miller, fearful of the effect of cannon fire on my father, had called during my absence and was standing behind my father's chair with Mrs. Byles. Andrew was close beside them, and they just stood and stared at that green hill across the river, while the coffee on the table went unnoticed. The booming of the guns was so loud that the contents of the cups moved in little concentric waves, and at the center boiled up in miniature brown fountains.

"There's no sound of drums from any part of the city," I told my father.

"It takes time to move troops," Doctor Miller said absently. "It takes time."

Mrs. Byles rubbed the palm of her hand upon her gray silk dress. "Why does it? Why does it take time? It didn't take the mob fifteen minutes to move against my house in Cambridge and wreck it; and look what's been done on that hill yonder in a few short hours! Breastworks dug and filled with men, and not a British general able even to think about moving that fast, let alone making regiments do it!"

"Let's hope they'll learn," my father said. "That's a great sight yonder: a great sight. These British officers need to know what Americans can do when they set their minds to it, and I hope this great affair before us will teach 'em."

Buell's voice spoke sharply behind us. "Well, it won't!" He had returned silently, coatless and drenched with perspiration, but over his shoulder he carried a bulging canvas sack such as sailors use for their belongings.

"Won't what, Tom?" my father asked.

"Won't teach 'em a lesson," Buell said. He lowered the sack to the floor, untied the cord that fastened it and from its contents drew a sea captain's perspective glass. Focusing it on the hill, he murmured in a faraway voice that if the man who owned it had been using it as he should on a morning like this, he'd never have lost it.

He studied the hill intently and made hissing sounds. "Yes, sir, by God," he said, "they're still digging over there; but over here there ain't a single British regiment moved off the Common! As for them at headquarters, they're all in the front rooms of the Province House, trying to make up their minds what to do. You can hear 'em arguing when you're as far off as the burying ground on one side, and clear way down at the end of Milk Street on the other. I walked right in at the back door with a letter for General Howe, and never even saw a soul on account of everybody being in the front of the house, hollering."

"A letter to General Howe?" my father asked. "Who wrote it?"

Buell lowered the glass and looked surprised. "Why, I did! You can't get into headquarters unless you have a letter for somebody. Besides, I wanted to be sure General Howe knew all the rebels had got themselves into a box they couldn't get out of. Of course General

Gage, being commander in chief, he'll just sit in his office and have
port brought to him; but General Howe'll have charge of the fighting, so he's the one I wanted to tell what to do."

"Good!" my father cried. "What did Howe say?"

"Couldn't get near him, Mr. Wiswell. Difficult. Besides there was
so much noise in the front rooms where he was, talking, arguing
and hollering orders at secretaries that were writing, why I just spent
most of what time I had in the back part of the building, and picked
up this glass and a few other odds and ends—just took the loan
of 'em, of course—and came away. Here, Mr. Wiswell: look at that
hill yourself and see if you ever saw a prettier sight."

My father took the glass and focused it. "Remarkable!" he exclaimed. "Remarkable, and a perfect demonstration of what to expect from men like that. They're determined to govern without
knowing anything about government; bound to fight battles without
understanding tactics or strategy. If ever men got themselves perfectly into a trap, those rebels have! They've failed to fortify the
landward end of the Neck, so their rear is open to attack; they
haven't even taken advantage of the highest hill on the Neck itself,
so an enemy force can get above them and fire down into them. I
suppose Howe's waiting until the Neck's crowded with rebels, so he
can capture all of 'em at once."

Buell seated himself on my bed and went on unpacking the canvas
bag; and as he did so he discoursed. "The mistake you're making,
Mr. Wiswell, is to think that Howe, being a soldier, is thinking about
soldiering first, last and all the time. Fact is, he's thinking about a
number of more important things."

"More important than destroying the rebels that are starting a civil
war in this country?" Doctor Miller asked.

"More important to General Howe," Buell said calmly. "You know
as well as I do that a squeak-voiced, turnip-headed female can be
more important to some men than health or happiness or fortune.
Howe's one of 'em. He ain't deaf, so he must have heard those guns
as soon as we did this morning, but before he could do anything, he
had to kiss Mrs. Loring good-by. You heard about him and Mrs. Loring yet? Oh my, yes! Yes, sir! Anyhow, they all say so."

"Gossip!" my father said. "Mrs. Loring has no bearing upon the
present situation."

"Oh, she hasn't, hasn't she?" Buell drew a round red cheese from
his bag, sniffed it, and tossed it to Andrew, who caught it and then

almost dropped it at the sound of a heavy detonation from the river.
"All I can say, Mr. Wiswell, you'd be surprised. Andrew, you slice
up that cheese. We'll have it all et up, and the rind too, before Howe
gets Mrs. Loring off his mind long enough to decide what to do
about the top of that hill."

He looked crossly at my father. "General Howe issues the orders to
the army in this town, and if you belonged to that army, you'd like
to get your orders from somebody that was thinking about war and
not about a woman, wouldn't you? I would, by God, and I'm certainly glad I ain't in that British Army, because for some little time
past, Howe's forgotten all about it. He's devoting all his energies to
trying to figure out how much Mrs. Loring means by what she's just
said to him, and how far he better try to go on the strength of it.
They tell me there's been a French lady dancer around Boston,
too—— But there! That might be scandal; I wouldn't soil my lips
with it!"

He drew a long-necked bottle from the bag, examined the label,
and looked hopeful. "This here's German wine! I never had any!
By Jolly, now, mightn't there be just the barest chance it'll agree with
me enough to let me feel how it feels to get drunk? It stands to
reason there's *some* kind of wine in the world would do that for me
without giving me the hiccups."

From the bag he drew five more bottles of the same type. "Used to
be Howe's," he said meditatively. "I thought if I left 'em there, Howe
might feel he had to finish 'em, and I wanted to get this battle started.
Mistake on my part; didn't help any. I saw case after case in the hall
on my way out, and one of Howe's servants was filling a basket with
bottles from one of 'em to carry along wherever the general goes.
Mrs. Loring must have told him not to go anywhere on such a hot
day without a dozen or so bottles of cool wine handy. They say she's
right careful of him."

The others in the room seemed to be paying little attention to
Buell, but at this my father glanced over his shoulder at him. "The
Mrs. Loring you speak of so lightly—would she by any chance be
Mrs. Joshua Loring?"

"That's the one, Mr. Wiswell. Mrs. Joshua Loring, Jr. She wouldn't
let her p'ecious General Howe go out at all on such a hot day if she
had her way, God damn her loving soul, if you'll excuse the term,
Mrs. Byles."

"I know her," Mrs. Byles said. "She's a sweet, kind woman, so innocent she never notices it when a man accidentally lets his arm bump against her hip. How many times I've heard Belcher say, when we were going to bed, that there's only one person blinder than the woman who pretends not to notice the pressure on her hip, and that's the man who thinks his laying-on-of-hands isn't seen.'"

"The Lorings came through from Dorchester the night we were driven out of Milton," my father said musingly. "Joshua Loring's high sheriff."

"His sheriffing's kind of gone bad," Buell observed. "He's able, though. General Howe saw ability in him right the first glance at Mrs. Loring. Appointed him commissary to the British Army, so Mr. and Mrs. Loring can always be right where the general is, and keep looking after his food and health, and be handy if he needs comforting. That's pretty near the only thing Howe's made up his mind about since he's been in Boston."

He jumped from the bed, went to stand beside my father's chair, and shook his fist at the silent green hill toward which black pellets of cannon balls still flew harmlessly from the fleecy puffs of smoke that jetted from Copp's Hill and the anchored frigates.

"Look at that!" he cried. "I ain't a soldier, but I'll kiss a pig if I don't know soldiering better than what those dunces over there do! Trapped themselves, haven't they?"

"Yes, they have," my father said. "There's no correct military principle on which their position can be defended."

"Think so too, Oliver?" Buell asked me.

"Of course I know nothing," I told him, "but I wouldn't choose such a position. If I were attacked by bigger men than myself, I wouldn't walk out on the end of a plank over water and wait for them either to hit me there or else to sit down on the shore end of the plank till I starved."

Mrs. Byles and Doctor Miller nodded emphatically.

"Well, that's the way it looks to you and me and all of us," Buell said. "But it doesn't look that way to Gage and Howe."

My father slowly raised his eyes to Buell's. "How on earth do you know that, Tom?"

"Mr. Wiswell, didn't I tell you I heard 'em arguing at the Province House? Clinton, Burgoyne and young Lord Percy kept telling Gage and Howe that those rebels over there have blundered into the nicest trap any fellers ever got into. They kept telling Howe he had complete control of the sea, and complete command of the rear and both flanks of that position yonder. They kept telling him that if he'd just get around behind those rebels, they wouldn't have a chance either to fight or to get away—not a chance!"

My father tried to raise the perspective glass to his eye again; but his hands were shaking. He let the glass rest upon his lap. "That's perfectly obvious, Tom. Surely Gage and Howe couldn't deny it."

"Well, sir, as near as I could get it, Gage and Howe just argued that this wasn't going to be a regular battle, so they needn't give it any regular thought. It sounded to me as though they figured no American would ever fight, and that this was the time to prove it. If I understood what I heard, Gage and Howe are possessed to show the world that Englishmen can scare any non-Englishmen to death by marching straight at 'em and shouting 'Boo!' "

CHAPTER X

THE rest of that morning was a sort of hazy hot dream. Not until noon did we hear the rattle of drums in near-by Hanover Street and the shuffling of marching regiments moving down toward the wharves from their camp on the Common. There was something about that hurried recurrent slapping of thick-soled shoes on a hard road that made my hands perspire and dried my tongue to the consistency of leather; that filled me with the same trembling, half-sick eagerness I had felt as a boy, when I crawled on hands and knees through underbrush to shoot my first moose.

We waited and waited, after that, for something to happen. George Leonard came in to share our windows with us. We talked and talked, wondering what would be the outcome of that long argument at British headquarters.

Two o'clock passed. Then there was a swelling of voices on all the housetops; an agitated sound made more significant by a thousand tense movements, quick changes of groupings and the flickering of gesturing arms and hands among the watchers.

A line of boats, packed with men, crept out from our side of the river and began to move slowly across the glassy strip of water that lay between them and those rising meadows of Charlestown where not long ago the peaceful cattle grazed.

In spite of the blazing heat of the cloudless day, the men in the boats wore uniforms of scarlet cloth, bound to them by heavy white crossed belts, and on their backs were strapped knapsacks that couldn't have weighed less than eighty pounds. All of us in my room, barring Mrs. Byles, knew the wrenching labor of carrying a dead doe out of the woods. Every one of those scarlet-clad soldiers

carried the equivalent of a doe on his back—so majestically arithmetical was the trained British military mind on this vital occasion.

The shape of Charlestown peninsula, as we saw it from our upper
windows on Sudbury Street, was that of an enormous muskrat, half
submerged, and swimming to the right. Farthest to the right was the
low swelling of the muskrat's head; a little behind was the higher
swelling of its shoulders; still farther back was the largest swelling of
all: that of its rump. Protruding from the rump, long and flat on the
water, like a muskrat's tail, was Charlestown Neck.

As I've said, the low fortifications thrown up by the rebels were
on the middle of the three swellings; and across the floating tail that
in reality was Charlestown Neck, more and more rebels coming for
the fight still were moving. Those distant tiny figures, like a choppy
and eccentric stream, irregularly flowed up over the rump of the
muskrat, then down upon his back, and, ascending again, were lost
among the walls of fresh earth upon the muskrat's shoulder.

My eyeballs smarted from tensely watching the line of rowboats
that seemed to crawl in a deadly lethargy, slower and slower and
smaller and smaller as they grew more distant, until they seemed
only toy boats almost standing still, with red-painted toy soldiers
motionless in them.

My ears ached from the banging of the guns; but within our room
there wasn't a sound except the heavy breathing of George Leonard,
the tapping of Mrs. Byles' cane and the spasmodic sound of Buell's
wrenching hiccups.

Now the world we lived in seemed to be half breathless silence
and half thunder; for as the lengthening line of boats moved obliquely
across the glassy waterway toward the head of the giant swimming
muskrat, the booming from the frigates and from Copp's Hill was
violent, but between the individual shots from the great guns, we
were conscious of profound silence: all the town around us was completely still. Not a sound came up to us from the streets, and the
thousands gathered upon the housetops were voiceless, and stood
or sat or leaned without motion, as if posed in some vast tableau.

What we most wanted to know was whether those slowly moving
boats would circle the nose of the swimming muskrat and pass along
its far side to the narrow tail.

Buell stood, almost leaning upon me; and in the interval between
two cannon shots, I felt inordinately irritated at the muted jerky

hiccupings that racked him. They seemed a disturbance, an intentional intrusion upon the drama, like coughing in a playhouse.

"Damn you, stop that," I almost said to him.

He seemed to feel something of this himself. "Excuse me," he said. "Can't appear to help it. Well, no matter. Look, there ain't a sail been shaken out on those frigates! I guess there ain't no question what that means."

Leonard turned on him, "Of course there is! They got a fair wind, haven't they? Why wouldn't it be good strategy to lie where they are till the last possible moment: then get under way in a hurry, move around to the Neck and bottle 'em up before they know what's happened to 'em? Why wouldn't it?"

I had a momentary faint hope that he was right: that perhaps those boatloads of soldiers would keep on around the muskrat's nose and that the frigates would soon set off to support them.

But he wasn't right. He was wrong; for the line of boats went straight to the beach at the base of the muskrat's head, and those red-coated figures flowed out along the sand like a widening pool of blood.

"There you are," Buell said. "Gage and Howe outranked Clinton and Burgoyne and Percy, so Gage and Howe won the argument. Gage and Howe told 'em Americans can't shoot, of course, and always run every time anyone fires a cannon at 'em, and turn pale and faint whenever they see a bayonet!" Again he made a hissing sound and turned from the window to sit on the bed, where I heard him opening another bottle of wine.

No sooner were the boats empty than they turned and rowed back to our side of the river, coming fast unburdened; and through the next hour we sat and watched an endless ferrying of scarlet infantrymen to the Charlestown shore; watched those who had been landed form into companies and regiments on the lower slopes of that lowest of Charlestown's three hills.

My father sighed shiveringly. "It can't be possible; they can't be going to attack that hill in front! They *can't* be!"

George Leonard spoke under his breath, "Never! Howe's a soldier. Gage—Clinton—Burgoyne—why, they couldn't do such a thing!"

Buell was close behind me again, smelling of wine and noisier inside. "They can too!" he said. "They can march right up the front of that hill, the way British gentlemen always do—until somebody learns 'em better."

"Never," George Leonard repeated huskily.

Mrs. Byles and Doctor Miller looked angrily at Buell, and I was angry at him myself for daring to speak what I feared was the truth.

"There's just a chance," my father said, "that they might be going to march around the peninsula, half on one side and half on the other, and join forces at the Neck."

Buell hiccuped. "Why should they march, when they can row around in boats? They'd be throwing men away if they *marched* around. Why, they'd lose five or six hundred! But if they *rowed* around, they probably wouldn't lose one. Not a damned one!" He looked earnestly at the bottle in his hand. "I doubt if I ever learn to be a drinker! Try, though!"

Not until that hot afternoon was at its hottest did the rowboats deposit the last load of soldiers on the beach. By then, on the top of the low muskrat head, the troops were drawn up in two long lines. Those two lines ran all the way across the head of the muskrat, as two scarlet hair ribbons might have spanned a girl's head from ear to ear.

There was no doubt now as to how those scarlet lines were going to attack; and in my room there was no more talk among us.

The two long lines moved down from the muskrat's head to his neck and began their ascent of the shoulder, which was the middle hill topped by the walls of brown earthworks. They moved with such smoothness, such precision in keeping their formation, that it was hard to believe they were composed of embattled human beings; and, as they surged upward upon the rising meadows, red coats and white breeches bright above the grass, they brought me the illusion that I beheld not men, but the stripes of a vastly wide red, white and green pennant, flung far across the face of the hill.

The moment that this wide pennant began to rise upward upon the hill, the gunfire from the frigates and from Boston ceased abruptly.

I found myself sweating as I had never sweated before, and I'd known what it was to sweat; for I'd swung a scythe on my father's farm in August; but never until now had I sweated until I shivered.

The long pennant of scarlet and white rose steadily: rose and rose until it seemed to us a man might have tossed a stone from it into the breastworks on the hilltop.

Then, as if the advancing scarlet lines had touched a trigger and released countless little mines, fleecy puffs of white smoke jetted from them with symmetrical regularity. The smoke was thick and white against the green hill: the men might have thrown expanding balls of cotton into the air, all at the same time.

To those in my room, the sound of this British volley firing came slow and long delayed—then we heard it: a muted pattering like the muffled popping of corn in a full popper.

But from the brown rectangle toward which the scarlet lines advanced, no white puff arose. The walls of earth were smokeless and still.

George Leonard got up suddenly. His chair fell over with a clatter. "Fire! For God's sake, fire—if you're ever going to!"

As if that had been a signal, the whole front of the breastworks on the hill spouted smoke.

On the instant the long scarlet pennant seemed struck by a sudden sharp wind. It shivered and fluttered; it undulated, thinned and thickened.

For a long moment it thus thickened, thinned and fluttered. Faint wisps of smoke rose from it, as though hot irons touched it lightly. Then its likeness to a pennant vanished.

The scarlet lines bent, broke and crumbled. Their edges flaked off and became scarlet human figures which fluttered leaf-like down the hill, dropping away from what seemed a long heap of scarlet leaves, a queer bright shadow of the original scarlet line—as if that line, in disappearing, had left its empty shell, red, upon the ground.

"Look!" Leonard whispered. "Look at the long piles! All those men in the grass—they're shot! One volley did for damn near half of 'em!"

He dropped the glass on the floor; fumbled for it stiffly. I picked it up and looked through it at the hilltop. It brought the twisted scarlet shadow close.

It wasn't a shadow, but soldiers in tangled heaps that writhed and heaved. Single figures reared up gropingly from the heaps and then sank back. I thought of the sounds that must be coming from those men, and at that thought my insides quaked; I thanked God we couldn't hear them.

I tried to ask whether anyone else wanted the glass, but my voice just croaked indistinguishably. Leonard awkwardly took the glass from me.

Nobody spoke. The scarlet shadow stayed where it was, but the moving scarlet figures went swiftly down the hill to the bottom; and there, like scarlet quicksilver, they gathered in blobs that expanded, contracted, swirled, thinned and gradually flowed again into scarlet lines that lay along the center of the little valley—lines shorter than those that had first moved with such smooth precision toward the silent earthworks.

Wisps of smoke were rising now from houses at the foot of the hill, and the guns on the frigates boomed wrathfully. The smoke from the houses thickened and spread, bellied out, billowed up into a dark cloud streaked with grays and yellows—a cloud that, constantly rising, drifted off to the eastward before the hot breeze from the west. It towered upward and hung against the sky in dark swags and folds, a half-drawn dusky curtain behind the bright green hill with its silent crown of entrenchments just above the scarlet shadow.

George Leonard looked at his palm. It was wet. He rubbed it against his thigh. "Charlestown's afire," he said. "Don't you want the glass, Seaton?"

My father shook his head.

Leonard took up the glass, got down on his knees and rested it on the window ledge.

He made a hissing sound. "They're going up again."

Buell hiccuped. "What's strange about that? Didn't they do it wrong the first time? They got to keep on doing it wrong, even if it kills every damned one of 'em!" His voice became politely formal. "I trust they have their packs on?"

"Yes," Leonard whispered.

"That's nice," Buell said. "Those packs weigh a hundred pounds, and if they took 'em off, they wouldn't be fighting the hard way. Those British generals wouldn't want 'em to win the easy way! Oh my, no!"

Mrs. Byles leaned heavily on her stick. "If they've got packs on," she said, "they've probably got 'em on for a good reason! General Gage and General Howe——"

Buell stopped her. "Excuse me, ma'am. I wish you'd go to bed so I can speak my mind! They ain't got a good reason for anything, ma'am. When they marched men to Concord and back, thirty-five miles, on the coldest night in April, they didn't let 'em have food or overcoats! And now, on the hottest day of the year, with only half a mile to go, they give 'em hundred-pound packs full of food and equipment for a week, and expect 'em to run up hill! Reason be God-damned, excusing me, Mrs. Byles!"

Mrs. Byles' lips were gray. "Buell," she said huskily, "give me a sip of that wine!"

Buell passed her an uncorked bottle, and she put it to her lips and drank thirstily without taking her eyes from those green hill-slopes lying so tranquilly beyond the towering, boiling pall of smoke that now poured up from the blazing houses of Charlestown.

The guns had stopped and the scarlet line in the valley was moving forward again—going up the hill with the same arithmetical neatness shown by those first scarlet lines a scant half-hour before.

"Jesus!" Buell whispered. "I can't watch this!" He went noisily away, but the next moment he was again at my elbow. "Can't not, either," he said. "Can't watch it and can't not."

Once again, as the moving line showed high on the hillside, white puffs jetted from it. The line drew close to the scarlet shadow; blended with it; passed on beyond it, nearer and nearer to the silent earthworks.

Leonard had the glass. "They'll get there!" he whispered. "They're almost there! By God, I believe they'll go over! They're almost— almost——"

Then he groaned.

From the whole length of the breastworks rose suddenly an almost solid bank of smoke, snow-white in the afternoon sun.

The advancing scarlet line might have been a taffeta ribbon, so sharply did it flutter, so suddenly was it torn to pieces. For a moment bits of it clung against the brown earth of the breastworks; then were blown away and hung tatteredly in threads and strings.

Red dots and patches showed where retreating men ran down the hill; but at the top another and higher scarlet shadow lay all along the front of the earthworks.

Leonard took the glass from his eye, fumbled for a handkerchief, and clumsily wiped the eyepiece. "Well," he said heavily, "if they try it again there won't be any left! Not any! There must have been three thousand of 'em started up that hill in the beginning, and look at 'em now! Can't those damned fools from the Province House be content unless they're every last one of 'em killed?"

Buell tossed an empty bottle from the window, and Leonard turned on him petulantly. "Don't throw things out of the window! You might hurt somebody!"

Buell took the perspective glass from him. "Wouldn't that be a shame on a nice day like this! Yes, sir; you're right! People ought to think more about doing things that might hurt other people! Throwing things out of windows, they might land on somebody's foot!"

He put the glass to his eye. "Yes, Mr. Leonard, you certainly are right about everything! Those soldiers started to get in their boats and go home, but somebody's got 'em to change their minds again. Yes, indeed! It's contrary to the rules of war to have anybody left when there's such a perfect opportunity to get 'em all killed! They're forming at the bottom of the hill again."

His voice grew sharper. "Yes, by God, and somebody's thought of something you'd never expected! They're taking off their packs —dumping 'em on the ground! Well, well! Taking off their packs! They're going to have a chance for their lives! My, my! I'll bet somebody gets himself court-martialed for permitting such unsoldierly and un-British conduct! Some officer must have a brother that's a private, and let him get familiar enough to mention you can climb a hill and get shot better without the weight of a yearling heifer on you. Yes, sir, I'll bet somebody gets up in Parliament and says some mighty sarcastic things about the modern soldier, who ain't good enough to fight battles the way his grandpa did, with two pounds of hair powder in his eyes and a big target over a vital spot. Well, anyway, they're starting! They're going up again—and they've left their packs behind 'em!"

His voice grew louder and louder. "They're·going up! By God, they're going to get there! There's nothing to stop 'em now! They'll rip the insides out of every bloody rebel that gets in their way!"

He drew a shuddering breath, looked surprised, and his eyes seemed to turn inward. "That stopped my hiccups! Give me another bottle, Oliver, quick!"

The scarlet line, pitifully thin by comparison with what it had been an hour earlier, had once more moved smoothly out of the valley and was now upon the hillslope. No bursts of white smoke came from it: it just went on and on, upward and upward, as silent as the earthworks against which it moved.

"They're brave men," Doctor Miller said. He hadn't spoken for an hour, and his voice sounded choked, as if he'd almost forgotten how to speak.

"Brave?" my father said. "They're the bravest men I ever hope to see!"

"Listen, Seaton," Leonard cried, "they're getting out the back side of that fort! There's a whole stream of 'em going across the big hill and down to the Neck!"

"It's not too late, even yet," my father whispered.

The scarlet line went up and up. It passed the first scarlet wind-row on the grass. Then it passed the second scarlet shadow, but this time no solid bank of smoke ejected itself from the breastworks. There were only scattered puffs.

"Ah!" my father sighed. "They must be running short! Short of powder: short of ball! They can't stand now!"

The scarlet line moved into the sparse smoke that came from the breastworks. Like a thin red wave it curled over the top of those brown embankments, and splashed redly down behind them, disappearing from us into a turmoil as appalling to us as if we saw it.

Above the enclosing square of the fortifications became visible a pale vapor that hung upon the air. The whole hilltop smoldered.

From the housetops of Boston went up a discordant high-pitched sound made up of innumerable cries of encouragement, desperation, anguish, elation, insupportable excitement.

Within my room on Sudbury Street I heard Mrs. Byles screaming encouragingly; saw her weeping as she screamed. Buell, in the intervals of drinking from his bottle, repeated thickly that he had known all the time what must happen if only they'd do as he said. Leonard, on his knees at the window, cursed excitedly and wiped at the eye-piece of the perspective glass with his handkerchief.

Even without the glass I could see drab figures pouring like ants from the rear of the earthworks, streaming off with unbelievable rapidity across the highest of Charlestown's hills.

Leonard got the glass focused at last. "The soldiers have got every last rebel out of the fortifications. They've caught 'em in a cross fire from there as they're running away! The rebels are finished! We've got 'em! They're going down by the hundreds!"

When he turned the glass toward the Neck, his voice shook. "Running! My God, look at 'em run! They're running like rabbits, trying to get across to the mainland!" His voice broke with excitement.

"Can you see any rebel reinforcements beyond the Neck?" my father asked.

"There aren't any," Leonard cried. "There's no reinforcements and no fortifications! Howe can put an end to that whole damned rebel army right now! All he's got to do's to keep on after 'em and there won't *be* any rebel army. He'll wipe it out, and you can all go back home!"

We sat there and sat there, waiting to see Howe start the remnants of his scarlet columns in pursuit, but never a scarlet figure moved out of the earthworks from which the rebels had been driven.

"Go after 'em!" Leonard cried again and again from the window, as if he believed he could be heard across the river.

He seemed to plead. "Aren't you going after 'em? Why don't you start! What's wrong with you? You can see as well as we can that you've got 'em if you'll only go after 'em! My God, why don't you go after 'em?"

They didn't go after them.

CHAPTER XI

THAT was the end of the Battle of Bunker Hill. We called it the Battle of Charlestown then, and the dead men were dumped into holes dug where they'd fallen, on the slopes above the town. The wounded were brought to Boston in rowboats that came slowly across the harbor all through that sultry Saturday night and all through the next day, which was a day of showers and much far-away thunder, as though the heavens grumbled at what they saw.

All of us who had horses and conveyances of any sort sent them to Long Wharf, and from there the wounded were driven to the hospitals; and I doubt that any city ever saw more dreadful sights or heard more horrible sounds than did Boston while those poor men passed through the streets.

Their cries and screams were sickening; and decent men and women, who couldn't avoid the thoroughfares through which the hurt men were carried, fled along them with averted faces, or stood with closed eyes and hands pressed over their ears, waiting for that agonized chorus to be distant.

I say decent men and women; for there were residents of Boston who couldn't take their eyes from the passing carts, but stood and gloated. I thought of such as these as ghouls, and that's how I still think of them.

Doctor Miller was one of the doctors who went to Long Wharf to help. I went with him to do what I could, and I could hardly believe that the things I saw had been done by my own countrymen.

Scores of carts and carriages stood in a line on the end of the wharf, and a billion flies darted and buzzed above the sorry nags that drew them. There was a constant fretful stamping of hoofs upon splintery planks, and a resultant mournful rumbling.

As the boats rowed in and rowed in, we could hear groans and lamentations far across the greasy, glassy waters of the harbor. Those sounds became piercing when the boats lay below us in the shadow of the wharf, and worse when their occupants were hauled up in fish baskets. A few among the basketloads were quiet; but only because they were dead. Some had died after being placed in the boats; and some were officers, brought back for burial, with their faces and bodies in the very contortions of the death agony of the day before. The dead were thrown helter-skelter in the nearest wagons, and the living wedged between them for comfort's sake. Dead and living alike were caked with blood, excrement and vomit in which sea wrack and sand from the Charlestown beach had hardened.

Doctor Miller, working with twenty other doctors, crawled on his knees among the groaning figures, a scalpel in his hand and shears hanging from his neck by a cord, while I kept near him, holding an opium box. Some of the poor men had torn open their clothes in their agony. Those that hadn't were given opium pills, and then the doctor slashed open their filthy, stinking uniforms with his shears. The sights he uncovered made even a doctor's face ashen.

"Nothing to be done," he kept saying, "nothing to be done! These men are alive, but they're torn to pieces inside! Almost every last one of 'em hit in the belly or the groin!"

With his scalpel he cut into the mangled body of the man over whom he knelt, and drew out a musket ball into the end of which a rusty nail had been driven. "That's the ninth of these," he said.

He ran his hand over his patient's blood-caked stomach. "Four—seven—ten—yes, ten buckshot holes! Ten buckshot holes in this man, besides what was done by that ball with a nail through it!"

He waved his hands despairingly at the countless flies that buzzed about us and crawled on the wounded man's contorted face, on his foul clothes, on his oozing wounds. "Put him in a wagon," he said. "He's got to be washed off before anybody can see what to do for him."

He looked down at the next man and shook his head hopelessly. "Nails!" he whispered. "What'll happen to this country, Oliver, if it falls into the hands of men willing to fire rusty nails into those who don't agree with 'em?"

Never until the wounded came back from Bunker Hill had I realized the lengths to which a determined minority will go in order to achieve its ends. For the first time I understood one of the fundamentals of warfare: that armies cannot be raised by nations or parties unless the rage of the people is first kindled by lies and name-calling.

The town was flooded with pamphlets and broadsides, issued by fanatic Sons of Liberty, in which all of us who remained loyal to the only constitutional form of government we had ever known were accused of every infamy and violence. We were tyrants; we were faithless; we were lost to shame; dead to honor. We were lawless, disloyal, corrupt, depraved, dissolute and profligate: most horrible of all, we were rich.

The rebels had seized and fortified the Charlestown hills so that Boston might be bombarded from them; yet those who resisted that attempt were called villains, scoundrels, monsters, devils incarnate, for daring to resist.

I found it impossible to think of the King's troops in Boston as Sons of Tyranny; and I knew beyond all question that my father and the other thousands who had been driven into the city by mobs were certainly not villains, scoundrels or monsters. They were the most peaceful of men, and they wanted exactly what many of the rebels claimed they wanted—a friendly adjustment of America's difficulties with England. It's almost unbelievable, now, to look back and realize that we'd have escaped all that war, all that misery, all that death and destruction, if it hadn't been for the persistent demagoguery of just one man—Sam Adams.

Mrs. Byles, goaded by the charges against us, was almost overwhelmed with a desire to give someone a piece of her mind.

I found her in my father's room, sitting bolt upright in a banister-back chair and fixing my father with a steely glare, while Buell sat beside her, listening so raptly that his lips followed her words in a sort of silent chorus.

She was openly contemptuous. "You men! Whatever these rebels say, you keep silent! Every last one of you's afraid to call his soul his own because of what the rebels may say about you. You're afraid, Seaton Wiswell, because of what may happen to your son if you say too much! You're afraid, Thomas Buell, for fear of what they may do to you if you say what you really think!

"You're letting noisy blatherskites frighten you into helplessness—

frighten all New England into helplessness! I don't understand you men! Belcher always said the best way to fight fire was with fire. He'd never have sat quietly and let this miserable Sam Adams call himself a patriot and in the same breath call us disloyal and Tories. You'd never have caught Belcher Byles forgetting the things Sam Adams said when he was a few years younger! Why, I myself remember a hundred things Sam Adams used to say! Belcher'd lie in bed, and tell 'em to me over and over, night after night! Sometimes Belcher'd harp on things so much that I'd almost wish I hadn't married him; but nobody ever forgot any of the things that Belcher harped on—I'll say that for him! I've heard Belcher quote what Sam Adams said about loyalty a thousand times. 'Whoever,' he said, 'insinuates notions of government contrary to the Constitution, or in any way winks at any measures to suppress or even to weaken it, is not a loyal man.' Sam Adams said that, and look what he's doing now!"

She applauded herself by rapping the ferrule of her stick upon the floor. "That's the man who's bawling that you and I are disloyal and unpatriotic! That's how Sam Adams has changed his tune in the last few years! Well, if I was a man, and Sam Adams lied about me the way he's lying about you, I'd change my tune as often as he did! I'd sign *any* paper! I'd swear to *any* agreement! I'd promise to do anything they wanted me to do! Then I'd do as I pleased."

She gripped her stick more firmly. "I declare to goodness, it doesn't seem as if *anybody* could be such a born fool as that minister down in Stratford, who was hauled before a committee and his life ruined just because he sprinkled water on a child and named it Thomas Gage. That man was a blasted fool! I declare, I get hot flushes every time I think what an idiot he was! The men on the committee were bad enough; but when I think of that minister, I could scream!"

She whacked her cane against the footboard of the bed. "Why didn't he lie! Why didn't he say he thought the child was being named for a greengage plum instead of a British general? 'Fight fire with fire,' Belcher used to say just before he blew out the light and came to bed, and Belcher was right. If I was a man I'd go up and see General Gage, quiet as a mouse, and have a private understanding with him. Next day I'd fill my pockets with all of Sam Adams' pamphlets, and I'd have the British throw me out of this city, pretending they couldn't stomach me. I'd go out into the country, damning all Tories, and I'd walk all the way to Newport just to see what people were saying! I'd have a good time doing it, what's more, and then I'd get on a British ship in Newport and come back here to Boston with enough food to keep my friends from starving to death, and make my report to General Gage on what the rebels are doing."

Buell slapped his knee and rose to his feet. "By Jolly," he whispered, "what's the matter with me, not to have thought of that myself! I guess I ought to use those Metallic Tractors on my own head!"

Buell left us a few days later, with a stock of Metallic Tractors rolled in a long strip of red flannel that had been neatly stitched into small compartments by Mrs. Byles; and in an inside pocket he carried drawings for a breech-loading rifle, fruit of three long nights of arduous labor in my bedroom.

"There," he said proudly, when he showed me the finished drawings, "with these drawings and the Metallic Tractors, there's nowhere I can't go and nobody I can't see. Even that old windbag General Putnam couldn't refuse to see me if I said I wanted to show him the plans for a breech-loading rifle."

"For God's sake be careful, Tom," I said. "Any military man familiar with firearms could trip you up, and if you were found out, you'd be hanged."

"No military man can trip me on these drawings," Buell said. "This is a breech-loading rifle that'll work. I've been thinking about it for five years, and no military man alive can find anything wrong with it in a mere five minutes or five hours—or five weeks, for that matter."

"If it'll work," I protested, "you shouldn't show it to rebels, should you? Mightn't they buy it and use it against us?"

"Oh my, no!" Buell said. "I could talk any rebel—that old flannel-mouthed Putnam, say—into believing that this breech-loading rifle of mine is just what the rebels need to win the war; but if Putnam tried to get the rest of the rebels to believe it too, he'd have to stop fighting us and take to fighting those he was trying to persuade."

"Why would he?" I asked.

"Listen, Oliver," Buell said. "What size shot do you use on partridges?"

"Number 9's," I said.

"Nines are too small," Buell told me. "I always use 6's."

I knew many gunners who used 6's and 7's on partridges, but they lost so many birds that I felt sorry for them. "If you'll only try 9's," I said, "you'll never go back to 6's. I can kill geese with 6's. For a bird as small as a partridge, 6's leave too many gaps in the pattern. When you use 9's, on the other hand, you have twice the chance of——"

Buell interrupted me. "That's why I ain't afraid of having the rebel army try to buy these drawings of mine. You think the feller who uses 6's on partridges is a misguided idiot; but those who've been using 6's on partridges all their lives know you're sensible enough about most things, but crazy as a coot about partridge-shooting. You probably swear by a 12-gauge shotgun, but you know as well as I do that the world is full of people who won't use anything but 10-gauges because 12-gauges ain't worth a damn. That's the way gunners and soldiers have always been about guns: for every hundred men that say a gun is the best in the world, there's always another hundred to swear it's the worst. No, Oliver: you needn't worry about me! I'll get all the rebels together and show 'em my gun, but they won't do a damned thing about it! Then I'll show 'em my Metallic Tractors, and they'll break their necks trying to buy 'em from me at three guineas a pair!"

When Buell returned, he came back from Newport in a British ship and with an enormous fund of news. Much of his conversation dealt with a gentleman named Benjamin Thompson, who had also boarded his ship at Newport and disembarked at Boston. So often did he quote Benjamin Thompson that I came to dislike the man, as people dislike a child when a parent constantly extols his virtues. I was glad, even, that I'd never have to meet Benjamin Thompson.

As my father had predicted, the dreadful mismanagement at Bunker Hill had ruined the military reputation of General Gage, so that he had been recalled to England and replaced by General Howe.

When Buell had reported privately to Howe, he came at once to see us, and not long afterwards two sailors from the *Siren* frigate left his baggage at our back door. His own personal bag was a small one, and contained nothing but a razor, a comb, two extra shirts, and two extra pairs of stockings, one gray wool and the other white silk. The white silk ones he gave at once to Mrs. Byles, saying that she might find the feet a little large, but that the quality would more than make up for their shortcomings.

Mrs. Byles scrutinized them closely. "English!" she exclaimed.
She looked up quickly at Buell. "I haven't seen a pair like these since
Belcher and I attended the captain's dinner on the *Inflexible 74*, sixteen years ago. These are quarter-deck stockings, young man, and
don't try to tell me they're not!"

"Certainly they are, ma'am. Those stockings belonged to an
admiral." He shook his head. "What's worse, ma'am, I traded a pair of
Metallic Tractors for two pairs of 'em. I tell you, ma'am, that's
shaken my confidence in the British Navy. I don't believe those
British admirals are——"

Mrs. Byles held up her hand. "I'd rather not discuss the matter.
Silk stockings are silk stockings, no matter how they're come by; and
I'm grateful for 'em, no matter whose they used to be." She stroked
them as they lay upon her knee. "It would have been nice if they
could have come from a rebel general, but I don't suppose rebels
have many extra pairs."

"Pairs!" Buell cried. "Why, they're lucky if they have any *shoes,*
even. I went through the whole rebel army, ma'am, and they got less
of everything than anybody'd have after being shipwrecked on a
desert island! Why, they got a company of Stockbridge Indians out
there, mostly wearing three feathers and a blue diaper around their
middles, and damned if they ain't got more on than most of those
rebels. Anyway, they don't look worse undressed."

Mrs. Byles looked incredulous. "Indians! You mean to say there's
Indians in the rebel camp?"

"Yes, ma'am," Buell said. "Stockbridge Indians. They hide in the
bushes near the water, mostly, and ambush British boats coming in
for sheep and fodder. They stuck so many arrows in one boat's crew
the other day that the poor fellers looked like pincushions."

Mrs. Byles waved her stick dangerously. "There you are! They're
using Indians themselves; but according to what *they* say, there's
nobody but the British even *think* of using Indians, and anybody
that has anything to do with anybody that thinks of using Indians is
nothing but a depraved assassin and a parricide! Isn't that just like
'em?"

She hitched herself forward in her chair. "What else'd you see in
the rebel camp, Buell? What kind of people are they?"

"What kind?" Buell asked. "I don't know as I can answer that,
ma'am, because I never saw any like 'em before—and a printer gets
to see about as rough characters as there is. I never saw folks as dirty

and nasty as they are; and what beats me is that the officers aren't any better than the men. Pretty often they're worse, because if they don't act worse than the men do, the men think they're getting uppity and won't obey 'em. According to what I hear, this General Washington they got to command 'em, they say he never goes near the Massachusetts troops without gargling his throat with spruce beer and hanging his clothes in a smokehouse when he gets back to headquarters. He's thrown a Massachusetts colonel and five Massachusetts captains out of the army for being cowards at Bunker Hill, and they say he'd throw out fifty or sixty more if it wasn't that the army'd get mad and go home on him, so't there wouldn't be anybody left in camp but himself."

"No *noblesse oblige!*" Mrs. Byles said scornfully.

"No, ma'am! Oh my, no—not unless some of the officers got 'em; but I didn't see any of the officers undressing, so I can't tell. And about the only thing they've got plenty of is grandfathers. There's more grandfathers to the square inch in that army than there is to the square mile anywhere else! It's just like a convention of dirty old grandfathers. It looks as if all the old fellers in New England that hadn't had anything to eat or anything to do, or any powder to put on their hair or in their guns, or anything to wash in for the last thirty-forty years, had got wind of what was happening, and come flapping down to Boston like a lot of buzzards, hoping to shoot somebody and sneak up and get some new breeches off him."

My father looked surprised. "All this must be rather trying to a southern gentleman like General Washington," he said.

"Trying!" Buell exclaimed. "It's just plumb damned exasperating! The general and his friends from the south, they ain't got a bit of use for being made an equal of Negroes and smelly old men with grease on their breeches and tobacco juice on their chins! Seems as if those southerners don't have the same ideas about liberty and all men being equal that Sam Adams does. It's more a figure of speech in the south, on account of all the slaves they got down there. In the south, when a man says 'Give me liberty or give me death,' he's usually got from two or three to fifty or so black people belonging to him that he can sell to somebody else if he takes a notion to; so what he means by he's got to have freedom or call in the undertaker, it's freedom for just a picked circle that's going to take the liberty of shooting anybody that argues different."

"Surely," my father protested, "you're not serious when you

say they have no powder! I assume that's a figure of speech on your part?"

"Oh my, no!" Buell said. "Those rebels ain't got more than a cup of powder apiece. If they had half as much gunpowder in their army as they have grandfathers that won't take a wash, they'd be dangerous —if they weren't so all-fired anxious to go home."

"Are you trying to tell us," Mrs. Byles asked heatedly, "that General Howe is letting his ten thousand troops be bottled up in this town by an army without gunpowder? If it's so, why doesn't somebody tell the old fool about it so he can attack instead of just sitting here?"

"I did," Buell said. "I did tell him about it. I went up to headquarters as soon as I landed this morning, and told him what I've just been telling you. Listen, Oliver: I made a great discovery. Generals used to kind of scare me, but they don't any more. All you got to do, when a general begins to talk as if he was thinking of having you shot, is to blow out all your breath. I tried it this morning when Howe looked sour, and he didn't bother me any more than old man Jeffers!"

"What did Howe say?" my father asked.

"Nothing. Looked as if he didn't believe me, so I sold him a pair of Metallic Tractors."

"There you are," Mrs. Byles cried. "That's the way any Englishman always looks at any American! Belcher always told me there's something about America that fuddles an Englishman's brains. Belcher always said when an Englishman comes over here, he takes our lies for gospel, neglects our wise men, and picks out an American fool to associate with, especially if it's a female. In times of war and trouble, if a smart Englishman comes over here, he can't be useful because some other Englishman who isn't smart gives him orders that get him killed right away. That does this country a great deal of good, because it leaves only the fool Englishmen to deal with!"

Mrs. Byles uttered a muffled sound and puffed out her lips peculiarly; if I hadn't known she was a lady, I'd have thought she'd inwardly either cursed or spat.

CHAPTER XII

So THERE we were, cooped up in Boston with a thousand men dying of wounds, two thousand dying of smallpox, and seven thousand British soldiers who might perish of sickness or starvation before they ever got out! Cooped up with thousands of Loyalists and a British general who couldn't even defeat an army that invited defeat: couldn't believe the information brought to him by people who'd risked their lives to get it for him!

That morning when I had seen the earthworks on the Charlestown hill, my heavy heart had suddenly lightened; I would see Sally Leighton soon—a hope gone by sunset!

Now the ugly, harried summer dragged away, and I saw only one possible chance of getting back to Milton—and Sally. My neutrality was gone; I'd seen too much, felt too much. I had thought that law-loving, peace-loving people like my father and myself could stand between the two parties: could keep cool heads and in quiet wisdom hold to a middle course, patient, inactive, impartial and with as little passion as dwelt in the bosom of Blind Justice herself.

This could not be, and I no longer wished it to be.

While my father continued ailing, as he did, I couldn't leave him; but my thought now was that as soon as he regained enough of his old strength to be left to Andrew's care, I'd join with other Loyalist soldiers under one of our own leaders—one competent to scatter these powderless fanatics before whom the indecisive Howe and his Englishmen remained so helpless. We Loyalist Americans ourselves would deal with this ill-omened, foolish uprising of our countrymen. We'd finish it—and I'd go home *to* Sally.

I've heard much about the misery and the suffering of those who spent that winter in Boston, but I've usually heard it from people who weren't there. Misery, in cold truth, is a weight less upon those who undergo it than upon the minds of those who see it; for he who is cold and starving is so busy in his efforts to obtain warmth and food that he has little time for self-pity, and endures his unhappy condition better than those who take it upon themselves to suffer for him.

In Boston that winter, moreover, we had a compensation: in spite of the scarcity of food and of fuel, we believed we had something to look forward to. The day must surely come, we still thought, when the mobs must be dispersed; when the courts would be opened and judges be allowed to sit; when every man's property would be as secure as it was before Sam Adams turned our whole world upside down with his determination to replace constitutional government by the rabble's whim.

Always and always in the back of our minds were our plans for returning to our homes—not immediately, of course; but next spring —or next summer; certainly eventually.

Since most people's pleasure in this life lies in anticipation, I'm not so sure that the Loyalists around us, in spite of their miserable situation, weren't happier than the wretched crew of rebels who had bottled us up in Boston and took such profound delight in our fruitless efforts to get firewood and bread.

As for myself, there came a day when I was happier, I think, than I had been for years; for at the very moment when the present and the future looked blackest to me—when even Buell was hard put to it to find enough wood to cook our scanty meals each day; when the funeral carts were thick around the burying grounds, and the general had forbidden the tolling of funeral bells, so that the incessant mournful din might not pound perpetually at our ears; when there was no leather in the city to patch our broken shoes; nothing to eat but fish; and when it seemed that this abominable winter would last forever in the God-forsaken town, sunshine fell suddenly upon me and warmed me through and through.

In a thousand imaginings I'd seen Sally Leighton's face turned toward me: not with kindness, but coldly and sometimes even with a kind of hate. Worse still, I'd thought of her as forgetting me; and worst of all—if she remembered me with regret or pain—my fancy. ings beheld her seeking consolation in the addresses of another.

Then, in the midst of all that darkness, I had a letter from Sally herself.

How it reached me, seemed itself a miracle. The rebels, in their efforts to keep food from us, maintained guards everywhere along the shores of the harbor; but here and there, in the country round-about, there were sympathizers with the Loyalists; and these, when they dared, sent flour, potatoes and information into Boston. The letter might have come through such a channel; I couldn't tell. All I knew was that Buell brought it to me one morning, saying it had been given to him by a man he met on the street.

He must have had more knowledge of it than that; for when he gave it to me he said, "When you want to answer this letter, let me know and I'll try to get hold of the feller who gave it to me. I shouldn't wonder if he could find a way to send it to the lady so that she'd be put to no trouble."

I turned the folded paper over and over in my hands. There was no address upon it, no writing visible to be recognized, yet my hope was so great that I feared to open it.

"It's all right," Buell said. "There's nothing in it to worry about. It's a nice letter. The feller that brought it in thought so too, and he couldn't read very well either."

"Dear Oliver: [she had written]

"I have so much to say and so little time to say it! I am well, as are all under this roof; and I hope, dear Oliver, that you, too, are well.

"I don't know what to think of all the things I hear. Everybody seems angry from morning to night—angry at everything, even at things that don't seem worth getting angry about. People repeat the most unbelievable rumors about those who used to be their friends, and it occurs to no one to doubt any of the stories. All around me people unhesitatingly believe dreadful things about British officers who surely are as amiable as they were before this trouble started. The same silly things are said about those who have been driven from their homes. I hear them about you and your father, Oliver, and have to sit silent, pretending to be busy with needlework. I'd come to your defense, dear Oliver, if any words of mine would help; but they'd only make things worse. If I didn't agree with them, they'd say I was British myself. They'd call me a Tyrant. That's the name, now, for anyone who holds contrary opinions. He's a Tyrant! You wouldn't want me to be a Tyrant, would you, Oliver?

"That's a thing that really frightens me, Oliver. People won't allow any good to be spoken of those they hate. They explode into sudden frenzies at everyone who doesn't openly damn all Tories, just as intoxicated men fly into unreasonable rages over nothing. It doesn't matter that those Tories may be thoughtful, brave men, like your father: they're shunned: spoken of with horror.

"That's why you mustn't write me, Oliver. Letters seem to have a way of falling into the hands of persons who are merciless in their suspicions. If you were to write me, I'd be in terror for days, fearful that somebody might have seen it and might be biding his time before accusing everyone in this house of being a friend of Tyranny —and all because you'd written me a letter! So don't write, dear Oliver. Perhaps, some day, you'll be able to send me word of yourself by someone trustworthy; but for my sake and that of every member of my family, please be careful!

"I'm afraid of something else, Oliver. I'm afraid those who've left their homes and gone to Boston won't even be allowed to stay in Boston. The rage at those who have abandoned their property is such that I truly believe they'd be torn in pieces if they should ever be deprived of the protection of the British military. This is a warning, Oliver, and not a rumor. If our party wins, you will have to go, and you must begin to think where.

"And this I must tell you: our friendship has existed too long to be wrecked by persons who won't listen to any arguments but their own. Our opinions differ, but on matters which aren't personal, and which must not be allowed to interfere with our friendship. Nothing can alter the fact that you're an American, just as I am; and even though we differ in our beliefs, we're both Americans still. You were my first friend; and though I'd hesitate to say it under other circumstances, you're still my dearest friend and will continue to be so, in spite of battles and bitternesses that may sweep away our homes and fortunes.

"Never, dear Oliver, did I think to put such words as these so openly and boldly upon paper; but they are truly the sentiments of my heart. No matter what the rules of propriety, I cannot, under these cruel circumstances, suppress them, even though you yourself may blush for me, thinking me unmaidenly in uttering them. If, as I fear, you should be forced to leave America I cannot let you go without admitting that I treasure above all else the words you have so often said to me. If I have seemed to hold them lightly, I have

only done so to conceal feelings I dared not reveal. Whatever your opinion about politics, I'm sure no contrary thoughts of mine on that same subject could ever change your sentiments toward me. In these days of our country's distress and our separation from each other, a closer union between us—if I may again speak so boldly—may be impossible. Nevertheless, Oliver, I know you're no different than before you went to live in Boston, nor do I permit myself to believe that the operations of war have changed your ever-too-indulgent opinion of me.

"Oh Oliver, I long for peace and an end to this madness that threatens to bring darkness and ruin to so many miserable mortals! When that end comes, Oliver, dearest Oliver, you'll find my affections still unchanged; and I dare to hope that if this missive reaches your hand, it will find place in a heart as faithful as my own.

"Sally."

'A heart as faithful as my own" . . . "to conceal feelings I dared not reveal" . . . "you will find my affections unchanged." So lingeringly and with such gratitude did I dwell upon those precious, healing words, dazzle my sight with them, that when I turned back to the beginning to read those touching pages all over again, I found that for the moment I couldn't read at all because of the happy fog in my eyes.

"Love thine enemy." Yes, but how many can do it? In the rapture of that day I could almost be glad that Sally Leighton and I were enemies, since we could. Love that loves an enemy must be strong.

CHAPTER XIII

B<small>Y THE</small> first of January there was no escaping the fact that unless Howe's army could dislodge the rebels from around Boston and make a foray into the interior for food, it would either have to starve to death or move away.

The logical place for it to go, my father said—and every other Loyalist in Boston agreed with him—was New York. Long Island almost to a man was loyal to the King and the Constitution, so that Howe and his army would be welcome there. Once Howe was safely landed on Long Island, the city of New York must immediately fall into his hands, and he would then have access to the interior of the country by way of the Hudson.

Why he hadn't moved to Long Island during the preceding summer, while the weather was still warm, was more than anybody—with the possible exception of Howe himself—could understand; and in Mrs. Byles' opinion, he didn't.

"Belcher knew Englishmen," Mrs. Byles informed us at supper one night. "Belcher told me, so I do too. He used to talk about Englishmen for hours and hours after we'd gone to bed. Thanks to poor Belcher, I can read what minds they've got like an open book. Howe wouldn't go when the weather was nice last summer because he didn't have enough ships; but one of these days you'll see him making the same trip with a lot more people and a lot less ships, and he'll probably pick the worst storm of the year to go in. It'll seem as if he'd waited for it. It'll be logical to him; but what's logical to an Englishman isn't what's logical to us. Whatever gave you the idea, Mr. Wiswell, that he'll do what seems logical to you? Anyhow, this isn't a logical war. According to most of the rebel leaders,

114

they're fighting because they object to bad laws they didn't have a hand in making; but they want to kill us for objecting to their worse laws that *we* didn't have a hand in making! Last summer the British set out to capture the rebels, and their logical way of doing it was to get 'em where they could be captured: then let 'em walk away. Now if it's logical for Howe to go to New York, that's the place he won't go! He'll put all his men on ships and sail for wherever's the most chance of being shipwrecked and getting everybody drowned. As it's winter, he'll consider it logical to steer for a place where anybody that didn't get drowned would be frozen to death. He'll go north."

"North!" my father repeated. "You don't think he'd go to Quebec or Halifax, do you?"

"I do indeed," Mrs. Byles said, "unless he remembers Hudson's Bay."

Buell's face brightened. "I wonder if there's any special food in Halifax that's good for a delicate stomach?"

Mrs. Byles eyed Buell pityingly. "There's nothing in Halifax but herring, Buell. What's worse, most of the herring is smoked. Belcher often told me about some smoked herring he ate on his fourth birthday anniversary, and could still smell on his own breath, if he ever got to panting much, after he was eighteen years old. I wouldn't advise smoked herring, Buell."

Buell looked mournful. "Don't they have anything that corresponds to potlicker up there? I ain't going to be sorry if we have to get out of Boston, because I can't stand much more of the salt-and-water soups and dogfish steaks we've been getting—excusing myself to you, Mrs. Byles, and certainly more the fault of what I've been bringing in rather than poor housewifery or malice on your part, I'm sure. Well, even if there ain't anything much in Halifax except smoked herring, I won't be much worse off there than I am here."

Mrs. Byles looked at him sharply. "You've heard something about Halifax, Buell! Out with it!"

"Why, it's nothing, ma'am," Buell returned. "Not a thing except that Mrs. Loring thinks she wants her p'ecious General Howe to take her to Halifax."

"P'ecious! Why do you use the word 'p'ecious', Buell? Have you heard Mrs. Loring address General Howe as 'P'ecious'? With your own ears?"

"Worse," Buell said. "Whose else would I hear it with? I've heard her call him—— No, I won't tell it! I'm a gentleman, and won't gag myself by repeating it. Anyhow, she must think there's something in Halifax besides——"

"Halifax!" Mrs. Byles' laughter was contemptuous. "Buell, you're an idiot! Mrs. Loring isn't happy unless she's gambling, and she gambles with gold sovereigns: not with fish. She'd look nice, wouldn't she, pushing a stack of lightly salted hake across a Wheel of Fortune and betting the red'll turn up. No, no, Buell: there's no attraction for Mrs. Loring in Halifax."

"Oh my!" Buell said. "What makes you think so, Mrs. Byles! If Howe goes to Halifax, he'll have to buy food in a hurry from Mr. Commissary Loring before he starts, won't he? And then when he left Halifax, which he'd prob'ly have to do eventually, he'd have to buy more food in a hurry from Mr. Commissary Loring—enough food to get him wherever he's going, wouldn't he?

"You know how it is in an army, Mrs. Byles: if you buy in a hurry, you buy a lot of things you don't need, a lot of things you can't use, and twice as much of everything as any sensible man would buy. That means that if Howe goes to Halifax, Loring'll make two or three times as much as he would if Howe went right straight to New York. Mrs. Loring wouldn't like that, would she! Oh my, no!"

Mrs. Byles tossed her head. "Buell, I hate a gossip! You've got no business sitting around the house on a nice winter afternoon, spouting venom like a cook over a hot stove! Why don't you go out and find us some venison? We haven't had venison for a week!"

Buell got up at once. "Venison's getting mighty scarce in this town, Mrs. Byles! You'd think there wasn't a damned pet left in——" He caught himself and coughed. "Well," he said, turning toward the door, "I'll do what I can."

There had been a time when Mrs. Byles had been inclined to question the savory stews that Andrew occasionally served us. Buell provided the meat, always speaking of it as venison. Sometimes it was tender and toothsome; at other times stringy and strong. I had known the worst when I met him one day on Queen Street, stopped to speak to him, and heard a muffled yowl from one of the large side pockets of his overcoat. He had looked embarrassed, but had told me frankly that a cat mightn't be as good as a dog for eating purposes, but was more nourishing than fish.

No matter what else was discussed, in those days, the talk always turned in the end upon food or fuel.

People often began conversations by speaking loudly of what the rebels intended to do—I got sick of hearing over and over again that Sam Adams was determined that America should be independent of Great Britain—and even now I can hear the interminably repeated discussions as I see again those gay gatherings at the Amorys' or the Pickerings' or the Faneuils', gay even though the ladies wore heavy pelisses at the dinner table; even though the gentlemen wore gaiters and greatcoats in the sitting rooms to keep from freezing; even though the principal dish of a dinner party might be a platter of fish cakes.

Always, in such a gathering, we discussed the question of what effect the committees that were intimidating almost every American town, condemning men unseen and unheard, would have on American morals and character.

Men shouted and pounded the table, and declared, by God, that those Extraordinary Tribunals would make America into a nation of cowards, bullies, chance-grabbers, hypocrites. But if anybody mentioned food in a whisper, they dropped all other subjects to join avidly in the talk of nourishment.

We babbled for hours of how a commander had demanded a thousand sheep from the rebels of Newport, but settled for fifty; of how a magnificent dish could be obtained by making flour into ribbons of dried paste, then cooking them in a bowl with the finely chopped breasts of sparrows; of how horse meat could be made succulent by slicing it thin and stewing it with oil, white wine and a few onions; of how, when spring came, one cup of beans could be made to do the work of four by baking them with dandelion shoots and bread crumbs.

Always, too, where old friends of my father gathered, there was unending talk of the fate that must inevitably overtake our country if that madman Sam Adams had his way.

Never, they argued, could those slovenly and improvident rebels gain their independence from England on the sea. By some unbelievable fluke they might gain it on land; but England still would rule the waves—and that in time would mean another war, and perhaps another and another.

Never, they insisted, could the American colonies, if independent of England, escape internal sectional war—on one side the slave-owning provinces of the south; on the other side the northern provinces to whom slave-owning had already begun to be repugnant.

But if, as they enlarged upon the horror, slaughter and ferocity of such a contest, somebody dropped a word or two about the relative edibility of sea gulls and sculpins, the whole table, as a man, fell eagerly to chattering upon this important subject; and before they were done, every mouth at the table would be a-water over the potential delights of sculpin-tail chowder.

Word had long since gone through the city that I was collecting material for use in a true account of our troubles with England. It was known, too, that my father had been a close friend of Governor Hutchinson, and that my purpose in going to Yale had been to learn how to help Hutchinson collect material to replace that which the mob had destroyed.

Consequently I frequently received usable information from our Loyalist friends—that George Leonard with his fleet of seven vessels had gone to Martha's Vineyard and presented the British case so successfully that some of the towns of the island, particularly Edgartown and Chilmark, had unanimously voted to furnish the British with fresh provisions and fuel; that Doctor William McKinstry's wife, Priscilla, a sister of Daniel Leonard, the lawyer and pamphleteer, had been forced to march around and around the liberty pole in Taunton because she dared to express the hope that our troubles with England might be peacefully concluded; that Chief Justice Peter Oliver had been so often mobbed that the King intended to make him the governor of a new province between the Penobscot and the St. Croix rivers; that Nathaniel Thomas, who had been driven out of Marshfield by the mob as had the hundred Loyalist neighbors who followed him to Boston, could get no word to his wife and children; and that she, held in Marshfield by this same mob, was selling all her silver and furniture in order to live; that the fifteen-year-old daughter of Benjamin Hallowell had been so abused and insulted by a mob that she had lost her reason; that Samuel Fitch had been in correspondence with friends in Vermont and had learned that eighteen thousand men had fled there to avoid military duty with the rebels; that William Isham Eppes, the stepson of Doctor Sylvester Gardiner, had enlisted in the Associated Loyalists to fight the rebels though only fifteen years old; that Elizabeth Dumaresq had been so reduced in circumstances by having her property seized that she had engaged herself as a servant to a lady going to the Sugar Islands.

In the beginning this information came to me haphazard; for all the Loyalists in Boston were scattered throughout the city, in many cases keeping their whereabouts a secret. In the end, as provisions became scarcer and scarcer, all these people, ourselves included, could get no food at all except from the King's stores; and from that time on I filled my notebooks with the first-hand stories of those who were enduring starvation, cold and the loss of their homes and property rather than side with the mob.

I can see now, after all these years, that little crowded room in the Province House; see the long line of Loyalists coiling from the door of the Province House around the upper end of Province Court, down Province Court to School Street and up School Street to Tremont; see that line moving almost imperceptibly forward through the long hours of those cold, gray winter days, up the steps into the Province House, and into the steamy little office in which Charles Stedman sat, handing out the slips of paper that entitled the bearer to draw one cup dried peas, one pound salt pork, one gill molasses, one pound hard bread.

Poor, unfortunate, honest Charles Stedman! How little I thought, when first I saw his candid, worried eyes peering up anxiously, as if to see into the minds of all those hungry men and women that shuffled past his desk—how little I thought that he and I would ever stand shoulder to shoulder to fight dishonesty and cruelty, as well as a common foe.

I liked him from the moment I met him; for when he saw my notebook, and learned the reason for the notes I was making, he took me out of the line and sat me down beside him; and never again, when I went to headquarters to get rations for my father, did I have to stand and shuffle, half frozen, around the endless upper end of Province Court.

He told me that he too hoped to be a writer; and generously he put at my disposal all the information he possessed. How rare that was, I was too young to know. Not until later did I learn that only writers who at heart are great are also generous.

Yes, I was young then: not only did I like Charles Stedman; I even liked Joshua Loring, the commissary general, Stedman's superior officer; for there never was a more polite and affable man than Loring. I liked Captain William Cunningham, the assistant provost marshal, who greeted Stedman so heartily each day, always asking in that smooth, melodious Irish voice of his, "And how many of our American cousins will be holding out their porridge bowl today, Mr. Stedman?" To look at Cunningham, with his broad shoulders, rounded outthrust chest, his florid face and his kindly, ready smile was to like him.

And of course I liked Benjamin Thompson, the young man with whom Buell had traveled back from Newport on the *Siren* frigate. Everybody liked Benjamin Thompson—liked him so well that he'd have gone far in this world, even though he'd been far less of a genius than he proved to be.

Yes, I liked them all—at first; and until the very end I think the most fascinating of the four was Benjamin Thompson.

Some people, by a sort of endless industry, seem to weave a web around themselves: a web that they're continually repairing and strengthening, like spiders. Into those webs their associates are forever stumbling, sometimes to be immeshed; sometimes merely to carry away a sticky strand that clings and clings embarrassingly.

Benjamin Thompson was a spinner of webs if ever there was one; and many a long year from now men will find fragments of his webs drifting across their faces or wavering from the rooftrees of their homes, and will be as ignorant of how they got there as I was of what he was doing during the days when I first knew him.

Stedman, I found, knew a vast deal about the Loyalists who came to him for food; but he only knew what they told him. For further information he had to go elsewhere—and that was how I got to know Thompson.

Often at the beginning of my friendship with Stedman, I sat beside him at his desk, helping him write orders for food; and a dozen times a day, after studying the application of a Loyalist who claimed to be without resources and to have suffered unduly at the hands of the rebels, Stedman would go quietly from the room. When he came back, he'd mark the applicant's card with a confidence he had previously lacked.

"Thompson says," he'd tell me, "that the Treats are getting food from beyond the rebel lines." Or he might murmur, "Thompson says the Cottons haven't a jewel or a stick of furniture left," or, "Thompson says the Jamisons can put their hands on £700 if they've a mind to."

There came a day when Stedman, half beside himself because of the throng of half-starved men and women clamoring for food, told me to see Thompson for him.

"Ask him about the names on this paper," he said. "They say they're without resources, but I can't be sure. They look too well fed to me."

I found Thompson in a dusty little room at the end of the hall. He was writing at a cluttered table, a dozen reports under each elbow; and since he was dressed all in scarlet, and since his eyes were cold and gray and still, I had a momentary impression of a beautiful scarlet spider crouching in the center of a gray web.

When I told him what I wanted, and handed him Stedman's notes, he took the paper, but continued to stare at me so intently that he gave the illusion of stealthily drawing closer.

"I believe I haven't had the pleasure," he said, and there was a lisping quality to his voice that I can only describe as dainty. "You're attached to Mr. Loring's department?"

"No," I said. "Mr. Stedman has been so kind as to help me get food for my father, and in return I've tried to be of some slight assistance to him. My name is Wiswell."

Thompson stopped me with an airy gesture. "You're no stranger to me, Mr. Wiswell. I'd be ignorant indeed if I didn't know all about Seaton Wiswell. I have it on good authority that his son"—he half rose in his chair to make me a graceful bow—"is laying the foundation of a career no less brilliant. I like your choice of a profession, sir! History lives when every other art is dead. I've been expecting a visit from you, and I sincerely hope to receive many more. I've a deal of information in this office, Mr. Wiswell, and you're welcome to it."

Everything about Thompson seemed vivid, warm, a little startling. His hair was a glistening auburn; a gay smile lurked constantly at the corner of his red lips; his flexible hands made fluttering gestures; but his adventurous eyes were as cold as May ice in the shadow of a ledge.

He studied the slip Stedman had given me. "Poor Mr. Stedman," he said. "I fear our Boston society must forever remain a mystery to so confirmed a Philadelphian! Here he's questioned the name of Clayton Meadows. The Meadows had next to nothing before they were driven out of Arlington, and they've even less now. Mr. Stedman must mistake pride for property. And he's questioned James Wadham. Let me see: James Wadham: James Wadham." He opened a lower drawer of his desk, fingered the leaves of a ledger, and raised slender eyebrows. "Dear me," he said. "I'd forgotten Wadham was supporting so many hangers-on. Stedman should give him all he asks, and whenever possible." He tapped his finger on the last name. "Ichabod Watkins gets nothing. If he gets nothing, he'll leave Boston and throw in his lot with the rebels, and that'll be a godsend."

He returned Stedman's note, and his manner changed. His cold eyes became as warm as his smile, and he leaned toward me as if to protect me. "What are your own circumstances, Mr. Wiswell? Is your father properly fed?"

"He's getting food," I said, "but not the sort he ought to have."

Thompson placed a hand caressingly upon my knee. "I understand that only too well," he said warmly. "By spring these rebels should be hiding in holes and corners, and our lean days should be over. Meanwhile, let me know if your father's fare becomes unbearable. Perhaps we can find a little hidden store of food for such a loyal subject as Seaton Wiswell."

He patted my knee reassuringly, flicked imaginary dust from his scarlet satin breeches, and placed a pensive forefinger against his cheek.

These are the things I find myself remembering most clearly about a man whose career was to be prodigious, though his name was then only Benjamin Thompson: his passion for scarlet garments of extreme cut; that peculiar combination of warmth and chill; those cold, still eyes; that affectionate smile; those fondling, airy move‐ ments of his hands, poised against his cheek, plucking imaginary nothings from the air, daintily touching his full red lips with a perfumed handkerchief. . . .

I turned to Benjamin Thompson for help sooner than I expected.

Two days after my first meeting with him, Buell went to the King's stores with the order Stedman had given me; and when he came back, his manner was so genial and expansive that I knew something unpleasant had happened. From my top-floor room I could hear him commenting gayly to Mrs. Byles on the generosity of His Majesty's commissaries.

"There's nothing too much for 'em to do for us Loyalists, ma'am! Why, if they had His Majesty himself pickled in one of those pork barrels, they wouldn't hesitate to let us have a piece of him, provided we had an order for it. Yes, sir, that Captain William Cunningham wouldn't stop at anything where an American's concerned. He'd give almost any American a piece of garbage from his own pail."

I lost no time getting downstairs; and as soon as I saw Buell's face, I knew my ears hadn't deceived me. His smile was almost wistful; but his eyes were opaque as paving stones, and his cheeks a mottled gray.

"What's the matter, Tom?" I asked. "They haven't cut down our rations, have they?"

"Oh my, no," Buell said. "Whatever put such an idea as that in your head, Oliver?" He slapped the basket he carried. "Why, I've got more in this basket than we've ever had before! Yes, sir; we've never had anything like this! I don't know whether or not I ought to let you look at it, Oliver. You might not want to accept so much from the King's stores." His eyes put me in mind of musket barrels, old anchors, muddy cables.

Mrs. Byles was sharp with him. "Don't try to be whimsical when you're angry, Buell! Let's see what you've got!" She hooked the handle of her stick beneath the piece of canvas tucked over the contents of Buell's basket, and whisked it away. On the instant my nostrils were assailed by a staggering odor of decay and corruption.

Mrs. Byles drew herself up. "Offal!" she gasped. "Take that carrion out of this house."

Buell looked at her coldly. "Awful? Why, Mrs. Byles, this ain't awful! You're just being whimsical yourself! It's good King's stores! It ain't half as awful as what some other Loyalists got."

Mrs. Byles pressed her handkerchief to her nose and spoke thickly. "Don't tell me, Tom Buell, that such meat as that comes from the King's stores! Meat like that's condemned, and they bury it!"

"Maybe they do," Buell said. "Maybe they buried this; but if they did, they dug it up again. Yes, sir; that prob'ly's just what happened! It does seem just the least little teeny bit gone—not enough to kill anybody, more than half—unless you stayed in the same room with it awhile. Put it up on the roof and it wouldn't hardly hurt you, unless you went up in the garret." He pushed the basket close to me. "Would you say they'd buried this meat, Oliver, or just left it lying out in the sun too long?"

I held my nose and stared at the gray meat. Its surface quivered and undulated, and one spot as large as a two-shilling piece was acrawl with fat white worms. They had a singular appearance of solidity, as if supported by innumerable millions of their fellows.

"I can't give this to my father," I said.

"You've got to if you eat King's stores," Buell said. "I guess you didn't notice the bread, did you?" He picked up a ship's biscuit and rapped it against the edge of the basket. As if by a sort of magic it changed in his hand to a mass of dust and squirming weevils. "There's potatoes, too," Buell added, "but they ain't as good as the rest of these provisions. They're so soft you can't pick 'em up."

Mrs. Byles' stricken gaze moved slowly from Buell's face to mine. "What's to become of us, Oliver?" she asked. "Rotten food and no wood to cook it."

I took the basket from Tom. "I don't know," I said, "but something's wrong. The British Army's in Boston, and the fleet's in the harbor. All those men can't be eating rotten food, and we won't. I don't know who's to blame, but I'll go to headquarters and try to find out."

"I can tell you who's at the bottom of it," Buell said. "It's that Captain Cunningham."

"You must be wrong," I said. "Cunningham's a gentleman—an officer and a gentleman."

"Now *you're* being whimsical," Buell protested; but he said no more when I took the basket from him and set off for Province Court to take advantage of the assistance Benjamin Thompson had so generously offered.

CHAPTER XIV

Wʜᴇɴ Thompson, in reply to my knock, shouted to me to come in, I expected to find him alone; but as luck would have it, Charles Stedman was seated astride a chair and had, I knew, been bending an appreciative ear to the brilliant conversation of that glittering and scarlet-clad young man.

"Oliver!" Thompson cried. "Just the man I want to see. You above all others will appreciate what I'm telling your friend Stedman. You're a man of imagination, Oliver, and you can assure Stedman that I'm on firm ground when I say the nature, essence, beginning of existence, and rise of the wind in general is due to nothing so much as nothing. That is to say, Oliver, nature abhors a vacuum; and when a vacuum, which is neither more nor less than nothing, exists, we then have——"

I put my basket on the corner of his table and whipped off the canvas covering. "Let's talk about the wind later," I said. "What about this?"

Stedman rose slowly from his chair, staring into the basket with a look that was half incredulity and half disgust.

Thompson drew his handkerchief from the breast of his scarlet coat, waved it beneath his nose, and looked with a cold scrutiny at my offering. "Interesting exhibit of still life," he said. "There's no danger of my forgetting it; so if you'll be kind enough to cover it, Oliver, we can discuss it as much as you please."

"Before I cover it," I said, "I want to be sure you understand that everything in this basket was drawn from the King's stores. Mr. Stedman gave me the order for it yesterday. Buell drew it to-day. This is what my father's supposed to eat."

125

"There must be some mistake," Stedman said. "Rations like this aren't being issued."

"These are rations," I said. "Take a good look at 'em." I picked up a paper cutter from Thompson's desk and pushed it into the slab of beef. A squirming heap of maggots came stickily away. "The bread's only a shell for weevils," I told them. "The potatoes are black slime."

Stedman turned away his head and coughed, but Thompson smiled urbanely. "Cover it up and take it away, Oliver," he said.

I lifted the basket from Thompson's desk, set it in the entryway and closed the door. Thompson, flirting his handkerchief beneath his nose, threw open the single window of the small room. Stedman, green-faced, sat down astride his chair and rested his forehead against the chair back.

"You can do better than that for Oliver, can't you, Charles?" Thompson asked.

Stedman raised his head. "Better? Of course I can do better."

"Yes," Thompson said thoughtfully. "It would be a mistake not to I'm afraid, Charles, we'll have trouble if this becomes common prac-tice."

Stedman looked puzzled. "Common practice! Surely you don't think our department would intentionally issue rations of that sort!"

Thompson said nothing.

Color flooded back into Stedman's face, and he rose to his feet. "Look here," he said angrily, "you're not implying, are you, that I knowingly permitted such rations to be issued? Good God, Thompson, you ought to know——"

Thompson drew slender fingers across his forehead. "My dear good Charles," he said, "don't take offense because I try to think aloud. Perhaps, after all, Oliver may have been unfortunate. Perhaps he was the only one to receive such miserable rations."

"That's not so," I said. "Buell told me that every Loyalist who drew food from the King's stores today fared about the same."

Stedman frowned. "It's not possible! Those in charge of the stores would have known!"

"They *did* know!" I cried. "A man can't be in a charnel house with-out knowing it, can he?"

Stedman stared blankly at me; then turned to Thompson, who contemplated the ceiling.

"Ah yes," Thompson said slowly. "I think perhaps we're both thinking the same thing, Charles. Those in charge of the King's

stores knew what they were doing—knew, and said nothing. It
seems obvious, does it not, that they acted under orders?"

"Orders?" Stedman whispered. "They acted under orders!"

The three of us were silent, cogitating. Then, from the passageway
without, there was the sound of footsteps and of a hearty voice that
shouted, "What's happened here? This is no place for dead bodies!
Damnation, Thompson! You'll be in trouble if you leave such stinking messes outside your door!"

The door burst open and Captain Cunningham stood framed in the
doorway against the dimness of the hall. His face was florid; his eyes
beamed upon us; the corners of his lips turned upward in a whimsical
smile; he was the personification of amiability, kindness, frankness.

"By Gad, Thompson," he cried, "your friends ought to be careful about their grave-robbing! Suppose General Howe put his foot
in that basket, Thompson!"

Thompson tapped a pensive knuckle against pursed lips. "We've
been studying that basket, Captain," he said. "Except for the odor,
we found it fascinating—really most amusing."

"You did, eh?" Cunningham said jovially. "Damned if I see how
you could study it without choking! What's in it?"

"See for yourself, Captain."

Cunningham stooped, lifted the canvas and peered beneath it.
When he straightened up, he wrinkled his nose good-naturedly.
"You Americans have a better sense of humor than I have. I hoped
I'd see a dead rebel at least!"

Thompson's smile was bland. "I'd rather hoped, Captain, you'd
find something familiar about it. Wiswell drew that meat from
the King's stores this afternoon. It occurred to me that if you were
there at all today, you'd certainly have remembered this meat."

Cunningham's smile faded and he looked horrified. "Mother of
God!" he cried. "You're never serious! We've had some dubious
provisions come to us from the fleet, as Mr. Stedman can tell you,
but I hadn't known we'd been saddled with anything like this! It
must have slipped in somehow. Who'd have believed it! Holy saints
and Virgin!" The gaze which he fixed on me was compassionate.
"And to think this should have happened to a friend of Mr. Thompson and Mr. Stedman! I'll give you a personal order on the stores,
Mr. Wiswell, and you can exchange these dreadful rations for
something more fitting."

"He wouldn't *exchange* 'em, would he, Captain?" Stedman protested. "We don't want provisions like that to go back into stores, do we?"

Cunningham's laugh was deprecating. "It's just my manner of speaking! Of course and of course we don't want it back in stores! Get rid of it in any way that strikes your fancy, Mr. Wiswell, and just draw more rations on my order."

He suddenly clapped his hand to his waistcoat pocket, looked startled, drew out a chronometer and stared wide-eyed at it. "Holy Saint Brendan!" he cried. "I'm late already! I'll send that order to Mr. Stedman's office by messenger, Mr. Wiswell. You can pick it up within the hour."

He gave us a cheery nod and went bustling from the room, as obliging a gentleman as ever I'd encountered.

Thompson stared thoughtfully at the table before him, and traced diagrams upon it with a slender forefinger. Stedman straddled his chair once more, looking as if he'd swallowed something that disagreed with him.

"Buell thought Cunningham was to blame for the bad provisions," I said; "but where he got the idea, I don't know."

Thompson said nothing, but Stedman leaped from his chair as though a pin had been thrust in him. "God damn it, Thompson," he cried, "I won't be a party to such goings-on!"

Thompson raised his eyebrows. "My dear Charles," he said, "aren't you letting your imagination run away with you?"

"Imagination!" Stedman cried. "Is it imagination that my department supplies the provost marshal with proper food for the Loyalists, but that the Loyalists receive highly improper food? Is it imagination that all these people who've given up their homes and their property in order to side with decent government are receiving victuals I wouldn't feed my dogs? Is it imagination that Captain Cunningham and Joshua Loring dine together at least three times a week? Is it imagination that Captain Cunningham, before he was made assistant provost marshal, had been willing to fatten his own purse out of the misery of his own countrymen? Why, damn it, Thompson, everybody in Philadelphia who knew anything at all knew Cunningham made his living by bringing poor Irishmen to America and selling 'em into slavery!"

"Come, come, Charles," Thompson said. "All these conjectures—all these old wives' tales—aren't sufficient to make out a case against our genial friend."

"Conjectures! Old wives' tales!" Stedman protested. "My home's in Philadelphia, Thompson! Surely there's no reason why I shouldn't be as well informed about other Philadelphians as you are about Bostonians! I know Cunningham's character, and I know he'll make money out of any position in which he finds himself. You don't think I'm blind, do you? Don't you think I know how Cunningham got himself appointed assistant provost marshal? *You* know, don't you?"

"My dear Charles," Thompson said coldly. "You came here from Philadelphia under the same unfortunate circumstances that brought all the rest of us here. Like all of us, you had no way of existing unless you could be helped by the government you were supporting; and you considered yourself fortunate to be given a position in the commissary general's department. If you lose that position, you'll have no other to turn to, and you'll starve! If you persist in giving tongue to disloyal gossip about superior officers, you'll inevitably be wholly out of employment—dependent on the bounty of a few of us like Wiswell and myself, who aren't exactly rolling in luxury; so it seems to me——"

Stedman, his face pale and his lips pressed tight together, stared angrily at Thompson. "Disloyal gossip? Disloyal poppycock! Loring told his wife he wanted Cunningham made assistant provost marshal. Nothing more was necessary. Mrs. Loring saw to it, and Cunningham was *made* assistant provost marshal! That's not gossip! That's a fact! Now the good food that our department has been trying to supply to Wiswell's father and all the other thousands of loyal Bostonians has vanished, and in its place is stinking meat and rotten potatoes and bread gone to dust with weevils. What do you have to say to that?"

Thompson shrugged his shoulders. "I have nothing to say to it, and neither will you, if you know what's good for you. Army commissaries are the same the world over, and always have been. Probably they always will be. If this rabble of rebels ever turns into an army, with proper officers and proper supplies of food, those that supply the food'll grow rich out of the needs of those who fight for 'em."

"But they shouldn't be allowed——"

"I agree," Thompson interrupted. "They should *not* be allowed; but the only way they can be stopped is by stopping war. I take it, Charles, you don't want the rebels to win. Presumably you wouldn't care to be governed by the same violent, intolerant mob that drove you out of Philadelphia?"

"Good God!" Stedman cried. "Never!"

"Exactly," Thompson said dryly. "My advice to you, Charles, is to go back to the commissary general's office and do everything in your power to help end this rebellion at the earliest possible moment. Hold your temper and your tongue a few months more, my friend, and the war'll be over. Then you'll be beyond the reach of the Cunninghams and the Lorings, and can speak your mind about them without endangering yourself."

He turned to me. "Oliver, I don't believe you'll have any further trouble over your father's rations. And since this conversation has taken place in my private office, I must ask you to treat it as strictly confidential. You have no way of knowing whether Charles is sure of his facts, and you don't want to be a party to sowing dissension in our ranks."

"If Cunningham's stealing food and selling it for his own and Loring's benefit," I said, "it seems to me the best way to avoid dissension is to bring the matter to General Howe's attention in the hope that——"

"Damn it, Oliver," Thompson said testily, "can't you understand what I've been telling you? Armies *must* have their Cunninghams and their Lorings! If you get rid of one Cunningham or one Loring, you'll find half a dozen patriotic citizens waiting to take his place. I must ask you to give me the assurance that you'll say nothing about what you've heard in this office today."

"Well," I said, "I suppose I must, but——"

Thompson jumped up and patted me on the shoulder. "That's right, Oliver! Just a little more patience and we'll move out beyond Dorchester Heights and send the rebels racing for safety. Just a little more patience, and we can all go back home—Mr. Stedman to Philadelphia and I to Woburn and you to Milton."

I hoped with all my heart he was right, because it seemed to me that my patience was almost exhausted. How little I knew, how painfully little I knew, of the patience—the strangling, deadening, heartbreaking, nerve-racking patience—that men must have if they are to endure a war.

"Just a little more patience," Thompson had told me, "and we can all go back home: we'll move out beyond Dorchester Heights and send the rebels racing for safety . . ."

That miserable winter dragged on and on and on; yet that move out beyond Dorchester Heights didn't come. What was worse, the Heights themselves remained empty and unfortified. Every Loyalist in Boston prayed for the occupation of those vital Heights—how vital every man knew who had heard the hoarse growling of the mob and felt its ruthless hands.

Boston lies on a straight line drawn between Bunker Hill and Dorchester Heights, and equidistant from each. Only a day or two before that hot June night when the rebels had thrown up their earthworks on Bunker Hill, General Gage had been planning to seize and fortify Dorchester Heights. Bunker Hill, seemingly, had diverted General Gage's mind; he had forgotten Dorchester Heights —a peculiar way to use his memory, for the Heights were still there, and most of the rest of us were remembering them acutely.

If the rebels could have held Bunker Hill, they'd have bombarded the city from it. Dorchester Heights offered them the same opportunity, and if they should have the sense to seize it, they could do what they wished with Boston. Consequently, ever since midsummer, there had been a constantly growing murmuring at the failure of the King's commanders to place men, guns and earthworks upon that hilly promontory before the rebels realized its importance to us —aye, and to them.

General Gage hadn't done it, perhaps because of his hundreds of wounded men; perhaps because of the smallpox that had laid low so many other hundreds; perhaps because he was a stupid man and kept putting it off, after the habit of stupid people.

But when Gage had been recalled and Howe had taken his place, Howe too had done nothing. Why not? every Loyalist wanted to know. Why not? my father asked. Why not? Mrs. Byles demanded Why don't they fortify Dorchester Heights? every man wondered. Why? For God's sake, why?

My own feelings being what they were, I went to Thompson about it.

"There isn't a Loyalist in Boston," I told him, "who isn't saying openly that all Loyalists were guaranteed protection when they came into this town, but that they're without protection so long as those heights are unfortified."

"Everybody's saying it," Thompson admitted. "Everybody but the general. He's been spoken to often enough, but he says the ground's frozen. Not the proper season, you see, Wiswell my lad. Frozen ground's ruinous to spades, and spades are King's stores! Waste not, want not! And we must have seasonableness above all things! Doing an unseasonable thing in war's like a breach of propriety. We must wait for an unfreezing."

"You don't have to dig in the ground to make fortifications," I said. "History's full of sieges in which breastworks were made of anything that would stop bullets. You could use hay bales."

"Oh yes: we've told him that." Thompson waved a graceful hand. "He looks fatigued when we speak of it. When a general looks fatigued, it's time to stop speaking, my dear friend. Generals always look fatigued when you tell 'em what they don't want to know. That fatigued look discourages open criticism and helps to ward off overexertion . . . yes . . . Mrs. Loring is a remarkable woman, Oliver. When General Howe's mind is fatigued by gabble about Dorchester Heights, she brings the light back again into the tired eyes; makes him forget all about such annoyances as war and fortifications."

"Well," I said, "with Dorchester Heights unfortified I'm uneasy about my father. He needs all the rest he can get, and if we're to have trouble because the general won't fortify the Heights, I want to know about it and move my father to a safer place. Let me know when you learn Howe's plans, will you?"

Thompson said he would, but that evening I had an experience that was far from encouraging.

My father, going over a bundle of legal papers in one of the chests we'd brought with us from Milton, found an abstract of title sent to him for an opinion months before by Ward Chipman of Cambridge, who had graduated from Harvard when he was sixteen and now, though exactly my own age, was regarded as having one of the keenest legal minds in America.

My father, who was punctiliousness itself, seemed perturbed at the thought that he'd sent Chipman the desired opinion but failed to include the abstract in his letter; so to put his mind at rest, I told him I'd take the paper to Chipman's house on Tremont Street. When he protested that it was late, I said I was glad for the opportunity of drinking a glass of wine with Chipman and picking up all the latest gossip about civil and military goings-on in Boston—for Ward Chipman was one of those gay, nimble-witted blades who somehow contrive to accomplish enormous amounts of work, and at the same time to be on good terms with everyone, as well as a seemingly indispensable part of every fashionable dinner party, tea party, ball and rout.

My father was clearly relieved at the suggestion. "It's probably of no consequence," he said, "but I won't deny I'd fret about it. Be sure to give it to Chip in person, and explain it was a wholly unintentional oversight. And say I hope to see him soon."

Knowing the Chipman house well, I went down the alley beside it to the door opening into the entryway adjoining the small room Chipman used as a library and study. The manservant who admitted me ushered me at once into the study, saying that Mr. Chipman, who had guests, had that moment gone to the gaming room on the second floor to see about the punch. When the servant left me to tell Ward, I sat in the dim, candlelighted study, trying to place the voices of the prattlers in the dining room. Some were English and vaguely familiar. I wasn't long in doubt; for almost at once I heard chairs being drawn back, and shortly thereafter the guests passed along the hall between the dining room and the front of the house. That hall ran at right angles to the dark little entryway by which I'd entered. I saw Jonathan Sewall, the attorney general, with one of the Pickman girls, her whitened hair towering almost a foot above her black eyebrows; General Timothy Ruggles and his wife; Colonel and Mrs. Edward Winslow from Plymouth; Mr. and Mrs. Pickman, who had only recently fled to Boston from Salem by separate and roundabout routes. Then I heard an affected scream, and a lady, laughing gaily, came suddenly into the dark entryway to stand in the study doorway, looking back at her escort, whom I couldn't clearly see. Other guests passed them. I saw that these two had an understanding, and wished to snatch a word with each other, after the fashion of lovers—and intriguers—since the world began. The woman was Mrs. Loring, the same pretty, smiling, dimpled Mrs. Joshua Loring who, on the night of April nineteenth, had sobbed so effectively to rebel officers at the barricades about the imminence of her pretended accouchement. Her mountain of powdered hair was dotted with little bows, as though a flock of butterflies had come to rest upon it, and she wore a billowing brocaded gown that might readily have fallen completely from her shoulders and bosom if she'd coughed unguardedly.

As she stood in the doorway, the room in which I sat was filled with a heavy odor of lilies of the valley—a flower I could never again smell with pleasure.

The man's voice, heavier even than the scent of the perfume, said, "I'll wager you've been forgetful again, my dear."

The lady spoke in a light, sweet, child's voice, that had both plaintiveness and excitement in it, as though something vaguely startling and almost indecent had happened to her—as though she had been the recipient of attentions that left her breathless, even though they were welcome.

"Forgetful?" she said. "I've never been forgetful of you, General, whatever I've been forgetful of."

"I fear," the heavy voice said, and I knew it now for General Howe's, "I fear you've forgotten your portemonnaie, so I've taken the liberty, in case you lose——"

Mrs. Loring was patently confused. "No!" she cried. "No—yes—no—why, dear me, I believe—yes, I actually have!" Then there was a little pause, and that miaouling child's voice with its suggestion of indecencies went on, "Oh, you thoughtful, p'ecious man! Oh, General! Oh, I protest! Oh, I can't let you! I vow I can't. Oh, you *are* p'ecious—so masterful! There's no resisting you, I vow! Just think! If I could double this, I could buy that p'ecious gold case!"

I heard the rumble of Howe's voice, and then an infantile protestation from Mrs. Loring, "Oh la! I'll do no such thing, you sweet thoughtful man! You've done enough already! I'll buy it my own self!"

There was a quick, thick silence, as perceptible, almost, as the scent of lilies of the valley that seemed to eddy about me.

Then Mrs. Loring said suddenly, in that strangely petulant infant voice, "I heard you tell Chip you'd see him tomorrow. You just cannot! Tomorrow's Thursday, and you promised I should have the whole day. You know you did, and Mrs. Coryell expects me to bring you! I absolutely promised you to Mrs. Coryell for dinner!"

"There've already been several such days," Howe's sulky voice said. "I have some pressing military matters to think of, my pet."

"Oh pshaw!" Mrs. Loring cried. "Always these military matters!"

"No, no!" Howe said. "Nothing like always! They've by no means had precedence during this charming dalliance!"

I could almost see Mrs. Loring pout, though her back was toward me. "Well, I've *got* to have you tomorrow; and the day after—Friday—you swore you'd go with me to the Ettricks'! I won't hear about military affairs when you've promised. I won't, I won't! I'll pout, I will indeed!"

The general made grumbling cooing sounds, but before he could turn those singular sounds into words, Ward Chipman's round and smiling face appeared beyond the general's shoulder.

"Hah!" the general bumbled. "Caught, eh, Chipman? Who can resist these fair Americans!"

"La!" Mrs. Loring said, "I'm bound you sha'n't resist me if there's any way to persuade you! Do, Chip, I implore you, lend your voice to mine to persuade the general to come to Mrs. Chandler's on Saturday!"

As she took the general's arm and drew him along the hallway, her gay, childish laughter was an indescribable blend of allure and foul suggestion.

Chipman stared after them, his expression a mixture of amusement and revulsion; then he came into the study and gave me a hearty greeting.

I knew then, beyond any question, that Dorchester Heights wouldn't be fortified on Thursday, Friday or Saturday. Howe wouldn't have time.

A week later Thompson gave me a first word of the staggering news that was to turn Boston into a madhouse.

Unexpectedly early in March, the rebels began a nightly bombardment of the city from their half-encircling camps that beleaguered Boston on its landward side. The nights were blustery and freezing cold; and from dark till dawn the distant guns boomed. Steadily, every minute or two, a shell would burst in the town— sometimes far away, with the noise of a cellar door violently slamming; sometimes near by, with a ripping crash.

Nobody in Boston knew the reason for this suddenly begun terrorization; but after three days of it we had the explanation, and the morning light answered our questions as it rosily illuminated Dorchester Heights.

Under cover of the darkness and the noise the rebels had drawn thousands of close-packed bales of hay to the hilltops and thus built a fort wherefrom long batteries of 24-pounders looked down on the British men-of-war in the harbor, and across to the unprotected houses of the town.

A white-lipped silence shut down over Boston at the sight of those guns in the embrasures of the hay fort; and when people spoke together, they did so in voices that were hushed and uncertain. Men looked with sick eyes at the fortified Heights, and were sicker when they spoke of Howe. Sickest of all were they when they thought of what could now befall them. After so long neglecting the Heights, would Howe, they asked each other, try to drive the rebels from them as he had from Bunker Hill, or would he refuse even to try?

Mrs. Byles longed loudly and often to be allowed to climb into her carryall and lead the attack, dragging Mrs. Loring with her. "Then, maybe, that fool of a Howe would come too," she said. But my father just lay silently on his bed, smiling a little. I think he knew all the time what was going to happen to us. As for Buell, he took on a stubborn, white-eyed look that reminded me of a balky horse.

In the afternoon, Thompson sent me a message to come and see him; then gave me the information that put me more than ever in his debt.

"Oliver," he said, placing his hand caressingly on my knee—a cajoling habit of his I didn't like, "we're all going to have to move out of Boston before long."

I'm afraid I laughed. "All of us? Even Mrs. Byles? Even my father, who can't walk upstairs alone?"

He waved his hand airily. "Of course, my dear friend, it won't be obligatory. I think Mrs. Byles would be comparatively safe, even with the rebels—if she keeps on talking."

"I don't," I told him. "Not if she talks as she would if they seize her property."

"They're certain to do that," he said. "Yes, on second thought it would be judicious for her to leave. As for your father, you'd be signing his death warrant if you let him stay in this town after the British move out and the rebels move in."

I stared at him. "Then it's settled, is it? The British are going?"

"Yes, Oliver; and if you and your father don't go too, you can expect pretty harsh treatment from the rebels. You've heard of Simsbury Mines, haven't you?"

"Simsbury Mines? I know they're copper mines, and in Connecticut. They're near Hartford, aren't they? What have they got to do with my father and me?"

"Only this," Thompson said. "The Connecticut rebels have generously squandered almost four hundred dollars making the old shafts and levels of Simsbury Mines into a jail for Tories. They've put iron bars and stone slabs over the shaft mouths, and they've built wooden platforms about thirty-five or forty feet down, in the caves the miners made when they dug out the copper. When a Tory's sent there, he's lowered to one of the platforms to stay till the war's over. It's a little damp, but they say it's warm in winter and cool in summer, and a sure cure for all sorts of skin diseases, including the itch. General Washington sent several Tories there a few days ago; and that's where you and your father'll be sent if you stay in Boston after the rest of us have gone."

"But my father wouldn't last a week in a place like that," I protested.

"No," Thompson said. "The rebels wouldn't wish him to. They don't wish any Loyalists to live; and in a year's time, if they have their way, none will. Let's be practical. When the army goes, I've got to go; you've got to go; we've all got to go. Otherwise——"

I interrupted him. "But what's Howe thinking of? He must have at least seven thousand effectives, all well armed and equipped; and the Loyalist regiments in this town would fight like devils if only the general'd turn 'em loose against this rabble that's been destroying everything we own! Why, the rebels *never* have enough powder; but Howe has enough to last for years! What's he trying to do? Just turn over all America to the rebels?"

"I don't know what he's trying to do," Thompson said. "Nobody knows. I hope to find out some day. Maybe if I ever get to England, somebody there can tell me; but maybe even the English don't know and never will.

"What I do know is this, Oliver. You may think troops will be sent to take Dorchester Heights from the rebels. You may even see the troops set out to do it. But the unfortunate truth, Oliver, is that they'll never get there. Dorchester Heights will never belong to us."

"How do you know that, Thompson?"

"Because I know Howe's our general; sorry I can't give you a better answer. Look at those rebel batteries of 24-pounders taken from the British in the surprise at Ticonderoga! Howe'll never go up the hill against 'em. On the other hand, we here in Boston needn't be afraid of 'em. The rebels have been giving us some hints in their night bombardments, to scare us; but too many of those who call themselves Patriots own property in Boston, and of course they're too foxy to destroy a town that they know as well as we do we're going to evacuate."

Still I couldn't accept it. "But why? Why, why, why? Why don't we——"

He stopped me. "Don't wait to ask any more questions, Oliver. You'd better be getting your father into as good a condition for departure as you can. I can make arrangements to have you put on board one of the transports, but my influence stops there. I can't do anything about your belongings. You'll have to look out for those yourselves."

"One of the transports?" I was a little dazed. "Where will it be going?"

"General Howe hasn't made up his mind about that yet," Thompson said, "but you'd better get your father into the warmest clothes you've got."

CHAPTER XV

Nor often does the whole population of a city fall into a complete frenzy of fear, irritation and breathless haste; but that was what happened to the inhabitants of Boston when Howe made public announcement that the town must be evacuated.

Never before, certainly, had Boston seen such an array of vessels as thronged the waterfront, from Copp's Hill to Long Wharf. They lay against the docks as tightly as they could be packed—schooners, brigs, snows, sloops and little sharp-ended pinks. Their masts were like a forest, as uncountable as the sparrows that roosted at night in the ivy of King's Chapel: scores upon scores upon scores of them—more than I had ever before seen in my whole life.

Thanks to Benjamin Thompson's warning, the few odds and ends we had brought into Boston from Milton were corded up and ready to go before the official announcement of the evacuation was made, and they seemed infinitesimal by comparison with the belongings Mrs. Byles designed to take with her. Her boxes, portmanteaus, sacks, packages and paper-wrapped parcels contained, simply, everything she owned. She was even ambitious of taking aboard ship the tall clock showing the moon's changes which had belonged to her grandfather Barrell.

She rooted out things she couldn't have seen for twenty years—pincushions, brooches of braided hair from the heads of favorite nieces who now were mothers, lace mitts in need of mending, mobcaps yellowed with age, mirrors, lectures written by her husband, from which she read snatches to us, unconsciously revealing that Belcher Byles' philosophical musings in the classroom were less pungent than those with which he favored his wife after they had retired.

She packed turkey carpets, books she had never read and never would read, different-sized hoops and panniers for all occasions, extra canes in case she broke her ivory-headed one, and little things that reminded her of Belcher—shoe buckles, bundles of letters, a terrestrial globe, his mahogany wigstand.

Our protests were unavailing. She spent the whole of March eighth rooting out those treasured possessions from holes and corners.

My father and I urged her to restrict herself to necessities, but she just continued to unearth the accumulated trash of a lifetime and pile it in the front parlor downstairs.

Buell, when he came home that evening, scanned the heap with a doubtful eye. "Ma'am," he said, "I've seen the embarcation orders; me and Oliver are assigned to the brigantine *Elizabeth*. So are you and Mr. Wiswell, and your servants Maggie and Andrew. We got no choice about what we go on. Your nephew George Leonard's vessels have all been requisitioned, so they ain't his any more. I was hoping we'd have one of 'em to ourselves, but we got to go the way we're ordered to go—on the *Elizabeth*. She's a transport, and there ain't anything allowed on transports except things that would do the rebels some good if left behind. Major Gorham and Captain Henderson and Captain White, they brought a lot of furniture when they came here, but they can't take it with 'em and they can't find any buyers for it, so they're burning it tonight. All over town people are burning their furniture."

"Buell," Mrs. Byles said, "where I go, Maggie goes, and so does that clock and wigstand."

"Not on the *Elizabeth* brigantine, they don't," Buell said, "and that's the one we're going on."

He seemed to consider the matter settled so far as Mrs. Byles was concerned. He drew some papers from his pocket and turned to my father. "I guess we'll be leaving pretty soon, Mr. Wiswell," he said, "because I just took these two proclamations from a pile I was printing for the general up at headquarters."

Both of the proclamations were addressed to Crean Bush, a commissary I'd often seen in Cunningham's company, and signed by William Howe. One ordered the inhabitants of Boston to deliver all woolen and linen goods to Bush, and announced that any person secreting or keeping such articles in his possession would be treated as a favorer of the rebels. Mrs. Byles, standing beside me to read the proclamation, said "Bah!" in a contemptuous voice.

The second proclamation, also to Crean Bush, was longer, and read:

"Sir,

"I am informed there are large quantities of goods in the town of Boston, which, if in possession of the rebels, would enable them to carry on war. And whereas I have given notice to all loyal inhabitants to remove such goods from hence, and that all who do not remove them, or deliver them to your care, will be considered as abettors or rebels, you are hereby authorized and required to take into your possession all such goods as answer this description, and to give certificates to the owners that you have received them for their use, and will deliver them to the owners' order, unavoidable accidents excepted. And you are to make inquiry if any such goods be secreted or left in stores; and you are to seize all such, and put them on board the Minerva *ship, or the brigantine* Elizabeth."

Mrs. Byles meditated frowningly. Then she turned upon Buell. " 'Unavoidable accidents excepted!' " she cried. " 'Authorized to take all such goods as answer this description!' Why, you fool, if you had that proclamation in your hand and claimed Crean Bush sent you, you'd have the right to seize everything in this house or any other house, and put it aboard any ship you wanted to put it aboard."

"Not aboard the *Elizabeth*," Buell said, stubbornly.

"Yes, even the *Elizabeth*," Mrs. Byles insisted. "But if the *Elizabeth* agitates you too much, you could use another vessel, couldn't you? You could! This proclamation gives you the right to seize anything you want to seize, doesn't it? Well, why not seize a vessel?"

Buell scratched his head and looked at her blankly. "Ah," he murmured.

"There's no two ways about it," Mrs. Byles went on. "I don't propose to burn up these things of mine, and I don't propose to let rebels have 'em! They're my personal belongings, necessary to my welfare. I've been guaranteed protection by the armed representatives of my government, and I'm going to have it, and I'm going to have the things I need!"

She went to a closet, burrowed in its dark recesses, and emerged backward, bent double and dragging a large basket that contained a complete washstand set of glazed earthenware vessels, the tops of two of them—a slop jar and a chamber—being fitted with porous knitted jackets of pale blue cotton to prevent either breakage or noise. "There!" she said. "Belcher's own, and I almost forgot 'em!"

Buell tried to be stately, thinking thereby to increase his weight with her. "Madam——" he began.

She pointed to the basket. "Every one of 'em necessities! I've got my own in a packing box; but suppose you drop that packing box, Buell, while you're carrying it?"

"Me?" Buell asked. "Me carrying it?"

"Yes, of course," she said. "You haven't anything of your own to carry, and you ought to be ashamed of yourself for not! You've got permission to carry along all the personal belongings you're a mind to, and look at what you're taking! You haven't even got that coat of tar the people out in Dedham presented you with, excuse me for mentioning it. Oliver and Andrew'll have to be getting Mr. Wiswell and their own things aboard, so who but you is to take charge of mine, Buell?"

He looked thoughtful.

Mrs. Byles went close to him and poked him in the ribs with the handle of her cane. "Don't be obstinate, Buell," she said. "I expect to reward you for seeing that all my things are stowed nicely aboard ship. I mean better by you than the donation of a shilling or two out of my scraggly purse. There's something right and handsome that ought to be done by an active man like you, especially since you've got permission to take anything you like."

Buell looked at her warily. "I won't carry that chamber," he said.

"No, and I wouldn't let you," she told him. "Hark to me, Tom Buell: there's been hundreds of rebel sympathizers move out of this town because they thought we might do to them as their mobs had done to us. It'd be right and handsome if we did, wouldn't it?"

"Yes, ma'am, it would!"

"Some of those rebel families that thought they'd better leave Boston," Mrs. Byles said musingly, "were disagreeable people. I wouldn't want to know more disagreeable and tiresome people than the Kirby family. Mr. and Mrs. Kirby and their daughters made a point of keeping track of people the rebels didn't like. What's more, it was surprising how often Committees of Vigilance took action against friends of the Kirbys. They were well acquainted with

Thomas Fellmore in Cambridge, and they'd spoken often of a nice silver ewer he owned. Well, a mob took action against old Mr. Fellmore, and drove him out and looted his house. Early the next morning the Kirbys came out to Cambridge and bought the ewer for a few pennies from the riffraff that had stolen it."

"They did?" Buell asked, interested. "Where is it now?"

"I don't know," Mrs. Byles said. "The Kirbys must have taken it with 'em when it was their turn to skedaddle out of Boston. I understand they took all their silver with 'em, but they must have had to leave a lot of other valuable things."

"Where?" Buell asked. "Where'd they leave 'em?"

Mrs. Byles seemed irritated at Buell's interruption. "Abijah Kirby," she went on, "was a mean old man, but always had good taste. Belcher and I used to take tea with 'em, for politeness, and Belcher used to say that if political opinions ever got worked up into war and deeds of violence, he'd like to be the first man to break into the Kirby home—he admired Kirby's taste to that extreme. You see, Abijah Kirby never stinted his wife and daughters on silks and jewelry, because he smuggled 'em the same as John Hancock did, and there were always bales of brocade in the attic—bales! You wouldn't be likely to know, Buell, but Mrs. Kirby was a Capen; proud, high-living people. The Capens didn't come to Boston till 1736, but they considered themselves real old residents, and always took care to have more family portraits than some of us who'd been here a hundred years longer. Why, Mrs. Kirby had eight paintings by Feke and Smibert and Copley that I'd be willing to claim as relatives my own self. They're nice pictures, better than money, and so's most of the furniture. So are bales of silk, for that matter, and I don't believe they had time to get much down from the attic. When I think of old Mr. Fellmore's ewer that he loved so much, it seems a terrible injustice for us to be chased out of Boston and to have the Kirbys coming back into their fine house to enjoy everything just as they left it, while we're suffering, with little to our backs, upon the stormy seas."

She looked dreamy. "I was passing the Kirby house only this morning, and noticed how it's all boarded up tight, except one window on the second floor that's got a nice strong trellis for vines leading up to it, almost like a ladder. As I say, they're a mean family, but I wouldn't have thought they'd be *that* stupid. Somebody ought to write to 'em about that window."

"Yes, they ought," Buell agreed earnestly. "Which side of the house did you say it was on?"

I never saw a town so full of pale-faced and haggard men and women perpetually running. Headquarters at the Province House was besieged by officers and civilians demanding to be told immediately the name of the transports on which they and their dependents were to sail.

All day on the ninth of March, and all that night, they ran in and out of the Province House; and during all that day and ensuing days and nights, the streets were full of shouting men, scurrying from their homes to the docks, and from the docks back to their homes again, trundling carts, trucks, wheelbarrows and handbarrows loaded with their personal belongings.

On dark streets men and boys fought over wheelbarrows and handbarrows, while on the wharves womenfolk sat guarding heaps of household goods—bedding, trunks, boxes, bags, oil paintings, stacks of books, rolled carpets, bird cages.

Carryalls and chaises, all loaded to overflowing and sometimes drawn by horses but more often by men and boys, rattled down Tremont Street and Beacon Hill as if the devil himself were between the shafts.

On the tenth the streets were crowded with army horses, clattering down to the horse transports, which that evening moved out from the wharves and were towed down the harbor by their boats.

On the eleventh Crean Bush began to carry out Howe's orders to remove from shops, residences and warehouses all goods that might be useful to the rebels when they returned to Boston. Bands of whooping roisterers, some in carts and some afoot, racketed up and down the streets. There was no telling whether they were soldiers, sailors or civilians, for some were in civilian dress and others in uniform; but there was no question that most of them were drunk.

They went bellowing through the town; and when the fancy struck them, they swarmed around a locked door or a shuttered window, smashed it and scrambled yelling through the breach. Shouts and crashings came from within those houses; then men charged out staggering, their arms full of useless things, clambered helter-skelter into their carts, and clattered wildly off.

For no discernible purpose except to make the nightmare worse, the British ships in the harbor opened fire on the works at Dor-

chester Heights and never stopped for twenty-four hours. The walls
of the houses shook, windows rattled in their casements and sleep
was as impossible as though one lay upon a giant drum that throbbed
to the thumping of a score of drummers.

Never once on that day did we set eyes on Buell, and not till the
following afternoon did we learn certainly where he'd been keeping
himself—though I'd ventured to guess, and hadn't been far wrong.

All the morning of the twelfth the streets had been aswarm with
drunken throngs of soldiers and sailors, just as on the day before;
and Mrs. Byles, fearful that one of the troops of looters might burst in
to seize her husband's wigstand and the rest of her treasures, had
moved an easy chair to the front hall.

There, tight-lipped and watchful, the resourceful lady sat most of the
day, until, just at dusk, a thunderous knocking shook the front door.

When Andrew's fingers fumbled for the door chain, Mrs. Byles
raised her cane above his knuckles. "If you let that chain slip off,"
she told him, "you'll hear from me!"

Again a fist thundered on the door. Andrew adjusted the chain,
drew the bolt, turned the key, and cautiously admitted a narrow
sliver of outer light.

On the instant, as if a shell had burst upon the steps, the door
flew open to the limit of the chain, half caught there; then the
chain pulled from its fastenings with a crash; the door swung back
against the wall to reveal, on the steps without, a group of men in
wrinkled pea jackets and hard black tarpaulin hats.

Andrew was thrown backward, a movement he arrested tem-
porarily by seating himself, without any wish to do so, upon Mrs.
Byles' lap. The group of men charged into the darkness of the
hallway; and Mrs. Byles' chair and Mrs. Byles and Andrew went over
backward with an uproar.

The men stared uncertainly at Mrs. Byles and Andrew, and at me
as I ran to help them. Then one of them peered through the sitting-
room doorway at the hill of boxes, packages and bundles.

Mrs. Byles, active within my assisting arms, struck at him with her
cane. "Get out! Get out of this house!" she screamed. She released
herself from me, sprang forward and brought down her stick with
a thwack on the tarpaulin hat of a hulking fellow who was pushing
forward into the sitting room.

The man removed the hat; examined the dent in its crown; then spoke sharply to his companions. "Come in! This here's what we want. We ain't got all night, so get it out to the cart!"

"You will not!" Mrs. Byles cried. "Out of my house with you! You're common sailor men, and my father was Elias Dexter Barrell of Salem! When captains spoke to him, they took off their hats and pulled hair out of their forelocks! Ordinary seamen never came in his office without knocking their foreheads on the step outside first. You take off your hats and troop out of his house! March!"

Two of the men removed their hats and looked into them. The one who had been struck, however, settled his dented headgear more firmly on his head with a slap of his horny hand and fixed a defiant eye on Mrs. Byles. "Now look here, ma'am: we ain't got all night, and I'll thank you to step away from in front of me before you get your feelings hurt by being lifted to one side."

"I warn you!" Mrs. Byles said, trembling dangerously. "You've got a dirty face, and on that account I'd hate to scratch it! But don't you lay a finger on me or anything in this house, if you ever expect to see again out of those big, bulging, bloodshot eyes of yours!"

"They are not!" the big man said defensively. "My eyes are not——"

"They are too!" Mrs. Byles cried. "Do you think I never heard my father talk to such as you? They're bloodshot and they're bulging, and you're nothing but a great big dirty Liverpool lime-juicer, dirty all over if the truth were known! If a man of my family were here, you'd be pitched out on your head, but you just touch one object in this room and I'll show you that even a female Barrell can take care of her own!"

"Now, now, Mrs. Byles," Tom Buell's voice came from the doorway and he stepped softly into the room. "What's the delay? Why isn't all this stuff packed on the cart? We've got three more loads to get down to the dock tonight—heavy ones."

Mrs. Byles sat down. "In the name of the great Jehovah," she said feebly, "if these sailors are yours, why didn't you tell 'em to say so, Tom Buell? You can tell by looking at 'em that they wouldn't have sense enough to say so unless you told 'em to. They came blundering in here in a way I'm afraid made me a little cool to 'em!" She tapped her cane against the knee of the man whose hat she had dented. "Come, come, my man; don't dawdle about! Do what you're here to do!"

He laughed harshly. "Not me! I wouldn't touch things that belonged to a Barrell! Such as us might soil 'em! For my part I wouldn't

even look at 'em with my great big dirty, bulging, bloodshot eyes!"
His companions agreed with him heartily and profanely, crowding
after him as he strode into the hall.

Buell stopped them. "No, you don't," he said. "You clap onto
that dunnage and stow it in the cart."

"Stow it in hell!" the enraged leader returned. "I can't be talked to
the way I been talked to, nor head-cudgeled the way I been, and
kiss the hand that done it. I don't like Americans. What bloody sort
of a place is it where they think they can treat you like a dog because they're female Barrells? A knight's lady couldn't have said
worse to us in England. You Americans may like to be tongue-lashed
and knocked about by people that's been created Barrells, male or
female; but Englishmen won't a-bear it. Me and my mates are going
back to our ship! What, hearties?"

"Aye," they shouted. "Big Joe's right! Damn the American's dunnage! Damn America! Off we go!"

"No, you won't," Buell said, his back to the front door. He took a
printed paper from his pocket. "You'll listen to this first. It's an order
issued by General Howe today. 'Any member of His Majesty's
forces taken in the act of plundering or of firing any dwelling house,
shop, warehouse or other building will be summarily executed. W.
Howe, Com. Chief.' "

"What concern is that of ours?" the leader said angrily. "You hired
us."

"I'm not so sure." Buell smiled at him. "I don't remember it. I just
happened to come home here where I live, and found you and your
men piling up all those goods yonder in the parlor, and aiming to
take them away—till I stopped you. Looks considerably like plundering to me."

Mrs. Byles' voice rose shrilly from the rear of the group. "Broke the
door chain when they burst in!" she cried. "Broke the chain, threw
Mr. Wiswell's serving man at me, knocked me over, and stamped in
rioting." She forced her way briskly through the group, pushing men
to right and left and slapping their legs with her cane. She stood at
Tom's side. "Mr. Buell, you go call the patrol! I'll keep these petty
rakehellies here till they come."

"Here she is again," the leader growled, beaten. "Why don't you
leave her in Boston? If she's here when the rebel army marches in,
all I've got to say is, God help the rebel army! Turn to, hearties! Get
this female Barrell stuff into the cart."

CHAPTER XVI

THE vessel Buell had found for us was a sixty-foot sloop that had been disguised by her rebel owner as a gundelow and housed in Clark's shipyard, next to Hutchinson's Wharf, there to remain until the British had left Boston and she could safely be brought out and put to work again without danger of seizure.

Armed with Howe's orders to Crean Bush, Buell had commandeered a working party of sailors, promised them a share of the booty with which he planned to load her, and with their help had unhoused her, run out her bowsprit, swayed up her topmast, bent on her sails, worked her around to Long Wharf and neatly squeezed her in between a brigantine and a topsail schooner, where she looked as inconspicuous as a six-inch trout between two salmon.

"This town's full of seamen who want to leave it," Buell told me, "so you'll have no trouble getting a crew. Hire as many men as you need to sail her, but be sure you can trust 'em. Thank God you've done some sailing yourself, so we don't need to worry about a captain."

"Buell," I said, "you'd better get a regular captain if you can find one. I've never handled anything bigger than Sally's little sloop, and if we're caught in a storm—as it's mighty likely we will be at this time of year—you'd all feel a lot safer with a seafaring man."

"Seafaring man be damned!" Buell said. "Sailing's just like anything else. If I know enough to stick type for a handbill, and have just a little common sense to boot, I can stick type in the biggest printing office in the world. If you can sail a dory around Dorchester Heights, you ought to be able to sail any other sort of one-masted vessel to Hell, Hull or Halifax. You've got common sense; and you can read, can't you? Get yourself a copy of Bourde's *Manoeuvering,*

148

and you'll know as much about navigation as most of the sea captains that sail in and out of Newport. If we get ourselves a regular sea captain, he won't be satisfied unless we give him half our cargo; and we'll need all of it for ourselves, Oliver! Without that cargo, we won't have enough between us, when we get wherever we're going, to buy food for Mrs. Byles. No, Oliver: you're the one that'll have to captain the *Osprey;* so get yourself a few honest sailors, and guard that sloop as if all our lives depended on her."

"They do, don't they?" I asked.

Buell nodded. "Yes, I guess they do. If the rebels ever catch us, I guess we're finished."

Those next four days were a little Purgatory—false alarms, intermittent harmless cannonading of Dorchester Heights by the British ships, retaliation by the Heights, not so harmless, mental agony, no sleep and hard work.

My father had grown frailer and frailer with each passing day of bad food and turmoil, and I had the dreadful feeling that if I left him for a moment, he might—and I dared not put it more plainly to myself—have dire need of me.

Yet there was nothing for me to do but leave him to Andrew and Mrs. Byles; for unless the sloop could be made ready for him, he'd be in as desperate a way aboard her as he would if we fell into the hands of the rebels to be harried and chivied through Massachusetts March mud to Simsbury Mines.

Two of the seamen I hired were Nova Scotiamen, deserters from Nova Scotia militia that had come down to help the rebels capture Boston. Their rage at the rebel army was profound; for the New Englanders had called them Holy Ghosters, had accused them of being halfhearted in their desire to drive the British from America, and had beaten them unmercifully.

Almost as bitter was the anger of these Nova Scotiamen at General Howe, who had failed to give battle to the hated rebels; and on the sloop, as we worked, I heard an echo of something Buell had told us months earlier.

"The rebels ain't had any powder all winter," one of the Nova Scotiamen insisted, "and there wasn't hardly a man in any regiment that didn't think he'd done his full duty after he'd been in camp three days. Those that got to camp Monday would be figuring how to leave by Saturday! What kind of a British general is it that couldn't figure how to wipe out a rabble like that?"

Then the man added, "So far in this war we've been on both sides and ain't seen a grain of sense in either of 'em. Give me Nova Scotia!"

I think that to be back in Nova Scotia these men would have gladly worked their way for nothing; but as I didn't then know we were going there, I offered each of them a fiftieth share in our cargo, which they accepted.

They helped me to find three more seamen, all from Loyalist localities—one from Marshfield and two from Rhode Island, a colony that had come closer to keeping its head and avoiding mob rule than any of its New England neighbors. Five men, I was sure, could handle the *Osprey* wherever she went, and I worked hard with them getting the little vessel ready for sea.

Like most Boston sloops, she must have carried coastwise passengers during her earlier sailing days; for there were six bunks in her small cabin, and a table at which ten people could eat—or on which two good-sized men could sleep.

The cabin looked to me as though it hadn't been used for years; for it was crusted with dirt, and when I walked across its floor, there was a juicy crackling beneath my shoes, and a breathless faint rushing sound from the myriads of insects that took cover.

After we had burned sulphur in the noisome little place, we pried open the ports and gave her an airing such as she couldn't have had since the day she slid off the ways. Then we scrubbed her with lye and swabbed her down with sea water, nailed new canvas over the deckhouse, so that she'd be tight in case of a storm, pumped her out, caulked her deck seams, slushed her rigging, and patched her sails where they needed it most.

We did all this work to the accompaniment of clattering hooves, shouting men, the rumbling of cart wheels on the wharf.

Several times each day Buell came hustling down among us, his face pale, sweaty and unshaven; his eyes red from lack of sleep; his hands and clothes crusted with grime. He had no time for idle talk and, while we worked, just flung me the barest outline of the news, all the while hoarsely spurring his own band of tarry hirelings to hurry, hurry, forever hurry: to hurry packing boxes, bulbous sacks and bundles from the cart to the *Osprey's* deck: to stow all this feverishly below hatches and trundle off with the cart again for another load.

Working half the night as well as all day, I didn't leave the sloop; and on the morning of the fourteenth Buell told me that all streets had been barricaded, in case the rebels should take it into their heads to try to hurry the army in its departure.

"Howe's issued a new set of orders," he said to me, as the two of us lowered through the hatch the last package of the day's first cartload. "I guess he had to do it, on account of the way some of the soldiers and sailors been behaving. They ain't used a particle of judgment, Oliver! Some of 'em even busted into houses that had people still living in 'em."

He lowered his voice. "The truth is, last night some of the dunder-heads didn't have any more sense than to go and bust into the house of some close friends of Mrs. Loring. Seems the house used to belong to some people named Kirby, and some of Mrs. Loring's friends had moved into it to see nothing happened while the Kirbys were away. From what I hear of the fuss she made, she must have left something she owned herself in that house—maybe something she didn't want her husband to see just yet, like a gold toothpick. They say she never uses anything but gold. I had a silver one once myself. A rich old lady gave it to me when I was fifteen years old, for politeness; but my grandmother took it away from me and gave it to the minister. Broke it all to pieces the first time he tried to use it. Eater! Anyhow, somebody made a terrible mistake not to know beforehand who Mrs. Loring's friends are among the dis-affected, and General Howe's got out another order saying that any soldier, sailor or civilian caught plundering will be hanged on the spot. He means it, too."

"For God's sake," I said, "be careful!"

"Careful of what?" Buell asked. "Do I take a single thing Crean Bush isn't taking or wouldn't take if he was along with me and my little party? Except Mrs. Byles' property, and goods that would be useful to the enemy, there ain't hardly a thing in our hold but what's wholly justifiable. Even those pictures of grandmothers and uncles, the rebels could turn into cash to buy ammunition with. Taking things they can turn into cash can't be called plundering. Plunder-ing's taking silk petticoats or gold and silver buckles off of somebody right while they're wearing 'em. If they've already been taken off and laid aside by the people that's wearing 'em, that's altogether different—under the laws of war."

He looked at me virtuously, reached under the back of his pea jacket and after some fumbling brought out a thin but heavy package. "Don't be nervous about this, Oliver. It's a gold patch box with a miniature of General Howe set in the lid and surrounded with diamonds. You put it away on this ship where nobody's going to find it. I don't want to have any more trouble with it, because look what it's stirred up already—getting Mrs. Loring so excited General Howe's got every street in the city all clogged up with barricades. You be careful with it, Oliver!"

On the fifteenth we were awakened by the hollow thumping of feet on the planks; and all through the morning troops poured onto the wharf above us, with beating drums, cased flags and bulging knapsacks—those cruel knapsacks, which, when loaded with the bare necessities of a soldier's existence, weighed a hundred pounds.

Regiments filled that enormous long wharf from end to end, leaving only a narrow passageway along one side; and a handsome sight they were in scarlet hats edged with white lace, scarlet coats finished with yellow, snow-white breeches, spotless black gaiters, stout shoes.

A regiment looked like a monstrous sleek scarlet dragon with thousands of rhythmically moving white-and-black legs, and I wondered with a sort of despair how in God's name this splendidly trained, magnificently equipped army could have been held prisoner by a throng of badly drilled, badly armed, badly officered civilians who were skilled at nothing but squabbling among themselves.

Apparently the soldiers and their officers too were as much at a loss as I, and almost as resentful, for they were the sourest lot of men I ever saw; and if looks could have burned, the town of Boston would have gone up in flames.

They stood there for hours, growling, grumbling; and when at last sick men began to come down in carts and I had received no word from Buell, I was desperate. I couldn't even send a messenger to Sudbury Street to find out how my father was, or what had become of Buell; because when I tried to do so, I learned that the entire population of Boston, barring the army, had been ordered to stay off the streets and in their houses until the troops had embarked.

In the afternoon the wind turned into the east, as it's forever doing in Boston, and whined and moaned through the rigging of the forest of vessels all around us. It was a bitter cold wind that kicked the waters of the harbor into a dirty chop; and after it had blown an hour, the drums thumped and rolled again, and the shivering troops went shuffling off the wharf and back to their barracks.

On the sixteenth Buell came alone to the wharf, dragging the partly filled cart. "Oliver, your father's the same; I just saw him," he said, and added hurriedly, "Lend me all your sailors. I found a beautiful little warehouse nobody else knows about, and it's got thirty kegs of brandy in it."

"Haven't you sailors of your own?" I asked.

"They've been rounded up and sent back to their ships," he said. "Hurry up, Oliver! The troops are loose in the town and raising hell everywhere. Let me have those men of yours before they break into that little warehouse."

I called the men from the fo'c'sle.

"Hurry 'em up," Buell said. "If I ain't been misinformed, it was John Hancock's own father that smuggled this brandy from the French Islands, and it ought to be worth ten pounds a keg for its own sake, and about double that on account of how John Hancock'll feel when he finds it's gone."

He climbed the ladder to the dock and stood looking down at us, shouting, "Hurry up."

"Go get that cart," I told the five sailors, "and sway it down here on the deck. Take off the wheels and pack the whole business in on top of the cargo; then make everything fast."

"You can't do that," Buell protested. "Do you want to leave thirty whole kegs of brandy—good, healthy brandy—for a damned lot of rebels that are wrecking our lives for us?"

"Go on up and get the cart," I told the men.

One of the Nova Scotiamen, a coil of rope in his hand, ran up the ladder, and the others followed.

"For God's sake, Oliver," Buell shouted, "what do you care what happens to John Hancock? Let me get just *half* of those kegs of brandy. Let me get just ten of 'em."

"Not one keg," I said. "As soon as the east wind stops blowing, those troops'll be back on this wharf again, ready to sail. I'm not going through another day like yesterday. Wherever we're going, we'll need that cart; and I won't have you running any more risks with it. This vessel's fit to be lived in, and I want my father and Mrs. Byles and Maggie and Andrew brought down here today—right now —and put aboard. What's more, I want you aboard yourself. You go get 'em, and get back here with 'em as fast as your legs'll carry you."

"I ought to have the cart for that, Oliver," Buell said.

"That cart doesn't leave this wharf," I told him. "You and Andrew can carry my father in a chair, and Mrs. Byles can walk."

Buell shook his head. "Walk?" he said wearily. "If she takes to remembering how much of a Barrell she is, she'll probably decide to roll! We'll likely be a good many days at sea, Oliver. When you think of how few times, all those days and nights, she's liable to stop talking, are you sure you're right about our not having just one teeny keg of that John Hancock brandy aboard to ease our hearing? If we had just one small, teeny——"

But I had ceased to pay any attention to him.

I thanked God, when dawn of the seventeenth arrived, that my father and Mrs. Byles were safe in their bunks; for the wind, though cold and damp, was a fair one, and the wharf above where we lay and all the other wharves in sight were bedlams.

Late on the day before, a little after my father and Mrs. Byles had come aboard, we heard that the rebels were moving down from Dorchester Heights and fortifying Nook's Hill, whence their guns could sweep the forest of vessels in the harbor as a scythe sweeps through hay.

We'd not long had this dismaying news when all the British war-craft in the harbor opened fire on Nook's Hill; and all night our whale-oil lamps shuddered in their gimbals; beneath our feet the decks trembled, shaken by the pounded air of explosions.

Before midnight the rush to the wharves began. Scattered figures came running out into the great wind-swept space; others followed them, more and more, scurrying up and down and everywhere like shadowy little animals driven from their holes by the impact of the cannonading.

With the coming of pale dawn we saw the wharf crowded from end to end with men, women and children; with light infantry regiments, grenadiers and artillerymen; with magnificently dressed officers surrounded by heavily laden servants; by sick men on carts, trundled along by sweating hospital helpers.

From all these people together came a high-pitched querulous gabbling. Women called to children and to husbands; officers shouted irritable orders to their men; frightened children wept piercingly; hospital doctors demanded passageway for patients borne in chairs and wounded soldiers on stretchers; draymen and barrowmen hoarsely bawled for gangway; sailors hung from yards and bowsprits to shout the names of vessels to the bewildered, harried throng.

I'd seen groups of people set off on long voyages, weeping to part from those they loved and scenes that were dear; but never before had I or anyone else on the wharves or in the ships seen a throng that would have peopled a whole city forced into exile and departing in despair, knowing not even the name of their destination.

I caught fleeting glimpses, like quick-moving shadows across a fire screen, of folk my father and I had known for years. Foster Hutchinson, a judge of the Supreme Court, peered down at me for a moment and somehow made me think of a ruffled hen surrounded by her brood. Clinging to him were his wife and nine children, eight of them girls; and while their father shouted at me to know where the brigantine *Millbanke* could be found, his daughters looked fearfully over their shoulders, as fluffy and frightened as newborn chicks.

Harrison Gray appeared above me, hunting the vessel to which he had been assigned. In his arms he carried his daughter, a slender, beautiful girl, who was too ill to hold up her head. Sally Leighton had known her well, and I wanted to run up the ladder to help them; but I didn't dare leave the sloop.

I saw Francis Green, one of the richest men in New England, who had served as captain in the Loyal Association of Volunteers. He had seven with him, women and children, and carried a spaniel under his arm.

Daniel Leonard, George's cousin, hurried by, herding his seven children before him, and close after him came Henry Hutton of the Custom House, with so many children and retainers I had no time to count them. Ward Chipman shouted anxiously to me, asking whether I'd seen Ed Winslow. It seemed to me that everyone I'd ever known was on that wharf. I caught glimpses of Robert Hallowell, Doctor Sylvester Gardiner, the Dumaresques, John Joy and his household, Archibald McNeil surrounded by a dozen dependents. I saw Benjamin Faneuil's family; Thomas Courtney's family; Leverett Saltonstall; scores of Winslows; General Timothy Ruggles and his family; James Putnam and half a dozen relatives; a number of Chandlers, Mrs. Flucker's family, several Debloises and any quantity of Allens, Lloyds, Phippses and Paddocks.

No matter how many of the troops clambered down ladders onto the transports, no matter how many civilians crawled antlike onto quarter-decks and vanished down companionways, the wharf was still as crowded at seven o'clock as it had been at five. Men still scurried here and there, shouting anxious inquiries to sailors. As fast as bundles vanished over bulwarks, more bundles appeared.

Then, toward eight o'clock of that furiously active morning, both the crowd and the quantity of bundles lessened. There were open spaces on the wharf; late-comers, running toward us, were suddenly conspicuous.

The open spaces widened, and heavily laden ships prepared to move out with great bellowings of "Aye, aye, sir!" and the screams of parents at children who were already attempting the ascent of ropes and ratlins.

It was strange to see the wharves look empty; for now upon them, far and near, there were only a few soldiers—rear guards and sentries hurrying in from distant parts of town.

"Buell," I said, "one of those transports is dropping her topsails. There's no use waiting for orders. They can't do anything to us, no matter what happens, so let's push off. Cast loose, and we'll move out into the channel."

But when we'd taken in our cables and stowed our ladder, we found we were pinned against the dock by the brig and the schooner on either side.

Everywhere sails were rising, and the clamor of voices—of captains and mates cursing their crews, of sergeants and corporals among the soldiers giving orders to their men, and of the exiles calling to one another from ship to ship—was drowned by the screaking of blocks and tackles.

Then, except for a running straggler or two, our wharf was bare; and between the forest of vessels and the wharf itself there was open, greasy, steel-gray water on which garbage floated. We were still impeded, however, by the vessels on either side of us, and our stern yet remained against the wharf.

While we worked with boat hooks and oars to free ourselves, we heard, far off, what seemed to be a kind of squealing in a woman's voice.

The sound grew louder rapidly, coming toward us; and then its origin became visible—a fluffily fair-haired middle-aged woman with petticoats and mobcap flying, two big bundles in her hands, and a little boy pantingly hanging to her as she ran. The bundles bothered her, and so did the child, who clutched tightly to his breast a yellow-faced black dog whose eyes were closed as part of an expression of profound annoyance; nevertheless the squealing woman, the panting boy and the annoyed dog made speed, and as they neared us the squealing became distinguishable as words of appeal, addressed to a transport now a hundred or more yards out into the harbor. *"Panther* ahoy! Wait, can't you? We're supposed to belong on the *Panther! Panther,* where are you going? Wait, *Panther,* wait!"

Panther, in stately motion, didn't even reply, though the squealing became more and more importunate. At the wharf's edge just above us the woman set down her bundles, drew forth a kerchief and waved frenziedly.

"Panther! You got to come back! Turn round and come back here this instant! I'm Mrs. Henrietta Dixon and Nathan! Sergeant Smith told me himself we were to go on you! I got a paper says my Nathan and I belong on you, *Panther! Panther* ahoy, ahoy, ahoy, ahoy!"

She seemed about to jump.

The *Osprey* was now the only vessel even near the wharf. "Hold hard," I said. "Put up the ladder, Buell. We'll have to take 'em aboard."

"There ain't room," Buell demurred. "And besides, look at her looks! Fluffy-haired kind of a puffed face! We don't want that little boy aboard; I can't be around children at all on account of my indigestion."

"Put up the ladder," I said again.

Buell obeyed. "Come on if you got to," he told the woman. "I bet you're always late! Step lively now!"

"Lively?" Mrs. Henrietta Dixon said, and looked down at him petulantly. "I don't choose to. I'm supposed to be on the *Panther."*

"You'll be supposed to be getting scalped by some of those rebel Indians in about twenty minutes," Buell said, "if you don't make use of this ladder. Hand me down the boy!"

The boy, about ten, didn't need to be handed down; he and his dog were upon the deck within five seconds.

"Now your bundles, Mrs. Henrietta What's-your-name," Buell called crossly.

"Oh my," she said, as she handed down the first one. "Be careful! Glassware!"

"In which one?" he asked. "Glassware in which?"

"In both," she told him, fluttering. "My best lamps! Irish, the best Irish glass."

"Irish glass? To wear on cold nights at sea?" he inquired bitterly. "Or maybe just for when you and your little Nathan get hungry? There! Don't wait up there to answer. You can tell us all about it during the next three or four months on the ocean. Get your feet on that ladder, can't you? Turn around! Ships' ladders are just the same as house ones: you come down 'em backward, just the same as you do ashore! Step lively!"

"Lively," Mrs. Henrietta Dixon repeated. "Oh my!" and diffidently she put a black-slippered foot upon the second rung from the top of the ladder, making plain to us that beneath a dozen petticoats she wore stockings striped red and white. "Oh my," she said, and her heart seemed to fail her.

"Lively!" Buell roared at her. "We don't care! You could be striped all over and we'd hardly notice! Lively, will you?"

"Oh my," Mrs. Dixon said once more, but descended to the deck, sat down upon it and asked for water. Then she shrieked. "Get him down first!" she cried, pointing to the ratlins, which little Nathan had already begun to ascend, while his dog looked up at him and barked protestingly. "Get Nathan down first, Mister Mate, please! After that you can bring me the water."

"Mister Mate!" Buell growled, turning to ascend the ratlins for Nathan. "Mr. Nurse! Mr. Watercarrier! If I ever take part in an evacuation of Boston again, damn my sore gizzard!"

CHAPTER XVII

ALL our vessels clung together, as if for company, as they moved slowly down the harbor; and their countless masts and spars and their gray sails, beneath the dark skies that go with Boston's east wind, were like a barren forest close hung with soiled linen—a forest from which arose a faint, dismal medley of far-off cries and sad creakings.

Yet there was something companionable in the very number of those masts, and I had no time to brood upon our mournful circumstances, for all of us knew there'd be no escaping dirty weather when we went out from the shelter of the islands and into the open sea.

So we stowed our gear as we went down the harbor, lashed our boats in their cradles and our oars in their racks, battened down hatches, pumped out our bilge, reefed the mainsail, did what we could to keep Nathan out of trouble, and willy-nilly learned the life history of Mrs. Dixon in her brief but frequent excursions from the cabin to scream at her son and to demand Buell's help in keeping him from harm.

She had successfully established herself with Mrs. Byles, I gathered, but still hesitated to speak freely in her presence. On the other hand, to Buell and to the sailors and to myself, she was chatteringly communicative, we being men and she more easily familiar of speech with our sex than with the other. This was particularly the case with her because hers had been the life of the tavern.

She was, in fact, the relict of the owner of the Golden Pineapple Tavern on King Street. After her husband's death she had catered to British officers because she found them gentlemanly and free with their money—when they had any. Her husband had been content to charge twenty shillings for a double bowl of punch, but she had raised the price to thirty shillings after his death and noticed no slackening in her trade.

I have no doubt she'd never have stopped talking that first day if, when we neared the harbor's mouth, the vessels hadn't borne off to the southward into Nantasket Roads, where a ship is sheltered by islands from sea winds and land winds. Ahead of us we saw vessels coming into the wind and brailing up their square sails, and the rattle and thump of anchor hawsers came clearly to our ears.

"Why, we're stopping!" Mrs. Dixon screamed. "Why are we stopping, Mister Mate?"

"So we can put you aboard the *Panther,* where you belong," Buell said sourly.

Mrs. Byles' mobcap appeared in the companionway when our own anchor went down. She peered at the thicket of masts and the array of black hulls all about us. "Mrs. Loring again!" she said. "I knew this would happen when I heard Mrs. Loring was aboard the general's ship! He can't make up his mind!"

And so, apparently, he couldn't; for Nantasket Roads, where we'd come to anchor, was only eight short miles from Boston as the crow flies; and we lay there for ten long, cold, dreary days, an enormous flotilla from which rose a perpetual haze of smoke as the galleys of every vessel worked at the task of supplying twelve thousand people with food.

From the beginning Mrs. Byles took kindly to Mrs. Dixon, as did my father—perhaps because she looked so helpless. I never saw a woman so incapable of doing anything neatly or quickly; but somehow she always contrived to make everybody think she'd do better next time—everybody, that is to say, but Buell.

Buell, to my surprise, was never far from her, whether she puttered about the cabin or scurried about the deck, following with squeals and outcries the unpredictable movements of Nathan. Buell grumbled at her, continually muttering complaints and never failing to tell her that whatever she did, thought or said was wrong; yet for reasons far beyond my limited powers of perception, she seemed to fascinate him.

Nathan was a limb of the devil if ever there was one. He was blessed with a sly grin and inexhaustible vigor, and was quick as a weasel—which creature, because of having eyes that tilted upward at the outer corners, he somewhat resembled.

There seemed to be, concealed within him, a lodestone that drew him to hidden valuables; and certainly he was persistently driven by an inner force to do whatever he shouldn't.

He found Buell's delicate engraving tools, and used the sharpest cutting instrument among them, first to remove a claw from his yellow-faced dog, and next to begin the removal of the mainmast from the sloop.

He had a habit of holding affectionately to his mother's hand, looking up into her face with that weasel smile of his; then, as a bright surprise, jumping suddenly upon one of her feet with both of his.

In the presence of Mrs. Byles and my father he somehow restrained himself; but he made life hideous for Buell.

When Buell, insufferably goaded, pursued his tormentor, the little boy would run yelping to the shelter of Mrs. Dixon's petticoats and pull them half off her, which seemed to appeal tenderly to the mother's heart.

"Brave little Nathan," she'd say, rearranging herself, and she undoubtedly took a curious pride in her offspring. "Think how little he is," she'd say, "and yet look what a condition he gets a great big grown man like Mate Buell into!"

She was right about Mate Buell's condition, especially when he leaped from his bunk shrieking, thinking a wet snake had joined him, and, fetching an ax to kill it, discovered coils of kelp, placed there for him by little Nathan—or when he found handfuls of mustard in our beans, or salt in the sugar, or nutmeg in fish sauce—and particularly when Buell's big round silver watch disappeared over the side because it just missed a sailor who had been so unfortunate as to displease Mrs. Dixon's pride and joy.

I spoke to Mrs. Dixon once—but only once—about transferring her and little Nathan to the *Panther,* which lay half a mile from us.

"*Panther?*" she cried. "Mr. Wiswell, I'd just as soon be rowed back to Boston and be tarred and feathered by the rebels! Look how that *Panther* treated me and Nathan when we were assigned to her—and the captain certainly knew it. Sailed right off without us, not showing a heart in any bosom and an insult besides! No indeed, Mr. Wiswell! I couldn't consent to it! I don't like your ship especially; but Nathan's happy here and we both of us hate that old *Panther!* No,

Mr. Wiswell, in spite of drawbacks, Nathan and I'll stay where we are, so we'll stop discussing it."

Thinking of Nathan, I refused to stop discussing it quite so promptly myself, and looked to Buell to join me in urging Mrs. Dixon to make the exchange. Nathan had just dropped Buell's hat overboard, and I thought he'd second me warmly. To my astonishment he only rubbed a place on his shin—Nathan had hit him with a belaying pin there the day before—and said, "Well, it's kind of choppy. Be pretty wet rowing her all the way over to the *Panther*; and besides, what's the use arguing with a woman! God knows I hate that Nathan, but they might as well stay!"

I find it impossible to describe the despondency that filled me at having to lie helpless and motionless, almost within reach of the Milton hills, but as far from them as though they were in another world.

Great Blue Hill and its four lesser companions lay like the humps of a monstrous saurian along the western sky; and at their foot, as if suckling at the parent range of hills, were the lesser bulks of Brush Hill and Milton Hill.

I could even see on Milton Hill a tiny pale patch that was our house; and to the right of it, near the dark row of poplars beside which Sally Leighton and I had sat eleven months ago, I imagined I could see a gable that was the Leightons'.

I was almost near enough to swim home, yet that home was in enemy country! It was, of course, my country too; and yet it was mine no longer, for it was in the hands of those who held me as their enemy—and by this time they were warranted in so regarding me.

On the twenty-seventh of March we woke to one of those unseasonable days when winter, weary of its long assault upon our eastern rocks and forests, sinks to its knees to rest.

There was still snow on Great Blue Hill, but the sun had more than a semblance of heat in that faded blue New England sky; and in the sudden, unexpected warmth of that sun, the air that rose from our open hatches was dank and icy.

The waters of the harbor were a satiny light blue, and the islands all around us wore a faint flush of green beneath their brown winter dress.

Perhaps this gleaming warm morning put new strength into the veins of General Howe; perhaps Mrs. Loring, sweetly capricious, longed to migrate like the birds; whatever the reason, flags went up on the warcraft ranged around the edges of our gargantuan flotilla, and their gigs came rowing down between the crowded vessels.

Officers with trumpets stood in the bows, shouting orders to the captains of the transports, and long before they reached us we could hear their voices along the lanes of glassy blue water: "This convoy will make sail for Halifax! This convoy will make sail for Halifax! Fast sailors will wait for slow ones! Don't lose your position by day or night! There's enemy privateers in these waters! Enemy privateers! All efforts must be made to avoid enemy privateers! Keep your positions day and night!"

An hour later all of us, ships, barques, barkentines, brigantines, brigs, schooners, sloops, pinks and longboats, moved out between Beacon Island and Point Allerton, a vast armada, sails gleaming whitely in the warm sun, pennants fluttering, high color against the bright sky. It must have looked, to those on shore, like the gayest and greatest regatta ever held; but my dour heart saw no gaiety in that sailing. The far white dot that was our house faded from my sight—and that was where Sally was! I was leaving her and leaving my own country, and how could a man who loved both leave either?

BOOK II

☆

New York

CHAPTER XVIII

W<small>E STOOD</small> out to sea, till the coastline itself began to fade; and as it grew paler, paler, almost invisible, I did what many another bereft soul in that fleet must have been doing, and wondered if the moisture in my eyes were not tears in a dream. If it was a dream, it was a bad one and went on to be worse.

The occurrences of the past year moved distortedly through my mind like the dark and senseless afflictions of a nightmare—the squalling mob that had tarred and feathered Buell; the unhappy long afternoon that changed to dusk while I sat and waited for Sally and she didn't come back to me; the plodding figures of the refugees who had poured across the Neck into Boston; the heat, the cannonading, the high pall of smoke and the scarlet windrows of senselessly murdered men, brutally murdered men, on the rising ground of that Charlestown meadow; the perpetual gunfire and cold of the hard and starving winter in Boston; the oft-repeated assurances that within a month—at the most within two months—the powderless rebels, who kept us from our homes, would be swept away, dispersed.

But they hadn't been dispersed. A score of times they should have been; but they hadn't been—and I was sailing away from Sally.

All that I had of her now was her letter—her one letter. Half worn out, it lay warm against my heart; and I had no need to bring it forth and read it. I could whisper every word of it to myself without that.

And how many times I tried to hearten myself with what she'd written last, I do not know: *"When the end comes, dearest Oliver, dearest Oliver, you will find my affections still unchanged. And oh,*

I dare to hope—yes, I dare to trust—that if this missive reaches your
hand, it will find place in a heart as faithful as my own."

By noon of that day, in spite of the orders of the naval officers, our
flotilla had divided. Forty of the larger vessels moved slowly away
from the remainder as though irresistibly drawn by a magnet. By
midafternoon there was misty distance between them and the great
mass of slower craft, of which the *Osprey* was one; and their hulls
wavered hazily above the crinkly dark blue chop kicked up by the
soft west wind.

By the time our riding lights were lit, their masthead lanterns, far
ahead, were like the yellow pin points of a distant city. More, the
slower group of vessels with which we had so far contrived to keep
pace was scattered over a great space of waters, and yet I could not
but see that they were all somewhat in advance of us, and steadily
drawing farther and farther away.

Remembering the orders trumpeted to us that morning, urging
us by all means to keep together, I was disquieted to realize that
the *Osprey* was, of all the vessels in that great fleet, the very slowest;
we were now, I saw, as I peered through the dusk, a mile behind
the rearmost of the others. Well—we were on her, and it could not
be helped.

It was eight bells when I turned the wheel over to Buell and went
down into the cabin. Little Nathan had already been given his supper
and, for a wonder, was sound asleep in his mother's berth. Overhead
the whale-oil lamp swung a little with the motion of the sloop, and
bright coals shone through the damper of the iron stove at the end
of the cabin. Beside my father's berth sat Mrs. Byles, knitting a gray
stocking and watching Henrietta Dixon and Maggie at work over a
savory-smelling pea soup. Mrs. Dixon looked bewildered, as though
she didn't know how the soup had got there or what was to be
done with it eventually.

The cabin was warm and cheerful, and I thought Mrs. Byles' face,
and my father's too, had become smoother in the short time since we
left Nantasket Roads; that the doubt and apprehension graven upon
them by the evil winter had almost vanished. It was hard indeed,
I thought, that a country could so treat good people of its own
that thousands of them should be happier outside of it than within it.

"Henrietta," Mrs. Byles said, "don't stand there looking as if you'd

lost your wits and wondering if you'd dropped them into the kettle!
You haven't and here's Oliver, so put the soup on the table!"

Mrs. Dixon made fluttering movements with her hands. I knew
she wanted plates, so I got them from the cupboard and gave them
to her. She took them and couldn't decide where to put them, her
mind seeming to be confused by the fact that she also held the ladle.

"Put the ladle back in the soup," Mrs. Byles said kindly. "Don't be
afraid. It's a nice gentle ladle and won't jump out at you if you'll
just——"

Mrs. Byles interrupted herself as Mrs. Dixon nervously dropped
the ladle into the soup with a splash. "Merciful God, Henrietta! I
didn't mean drop the whole ladle in! People usually leave the handle
sticking out over the edge of the kettle so as to—— There, let it
alone! I'll do the fishing!"

Mrs. Byles rose, used her knitting needle to find the ladle, worked
it up to stand against the side of the kettle, then cleaned the needle,
so to speak, with her tongue.

"Damned good duff, or lobscouse, or whatever they call soup on
shipboard," she said, "since now it's appropriate to talk sailor language. I don't know how it happens, Henrietta, but you do everything entirely wrong and yet come out right. While I watched you
making this soup, I was sure I wouldn't want nourishment until
breakfast tomorrow; yet by the taste of it I never gave Belcher a
better."

"Never what?" Mrs. Dixon asked, flustered.

"Never mind," Mrs. Byles said, and turned to my father. "She's
full of luck, Seaton. That's the explanation. When you go to London,
you'd better take Henrietta for luck."

I crumbled common crackers into the pea soup and tried it. It
was good pea soup, so Mrs. Byles was at least partly right.

"What's this about London?" I asked. "This is the first I've heard
of London."

My father looked happier than I had seen him in months. "It's
just come to me, Oliver," he said. "If Mrs. Byles and all these others
lose everything out of loyalty to a government that can't protect
them, then they have a just claim on that government. Unfortunately
governments seldom recognize just claims unless they're presented
in person, and sometimes not even then. Unless Mrs. Byles wants
to spend the rest of her days begging or living on charity, she'll have
to go to London and present her claims. As I see it, it's my duty to

go there myself and argue the cases of those who'd otherwise not be properly represented. I'm sure I could persuade Ward Chipman to associate himself with me in such an enterprise."

Mrs. Byles raised inscrutable eyes to mine, and for a moment the thought was in my mind—irrelevantly, I supposed—that she looked as she had so often on winter evenings when she described to us the deathbeds of Barrell after Barrell.

"Yes, your father's going to London, Oliver," she said gently. "We'll all go to London. I've always wanted to see England in the spring."

My father sighed, yet still smiled. "It must be a little like Milton—the loveliest countrysides. I mean the loveliest countrysides of England must be a little like ours."

"A little like Milton!" His voice brought to me with almost unbearable poignance those five blue hills: that rich and rolling hillslope from which we'd been banished because we preferred to settle our troubles by argument rather than by bloodshed.

All the things I'd tried to forget—the scent of marsh heather and the sound of locusts that came up to us on warm nights; the faint fragrance of apple blossoms mingled with the odor from a burning candle when I read in bed on spring nights; the feel of Sally's hair upon my cheek and her hand in mine—all these came washing into my brain like a bright flood. Was it possible, I wondered, that I was to spend the rest of my days in alien lands and never again know, except in memory, the scenes and scents I loved?

"London?" I said huskily. "How could we—where could we find——"

Mrs. Byles' voice was firm. "As soon as we reach Halifax, I'll sell Belcher's mahogany wigstand and whatever else need be. The only thing I won't sell is Mr. Copley's portrait of Belcher, no matter what I might be offered."

Mrs. Dixon's fingers fluttered about her lips, as they often did when she was making up her mind to say something. Then she addressed me plaintively. "How much does it cost to get to London from wherever we're going, Mr. Wiswell? I'd like to go by stagecoach if possible, and I could sell my Irish-glass lamps for seats for Nathan and me. I'd like to make some provision for Nathan, if I should get worn out and die. He's a loving child, if you see beneath his little pranks. When his poor sick father knew he was going to leave Nathan and me, he cried and cried."

Too distinctly I heard Mrs. Byles hoarsely whisper the words, "From joy!" and I hastened to intervene.

"Now, now," I said hurriedly, "we needn't be talking of selling things. The hold of the *Osprey's* pretty well stored with confiscated resources of the rebels, collected by Buell, and I haven't a doubt that he feels we're all part owners—at least to some extent. I'm sure that Buell——"

The door of the companionway slammed, and Buell himself burst in among us. "Oliver, there's a vessel without lights ranging up on our starboard beam! She's edging us——"

I got him by the wrist and may have squeezed it harder than I intended, for he choked.

"It's only one of the warcraft that's convoying us," I said.

I turned him back to the companionway and pushed him up it. "I'll have a look, Father, to make sure," I called over my shoulder, and I laughed. "The captain has to be on deck, you know, when sailors see ghosts." With that I followed Buell up the steps.

"I tell you she's crowding us, and she's not one of the convoy," Buell said angrily, "and what in hell would any of our vessels be traveling without lights for?"

"Keep your mouth shut," I said. "I can't have you worrying my father unnecessarily."

"Unnecessarily!" Buell cried. "Look at that, will you?" He pulled me under the main boom. Andrew and the whole crew, barring the helmsman, stood at the starboard rail, staring at a tall schooner, half again as large as the *Osprey*. She was abreast of us, so close that I could have tossed an apple aboard; and she was cutting so sharply into our course that if we kept on as we were, she'd be foul of us in five minutes.

There wasn't a light aboard her except a faint gleam from the binnacle; and though she was dim in the starlit gloom, I thought I could see, in her waist, the shifting bulk of gun crews. Far, far ahead I saw the wavering lights of the last of our sister vessels; but behind us and on each side I could see nothing but the black void of an empty ocean.

"Yes, she's after us," I told Buell. "I'm going to go off before the wind. If we keep on, she'll run us down; but there's just a chance we'll miss her if we go off."

I ran to the helmsman; together we pushed the tiller hard over. The

Osprey's bowsprit swung abruptly toward the strange schooner, from whose decks came a sudden angry shouting.

I half expected our bowsprit to catch in her ratlins; certainly I thought a gun would bellow at us as we hung bow on to her, in a position to be raked if she chose.

Neither thing happened. We missed her because of her speed and our own slowness; and no doubt she didn't fire for fear of bringing down a British war vessel on her. She just paid off before the wind herself, and in five minutes' time was close astern of us.

"It's no good," I told Buell. "I'll jibe when she's close on to us; but in the end she'll catch us. I think I could keep on dodging her if she were square-rigged; but I can't do anything against a schooner."

"Oliver," Buell said quietly, "if she catches us, I ain't going back. I've had a mob's hands on me once, and once is enough. I'd rather take a plank and jump overboard."

"You can't do that," I said. "This water's too cold and you wouldn't last twenty minutes. If we're taken, you can pretend to turn your coat and join 'em."

Then, so sick at heart that my voice was sickly too, I added, "Anyhow, we won't give up till we have to. While there's life, I've heard, there's hope—and this, unhappily, looks like a chance to prove it."

From the stranger behind us came a hoarse bellowing. "Heave to or I'll blow you out of water."

One of the Nova Scotiamen touched me on the sleeve. "If we're taken, Captain, Hal and I'll be shot. We deserted."

"No," I said, "they won't shoot you. They wouldn't shoot their own countrymen. The worst they'll do to you is send you to Simsbury Mines."

The Nova Scotiaman laughed harshly. "They're shooting 'em," he said, "unless they give 'em a thousand lashes. It's all the same in the end, except it takes you three weeks to die when you get a thousand lashes."

"Well," I said, "there's no help for it. We've got three women aboard." I thought of my father, but didn't mention him. "We've got three women aboard," I said again, and with that I pushed the tiller over and brought her into the wind.

"Lower the jib and stays'l," I called, expecting to have to do it myself; but Buell and the Nova Scotiamen, moving slowly, did my bidding.

As we lay there wallowing, I heard Nathan yelping at the top of his lungs in the cabin; and my despair was black as I faced the deadly truth. These twelve people—my sick father, three women and a child, the five sailors, Buell and the poor servant Andrew—had trusted to my seafaring knowledge, had put their lives in my hands, and I had failed them.

The schooner rounded into the wind off our lee bow and slowly drifted back toward us.

"Throw us a line," shouted a voice from the quarter-deck, "and when we're abeam, throw us another. I'll take all of you aboard this ship."

Nathan's howls seemed to pierce my ears.

The cabin hatch slid open with a sound of grating, and I saw, framed against the dim light from below, the head and shoulders of Mrs. Byles. She called to me, "Oliver! Oliver, you'll have to come down here! It's your father!"

CHAPTER XIX

I SLAPPED Buell's shoulder fiercely. "Steady!" I said. "Do everything they tell you. Don't do or say anything to make 'em angry! Don't talk at all! Don't let any of the men speak! I'll be back and do the talking."

As I turned and ran for the companionway, the taffrail of the schooner was so near that I could see the staring eyes and dim faces of men preparing to board us; I saw the yawning muzzle of an 18-pounder thrust from a cabin port.

Mrs. Byles had waited for me on the steps of the companionway. "It came so suddenly, Oliver," she said. "I think it would have happened anywhere."

I brushed her aside and went down into the cabin. Mrs. Dixon was stooping over my father, while little Nathan, yelping, struck her upon the buttocks. I tossed him into his bunk on the far side of the cabin; then pulled Mrs. Dixon away.

One half of my father's face seemed to have slipped from the other half, as a waxen mask might have drooped if a warm sun had shone against one side. There was a claylike pallor to his skin; beneath his half-drooped eyelids I could see only the whites of his eyes; his lips had thickened and on them was a scum.

I stared and stared at that loved face so unrecognizably distorted. I could only stand there faltering as I vainly tried to whisper "Father!"

Then I seemed to wake; I pulled the bedclothes from him and felt his heart. It fluttered faintly, and his body was cold and wet, as though he had lain in sea water. I picked up his legs and raised them in the air, as Doctor Miller had told me to do; then lifted him in my arms and held him head downward.

"What brought it on?" I asked Mrs. Dixon.

She gnawed her finger tips helplessly. "Nothing," she said. "I was sitting beside the table—no, I was standing beside the stove—no, the table—I was sitting at the table—and Mrs. Byles was saying something—I can't remember what, when——"

Mrs. Byles' cane appeared from nowhere, poked Henrietta in the ribs; and Henrietta, staggering backward, fell into the bunk where Nathan lay.

"He knew what was up, Oliver," Mrs. Byles said. "He understood they'd caught us."

From overhead came the clatter of running feet.

Mrs. Byles wiped my father's lips. "That's enough, Oliver," she said. "Put him back in the bunk and raise the mattress a little at the foot. Don't give him a pillow."

She lifted her cane and shook it. "Why couldn't God have sent us somebody except William Howe! He killed a thousand on Bunker Hill, and it'll be God's wonder if he doesn't kill us all before he's through with us!"

When I laid my father in his bunk, I saw one of his eyelids flutter, and heard a sound like porridge bubbling in a kettle. I knew he was trying to say something, but when I put my ear close to his lips, I could scarcely understand a word he said—not only because he mumbled, but because of an angry shouting from above, the crunching of the schooner against the *Osprey's* bends, the yelps of Nathan and the snifflings of Henrietta Dixon. From my father I caught the words "convictions", "intolerance", the word "loyal", but aside from that only a thick whispering, unintelligible though I strained desperately to hear.

While I knelt there, holding my breath, feet clattered on the companionway and two sailors clumped into the cabin, pistols in hand. They wore stocking caps, ragged old pea jackets and striped Osnaburg trousers rolled high above bare knees. Both had long horse faces, expressions half sly and half querulous, and jaws that moved rhythmically, as if they chewed cuds. From the odor that accompanied them, they might have carried old fish in their pockets.

As they stepped through the door, Nathan's yellow-faced dog came out from under Nathan's berth like a dark thunderbolt and without a sound sunk his teeth into the bare leg of the first sailor. The sailor shouted angrily and brought his pistol down on the dog's head—

brought it down a second, third and fourth time, till the dog lay on the floor, kicking feebly.

Nathan, hidden in the berth, made choking sounds, and I knew his mother was holding him.

The sailor wagged his pistol at us. "Take your duds and get on deck! Cap'n wants all hands shifted without loss of time."

I stood up. "My father's sick," I said. "He can't be moved."

"Oh yes, he can," the man said. "What's the matter with him?"

He moved to the side of the bunk, pulled back the bedclothes, and looked at my father. "It's a fact he don't look any too pert," he said, "but he's got to go. Get him up!"

I took a deep breath and swallowed hard. "Where are you from?" I asked.

"That ain't neither here nor there," the sailor said. "If there's any questions asked around here, we aim to ask 'em." He exchanged glances with his companion, and they both cackled.

"You sound to me as though you came from the North Shore," I said. "Salem, maybe, or Beverly. I'm from Milton myself. My father's had a shock. You surely don't want to do a thing that would kill a helpless man."

The sailor suddenly began to shout irascibly. "You're all a damned pack of Tories! We can't stand here and listen to you all night! Get that man on deck and over to our vessel! If he can't walk, carry him on the mattress."

Mrs. Byles stepped over Nathan's dead dog, pushed between me and the sailor, and looked up at that lantern-jawed face above hers. She just looked up at him, but there was something in her look that silenced him and made him scratch his chin.

Mrs. Byles went to my father and touched her fingers to his cheek. Then she bent over and looked into his eyes.

She straightened up and came back to stand between me and the sailors again. "I'm sorry, Oliver," she said. "He's gone."

"Gone?" I began to shake. "Why, no: he spoke to me only a moment ago! He can't be——" I couldn't say the word.

"Yes." She was crying now, and put her arms about me. "Yes. Poor boy. Poor boy!"

I had the feeling that my outer body was a rigid shell, and that my whole inner self had passed into a cold and dark chamber, around which my thoughts stumbled rapidly and without emotion. I had quick irrelevant glimpses of my father, seated in his carriage, return-

ing the salutes of his fellow townsmen as the horses made their slow
ascent of Tremont Street; standing in court, impressive in formal
black satin, to argue a case before the chief justice; sitting on the
far side of our marble-topped library table in the light of the yellow
lamp, eyeing me attentively as I read to him from the difficult pages
of Plutarch; wading thigh-deep in the upper reaches of the Neponset
River and looping a fly beneath overhanging willow branches. . . .

"Poor boy! Poor boy!" I heard Mrs. Byles say again.

I felt like pushing her away. I didn't want her sympathy. I didn't
want anything except an opportunity to make somebody pay for
the injustices, the inhumanities that my father had suffered.

Then, as we stood, I heard an angry bellowing from above; it
seemed to come from the schooner. I was only half conscious of it,
and yet it hurt my ears.

"If the man's dead," one of the two sailors said harshly, "haul him
out and put him over the side. You can't put him aboard us if he's
dead." He spoke to his comrade. "Make sure if he's dead, Abijah."

"Dead?" the one called Abijah said. He felt my father's wrist;
poked the poor fallen chin with a gnarled forefinger. "Ha! You
needn't worry! He's dead. Dead as a coffin nail! Gives us one less
Tory to bother about, I guess."

Mrs. Byles was stroking my shoulder. "Poor boy, poor boy."

"Come, now; be done with this," the first sailor said. "That's the
captain you heard hollering. Get up on deck and climb over onto
the schooner. The captain don't like to wait. No dawdling, now!"

I looked at the stilled face upon the pillow and saw that it was
strange to me, bearing but the faintest semblance to my father's
when he lived. His spirit had lifted out of that body and was flown.
Knowing that, I knew not what I meant to do; but I did know I
was free to get myself killed if I chose.

I made two strides to my bunk, took from beneath the pillow a
loaded pistol I kept there, thrust back the nearer of the two sailors,
leaped to the companionway and ran on deck. Men from the
schooner were jumping from their higher bulwarks and clattering
upon our deck, and in the starlight I made out the figures of Buell,
Andrew, the Nova Scotiamen and the three other members of our
crew, still standing on our quarter-deck where I had left them a few
minutes before. I hadn't any plan; I only knew my father was dead
and I free to get myself killed.

I shouted Buell's name loudly, ran for the bulwarks, jumped for the schooner's main shrouds and then was aboard her, not knowing how or, consciously, why.

On her quarter-deck I saw two figures, one a boy in stocking cap, at the wheel; the other a lumbering pea-jacketed man who leaned upon the bulwarks, bending down to see what took place on the *Osprey,* and bellowing fiercely, "Where's that sloop's captain? Bring me her captain! You God-damned lubber-headed landsmen, bring me her captain!"

I reached him just as he was straightening up, hit him as hard as I could on the side of the head with the barrel of the pistol, and caught him around the throat with my left arm so that he didn't fall. Buell, who'd followed me, took the boy at the helm by the throat and so held him.

At the top of my lungs I shouted, "If any man of this vessel so much as moves, while I'm speaking, by God I'll shoot your captain through the head!"

CHAPTER XX

Still, even with the captain's head under my arm, ready
to be shot, I had no plan that I knew when I made my threat; and
when I swore I'd shoot if there was movement while I spoke, I
didn't know what I was going to say. I did know, though, that I'd
die rather than let these rebels have their will of the *Osprey* and
of me.

"That's it!" Buell's voice behind me was tense. "Don't let 'em
come back on the schooner, or they'll rush us! For God's sake keep
'em on the *Osprey!*"

That gave me my plan; my head was clearer and I saw what I
must try to do.

"Get a rope," I said to Buell. "Make a slipknot and a noose at
one end."

"Aye, aye, sir!"

Buell pushed the boy into the scuppers; and then I saw, coming
toward me upon the schooner's deck from forward, a long-armed,
heavy-shouldered sailor.

"Cap'n Soule," he called as he came near. "What's wrong, Cap'n
Soule?"

"The captain can't speak; come and see," I said; and, when the
man did, Buell took him from behind and I, with the pistol semi-
circling from his chest to the captain's head, gave him orders.

Buell had the rope; he fitted the noose around the captain's neck
with the knot under the ear. Then I made the seaman take the captain's body in his arm and lift him. "Hold him as high as you can,"
I said. And Buell, with the rope taut, made fast the other end of it
to the ratlins overhead.

179

"If you let him drop an inch," I told the seaman, "he'll strangle. If I have to shoot you, you'll both die."

On the *Osprey* the men from the schooner, astounded—though not more so, I think, than were Buell and I ourselves—stood like dark statues, yet were not stiller than Andrew and our own crew.

"I want my people aboard this ship," I called. "The rest of you stay where you are. Andrew!"

Andrew moved out from the little knot on the *Osprey's* deck. "Yes, Mr. Oliver."

"Take two of our men," I told him. "Go to the cabin and bring my father. Send Mrs. Byles, Mrs. Dixon, Maggie and Nathan before you. If anybody opposes you, shout my name once—just once! That'll be enough. Go, Andrew!"

In five minutes my father's body, wrapped in a sheet, lay on the schooner's quarter-deck, and grouped around the tiller were my five seamen, Andrew, Mrs. Byles, Mrs. Dixon, Maggie and Nathan.

The two vessels, in spite of their restless rocking and the faint creakings of their booms and tackles, were silent; the dim shapes upon their decks now neither moved nor spoke. I went to the taffrail, saw pallid faces looking up at me from the *Osprey*.

"Listen hard, you men from the schooner," I said. "If any one of you doesn't hear me distinctly and makes a mistake, it may cost all of you your lives. This dead man on the deck is my father. He died of shock when we were boarded, and because of his death, it's all the same to me whether I live or don't live myself. You'd better bear that in mind. I intend to hold this vessel. I'm going to sail her to Halifax, and I'm going to take your captain and your mates with me. The rest of you'll have that sloop, with your sailing master to navigate for you. You'll work the sloop to Halifax. If both vessels reach there safely, I'll see to it that every last one of you, from captain to cabin boy, goes free. I'll do more than that. The sloop is private property. She's mine to dispose of as I see fit. I'll give her to you, and guarantee you'll be allowed to go safely out of Halifax in her."

Then I leaned out over the taffrail and spoke slowly. "You've heard me! God help your captain and your mates if you fail to bring the sloop safely into Halifax! See you get her there; for if you don't, I swear I'll hang 'em; and if I do, yours is the blame: yours and nobody else's! That's not all. If a hand is laid on the cargo of that sloop, or anything in her hold damaged, you and your officers'll go to prison for the rest of this war."

I turned to Buell. "Bring the two mates to the quarter-deck. Tie one of 'em and let the other hold the captain."

"That's one of 'em holding up the captain," Buell said. "The other's on the *Osprey*."

"Bring him here," I ordered. "Then tie him up, put the rest of the schooner's crew aboard the sloop, cast her off and hoist our jib and stays'l. We don't want this to be the last vessel into Halifax."

We left the *Osprey* behind us as though she were anchored, and as we bore off to the north-northeast, I realized that in my ears there was the sound of weeping. It came from Mrs. Byles, who sat upon a coil of rope beside the body of my father.

"If he could only have lived just this little time longer, Oliver!" she said. "If he could just have seen what you've done, and known what a valiant son he had!"

Valiant! The word mocked me, for I knew myself to be anything but valiant. What I had done, I had done in a fit of insane bitterness, not with cool courage, not with brave quick thinking, not with presence of mind—but with the absence of it. Because of a staggering thunderbolt of luck I had succeeded—but the success wasn't complete yet.

I turned to where, beside me, a bulbous-shaped mass rose from the deck into the darkness overhead—the wobbling and panting figure that clutched another and held it supported.

"You're the first mate?" I asked.

"For God's sake——" the man gasped. "For God's sake——"

"He's the second," Buell said. "This man Andrew's holding is the first mate. Don't worry; we got his elbows tied."

"Hark ye," I said to the man Andrew held. "I'd like to cut down your captain and give him decent treatment for the lump he's got on the side of his head. That rests with the captain himself, and with you and the second mate. The captain's coming back to his senses— I see his hands beginning to move, but we can tie them. Then if the three of you care to make trouble, I'll give you and the second mate turn and turn about holding up the captain where he is until we reach Halifax. There might be a day or two of rough weather before then; that would make hard holding, I take it! I'll give you your choice. Either you two, turn by turn, keep the captain in the air as far as Halifax, or I'll parole all three of you. Give me your oaths to do nothing whatever to hinder this schooner from reaching Halifax and I'll let the captain down."

The first mate, surly, seemed to wish to be oratorical. "You're a damned Tory! Think I'll give my oath to a damned Tory? You beat us by a dirty cowardly trick! You're bloody renegades, trying to betray your own country, sneaking out into the devil's darkness, hoping to crawl back behind British regiments to plunge the poisoned dagger into the land that gave you birth! You're a pack of cowardly——"

He was interrupted by strangling sounds from overhead.

"What's the captain want?" I asked Buell.

"I ain't sure," Buell answered. "I think I kind of make out, though, that he'd like the arguing to quit and paroles to be given so he can stop choking to death."

By the light of a lantern Buell and I sewed my father into a stays'l with an eighteen-pound shot at his feet; then, after a little while, I had the captain of the schooner brought to me. "Is there a Bible on board?" I asked him.

"No, there ain't!"

Mrs. Byles came forward, knelt, and put her hand upon the dark roll of canvas. "Into thy hands, O Lord," she said, "we deliver Seaton Wiswell. Grant to us all, as you did to him, the will to stand firm against intolerance and to make no peace with oppression."

She rose and stepped back. "Let it be Andrew, his old servant," she said. "Andrew and Buell."

As if reflected in a darkened mirror, I saw Andrew and Buell raise the clumsy cylinder and rest it upon the bulwarks.

In my mind, then, there were thoughts of a thousand things I could have done for my father and hadn't. Ah—and the thoughts of the things I hadn't said to him! Never once had I told him how I admired him, loved him. My whole life seemed to have been spent in taking all from him and giving nothing! Why hadn't I once—just once—told him what I so deeply and truly knew him to be—the best and wisest man in the world? No such word had ever come from me—and there was that black sack, in the darkness, on the dark bulwarks!

"Into thy hands, O Lord!"

The schooner lurched in the uneasy chop; and then, where that long sack had rested, there was only dim vacancy.

CHAPTER XXI

THE harbor of Halifax is like a beautiful broad river. It lies between long ranges of hills, guarded from the ocean by islands wedged into the harbor entrance almost like melons jammed in the mouth of a sack.

When we passed through the southern channel on the morning of the first of April and opened up the harbor, it had the look of an enormous marine fair. Not only was the water studded with score upon score of newly arrived craft of every description, their sails hanging slack to dry, their yards cocked every which way; but the calm ocean behind us was dotted with sails, some near, some barely discernible on the horizon, and all converging on that harbor mouth.

Just inside the islands were three frigates, so situated as to intercept every vessel; and as we stood in past the nearest of the three, we were hailed harshly from her quarter-deck.

"What schooner is that?"

"Private armed schooner *Badger*," I said. "A prize out of Chelsea."

"*Badger?*" the harsh voice bawled. "Prize? Prize to whom? Haul your wind, sir! Come over here and let's have a look at you!"

I lowered a boat and did as ordered; and when I went up over the frigate's side and turned to salute the quarter-deck, I found a group of officers gathered at the head of the companion, staring at me.

They looked at me haughtily when I mounted the gangway to stand among them. One, a lieutenant, had a paper in his hand, and he snapped "Name!" at me as he might have snapped at a dog. The captain eyed me coldly, and the coldness of his glance turned to suspicion when I said "Wiswell; sloop *Osprey*."

183

The captain looked sharply at the lieutenant with the paper. *"Osprey?* What armament?"

The lieutenant shook his head. "Not armed, sir. Crew of five."

The captain turned to me, frowning. "Sir, are you telling me you and five others captured an armed schooner? How many men aboard her?"

"A captain, two mates, a sailing master, three prize masters and thirty-two men, sir. She'd already manned out one prize with eight of her crew."

The captain grunted. "Come, come! In what manner do you claim you accomplished this prodigy?"

I looked him in the eye. "My father was aboard the *Osprey* when we sailed. He was ill. He'd had a shock last April. When the schooner hove us to, he had another and it killed him."

The red face of the captain, with its beetling eyebrows and triple chin, faded from my gaze. I saw my father's kind eyes and wry smile—then heard those last whisperings of his: "convictions", "intolerance", "loyal".

The captain shouted at me angrily. "That captured a ship, did it? Your father died, so that gave you a schooner, her officers, crew of thirty-two men, and all!"

"Yes, sir. Because when my father'd died, I didn't know what I was doing, so I went aboard the schooner and contrived to get my hands on her captain. I arranged to kill him if any of his men moved, so none moved. That was all there was to it. She didn't need a crew of thirty-two to sail her, of course; a great part of them were for fighting. She handles easily, and we had no foul weather."

"Quite a tale," the captain said, grunting. "Quite a tale."

"On the other hand, sir," I suggested, "there's the schooner. If you'll trouble to glance——"

One of the officers who stood about us laughed. "That's true, sir. It's hard to deny the schooner, and the young gentleman seems to be in command of her."

"God bless my soul," the captain said. "But what did you do with her officers and thirty-two men, eh? You and your crew of five haven't got 'em in your pockets, have you? Where'd you put 'em?"

"I kept the captain and his mates aboard the schooner with me, and put the crew and the sailing master on my sloop with orders to bring her into Halifax."

"Well, damn my soul," the captain said, and puffed till the free air about our heads smelled like an alehouse. "You're not such a fool as to expect ever to see your sloop again, are you?"

"Yes," I replied, "I am. She's slow, but she'll be in."

"She will? Why?"

"Because I told them that if they didn't bring her into Halifax within forty-eight hours after I got here, I'd have the captain and his mates hanged."

"Hanged?" The captain puffed again; then he said, "Very good! Bring 'em up! Bring up the rebel captain and his mates. If your sloop doesn't come in, I'll hang 'em for you! If it doesn't come in in the next forty-eight hours, I'll hang 'em. If it *does* come in, I'll send 'em to England and have 'em put in Mill Prison. The crew I'll——"

"No, sir," I interrupted. "The captain and the mates will have to remain on the schooner. I promised——"

The captain whirled to face me. "Tut, tut, man! Let's have less talk! Send 'em up, and if your sloop comes in, I'll put all men aboard her in my cable tier and they'll go along with their officers to England and Mill Prison."

"You can't do that, sir," I said. "I promised they'd go free if they brought the sloop in safely. I promised 'em the sloop for their own."

"*You* promised them!" the captain cried and his chins seemed to swell. "Who are you to be promising? They're rebels, aren't they? They've defaulted in their sacred duty to their king, and they're entitled to no consideration."

"That may be so," I admitted, "but the only way I could get my sloop and its cargo to Halifax was to pass my word. I passed it, and that's the end of it. If that's all clear, sir, I'd like to unload my passengers and look for a place to live."

He glowered at me. "If I'm to believe your story, you're bringing a boatload of rebels into this harbor where they can see exactly how many ships we've got, and you propose to let the scoundrels calmly sail back home with the information! Yes, and in a vessel that we ourselves need for transport duty! No, sir; no, sir! You can't do it!"

"I think you're mistaken, sir," I said reasonably. "The sloop belonged to my first mate and me. All we've got in the world is in her. She's ours to sink, sail or do with as we please. The schooner's ours, too, because we and nobody else took her. If there's any doubt in your mind about my right to either vessel, I'll ask you to see General Howe about it. We've been subject to his authority in Boston; we left Boston on his orders; and meaning no offense, Captain,

I don't recognize any other authority until he commands me to do so."

"My God, what's here? A damned lawyer?" The captain glared. "From Boston of course! I know 'em! Tickle one of their fat house-maids in the ribs and they appeal to the commander in chief! Splash a drop of mud on their doorsteps and they write to His Majesty's ministers! That'll do, by God, sir, damn you! Proceed to your anchorage! General Howe! You'll hear from General Howe, and be damned to you! Get off my ship!"

As I went over the side I heard profane growling from the quarterdeck: "Damnation Yankees! Damned upstarts! Damned arguing upstarts! Talk you dead, give 'em a chance! Damned yelping Yankees! Damned God-forsaken upstart yelping Yankees! Damn every damn last damned mother's damned son of 'em! Good riddance!"

This was the comradely appreciation we had for taking a rebel privateer, and it wasn't unique, I found later, in my association with Englishmen. I should have seen it, indeed, as a foreshadowing.

CHAPTER XXII

THE bedlam of Boston during the evacuation was as nothing to that which Buell and I found when we went ashore in Halifax to report our arrival; and I was thankful that there was no pressing necessity for us to find a place to live in the town.

Lodging houses, taverns and every space of open ground crawled with troops and Bostonians, as a fruit tree crawls with locusts during a plague; while men hunting food and a place to sleep snarled and fought on the streets like dogs.

Half the houses we passed had sentries posted before them—to guard against homeless people rushing in and taking forcible possession. The windows and doors of food shops were barricaded; and grenadiers in red coats and black gaiters paced watchfully before every lumber yard. The common in the center of town was like a crowded fair; for tents stood in rows on every part of it; soldiers labored, paraded, sang and roistered around and among the tents; and wherever we looked, we saw lines of civilians standing in front of houses and tents, as people wait to enter a peep show.

They were waiting, we found, to be assigned to lodgings, to receive orders for tea, coffee, tobacco and provisions from the King's stores, or to seek the services of soldiers to aid them in carrying goods from the docks.

We found the provost marshal's quarters in the center of the common; and they were so besieged by citizens of Halifax as well as by refugees that a double row of sentries were stationed outside, so that everybody who wished to enter was forced to form in line and pass between those two scarlet rows of guards.

From the length of the line, I thought we must be the last to

187

arrive for that day; but we'd been there not more than five minutes and had moved forward only a few steps when there were more behind us than in front—grimy, haggard men and a few draggled women, many of them looking as if they'd not long since been seasick.

The man behind Buell and me was Samuel Fitch, advocate general of Massachusetts, who had gone out of his way in Boston to be kind to me because he too had once been a student at New Haven. Unlike most Yale graduates, he was highly esteemed in Boston, and had even been given an honorary degree by Harvard—a college that regards the education acquired in other institutions of learning as worthless, if not a downright detriment. From the appearance of his clothes, he had slept for weeks in a muddy gutter; and when he spoke to me, he sounded collapsed inside.

"How fast is the line moving, Oliver?" he asked. "Do you think we'll have to sleep on the docks?"

"I don't think so," I said. "If the worst came to the worst, you could probably bribe a soldier to let you use a corner in his tent."

Fitch nodded vaguely. "Yes. My furniture's on a warship, and when I get it, if I do, perhaps I can sell a little."

He scratched thoughtfully at stains on the front of his coat. "I want to get Mrs. Fitch under a roof. She had a bad spell coming up. I thought I might lose her."

He shook his head and looked at me helplessly. "We had thirty-five in our cabin, Oliver. Thirty-five in a space intended for eight."

I had a thought. "If Mrs. Fitch and you can't find lodgings in the town, we have a schooner that'll be glad to welcome you, sir."

"Thank you, my boy, but wouldn't it be an inconvenience to your father? I hope, by the way, his condition is better than when I last heard."

"No," I said, and told him.

He was sorry—genuinely, I could see—and spoke of my father's fine mind and lofty character simply and touchingly. "What a need has America of men like him!" he said sadly. "America—America that loses them not only by death, but by driving them away." Then he was silent for a time, his gaze upon the ground; but afterward he looked up and seemed dazed at the sight of the bleak Nova Scotian hills. "It's hard to remember," he said apologetically, "that we aren't in Massachusetts any longer."

His voice sank to a whisper. "What do you think will happen to us, Oliver? What did your father——" He stopped abruptly, his fingers fumbling at his lips.

"Father didn't know," I said. "He only knew little men were being pushed into high positions, as always happens in revolutions. I think he thought they'd bring misery and destruction to everybody except themselves."

Mr. Fitch drew a quivering deep breath. "Think of it," he whispered. "Only a few years ago our country was the happiest and most contented on the face of the globe. Now it has no government, no credit; no law-abiding man can speak his mind without being in danger of losing his life!"

I had no heart to answer him, and I was glad when Buell touched my arm and, by drawing me toward the upheld tent flap of the provost marshal's marquee, excused me for not trying to answer the unanswerable.

In the moment of entering, Buell turned sharply toward me and trod upon my toes, as if seized by a sudden change of heart. When I impatiently pushed him forward, he hung back, muttering. "Damn it, Oliver," he whispered, "I stumble into that fish hawk wherever I go! Be careful, Oliver!"

I moved ahead of Buell and saw the reason for his displeasure. Four uniformed clerks sat at a long table, and behind them, striding up and down like a smiling, handsome actor in the role of Mercutio, was Captain William Cunningham, whom I had last seen in Benjamin Thompson's office.

At sight of me, he stopped his pacing. "Mr. Wiswell," he cried, "this is indeed a pleasure!" He beamed upon me, and smiled with equal friendliness at Buell. To one of the clerks he said, "Let me have the papers on Mr. Oliver Wiswell and Mr. Seaton Wiswell." To me he added, "I'm mighty glad you've arrived safely, Mr. Wiswell! Holy Saint Brendan, but it was a lucky thing we had no more than a capful of wind! You had no trouble, I take it?"

Without waiting for an answer, he took a paper from a clerk's upraised hand and read from it, "Sloop *Osprey,* Oliver Wiswell, Seaton Wiswell, Mrs. Belcher Byles, Mrs. Henrietta Dixon transferred from His Majesty's Transport *Panther.*" He slapped his thigh. "By God, Mr. Wiswell, your father must have used all his influence to get *her* aboard the *Osprey,* eh? Ha, ha! Yes! Let's see: Mrs. Henrietta Dixon,

Nathan Dixon, Thomas Buell." He studied the paper. "Who's this Buell?"

His mention of my father robbed me of my voice, so I just took Tom by the elbow and drew him up beside me.

Cunningham nodded amiably. "Ah yes! Buell! I thought his face was familiar. I trust, Mr. Wiswell, that all your other passengers are present and accounted for?"

"Oliver's father died four days ago," Buell said. "The rest of us made out all right, thanks to getting fewer maggots in our food than we'd been getting in Boston."

Cunningham ignored Buell and gave me a compassionate look. "Your father died!" he exclaimed. "Devilish hard! Damned unfortunate! Ah—where's the *Osprey* lying?"

"We didn't come in the *Osprey* after all," I said. "We had to make a change. The night we left Boston a rebel schooner, the *Badger,* undertook to board us. We had the good fortune to take her, so we're in the *Badger;* not in the *Osprey.* She's lying in the south-southwest section of the inner harbor."

Buell was openly annoyed. "What do you want to mislead Captain Cunningham for? He'll think you ain't able to stand up for your rights! It wasn't good fortune that took the *Badger.*" He turned to Cunningham. "He went up onto that quarter-deck like a starved catamount, and I thought by God he'd tear that captain's head right off his shoulders!"

Cunningham stared at us silently and seemed to cogitate.

"You're provost marshal, sir?" I asked.

"Yes," Cunningham said heartily. "Unexpected promotion, and not without its difficulties. Why do you ask?"

"I had a little trouble when I entered the harbor," I said. "The *Scorpion* frigate brought me to, and the captain ordered me aboard. He seemed to think I'd exceeded my authority in disposing of the rebels as I saw fit."

Cunningham's face lighted up. "Did you hang 'em?"

"No, sir," I said. "When I took the *Badger,* I boarded her with my own people. I put the rebels on the *Osprey* and ordered her to follow me into this port."

"Should have sunk her," Cunningham said brusquely.

"I couldn't, Captain," I said. "I needed her. She was an armed schooner and valuable. Since I'd taken her in a fair fight, she belonged to me and my people. Yet all our belongings were aboard the *Osprey,* and I didn't have time to transfer 'em to the *Badger*. I kept the *Badger's* captain and officers as hostages. I've got 'em here in Halifax with me. I've promised to hang 'em unless the rebels bring the *Osprey* and all our belongings safe into port."

Cunningham smiled at me benevolently. "Good! Very clever indeed, Mr. Wiswell! Turn 'em over to me and I'll keep 'em till the *Osprey* comes in. Then I'll hang 'em for you—hang those on the *Osprey, too.*"

"I don't think I've made myself clear, Captain," I said. "I promised the officers and crew of the *Badger* that if the *Osprey* were brought safely into Halifax, I'd set 'em free—and give 'em the *Osprey* for their own."

Cunningham snorted. "Of course you had to tell 'em something like that, Mr. Wiswell; but a promise to a rebel doesn't have to be kept. Didn't the rebels break all their promises when they became rebels? Indeed and indeed they did, my boy! They'd promised to obey our laws, support our government and refrain from treachery; yet look at 'em! Defying our laws, doing their bloody damnedest to destroy our government, and stabbing us in the back whenever and wherever they can! No, no, Mr. Wiswell: don't think you have to keep promises made to renegades!" His smile was almost paternal.

"That's a mighty nice point, Oliver," Buell said. "I don't know as I'd feel free to murder rebels on the strength of it—not without debating the matter more fully; but it opens up a lot of ideas that might be useful." He stared raptly at the striped canvas roof of Cunningham's marquee.

I looked closely at Cunningham, wondering whether I was so thick-witted that I had failed to recognize a jest in his words. His lips were still curled upward in that kindly smile of his, but his eyes were serious.

"I don't believe I could quite see things that way," I said. "Those men were fighting fairly, according to their lights, and I wouldn't feel right unless I kept my promises to them."

Cunningham's face was suddenly crimson. "You wouldn't feel right? Good God, Wiswell! Those rebels were doing everything they could to disrupt the British Empire, and yet you propose to let them go free, so they can ambush us again! Are you mad?" His voice had risen, and his hands, I saw, were shaking.

Buell touched my arm. His eyes were innocent. "Couldn't we compromise, Oliver? Captain Cunningham wants to hang 'em, and you promised to let 'em go. Seems to me I promised to let 'em go, too. Maybe if we cut out their tongues, Captain Cunningham wouldn't mind if they were turned loose."

Cunningham whirled on Buell. "I'll have no God-blasted levity! What right have you to inject yourself into this discussion?"

Buell scratched his head. "What right? Let's see now: the *Osprey* was my sloop, and we wouldn't be having this discussion at all if it wasn't for the *Osprey,* would we? What's more, the *Osprey* was loaded with food I gathered up in Boston; and after some of the experiences I'd had there, I figure I got a right to inject myself into any discussion that might tend to deprive me of food. You'd scarcely believe the things that used to happen to food in Boston, Captain, if you didn't keep your eye on it and protect it every second! It wouldn't surprise me at all to learn that some of those commissaries in Boston were just plain, ordinary, grave-snatching, child-robbing, pocket-picking, yellow-livered, light-fingered thieves! No, sir: I ain't going to relinquish my right to discuss my food—not without doing a little yelling."

Cunningham looked from Buell to me and back to Buell again. His face grew less crimson and his breathing less audible.

"Now, now," he said, and once again he smiled. "Nobody's trying to rob you of your rights, but military discipline must be maintained, Mr.—Ah—" he consulted the paper in his hand, and added—"Mr. Buell." He made the name rhyme with mule, and the dislike of Cunningham that had smoldered within me since the day I met him in Thompson's office burst suddenly into a blaze.

He turned to me. "Here's another thing you'll have to consider, Mr. Wiswell: that's freehandedness with rebels. We can't be too freehanded when dealing with them, can we? Sloops now, for example! Sloops are valuable! We don't want to make outright presents of a sloop to them, do we? We can hardly do that, can we, Mr. Wiswell? I put it to you!"

"A sloop more or less oughtn't to make much difference," Buell said. "When General Howe evacuated Boston, he left forty-eight cannon, two tons of powder and a shipload of army supplies where the rebels couldn't overlook them, didn't he?"

"Even if he did," Cunningham said quickly, "he didn't do it purposely. It wasn't a deliberate attempt to help the rebels. Rebels deserve no consideration. Those who're captured ought to stay captured—not be released to fight again. We're fighting rebels in order to destroy 'em, aren't we? And the way to destroy 'em is to destroy 'em, isn't it? I think I may say that's the logical way of looking at it."

"So that's logic, is it?" Buell asked. "I thought you had to go to college to learn logic, but I see you don't. I can talk logic as well as anyone. The way to keep a promise to rebels is to keep a promise to rebels. The way to get an army to release prisoners is to get an army to release prisoners. The highest authority in an army is the highest authority in an army."

"Captain," I said, "I'm afraid we're talking at cross-purposes, and since I'm not in the army, I think I'll have to take this case to General Howe."

"Oh, Mr. Wiswell," Cunningham protested, "you wouldn't bother the general with a little thing like this, would you?"

"Little?" Buell asked. "If Oliver and I were fixing to kill you and thirty-five of your friends, it wouldn't strike you as being so damned little, would it?"

Cunningham laughed heartily. "Well said, my boy! If Mr. Wiswell feels he must see the general, then he must see the general. That's only logic. I'll go with you myself, Mr. Wiswell!" And in spite of my protests, he did.

General Howe's headquarters were in a mansion that must have cost the profits of a score of fishing voyages. It was even more crowded than the provost marshal's had been; but when Captain Cunningham murmured a few words to a gaudy young aide, we were taken at once to an anteroom in which a dozen clerks scratched busily with quills at orders, letters and reports; and almost immediately thereafter we were shown into a large corner room whose windows looked out on the common and the whole long length of the harbor.

The room had a tarry, stuffy odor from the fire of cannel coal that burned in an open grate; and the general, who sat behind a heavy desk and raised sleepy eyes to us as we came in, seemed to fit that smoky, stuffy atmosphere.

He was a bulky man with an olive complexion, a broad nose and thick, sulky lips. It was a slack and self-indulgent face—the face of a man whose clothes should have been wrinkled; whose wig should have been askew. Instead of that his wig was a gleaming white and his blue coat and white silk waistcoat were as immaculate as his face was sullen.

"What's this, Captain Cunningham?" he said heavily. "You're provost marshal! Should you be running all over Halifax at a time like this?"

Cunningham was affable and offhand. "Not at all, General; and I wouldn't be, except for an unusual case. Most unusual."

"Unusual, eh?" the general said testily. "Whole damned business is unusual. Curse it, Captain, d'you know these confounded fish peddlers are doubling the price of food and lodging every half-hour? Unusual! By Gad, Captain, it better be! Come, come; out with it!"

"It's largely a case of misunderstanding on Mr. Wiswell's part, General," Cunningham said. "I fear he hasn't grasped the military situation. He not only proposes to set free a number of rebel prisoners, but he even wishes to make them a present, without official approval, of valuable property—property that would be of more than a little use to us."

"Indeed," the general said, and he looked more amiable. "First highhanded; then freehanded." His heavy stomach jerked convulsively in what I took to be a sort of self-applause.

"Captain Cunningham ain't starting at the right end, General," Buell said. "He ain't told you what happened, or anything. Oliver ain't highhanded nor yet freehanded. And if he ain't grasped the military situation, it was because he was on the deck of a rebel schooner, grasping the captain by the neck and pushing a pistol into his gizzard. He certainly grasped that captain, General!"

The general looked coldly at Buell, who made a sort of disarming gesture, as if he lightly brushed a fly from before his face with the back of his hand.

"What's more," Buell continued, "we don't know what Captain Cunningham's talking about when he talks about getting official approval of giving away valuable property. That valuable property, General, is a sloop, and the sloop's mine. I bought it in Boston. Since when have you had to have official approval to give away personal property? Oliver Wiswell's going to give my sloop away because I told him he could."

The general looked disgusted. "You're wasting my time! I haven't the vaguest idea what you gentlemen are talking about. Suppose you give me your version of the situation, Mr. Wiswell. Who are the rebels you're freeing, and why are you giving them a sloop?"

While I haltingly explained my case, the general sat glowering somberly; and I, watching the apparent effect of my words upon him, grew sure that as a human being he was as unpleasant as he was incapable as a commanding officer.

In this I was mistaken. He was by no means an invariably disagreeable man, as we soon discovered, and I think I ought to say here that although William Howe was more instrumental than any other man in losing America for the British, he was kindly at heart, and as brave a soldier personally as ever lived.

When I had finished, the general looked glum and cast an uneasy glance through the window toward the harbor entrance. "Good God, Captain Cunningham," he cried in sudden irascibility, "look at 'em! Eleven, twelve, fifteen more in sight, and seven dropped anchor in the last ten minutes! Get back to your post! Double your sentries tonight, and shoot all looters. Come, come, Captain! There's no time to be lost! Be off about your duties, and I'll take care of Mr. Wiswell's case."

When Cunningham had gone, Howe fingered his heavy underlip as if probing it for a cold sore. "Sorry to hear about your father, Mr. Wiswell," he said. "I know he was highly spoken of in Boston. Haven't I heard cases were often sent to him from England for an opinion?"

"Yes, sir."

"Drat 'em, these Americans!" Howe said. "Why didn't they *use* men like that instead of driving 'em out and destroying 'em?"

"Well, sir," I said, "they don't seem to have any use for those that aren't violent and crackbrained; but I guess there's nothing to be done about it."

Howe eyed me curiously. "Nothing to be done about it, eh? That sounds odd, coming from a man who's lately captured a rebel privateer in the manner just outlined to me. What would be needed to rouse you to take more active remedial measures, Mr. Wiswell?"

"Rouse?" Buell said. "I think you'll find we're all roused enough—if we could find the right leaders."

The general lowered his head and examined Buell coldly. "Have I had the pleasure of your acquaintance?"

"I don't know, General," Buell said. "I printed your orders in Boston, and before I got to be your printer I was tarred and feathered. That kind of roused me, and I been having a little private war with the rebels ever since."

He seemed innocent and helpless. "When I start a war," he added apologetically, "I'm so roused I like to finish it. Mr. Wiswell's that way too."

He went on to brag of me, as he usually did when he got the chance, leaving me to stand hot and embarrassed, not daring to protest lest I seem to exhibit an offensive mock modesty.

He described floridly my services to himself in taking him from the mob and, continuing rapidly, he elaborated upon Cunningham's brief account of the capture of the schooner and my part in that affair.

"If it hadn't been for Oliver Wiswell," he finished, "God knows what would 'a' happened to our ladies on board; and as for the rest of us, we'd all been slaving in Simsbury Mines by this time. That's all I have to say."

"Is it?" The general looked at my flushed face. "I've no doubt Mr. Wiswell's glad to hear it." Then his heavy eyelids drooped; his lower lip hung slack; he seemed to forget Buell.

"Am I to understand, Mr. Wiswell," he went on, "that it's your desire to take up arms against the rebels?"

I shook my head. "My father distrusted and hated the mobs that were ruining America, and so do I. The rebels aren't all mobsters, though, sir; there are neighbors of mine among 'em, and they believe they're doing the right thing. I couldn't take up arms against my neighbors."

Somewhat incoherently I added, "I went to Yale, sir, and I understand there are as many Yale men among the rebels as among the Loyalists. I'm a New Englander, and I don't want to go to war against other New Englanders. After all, they're my own people."

The general glanced out of the window. "Ah, then you didn't go to war against the crew of the *Badger*."

"I don't think that was war, sir."

"No? To my mind it seems to bear some resemblance, Mr. Wiswell. How do you account for your actions?"

"I think I was out of my head," I told him.

The general coughed. "Unfortunate you didn't stay that way. Let me ask you a question. Do you think the American colonies can be properly governed by the rebels?"

"No, sir," I said, "and I'd do almost anything to stop 'em. They'd turn our country into a madhouse! They're ignorant of government and finance; they hate tolerance, education and discipline as they hate rattlesnakes."

Howe rose from his chair. "So I could count on you, could I," he asked, "as long as you didn't have to carry a musket against your fellow countrymen?"

I spoke from my heart when I said that he could.

"Then I'll ask you to keep your own counsel and await my instructions," Howe said. "We won't be long in Halifax; and when we move, I'll take you with me. I have something in mind for you— something that might be of advantage to those neighbors of whom you're so fond, and might perhaps help to end the frenzy that has driven your countrymen insane. You'll hear from me."

"We will?" Buell asked. "Both of us will?"

The general looked at him coldly. "Possibly," he said. "Provided you're both out of jail—where I don't mean to imply there's any chance of Mr. Wiswell's being."

"Thank you, General," Buell said gratefully. "I'll be wherever he is."

CHAPTER XXIII

THE *Osprey* came to anchor under our lee quarter a little after dawn on the following morning, amid a bellowing so outrageous that it brought all of us on the *Badger* from our berths.

When I came on deck, I was met by Captain Soule, his fringe of whiskers abristle and his eyes ablaze. "Captain Wiswell," he said, "the British Navy's making free with my crew in spite of all your promises!"

I pushed past him, went to the lee rail and saw the longboats of two frigates beneath the *Osprey's* counter. In the bow of one a red-faced lieutenant shook a clenched fist at the silent men who stared down from the *Osprey's* quarter-deck and waist.

I heard him shout "To Mill Prison for this, by God! Damned high-handed disregard for orders! You'll get a thousand lashes for this, every bloody damned last bloody one of you! Hoist your bloody anchor, damn you, and follow us back to the frigate!"

Mrs. Byles came to stand beside me and rapped with her cane upon the deck. "That's strong seafaring language, Oliver," she said, "but I'll thank you to remember that Belcher's wigstand and my clock and all the rest of my belongings are still aboard that sloop! Don't let those swabs outtalk you!"

Henrietta Dixon looked imploringly at Buell. "My lamps!" she cried. "My Irish-glass lamps!" she hiccuped and wept; and young Nathan, pressed against her skirts, set up a sympathetic roaring and pounded her ample hips with clenched fists.

"Lower a boat," I told Buell. "We'll take Captain Soule ashore and talk to Cunningham. On our way I'll say a word to the young gentlemen in those boats."

When, a little later, two of our seamen rowed me over to them, with Buell and Captain Soule sitting beside me in the stern of our boat, I felt I'd seldom encountered a more icy staring.

"By what right," one of the officers said, "do you issue orders to this sloop? Don't you know Halifax harbor and all adjacent waters are subject to His Majesty's Navy?"

"Yes, sir," I said, "but the sloop carried my people out of Boston with General Howe's army. I've explained the situation to General Howe, and the matter's in his hands."

"Damnation, sir," the lieutenant cried, "we ordered her to heave to, but she kept right on running! If she hadn't been headed into a crowded harbor, we'd have blown her out of water."

"They couldn't heave to," I explained. "They were running in on my orders. If they hadn't obeyed my orders, their captain would have been hanged. Their captain's here with me, and I'm taking him to the provost marshal, so he and his crew can go back to Boston without interference. I'll be obliged if you let matters remain as they are until I've seen the provost marshal."

With that, assuming an assent I briskly affected to take for granted, I signed to the oarsmen and they rowed us rapidly ashore, where I wasted no time escorting Captain Soule to the provost marshal's quarters.

Captain Cunningham greeted me as expansively as though I were a long-lost friend.

"So you talked the general into it, did you?" he asked jovially. "You've a tongue of gold, my boy—a tongue of gold!"

He picked up a paper from his desk and handed it to me:

"Because of promises [it read] *made by Oliver Wiswell to the officers and crew of the rebel privateer schooner* Badger, *the officers and crew shall be allowed to proceed from Halifax without molestation in the* Osprey *sloop, and, if halted by His Majesty's cruisers prior to their arriving at their port of destination, shall be allowed to continue without interference.*

"W. Howe, Com. Chief."

"I'm mighty glad to have these orders," I told Cunningham. "Mighty glad! The *Scorpion* frigate sent two lieutenants and two boatloads of men in pursuit of the *Osprey* this morning because she persisted in running alongside of me instead of heaving to where the

Scorpion thought she should. His Majesty's naval officers haven't a high regard for anyone's wishes but their own, but I think these orders will settle the matter."

Captain Cunningham came around his desk, placed his hand affectionately on my shoulder, turned me toward the entrance of the marquee, and motioned Captain Soule to precede us.

When Soule had gone out, Cunningham halted me. "Mr. Wiswell," he said seriously, "a general's orders are a general's orders, and as such they command respect and obedience from any man in his army; but as you've seen, the navy's a law to itself. I can see you've set your heart on having these rebels of yours go safely off, but unless the proper precautions are taken, I fear they may have difficulty."

"I don't follow you," I said. "This order specifically instructs——"

Cunningham tightened his grip on my shoulder. "I know, I know," he whispered, "but take my word for it, Wiswell: it's better to be safe than to be sorry. The only safe way—I'm sure you'll understand me, Mr. Wiswell—is to have a private understanding with the two naval lieutenants you mentioned. I don't for a moment suggest that you do it yourself. I'd consider that dangerous. If you want it done—and I strongly advise it—I'll be only too happy to act for you."

I couldn't believe I'd understood him. "A private understanding? You don't think, do you, that two naval officers would——"

"Oh dear me, yes," Captain Cunningham said. "The poor young men have almost no private means of their own. As I understand it, you brought a deal of provisions from Boston, and a few boatloads might make all the difference. If I were you, I'd part with all I could afford."

I pretended to consider Cunningham's suggestion. Then I shook my head. "I can't do it, Captain. That food and the rest of the *Osprey's* cargo isn't mine. It's only held in trust by me for Mrs. Byles, Mrs. Dixon and my friend Buell. I'm afraid I'll have to see the general again and let him know that naval officers are taking bribes."

Cunningham looked shocked. "Bribes! They wouldn't be taking bribes! They'd merely be accepting a little present from a well-wisher! You've misunderstood me, Mr. Wiswell! Just forget the whole thing, and I'll send one of my men as far as the harbor's mouth with the *Osprey* when she sails."

He clapped me on the shoulder, gave me the friendliest smile imaginable, and waved me lightly toward the muddy streets of Halifax.

We laid the *Osprey* alongside the *Badger* schooner, lashed her there, and the two crews toiled all day transferring cargo from the sloop to the schooner. So amiably did they labor together that no stranger could have told which were the rebels and which the Loyalists; and I, watching them, thought that if only enemies could be given work to do in common, there'd be an end to war.

Mrs. Byles and Henrietta Dixon sat beside the hatch, Mrs. Byles triumphantly calling out the bales and bundles as they came aboard, and Henrietta Dixon writing them in a commonplace book.

"Twenty bolts of taffeta," I heard Mrs. Byles say.

"How do you spell 'taffeta', Mate Buell?" Henrietta asked. "With a 'y'?"

"Three thousand sheets of Japan vellum," Mrs. Byles announced.

"What's vellum for, Mate Buell?" Henrietta asked.

"Two hundred pairs of ladies'——" Mrs. Byles began; then lowered her voice. "Ladies' pantalets," she whispered to Henrietta; then again spoke loudly. "Nothing to interest you, Mate Buell. Kindly step to a distance."

He didn't, but peered over Henrietta's shoulder as she wrote.

Mrs. Byles covered the terrible word with her hand.

"Mate Buell!"

He sighed and returned to his work.

Towards sundown the *Osprey* left us, her officers and men shouting hoarse and friendly good-bys to us across the steel-gray water; and that night we accepted the *Badger* schooner as our permanent home in Halifax—and a cozy home we had by comparison with some of those in which our fellow fugitives from Boston were forced to live.

In our hold we had the potatoes, dried peas, salt pork, flour and molasses picked up by Buell in Boston; and in the cabin ticked Mrs. Byles' tall clock showing the moon's changes and the days of the month. Lashed to the cabin beams by Buell, to keep them from the questing fingers of Nathan, were Henrietta's lamps of Irish glass; and beside the stove, protected by a spare stays'l, was Belcher Byles' wigstand, holding within it a bucket of drinking water.

Thanks to Buell's foresight, our fare was almost princely; but unhappy indeed was the lot of our fellow refugees upon the land.

General Howe and his army remained in Halifax for two months, and during those two months the Boston refugees were never once comfortable, were almost never warm, and usually never knew whether the next day would find their stomachs full or empty.

Almost without exception those refugees were penniless; and their only means of livelihood was to sell the few belongings which they had been so fortunate as to save. Thus the streets of Halifax took on the appearance of a vast fair; and people I'd known all my life sat in little makeshift booths along the sidewalks, offering to the reluctant citizens of Halifax the clothing, paintings, furniture and silver that so recently had graced homes on Tremont Street and Beacon Hill.

We heard strange tales of the abilities that suddenly developed in some of the unfortunates. Most of them could do nothing but sell what they had; and when their small stores of possessions were gone, and their money too, they begged or borrowed where they could. A few, though, were different. By swapping, bargaining, buying on credit; by taking advantage of every opportunity, and creating opportunities where none existed, they increased their meager store of salable articles: increased them, had a few shillings to spend, and somehow found a way to rent rooms in which their precious stocks might be locked of nights.

I learned then, beyond question, that if all the property in the world were distributed, and an equal share given to everyone, the bulk of mankind would soon be destitute, and a few would have everything.

Buell, alas, was not one of the few. He was constantly in touch with the most needy refugees, since he had suggested to General Howe that living quarters be provided for them in crowded Halifax by removing the cabins from transports and erecting the cabins on the hillslopes above the harbor; and the general had not only agreed to the operation, but had seen fit to put Buell in charge of it.

Each cabin brought ashore was instantly surrounded by clamorous refugees, all penniless and in fear of freezing to death during the coming winter. Buell's earnest simplicity forced him to listen with reluctant understanding to their troubles, and he was forever grumblingly attempting to lighten their sufferings.

He was always indignantly discovering somebody for whom we had to provide—always angrily coming across a family of six or seven Loyalists wretchedly sheltered in a ragged tent, or an aged couple who had lived on half-rotten potatoes for a month, or some old gentleman who couldn't go out in the daytime because of lacking enough to cover his nakedness.

"Damn it, Oliver," he said, "we'd ought to be allowed to keep our money for ourselves! All these people had the same chances to help themselves to rebel goods that we did, and they should 'a' done it! There ain't one single damned reason why we need to give 'em a penny; and not a shilling would they get out of me if they were back in Boston! Still, they never damaged us, and the rebels did; and since we stole all this stuff from rebels, I suppose we've got to let these people have some of it. I dunno what'll happen to us if this keeps on! Smoked herrings certainly raise hob with my disposition, and I been hoping to save enough so I could go to South Carolina and improve my health with potlicker, corn bread and chittlings; but the way it looks now, I won't be able to go anywhere unless General Howe takes me along."

The drain on our resources became so great that I was forced to protect Mrs. Byles and Mrs. Dixon by putting Buell on a rigid allowance of two shillings a day. I say *our* resources, because Buell insisted that I should have one half the proceeds from the sale of the supplies he had loaded aboard the *Osprey* at Boston.

He readily agreed to this interference with his freedom of action because of his fear for the future of Mrs. Byles and Mrs. Dixon.

"There's no telling what'll happen to us, Oliver," he said. "General Howe thinks there won't be any more rebellion after we've reached wherever we're going when we leave here; but God knows why he thinks so! Bunker Hill ought to have ended the Revolution; but thanks to this same General Howe, it didn't; so what makes him think he'll do better next time? Once a damned fool, always a damned fool! It wouldn't surprise me if the Revolution lasted as long as Mrs. Loring, and she's a young woman still.

"Now s'pose the Revolution *does* last forever, or s'pose a rebel mob catches us, or s'pose we choke to death some morning on these damned stinking herring! What'll become of Mrs. Byles and Henrietta if they don't have us to lean on? Maybe Mrs. Byles could make out somehow; but Henrietta, she'd just be plumb lost. If they want to stay out of debtors' prison, they'll have to go to England, the way your father said, and put in claims for the property they lost when the rebels drove 'em out of Boston. That means somebody's got to pay their passage, and they'll have to have something to live on in England, and they'll need money to hire a lawyer; so there just ain't any help for it: they got to be provided for, and we're the ones that have to do the providing."

With each passing week he became more and more infuriated by the helplessness of Henrietta Dixon; and as his fury grew, her helplessness became more apparent. Whenever he went ashore, he was in a constant fever to get back to the schooner to find out, as he put it, what damned fool thing she'd done; and when he was with her, he was perpetually shaking his head over her blunders. What it was that ailed him, he didn't seem to know; but since his symptoms were unmistakable, I wasn't surprised when he proposed, on the eve of the army's departure from Halifax, that all funds remaining from the sale of the *Osprey's* cargo be placed in Mrs. Byles' and Mrs. Dixon's hands for safekeeping.

"I don't care what you do with it," I told him. "It's really yours; but if you feel Henrietta's incompetent, I should think you'd hesitate to burden her with all this financial responsibility."

Buell looked embarrassed. "Oh," he said carelessly, "she ain't incompetent about *everything*. Now if I really set out to drown that Nathan of hers, the way I'd like to sometimes, she'd take care of *him* all right in spite of the best I could do; and if anybody—you, say, or —or—well, General Howe, say—undertook to be free and easy with her—wanted to squeeze her, mebbe, or kind of do a little general handiwork—I dunno as I make myself exactly clear, Oliver, but——"

"I think I see what you're getting at," I said.

Buell looked relieved. "Well, when anybody tries anything like that, she ain't incompetent." He looked regretfully introspective. "No, Oliver, on some points she's mighty competent and muscular. To continue, though, money's another point she's competent on. Seems to me we'd do as well to let her and Mrs. Byles take care of our funds as to put 'em in the Bank of England. Of course I wouldn't try to steal from the Bank of England; it wouldn't be reasonable; but I wouldn't undertake to steal from Mrs. Byles and Henrietta unless I was ready to see my Maker—which isn't the case."

He came closer and spoke behind a cupped hand. "Besides, Oliver, we don't need money, so Henrietta and Mrs. Byles might as well have ours. I thought up a way to get more—as much more as we need— when we get where we're going." He glanced cautiously over his shoulder.

"As much as we need?" I asked.

He nodded and drew a soiled slip of paper from his pocket. "Look at it!" he exclaimed contemptuously. "Rebel money! That's an eight-dollar bill. Look at that pine tree! Ain't it terrible? Looks like a suppository! I could engrave a plate like that in half an hour with a hatchet; and I could print a thousand of 'em in the time it takes you to shave, pretty near. It'll be a real pleasure, Oliver, to trade a bundle of these to a rebel for ten dollars in real money—when you hear from General Howe, and if I'm still out of jail, like he said."

I did hear from General Howe, but not until the end of May. Late one afternoon, when the slanting rays of the sun brightened the misty green halos that had just appeared upon the elms and maples of that bleak northern town, a boat rowed under our counter with one of Captain Cunningham's aides in its stern sheets.

"Captain Cunningham's compliments," he shouted to me. "The general's asked your whereabouts, and Captain Cunningham suggests seeing him as soon as possible. He mentioned tomorrow morning."

"If he said 'as soon as possible'," I told him, "I won't wait till tomorrow. I'll go back with you if you'll give me a minute to make myself presentable."

Without waiting for an answer I ran to the cabin, with Mrs. Byles, Henrietta Dixon, Buell and Nathan close at my heels.

"Wear your frilled shirt," Mrs. Byles panted. "Henrietta, bring me the brush! Get the sponge and look for spots on Oliver's blue coat! Oliver, I think you'd better wear Belcher's brooch. It'll be very genteel against those frills."

Henrietta Dixon, noisily opening and closing the drawers beneath my berth, burst into tears.

"Now what's the matter?" Buell asked her. "I never saw such a woman! Always laughing when you ought to be crying, and crying when you ought to be laughing!"

Henrietta snuffled, shook her head, and went on opening and closing drawers.

"You ought to be glad the general's taking notice of Oliver," Buell went on. "It probably means we'll both of us have a chance to do something worth doing instead of lying here in this harbor, eating smoked herring and being nursemaids."

Mrs. Dixon turned on him. "If you know where that sponge is," she said, "get it! I've had all the talk I can stand!"

While Mrs. Byles helped adjust my frills, Henrietta moved helplessly about us, hiccuping and snuffling; and Buell, muttering to himself, rubbed at my coat with the sponge.

"When he sees this frilled shirt, Oliver," Mrs. Byles said, "he'll know you're fit to go wherever an Englishman could go, and do anything anyone could do."

"You want 'em both to go," Henrietta said accusingly. "You know you do!"

"You'll hold your tongue," Mrs. Byles said, "or you'll never travel to England with me!"

"Look here," I said, "I don't know the reason for this display of emotion; but I'd like it stopped. No people ever got along better together than we have aboard this schooner for the last two months, and that's how I'd like to remember our last days together."

"Here's your coat, Oliver," Buell said heartily. He helped me into it, glared at Henrietta Dixon and noisily pushed me on deck; but noisy as his movements were, they weren't noisy enough to drown the renewed snuffling of Henrietta Dixon, or Nathan's howls of sympathetic sorrow.

CHAPTER XXIV

I DETESTED Halifax for more reasons than one, and I always went ashore reluctantly, knowing I'd encounter scores of Bostonians I knew, all urgently in need of assistance I couldn't give. Now that Howe had asked for me, I was eager for once to climb the slippery ladder to the central dock; but even still my eagerness was shadowed by the dread of again seeing the hopeless glances, the weary dejection, of all those poor banished souls.

Cunningham's aide, an amiable young man, climbed the ladder close behind me; and when he reached the top, he shouted angrily and darted past me toward a throng of men who stood idly in the broad space at the dockhead. "Get yourself to one side or the other," he ordered brusquely. "You've been told not to hang about here where you're forever underfoot! Why don't you obey orders? Where's your captain?"

When none of the men answered, the aide snapped, "Any officer'll do! Push one of 'em out and let him talk!"

Every one of the men was literally in rags—rags that would have made any scarecrow look well dressed. Some were shirtless; some shoeless. In place of stockings, most of them wore sacking tied at the ankle and below the knee. Their breeches were patched with odds and ends of cloth cut from curtains, bags, women's dresses.

One of these grotesques gave the aide a halfhearted salute. "They're all of 'em gone to try to get us some clothes and tents," he said.

"Why," I said, "those men are Americans!"

"They're a bloody nuisance," the aide said. "They've been here three days, underfoot every damned minute!"

I went closer to the scarecrow figures. "Are you a military organization?" I asked. "Where are you from?"

They spoke up cheerfully enough. "New York Volunteers," they said, and a score of voices named their homes—"Bloomingdale, Hoboken, Princeton, Dobbs Ferry, Poughkeepsie."

I singled out the man who'd replied to Cunningham's aide. "Am I to understand you've come here to offer your services to General Howe? How'd you get here, if you've only been here three days? How's it happen you've no uniforms or equipment?"

"There ain't any way we can get anything," the man said, answering my last question first. "When the rebels put us out of our homes last January, they didn't give us time to sell anything, or get our hands on any money, so ever since we've had to get along on what we wore when we got away."

"Captain Grant and Captain Campbell, they formed us into companies," another ragged soldier said. "We fought the rebels when they were burning Loyalist farms, but when they got to outnumbering us ten to one, we had to run for it. Captain Grant and Captain Campbell, they led us across to Staten Island and got us out to the King's ships at Sandy Hook. We lived on 'em three months, till they sailed up here a week ago."

"How'd it happen the ships' officers didn't supply you with clothes?" I asked.

The men stared at me blankly. One of them said, "I guess they didn't have any to spare."

Captain Cunningham's aide undertook to explain the situation. "They're not on any establishment, Mr. Wiswell. They haven't even been reviewed, nor are their officers regularly appointed. They just appeared here a few days ago, and there isn't anything they don't want! Morning, noon and night they're standing around while their so-called officers ask for this and that and t'other."

I looked at him hard, wondering if he could be speaking in all seriousness. I saw that he was.

"Where can I find your officers?" I asked the ragged men.

They shook their heads. "They're on the go all the time," one said. "Captain Grant and Lieutenant Hewlett, they're usually around the commissary general's. Captain Campbell and Lieutenant Taylor, they spend their time waiting in officers' tents."

Cunningham's aide laughed harshly. "Keep clear of those officers,

Mr. Wiswell: if you ever run into 'em, they'll dry you up telling you their troubles."

"Here's Lieutenant Hewlett now," a man said.

A young man about my own age, wearing a threadbare blue uniform coat patched at the elbows and on the cuffs with scarlet, trotted onto the dock. From his belt hung an old iron-hilted ship's cutlass. "All right, men," he shouted. "The captain's got twenty fathoms of cod line for us, and a thousand feet of lumber; also permission to pitch camp. Fall in!"

The ragged soldiers gabbled excitedly and formed themselves in line.

I spoke to the lieutenant. "Lieutenant Hewlett, my name's Wiswell. I'm from Boston, and I'd certainly like to help you if I can. How does it happen these men of yours can't get decent clothes?"

Hewlett ran a quick eye over me. "Well, Mr. Wiswell, we're not on the establishment. If we can get on the establishment, we'll probably be all right."

"Have you seen General Howe?" I asked.

"We saw one of his aides," Hewlett said. "He couldn't do anything, but we'll be all right if we can get a crack at the rebels. We'll take their clothes—if they have any." He eyed the long line of ragged soldiers who waited for orders. "You'll have to excuse me, Mr. Wiswell. These men haven't had any food today. I want to start 'em catching some fish." He gave me an abrupt nod, shouted "Left, *heel!* Forward, *hup!*" and ran to the head of the moving line.

Ignoring the murmurings of Cunningham's aide, I hurried off toward headquarters, seething with rage at the stupidity of armies and army officers.

I grew cooler while I waited for my audience with the general; for he was at dinner when I arrived, and that function was so interminable that nothing could have stayed hot for so long a period.

Not until eleven o'clock did he come heavily into his office. He came steadily enough, but his eyelids drooped, as if he were ready for bed; and he was as redolent of wine as though he had swum in it, clothes and all.

He had me before him at once, and as he stared at me, he rubbed the dark circles beneath his eyes with a puffy forefinger. "Sorry to keep you waiting a few moments, Mr. Wiswell," he said. "Didn't expect you until tomorrow, but it's well you came tonight. I've just now discussed your case with our new commissary of prisoners—a fellow townsman of yours: Mr. Joshua Loring." His attitude was overcareless. "No doubt you know Commissary Loring?"

"Only slightly," I said. "My father was better acquainted with him and his lovely wife."

The general coughed and adjusted the gold gorget at his throat. "Now, Mr. Wiswell," he said, "you're not inclined to be a fighting man as yet, but you want to help your country escape from the clutches of demagogues who are ruining it. You're an educated man, able to understand what you see; able to put your thoughts accurately into words.

"When we leave here, Mr. Wiswell, we're going to Long Island, and in a few weeks, in all likelihood, the city of New York will be ours and the rebellion of your fellow countrymen ended. According to the information I've received, the Loyalists on Long Island and in New York greatly outnumber the rebels. It's also my understanding that since the rebels have an army, even though it's a bad one, and since the Loyalists haven't, the rebels are making life miserable for everyone on Long Island, just as they did for those in Boston. As you well understand, Mr. Wiswell, that's not a pleasant situation."

The general paused and eyed me sleepily.

"Yes, sir," I said.

"Well," Howe said, "there it is. The rebels are raising the devil, but I don't know the details. I want you to get them for me. I want to know who's bulldozing the people that stand for orderly government. I want to know who's lodging the information, leading the mobs, and terrorizing decent, law-abiding people on Long Island and in New York. What are they doing to those they throw into jail?"

The general's fist thundered on the table. "By God, Wiswell, I'm a long-suffering man, and I'll take no advantage of those who're standing up for their beliefs; but I won't see honest men treated like felons without raising a hand against those responsible for it!" He leaned forward and fixed me with heavy-lidded eyes. "Will *you*, Wiswell?"

"No, General."

"No, nor anybody else," Howe said. "If we drive the rebels out of Long Island and New York this summer, as we shall, I'll not have those informers and those leaders of the mob nipping at our heels like ill-tempered dogs. What's more, the rebels I capture will be treated as our own people have been treated—no better and no worse.

"That's what you've got to find out, Wiswell: how they've been treated. How, where, why and by whom. I know it's not an easy task. In fact, it's one of the most difficult of wartime operations, but a highly necessary one. It calls for education, judgment, dexterity, quick thinking. Now then: do you think you can do it? Can you find out what I want to know, and write it all down in a clear and ample report?"

"But if I were in the army," I said, "the rebels wouldn't allow me to——"

"You wouldn't be in the army," the general said sharply. "You told me yourself you didn't want to be. You'd be loosely attached to the commissary for prisoners, and you'll be particularly assigned to the needs of Loyalists. You'll go along with us when we move to Long Island, and ostensibly you'll be under Mr. Loring. Mr. Stedman will also be under Mr. Loring, and I think you work congenially with Mr. Stedman. In reality, you'll be answerable only to me, and you'll bring your written and other information to me. I'll expect you to make me fully acquainted with what the Loyalists are saying as well as how they're being treated. I'll expect you to gather all the information you can—and to help you, you can have that man of yours: that person the rebels tarred and feathered. Bowel, wasn't it, or some such name?"

"Buell," I said.

"Buell or Bowel: all the same," Howe said testily. "Of course, I can't pay him as much as I can you, but——"

"Nothing," I said quickly. "I need nothing, and neither does Buell. I'll do whatever I can to help any mistreated countryman of mine, and so will Buell; but not for pay, General."

"No compensation, eh?" Howe asked. "So much the better; so much the better! There'll be times, no doubt, when you'll be playing a lone hand—rowing your own canoe, I believe you Americans say—and funds might be difficult for you to obtain if you had to depend on Mr. Loring. As you can see, Wiswell, you'll be a member of my own staff, in a way: yet you won't be in uniform, and I won't be able to protect you in certain contingencies."

"I think I understand," I said. "That means I'll be a spy, doesn't it?"

"Do you have moral scruples against spying?" Howe asked politely.

"None, sir."

"I'm glad of that," Howe said. "The best and bravest officers in every army have always been proud to obtain for their commanders the intelligence without which a campaign must fail. You can call your duties whatever you wish. All I can say is that I'm asking you to perform work that I'd by no means entrust to anyone—the work of getting intelligence which, if obtained, will secure your own countrymen against brutality and outrages."

"There's just one thing, sir," I said. "If Buell and I do the work you've chosen for us, I'd like to be sure you'll trust us."

The general frowned. "Come, come, Mr. Wiswell! How'm I to interpret that!"

"As a respectful request, sir," I said. "If Buell and I bring you information that you don't like—information that doesn't agree with your ideas—I wouldn't want either of us to be punished or discredited for doing our best. In other words, sir, if you consider us fit to run risks for you, I want to be sure you're prepared to believe what we say. I want to be able to make any sort of report, so long as it's true, and not have to guard against being too frank."

"Nonsense," Howe said. "The truth is exactly what I want, so consider all your doubts ended."

"In that case, General," I said, "I'd like to make a report right now on two companies of Loyalist troops that I just saw. They're New York Volunteers. They fought to keep Loyalists from being mistreated; and when they were outnumbered, they took refuge on——"

"I've heard about them, Mr. Wiswell."

"But they're half naked," I protested. "They're Americans, offering to help you put down a rebellion, and nothing's being done for 'em—nothing! They're not being clothed, not being decently fed."

"You don't understand, Mr. Wiswell," Howe said. "These men aren't on the establishment."

"Establishment be damned, sir!"

"Ah yes," Howe said, "but if no provision is made and no fund established from which these men may be clothed and accoutered, and I clothe and accouter them, I become personally responsible."

"There must be a way around, sir," I protested. "You owe it to every Loyalist in America to see that these troops receive a cordial welcome and ample support. Nobody will ever believe that so powerful a general as yourself could possibly lack the power to furnish common necessaries for two hundred men—unless he was unfavorably disposed toward all Loyalists."

"Mr. Wiswell," Howe said, "you no doubt mean well, but your knowledge of army procedure is abysmal. Your duty ends when you supply me with the information I want. The New York Loyalists are my affair. From you I want information concerning conditions on Long Island. Is that clear?"

All that was clear to me was that the war, in which I'd hoped not to be caught, had me by the heels, and that I'd better make the best of it.

In the two weeks that remained to us before we sailed from Halifax, Buell, stirred to new heights of energy by the belief that he was leaving the hated smoked herring of Nova Scotia forever behind him, sold the *Badger* schooner for £600, disposed of the *Osprey's* cargo for another £1100, established my father's servant Andrew and Mrs. Byles' Maggie as the owners of a restaurant, obtained temporary quarters for Mrs. Byles, Henrietta and Nathan in rooms vacated by two of Howe's young officers, took passage for them on a barkentine for Bristol, and built for himself a little hand press that, when dismantled, filled less than a quarter of a seaman's chest. He set up the press in Mrs. Byles' bedroom, and spent his spare moments striking off eight-dollar Continental notes and simultaneously advising Henrietta what to do when she reached London.

"You want to remember, Henrietta," he said, "that I've traveled, and you haven't; and you want to remember, too, that most travelers have one thing in common. Of course, I'm different, Henrietta, but I'm unusual." He looked at her significantly as he pulled the lever of his press. "I'm different, Henrietta," he repeated, "but you probably won't appreciate it till we're separated. Then you'll remember how different I was from all the others."

He removed an eight-dollar note from the press, examined it admiringly, and dropped it carelessly in a market basket which stood beside him, already half filled with newly printed Congress money.

"I'm different," he repeated, adjusting another sheet of paper in his press, "but all the others are alike: let 'em travel in strange places, and they want the food they had at home. When a Bostonian goes to Philadelphia, he wants beans and scrod. When a Nova Scotiaman goes to Boston, he wants smoked herring. When a Philadelphian goes to Albany, he's always whining for scrapple. And when an American goes to foreign parts, he's forever wishing for American food. It don't matter how good the cooking is where he goes: he'd rather have worse things, if so be he'd ever had 'em in America.

"Take ham and eggs, Henrietta: put an American in heaven, and he'd rather have ham and eggs than what the Good Book calls this nectar and ambrosia of the gods. He'd rather have one drink of hot buttered rum than a gallon of those liquids. You tell an American in London where he can get corned-beef hash, or finnan haddie, or salt fish and pork scraps, or tongues and cheeks by merely running five miles, and he'll run five miles every day.

"Bear that in mind, Henrietta, and get yourself a tavern in London—just a neat little place where Americans can get Indian pudding, hash, fish balls and baked beans, and they'll probably have to call out the troops to scatter the mobs of Americans that try to break down the front door."

Mrs. Byles thumped her cane upon the floor. "Buell, you never spoke a truer word. I remember how Belcher wasted away on mutton and cold potatoes in England! When I made him a fish chowder, he broke down and cried! We'll have a tavern in London, Tom Buell; and if you and Oliver ever come to see us, there'll be nothing lacking to make you think of Boston—nothing but a mob to tar and feather you, and an army of grandfathers to chase you every time you set foot outdoors."

Buell, finished with his money-making, wiped ink from his press with a rag moistened with acrid-smelling fluid. "We'll come fast enough," he said. "You've given me an idea. I've been idling away my time too long! Starting tomorrow I'm going to collect the most useful things any man could have if he's forced to live anywhere near an army—autographs and orders. Six months from now I'll be able to write my own orders and order myself anywhere any general takes a notion not to send me."

He looked significantly at Henrietta Dixon and added, "So bear in mind, if you feel inclined to forget old friends when you're in London, that every footstep may be that of Thomas Buell!"

We left Halifax on the eighth of June, after a night of cheering, toast-drinking and gaiety such as Halifax had never before seen, and never, I was sure, would see again.

Somewhere and somehow Buell had obtained a case of champagne in the hope that it would rest gently upon his eager stomach; and we dined royally on pork pie, roast goose and bread pudding at the Royal George Tavern before embarking aboard the *Greyhound* frigate.

We drank scores of toasts, I seem to remember: toasts to Halifax because we hoped and believed we'd never see the place again; toasts to the peaceful life that lay before Mrs. Byles and Mrs. Dixon in England; toasts to the imminent downfall of Sam Adams and all his crew of rabble-rousers; toasts to the Loyalists of America, who had sacrificed their homes and fortunes rather than submit to the rule of the mob; toasts, toward the end, to little Nathan, who slept beneath the table, overcome by the innumerable sugar loaves, surreptitiously soaked in champagne, which Buell had fed him—and at the end of each toast I drank a silent one of my own to Sally Leighton and the day, now near, when I should climb again the slope of Milton Hill to find her dark eyes as kind and her hand as soft in mine as they had been before politicians wrecked our lives.

Between toasts, Mrs. Byles told us strange tales of Belcher and of girls she'd known in cloistered Cambridge. "Never a one of them," Mrs. Byles said darkly, pounding her stick upon the floor, "never a one of them but had a secret indiscretion locked within her bosom, a secret she carried with her to her grave."

"And how," Buell asked, "how did you know it?"

"Found out about it," she replied, hiccuping openly, and added, "they were just like me, only I've got three or four I'm carrying to my grave, but nobody's ever going to find out about them."

Henrietta Dixon became the soul of helplessness. At the thought of Mrs. Byles' unnamed indiscretions, she wept and rocked in her chair; came to rest, sobbing, against Buell's shoulder. Yet when Buell, trying to comfort her, placed her across two chairs and said what she needed was to have her stays loosened, she sat up suddenly and fetched him a clout that hurt both his feelings and his nose.

"That ain't right of you, Henrietta," he said reproachfully. "I wasn't going to do it myself." Doubtless he saw Mrs. Byles, just then, as plural; for he added, "I was going to ask one of the ladies to do it."

"Which one?" Mrs. Byles inquired earnestly. "Me or me?"

When, later, we went to the wharves, Mrs. Byles and Henrietta Dixon went too; and the whole population of Halifax seemed to move with us, laughing, shouting and cheering in gay certainty that this was the beginning of the end of the tribulations that had so long oppressed America.

The fleet of transports and warships were ranged before the wharves like a bristling curtain on which burned a thousand flares; and across the wriggling fiery reflections in the black water moved flatboats by the hundreds.

Scores of tar kettles blazed on the wharves, and in their smoky glare the whole population of the city waved and shouted last good-bys to the torrent of uniformed men who cascaded down over the edge of the wharves and into the waiting flatboats.

I saw again, as I had seen in Boston, the families of James Putnam, John Joy, General Timothy Ruggles, Daniel Leonard, Ward Chipman, Edward Winslow, Dr. Adino Paddock and other old acquaintances; saw the Lorings and the Hallowells; saw Gardiners, Faneuils, Courtneys, Fluckers, Debloises, Greens, Chandlers, Grays; but the womenfolk were no longer in a panic: no longer running away. They were gay in the knowledge that their men were on their way to fight for and recover their freedom and their homes.

In this departure there seemed to be no sadness: only an eager anticipation. I felt Henrietta Dixon's wet lips upon my cheek; smelt the lavender on Mrs. Byles' cap as she stood on tiptoe to kiss me good-by. Then Buell, singing lustily, fell into the boat beside me, picked himself up from the bottom, fell down again and came to rest across my knees. "Oliver," he said earnestly, "I wouldn't wonder if there was something in those Perkins' Metallic Tractors after all! I got fifty pairs of 'em wrapped in a cloth and tied around my waist, and for the first time in my life, Oliver, I ain't hiccuped once! I'm good and drunk!"

CHAPTER XXV

GENERAL HOWE may have been reckless at the gaming table and ardent in his affairs of the heart; but in war he was as careful and methodical as an old lady preparing for bed. Nay, he was more —he was as reluctant as a fledgling the day it leaves its nest.

The morning of the twenty-third of June was shimmering and steamy; and as we drew close to the low blue shores of Long Island and the misty islands guarding New York Harbor, the flagship of our fleet came to anchor. So, too, did the *Greyhound* frigate, on which Buell and I had left Halifax, and the three sloops-of-war that had kept up with us.

Why we should lie a good three miles from shore, rocking slowly on an oily swell, was a mystery to everyone aboard the *Greyhound;* but there we lay all night, rolling and screaking. Little sloops, manned by Long Island Loyalists, slipped past us like shadows; from them spectral voices hailed our quarter-deck, asking where they might find General Howe; and we could hear splashings and far-off tappings as they mounted the ladder of the general's vessel.

In the morning we moved onward in light airs to the Narrows, and dropped anchor close to the green and rolling shore of Staten Island. Only a mile away, across the Narrows, was the tip of Long Island; and on the high land at its end we could see a rough fort and guns. That fort on Brooklyn Heights looked across at the houses of New York just as the rough fortifications on Bunker Hill had looked across at Boston; and to all of us it seemed apparent that when the rest of the army arrived from Halifax, the Heights of Brooklyn would be as easy to capture from the rebels who had so foolishly fortified them as Bunker Hill should have been.

But Howe, as I have already said, was cautious—as cautious as a wary old rabbit stealing out at dawn with quivering nose and oscillating ears to feed upon a row of dewy lettuces.

For five long, hot days we lay off Staten Island doing nothing, while Buell made himself a padded weskit with eight-dollar notes basted between two layers of silk that I recognized as once belonging to a skirt of Henrietta Dixon's. He hummed as he worked, and I knew that the sentimental value of that vest far outweighed the counterfeit currency and the Perkins' Metallic Tractors it concealed.

On the morning of the twenty-ninth the remainder of our fleet came in; and all day long those ships, barks, barkentines, brigs and brigantines appeared as faint white pin points in the far haze to the eastward. The white specks became white oblongs; grew into tall pyramids of gleaming canvas; and at last, flags aflutter and bulwarks lined with cheering freight, came into the wind and dropped anchor amid the great fleet that ringed the end of Staten Island with a halo of yellow masts and spars.

Buell's weskit-making was premature, for instead of crossing over to Long Island to drive the rebels from their fortifications, Howe disembarked his whole army on Staten Island—piled them ashore in squads, companies, brigades, regiments and divisions, until every sheltered green meadow on the island was transformed into a town of tents—a town in which drums rolled all day and long lines of scarlet-clad men drilled and drilled; in which bored soldiers dickered, wrangled, gambled, fought, drank, cursed from dawn to dark; in which their women sang and hoarsely laughed the long nights through.

During our first few days on Staten Island we lived in a fog of rumors that seemed almost tangible—a sort of miasma above those towns of tents and marquees. All through those days a heat mist rose from the land, shrouding the distant small houses of New York and even the near-by shores of Long Island in a gray haze; and that haze, oppressive as it was, was less oppressive than the rumors.

The worst of the rumors said that the colonies had finally and irrevocably declared themselves independent of Great Britain, so that all hope of compromise between England and America was at an end; that the mobs in the colonies had effectively gained the

upper hand; that those who disagreed with them would be proscribed and banished, their property seized and sold to the highest
bidder and their leaders put to death; that men and women throughout the colonies, by means of outrageous lies, were being incited to
look upon every Loyalist as a monster of depravity and cruelty;
that any Loyalist who dared bear arms in defense of his beliefs
would, if captured by the rebels, be first tortured and then hanged;
that rebel regiments were a plague upon the country, robbing, burning and committing every conceivable outrage upon friend and enemy
alike; that General Howe, by so long delaying his departure from
Halifax, might be obliged to wait a year before he could start a campaign against the rebels; that at Howe's first attempt to land upon
the mainland, the rebels proposed to destroy every town along the
seacoast and retire to the shelter of the mountains.

The rumors were bad enough; but they were only rumors, half
believed. The truth, when I was summoned to General Howe's headquarters to hear it from the lips of Frank James, seemed even worse.

My summons came from Joshua Loring, commissary of prisoners,
and as soon as Buell heard what Loring's servant had to say to me,
he at once began to put away his engraving tools with which he
had been working on a plate for a new forty-dollar bill.

"Thank God it's come at last, Oliver," he said. "If those eight-dollar
bills of mine are only worth a dollar, and a forty-dollar bill is only
worth what an eight-dollar bill used to be worth, we'd soon have to
carry our money in a cart if we wanted to buy anything bigger than
an awful little sheep. Not another pair of Perkins' Metallic Tractors will I ever sell for paper money! Hard money, or something
good to eat, is all I'll ever take for Metallic Tractors till this war
is over!"

As we hurried between the long avenues of tents on our way to
the farmhouse occupied by General Howe, he continued his grumbling
about rebel money. "Even if the rebels hadn't tarred and feathered
me," he said, "I'd hate 'em for what they've done to money. They've
started the most expensive thing there is—a war—without having
enough money to begin with, and they think they can make all
they need by just printing it. Well, Oliver: that ain't the way it works.
The more they print, the less they'll have; and those that lose the
most are the ones that have the least to lose—just the ones that think
they're going to get the most out of fighting a war. I ain't got any

objection to taking something away from folks that have plenty,
provided I don't hurt anybody else when I do it; but I don't approve
of stealing from people that don't have anything to begin with,
especially when it obliges me to come back and steal from 'em again
and again, every time having to steal twice as much as I stole before.
All in all, and coming down to the hard facts, the simple meaning of
it is, the more money the rebels print, the more I got to print myself, till it might come to be a hardship."

"Stop worrying about rebel money," I said. "Unless every Loyalist
is wrong, it'll be no better than the paper it's printed on in a few
weeks' time."

"That's all it's worth now," Buell said. "That's all it'll ever be
worth, after a few more people find out what it's worth, meaning
nothing. My forty-dollar bills are just as good as Congress' forty-
dollar bills, neither me nor Congress having anything to make 'em
good with, so I got just as much right to issue 'em as Congress has.
The rebels called themselves a government, didn't they, even though
you and I and a million other Americans didn't want 'em to do it, and
knew they hadn't any business to? All right: I'm a government, too,
Oliver! I'm the government of New India, up on Passamaquoddy
Bay! This money of mine, it's the legal currency of New India, and
I raised it by taxing myself. If I was a private individual, I'd be more
careful; but being as I'm a government, I'm privileged to make a
God-damned fool of myself in any way I choose, especially by spending a lot more money than I've got or ever will have, and promising
to do things that I ain't got a chance of doing."

Buell was like that: Whenever he put his mind on anything,
whether it was money, Henrietta Dixon, his indigestion, or the potlicker of South Carolina, he theorized about it until his listeners'
numbed ears refused their proper office of conveying meanings to
the mind, and heard but vacant sound.

I was still hearing that kind of sound when we arrived at the
general's headquarters. The scene here was calculated to quiet the
fears of those who thought the rebels would long continue to print
their worthless currency.

The slopes on either side of the farmhouse were dotted with tents.
Tents stretched off to the westward and to the eastward as far as we
could see, and the strip of blue water between the tent-flecked fields
of Staten Island and the opposite Long Island shore bristled with the
masts of transports, sloops-of-war, frigates and ships of the line, and

with scores of lesser craft—sloops and flatboats belonging to Loyalist sympathizers from Long Island.

There was an air of confidence about the scores of officers, soldiers and civilians who bustled in and out of The Rose and Crown farmhouse, and most assured of all in appearance was the commissary of prisoners, Joshua Loring, who stood near the front door talking with a tall man who seemed made up of knobs.

This knobby man was so gangling and so awkward that he looked artificial, as though he'd been sawed out of wood and nailed together by an inept carpenter. On his knobby head was perched a cloth cap too small for him; and up and down his long throat, when he spoke or swallowed, which was often, surged an Adam's apple the size of a plucked woodcock.

His neck was too thin for his shirt; his arms were too long for his sleeves; his breeches too small for his legs. His knees and wrists were knobby and so were his large fingers, whose joints he cracked sharply as an aid to thought and conversation.

Loring, I saw, had put on weight since that unhappy night when we had overtaken him and his pretty wife outside the barricades in Roxbury; and there was a smug and arrogant look about him, as is often the case with men who have unexpectedly acquired great power or great wealth.

He greeted me with an excessive affability that gave me the feeling he was inwardly dwelling upon the £6,000 a year that General Howe was paying him.

"The general made a point of having you come here to meet Mr. James," he said, and airily waved a hand toward the knobby man. "Mr. James of Long Island. Mr. James has worked miracles in our behalf, and I think the general hopes he'll be of service to you."

Joints cracked in James' hands. His Adam's apple moved; he worked his neck as if to free it from his already loose collar, and stared at the heavens with a seaman's calculating eye. Never a word did he say to me or to Buell; and from the innocently wide-eyed stare which Buell gave me, I knew he suspected that the services we were about to receive from Frank James would be negligible.

Loring led us at once into headquarters, waving aside the gaudy young aides who tried officiously to be parties to our entrance; and when he pushed us into the front room, we found General Howe standing with a hulk of a man at the window that looked out across the Narrows to Long Island. When the general and his visitor turned to look at us, I was conscious of a vague resentment that Howe should be on terms of familiarity with such a man. Not only was he loutish in his appearance, with a thick nose, thick lips, bad teeth and the same sort of slyly malicious grin upon his heavy features that I'd seen on half-witted boys who delighted in torturing harmless birds or helpless puppies, but he was dirty and disheveled. His old green uniform coat was streaked with the remains of past meals; his hair couldn't have been combed for days; his hair ribbon was more of a string than a ribbon; his stockings were wrinkled and his shoes broken; and worst of all, he had a pungently dirty smell that seemed to be a blend of old, old alehouses, rank tobacco smoke, sweat, ammonia, uncleaned harnesses and damp old clothes.

Howe gave us a negligent wave of his hand and spoke to the knobby-featured Frank James. "Good! Good! Glad you're here, Mr. James! Sit down; sit down! Sit down, all of you. We've several things to discuss, Mr. James. You've met Mr. Wiswell and Mr. Buell, I see. This other gentleman is Colonel Robert Rogers, who proposes to do us a great service. I need your help for all three of 'em."

James took off his hat, perched himself upon the edge of a chair, and clasped his enormous fingers tight around the chair arm. His long neck and legs seemed to fold into his clothes like an accordion; his Adam's apple was concealed by his neckcloth; and his blue eyes fastened sharply and eagerly upon the general. He no longer seemed knobby and gangling, but capable and resourceful.

"Mr. James," the general said, "I've heard from Captain Barton of the assistance you've given him in holding the rebels in check on these waters, and I'm as indebted to you as he is. If I've been correctly informed, you've confined your activities largely to Jamaica Bay and the waters around Long Island for the past six months, and aren't familiar with what's going on ashore."

James took a firmer grip on the arm of his chair. "General," he said huskily, "there's nobody that sails out of Long Island that isn't familiar with what's going on. The whole damned island, begging your pardon, is being terrorized by two regiments of rebel militia and that hellion Christopher Duyckinck's mob. We've tried to avoid a war, General. We've submitted to having our arms seized, to being spied on and tattled about by dirty loafers that couldn't get into the front door of a decent man's house; we've seen our best men sent away to rot and starve in jail; had our boys forced into that rotten rebel militia at the points of bayonets; had our farms plundered and our cattle driven away by thieves that call themselves rebel cavalry! We've been threatened and yapped at by committees that don't even know how to run a henhouse properly; and a good part of our men are hiding on the brush plains and in swamps, so they won't be rounded up and sent to Norwich Jail or Simsbury Mines or some worse place—if there is any."

He drew a deep breath, and his Adam's apple leaped momentarily above the line of his collar. "That's what's going on, General, and that's why four men out of every five on Long Island hope to God you won't waste any time getting over there with your army."

The general nodded heavily. "All in good season, Mr. James," he said. "All in good season. Everything you say I've heard before, and I think you'll find the burdens of your unhappy island will soon be lightened."

Colonel Rogers spoke in a thick, clabbery voice. "You say they're hiding in the swamps? If I were to lead 'em out, General——"

Howe shook his head decisively. "You're to raise your Rangers on the other side of the Sound, Colonel Rogers! I'm in no position to arm those men in the swamps, and I want to find out certain things about 'em from Mr. Wiswell. You let Long Island alone for the moment, Colonel."

Rogers laughed vacantly. James relinquished his grip on his chair arm and wiped the palm of his hand against his knee.

The general turned back to James. "No doubt, Captain, you've had the pleasure of meeting Judge Jones of the Supreme Court."

James' brick-red face grew darker. "There ain't anybody on Long Island that don't know Judge Jones! There never was a finer man in this world! The rebels took him away from his wife and his family, sent him over to Connecticut and threw him in Norwich Jail! Yes, and Daniel Kissam and Judge Daniel Horsemanden, and Governor Cadwallader Colden and his son, and Lindley Murray, the best Quaker that ever lived, and John Rapalye, and the Hewletts——"

"Yes, yes," the general said, "so I understand. And are you also familiar with what has happened to Judge Jones since he's been in Norwich Jail? How has he been treated?"

"His family hasn't heard from him," James said.

The general nodded. "That was my understanding. What happened to Kissam?"

James' knuckles cracked loudly. "There's no way of knowing, General."

Howe got up from his chair and went to the window to look across the Narrows at the hazy fortifications on the Heights of Brooklyn. "No way of knowing, eh? What about all the Loyalists that have taken refuge in the swamps of Massapequa? What about the four hundred Loyalists who deserted from the rebel militia to hide in the brush? What about the Loyalists lodged in Kingston Jail? Who are the rebel informers that are driving honest, peaceful, law-abiding citizens from their homes and families?"

He whirled to shake his fist at James. "Who are they? Name those informers!"

James moved uneasily on the edge of his chair. "They've been mighty careful not to let themselves be known, General."

"Well, I've got to know," Howe said. "I want to know the condition of the Loyalists in the Hempstead swamps, now that the rebel militia has hemmed them in. How many have been killed for refusing to follow the leadership of blacksmiths, butchers, shoemakers, farm hands? How many are dying with fevers? How many are starving to death? Do *you* know?"

James shook his head. "No, sir."

General Howe thrust out his underlip. "Then you're not as familiar with Long Island as I could wish." He rapped a fat forefinger against his palm. "I propose to know those things, Captain James! Mr. Loring's my commissioner of prisoners, and he'll have to know them, too. When my army moves over to Long Island to drive out the rebels, I want to know who our secret enemies are. If they're maltreating our people, I want to put an end to it. Those rebels can't behave like barbarians, and at the same time make the world think all the barbarities are on our side! I'm sending Colonel Rogers to Connecticut to raise a corps of Rangers, and I'm sending Mr. Wiswell and Mr. Buell into the Long Island swamps to find out exactly what's happening there. You're to get them safely across to Long Island, Captain James, and set them safely on their way. I want all three of them landed on Long Island tonight. Will you do it?"

James looked around at us. His Adam's apple rose and fell. "I can land them safely, General," he said; "but I don't know how long they'll be safe."

Buell and I, in company with Colonel Rogers, left Staten Island at midnight that night on Frank James' sloop.

Before we started, Buell had outlined his plans to me. "There's

one thing I don't want, Oliver," he said, "and that's to make people
suspicious. These rebels are the suspiciousest people there are, except for those who don't want to get into trouble with rebels. The
way I look at it, there won't be anybody who ain't suspicious of us if
we try to keep out of sight or hide behind a bush every time we see
anyone. What's more, we're supposed to be talking to people: not hiding behind bushes or keeping out of everybody's way. Ain't that
right, Oliver?"

"Yes," I said, "but Captain James knows all the Loyalists on the
island, and we'll be passed from one to the other until we get where
we're going."

Buell looked dissatisfied. "That don't give me any chance to talk
to rebels," he objected. "If I can't talk to rebels, how can I sell any of
my Metallic Tractors or spend my good Congress money? A Loyalist
wouldn't want either—not without you tied him up and rammed 'em
down his throat! No, sir, I got a better scheme than yours!"

I knew from experience that Buell's ideas were frequently worth
hearing, so I just waited for him to explain.

"The way I see it," he went on, "the best way to keep people away
from you is to make a kind of a nuisance of yourself; and the best
way to keep people from paying attention to you is to keep pushing
yourself in front of 'em. Just suppose I kept coming around your
front door two or three times a day, knocking and hollering to be let
in so I could sell you something. How'd you feel about me?"

Since the answer was obvious, I said nothing.

"Yes, sir," Buell continued, "you'd certainly hate me; and if you
ran into me on the street, you'd most likely look the other way.
Well, Oliver, I've got me a bell—the noisiest scissors-grinder's bell
I can find—and a scissors-grinder's box with a nice little round, red
scissors-grinder's grindstone fixed on it, to strap on my back. I've put
a false bottom on the box and packed all my money underneath it,
and I'm going to go all around Long Island, ringing my bell and hollering till everybody'll wish I was dead! I'll sharpen scissors, shears,
bayonets and razors, mend clocks, brooches, or busted shoe buckles;
solder pans, sword hilts and kettles; fix anything that needs fixing
or buy anything that anybody's willing to sell. How's that, Oliver?"

"That's all very well for you," I said, "and I think the idea's a good
one; but if that's the way you want to travel, we'll have to part
company. I want to see Loyalists; and I want to go to 'em well
recommended, so they won't have any hesitation about talking to me."

"That's all right," Buell said cheerfully. "You go see your Loyalists, and I'll just go hollering along the road. If you need me, you won't have any trouble finding me on account of my bell. If you let me know where you're going to be each night, you'll have to be deaf not to know where I am."

Anticipating a hard day on the morrow, I'd have been glad to sleep during our trip to Jamaica Bay on James' sloop, but Colonel Rogers wouldn't have it so. He wanted to drink; and even more than he wanted to drink, seemingly, he wanted to talk in a thick, braggart voice of past exploits, military and amatory.

He came aboard the sloop in an alcoholic aura, and the first question he asked was whether anyone had any rum. When James admitted to having a bottle or two in his seaman's chest, the colonel jovially pressed him to bring it out. It was a chest with four large bottles and eight small. Two of the large ones were filled with rum, another with apple brandy and the fourth with port. Rogers drank over half of them himself, after which he gaily commandeered Buell's small supply and then my own. When everything else was gone, he willingly contributed his own canteen, which held a gallon and was filled with rum.

That clabbery voice of his went thickly on and on, pausing only when he drank; and at the end of each drink he contrived to exhale so gustily as to drown out any other speaker. Thus he held the floor, with small exceptions, all the night.

He told the tallest tales I'd ever heard—of the superhuman abilities of Rangers he had led in the Old French War; of marches, performed by him and his men, of six hundred, eight hundred, a thousand miles through trackless forests; of distinguished statesmen who had cruelly wronged him and kept him from performing tasks of incredible magnitude; of books and plays he had written, great men he had known, far-off places he had visited. As I might have spoken of Governor Hutchinson and Soame Leighton, he spoke of the King of England and how the King had said to him, "Colonel, I believe you've got the answer to our troubles."

There was no telling whether he was making up his stories out of whole cloth, or whether all these strange things had actually happened to him. He was so casual in speaking of marvels that I only half believed him.

There was something disgusting about him, too, that destroyed confidence. That soiled, red-eyed hulk of a man talked about the thousands of streetwalkers in London with a reminiscent smacking of his thick lips; and whenever he spoke of Indian tribes—as he frequently did—he went into vivid details of the peculiarities of the women of the different tribes. He told us, with relish, innumerable shocking things about the women of the Sioux, of the Mandans—who, he insisted, were descended from Welsh tribes who had come to America long centuries ago. He claimed to have fought as a general in the army of the Dey of Algiers, and to have had six women in gauze pantaloons allotted to him by the Dey.

As he talked, he drank and hiccuped and belched, and Buell became more and more restive. In the end he broke in by main strength on Rogers' alcoholic maunderings.

"You ought to be careful how you take up with so many women," Buell said, "or you'll get sick. You ought to——"

"Sick!" Rogers bellowed gaily. "You don't know anything about being sick! What's a little sickness, anyway! Why, they got me down into the Carolinas a few years ago to fight the Cherokees. I went to Ninety Six, right on the edge of the Cherokee Country, and I showed those Cherokees more about fighting in a month than they'd learned in a thousand years! Well, sir, I was as good as king of that country around Ninety Six; and what I don't know about Cherokee women ain't worth knowing! They're the best of the lot! Yes, sir, they're almost white, and near as tall as I am, and they ain't fat! No, sir, there ain't a spare ounce on 'em, the way there is on Winnebagos and Sac and Fox women, and they don't toe in. Still and all, they're strong as horses, and they're pretty! Yes, sir, they're pretty as pictures, and they live in white houses, all white clay, white as snow. There ain't any Indian women anywhere can touch 'em. There's just one trouble with 'em: they've seen too much of traders from hot ports, and runaway Negroes from Charleston and Savannah. You don't want to go to Ninety Six, or have much to do with Cherokee women, unless you've got plenty of calomel and black salve with you to take care of the sores!"

He took a mouthful of rum, washed it around in his mouth with a sound as of many waters, swallowed it, and hiccuped sonorously.

"What you should 'a' had," Buell interjected, "is a pair of Perkins' Metallic Tractors." He drew a pair from his pocket and explained their miraculous properties at great length, while Rogers stared at them out of pouchy eyes.

"Will they cure a headache after you've had too much rum?" Rogers asked.

"I don't know," Buell said. "I practically ain't had any experience with headaches from rum. But they're great things for rheumatism, toothaches, sore ankles and the itch. There ain't a case of the itch they won't cure, if you have faith in 'em and use 'em steady."

"You don't say!" Rogers exclaimed. "What's a pair of 'em worth?"

"Doctor Perkins, who invented 'em," Buell said, "sold 'em for five guineas a pair, but seeing who you are, I'll let you have these for three."

Rogers shook his head regretfully. "I can't spare that much money, but I'll trade you for 'em. I see you're a man who's interested in inventions, and I'll trade you an invention I picked up in Newport some years back. This invention is sure death to cockroaches and bedbugs."

"I don't believe it," Buell said promptly.

"You'd believe it if you saw it, I suppose," Rogers said.

Buell admitted reluctantly that he would.

"All right," Rogers shouted thickly. "That's a trade, then! If my invention kills 'em, you'll trade me a pair of Perkins' Metallic Tractors. That's agreed, is it?"

"I suppose it is," Buell said. He seemed suspicious, but somewhat bewildered, perhaps because of the rum he'd had.

"Captain," Rogers said to Frank James, "there never was a sloop that wasn't stocked with bedbugs, and you must have plenty of 'em in your mattress. Get me a fat one, will you?"

James turned over the tiller to me and went below. When, in a few moments, he came back, he held between his thumb and forefinger a fat, struggling, dark-red bedbug.

"Hah!" Rogers cried. "Now we'll see!" From his pocket he drew two pennies. On one he placed the bedbug, and over the insect he placed the second penny. Then he pressed hard; a snapping sound came from between the coins, and our nostrils were assailed by the unmistakable musty odor of a crushed bedbug.

Rogers handed the two coins to Buell, and simultaneously removed the Metallic Tractors from Buell's unresisting fingers. "There you are, my boy," he roared. "There ain't a cockroach or a bedbug on earth that can't be killed with that invention!"

Bellowing with hoarse merriment, he drank deep from his canteen, belched resoundingly, and lowered himself to the deck beside the mast. "I'll just rest my eyes a minute," he said. He sighed like a tired dog and was instantly asleep.

The gray dawn found us snugly tucked against the sandspit that shelters Jamaica Bay from the ocean. How Captain James, on a dark night, found his way between the sedge-grown islets of that pleasant harbor will always be a mystery to me, and perhaps Buell was right when he said James did it by cracking his knuckles and listening for the echo.

All through that hot day James kept the three of us out of sight in his cabin. He drew maps of the island for us and put down the location of the homes of influential Loyalists—Simonson's tavern at Hempstead; Captain Hewlett's on the Hempstead road; Captain Archibald Hamilton of Flushing; Doctor Samuel Martin of Hempstead; Doctor Charles Arden of Jamaica; David Mathews of Flatbush, mayor of New York.

At nightfall he took us ashore, led us along the sand bar to a path through the sedge and started us off on the road that led past Captain Hewlett's house to Demott's Mill Pond and Hempstead. Thanks to his diagrams and instructions, we could have drawn a trustworthy map of that part of Long Island with our eyes shut.

"You'll be close onto Hempstead by dawn," James told us. "Look for the mill at the head of the pond, and if there's a sheet hanging from an upper window, hide in the swamp. If there ain't, see the miller, Demott. He'll send you wherever you want to go. You can always hide by the roadside if you hear anybody coming at night; and Demott'll tell you how to travel—if you have to."

He left us, and I turned to Colonel Rogers, to see what his plans might be. To my surprise, he was gone. Save for the scent of stale alcohol and tobacco and of sour sweaty leather that clung in my nostrils, I might have thought that the colonel had been nothing but a distorted ghost of a one-time hero.

CHAPTER XXVI

Dᴜʀɪɴɢ our long, dusty walk that night, not a sound did we hear to indicate that we were passing through a part of the country plentifully populated with rebels and informers constantly at war with their even more numerous Loyalist neighbors—and not a sound could any ear have heard from us, for we walked softly in the dust; and Buell, with his scissors-grinder's box upon his back, kept his boasted bell in his coat pocket and had muffled the clapper in his big red handkerchief.

We saw distant lights while the night was young; heard the far-off barking of dogs as we plodded on through thick darkness heavy with the scents of July—bayberries, salt marshes, hay fields, barnyards.

In the small hours we crouched by the roadside to let an occasional cart creak past, the drivers as silent as dead men. We suspected, from what James had told us, that they were provision carts sent by loyal inhabitants of the island to help feed the fleet behind us.

Around three o'clock a sonorous croaking of frogs told us we had reached Demott's Mill Pond; and there we waited in the bushes, fighting mosquitoes, until the east grew pale and the blackbirds in the brush along the pond, coming to life with weak chirpings, clambered clumsily up and down the marsh grass as if stricken with rheumatic pains.

Buell, peering cautiously above the bushes, wasn't satisfied with what he saw. "There's no sheet hanging on this side of the mill, Oliver," he said, "but who knows what's on the other side? I'll go see, and don't you move. You wait here till you hear my bell ringing. That'll mean there's no sheets on the other side and that it's safe for

230

you to come ahead. It'll also mean everybody in the house is awake, and that you'll have something to eat as soon as you get there."

He hoisted his scissors-grinder to his shoulder, took his bell by the clapper, and trudged off through the dawn mist toward the dim gray stone building at the head of the pond. Five minutes later, I heard the bell clanging the measured irregularities peculiar to scissors-grinders, and hurried down the road to be with him.

When I reached the gate, I found Buell standing in the mill yard, ringing his bell like a man possessed and staring raptly at the brightening eastern sky as a violinist stares into space while wielding his bow. In the open door, tying his apron and staring suspiciously at Buell, was a stout, ruddy man with a pale nose and jowls the color of fresh beef. He scratched his head and looked from Buell to me.

Buell suddenly stopped his ringing and pointed his bell abruptly at the miller. "Any scissors to grind?"

The miller shook his head. "Ain't you on the road pretty early?"

Buell's bell clanged. "What's hours got to do with scissors-grinding? I grind as well in the morning as in the afternoon. Got any scissors to grind?"

The miller still studied us.

"Any knives?" Buell asked patiently. "Any axes, scythes, saws, hatchets, hoes? Any bayonets to sharpen?"

The miller narrowed his eyes. "How'd you get here? By way of New York or across the Sound?"

"What difference does it make?" Buell asked. "I grind shears and grind 'em well. I sharpen scythes or sickles or anything you've got. Ain't you got *anything* to be sharpened?"

"I might have," the miller said reluctantly. "How much do you charge?"

Buell looked relieved. "That's all I wanted to know." He turned to me. "Frank James said if we could satisfy Demott, we could satisfy anyone, so I guess we're all right. What you got for breakfast, Mr. Demott?"

The miller yawned and stretched, at ease for the first time since he'd seen us. "There ain't much in the house," he said, "but I'll try to see no friend of Frank James leaves here hungry. You can have hot ale and sour-milk cheese and new bread, and maybe a little sausage and blueberry pie."

"That's pretty near all we need, Mr. Demott," Buell said heartily. "My digestion ain't what it ought to be, and personally I can't eat more'n half a pie for breakfast, and maybe a dozen sausages. More might give me trouble."

"When's Howe coming?" Demott wanted to know before I had a chance to say a word; and all the members of his household, as we met them, asked the selfsame thing as soon as they learned who we were.

Indeed, that was the first question on the tongues of all the Loyalists we met in those next few weeks. They had been harried, spied on, lied about, informed against, robbed and insulted; and they longed achingly for Howe and his army, so that they might be freed from the oppressions and the restrictions of Congress, mobs and committees.

"By God," Demott said, filling our pewter mugs with steaming ale, "there's no telling what'll happen to the people on this island unless Howe gets here pretty quick! We're all of us under suspicion, and they can't put *all* of us in jail, the way they have Cadwallader Colden and Judge Jones. The jails are full, and so are the swamps and the brush. I guess they'll have to kill a lot of us if Howe doesn't come pretty quick."

He dropped so heavily into a chair that the floor shook. "How long before the general figures on getting here?"

"Nobody knows," I said. "His officers think he ought to bring his army across and start fighting before the end of July, but he doesn't often do as his officers think he should."

Demott looked stricken. "What'll become of us? We can't resist unless we're organized, and we can't organize without a central head. That means we'll be helpless till Howe gets here."

I knew he was suffering from that same miserable feeling of impotence that had oppressed us in Massachusetts when the mobs played hob with us and we had been unable to resist.

"He'll be here eventually," I said as reassuringly as I could. "After all, you're no worse off than Loyalists in New England."

Demott sighed. "I suppose not. I suppose we must be even better off, or there wouldn't be so many Loyalists pouring into Long Island from all the eastern provinces. Scores of 'em cross the Sound every night. That's one of the things that bothers us. The rebels won't take the trouble to send a regiment against a few men hiding in a swamp; but when there's two thousand of 'em in the swamp, they're worth capturing. There must be fifty Massachusetts Loyalists in that swamp over yonder"—he swung a hamlike fist toward the west window of the kitchen—"and maybe another hundred from Connecticut and Rhode Island, to say nothing of all who've been hunted out of towns around here by those damned horse thieves the rebels call militia!"

"Have you been in to see how they're getting along?" I asked.

"Not me," Demott said, "and don't you, either—not unless you have to! I guess it ain't comfortable. I don't see how they stand it." He looked reflective. "Of course, it's probably better than having a mob get hold of you."

"I'll have to go there," I said. "The general wants to know what's happening to 'em. What's the best way of getting in?"

"There's only one way," Demott said, "and if you insist, I'll show it to you tonight. You'll have to go in with the night's crop of Loyalists who come down from the Sound after dark."

"I'd rather go by myself," I said, "and this morning. I've got to talk to those men. The sooner I see 'em, the sooner I can find out what the general wants to know."

"Maybe so," Demott agreed, "but if the general really needs the information, you'd better do what I tell you. Otherwise he might not get it—and we want him to have the information even more than you do. Look, Mr. Wiswell: there hasn't been a day, during the past year, that we've felt safe. There's never a morning that we aren't afraid we'll be hiding in the swamps before night. A year's a long time, Mr. Wiswell—a mighty long time to be at the mercy of any cheap rascal that chooses to lead a gang of armed good-for-nothings against anyone he happens to dislike."

Buell helped himself liberally to sour-milk cheese. "Haven't you got enough people to make a gang of your own?"

"Certainly," the miller said. "This island is three-quarters Loyalist; but we can't do the things the rebels do. They send in militia from other colonies, or bring their mobs from New York. They have no homes here; no families; no belongings except what they have on their backs. We have! If we fight 'em, they seize our cattle, burn our barns and houses, and drive our families across the Sound. I can name hundreds of people, right in this neighborhood, who've been up to their necks in misery and ruin for over a year, just because they were known to be against rebellion. I hate to think what's going to happen if the Loyalists of this island ever do somehow contrive to band together and lay hands on the mobs and committeemen that mistreated such men as——"

He was interrupted by a shrill cry from the head of the stairs. "Daniel, Daniel! Foot soldiers coming around the bend at the lower end of the millpond!"

Demott groaned and struggled to his feet. "Hang out this sheet!" he shouted. To me he said urgently, "You and your friend better hide in a cornbin in the mill. You can dig down in it and breathe through a tube."

"Not me," Buell said. "I'm a peaceable scissors-grinder, and no one can prove different!"

"No cornbin for me," I said. "I'll take to the swamp."

"You can't! You don't know your way around! You'd have a bullet through you before night! Damn it, Mr. Wiswell, can't you understand the rebels are trying to capture all those men in the swamps, so they can force 'em into the rebel militia and put 'em to work making forts?"

"I understand," I said, "but I didn't come here without a plan."

Buell looked indignant. "Plan? Why didn't you tell me, Oliver?"

"It's so simple you might not have approved of it."

Buell was disgusted. "You'd ought to told me, Oliver! If we get separated——"

"We won't," I said. "Get outside and sharpen something, or you'll be in the militia yourself."

He swung his sharpening wheel to his shoulder, snatched a knife from the table and his bell from the floor, ran from the house, and immediately, in the front yard, his bell began to ring and his voice to bellow.

To Demott I said, "Give me the use of one of your blankets till the rebels have gone. I need a blanket, a strip of old linen and a lump of suet the size of a robin's egg!"

Demott stared at me, then ran to the stairs. In his absence I unbuttoned the knee band of my breeches, pushed down a stocking, took the loggerhead from the kitchen fire and held it close to the flesh above my knee. Beneath the hot iron the flesh rose in an ugly-looking welt that would soon be a blister. When Demott brought me the blanket, linen and suet, I folded the suet in one end of the linen, laid it on a hot brick beside the oven until it was melted; then pressed it over the blister and wrapped the linen around my leg. The soft suet, forced out by the pressure of the bandage, was a dirty, unhealthy white against the flesh.

As I went into the yard, thus bandaged, Buell rolled an appraising eye at my leg, but kept on with his bellowing and grinding.

Approaching us through a haze of dust that overhung the road was a long column of men—a slovenly column that marched irregularly and out of step, so that it had the look of a gigantic centipede whose feet hurt.

I lowered myself against the wall of the mill in a sunny spot and spread the blanket over my legs.

The column drew closer and closer, and from it rose a sound of babbling, a kind of chattering such as might come from a cage of animals. At the head of the column, on a sway-backed cart horse with shaggy fetlocks and droopy head, rode a paunchy, red-faced man. He had an upturned nose and little eyes that peered out from between fat lids, and looked surprisingly like a pig on horseback.

At a bellowed order from this porcine leader, the long line of men halted and shuffled their feet in the dusty road. There may have been five hundred of them, and they were as scurvy-looking as those citizen soldiers who had stared surlily at my father and me on the night we were driven out of Milton. For the most part they were pockmarked; their hair hung lankly from under sweat-stained hats; many were stockingless; and their coats were patched and foul. Even from where I lay I could hear them cursing purposelessly.

As the pig-eyed leader rode into the mill yard, Demott appeared in the doorway. He seemed pleased at the sight of the paunchy rider, and greeted him heartily as Colonel Birdsall. "What brings you here at this time of day, Colonel?" he asked.

"You know damned well," Birdsall said. His voice had a squealing resonance something like that of a sow impatiently crying out for food. "I'm after the damned Tories hiding in this swamp; and I think you know a good way in, Demott!"

Demott was indignant. "I'm a law-abiding citizen, Colonel! You've never had trouble with me, and you never will! It'd be as much as my life is worth to do anything for a Tory. No, Colonel, I'm hiding no Tories!"

Birdsall yelped contemptuously. "Pah! You can't live on the edge of this swamp and not know what goes on in it! Do you deny there's Loyalists hiding in here?" His little deep-set eyes roamed to Buell and me.

Buell, seemingly uninterested in the fat colonel, pedaled so furiously at his wheel that a stream of sparks flew from the edge of the knife

blade on which he worked. The colonel leveled a stumpy forefinger
at him. "You, there! You ain't a native of these parts! Where you
from? What you doing here?"

Buell ceased pedaling, ran his thumb over the knife blade, and
held it, point first, toward the colonel. "Me?" he asked. "Why, I ain't
doing nothing! I'm just sharpening this knife."

"I can see that," Birdsall said. "What I can't see's where you're
from. You don't belong here, and I want to know how you got here."

"I'm from Massachusetts," Buell said, "which ain't no place for
an honest scissors-grinder."

"Why not?"

"Because there ain't anything left to sharpen in Massachusetts. They
sharpened up all their axes, hatchets and bayonets for the British
five years ago. Why, Colonel, you could walk half across Massachusetts, ringing your bell all the way, and not get more'n two
knives to sharpen! What's *your* trade, brother, when you ain't a
soldier?"

"Who, me?" the colonel asked. "I'm a drover."

"Well," Buell said, "how'd you like it if you drove a lot of cows all
through this province and never found a butcher to take 'em off
your hands? You wouldn't like it, would you?"

"Beef ain't knives," Birdsall said. "People have to have beef, but
they can sharpen their own knives. What you say don't explain
nothing! What brought you here?"

"Why, Colonel," Buell said, "everyone in Massachusetts knows
folks on Long Island are whetting their knives for each other. When
I heard all you people were just waiting for a chance to cut each
other's throats, I hurried right over here to get some of the trade. I
figured that if people want to cut each other's throats, they ought
to be helped to do a good clean job. As a drover, you've had dealings
with butchers, and you know that's plain ordinary horse sense."

The colonel looked doubtful, but kicked his mare in the ribs and
moved over to stand above me. "Who's this? Demott, who's this?
He's *another* stranger! By God, Demott, you claim you don't know
what's going on in that swamp; yet there's always a stranger or two
around your house—someone who can't account for himself. Who
is this man?"

I spoke up in a voice of high complaint. "Colonel, I'll tell you who
I am, and what's more, I think it's your duty and the duty of every
compassionate man who hates King George to do something for

me. . . . Even this miller here grudges to let me lie on his ground! If you want to know where I'm from, I'm from a British ship! I was sick and they wouldn't let me stay aboard."

Birdsall made a squealing protest. "You're a damned fool if you think I'll believe that! You don't catch Ben Birdsall believing it! British surgeons may not know how to take care of their sick, but they generally pretend they do!"

He leaned from his horse and poked me with the switch he carried. "What's the matter with you, you damned ministerial tool!"

I rose on one elbow. "Only a little sore on my leg that doesn't amount to anything."

"Sore? A little sore? What kind of a little sore? You mean to say the doctors on your ship drove you off because you had a little sore? Let's look at it!"

I threw back the blanket from my leg. Above and below the bandage were scaly white excrescences, extremely unhealthy-looking.

"Hm," the colonel said. "What's the matter with it? That oughtn't to bother a doctor that's worth his salt! What did they say it was?"

I covered my leg and looked around me in what I hoped was a hunted manner. "I don't believe they knew," I said.

"Gammon!" Birdsall cried. "Either they knew or they didn't! Speak up! What did they call it?"

"Well, sir," I said, "I don't think it's true. I've never been anywhere a man could get it. I don't think it's true that I've got it!"

"By God!" Birdsall whispered. "Leprosy!" He reined back his horse. "Was that what they told you you had? Leprosy?"

I swallowed and tried to groan realistically. "No, Colonel! No! They didn't say so! They didn't come right out with the word, anyhow!"

"Demott," Birdsall shouted, "get this man away from here! Give him a bag of potatoes and see he leaves at once! Understand? Get him away from this neighborhood or I'll burn your mill!"

He urged his clumsy cart horse to a trot; and as he shouted orders to his line of scarecrow troops, he repeatedly looked back over his shoulder at me in a way that was a tribute to my blister and the sincerity of my acting.

From a distance we watched Birdsall send flanking parties of militiamen around the swamp; faintly heard his bellowing voice ordering other parties to go straight in.

"Dead or alive!" we heard him shouting. "Drive 'em out dead or alive! . . . Dead or alive!"

All through the morning and the early afternoon we heard far-off shouts and shots—single detonations; ripples of musketry fire; then long silences, during which I pictured sullen, sunken-cheeked militiamen prowling from bush to bush in that dark and watery swamp, to stalk fellow countrymen as they'd have stalked wild animals.

Toward sundown they came out again, hallooing and cursing, splashed with mud and scratched with brambles from head to foot. They had, they told Demott exultantly, killed one and taken three prisoners. The hunted Loyalists, they said, had run from them like water rats; but how many there were, or why the rest had escaped, they were unable to say.

Before that night was over we found out for ourselves.

CHAPTER XXVII

W<small>E LAY</small> in the brush behind the mill until Birdsall and his men went shouting down the road; and when they had gone, the whole world—except for the diapason of sound from innumerable frogs—seemed empty of life. But Demott had told Buell and me to stay where he'd put us in the scrub behind the mill; and so we waited, with the scent of bayberry coming to us in waves, as though this war-tormented island sighingly sought our sympathy.

Not until ten o'clock did we hear stirrings and faint tappings above the all-pervasive frog chorus, and soon thereafter we saw a lantern swing in circles near the darkened mill. That was the signal for which we waited, and when we hurried to the mill yard, we found dim figures standing there in silence.

Demott himself wasn't among them, and when one of his women-folk came out with a lantern shrouded in a bag, I remembered with what obvious sincerity Demott had sworn to Birdsall that he had never seen a Loyalist in the swamp.

Without a word being spoken, the woman turned her back upon the mill and walked into the darkness. Buell and I followed her, and one by one so did the blurred figures that had been waiting. She led us upon a path that constantly grew softer and wetter, and when she slipped the bag from her lantern and waved it, we saw, far ahead, a yellow pin point of light.

As we drew closer, the pin point became a lantern, held by a cadaverous tall man whose breeches clung to his bony legs as if he'd been wading waist-high in a river. He stood in the stern of a sedge boat—one of the flat-bottomed square-ended craft used by Long Islanders for transporting hay crops and carrying heavy burdens

through their interminable marshes; and resting against the swampy
shore of the black stream were five other sedge boats, in the stern
of each of which sat a hollow-cheeked man peering intently and
suspiciously at us. Across their knees lay short-barreled muskets.

"How many?" the man with the lantern asked, and without waiting for an answer he added, "Did you get the medicine? Did you
get the bandages?"

Our woman guide spoke up. "I got two sheets and a pail of mutton
tallow," she said. "It'll have to do."

The man groaned. "Bring rags tomorrow if you can't get sheets.
We could use six sheets. Bring cinchona bark, too. The fever's bad."

The woman pushed me forward. "This here's Mr. Wiswell," she
said. "Dan says you're to take special care of him, because he came
over from Staten Island to find out what's happening to you."

"From Staten Island?" the man repeated blankly. Then, in the
light of the lantern, he suddenly changed. His eyes glittered; his
emaciated limbs seemed to strengthen and take on more substance;
he stood straighter. "He came from Staten Island?" he cried. "When's
Howe coming?"

"Soon," I said, "soon! Soon, I think."

At that the man groaned. " 'Soon!' That's all we've heard for the
past six months! Well, get in, Mr. Wiswell, and your friend too. How
many in all?"

"There's eighteen," the woman said. "All forwarded and vouched
for by Mayor Mathews."

Our half-seen company entered the sedge boats with a sound of
thumpings and splashing. I found myself seated in two inches of
water smelling strongly of fish; and behind me sat Buell, growling
at the difficulty of keeping his scissors-grinder dry. The man set his
lantern on the back thwart, picked up an oar and pushed his boat
away from the bank. Facing backward and never once looking ahead,
he sculled us into the swamp; and behind us the other sedge boats,
each with a dim lantern in its stern, followed around sharp turns and
through sedgy passageways like a sluggish and dimly phosphorescent
marsh monster phlegmatically traversing familiar waters.

We seemed to float on a river of drumlike rumbling—a frog chorus
so vast that it had a sort of solidity. We moved, too, in a dense cloud
of insects whose wings made a constant shrill whining accompaniment to the resonant song of the frogs. Those damnable bugs were
like dust or smoke, and filtered through every aperture, no matter

how small. When I opened my eyes, they dashed against my eyeballs.
When I opened my mouth, it was filled with their fluttering wings.
They were in my nose, ears, hair—down my neck, up my sleeves;
and I felt them crawling far down inside my clothes. They pierced
me with little hot itching thrusts, with slow malignant bites, with
sharp vindictive stabs. When I brushed them from one part, they
attacked in a score of others, tormenting me beyond endurance.

"You'll get used to 'em," the boatman said. "You got nice rich
blood, and if there's anything those critters like, it's fresh meat!
When they've sucked a few quarts out of you, you'll be like the
rest of us, and they won't bother you so much. Where you from, Mr.
Wiswell?"

"Milton," I said, "but for the last three months I've been in Halifax
with General Howe."

The boatman spoke explosively. "What's he waiting for! For
God's sake, why don't he come! Does he want to find us all dead
when he gets here?"

"I think he wants to be sure nothing goes wrong," I said. "He's
waiting for his brother, the admiral, and the fleet from England."

"By God," the boatman said, "we wouldn't need him or his brother
or the fleet if he'd only send us a few officers that knew how to fight!"

He spat violently in the water, and a bullet would have made less
of an impact. He poled onward, silent for a time. Then he said,
"We've got some Boston men in here with us. They say Massachusetts
committees are seizing the property of everybody that left their
homes, and selling it for next to nothing to those the rebels favor.
They say Sam Adams figures on having all you Massachusetts folks
banished for good; proscribed, too, so you can be shot in a hurry
in case you take it into your head to go back. This General Howe,
he'd better not waste much more time."

"Banished and proscribed?" Indiscreetly I laughed aloud; and the
opening of my mouth filled it with those horrible bugs. I sputtered
them out. "Aren't we banished and proscribed enough already?"

The boatman slapped his sculling oar. "Now I come to think of
it, one of those Massachusetts fellers—I disremember his name—was
from Milton, same as you. He asked two or three times if we'd heard
of anyone named Wiswell. Yes, sir, that was the name: Wiswell!
Could it 'a' been you he was asking about, Mr. Wiswell?"

Hope shot up within me, as smoldering leaves burst into flame;
then died again. Would I hear something of Sally—even something

from her? No, I wouldn't! After what had happened to me in the past year, I knew more than to hope. The whole world, in the words of that gay old song, was turned upside down. Nothing could come out right. I only grunted in answer to the boatman and settled myself down into the wetness in which I sat.

The Aristophanes chorus of croaking was a solid sound all about us, dimming all other senses except the afflicted one of hearing, till I croaked grotesquely myself, in protest, "Hold your tongues, you damned frogs! Can't you be quiet just an instant, for God's sake?"

At one moment the marsh before us was as black as the bottom of a well; the next moment the boatman sharply turned us against a wall of sedge, thrust hard, and we passed rustling through tall grasses and came into a pool on the far side of which blinked scores of lights, like fireflies above a meadow.

A dozen smudges smoldered among those flitting lights, and smoke from them lay in a dimly seen blanket above our heads. As the lantern in our boat cleared the wall of sedge behind us, an eager babbling arose from the shore and I had the singular and unexpected feeling that here was a haven in which I would be both safe and welcome.

Individual voices came clearer to me from among those moving lights. "What about Howe?" "Any troops landed yet?" "When's Howe coming?"

The boatman flourished his sculling oar. "The general's sent a man to see us," he cried. "I got him here—here in this boat."

The shouting on shore faded to a whispering like that of dead leaves on an autumn night.

With a sharp twist of his sculling oar the boatman drove the nose of our little craft onto dry land, and I found myself looking up into a semicircle of gaunt faces. The light of many lanterns showed eye sockets black and bearded cheeks hollow, so that these hunted creatures had the look of dead men standing upright—yet all the eyes glittered with the hope that my coming brought.

As I stepped ashore, I heard the boatman ask, "Where's the judge?" heard someone say, "They're bringing him down."

Buell climbed from the boat, swung his scissors-grinder after him, put it down behind him and sat upon it. I heard the other boats grate against the sedge bank; heard their boatmen muttering orders; felt their occupants moving up the bank and coming to a halt behind me; but still that half-circle of hollow-eyed men stood like a wall before us.

"You don't suppose, do you, Oliver," Buell asked, making a pretense of anxiety, "that these people don't want us around here? Maybe we ought to go back and tell Howe there ain't any use trying to find out what's happening to Loyalists on Long Island."

A sharp voice answered. "If you're the man General Howe sent to us, you're welcomer than ice to hell; but nobody gets into this swamp without we know who he is. Judge Hendon has to talk to each man. If you'd ever had a mob after you, you'd know why."

"Brother," Buell said, "I've had more tar on me than you could get on a barn roof."

The circle of men swayed and muttered. From far behind them we heard a commotion and shouting. The shouting proved to be one sentence, oft-repeated: "Make way for the judge! Make way for the judge!"

The half-circle opened, and through the lane thus formed came two men carrying a third who sat in a chair made from birch poles. When the chair was put down, the half-circle closed behind it, and the two bearers stood on either side, with lanterns raised shoulder-high.

Our boatman stepped forward. "Judge," he said, "this here's a Mr. Wiswell, vouched for by Demott. He and a friend want to find out what's happening here, so they can take back word to General Howe."

The judge was a frail old man with white hair and a thin ascetic face; but I could see he was seriously an invalid, for he was obviously unable to rise from his chair, and his hands were twisted as if his fingers had been bound against his palms for a long, long time, until they were stiffened and useless. His eyes, however, were quick and young, and his voice was as gentle as his smile.

"We're honored to have you here, Mr. Wiswell," he said, "and we welcome you and your friend—I don't believe I heard your friend's name, Mr. Wiswell?"

Buell spoke up briskly. "Thomas Buell, printer, repairer of military arms; maker of fashionable ornaments for military caps and cartridge boxes; painter and gilder of escutcheons; engraver of seals, dies, punches and copper plates; marker of silver plate with elegant ciphers and arms; cutter of blocks and ornaments for printers; maker of models for canal locks, paint-grinding mills, machines for cutting and polishing crystals and precious stones; agent for Perkins' Metallic Tractors, claimed by Doctor Elisha Perkins of Norwich, Connecticut, to be a sure cure for rheumatism, gout, black spots before the eyes, dizziness and the itch."

The judge stared contemplatively at Buell. "Indeed! Indeed, Mr. Buell! I'm a sufferer from rheumatism myself. Am I to understand that you know of metallic substances that will cure me?"

"Not me, Judge," Buell said promptly. "Those Metallic Tractors ain't good for one damned thing—except to prove that anyone who believes in 'em is a natural-born rebel."

Obviously relieved at Buell's answer, the judge turned back to me. "Your home is in Boston, Mr. Wiswell?"

"Milton," I said. "I lived in Boston a year after we were driven from our house."

"I had great respect for a gentleman of your name, Mr. Wiswell," the judge said. "Perhaps you're related to him. I refer to Mr. Seaton Wiswell."

"My father," I said. "He—he——"

I couldn't go on. The unexpected mention of my father's name by this kind old judge, the presence of this distinguished and harmless gentleman, bent and crippled with rheumatism, in a mosquito-ridden swamp, the hollow eyes and sodden, tattered garments of all those men before me, tightened my throat so that I could neither speak nor draw a full breath.

The judge's eyes darted over the men who stood behind me, then came back to mine again. "I'll expect you later in my hut, Mr. Wiswell," he said. "We're somewhat restricted in our hospitality; but we can offer you loyalty and friendship. That's *something* in these troubled days, as you've doubtless learned by now."

When we moved aside, the refugees who had accompanied us in the sedge boats came up one by one to offer their credentials. How, the judge asked each one, had he come to Long Island? With whom had he come? Where had he landed and when? To whom had he gone, and who had told him to go there? By what road had he traveled to Hempstead? Where had he stopped on the way? Had he seen any rebel militia?

Having satisfied himself about such details, he went deeper into each man's life. Where was he born? Where had he lived before coming to Long Island? Why had he decided to leave his home? Had the rebels attempted to persuade him to join their party?

On learning where each man lived, Judge Hendon summoned from among the onlookers someone from the same town or near it, and directed him to ask questions of the newcomer.

Our boatman, standing at our shoulders, enlightened us in a hoarse whisper. "The judge tripped up three of 'em last week. Rebel spies, they were."

"What happened to them?" I asked.

The boatman looked surprised. "They're still here. You'd oughta talk to 'em about how things are. They get better food and more of it than the rest of us. Of course, we can't let 'em get away, because if we did, they'd show the rebels how to get at us, and we wouldn't last long."

The stories that the judge drew from the men who had come with us from Demott's were in all likelihood not different from scores of those I had heard in Boston; yet their simplicity made them seem new and horrible.

Thomas French had been seized by Birdsall's mob on Long Island, sent across the Sound and put in Simsbury Mines. The two companions with whom he attempted to escape had been caught under water and drowned. Edward Beekman of Norwich, Connecticut, had been tarred and feathered and the sight of one eye destroyed. Charles Holcomb of Worcester, for daring to urge his neighbors not to take up arms until all other methods of reconciliation had failed, had been chained to a cart and driven over rocky roads until something inside him burst and he was left for dead beside the road. Arthur Downs of Stonington, charged with helping Loyalists seek sanctuary on Long Island, had been towed to sea in his sloop, his sloop scuttled, and he left to drown or get to shore by long swimming. Edward Johnson of Kingston, New York, for trying to lighten the lot of Loyalists sent to the jail in that town, had been hoisted halfway up a liberty pole by the heels, left there all night, and lowered as dead in the morning.

When the last man had spoken, the silent audience moved restlessly; and its whisperings were like a prolonged hiss of anger.

Judge Hendon half raised one of his distorted hands. "Kingston Jail," he said. "Weren't several gentlemen from this part of Long Island sent to Kingston Jail?"

"I only heard about one," Johnson said. "He's the one that got me into trouble—Governor Colden. They had him in a room with five other men. The rebel militia stole his coat, so he didn't have anything but breeches and shirt, and he got the fever and had to sleep on a stone floor without coverings. They didn't give him any medicines or even enough drinking water, and I just couldn't see an old man like the governor, who'd never done anybody any harm, treated like that. I took him some clothes and medicines, and a blanket and a mattress, and on that account they burned down my store and I heard they were going to put me in Simsbury Mines; but I didn't propose to rot away in that hole in the ground, so I came here."

"In your opinion," the judge asked, "was Governor Colden treated worse than other Loyalists in Kingston Jail?"

"Oh no, sir," Johnson said. "Some were treated worse; lots worse! Some had all their clothes stolen, and wore flour sacks. There's a fever room in the jail, and when a man gets fever, he's put in it with a pan of potatoes beside him. That's all he gets to eat. If he doesn't have the strength to eat, he doesn't get anything."

"Are they allowed to have exercise—permitted to walk in the town?" the judge asked.

"My goodness, no!" Johnson said. "If they were let out, half the womenfolk in town'd give 'em clothes and food. That ain't allowed! Folks that are such skunks as to want peace and the right to speak their minds shouldn't get food and clothes! No, sir; they sit right there in their little coffins of cells, gasping with heat in summer and freezing in the winter! By God, Judge, can't something be done to get our people out of Kingston Jail and all the rest of the jails to the eastward?"

His voice shook and became shrill. "They haven't done a damned thing, Judge; not one damned thing! There's an awful lot of mighty fine men in Kingston Jail, Judge! Can't something be done for 'em?"

"Possibly," the judge said cautiously. "We'll hope for the best. Meanwhile, try not to bear malice. I want all you newcomers to make yourselves useful. You'll be helped to get settled, and you'll be expected to help us in return. Sometimes one of the most valuable things you can give us is cheerfulness. If only we can have that, we'll contrive to endure what we must."

He motioned to his chair bearers, who picked him up. The silent audience separated to let him through, and we moved slowly after him in a grotesque and insubstantial pageant.

CHAPTER XXVIII

As the crowded half-circle dispersed, I began to have an idea of the size of the company that dwelt within this swamp.

Scores of dark figures, dimly seen in the lantern light, moved before me; and as we walked beside the judge's swaying chair, I could see them carrying their lanterns to little huts built in the brush beyond the open parade across which we moved. The parade was crowded, like Boston Common on a Saturday night.

They seemed a different breed from Colonel Birdsall's militia—more alert, more determined, more resourceful.

"It wouldn't be difficult, would it, Judge," I asked, "to defeat a regiment of rebels with these men here?"

"No," Judge Hendon said, "it wouldn't! You haven't met the young men who are kind enough to act as my chair bearers. The one in front is Stephen DeLancey. His uncle's General Oliver DeLancey. The one behind is John Barbarie. John and Stephen say that Birdsall's and Duyckinck's militiamen are no better than mobs, cowards at heart. They think they can train the men in this swamp to whip ten times their number of rebels; but I can't permit it, Mr. Wiswell. There's no doubt these men have the quality and the determination to whip Birdsall and Duyckinck, but they'd never be able to protect the thousands of unarmed, unorganized Loyalists on Long Island."

"Those damned rebels splash around like a lot of pigs," Barbarie said. "They talk like pigs and smell like pigs, too. If Stephen and I'd been free this afternoon, we could have killed twenty of 'em without firing a gun—the way you'd kill pigs."

"Yes, and gained nothing by it," Judge Hendon said sharply. "Dead men help no one, not even those who kill them!" He leaned

247

forward and spoke to Stephen DeLancey. "We'd best go by way of the hospital, Stephen."

DeLancey bore to the right, and we saw before us a long hut, roofed with leafy boughs, but without sides. On each corner post hung a lantern, and by this faint light I saw a score of figures lying on beds of leaves. They were covered with tattered blankets, bed ticking, flour bags, old coats. A few lay silent, staring up at the leafy branches overhead; others tossed and turned, sighing and groaning.

"The rebels do all they can to keep us from getting medicines," the judge said. "They aim either to kill us, or capture us and force us into the rebel militia; but it seems as though our men just won't die till Howe gets here to set us free."

A dark figure rose from his knees at the far end of the long hut and came toward us. "Judge," he said, "we've got to have more men to take care of these people. They're being eaten alive by mosquitoes, and their fevers can't be kept down. Bonner just died; and I'll lose a dozen more if I can't have another ten men to trickle water on 'em and keep off the mosquitoes."

"Bonner," the judge said thoughtfully. "He got here just yesterday, didn't he? Wasn't he the one who was going to be married next week?"

The doctor looked doubtful. "Maybe so. He had five buckshot in the small of his back, and another lodged in his skull." He gave us a quick glance; then said to the judge: "When's Howe coming?"

The judge seemed not to hear him. "This is Doctor Rounds of Islip, Mr. Wiswell. The rebels drove away eighteen horses belonging to the doctor, and obliged his wife and his daughters to take refuge in New Jersey. It's hard on the doctor, Mr. Wiswell; but it's our good fortune. Probably half of us would be dead if we didn't have him to look after us."

He touched young DeLancey. "Take me out to the parade, Stephen. We'll get those ten men for the doctor." To the doctor he added, "Come to my hut when you've made your men comfortable for the night. I'll have Mr. Wiswell with me, and we'll be even more eager to hear what he has to say than he'll be to talk to us."

As we moved out to the open space, the judge repeated name after name to DeLancey, who snapped them out in a voice that must, I thought, be audible on Staten Island.

That done, the judge took us to his own hut, which, like the hospital and all the other shelters, was nothing but a roof of branches

supported by four tree trunks. To my surprise, the hut already had
an occupant, and it had a ready-made audience too; for on every
side of it sat and stood scores of Loyalists, their eyeballs white in the
lantern light; and their hands, perpetually brushing at mosquitoes,
made a pale flickering, as of a half-moonlight upon restless water.

Barbarie and DeLancey put down the chair beside the occupant
of the hut, who was lying on a thick mat of sedge. In the light of
the lanterns his thin face had a waxy pallor, but his black eyes
sparkled and his lips were curved in a smile that was both patient
and sardonic. The judge leaned down and looked at him, seemed
reassured by what he saw; then said to me, "This is the Reverend
Edmund Lane, Mr. Wiswell. One of these days he'll be a bishop,
but we almost lost him this afternoon, because he thought the rebels
wouldn't shoot their own countrymen. We took four buckshot out of
his shoulder."

Lane moved his hand in a small gesture that took in all the
men outside the hut. "They've come here for news, Judge. You'd better arrange to give it to them, or they'll stand around all night, waiting."

The judge turned to me. "Mr. Wiswell, have you any information
for us in regard to General Howe's plans, and when we may expect
him to move to our relief?"

"No," I said, and I spoke loudly, so that I might be heard at a
considerable distance. "I'm sorry. I'm not a carrier of information,
but a seeker for it. I don't know the general's plans, or how long
he may be delayed before attacking. My instructions are only to find
out your numbers and the conditions under which you live, and
report on 'em to the general."

I heard voices muttering in disappointment, and then, after a
moment or two, the word "Declaration". It was repeated from here
and there, "Declaration, Declaration," until it became a general insistent outcry. "Declaration! Declaration!"

The judge looked at me apologetically. "We've all heard Congress
issued a Declaration of Independence a short time ago, but nobody
can tell us what was in it. Can you, by any chance, tell us what it's
about?"

"Well, sir," I said, "I can give you a general idea. I can't recite it for
you; but two sentences stick in my mind and I can say 'em for you
word for word. Every Loyalist, almost, knows its first sentence—
'When in the course of human events it becomes necessary for one

people to dissolve the political bands which have connected them with another, and to assume, among the powers of the earth, the separate and equal station to which the laws of nature and of nature's God entitle them, a decent respect to the opinions of mankind requires that they should declare the causes which impel them to the separation.' "

Somewhere among the close-packed circle of listeners a man laughed abruptly, and the laughter spread as a ripple progresses upon the surface of a pool.

Judge Hendon raised his hand and the laughter died away. "Do you know who wrote the paper?" he asked.

"Thomas Jefferson, I'm told, sir."

The judge nodded. "I see: I see. You said 'one people', did you not? 'When it becomes necessary for one people.' " He made an exasperated movement. "Four fifths of the people on this island are loyal. Two thirds of the people in New York and Pennsylvania are loyal. More than half the people in all of North America are loyal. It looks to me as though Mr. Jefferson hasn't a high respect for the opinions of mankind—not if he wants mankind to think that I, and all the others who have fled to the security of this swamp, and another million of our fellow countrymen, are not people."

"You'll be equally interested in the other sentence," I said. "It reads, 'We hold these truths to be self-evident, that all men are created equal, that they are endowed by their Creator with certain unalienable rights, that among these are life, liberty and the pursuit of happiness.' "

"Well, well!" Judge Hendon said. "So all men are created equal! So they're endowed with the unalienable rights of life, liberty and the pursuit of happiness!" He shook his head. "I suppose we, in this swamp, are supposed to be in possession of our liberty, and engaged in the pursuit of happiness, since Mr. Jefferson declares them to be our unalienable rights."

An angry muttering rose from the crowd of listeners.

The Reverend Mr. Lane raised a protesting hand. "No profanity, please! Model yourselves on Judge Hendon. Don't make matters worse by speaking indiscreetly or with improper heat."

"Oh my, no!" Buell said. "When the neighbors tar and feather you, don't ever call 'em anything worse than 'the said neighbors'. If you get too hot about it, you can relieve yourself with 'whereas' and 'feloniously'. Like this: 'Whereas the said neighbors did feloniously tar and feather my aforesaid hide, including my aforesaid hair, my said nose and aforesaid fingernails, therefore know all men', and so on. Yes, sir; we got to keep our passions down!"

I went on hastily. "Those two sentences are the only ones I can quote exactly, but the document speaks of the abuses suffered by residents of North America at England's hands. It says that the King of England has refused his assent to wholesome laws, and plans the establishment of absolute tyranny over these states."

"That's not so," Judge Hendon said. "No colony has ever been prevented from making any law it wished. The only thing they *haven't* been allowed to do is to issue fraudulent currency and declare it legal tender. Can you give us a better example of royal tyranny and brutality, Mr. Wiswell?"

"Well, sir," I said, "the document says the King has called together legislative bodies, at places unusual, uncomfortable, and distant from the depository of their public records, for the sole purpose of fatiguing the Patriots into a compliance with his measures!"

"Yes," the judge said meditatively, "a legislative body *was* moved in Massachusetts. It was transferred from Boston to Cambridge so the legislators might be protected against mobs. I find myself strangely lacking in sympathy for Patriots who admit they can be 'fatigued' into complying with measures of which they disapprove! I fear it's a feeble and sickly patriotism that wilts before such dreadful hardships as undertaking the long, long journey between Boston and Cambridge! I don't much care for it as an argument justifying a national rebellion against constituted authority and embarking on a civil war!"

Every man without that hut was now as silent as though carved from stone.

"Another abuse mentioned," I said, "is that the King has erected a multitude of new offices, and sent swarms of officers to harass our people and eat out their subsistence."

The judge looked irritated. "Five new commissioners were appointed for this whole country, and fifteen or twenty clerks to go with them. Those are the swarms who harass Americans and eat out their subsistence! How do they compare with the packs of rebel militia that pull down our homes, maim our cattle and make the lives of our womenfolk a perpetual nightmare!"

"Well, sir," I said, "the paper says America is opposing with manly firmness the King's invasions on the rights of the people."

"Since when," Judge Hendon asked, "has a government been able to maintain its integrity without putting down rebellion and mob rule? All these so-called measures of repression were provoked by popular outrage! Doesn't this document anywhere hint that a government must protect its officers from assault and their houses from being sacked, its loyal lieges from being tarred and feathered, and the property of merchants sailing under its flags from being thrown by lawless hands into the sea?"

"No, sir," I said.

He raised his crippled hands in a half gesture of disgust. "I've heard enough! From the beginning, twelve years ago, the rebellious agitators against England have consistently disavowed any desire for independence. For twelve long years the rebel leaders have solemnly affirmed and reiterated that they only wished to obstruct and defeat a weak ministerial policy, thereby to secure a redress of grievances. At every opportunity they vowed they abhorred the thought of independence! James Otis, Alexander Hamilton, George Washington, John Dickinson—all of them said independence would be a calamity and a crime. On this ground they secured the help of Pitt, Burke, Conway, Barré. Now they've turned traitor to those who helped them. Pitt, Burke and all the others have been made parties to a disruption of the British Empire. The men responsible for this Declaration are political hypocrites, as those of us who disagree with them have always charged. While openly disavowing a wish for independence, some of them must have been treacherously working with that end in view all the time!"

He leaned forward in his chair. "Take word to General Howe for us, Mr. Wiswell, that the rebels are in a position where they must be utterly destroyed if they're attacked soon. *Our* country is at stake, Mr. Wiswell. The war these rebels are forcing upon us is neither just nor necessary, because without it neither their freedom nor their happiness would be impaired or imperiled. In this colony, which is overwhelmingly loyal, rebellion was instigated and made inevitable by three lawyers—all demagogues and unscrupulous users of cunning chicanery and falsehood: the uncouth, bigoted, savage, violent, sullen William Livingston; the sycophantic hypocrite William Smith, Junior, who unhesitatingly sacrifices friendship, honor, religion or his sacred word to pride, ambition or avarice; and a violent and acrimonious madman, John Morin Scott; by a liquor dealer and son of a convict, John Lamb; by a slop-shop keeper, Alexander Mc-

Dougall; by a sailor-fish-peddler-alehouse-keeper, Isaac Sears; by a bail-jumper and a coward at Quebec under fire, Donald Campbell; by Peter Livingston, whose low cunning and avarice have earned him the name of Jew Peter.

"If these men have their way with us, the population, instead of employing themselves in peaceful occupations, will engage in costly and endless struggles for political offices and grants from the public treasury. Assemblies will be tumultuous and disorderly; the voices of worthy and modest men will seldom be heard; the bold, the ambitious, the artful will hold sway. Alcibiades will rule and Socrates will be martyred, as the Smiths proposed to martyr Doctor Myles Cooper, president of King's College, by shaving his head, slitting his nose, stripping him naked and turning him adrift! Themistocles, Xenophon and Aristides will be banished; great Pericles will be fined and his sons put to death when laurels should be their reward. Our futures and our lives depend on leadership, Mr. Wiswell. That's the word we want taken back to General Howe."

Judge Hendon, his twisted hands held tight against his breast, stared into the steamy darkness of the swamp with the rapt gaze of a prophet.

The Reverend Mr. Lane sighed. "Put out the lanterns," he told Barbarie and DeLancey, "and have someone cut green grass for the smudges. We need all the blood we've got if Birdsall and his men take a notion to come after us again tomorrow."

Dim, silent figures moved slowly away. A black depression weighed me down.

My thoughts and fears must have come out from me like a dark cloud, for the judge said: "Remember, Mr. Wiswell, nothing's ever as hopeless as it seems—not even death. You might tell General Howe that no matter what happens to us, we'll never lose courage."

He looked up suddenly. "Who's that?"

A voice spoke from the darkness beyond the hut. "Eben Drake of Milton, Judge. I'd like a word with Mr. Wiswell."

I didn't wait to hear what the judge said, but darted from the hut toward the dark figure standing outside. "Are you one of the Drakes from Brush Hill Road?" I asked, and in spite of myself my voice shook.

"I certainly am," he said. "I worked in Vose Leighton's store, Mr. Wiswell. I had to leave because my uncle Robie worked for Mr.

John Chandler up in Worcester. Everybody that had anything to do with the Chandlers was driven out, Mr. Wiswell. The Chandlers had too much money."

"I know," I said. "Were the Leightons well when you left? How was Soame? How was Mrs. Leighton and the other boys; how was —how was—how were they all?"

"I dunno, damn 'em," Drake said. "They're in the army—the rebel army; and I hope they get their come-uppance! There ain't but one in the whole damned family I'd turn my hand over for, and she's why I wanted to see you. She thought you might come to Long Island sooner or later, so she gave me the money to get here—and this for you."

He gave me a little damp wad of paper, uncertainly said, "Well——" and drifted away in the darkness. I hurried back to the hut and, with trembling hands, rekindled one of the lanterns. The letter was discolored with grime and perspiration; the ink upon it almost illegible from innumerable wettings and dryings.

I was conscious, as I scrutinized the faded writing, that Judge Hendon, Mr. Lane and Buell were watching me when I put the precious document on the top of Buell's scissors-grinder to steady it, and as I held the lantern close above those blurred words, Buell tried to take it from me. "You'll spill the oil out of that lamp, Oliver," he said, "and first thing you know you won't have any letter at all. Why don't you let me read it for you? I've had practice reading messy writing."

"I can read it without assistance," I said.

"Oh, private matter," Buell said, and added slowly, "I see, I see." The others also seemed to see; for they ceased to stare at me, and I had the letter to myself.

I made out the words "Dearest Oliver." My eyes cleared; my hand grew steadier; sentences that had seemed a hopeless blur became readable.

"Dearest Oliver," [she had written] *"Two weeks ago I had a beautiful experience. I'd just stepped out of our gate upon the road when a strange man, all the color of dust, came from some bushes across the way, where he seemed to have been lurking. At first I was a little afraid of him, because there was no one else in sight; but his manner was respectful and he touched his ragged hat. He asked me if my name wasn't Sally Leighton; and when I told him Yes, he spoke to me quickly in a low voice and said, 'There's a friend of yours whose*

name begins with O, and he asked me to tell you that he was well and hopeful, and to say that nothing's changed or ever will be.' He was gone down the road before I could utter a word in answer; but oh, Oliver, I knew you'd sent it—and thank you, thank you, thank you! Inside me I've lived in sunlight ever since I saw the dust-colored man! You mustn't write to me, remember; but, oh, perhaps there'll be another dust-colored man some day?

"*How often, oh, how often have I wished to write you during all these long, cold months; and how often have I longed for word from you. Now spring is here, and every scene and scent and sound reminds me of spring days we spent together.*

"*I have never seen such vast flocks of Old Shags flying north: there have been thousands and thousands, in long lines, like those we saw the day we sailed to Hingham and caught the eels and made the stew. Father says this means we shall have a hot summer. Probably so, because there have been rings around the sun for two weeks, and never a drop of rain.*

"*The willows along the river in Dedham smell like honey, Oliver. Do you remember the day you put the mouse on the shingle for me and floated it down over the pool where the sulky big trout lay, and how we thought he'd swallowed the shingle when he struck?*

"*Of course you remember Pie Benjamin, the town idiot? He stood outside our house every day for eight days, making whirling motions around his ears with his forefinger, and then I remembered that either you or your father had always given him a shilling every spring so he could have his winter hair cut off. I was deeply touched that he should have come to me, and I gave him a shilling for you, Oliver.*

"*Albion, Soame, Steven, Jeremiah and John have gone south with their regiments. Everybody says that the British are about to leave Halifax, or have already left. It's common talk that they're going to Long Island—that all their sympathizers are going with them. That's why I'm sending this letter by Eben Drake. He knows you because he worked in Father's store for six years, and saw you often. I'm hoping he'll come across you on Long Island, for if you're as eager to have a word from me as I am to hear from you, you'll be glad for it.*

"*I wonder, dear Oliver, whether you know all the things that our brave army has learned. I am sure that if you knew the cruel things your associates have been guilty of, you would have a change of heart. The Ministry is arousing the black slaves of the south to attack us,* and employing savages to make uncivilized war upon our frontiers. The Ministry has sent Hessian mercenaries to butcher us. These hirelings have been told that if they allow themselves to be captured by Americans, their bodies will be stuck full of pine splinters and then slowly burned to cinders. Was anything ever more horrible, Oliver?

"Oh, my dear! I can write no more; but you will understand and hear me crying out to you—see all the words that rest unwritten in my heart. Dear, dear Oliver, I'm your

"Sally."

CHAPTER XXIX

I READ the letter the first time as a child reads a tale, seeking the passages that delight him. She had longed for word from me! She thought often of me! She still was my Sally!

I drew a deep breath and read the letter again; and this time phrases came out from it and struck upon me with hammers: "you would have a change of heart", "cruel associates", "arousing the black slaves of the south", "see all the words that rest unwritten in my heart".

When, for the third time, I read the letter through, I seemed to be in a fog of puzzlement.

Buell touched my arm. "Don't you hear the judge speaking to you, Oliver?"

"My apologies, sir," I said. "I—I didn't hear."

"You've had troublesome news, Mr. Wiswell," the judge said. "Is there anything I can do?"

I fear I spoke brusquely. "Nothing! You can do nothing! What can you do when a person doesn't see things as you see them?"

"What can you do?" the judge asked. "You can do this, Mr. Wiswell: you can remind yourself that if the lady—and of course it *is* a lady—doesn't see things as you see them, it's because she doesn't know the truth. Yet she's obviously a true lady and a reasonable one. Otherwise she'd never have written things that first made you smile as you did, even while she wrote words that later hurt you."

I couldn't say a word.

"And of course she loves you," the judge went on, "because she's trying to help you. She's careful to season advice with gentleness, and that's not easily done. I suspect you're fortunate in your choice."

"I'm fortunate if I can hold her," I said, "but how can I hold her when she's forever hearing that you and I and all these men in the swamps condone cruelty and butchery? My God, Judge, do men believe whatever lie they hear about an enemy?"

"Always," the judge said. "Suppose, Mr. Wiswell, you read me part of your letter—I mean the part that hurt you. I know what it is to be separated from those held dear. It's a sort of torture that's always increased by doubts."

When I did as he suggested, Judge Hendon caressed one crippled hand with the other. "I thought it might be like that, Mr. Wiswell. Your lady has heard the old shibboleths of war—all the old accusations that were made, no doubt, by the Medes and the Persians against their enemies; by the Phoenicians; by the armies of Julius Caesar. She's mistaken, Mr. Wiswell; and all she needs, I think, is your personal assurance that your side of this struggle is supported by arguments that are far from weak; that its motives and sentiments are far from base; and that the devotion and self-sacrifice shown by those who support it are not unheroic.

"You've been hurt by the lady's suggestion that you turn to the rebel viewpoint; but I think you can make her understand that a cause which is embraced and cherished by so vast a portion of American society, regardless of obloquy and disaster, can never be turned out of court summarily and contemptuously.

"It's clear from the lady's letter that the rebels are branding us to the whole world as execrable, and insisting that there is neither patriotism nor decency outside the rebel ranks.

"Well, Mr. Wiswell, you can't very well extol your own decency and patriotism; but if your lady can hear the truth from your own lips, she'll recognize it; for every true lady is by nature a Loyalist. We are the people who have land, belongings, position, and we're standing by our guns in opposition to the people who have nothing. We're the conservative people; and what has been true of conservative people in all ages and all lands is true of us. We dissent from extreme and injudicious measures, from violence, from oppression, from revolution, from reckless statements and misrepresentation. We can't stomach liars, bullies or demagogues, or leaders without experience, ability or sound judgment; and in the end the lady you love will never love you less for holding to such beliefs.

"There's no denying that within our ranks are a fair portion—and in this statement I'm again conservative—of the cultivation, of the moral thoughtfulness, of the personal purity and honor that exist in the American colonies. I've seen a list, Mr. Wiswell, of those in your native Massachusetts who will probably be proscribed and forever banished for no reason except that they have been conservative men. There are hundreds of them, and not one a tyrant; not one a profligate; not one a man of small consequence. Their names are those of the oldest and noblest families whose diligence and abilities founded and built up New England. They are the most substantial and influential men in Massachusetts—men of the highest integrity. Their attitude is inspired by conscientious conviction; persisted in despite all the outrages that have been done against them, and despite all the outrages that they still must suffer.

"Conservatives aren't braggarts as a rule, Mr. Wiswell; but you can safely tell your lady or anyone else in the world that the side you have chosen has so much solid fact and valid reasoning behind it that any intelligent and noble-minded American can with reason take that side, and stick to it, and go into battle for it, and if necessary die for it: even imperil all the interests of his life in defense of it without having either his reason or his integrity impeached. You never need fear that your lady will ever believe otherwise, once she hears your case from your own lips."

The words of the old judge gave me new courage. In spite of the tumultuous croaking of the frogs, the shrill whining of the mosquitoes, the dank moisture of this miserable swamp, and the hard bed on which I rested, my sleep was more profound and freer from distracting dreams than it had been for many a long and weary night.

CHAPTER XXX

W<small>HEN</small>, two weeks later, I sailed back to Staten Island with Buell and Captain James to deliver my report, the broad sweep of bay between Long Island and Staten Island held what I was sure was the greatest fleet ever assembled; and James was jubilant.

"The best army on earth couldn't stand against the force already piled into this harbor," James said, "and there's more coming! All of Sir Henry Clinton's men sailed in here on thirty-five transports just a few days ago, after catching hell at Fort Moultrie; and there hasn't been a day since then that ships haven't come in from Jamaica, Florida and the Mediterranean."

He wagged his head. "Those British must have a warship in every port that holds more'n fifty gallons of water! When all of 'em get here, there ought to be enough to take all of New York without firing a shot."

"All of 'em?" Buell asked. "There can't be more than six other ships left in the whole world, I'd think."

James looked pained. "The admiral ain't here yet, even," he said. "He's the general's brother. You ought to know as well as I do that an admiral won't go to sea in any warship smaller than Fraunce's Tavern, or make a move without having a hundred other ships go along. When the admiral gets here, the ships'll be packed into this bay like plover in a barrel. Then we'll chase those damned rebels back where they belong—back to making shoes and spreading fertilizer."

"Why isn't the general's brother here?" I asked. "When's he expected?"

"God only knows," James said. "He and his fleet left England thirteen weeks ago; but where he's been all that time, and what he's been doing, there's no way of finding out."

"He must be quite an admiral," Buell said thoughtfully. "If he takes more'n three months to sail across the Atlantic Ocean, I don't know as I'd like to be depending on him to get me out of a Hempstead swamp."

We felt more cheerful when James put us ashore on Staten Island, for though there had been tent towns upon it when we had left it in July, there had also been broad meadows of tall grass between the encampments: meadows starred with buttercups and daisies.

Now there seemed to be only endless row upon row of tents; and among them and around them moved soldiers in scarlet and white, as innumerable as the leaves that whirl down from maples in an October gale.

The Rose and Crown farmhouse had stood in an open field when we last saw General Howe; but today marquees and tents were ringed close about it, as the houses of Boston encircle Faneuil Hall. To get inside that farmhouse was even more difficult than penetrating to the heart of Hempstead swamp; for a sentry barred every door, and throngs of officers in scarlet, white and gold stood in the yard, on the doorsteps and in the entryway within, all of them irritable and smelling of sweat and smoke, and almost all of them contemptuous of mere civilians like Buell and me.

Sentries and officers alike looked amused when I asked that my name be taken to General Howe. He was, they said indifferently, at a council of war, and there was no knowing when the council would be over.

"You'd better go see Loring," Buell told me. "If we don't get in to see the general for a week or two, Judge Hendon and those friends of his might all be killed. If Howe wants to wreck the British Empire by sitting here and doing nothing, I suppose that's his lookout; but I kind of took a fancy to that old judge, and feel as if he was our lookout. You get Loring, Oliver! I'll stay here and keep an eye on what happens."

He did more than that; for when I returned an hour later with Loring, Buell was the center of a knot of British officers, to whom he was holding forth on the peculiarities of rebel currency.

"These forty-dollar notes," he said, "ain't worth forty dollars as money, of course; but to collectors I shouldn't wonder if they'd be worth a lot more than forty dollars some day. No matter how you look at 'em, they ain't a bad investment—if you buy 'em right, the way you can from me. If you gentlemen beat the rebels when you cross over to wherever you're crossing to, there won't be any more of this rebel money issued. It'll be rare, and therefore valuable. If the general decides he ain't going to cross over and do any fighting, the rebel government will be as good as any government, and its money just like regular money everywhere. That means it'll be worth forty dollars."

"How much did you say you were asking for one of those forty-dollar bills?" an officer asked.

"Ten shillings hard money," Buell said.

"I'll give you five."

Buell looked shocked. "Oh my! I couldn't do that! Oh my, no! I worked too hard for this money to throw it away! I don't believe you gentlemen understand what I'm offering you! Of course it don't make any difference to me if you don't know enough to buy 'em, because I can use 'em for money when I go back to Long Island. The only reason I'm letting you have any of 'em is that I'm grateful to you gentlemen for coming over here to help us. I want to do you a favor; that's all."

The officer handed him ten shillings, and I saw others of those about Buell absent-mindedly feeling in their pockets, as men do when contemplating a purchase.

I went on into headquarters with Loring; but not even Loring's influence was sufficient to get me into the general's presence that day. Not until the following noon, after long hours of waiting, were Buell and I admitted for an interview that I considered far too brief.

"Go back at once," Howe interrupted, as soon as I'd handed him my written report and told him the merest fraction of our experiences, "go back to Long Island at once!

"Take word to those men in the swamps not to lose heart. Tell 'em that when I reach Long Island, I'll put all of 'em in Provincial corps, officered by Provincials. They'll be provided with clothes, equipment, food, pay. Spare no efforts to arouse their enthusiasm, Mr. Wiswell! We can use those men; and besides, I want to get 'em under military control before they try to revenge themselves on the rebels. So go back at once, Mr. Wiswell. At once! Rejoin me as soon as the army lands on Long Island, and report to Mr. Loring."

"Can you give me an idea when that might be, sir?" I asked.

"Don't worry your head about that, Mr. Wiswell," Howe said. "It's enough for you to know that I'll be there eventually."

"No, it ain't, General," Buell said promptly. "It's hot as hell in those swamps, and the men's breeches have rotted away. If they got to stay there till frost, they'll freeze. If you ain't coming over for a few months yet, I'd like to take 'em some knives so they can cut a few rebel throats and get themselves whole breeches and warm blankets as a Christmas present. You ought to give 'em just a hint, General, so they won't——"

The general stopped him with an upraised fat hand. "You can tell 'em I'll be there before Christmas," he said, and no doubt he thought he was being facetious. To me his words lacked humor, and carried a threat of more delays like those that had already been so costly to his cause, which unhappily was also ours.

James took us back to Jamaica Bay; and as we lay on the deck of the little sloop in the hot August sunshine, Buell discoursed profoundly concerning commanders in chief.

"The general of an army," he said, "is an army's soul, and an army without one is like a wife without a husband. That's why a commander in chief always sends others to do dangerous things for him, and takes all the credit if they're successful.

"He's the only man in an army that can have any ideas, so it wouldn't be military for him to consult any other person's convenience, or to take anybody else's opinion about anything if the opinion ain't the same as his own. A general has to be awful secret about his plans; and he has to be silent and sulky, or else people might get to think he wasn't being secret. If he ain't got any plans at all, he's obliged to be sulky and silent, too, so folks'll think he knows everything there is to know.

"Generals most generally don't often get their distinguished rank because they're the best fighters, but because of being left-handed relations of a king or friends of a left-handed politician. Naturally they ain't smart enough to promote smart soldiers just because they're smart, and that's why you never find smart officers around a commander in chief.

"One of the few things a commander in chief knows is that soft living makes soft soldiers. That's why he gives his men bad food and not enough clothes—so they won't get soft and refuse to fight.

He figures desperate men are careless about their lives, so he figures his army'll fight best if all the men in it wish they were dead to begin with.

"A commander in chief has to be mighty careful, too, not to be too hasty and win battles too quickly, because if he does, the war might be over before he'd provided for all his relations and lady friends."

He philosophized similarly throughout the voyage, and relapsed not into silence until we were once more ashore and on our way to Demott's to carry Howe's message to Judge Hendon, Mr. Lane and their Loyalist friends.

From Demott's we bore off to the eastward through the great brush plains to Massapequa, where other hundreds of Loyalists were congregated in the tortuous waterways that empty into Massapequa Creek; and from Massapequa we continued on to Islip, where more Loyalists had built themselves a maze in the brush and lived at the heart of it. So skillfully was the maze constructed that rebel mobs and regiments dared not even try to penetrate to its center for fear of being ambushed.

Then we turned north and back toward the western tip of the island, stopping to give Howe's message to our hunted fellow countrymen living in the Sunken Meadows and among the circle of hills south of Huntington—one of them a veritable mountain over four hundred feet high, on the top of which a guard of Loyalists watched day and night for signs of approaching rebels.

We told the Loyalists south of Oyster Bay, and in the winding sedge swamps near Great Neck and Flushing; then, traveling only by night, we set our course for the shores of lower New York Bay, where we could lie on the slopes south of Brooklyn and look across to Howe's camp on Staten Island.

When we first came to Long Island in July, the little towns had seemed peaceful, even though they weren't; farmers had been busy in their fields; the roads were tranquil enough.

But now all that was changed. Along every highway traveled companies of rebel militiamen, constantly looking apprehensively over their shoulders at the ships that thronged the Narrows between Long Island and Staten Island. The militiamen had reason to look apprehensive; for in a few days' time those ships had multiplied until their very numbers were menacing and eye-arresting, as is a black cloud athwart the heavens.

Before every farmhouse, all day long, stood men and women and children, gathered in knots to stare at that enormous fleet, whose equal no person there had ever before seen, or ever would see again.

Far in the distance, as we lay concealed in the brush on the hill-slopes, we saw scouting parties of rebels moving down to the shore from the Heights of Brooklyn behind us, settling themselves in vantage points which they thought would be useful for the repulse of landing parties; then, as if aware of their own insignificance in that vast panorama, rising, mere midges on an ocean's rim, and raggedly moving on to fresh positions.

Water, earth and air seemed to quiver with impending battle. To our ears came slow irregular pulsations of distant guns, now from the Jersey shore, blue in the heat haze to the westward; now from New York itself, which was screened from our sight by the rising land of Brooklyn in our rear.

From the swarm of vessels between us and Staten Island rose an unending buzzing such as sounds within a nest of angry hornets—a buzzing made up of the rolling of innumerable drums, the piping of countless whistles, the cries and shouts of many men, the creaking of myriads of blocks and tackles, all blended by distance into an ominous humming.

At night, when we ventured from our hiding places to visit farm-houses for food, the campfires and the lighted tents on Staten Island were like a low-lying, rosy cloud hovering above the galaxy of stars that were the masthead lights, riding lights and binnacle lights of that tremendous fleet.

The farmers upon whose doors we furtively tapped were Loyalists at heart, every last one of them. They were white-faced with fury at the outrages perpetrated upon them by the rebel militia, dubbing them "thieves", "harpies", "brigands", "footpads"; and their craving for relief racked them physically, as thirst racks a wanderer in the desert.

"When's Howe coming?" they whispered to us as they gave us chickens and bread. "What's he waiting for? We heard he was coming yesterday! When's he coming?"

Knowing us to be Loyalists, they waved aside our offers to pay; but Buell always left a memento, as he called it, in the form of Continental notes. A chicken, he insisted, was worth at least one thousand dollars in Continental money, and a loaf of bread one hundred dollars. An egg, in his opinion, had a value of forty dollars; and he said a cow ought to bring at least twenty thousand.

On the morning of August twenty-second our long waiting ended. We wakened, in our brush shelter, to a hot, cloudless, brilliant morning and to a distant rumbling that made me think for a moment I was back in the swamp at Hempstead, listening to the dull booming of the frogs.

But it was cannon fire, not frogs; and when we peered from our hiding place, we saw that all the hundreds and hundreds of warcraft that dotted the water between us and Staten Island were hoisting their sails and moving like bits of shining white glass in a kaleidoscope. All around them rowed innumerable flatboats, so that there was restless movement everywhere—even upon the Staten Island meadows. The white tents upon those distant slopes seemed to slip about and quiver. Whole acres of them wavered and flattened, as though pressed down by an invisible hand; then the little squares of canvas seemed to shrink; and where the tents had stood, appeared splotches of green which flowed together and became open fields.

Below us, on the Long Island shore, straggling columns of rebel militia, drab through a faint fog of dust, moved slowly between fires that kept pace with them, erupting plumes of dark gray smoke.

"Damned rebel horse thieves!" Buell said. "They're burning all the hay and fodder! Well, brothers, enjoy yourselves while you can, because the next thing that gets burned will be your own backsides!"

He made his usual morning toilet, picking straws from his stockings, tightening the kneebands of his breeches, rubbing his eyes with his knuckles, thrusting his fingers through his unruly hair, and scrubbing his teeth with the frayed end of a twig dipped in salt.

I agreed with Buell. Certainly no force that the rebels could muster, no fortifications that they could erect, could stop for a moment the tremendous fleet of warcraft maneuvering in the Narrows, or the great army of scarlet-coated soldiers that we could see flowing like distant blood-red ribbons down across the meadows of Staten Island toward the shore.

Along that shore, like a black fringe, were flatboats, score upon score of them; and the scarlet ribbons, as we watched, flowed smoothly down and filled them.

"Yes, sir," Buell went on, "this time Howe's got 'em where he wants 'em! The fleet'll get between New York and Brooklyn, and the army'll get behind Brooklyn. The rebels'll be pinched between 'em, and this time there won't be any place for 'em to go! Come on, Oliver! We've waited a long time for this, so let's go down and watch it happen."

As we cautiously made our way closer and closer to the lower bay, taking advantage of every hedge, bypath and stand of trees, the far-off roar of a signal gun pressed our eardrums; and those narrow waters, alive as they had been up to now, awoke to an even more tumultuous activity.

We saw bateaux and row-galleys move out from the Staten Island shore, oars all aglitter in the brightness of the morning; and behind them, like a gigantic flag striped blue and white, close ranks of white boats moved over the blue water. From the bows of the bateaux and row-galleys jetted puffs of white smoke that swirled back upon the boats as rain clouds swirl about a mountain, and from those clouds came the thunder of great guns. The striped flag of boats, driven by oars that flickered through the smoke, moved toward us like a miniature thunderstorm.

On the Staten Island shore, scarlet-coated soldiers still poured into flatboats; and through the alternately thinning and thickening smoke above the approaching flotilla, we could see the flatboats moving with the regularity of machines to the sides of transports; see thin scarlet streams ascending from the boats into the ships like scarlet ants flowing fumblingly over the rim of a flowerpot; see the sails of the transports rising. While we still hurried toward the road, the transports moved out from the Staten Island shore to follow the flotilla of boats. There were so many of them that the whole horizon seemed packed with their white sails.

We knew, long before we came to it, that we were near the main road along the bay; for from it rose the gabbling of innumerable voices. They were those of the men in the militia regiments we had so recently seen from higher up on the slope; but now those men were hurrying pell-mell back toward Brooklyn, a disorderly rabble.

They were in a panic, throwing away their packs, pushing their muskets behind fences, ridding themselves of cartridge boxes and all the little things that seem, to panic-stricken men, to impede them in their flight. Their eyes were staring; their faces white and sweaty; their mouths agape, as though they lacked the strength to close them. Where their officers were, God only knew.

When the last of these frightened soldiers had disappeared toward Brooklyn, Buell and I came out into the road. Ahead of us, as far as we could see, hayricks, corn shocks, wheat stacks and piled fodder smoldered and blazed. We saw men run into the road, stare momentarily in our direction, then fall to work upon the blazing piles with flails, pitchforks, buckets of water. Whole families stood huddled in farmyards, watching us as we drew near—fearful, of course, that we might be rebels; unwilling to make open display of their sympathies before men who might drive them from their homes.

When Buell waved his hat at them and bawled "Howe's coming!", all those doubtful people magically changed. They raced, shouting, to their homes; scurried out again, their eyes all shining; signaled to unseen neighbors; poured out into the road behind us to hasten toward the ever-louder cannonading.

When at last we turned the point that had shielded Gravesend Bay from us, we came upon a spectacle that still in my mind is unequaled for magnitude and grandeur.

Line upon line of boats, filled with soldiers in blue coats and in red coats, moved across that shallow sheet of water. Behind them, from an endless double row of transports, scarlet-coated men flowed down into waiting bateaux. Beyond those lines of transports were other vessels under full sail, their bulwarks and ratlins studded thick with soldiers. Wherever we looked there were boats, men, ships; ships, men, boats; longboats packed with soldiers; flatboats laden with horses; sedge boats and bateaux carrying cannon; gundelows, schooners, brigs, barks, ships, every last one acrawl with men.

We hurried around the curving shore of the bay to the long white beach where this enormous force had already begun to land. The soldiers in blue who had filled all those first boats, I then saw, were the Hessians of whom everyone in America had heard so many conflicting stories, most of them unpleasant.

I expected them to be fierce, hard-faced, brutal men. Instead of that they were boys, downy-cheeked boys, weighted with equipment so bulky and heavy that rivulets of perspiration ran down their flushed cheeks.

They were working like farm hands, carrying knapsacks, powder barrels, rolled tents and stores of every description to high ground; and as we hastened past them, looking for the presiding genius of this vast movement of troops, they stared white-eyed at us, as a skittish colt might eye a bear cub. It dawned upon me that they must have heard even more terrifying stories about us than we had heard of them.

"Oliver," Buell said, "those Hessians don't look extra bright to me. I got a notion I could do real well for us if I stayed around 'em a few days." He went to one of them, drew a forty-dollar note from his pocket, held it before the Hessian's startled eyes and raised four fingers. "Four shillings," he said with exaggerated distinctness. "Forty dollars, four shillings."

The Hessian just stared at him; and others of his comrades stopped to peer open-mouthed at the forty-dollar note.

An officer appeared from nowhere to strike the soldier sharply across the back with a cane, and shout gutturally.

When the boy shied away, Buell caught him by the wrist and put the forty-dollar note in his hand. When we went on, all the Hessians, officer and men alike, looked over their shoulders at us as at something dangerous.

"By God, Oliver," Buell whispered, "did you see that boy's face when the officer hit him? Why, he didn't mind being *hit!* He was just a little ashamed of being caught talking to us!"

The beach and the grassy meadows at the end of the bay were a turmoil of British light infantrymen and troops of cavalry. Cavalrymen pushed and hauled their horses off the flatboats that had brought them ashore. Horses squealed with terror; plunged off the boats in showers of spray; swam to shore with laid-back ears and staring eyes; shook themselves on the beach; rolled on the grass; while sweating light infantrymen scuttled cursing among them, forming themselves into companies.

Between the Hessians and the light infantrymen, on rising ground, was a platform built of planks laid upon a score of beer kegs. On the platform stood a sort of desk, also made of planks on beer kegs; and at the desk, watching the troops that poured unendingly ashore, was handsome young Lord Percy. Close to him, on the platform and all around it, were aides with maps, uniformed clerks with open notebooks and eager officers all smiles and good nature, as men are when embarking on an adventure that offers them certain success and possible fame.

Among the throng was Captain Cunningham, his red face bent over a map; and when I pushed through the crowd and reported myself, as Howe had told me to do, he was amiably casual. "Wiswell, eh? Well, well! Yes, yes! I've been expecting you! Now see here, Wiswell, what's the name of that place where all those fellows live in a swamp?"

"Hempstead?" I asked. "Massapequa?"

"Precisely," Cunningham said. "Never heard such names as they have in this damned country! How do you ever remember them? We've got to go there, Wiswell."

"To Hempstead? To Massapequa?"

"With a troop of dragoons," Cunningham said. "I'll see to your mount."

Buell made sounds of protest. "I ain't used to horses, Oliver," he said. "You go, and let me stay here and see what happens. Maybe I can have a few business dealings with those Hessian officers."

Cunningham looked incredulous. "Not used to horses? Thought everybody was used to horses!" He turned contemptuously from him. "Now then, Wiswell," he said, "the general's orders are to let all those swamp fellows see what we look like. Put heart in 'em if they need it, eh? Show those damnable rebels they'd best have a care, what? We'll start at once, so we'll be back here before anything happens."

No Roman emperor, returning victorious from his conquests, ever received a more wholehearted welcome than did our little troop of cavalry in that ride to the eastward, away from the satiny blue of Gravesend Bay and all those hundreds of ships and flatboats.

From every farmhouse we passed, from every little village and crossroads settlement, rejoicing Long Islanders poured out to see us go by, and their welcome was as sincere as it was tumultuous. Girls pelted us with flowers; small boys ran leaping and shouting beside our stirrups; young men and old men too kept pace with us to ask how many had come ashore with Howe; to tell us that Heard's regiment of rebel militia had hurried away to the northward earlier in the day; that Birdsall's militia had disbanded only that morning; that Duyckinck's New York mob had stolen boats and embarked for safety on Great South Bay.

Whenever the troops stopped to rest and to water their horses, farmers hurried to us with offers of forage and food. They brought kegs of beer in carts, barrels of cider, crates of chickens, firkins of butter. They slapped our horses' flanks, rubbed their sweaty shoulders with handfuls of grass, readjusted our stirrup leathers, made little fondling gestures.

But their welcome was pale indeed by comparison with that which awaited us at the swamps.

We reached Demott's mill late in the afternoon, to find Demott and his family clustered at the gate around a barrel of beer on a sawhorse, and Demott himself almost inarticulate with excitement. "Oh, by God, Mr. Wiswell," he shouted, "tell 'em to get off and take any damned thing! Anything we got! Have some pie! Have some corn, oats, beer, cheese? How about a sheep? Birdsall's gone, God damn him! He and his men went through here an hour ago—took my last two horses and set fire to my barn!"

"We want word sent to Judge Hendon," I said. "Captain Cunningham wants to talk to the judge and his men."

Demott laughed boisterously. "It's sent already! We knew what had happened when Birdsall's men came through, and I sent word as soon as they'd left! You don't think I'd leave 'em rotting——"

He broke off; turned his head from us; then ran to the rear of the mill to stand listening. The frogs were croaking again, and the resonant chorus of those grumbling millions seemed to fill the air about us to the exclusion of all other sounds.

Demott looked around meaningly, his fat face split by a grin. Above the rumbling of the frogs we heard a distant splashing; the sharp rap of wood against hollow wood; a far, far, faint shout.

Out from the brush beyond Demott came a man who might have been a familiar spirit of marshy obscurity and damp. He was thin, dark, twisted, like the root of a swamp tree. His hair had the lankness of wet weed; his face was drawn, swarthy, unshaven; his clothes seemed soggy, like waterlogged bark. He stopped dead and peered at us.

Then he spun about and ran back into the brush, shouting, "They're here! They're right here now! They're here! They're here!"

The brush waved and swirled, as if a storm whipped it, and the men from the swamp burst from it, hollow-eyed, haggard, clothed in rags or in garments that hung upon them like those of scarecrows in a tempest. They ran toward us, shouting hoarsely and exultantly, and Demott was engulfed by them as by a flood.

I saw Judge Hendon, supported by young Barbarie and Stephen DeLancey, emerge from the wall of undergrowth, and the Reverend Mr. Lane—good Doctor Rounds, too, and all the kind gentlemen who had shared their food and shelters with me for so many days. They came out and came out; poured through the mill yard and into the road; dodged between our horses, and under them. They pressed close to us on every side, waving limp hats and laughing jubilantly.

When our horses shied and sidled away from them, their hands reached out to hold our bridles. The faces of those near us were contorted, as if by pain or violent exertion; but from the smarting in my own eyes, I knew their grimaces were joyful.

CHAPTER XXXI

Cunningham seemed genuinely moved at the happiness of all these persecuted men, and when he spoke to them, he was almost inarticulate.

"The general sent a message," he said. "Heard all about your misfortunes in this swamp—dreadful place! Worse than we'd imagined. Afraid some of us thought Mr. Wiswell's report somewhat exaggerated, but not at all! No, no! Far from it, far from it!"

He cleared his throat, seemed to rack his brain for further thoughts, and went on fumblingly: "The general presents his compliments—very appreciative of your loyalty—wants your assistance —if you're willing to give it, I mean to say."

A drawling voice spoke from the back of the throng. "We'll help the general if he'll lend us a pound of powder."

The men around us shuffled their feet in the dusty road and stared soberly at Cunningham.

"Oh dear me, yes," Cunningham said quickly. "You'll have whatever you need."

"That's a pretty big order," another voice said. "Maybe you ain't noticed how much we ain't got."

Cunningham spoke heartily. "I have indeed! We'll supply all deficiencies—all! Powder, muskets, uniforms, boots——"

An awed voice echoed the words. "Boots!"

"Boots," Cunningham said firmly.

"Any rum?" a new voice inquired.

Cunningham looked contemptuous. "Rum! You'll have lashings of it! What else do you need?"

"Nothing but a good general," a man drawled.

The ragged, haggard company, hitherto sober and silent, laughed dryly. Captain Cunningham smiled too, but somewhat sourly, I thought.

There was a movement among Cunningham's audience. A passageway opened through the crowd, and DeLancey and Barbarie brought Judge Hendon forward in his chair. The old judge raised a twisted hand in a queer half-salute.

"You won't misunderstand these pleasantries, I hope," he said to Cunningham. "Men say unexpected things, I fear, when they've had to hide in swamps for months."

Cunningham stared down at the old man and grinned lopsidedly. "So they kept you in this swamp for months, did they? Well, they'll be paid back, never fear!" His voice was almost kindly as he added, "There must be something about the air of this damned country that makes Americans behave like wolves."

The judge eyed him thoughtfully. "We're Americans, Captain, just as the Huguenots were Frenchmen; just as the Cavaliers, in England, were Englishmen."

Cunningham smiled vaguely. "No doubt," he said. "No doubt. But that was long ago, and this is now."

"Civil war's civil war," the judge reminded him. "It always has been and always will be. Intolerance brings it on, and intolerance is the greatest curse of every land, though every man likes to think his own land is free of it."

With a helpless movement of his twisted hands the judge seemed to change the subject. "You say General Howe wants these men's assistance, Captain. Well, I can speak for them. They'll fight the rebels, and they'll fight as well as any troops ever fought. But there's one thing on which they insist, and we may as well have it understood now. All these men are refugees from American rebels, but *they're* Americans too, and they don't want anyone to forget it, ever. It's their wish and determination, Captain, to fight only as Americans, and only under American officers."

Before we rode on to Massapequa, Cunningham had agreed to all Judge Hendon's suggestions for the welfare of his men, and the men themselves had marched off in a body toward Gravesend Bay, dry-footed, many of them, for the first time in months, and every last one of them eager to repay with interest a few of the things that had been done to them. The way they repaid it, after they had been incorporated in DeLancey's Loyalist Battalions and the New Jersey

Volunteers, is as shining an example of fortitude as any nation's history can show.

On the twenty-fourth of August we came back again to the western end of Long Island, and we rode at a canter; for ahead of us, to draw us onward, was an unending slow hammering of heavy guns.

"Can't be a battle," Cunningham said repeatedly, as if to reassure himself. Then he would rake his horse with his spurs and bark sharply at his troop, urging them to make better time—though no troopers could have made better.

I never saw a man as fearful of missing anything as Cunningham was of missing the battle that would destroy the rebels and end the war. "Those bloody damned rebels! Those damned bloody Americans!" he murmured, over and over. He constantly licked his lips as a man does when he anticipates a sensuous pleasure.

A range of forested hills cross the western end of Long Island, sheltering its tip and the Heights of Brooklyn from the monotony of the brush plains to the eastward; and the cannonading, we found, was coming from those timbered heights.

From afar, as we rode, we saw a smoke haze above the level country between us and those hills. It was the smoke from Howe's main camp—a camp which, when we reached it, seemed to stretch almost all the way across Long Island.

Cunningham made choked sounds of relief when we caught our first glimpse of that enormous camp. "Upon my word, Wiswell," he said, "I was startled when first I heard those guns! 'Cunningham,' I said to myself, 'your luck's run out! You've waited months to pay those rebels back for what they did to you in Philadelphia, and now you've missed the end of it because you had to do a good turn for a few bloody ragamuffins in a swamp.' That's what I said, Wiswell; but by God I believe I was wrong! I believe I'll be in at the death after all!"

Everybody in that enormous camp shared Cunningham's confidence; and even Buell, when I found him near Joshua Loring's headquarters, was so much a picture of assurance that his greeting to me struck me as almost patronizing.

"Welcome back, my boy," he said. "Have a nice little trip?" He flicked ash from a cigar and examined the tip with the eye of a connoisseur.

"What's happened to you?" I asked. "You must have found food that agrees with you."

"I have, Oliver, but not enough to live on. I had just the merest taste of it when I had dinner with General Howe, and I——"

"Dinner! You had dinner with General Howe!"

He waved his cigar beneath my nose. "This is one of the general's, and there's more of 'em in the tent. Let me tell you about that food I had at the general's. Patty de foy graw, they call it. Made out of German geese's lights or livers, but tasty. I've been thinking I might settle on Long Island when the war's over, Oliver, and raise geese. It's as nice a place for geese as there is, and there ain't any bird as entertaining as a goose. I got it all planned out: I'd encourage my geese to eat too much, so they'd have big lights and livers to make patty de foy graw out of. They'd be bad-tempered, of course, with their livers all swelled up; but I'd have a few for pleasure and company, and wouldn't let 'em eat so much. I've been studying geese, Oliver, and——"

"Just a moment," I interrupted. "How'd you happen to dine with the general?"

Buell gazed dreamily into space. "They lay their eggs in an open field, Oliver, and build little fences of paper around 'em. And you'd never dream how they do their mating. Unless they have a puddle of water they——"

I shook him from his dreams of geese. "What about the general? What about that battle?"

Buell passed his hand across his brow. "That's right. You haven't been around here for a couple of days, have you? Let's see, did I tell you about getting rid of all my forty-dollar notes?"

"You've told me nothing," I said; "nothing but some nonsense about geese and a lie about dining with the general."

Buell seemed puzzled. "Didn't I tell you about going inside the rebel lines? Didn't I tell you about the third road through the hills?" He caught himself, placed a finger warningly upon his lips, and glanced furtively over his shoulder.

His actions exasperated me. "Look here," I said, "I want to know what Howe's doing to put an end to this rebellion! Tell me what you know—if you know anything."

"Well," Buell said, "get rid of your horse and come over to the tent. It's the one right behind Commissary Loring's. There's four geese tied to its tent pegs—two on each side. I'd like to get you more interested in geese. They're mighty cute, Oliver, and they're an awful lot like people, only not so harmful."

When I had turned my horse over to one of Loring's servants, I pushed through throngs of soldiers and women camp followers, all of them gabbling and laughing like sight-seers on a picnic. Well to the rear of Loring's marquee stood a tent outside which three fat geese, fastened to tent pegs, stared haughtily at the sky. In the tent opening stood Buell, beneath his arm a fourth goose that looked reserved and a little drowsy.

"Come right in," Buell said, "and have a cigar. Stedman ain't here, but we'll have Old Put for company." He offered me a cedar box the size of a field desk. When I stretched out my hand toward it, the goose hissed terrifyingly and struck a hammer blow at me. The three geese outside the tent honked brassily.

Buell shook his goose and spoke sharply. "Stop it, Put! This here's Oliver." To me he said, "Old Put's my pet. He's named for that rebel general Putnam. Looks just like the general, he does: grumbles like him, lisps like him, waddles like him, putters around like him, but knows more. Better educated! I tell you, Oliver, you ought to make a study of geese. It'll help you a lot when you write your history. They're the most peaceable birds there are, and if any other bird starts a fight near 'em, they can't rest till they stop it. At the same time, they don't like strangers, and don't want 'em around. One mean-feeling goose'll tackle ten others, and he don't draw the line at little birds, either. He'll peck a lady duck or a baby duckling to pieces, and not feel any sorrier about it than a general would. They get attached to you if you take their fancy, and follow you around like a dog, hoping you'll do something to laugh at in a fond way. Old Put knows you're a friend of mine now, and you'll find he'll be real kind to you. Sit in your lap for hours, Old Put will—if you'll let him."

"I won't let him," I said. "How'd you happen to have dinner with General Howe?"

"You're totally wrong about geese," Buell protested. "If it wasn't for these geese, I don't know as I'd dare to tell you about the general and the third road through the hills and all the rest of it, for fear somebody'd overhear me. But with these friends all round me, there can't nobody come near this tent without being honked at. No, Oliver; a friendly goose is more than comfortable; he staves off danger. Look at Rome. One night, a couple of thousand years or so ago, when the enemy was sneaking up on Rome, with every-body asleep except one true-hearted goose——"

"Did General Howe let you in to wash the dishes?" I interrupted. "Was that how you got these cigars?"

"Me? Did you ever see me wash even my own dishes?" Buell looked indignant; then kissed the top of the goose's head. "Sweet thing!" he said. "No, Oliver, I had dinner with the general because of finding that third road through the hills, and I found the third road through the hills because I had to get rid of my forty-dollar notes to the rebel army, or not get rid of 'em at all."

He went to the tent opening and pointed to the range of wooded hills that lay to the westward of the camp. "See those hills, Oliver?"

I just looked at him.

"Over behind those hills," he said, "there's a fine big valley, all meadowland and little groves of trees. It's the western tip of Long Island, and at the very end of the valley there's a point of high land—Brooklyn Heights—that looks across to New York. The rebels have built a fort on that piece of high land, and put ten thousand men in it, and all their best generals." He looked apologetic. "Of course, the word 'best' don't mean much when applied to rebel generals. Ten of their best ones don't know half as much as a colonel out of any other army."

"Have you seen the fort?" I asked.

Buell spoke patiently. "Certainly I've seen the fort! It ain't worth a damn. When Howe puts ships on one side of it and a few regi-ments of regulars on the other, it won't be any more use than a toy fort made out of kindling wood. The ten thousand men inside it won't have any place to run to, so they'll have to surrender, gen-erals and all." He puffed contentedly at his cigar.

"Nonsense!" I said. "No rebel general would send an army over to this island and risk a battle in a place from which he couldn't retreat if he needed to. Only a fool or a madman would do such a thing!"

"Well," Buell said, "generals wouldn't be generals if they acted like ordinary human beings. Washington *has* sent an army over here, and he's put General Putnam in command of it; and Putnam's going to have a battle on his hands, whether he wants it or not. That Putnam, he stutters and putters and talks with a lisp, and tries to make up for it by telling everybody how good he is; and somehow or other, God knows how, he's got everybody believing him. He even claims he won the battle of Bunker Hill, and they even believe *that*.

The truth is, Oliver, he's never won a victory, and never even fought a battle, so Washington's put him in command of all the rebel troops on Long Island. That gives you kind of an idea what we'd have got from the rebels in the way of government if they'd won this war."

"But if the fort's defended by good soldiers," I said, "the general doesn't need to be a good one. Look at what happened at Bunker Hill!"

"This is different," Buell said comfortably. "If they're licked here, they'll have to stay licked—and that's what they're going to be: licked!"

"It must be a trick," I protested. "Probably Washington's making a feint with a part of his army, so the other part can steal out of New York and get safely away."

Buell looked at me compassionately. "Oliver, you're like a lot of people. You don't know a damned thing about the rebel army; yet you feel free to tell me all about it. I'll thank you kindly not to tell me what the rebels intend to do, and why they'll do it—not till you go to see 'em and find out for yourself, the way I did. No, Oliver: there's an awful good reason why that fort full of rebels ain't here as a feint."

"What is the reason, Tom?"

"Because there practically ain't any rest of Washington's army! It's all in that fort on the other side of those hills."

"Do you mean to tell me that if that fort should be captured, there wouldn't be any more rebel army?"

Buell was patient with me. "That's what I'm trying to say, Oliver. Why, you'd never believe the damned-fool things those rebels have done!"

"If they've failed to provide a means of escape in case of defeat," I said, "no other mistake they could make would be worth noticing."

"You're wrong, Oliver," Buell said. "I kind of half wish you'd got a coat of tar and feathers yourself, so you'd understand what terrible fellers those rebels are! Look, Oliver: they not only sent their whole army over here onto this island and cooped it up so it couldn't get away, but Old Put took his very best troops out of that fort and sent 'em over onto these hills."

He held back the tent flap to let me see the wooded Heights whence came the intermittent booming of the big guns. "There's two passes in those hills, Oliver, and the best rebel troops are guarding 'em, miles away from their fort, so to keep Howe from marching through the passes and getting into the valley in front of the fort. How's that for plumb damned idiocy or whatever you want to call it?"

"If they did that," I said, "the passes are probably narrow and easy to defend."

Buell impaled the butt of his cigar on the point of his pocketknife, so to get the last available mouthful of smoke. "That's right, Oliver. They *are* easy to defend. I wanted to get across those hills, but I wouldn't have gone through either of those two passes! No, sir! Not while Howe's guns are firing cannon balls through 'em, the way they are now, just to keep the rebels diverted, and while the rebels are sitting up there behind those trees waiting for Howe's men to show their heads. Oh my, no!

"What I wanted, Oliver, was a nice quiet road through those hills— a road that didn't have any rebels on it, or any cannon balls whizzing through it. What's more, Oliver, I found it."

His outstretched hand and extended index finger swung from left to right, tracing the serrated outline of the ridge to the point where it was dim in the August heat haze.

"I went prowling along the foot of that range of hills, Oliver, figuring on going all the way to Long Island Sound if I had to; and away over yonder, halfway to the Sound, I found just what I was looking for—a nice, peaceful, quiet pass. I walked right through it with my scissors-grinder on my back, and came out in that big valley without anybody so much as saying Boo to me. Nobody stopped me when I crossed the valley, and I went right up to the fort and hammered on its front door with my bell; and the rebels came out with knives and bayonets to sharpen. I worked till dark sharpening 'em and buying their loot.

"I bought three paintings, two silver teapots, a horse and eighty-seven dollars in hard money, all for thirty-nine thousand dollars that I'd printed myself. Then I got on my new horse, went back to my nice quiet pass, bought four geese with my last fifty notes and two hard dollars, and came through the hills again just as simple and easy as kiss your hand." Reluctantly he removed the remnants of his cigar from the point of his knife.

I couldn't believe I'd understood him correctly. "You found an unguarded road that took you around behind those hills? A road that let you get between two rebel forces?"

"That's what I did, Oliver. And as I said before, the best of all the rebel regiments were up in those hills, watching the two main passes. I got in behind 'em. There wasn't anybody in the fort but militia consisting of grandfathers and little boys that ain't interested in much of anything but going home."

Buell's astounding statement made my spine tingle. The unguarded pass he had discovered would permit an army to get in behind the pick of the rebel forces, cut them off from their base, and destroy them utterly.

"So that's why you had dinner with Howe," I said. "Did he believe you? I can hardly believe you myself! How can those rebels be such fools as to invite extinction?"

"They were fools at Bunker Hill, weren't they?" Buell asked. "They got themselves into a corner there, if you remember. What they've done here ain't much different from what they did at Bunker Hill, except that at Bunker Hill they had a neck of land they could escape over. Here they ain't even got a neck of land. If they want to get away they'll have to swim. As for Howe, I don't know whether he believed me or not. He didn't take me into his confidence. In fact, he didn't even thank me for telling him about that third road. That's how I happened to get this box of cigars. I figured I was entitled to something for bringing him all that information, so when he went out after dinner—probably to tell Mrs. Loring what I'd told him—I picked up an extra box of cigars I was sure he didn't want and went out myself."

We sat in that hot little tent, listening to the near-by muted gabbling of Buell's geese; to the slow thudding of the guns on the wooded slopes before us. There seemed to be nothing more to say.

If Buell was right, and if Howe believed him, the rebel army was doomed.

Thoughts and hopes raced through my brain, and they were all of Sally.

CHAPTER XXXII

The twenty-sixth and twenty-seventh of that August—the August of 1776—will never be forgotten by any man who took part in the events that, on those days, turned the western tip of Long Island into a country of nightmare—a land where gorgons and hydras and chimeras dire would have seemed commonplace.

Again and again, during the dark early-morning hours of the twenty-sixth, Buell, Stedman and I were wakened in our hot little tent by the ripping rattle of far-off musketry fire. At dawn, drums began to roll all round about us, so that we were the center of a humming like that of a giant beehive; and at sunrise, while we were making a meal on a dubious mixture of salt pork and dandelion greens concocted by Buell the night before as a sop to his delicate stomach, one of Joshua Loring's servants scratched at our tent flap and demanded the immediate presence of Mr. Stedman to act as interpreter for the commissary of prisoners.

Buell immediately carried his dish of pork and greens outside the tent and put it before Old Put, who made short work of it. "We'll all go over," Buell said. "Loring gets the best food there is, on account of his wife being so helpful and companionable with the general, and I'd like to pick up a little of it. What's more, Loring picks up a good deal of information in one way and another, and the sooner we find out what this drumming's about, the better. There's something serious afoot to get Loring out of bed at sun-up."

Buell was right. Loring's marquee was crowded with aides and assistants, filling out requisitions, compiling long lists of foodstuffs and forage, and dispatching orders and letters. Loring himself, pale and perspiring, was listening distractedly to the guttural protests of two Hessian officers.

"Good God," Loring cried at sight of us, "tell me what these men want! Mr. Stedman, I beg of you, find out what's the matter, and promise them anything to keep them quiet! Anything! Good God! As if I didn't have enough to do with a battle in prospect—a battle, and the whole rebel army likely to be made prisoner."

The Hessians, Stedman quickly learned, were profoundly disturbed over the indecent and barbarous fighting hours of the rebels. They fought and, like snakes, crawled in ditches and behind bushes at hours when all decent soldiers should be in bed, and so had contrived to capture two Hessian outposts. The two Hessian officers wanted their outposts recaptured.

Loring, as always, was all suavity. "Say to the gentlemen," he told Stedman, "that there'll be no more rebel army by tomorrow night. Their outposts will be recaptured. Everything shall be done as the gentlemen wish! No more crawling in ditches and behind bushes! My word for it! Get rid of them, Mr. Stedman!"

When the Hessians at last were gone, Loring told us the news, and his pale, clamlike eyes glittered with excitement when he spoke of prisoners—and well they might, for a commissary of prisoners can become a Croesus if permitted to purchase supplies for a sufficient number.

"We attack tonight," Loring said. "My orders are to send three men with the van, and the three are Mr. Wiswell, Mr. Stedman and Mr. Buell. You'll be needed as soon as prisoners begin to be taken, and your duties will be to assist in collecting them from their captors, and conducting them into whatever enclosure the provost marshal, Captain Cunningham, prepares for them. You will question them to obtain information as to the position of the enemy upon the field of battle, and see that this information reaches the proper officers at the earliest possible moment. Later, of course, your duties will be to assist the provost marshal in seeing they're properly lodged and fed. You'll move out with Sir Henry Clinton and the advanced guard, and he'll march at nine o'clock tonight. He'll be followed by Lord Percy with thirteen regiments and the artillery. Lord Cornwallis will lead the reserves. General Howe will march with Lord Percy."

"Are we going by my road?" Buell asked.

Loring ignored him. "The route's a secret, and so's the whole movement. Say nothing to anybody during the day, and report to

Sir Henry Clinton's headquarters staff at dark tonight. Leave your tent standing. No tent in this camp is to be struck. If the rebels should find out what we're doing, it might cost us dear."

When we left Loring's tent, Buell was jubilant. "So we leave our tents standing, do we? Do you know what that means? It means we're going to use my road—that third road! It means there's no rebel troops anywhere near it. It means we'll get in behind the regiments Old Stuttering Put sent out on those hills. Yes, sir, that's what it means; and another thing it means is that we'll capture their fort and their whole damned army; and by tomorrow night that General Washington of theirs is going to be saying, 'This is what we get for tarring and feathering Tom Buell.' "

That night march of Howe's ten thousand troops—light and heavy dragoons, light and heavy infantry, artillery, ammunition wagons, commissary wagons laden with food and even the greater part of the women who followed the fortunes of those ten thousand men— was as splendidly executed a piece of military maneuvering as any general could have planned or any army performed.

Buell, as the day drew to a close, seemed more worried about his geese than about the battle into which we were going. "If they were anything but geese," he told me, "I'd kill 'em and we'd take 'em with us and eat 'em; but I just ain't got the heart to kill a friendly goose. I'd as soon think of killing a little white dog that depended on me. I hate to leave 'em here, too, because the camp followers of this army ain't got any morals to speak of. They'd steal anything if they got a chance—and a goose is awful tempting. If I lost Old Put, I'd feel like I'd lost an uncle. By rights oughtn't I to take him with me when we march?"

"Take a goose into battle?" I said. "Not if you're going with me!"

Buell wanted to argue the point. Nearly every British officer, he reminded me, had brought a dog to America and took him wherever he went. A large number of the soldiers had brought women with them, and the women traveled with the baggage train as a matter of course. Why, therefore, wasn't it right for him to take Old Put?

"Public opinion," I said. "Taking a dog anywhere with you's all right, and even women look less out of place in a battle than geese would. But a goose just wouldn't be understood. You'd be criticized."

"I've been tarred and feathered," Buell said. "What do I care for a little criticism!"

"Think of your descendants," I told him. "What'll they think, a hundred years from now, when they read in history books that you wouldn't fight for your principles unless you had a loving goose beside you?"

Buell snapped his fingers. "I don't care *that* for my descendants! What use are they to me? I won't take Old Put, but don't think you talked me out of it. I'm leaving him here totally because something might occur that'd later make him regret accompanying me himself. If he lost a leg or something, he might feel that way, and I don't want anything to interfere with this friendship."

While I shaved and washed my clothes, as everyone should before a battle, Buell dug a pit for the geese in one corner of our tent. At the bottom of the pit he put his scissors-grinder, pushed the outraged and complaining geese between its legs, added two loaves of bread and a bucket of water, and on top of the scissors-grinder arranged his pocket printing press and the few meager possessions we had accumulated in the roving life we'd led since we left Milton.

When, at dusk, we tied down our tent flap and went to get our horses, Buell was depressed. "War's a terrible thing, Oliver," he said, "because it makes everybody crazy and willing to do anything at all. A general steals a country or a city, and a common soldier don't hesitate to steal anything he can get his fingers on. All the rebels steal from everybody, and these damned British not only'll steal, but talk high and mighty while they're doing it. I ain't so sure, Oliver, but what the whole world's sinful. Maybe everybody ought to be destroyed, so Europe and America could begin over with just nice animals for populations."

As we moved toward the flatlands to the east of the camp, where we had been told the staffs of General Howe and General Clinton would assemble, the road and the fields on either side crawled and surged with men, horses, wagons; with hurrying aides, slow-moving officers, troops of dragoons, women camp followers.

As we rode farther and farther to the eastward, we found regiments standing beside the road in long, long, dim lines; and against the background of this darkling human hedge, aides trotted backward and forward.

Buell's pessimism was profound. "I hope I never have to be in an army," he said, "but if I do, I'll be in the cavalry and nowhere else. I don't know where people get the idea armies spend most of their time marching and fighting, when what they mostly do is stand around and wait, loaded like a jackass, while some damn fool of a general's aide gallops up and down in front of 'em, covering 'em with mud and horse manure!

"If I've got to spend half my life waiting for a general to make up his mind, the way soldiers do, I want to sit down to it; and God knows there's no place to sit down in an army except on a horse! I hate horses; but there's some things I hate more, and one of 'em's standing around and waiting for a general."

It seemed to me we rode past miles of waiting soldiers before we came to two hillocks on which shrouded lanterns were partly screened by shifting, hurrying figures. At the foot of the nearer knoll a sentry halted us. I gave him the countersign for the night, adding "From the commissary of prisoners, to march with General Clinton."

The sentry pointed to the other knoll. "General Clinton's over there. This here's General Howe."

We dimly saw the two commanders working with clerks and aides and orderlies, with colonels and majors, commissaries and sergeant majors, guides and adjutants, to make sure all was ready.

Around the hillocks were companies of light infantry in short jackets and tight leather hats. They carried short muskets, little longer than pistols, and their knapsacks were mere nothings by comparison with the dreadful packs we'd seen them carrying at Bunker Hill.

On Clinton's knoll we found Cunningham waiting for us, and we sat with him, shivering in the night damp and listening to army aides reporting on the readiness of those long lines of men upon the road behind us.

How those endless lines could be moved in the darkness without deafening uproar and hopeless confusion was beyond me; for I wasn't a soldier then. Even at a later day, when I *was* a soldier and had learned to look on night marches as one of life's disagreeable but unavoidable necessities, I often thought back to that night march of Clinton and Cornwallis, Percy and Howe, as one looks back at a great performance on the stage, or brings to mind one of those rare and perfect happenings that men count themselves fortunate to have seen.

Clinton, stooping over a map, looked to me like a wealthy Bostonian studying his investments. He was short, fat, big-nosed, and had a habit of pursing his lips as though in contemplation of a wallet too meagerly filled. I knew little about Clinton then, except that he had opposed the costly tactics of Gage and Howe at the battle of Bunker Hill; and I had the unpleasant feeling, as I watched him receiving the reports of aides and stabbing a pencil at his diagram, that he might lead us into trouble before the night was over.

Buell had the same feeling; he grumbled beneath his breath as he watched Clinton. "If he's going to take us through that pass of mine," Buell said, "he better forget that pencil and start moving! That pass is just about wide enough for him and one small horse."

He turned to Stedman. "How many'll travel this road with us, do you think?"

"Not less than ten thousand," Stedman told him.

"Ten thousand," Buell echoed. "Well, figure it out for yourself. If that pass of mine only lets 'em through one at a time, it ought to take about five seconds for one man to go past a given spot in it. That would mean twelve men a minute, or seven hundred and twenty men an hour. Ten thousand men would be fifteen hours getting through, and that fifteen hours don't allow for cannon getting jammed in the middle of the pass, or generals stopping to drink a bottle of wine and have their boots polished so they'll look good in the battle. Here it is pretty near nine o'clock, so it looks to me as if this army wouldn't get much of anywhere till day after tomorrow!"

I saw Clinton straighten up from his diagram and make a small gesture to the officers around him. The whole knoll was suddenly in a tumult of movement; mounted officers clattered off; all about us were faint hallooings, as if partridge hunters in deep woods shouted with repressed voices to fellow hunters.

The light infantrymen were on their feet, moving from between the knolls, and beyond them I heard the clattering of innumerable horses.

No one, I suppose, can know what a night march is like unless he's been in one himself. Exasperation constantly floods the breasts of those who take part in it—exasperation at the endlessness of the night; at the depressing pangs of hunger; at the oft-repeated and seemingly useless halts; at the impossibility of knowing what lies in the darkness just ahead and on each side; at the fits of shivering that weaken knees and set teeth to chattering; at the gallopings of aides to front and rear; at the enigmatic whispered reports delivered by messengers from the head of the column; at the stupidity of those behind, perpetually blundering into those ahead during halts; at the unexplained loud shouts, the ear-piercing whinnying of horses, the unavoidable tumult of the moving army that seemingly must bring down upon the helpless column the withering fire of enemy guns.

At ten o'clock we were marching and halting and marching. At eleven o'clock we were halting and marching and halting. At midnight we were doing the same thing. We passed dim farmhouses, their occupants herded together beside the road under the guard of light infantrymen.

The night air grew colder and colder, as if our slow progress to the north were taking us from summer into autumn.

"Yes, sir," Buell said, "we're heading for my pass—that third road; but at the rate we're going, they'll hear about it in Boston before we reach Brooklyn!"

At two o'clock in the morning our forward movement seemed to stop for good. Buell impatiently heaved himself about in his saddle; and I, too, was bitterly resentful at our failure to get forward and within reach of the rebels.

We were beside a tavern. Around it a few light infantrymen stood on guard; but the rest of the light infantry and all the dragoons had gone on ahead. We could hear, within the tavern, voices raised in argument; but over what, we couldn't know.

We may have waited an hour when we heard shouts and laughter far ahead. Out of the darkness came a squad of dragoons. "Only five horsemen stationed in the pass," we heard them shout. "Captured all five! Not another damn soul anywhere around! The whole pass is open!"

They clattered to the tavern to report to Clinton, while we waited and shivered.

Dawn was close; stars were faint in the dark sky. Before us we could feel the loom of black hills—the long and dangerous hills that barred us from the rebels. I wondered how a man could stand the delays and disappointments of a soldier's life unless his brain was partly atrophied.

When the true dawn came, we moved at last, on and up into those dark hills; and looking back, as we mounted the slope, I saw for the first time, stretched out upon the plain behind us, the whole extent of the army that Clinton and Howe were leading against the rebels. Infantry regiments, grenadiers, artillery, Hessians, baggage train, camp followers—they were strung out across the flat fields like a mile-long caterpillar. It seemed a ghost of an army, moving silently in a faint pall of dust; and in the gray dawn light the canary-colored waistcoats, white breeches, black gaiters, scarlet jackets, blue jackets, green jackets, were all a toneless drab.

When we entered the pass, I saw it had been widened to let us through; on both sides were windrows of felled trees.

"By God, Oliver," Buell said, "look at those trees! They weren't chopped down; they were *sawed* down, so to make no noise! I tell you this General Clinton knows a thing or two! He's——" He seemed to catch himself, and laughed scornfully. "Listen to me run on! I must be getting weak-minded! A general's a general, and that's all there is to it!"

The pass, topping the ridge, turned westward; and we, wheeling to the left, began to descend the inner slope on a long downward slant.

Two aides clattered past us. "The rebel army's on this ridge," they shouted. "Move fast! Move fast! We've caught the whole rebel army on this ridge! We've got to get down behind 'em quick!"

This heavily wooded ridge, which we had just crossed by the neglected third road, was the main position of the rebel army. Our night march had taken us out beyond where they lay about the mouths of the other two passes, waiting to be attacked; thus we had outflanked them, and were now heading downward into the plain behind them.

Buell's horse jostled mine, and I felt his elbow against my ribs. "It ain't true, is it, Oliver? I never really believed it could be done! I never thought there'd be an end to all those miseries—tar and feathers . . . broken printing presses . . . burned barns . . . driven out of Boston . . . proscribed . . . chased into swamps . . . turned into counterfeiters . . . damned near destroyed. . . . Do you really think our luck has turned? Are we really going to pay 'em back today—right now—for all they did to us? It's a dream, isn't it, Oliver?"

"No," I said, "it isn't!"

And it wasn't.

CHAPTER XXXIII

THE rocky road, gullied by past rainstorms, slanted steeply down through the woods. We, marching to the westerly, descending into the plain, had to our left and above us the hill forests that held the principal fighting force of the rebels; and lo! two miles to our right, across the plain, we beheld the fort that was their base. Not only was the plain between their base and them, but so were we!

Below us the tip of Long Island was spread out like a giant triangular map, its far edges outlined by the blue waters of New York Harbor. It was a rich and rolling triangle of scattered farms and maple groves. In the golden light of the newly risen sun, the barns, the trees, the hillocks cast long black shadows across fields of ripening wheat. On all that expanse of plain no figure moved. The fort was silent.

Men behave unexpectedly when going into battle—are concerned with small things; laugh easily; seem gifted with an acuteness that at other times they lack. When we started down that rocky path, all the scarlet-coated officers who rode before us might have been out for an early-morning canter in a park; for they listened deferentially to their neighbors; spoke with exaggerated politeness; held their reins unnecessarily high, to guard their horses from slipping on loose stones; affected a lack of interest in that silent fort in the haze to the right of us.

I marveled that the others could be so calm when my own heart pounded with excitement; that even Buell should seem unmoved. Then he pushed his horse close to mine. "What do you do to keep from getting scared, Oliver?" he asked. "I feel bad inside, like jelly."

I felt a great relief at his words, for I suddenly knew that all the carelessness and indifference of the generals and colonels and majors and aides in front of us was assumed—that they, like myself and Buell, were torn and racked within by the fever of war.

That's all war is—a consuming fever: a period of delirium and insanity, of misery, disappointment, discomfort, anxiety, despair, waste, weariness, boredom, brutality, death; and yet to every man in every war there comes a day worth living for: a day when a lifetime of excitement is packed into a few short hours.

This, I think, was such a day.

While we were still high on the slope, the guns came thundering down the road, forcing all of us into the underbrush on either side. Gun after gun, caisson after caisson, bounced and crashed past us like a succession of thunderous cyclones. To the tune of this crashing, the officers around me fumbled in their saddlebags for food; and while they ate, their eyes wandered, hunting and ceaselessly hunting for signs of the rebel forces we were stalking.

Buell, gnawing a cold chicken that he had obtained in some mysterious way, pointed with its carcass toward General Clinton and his staff, hazily visible to us through the dust that hung in the wake of the guns. "They don't know where the rebels are, Oliver," he said. "Look at 'em look! We know as much as they do! Do you think they've got away, Oliver? Look at that valley! Not a sign of life in it! I'll bet they got away!"

Two scarlet-coated officers turned contemptuous stares on Buell, who looked apologetic. "I s'pose I ought to say we got the situation well in hand, the way generals do when they're lost in the fog; but I ain't a general. If those rebels ain't got away, where are they?"

Where were they, indeed! That distant fort out of which ragged rebels had poured only two days earlier, to let Buell sharpen their knives, seemed devoid of life as a church on a weekday morning.

Below us, at the foot of the hill, dragoons—scarlet toy soldiers on midget horses—rode from the cover of the trees into the open road, almost as though a child had fastened them to strings and was drawing them forward. Alongside them moved light infantrymen. From where we were they seemed to move slowly, like a stream of blood crawling sluggishly along the narrow channel through the green wheat.

All the guns had gone by, and dust hung like a dry fog in their wake. The dust was heavy with the scent of the fire struck from the rock by their wheels. When we moved on into that dust, our horses slipped and stumbled on the rocky road. The officers before me swayed jerkily in their saddles as if jolted by the tumult of sound that still came back to us from the artillery wagons.

Through the opening in the trees we saw two guns come out upon the plain, their horses elongated in a gallop, and move off the road into a field of wheat. A ball of white smoke burst from the muzzle of one, and the wheat before it flattened and fluttered. While I waited, mouth ajar, for the roar to reach me, the other gun jetted smoke; and the double boom of the two discharges drove my ribs against my heart.

Buell's voice was hoarse. "That's the signal, Oliver! I heard 'em say so up ahead. That's the signal; we're through the pass, so those outside the other passes can attack—if there's any rebels here to *be* attacked. Damned if I don't think they've all run home!"

He was wrong. He had no more than spoken when, far along the ridge on which we stood, volcanoes of gunfire erupted. I could see no smoke, but there was something solid and tangible about those two patches of gunfire. They were like two mountainous islands of sound: two towering thunderous columns, shot through with the lesser sharp rattle of musketry.

The dusty riders before me, suddenly, ceased to be dim and colorless, and were brilliant against a shining background of gold and green. We were no longer in the shadows of the forested pass, but out in the valley among the wheat. Dragoons, drawn up beside the road, were not the toy soldiers we had seen from higher up, but giants of men in the clear light of early morning.

The straight road before us slanted away from the hills through which we had just passed, as the gaff of a raised mainsail slants away from its supporting mast. It ran straight as a string through the rolling fields, on its left the darkly wooded hillslopes from which the two pillars of gunfire still rose undiminished. Far, far ahead, along that road, scarlet-coated dragoons and light infantrymen flowed smoothly onward, disappearing over the crests of hummocks and flowing up again to rises beyond.

Behind us, out of the forest, poured an unending stream of infantry regiments.

Officers near us shouted and pointed. Ahead of us dragoons and light infantrymen had broken from the ranks and were moving swiftly through the wheat toward the dark hills on our left.

Buell stood in his stirrups. "There they are!" he whispered. "Look at 'em! This is the last battle *they'll* ever fight!"

A long line of dark figures had come out of the woods, advanced a short distance into the wheatfield and halted, so that they had the appearance of far-off scarecrows. More dark figures trickled out to join them. They all moved indecisively, seeming to drift in the direction of the pass we had so recently left. From that pass the wagons of our baggage train were just emerging, along with a horde of figures that I knew to be women camp followers and the strange human derelicts that follow an army, even into battle.

The little groups of scarecrows ceased drifting, broke apart, reformed into other groups; broke again and moved swiftly back into the forest.

The squad of dragoons from our column had far outdistanced the light infantrymen. Their closely massed horses slid upward through the green wheat; slipped smoothly and silently into the forest after the vanished scarecrows.

Surprisingly, then, the small dark figures reappeared at the edge of the forest, scurrying into the open like frightened insects. From the advancing thin line of light infantrymen rose puffs of white smoke. The distant dark figures halted and wavered.

Dragoons came out from the trees at a gallop, and the little dark figures resumed their scurrying. I could see the flashing of sabers as the dragoons chased them: see the small dark figures flow down the hill, as if to throw themselves among the light infantrymen. The puffs of smoke thickened. Miraculously the dark figures dwindled in number, dwindled and dwindled. Where there had been forty, there were twenty-five; then fifteen; a moment later there were none at all, and the dragoons turned and rode back into the forest.

Buell was indignant. "Why, those rebels never even made a fight!" he cried. "They just let themselves be killed!"

"They're not all dead," I said. "Some may be, but the rest must be crawling through the wheat like wounded partridges. I'm going to move ahead with the column. You go on out there and see that those prisoners are brought in safely."

"Me?" Buell asked. "I want to see the rest of this battle."

"You'll see enough battle before the day's over," I told him. "Do as I say, and talk to the prisoners while you're bringing 'em in. Find out all about 'em." I gave his horse a cut across the rump; and Buell, still grumbling, cantered toward the slope where the light infantrymen moved uncertainly in the field in which the dark figures had vanished.

Until some of those dark little figures had been brought in for questioning, there was no way of knowing who they were—barring the fact that they were rebels—or what they had been doing so far away from the two tempests of gunfire that continued to boom and thunder on the ridge at our left.

Cunningham, who was just ahead, looked round at me, his red face split by a grin; and when he saw me riding alone, he reined in his horse and waited. "By gad, Wiswell," he said, "the whole thing's working like a chess problem. Upon my soul, I believe they've done the exact things I'd have wanted them to do if I'd planned the battle for them myself. The general's making for that little village ahead of us—Bedford. He'll establish headquarters there, and you and I'll continue on till we find the proper place for prisoners. We'll have as many as we can handle before this day's over!"

"Those men who came out of the woods just now," I said—"what were they doing there?"

Cunningham spoke contemptuously. "Making fools of themselves, for one thing! I suppose they think they're the left wing of the rebel army—which has no business out on this ridge to begin with. They must be the left wing, because the center's guarding the middle pass through these hills, where all that banging's coming from, and the right must be guarding the pass at the end of the ridge, close to the harbor, where you hear the rest of the banging. Yes, Oliver, I really think those men we saw belong to the left wing; and if so, the rebels' left wing was in the air, where no wing should ever be. A wing ought to be anchored to something. In this particular case, to be of any assistance at all, a left wing should have been anchored to the pass we came through, so to fight us off when we started to move in behind them. God knows who put those men where they were, but whoever did it ought to be court-martialed and shot. What's more, the men themselves don't deserve much mercy, because they let themselves be surprised. In an army, Mr. Wiswell, that's a worse sin than murder."

"What makes you so sure this'll work out prettily?" I asked him. "Bunker Hill should have worked out prettily, but it didn't."

"That's true," he admitted, "but that was due to a piece of stupidity that couldn't happen again. Here there's no way for things to go wrong. The Hessians have attacked the middle pass on the other side of the ridge; General Grant's attacked them at the far pass. When they learn we're behind them, there'll be nothing for 'em to do but run for their fort. When they do, they'll run straight into our arms. We'll have the whole of 'em in our hands by nightfall—all of 'em, and the fort to boot, and that'll be the end of the rebellion."

On rising ground in the center of the rolling plain through which we rode was a group of small farms and outbuildings, clustered around a crossroads. When we reached this little settlement, it was aswarm with dragoons and light infantry. They were around the houses, in them, behind them: a tangle of shouting officers, worried-looking men, restive horses.

A sentry motioned us into a farmyard. The tumult was deafening. A battery of four guns stood at the rear of the yard, pointing toward the dark hillslopes. Artillerymen scuttled about them like blue beetles.

We saw Clinton swing himself from his horse, pull at his breeches as if fearful they might have stuck to his fat legs, yawn cavernously, walk close to the four guns and stand there scratching his rump and looking out across the valley toward the hills.

He had a good view, for the farmhouse was on a hill, and about in the center of the triangular tip of the island. Far to the left was the pass through which we had come. Regiments were still pouring down from it, filling the slanting road through the wheatfields.

Straight ahead of us, less than a mile away, the hills were notched by what I knew to be the middle pass.

Off to the right the ridge of hills ran down into New York Bay and ended in flat brown marshes cut by shining blue creeks and inlets.

A mile to the rear were the log walls of the fort on Brooklyn Heights—walls so silent that they seemed as useless as they did harmless.

Clinton turned back to the farmhouse and thrust his head into an open rear window. He seemed to like what he saw, for he called his aides, went around to the door and vanished from our sight. The farmhouse was no longer a mere farmhouse. It was headquarters: mysterious and awesome source of life and death, victory and defeat.

The chaos of the crowded farmyard merged into something like order. Officers' horses were led to a rail fence and picketed. The gun crews, having arranged the four cannon to their satisfaction, leaned idly against wheels and limbers. Knots of generals and lesser officers whispered together and constantly turned their heads to watch that newly glorified farmhouse.

When another group of gaudily dressed officers rode into the yard, Clinton thrust his head from an upper window and shouted at them irascibly, as Vose Leighton had shouted at me and his sons when we, as little boys, disturbed him by our play. "Not here!" he cried. "Don't stop here! Keep moving toward the bay! Hurry up about it, unless you want the rebels to run clean around you and get away! Go right on down to the water!"

Major generals and brigadier generals turned and stared indignantly at the columns of infantry that had halted outside the yard. Young officers waved their arms and shouted. The columns shuffled forward. I saw the men wink at each other, secretly pleased by the irritation of Clinton and his generals, and knew they were in high spirits.

Aides ran in and out of the farmhouse. One of them came to Captain Cunningham and handed him a slip of paper. "The general wants the prisoners well guarded," the aide said. "They'll be embarrassing if you don't look out. He's assigned Captain Evelyn of the dragoons to this duty, with a squad of dragoons, a field piece and two companies of infantry. He says to put the camp between the main roads, so it'll be easy to reach."

He saluted and hurried away.

The hour was nine o'clock. From then on the battle of Long Island became for me a series of disconnected sketches—vignettes of heroism and desperation; of cowardice and panic; of stupidity and ignorance; of a veritable travesty of war that made me ashamed for my rebellious countrymen, enemy to them though I was.

CHAPTER XXXIV

Acting on Cunningham's orders, Stedman and I laid out the prisoners' camp in a sort of amphitheater among knolls. We had the help of Captain Evelyn, who was young, a trifle stooped, and extremely lackadaisical in his manner, as if he'd never given anything a minute's thought. That manner of his was deceptive, for he seemed to know exactly what to do, as if by instinct. While we placed gun crew, dragoons and infantrymen at commanding posts around the hills, the lowland all around us was aswarm with scarlet-coated regiments.

Cunningham viewed our labors complacently. "Grand," he said, in his oily voice. "A grand place for rebel prisoners! If they try to escape, we can mow 'em down like cattle!" His face was suddenly scarlet. "See you do it, too! If they show their teeth, give 'em a foot of bayonet in the ribs before they have a chance to bite!"

The flush left his face and he beamed upon us. "If you need me, I'll be at headquarters." He turned on his heel and swaggered off, a fine figure of a man, but one that I found increasingly repellent.

I couldn't have said when the battle began, any more than I could say when the distant rumble of thunder becomes a thunderstorm.

The sound of gunfire that had hung so long above the two guarded passes had grown louder and still louder. This, we knew, was because the British attack was being pressed on the opposite slopes of the ridge. The British forces were like the two blades of a gigantic pair of scissors. We in the plain were one blade; and the other, on the far side of the ridge, was doing some sharp cutting.

Surprisingly, then, the sound of gunfire no longer came from about the passes, but from the fields before us. Drifts of smoke appeared above the waiting scarlet regiments. The guns on the hillocks leaped as they bellowed.

Then I saw the rebels coming down from the forest on the ridge —pouring out in tens, twenties, hundreds, uncountable hundreds; unformed mobs, running, hiding in the wheat, taking shelter behind trees, dodging behind fences, all hurrying toward us, hopeful of passing us and reaching the rebel fort.

At first the scarlet regiments held their formation. They were like a long scarlet fence that held back all those scattered groups of fleeing rebels. Then the scarlet regiments, too, broke apart, and the wheatfields at the foot of the hillslope were dotted with slow-moving red figures eddying at the edges of thickets, fumbling along ditches, prodding before them with bayonets, as men prod with pitchforks at new-cut hay.

I knew the rebels were hiding in the fields; the scarlet infantry-men hunting them through the wheat. The rebels were being destroyed: no doubt of that; and for fifteen long months I'd been hoping for such a thing to happen; yet now that the destruction was taking place, I was conscious only of a consuming weariness: of an overwhelming desire to sleep a little, and to find, when I waked, that those scarlet battalions had forever vanished, that the long black guns didn't exist, that the sharp, thick taste of gunpowder was a thing of the past.

The complete ruin of the rebels was what I'd hoped for, but now I didn't want to see it; I didn't even want it to happen—because these running, hiding men were no longer the lunatics and bullies who had killed my father: they were just helpless Americans, as my father and I had been.

The voices of our dragoons and infantrymen became shrill. I saw them pointing across the valley. Then Buell, surrounded by a throng of men on foot, came around a knoll and signaled to me.

"Where do you want 'em, Oliver? This is only the beginning of 'em! The Hessians are driving 'em out of the hills like cattle!"

The men around Buell had the whipped look of vagabonds or idlers. Their faces were unshaven, their coats tied to their belts with raw-hide thongs or hazel shoots. They wore ancient leather breeches, sweat-stained hickory shirts. The stockings of those who had stockings hung wrinkled around their shoe tops. There were thirty-seven of them.

"Do you mean to say," I asked Buell, "that only thirty-seven prisoners were taken in that first charge?"

"Thirty-seven's a lot, Oliver," Buell said. "They run like rabbits! They dodged back into the woods and ran around us, over to the middle pass. You'll get 'em in bigger bunches pretty quick."

Captain Evelyn rode up behind me, followed by his squad of dragoons. "Good God," Evelyn said, "these aren't soldiers, are they?"

Buell slid groaningly off his horse, and felt tenderly of his buttocks. "Everybody claims they're soldiers, including themselves," Buell said, "so I guess they must be."

"If they're soldiers, how'd it happen no officers were captured with them?" Evelyn asked.

Buell looked surprised. "Good land, Captain, most of 'em *are* officers!" He pointed to a sour-faced man chewing a blade of grass. "That there's a lieutenant colonel." He indicated another with fat, red cheeks, a rosebud of a mouth, and clubbed hair tied with a boot-lace. "That there's a major. We got four captains, too, and three lieutenants. Most of those with stockings are officers."

Evelyn, his gorget, brass buttons, saber and regimental insignia glittering like newly burnished gold against the scarlet of his uniform, looked incredulous; then saluted the lieutenant colonel and the major. "Fortunes of war, gentlemen," he said. "You're well out of it, if you don't mind my saying so."

The rebel officers eyed him stonily.

Evelyn turned a questioning glance upon Buell. "These men are frightened," he said. "Did anything happen to 'em while you were bringing 'em in?"

Buell looked disgusted. "Not a damned thing. On the way over here we passed those two companies of New York Volunteers—the ones that came to Halifax in May. They still ain't got any clothes, and if these fellers had been wearing anything decent, they'd 'a' undressed 'em. Can I go back and watch the Hessians chase the rebels, Oliver?"

When he left me, I spoke to the prisoners. "If you behave your-selves," I told them, "you'll be well treated, and at the earliest oppor-tunity you'll be exchanged. If you don't behave yourselves—if you try to escape or disarm your guards—you'll have to take the conse-quences."

They stared up at me as if they didn't propose to understand. Evelyn leaned on the pommel of his saddle, staring down at these sorry-looking soldiers. "No offense meant, Colonel," he said, "but I'd very much like to know how you came to find yourselves in such a precarious position this morning."

The colonel looked sullen. "It wa'n't our fault if we didn't have enough men! You had five times what we did. That's all there was to it!"

"I'm afraid that explanation doesn't go back far enough," Evelyn said. "I'm particularly interested in knowing how your army came to be on Long Island. What puzzles me is how your general thought he could defend a land-and-water front of nearly thirty miles against a vastly superior force free to attack where it pleased. Good God, gentlemen, your thirty-mile lines were open to attack on the rear, both flanks and the front, and on top of that they were cut in two by a navigable channel!"

The prisoners just looked angry.

Evelyn took off his shining dragoon's helmet and scratched his curly fair hair. "I'm really interested, you know. We've had strange generals in our own army—got us into all sorts of uncomfortable fixes, I'm free to admit; but this beats anything I ever heard! Why, no matter where we chose to attack, gentlemen, we had you! You had no possible way of stopping us! You had only a third as many troops as we, and most of them militia, untrained and unreliable. You had no ships, no artillery, no cavalry. Think of it, gentlemen! No cavalry! It was an army without eyes! We could have gone up on Manhattan Island, landed there and swept you into the river as with a broom! I wish you'd give me an inkling, as one soldier to another, why your general should have tried to hold New York in the first place! Why should he have come over here to Brooklyn when he lacked half enough troops to do it properly? Why did he divide those troops in such a way that we cut you in two, as we're doing at this moment?"

The rebels were gray-faced. "Just because we're prisoners," the colonel said, "ain't no reason to insult us! General Washington's in command of this army, I'll have you know!"

Evelyn looked pained. "My dear good man, I haven't the slightest wish to insult you! I'm a soldier, deeply interested in military strategy and tactics. No matter who your general is, his blunders today have been monumental! I feel free to say so, just as I'd feel free to criticize miserable leadership in my own army. That's what you've had— miserable leadership! I don't know how much of an army your general will have left in a week's time; but I'm sure it won't be large— and that, gentlemen, will be exactly what he deserves."

One of the prisoners spat the word "parricide" at him.

Evelyn looked puzzled. "Parricide? Parricide? You mean I'm in rebellion against my parents, intending to be their assassin?"

"No, no," I said, and explained, for I'd heard the epithet before. "It's a little peculiar; 'parricide's' just a word they have for everybody not on their side. They know it means something unpleasant, but they're not etymologists."

He nodded, murmured "parricide" ruminatively, and gathered up his reins. "How do you want these prisoners handled, Mr. Wiswell? Let's not waste time on 'em when we can see the finish of Mr. Washington's army from one of these knolls."

"I'd like the officers and men separated," I said. "Keep the officers at one end of the camp, the men at the other. The men should be divided into small groups, so they can be easily questioned."

Evelyn repeated my wishes to his dragoons, and added sharply, "If they attempt to escape, they're no longer prisoners: they're rebels and enemies. You'll order them to halt; and if they don't halt, use your sabers. If that doesn't stop 'em, they're to be left to the infantry. Repeat these orders to every new group of prisoners as they're brought in."

When my duties permitted, and I'd sent my first reports in to Clinton's headquarters, I was glad to follow Evelyn to the high ground that rimmed the camp—glad to get away from the rebel prisoners. They were sullenly bitter, angrily resentful of any attempt to be friendly. They seemed to revel in churlishness and ignorance.

When I stood on the hilltop with Evelyn and Stedman, I felt hemmed in by a steadily contracting ring of musketry fire.

Evelyn made faint sounds of wonderment. "By God," he said, "there's a sight you wouldn't see in a dozen wars!"

The wheatfields between us and the range of hills were covered with moving figures and fleecy puffs that bloomed and faded. The God of War might have come down from Olympus and with a lavish hand sown toy soldiers and balls of cotton from end to end of those broad meadows.

The upper fields were covered with blue-coated Hessians; the lower fields dotted with scarlet infantrymen. Between those two loose bands of scarlet and blue were hundreds upon hundreds of dun-colored figures—rebels, caught between the Hessians and the infantry. They swarmed confusedly up and down between the scarlet band and the blue band, like frightened minnows in a ditch.

We could see them hide in the wheat; then rise and run again. Wherever we looked we saw those dun-colored figures, running, running, running; saw groups of them surrounded and engulfed by larger scarlet groups or blue groups.

Evelyn groaned at the spectacle. "We've caught the whole center and left of the rebel army, and I'm not there! Look at those Hessians stab the wheat with their bayonets! There's a whole army being wiped out; and here I am, standing on a hill, guarding prisoners!"

"You really think the rebels are caught?" Stedman asked. "Isn't it possible they might escape somehow?"

Evelyn looked shocked. "Escape? How *can* they? The whole left and center's gone! Those men out there are nothing but a panic-struck mob, as good as dead or captured, right this minute!"

"I hope to God there's no mistake this time," Buell said. "I want to get back to my geese!"

Evelyn turned to look toward the shimmering waterways of the marsh at the extreme right. Near the edge of that marsh, scarlet columns were deployed in the fields, waiting. "It's true," he said, "that the rebel right wing hasn't yet come out of the hills; but when it does, it'll be trapped just as the left and center have been."

Around the shoulder of a near-by knoll streamed a procession of rebel prisoners. They came toward us in squads and straggling groups. Some were herded along by infantrymen; some watched over by Hessian officers; some guarded by dragoons with drawn sabers. Some, I even thought, were urged onward by women; and although I knew it wasn't possible, I imagined I saw the women striking with sticks at those they escorted.

When I went down to meet them, I began to fear that our camp was too small for our prisoners; that all of Long Island would be needed to hold them; that not even an entire regiment of infantry would be sufficient to guard them.

They poured between the sentries in an endless stream, haggard, wretchedly clothed, soiled beyond words. They had bayonet wounds in their buttocks, in the backs of their legs. They were hatless and coatless, smeared with dust and grass stains, their pale faces streaked with sweat. They seemed unwilling to look at their companions, much less at us, their captors.

Buell forced his horse through the line of draggled, white-faced prisoners and drew up beside me. He flung a gracious word to those he had just left. "All right, boys. You're safe now! Don't be worried! I won't let the Hessians do anything to you."

He turned back to me, and his face was serious. "Christ, Oliver," he whispered, "I don't want to see anything like *that* again!"

He mopped his forehead with his sleeve. "They weren't men any longer, Oliver! They were just animals, squeaking and running! There wasn't hardly a one of 'em that lifted his hand to save himself or anyone else."

He lowered his voice. "I'm kind of ashamed to tell you what I saw, Oliver. We've captured regiments from all over—Rhode Island, Massachusetts, Connecticut, New York, New Jersey; and no matter where they came from, they were all alike! They ran and they ran! They hid under bushes, and tried to crawl into fox holes. If ever an officer tried to make 'em stop and fight, they squealed like scared woodchucks under a wall! The women camp followers went out from our baggage train with clubs, kicked those Patriots out from the wheat and took 'em prisoner!" He shook his head. "Patriots! Don't it beat hell, Oliver, the labels men put on themselves?"

He was silent and so was I. We sat there together, watching the pallid prisoners hurry past the sentries and into the campground, like lost souls crowding with a sort of miserable relief toward Charon's ferry.

The rout of the rebel left and center was an overwhelming one; but it was drab by comparison with the drama when the rebel right wing, at noon, came down off the ridge and set out to skirt the marshes that lay between them and the fort on Brooklyn Heights. I watched it with Evelyn, Stedman and Buell from the highest knoll at the rear of the prisoners' camp; and rebel officers, one by one, came out from the hundreds of silent prisoners to mount the knoll and stand near us, staring and muttering. What they saw made them look sick, and no wonder; for this was the end of all their schemes and all their labor—an ignominious end brought upon them by reckless leaders.

The road down which the rebels poured ran in a half-circle around the marsh. Abreast of that half-circle were our light infantry regiments, grenadiers, Highlanders, squads of dragoons and a dozen heavy guns.

The rebels themselves had a different look from those who had come down from the center pass; for they marched in formation instead of running in a mob; and even when the heavy guns and the infantry and the Highlanders opened fire on them, the marching battalions held together as long as was humanly possible.

Evelyn turned and looked down at the rebel officers who stood near him. "What's that regiment in brown?" he asked.

Not a rebel would answer.

"Move up ahead of us if you can't see, gentlemen," Evelyn said. "That brown regiment's going to attack!" He leaned forward to tap one of the prisoners on the shoulder. "I beg your pardon," he said, "but that regiment in brown's behaving extremely well, you know!"

The prisoner ignored him.

Evelyn raised his eyebrows. "Come, come, gentlemen: I'm not trying to pry military secrets from you. I'd like to give credit where it's due, that's all."

"They're Smallwood's Maryland battalion," one of the officers said huskily.

"Maryland, eh?" Evelyn said. "Well, they'll never see Maryland again! They're attacking Cornwallis' whole division, so to give the others a chance to escape. Too bad! Too bad! They're brave men, and this'll be the end of them."

Evelyn was right about their bravery. That little brown battalion marched against the long curved line of scarlet regiments as smoothly as any body of men ever moved on parade; and far behind them the throng of rebels that had come out of the hills ran desperately to save themselves. They straggled down from the wheatfields into the marsh; floundered through the pools and mud and winding watercourses; plunged headlong into the creek that curved through it like a silver sickle.

In defense of the fleeing hundreds the little brown column came on and on. The scarlet line toward which it moved jetted smoke; the guns on the hillocks wreathed themselves in fleecy clouds; the brown column seemed about to be engulfed and overwhelmed in thunderings.

The marsh beyond that little column crawled with retreating men. We could see them leaping from tussock to tussock; sinking in the mud to their knees when they missed their footing; plunging to their armpits in the marsh pools and beating the water to get free; blundering in the creek, vanishing in deep water, struggling onward with flailing arms.

The rebel officers around us groaned and cursed. Probably, like myself, each one watched with strained muscles the fortunes of one out of those hundreds who labored in the marsh.

"He can't get out," Buell shouted in my ear. "Look there, Oliver! It's up to his shoulders! Up to his neck! Christ, Oliver, it's into his mouth—into his mouth——"

I didn't see the man Buell saw, but I saw another—saw him too clearly. He labored through a marsh pool; fell in a hidden waterway and slowly emerged; rested awhile on hands and knees; painfully rose; gropingly gathered up his musket and knapsack.

I could imagine the heavy mud upon his legs, and how it stank; the sweat in his eyes; the dryness of his throat, holding air from his lungs. Almost I could hear him gasp for breath.

He swayed on the brink of the creek; fell forward into the water, floundered to his feet and stood thigh-deep in the stream. He moved forward. The water was up to his waist; up to his chest. When it reached his armpits, he stood motionless, looking upstream and downstream at his fleeing fellows.

Then he struck out for himself, swimming slowly. I was sure he wouldn't make it; for as he swam he rolled like a sick fish. When his head dipped under, I knew he was done, though his arms made swimming motions still. After that his head came up once; his arms rose and fell. Then he was gone, and I found myself standing in my stirrups and shouting, as if hopeful of persuading one of those distant fugitives to save that dying man.

The rebel officers around us stared dejectedly at that thunderous panorama—at the dark little figures wallowing across the marsh in the direction of the fort; at the curved lines of troops on the inner edge of the marsh; at the scarlet regiments hurrying to overtake those who had passed the marsh and were straggling toward the earthworks on the Heights.

The brown battalion had re-formed in the shelter of a grove, and once more was marching against the scarlet lines. The end of all this confused marching and running and banging, I felt, was near, and my heart beat harder.

Evelyn walked his horse out in front of the rebel officers. "I'll ask you to go down with the rest of the prisoners," he told them. "Your whole army's on the run, and the prisoners might start running too. It's your duty to see they don't. If they should, we'd be bound to stop 'em, and you wouldn't want that to happen."

Unprotestingly those hatless men in soiled shirts and homespun breeches slowly gave ground, but their eyes remained fixed until the last possible moment on the brown battalion marching against the guns and the long scarlet lines.

I couldn't turn my gaze from those brown lines. Their advance slowed; the lines seemed to thicken and thin. They wavered and swirled; and then, in a moment, there were no ranks at all: only a mass of brown figures running away, running toward the marsh. As they ran, the regiments that had opposed them began to move, as if stirred to life by the flight of the men in brown. The guns on the hillocks stirred and crawled like black beetles toward the Heights of Brooklyn. The scarlet lines ringing the marsh straightened and set off past the lumbering guns, all pointing toward that silent fort upon the Heights.

I turned to Buell. "Well, Tom, they're getting what they deserve, I suppose. When I think of all they did to my father and to you and to all those others in Boston——"

I saw he wasn't listening. He was staring at the rebel officers moving back toward the throng of prisoners in the amphitheater below.

"What's the matter?" I asked.

"I ain't sure," Buell said. "One of those fellers doesn't look quite right. From the way he's eyeing you, I sort of thought he might have a pistol in his pocket—and might be thinking of using it on you."

I looked where he pointed. Among the rearmost of the rebel officers, staring at me with a look so like Sally's that it wrung my heart, was my boyhood friend, Sally Leighton's brother Soame.

CHAPTER XXXV

A FAMILIAR face from home, even that of a bitter enemy, unexpectedly seen in strange surroundings, brings pleasure, at least for the first moment, to any man—which proves, I suppose, that all men are well disposed toward one another by nature, and only hate when poisoned by ignorance, stupidity, knavery, lies, sickness, love or war.

If Soame Leighton had, in days gone by, been nothing more than a neighbor, my heart would have leaped at sight of him; but he was vastly more than that. He was Sally's brother, and in my excitement, when I saw him, I shouted his name as though he were still my dearest friend and not a sympathizer, at least, with the mob that had driven my father and me from Milton.

I swung myself from the saddle, tossed my reins to Buell, ran to Soame and caught him by the shoulder. "Soame," I cried, "why didn't you tell me you were here? Are you hurt? Are you all right?"

He pulled away. "If it's all the same to you, Oliver, don't bother about me. Just let me alone."

"Nonsense, Soame!" I protested. "We've been friends! Nobody's going to be such a fool as to think hard thoughts of you because one of your friends holds different opinions."

Soame glanced at the other rebel officers who stood near us, seemingly oblivious of our conversation. To me he said, "Different opinions! Is that what you call it when you try to stab your mother to the heart?"

I'm afraid I laughed. "Listen to me, Soame," I urged. "People don't stop being civilized human beings because they're at war!"

Soame looked at me oddly. "Don't talk to me, Oliver! Please don't talk to me! If you do, I'll be under suspicion of being friends with Tories and traitors."

To my distress his face twisted, reddened, seemed to swell; tears welled into his eyes and ran down his cheeks. "By God, Oliver, we *aren't* friends any more!" He sounded half strangled. "You're on their side, and they hit us from behind! They didn't fight fair! Then those damned Hessians came up the hill on the other side, and down on us through the woods! They pinned our men to trees with bayonets! I saw one of 'em stick a bayonet clean through Allan Sawyer's stomach and into a maple! You knew Allan Sawyer! He lived in Roxbury!"

The other rebel officers were listening, their faces hard and hating. "What are bayonets for?" Buell asked. "You have 'em, don't you?"

"Be still, Tom," I said.

Buell sat straighter in his saddle. "Why should I? He called us traitors! No man's a traitor for trying to save his country from Sam Adams—from people who kill you if you don't think the way they do! How are we traitors for being loyal to our government instead of joining the mobs? And what's unfair about attacking an army in a place it forgot to protect itself? What made these Patriots start a war if they wanted to have everything their own way—if they only wanted to fight according to their own rules? That ain't the way wars are fought!"

The rebel officers looked murder and sudden death at Buell, and the stupidity of this rage of theirs irritated me.

"That's the unfortunate truth," I told them. "You gentlemen are officers, supposedly able to recognize military facts when you see them. You've been outgeneraled and outfought, but you're trying to put the blame everywhere except where it belongs—which is on yourselves and your generals. I'll have to ask you not to insult our intelligence in such a way. I'll also ask you to leave me alone with Mr. Leighton."

Buell handed me my horse's reins, and the soiled and draggled officers moved away before me without a word, their faces still defiant; and Soame, left alone with me, stared at the ground.

"Soame," I said, "I'd help any Milton man, even if I didn't know him well. But you aren't just a Milton man, Soame: you're Sally's brother! Even if you don't want to be helped, I'm going to help you. How's Sally, Soame?"

"Just a little fool," Soame said. "Your property's seized; and if you come back to Milton, you'll be shot if you're caught. You're worse than dead, and yet she won't give you up! She's turned nun over a man she'll never live with—a man who isn't an American any more!"

Guns were booming, muskets rattling, and men dying in the marsh over yonder, but I had a moment of sheer delight. "Thank you, Soame," I said. "I'll chance being shot when I come home to Milton, and of Sally's never living with me!

"Look at this battlefield around us! Every last rebel regiment on the run! Before night all that's left of General Washington's troops will have the British Navy on one side of 'em and Howe's whole army on the other! Did Sally give you a message for me, Soame, in case I happened to be the one that got captured? By God, I believe she did! Where is it?"

"She never expected we'd lose this battle," Soame said. "She never thought we'd be stabbed in the back, as we have been."

"Where's her message, Soame?" I said again.

Soame sounded bewildered. "Nobody thought we'd be beaten, Oliver. Nobody thought the troops of a foreign tyrant could win from us! Even now I don't *feel* beaten! I can't understand how it happened!" His anger returned. "If I'd known it would be this way, I'd never have let Sally write you! If she'd persisted, I wouldn't have carried it!"

"Yes, but she did, Soame! And what's more, you carried it. Give it to me!"

Reluctantly he brought out a little wad of paper, black with dirt and moist with perspiration.

I left Soame and went to the top of the knoll where I could be alone. The far-off roads on both sides were filled with troops, marching toward the fort on Brooklyn Heights. The fields were sprinkled with regiments re-forming to the sound of distant drumbeats after their man hunt through the wheat. The cannonading and musketry fire had ceased, and the sound of far-off drums was like the humming of a myriad of hornets.

As I worked with shaking fingers to unfold the worn and grimy letter, I was only dimly aware of that confused, tumultuous landscape. I knew the battle was won. and was vaguely conscious a peculiar pallor had come upon the groves and fields, preluding an approaching storm—but I had Sally's letter! It was written in pencil.

"*Dearest Oliver:*

"*Was anything ever so torn as this poor heart in my breast! All about me are unhappy people, telling me that I should be happy too in the triumph of the good cause; and so I should be, Oliver dear, did I not too well know what that cause's triumph means to you. Washington's soldiers have sworn to die rather than permit the troops of a foreign tyrant to occupy so much as one inch of American soil; and my father says that this splendid army of Washington's is unconquerable; and so by now, as all aver, the armed forces with which you, dear Oliver, are associated must be flying in defeat, or prisoners.*

"*Oh, Oliver! Can I rejoice when I know how black this hour's defeat must be for you! Were it not for that, I could think it glorious that those foreign invaders had been driven into the sea by the brave defenders of our soil. I hear the word 'glorious' a dozen times an hour, and children run huzza-ing up and down the road—and so would I if I knew that you were safe and coming home!*

"*All my brothers have promised me upon their sacred honor that if you are among the prisoners, no harm shall come to you.*

"*Oliver, I have* felt *the answer to my prayers for you. Those prayers have been so constant and so deep, I* know *the worst thing that can have happened to you is that you are prisoner. Assurance from on High has told me so. Something flutters in my throat when I think that you will not be long a captive; for this great victory of General Washington's will end the war; and then kindness and understanding and peace will take the place of the clash of arms. The great cloud of anger will roll away and all men will be friends again. Righteousness and mercy will prevail in the land, and you will be free.*

"*This hour will be dark for you. Let me share its darkness with you; but believe me when I tell you that the dawn is coming fast. I know that you have done what your conscience bade you do. You have struggled for the right as you saw the right, and I could* not *be prouder of you.*

"*To think the war is over! To you, Oliver, it may seem that you will come home defeated; but there is one poor heart to whom you will come as its victor, and in triumph. It is the heart of your*

"*Sally.*"

Dear, dear Sally! Sweet, faithful, understanding Sally! I folded the letter, buttoned it tightly against my heart, came back to Soame and put my arm across his shoulder.

"Soame," I said, "you've been misled. Those who started this war told you you'd got to defend your homes against a foreign tyrant. You didn't have to do anything of the sort, any more than you'd have to defend your home against me; but they kept at you till you believed what they told you. Then they sat comfortably and safely in their houses while you tried to fight without proper food or guns or clothes—and without knowing how to fight! You've been sadly deceived, but your troubles are almost over—and so, I think, are mine. I'll see what can be done, Soame, so don't——"

Soame, I suddenly found, was staring beyond me with a look I knew of old—a look that meant he didn't like what he saw.

I turned to see Captain Cunningham close behind me, a queer half-smile upon his ruddy face. "Well," he said, "isn't this a little unusual —enemies falling on each other's neck during a battle?"

"Captain," I said, "you're just the man I want to see. I was going to headquarters this minute to look for you."

"Good enough," Cunningham said heartily. "I was afraid you might conceal the communication that just passed between this gentleman and you!"

"Communication?" I said blankly. Then I realized he was speaking of Sally's letter. "That wasn't a communication, Captain. That is to say, it was wholly private. I mean—— Look here, Captain, don't misunderstand this! Captain Leighton's an old friend of mine. He's a neighbor from Milton."

"Ah yes," Cunningham said. "And for months, no doubt, he's been carrying a letter for you!" He seemed genuinely amused. "That's unusual, to say the least, Mr. Wiswell. Suppose you let me glance at this letter—this harmless personal letter."

"Does he go through your pockets each night?" Soame asked me pleasantly.

All the ruddy color in Cunningham's face paled to a greenish yellow, then reddened rapidly. "Oh," he said, "so that's the tone a rebel takes when he's stopped in his efforts to betray his country."

Soame's voice was careless. "That's the tone any man takes when he hears a friend insulted."

Cunningham's eyes were like our blue New England marl that turns the sharpest drills. "Wiswell," he said, "your duty's to keep

prisoners from escaping—to prevent 'em murdering us or any more
of our men: not to put your arms around their necks and accept
documents from 'em. I'll have a look at the paper this man gave
you."

I wondered if I could be hearing him correctly. I looked at my
hand and saw it was really mine. Everything around me was real:
the sky was a heavy gray, and the wind, which had backed into the
northeast, was moist and cold against my face—sure sign of a northeaster. The prisoners below us in the camp were huddled in the
center of the amphitheater; and I could hear the idle talk and
laughter of the dragoons and infantrymen who guarded them. From
all about us, far away, came fitful musket shots and the occasional
thudding roar of a great gun. No: nothing was unreal. Soame was
real, my letter from Sally certainly was real, Cunningham was real,
and he really had said what I thought I'd heard him say.

"You can't have it," I told him. "It's a personal letter."

I had a momentary glimpse, in Cunningham's eyes, of something
I didn't understand: something dark and inhuman, unlike anything
within my experience. Yet he seemed to dismiss the matter. "Tut,
tut," he said lightly, "you Americans are too damned serious! That's
dangerous, Mr. Wiswell! Some day we might misunderstand each
other."

I was too confused to do more than gawp at him like any country
bumpkin.

"You said you were on your way to headquarters to see me," Cunningham went on. "No doubt you wanted special favors for your
friend here. Was that it, Mr. Wiswell?"

"Yes, Captain, I wanted a parole for him."

"Ah yes," Cunningham said, "a parole. Well, Mr. Wiswell, run
along to headquarters and see what they'll do for you there. See the
general." His eyes twinkled good-naturedly.

"Don't do it, Oliver," Soame said. "This battle's not over yet.
Don't ask a soldier anything in the middle of a battle: he doesn't
know what he's doing."

The chameleonlike changes in Cunningham's manner had frightened me. I swung myself into the saddle and leaned forward to shake
Soame's hand. "I'll be back as soon as I can," I said. "The war'll be
over tomorrow and we'll go back to Milton together."

CHAPTER XXXVI

The farmhouse that Clinton had chosen as his headquarters had been neat as a pin when I had left it at nine o'clock in the morning. Now, three hours later, it seemed on the verge of rack and ruin.

Why war soils and disarranges whatever it touches, I cannot say; but the farmyard around headquarters was a sample of what war does in almost the twinkling of an eye.

Horse droppings were everywhere: the air stank of ammonia, sweat, rancidness. The once-grassy yard had been chopped and churned into dust and mud; and half-embedded in its puddinglike surface were bread crusts, old shoes, scraps of paper, bits of harness, chicken feathers, hats, empty powder bags, stray stockings, broken belts, soiled rags. In one corner of the yard was a dead horse, and against the front steps of the farmhouse lay the body of a cat.

War does similar things to men's brains.

I expected, when I rode among the officers, aides, commissaries and hangers-on who thronged that soiled and cluttered enclosure, to see every face wreathed in smiles; to find the gaiety of victory on every side; to find General Howe flushed with success and glad to give me a parole for Soame Leighton.

Instead of that, the whole company had a stricken look. Some were pale and silent; others red-faced and indignant. A few, openly raging, seemed upon the verge of apoplexy.

A knot of officers, Stedman among them, stared silently at a captain in their midst. The captain's contorted face was streaked with mud and powder stains; his scarlet jacket, beneath his arms and between his shoulder blades, was almost black with sweat; his boots were clay-stained, scratched as if by matted brambles. Around every button and buckle on his boots and breeches wisps of redtop had tightly wound themselves. His voice, when he spoke to those about him, shook and was shrill, so that I thought he must be either drunk or mentally affected by what he'd been through.

"God damn it," he shouted, "can't *someone* make it clear to him? We can walk right into their bloody God-damned fort and hack 'em to pieces with bayonets! He *can't* stop us *now!* He's got no right to order us back when we're on the verge of wiping 'em out!"

He appealed directly to one of the silent officers before him. "For Christ's sake, Colonel, can't you talk to him? Can't *somebody* talk to him? We've earned a victory over these damned rebels, and he's got no right to keep us from it!"

The colonel stared at him with eyes like oysters. "The general's issued his orders, Captain. No assault's to be made on the fort to-day."

The captain's voice was almost a scream. "But my men were practically *in* the fort! Ten regiments could have walked in there without losing a man! Doesn't the general want to finish this war, for Christ's sake?"

The colonel eyed him stonily. "I suggest you be more guarded in your speech, Captain. Not even a victory like this one gives us immunity from court-martials."

"Victory be damned!" the captain shouted. "Where's the victory if enough rebels get away to fight again? There's still part of an army in that fort, and the best of their generals, such as they are. Washington's there; Putnam's there! For God's sake, Colonel, I beg of you to make a personal plea to General Howe! We've got seven hours of daylight to wipe 'em out!"

A score of voices chorused approval. "He's right!" "The captain's right!" "Don't give 'em time to recover!" "Wipe 'em out this afternoon!"

All the cannonading and excitement of the past fifteen hours seemed to have addled my brain. I understood the words I heard, but couldn't seem to grasp their meaning. I even forgot I had come here to get help for Soame Leighton. I climbed from my horse and drew Stedman from the circle of officers around the angry young captain. He looked both exasperated and contemptuous.

"What happened?" I asked. "Is Clinton dead? Howe'd never take the command away from him, would he, considering how Clinton's plans turned out?"

"Clinton never was commander in chief," Stedman said. "Howe's commander in chief. A commander in chief can't let a subordinate general get credit for a victory."

The oyster-eyed colonel was talking again. "I suggest, Captain, that you return to your command without loss of time and withdraw from in front of the fort. I heard the general's orders. Our lines at all points must be at least seven hundred yards from the rebel outposts."

The captain thrust his clenched fist within an inch of the colonel's nose. "God all bloody mighty, Colonel! The general can't understand what's happened out there! Those rebels are huddled into their fort like hens in a barn with a fox outside! There isn't a blasted thing they can do to stop us, Colonel! I swear to God that when I got the general's orders and halted my men, they damn near trampled over me! Some of 'em were so mad, they cried!"

He pressed his lips together and made a strange, choked sound. His own eyelids, I saw, were red and puffy: his eyes shining with angry tears.

Stedman looked at me and lifted his hands in a gesture of helplessness.

"I still don't understand," I said. "What's General Howe's reason for not attacking?"

Stedman snorted. "He's mentioned several. One is the fort's so easy to take, he'd be wasting lives if he assaulted it. He prefers to take it by regular approaches."

"Regular approaches!" I cried. "What's he mean by that?"

Stedman shook his head. "I'm not sure. I think he means he prefers to wait for the warships to sail upstream until they're between New York and Brooklyn, in a position to bombard the fort at short range. Then those in the fort'll have to surrender or be blown to pieces."

"But the wind's northeast," I said. "Doesn't the general know the wind's northeast? Doesn't he know that when the wind backs into the northeast after a beautiful clear day like yesterday, we're in for a northeaster? Doesn't he know a northeaster usually blows three days —sometimes five—at this time of year?"

The group of officers turned to listen.

The colonel spoke up sharply. "What difference would it make if he *did* know it? He's sent out repeated orders not to attack that fort today! He can't rescind those orders."

"Why not, for God's sake?" I asked. "Why can't he rescind them? If a northeaster blows four or five days, his ships can't possibly get up the river to help him! He'll have to lie right where he is, sopping wet. He can't move!"

"Neither can the rebels," the colonel said.

"What makes you think they can't? You didn't expect 'em to occupy Bunker Hill, but they did! You didn't think they'd fortify Dorchester Heights, but they did, and you had to leave Boston as a result."

The colonel grunted, then favored me with a view of his back.

The young captain looked imploringly at the colonel, made a muffled sound of disgust, turned on his heel and went to his picketed horse.

Two sullen-faced aides bolted from the farmhouse door and ran toward their own horses.

The captain looked hopefully at them. "Any change in orders?"

"Yes," one of the aides said. "Don't be so long moving back from in front of that fort! How many times do you have to be told to move back before you move back? The general says he'll have someone court-martialed if all regiments don't move back as ordered."

The two young men swung into their saddles and clattered out of the farmyard.

The captain climbed heavily onto his horse, gathered up his reins and followed dejectedly, bent over in his saddle, as though suffering from a stomach-ache—which I have no doubt he was. I had the beginning of one myself.

The other officers in the farmyard stared at the ground.

I smothered my inclination to curse these imperturbable Englishmen—to speak my mind about a general who could order his army to sit idle all through an August afternoon, while the fruits of a hard-won victory rotted before his eyes. I'd have to wait until tomorrow, I knew, before speaking to the general about Soame Leighton.

Rain began to fall at dusk. By nine o'clock at night a northeaster whipped sheets of wetness into our faces; and when the sad dawn of August twenty-eighth broke, the waiting army on either side of us was obscured in gray veils of moisture that thickened, thinned and thickened.

The rebel fort, less than a mile away, was wholly lost behind curtains of rain. There were no tents for the prisoners; no tents for the army; no fires for cooking. How any infantryman, exposed to that downpour, kept his powder dry was beyond my understanding. Yet some did; for all through the day men worked at digging trenches from which the fort would eventually be attacked; and the diggers were supported by infantrymen who kept up a continual spatter of musketry fire. From the fort, too, came answering musketry fire and the occasional roar of a great gun.

An infantry regiment stood guard in the rain around our prisoners; and Buell, Stedman and I sheltered ourselves as best we could in a little woodchuck-hole of a cave we had dug near the top of the knoll.

"If Howe stays here long enough," Buell said, "he might learn something about America. Bunker Hill taught him not to attack in front, and it looks as if he'd never forget that lesson. Now he's learning about northeasters, and I'll lay odds he'll never be caught out in one again."

"He'll never learn," Stedman said. "Teaching an Englishman about America is like teaching a foolish girl how to be a good wife. A foolish girl might learn to have supper on time; learn to laugh whenever her husband said something he thought was funny; but she'd forget not to be angry when her husband spoke lightly of her mother. If Howe remembers about frontal attacks and northeast storms, he'll forget something else."

That was the truth of it. All through the twenty-eighth the rain trickled down our necks, filled our nostrils with the musty odor of soggy wool, made our shoes into water buckets in which our feet squelched and felt shriveled.

All through that night we dozed fitfully in waterlogged restlessness.

All through the twenty-ninth drifting rain poured down from gray clouds caught like smoke in the tops of trees.

That night the rain stopped. Stedman, making his rounds of the prisoners' camp at dawn on August thirtieth, woke us with good news. "The wind's shifting," he told us. "There's a fog over everything, and it smells of the sea. We'll get 'em today!"

I crawled from our shelter and went to the top of the knoll. Everything around me was shrouded in a cottony mist smelling of clams and wet mud

While I stood listening and trying to see through that vaporous blanket, I heard, far, far away to the right, a musket shot, thick and cottony as if fired beneath pillows. A drum beat with a ghostly quality, as if the drum were filled with water. There were more musket shots, and a hurried spongy thumping from other distant drums.

Buell came to stand beside me, yawning cavernously. He listened to the drums, tilting his head this way and that. "Hell, Oliver," he said, "there's something wrong! There's a regiment moving out—moving toward the rebel fort. They're hollering! That ain't right, is it? They wouldn't be letting the rebels know they were coming, would they?"

I knew he was right. There was something sinister about the silence of the rebel fort. Why, when the rain had stopped, when dawn had come, when drums were beating and regiments were noisily on the march—why, at such a time, should that fort and those lines from which muskets had rattled all through the drenching rain of the past two days be as silent as though every rebel were dead?

An aide materialized from the fog and made for the entrance to the camp, his horse's hoofs making sucking sounds in the churned mud of the path. I ran toward him; and when I reached his side he leaned down to whisper his message, as if fearful that some of the prisoners might hear.

"You're to take special precautions with the prisoners," he said. "The rebels got away! All of 'em got away!"

I didn't believe him. "They *all* got away? They couldn't!"

"They all got away," he repeated. "They crossed the river to New York in rowboats last night and this morning. There isn't one of 'em left. Not one!"

"You mean to say the whole rebel army got away? That all those men escaped across the river without General Howe's knowing anything about it?"

The aide's voice was suddenly exasperated. "That's exactly what I mean! They all got clean away! Every God-damned one!"

CHAPTER XXXVII

THE escape of all the rebels, in the very moment of their overwhelming defeat, sent every man in Howe's army into a despairing fury. The entire rebel army had been routed, their generals had been cornered and revealed as utterly incompetent, their rebellion had been crushed—and then, thanks to the sudden stubborn inactivity of General Howe and of General Howe alone, the cornered army, the helpless generals, had escaped: the crushed rebellion was again alive; and all the efforts, all the bravery of the troops Howe had led, had gone for nothing.

Even worse was the despair of the Loyalists. The two companies of New York Volunteers who had unprotestingly gone cold, hungry, unclothed for months in anticipation of this day, and fought so valiantly against the rebels that Howe had commended them in his orders, were like men in a daze. They acted stunned, as if they'd been hit on the head. The same thing, we heard, was true of the thousands of persecuted families on Long Island, in New Jersey, in New York, and across the Sound in Connecticut and Rhode Island.

Buell spoke weakly enough for all of us when he put some of the blame on Mrs. Loring. "My God," he cried, "we'll never win a battle unless we do some woman-killing first! Howe can't go anywhere to do anything without going back to see what Mrs. Loring's doing! Damn Mrs. Loring! Damn her blue eyes; damn her lips; damn her fat little switch-tail! Ain't it a hell of a thing to think that if she'd been ten years older, and her bottom ten inches bigger, Howe wouldn't 'a' looked at her, and the war'd been over!

"I s'pose there'll be statues some day to the noble heroes that got the rebels out of a hole at the battle of Long Island—to General

Washington, who put 'em in the hole to begin with, and that old blatherskite Putnam, and all those damned fool generals who hid under fences in the wheatfields; but they ain't the ones who ought to have the statues, Oliver! Nobody did a damned thing for the rebels at the battle of Long Island except General Howe and Mrs. Loring, and nobody else ought to have a statue!

"Yes, Oliver, I suppose there ought to be one statue of Mrs. Loring squeezing the last drop of champagne out of one of the general's wine bottles, and another of her squeezing the general while the rebels escape.

"The truth is, Oliver, that up to now Mrs. Loring's done ten times as much for the rebels as all their generals and Congresses and regiments put together! Why, damn it, Oliver, there wouldn't *be* any rebel generals or army except for Mrs. Loring! If there'd been *two* Mrs. Lorings, the rebels would have King George in a cage on Boston Common, with little boys poking sticks at him, by this time! Damned if I don't think it would be a mighty patriotic act to send her a bottle of champagne with something in it, like the Borgia family used to do to their friends!"

Stedman, equally angry, was less pessimistic. "They still can't get away," he insisted. "They'll try to hold New York, and it just can't be held. Howe made a terrible blunder when he refused to let the fort be attacked; but he *can't* make that mistake again. The next time he corners 'em, he'll wipe 'em out; and he's bound to corner 'em in New York if they try to stay there."

The story of the night retreat of the rebel army from Brooklyn, as Stedman learned it, was almost unbelievable.

General Washington sent a regiment of Marblehead men to scour the waterfront of New York for rowboats. That regiment of skiffs and dories, rowed by men who had been mariners from birth, had crossed to Brooklyn in the storm; and when the rain slackened on the night of the twenty-ninth, Washington had marched his whipped regiments out of the fort and down to the boats. The undisciplined, unruly soldiers had trampled each other in their panic: had climbed over the shoulders of their comrades in their eagerness to escape; yet all of them had been safely dumped into the boats and ferried across to the lower tip of Manhattan Island.

The behavior of the rebels in the weeks that followed was bad enough; but that of Howe was worse.

When the wind changed and the admiral's ships were able to move up the East River and the North River, and to trap the rebels on the lower end of Manhattan Island, Howe wouldn't move.

He had to make new plans, Stedman told us, and he laughed when he said it.

"Plans!" Buell shouted. "What sort of plans does he have to make that are any harder than I'd have to make if I was going out to rob an apple orchard! Plans be damned! All he's got to do is sail his troops up the river and let 'em go ashore! The minute he does that, he'll have the rebels boxed up on the tip of the island, with warships anchored on three sides of 'em, and Howe's army on the fourth!"

"That's pretty near the truth," Stedman said.

"Pretty near!" Buell cried. "Hell, it's exact! Any pink-cheeked leftenant in Howe's army that ain't hardly out of diapers yet could plan how to capture New York and every last rebel! You don't even have to be a soldier to plan how to do what Howe wants to do! Why, damn it, I could plan it myself, and plan it a lot easier than I could figure how to get rid of eight dollars in counterfeit rebel money!"

"I know one thing," I said. "I came here to see the finish of the rebel army, and I've seen about all I can stand. Howe delayed, delayed, delayed, until the summer was almost gone; then he outwitted and battered the rebels till they were ready to surrender to sixteen dragoons and a wooden cannon; then he sat down and let 'em get away! Now he's doing nothing again at the very moment when he could make himself immortal by one quick move. I can't sit here any longer and watch this fool play into the rebels' hands. I've got to do something that'll be useful—go where everything isn't being botched and bungled."

"You can't go now," Stedman protested. "You'd be leaving at the exact moment when things must change for the better. The next time Howe moves, the rebels can't possibly dodge him. They won't be able to row away, because of the warships. They won't be able to fight their way through Howe's army, because they have no guns, no cavalry, no generals that know what to do, no army capable of following instructions."

"I've heard all that before," I said. "I used to believe it, but I don't believe it any longer."

"I feel about the way you do, Oliver," Buell said, "but if I was you, I'd give it one more try. I heard somewhere that the third try never fails, and Howe's next attack on the rebels will be the third one. He let 'em get away after they were licked at Bunker Hill, and he let 'em get away after they were licked at Brooklyn; but it ain't possible he'll let 'em get away again! He's a bastard in more ways than one, Oliver; but he can't be *all* bastard."

He looked at me owlishly. "Ain't it strange, Oliver, that nobody's given the general a title for what he's done over here? I could think up some good ones for him."

After the manner of all men in all wars, we laughed immoderately at some of the names Buell thought up for Howe; and we even helped him with such whimsical masterpieces as Lord Snore of Neverup; Lord Howe of When; William Howe, Duke of Dally; Lord Lingerloring . . .

We didn't know the half of it!

Against my better judgment, I waited for Howe to move once more, and the waiting was a nightmare.

Day after day, for more than two weeks, while summer waned and winter's inactivity came closer, the whole army camped on the tip of Long Island, looking across to New York. In addition to the agony of waiting, the prisoners supposedly in my care were hungry and mistreated, and I could do nothing about it.

For two days after the battle all the prisoners were crowded into a small farmhouse in Bedford and kept closely confined, though I was unable to learn why, other than that Cunningham desired it.

Cunningham took perverse delight in making the captured rebels miserable mentally as well as physically. If the dimensions of a room for prisoners were twelve by twenty feet, he quartered fifty in it. Into such a room forty men can wedge themselves at night, provided they lie tight against each other, and roll over together on a given signal. Fifty, however, are too many; but Cunningham took visible pleasure in seeing fifty trying to live in such a room.

Somewhere he had picked up, as servant, pet and confidant, an enormous jet-black Negro called Sip, after—as Cunningham genially explained—that celebrated Negro, Scipio Africanus. Stedman and I were at a loss to know whether Sip's sense of humor was so abnormally developed that everything seemed humorous to him, or whether, like Cunningham's, it was merely warped. No matter what Cunningham did or said, Sip was quick with shrill laughter—unless warned by Cunningham to be silent.

Cunningham visited the prisoners only when he'd been drinking. Thus he usually came to see them at hours when Stedman and I were at work on other things. When we wished to find him in order to correct the abuses for which he was responsible, nobody ever seemed to know where he was.

The second day after the battle I rose early and went to the prison house to make sure the doors and windows were opened as soon as possible; and while I stood there, trying to close my ears to the curses and recriminations of the prisoners, Cunningham strode into the yard, followed by Sip. He was steady enough on his feet, but his lips had a loose look, as if they might at any moment slip and slide to any part of his face. His eyes were red, as though the wine he had consumed had flooded into them. Evidently he had made a night of it and wished he hadn't.

"Who opened those windows?" he asked. He passed his hand over his mouth, stared hard at his palm; then focused his eyes on me. "Oh, it's you, Wiswell! Don't you know these rebel scoundrels? Cowards! Stab you in the back! Have those windows closed!"

The prisoners heard him all too easily; a shout of protest and hatred came from them.

Cunningham gave me a patronizing look. "Hear that? Close the windows, Wiswell, and nail 'em shut!"

"Captain," I said, "there's too many prisoners in those rooms. I had the windows opened. The prisoners'll die if you nail the windows shut."

"Let 'em," Cunningham said. "Damned small loss to the world if every damned American died."

"That's open to argument," I said. "Each prisoner, if alive, can be exchanged for one of your own army. Also we're responsible for prisoners, just as a parent is responsible for a child, even though the child isn't all it ought to be."

"Oh, come now!" Cunningham cried. "D'you mean to say we're responsible for rebels? Most emphatically not, Wiswell! They forced themselves on us, didn't they? Certainly they did, because they were too scared to run away! We're not responsible for 'em any more'n you'd be responsible for thieves that broke into your house!" He turned to the huge Negro. "Sip, where's that rope?"

The colored man drew a coil of hemp from beneath his ragged jacket.

Cunningham took it and studied the noose at its end. "Splendid bit of hemp," he said. "Flexible but strong! Chokes nicely without unduly shocking. It's had a deal of use, I'd say. How many hanged with it already, Sip?"

"Lan' sake, Cap'n," Sip said, "I lost count!"

"I feared so," Cunningham said. "Ah well: no harm done, but don't make mistakes like that when you start hanging 'em in *this* house!"

Sip laughed understandingly.

"Sir," I said, "I don't think these men should be smothered at night, starved during the day, or frightened by empty threats at any time."

Cunningham moistened his lips, and his smile seemed to undulate upon his lower face. I might have thought of that smile, once, as genial. I knew better now.

"Empty threats, eh?" Cunningham asked. "You Americans should get about a bit, to learn what's happening! Why, my young friend, there's scarcely a house in New York that hasn't been pillaged by these miserable rebels. They're soldiers, and under military discipline; yet they pillage their own people! Damn it, sir, the rebel general Washington has to have about a thousand of 'em lashed to ribbons every day for thievery and worse! Oh yes; worse! Damn it, Wiswell, hanging's kinder treatment than they ought to get!"

From one of the windows of the jail came a gay and mocking voice —that of Soame Leighton. "The captain's an authority on thievery, Mr. Wiswell. He steals our rations, and replaces 'em with maggots and weevils packed in stinking meat and rotten bread."

A roar that was part applause and part hatred came from the jail windows. I heard the words, "Irish slave-driver!" "Food-snatcher!" "Thief!" "Murderer!"

Cunningham went suddenly crimson and, all in a moment's time, sickeningly white. He slowly turned his head to look at me, and his eye sockets had a sooty look against his parchmentlike skin. Yet he continued to smile, even then. "Seem to know your name, Wiswell!"

He went closer to the prison house, his sooty black eyes fixed upon the faces at the windows. "And are the maggots to your taste, gentlemen," he asked, "or are they smaller than those you're accustomed to in your cozy homes?"

Soame Leighton's mocking voice sounded clear above the hooting of the other prisoners: "We don't like 'em, Cunningham! They're too gamy! They must have been brought up inside Englishmen and

Irishmen that haven't opened their heads to a new idea since 1692!"

Cunningham turned to me. "Call the guard, Mr. Wiswell."

"Captain," I said, "they've had bad treatment since the battle. They don't——"

"Call the guard!" he shouted. "Can't you hear me tell you to call the guard? Can't you God-damned Americans do one damned thing you're told? Call that guard, or by God you'll regret it!"

"Sir," I said, "that prisoner——"

"You'll call the guard, Wiswell," Cunningham whispered, "unless you want to see that prisoner skinned alive! I recognized him. You want to make a pet of him, don't you? I suppose you think pets always escape, eh? Well, this pet won't! Call the guard, Wiswell, before I lose my temper."

I called the guard. A corporal, followed by six men, marched through the gate and to where we stood. The corporal saluted.

Cunningham beamed at the corporal in a manner I can only describe as fatherly. "We're moving a prisoner or two. What are you loaded with?"

"Ball," the corporal said.

Cunningham looked dubious. "It's not enough, boys. Load with buckshot."

"Shall we draw the ball?" the corporal asked.

"No indeed," Cunningham said. "Leave the ball and put six buckshot on top of it." He smiled up at the windows of the jail. Those windows were silent now—so silent that the dry rattling of the buckshot rolling down the barrels was loud in our ears.

The corporal's guard, their loading finished, stood rigidly in a line.

Cunningham looked pleased. "Take positions on either side of the doorway," he said. "If there's any demonstration, shoot at their stomachs." He winked at me and strode to the jail door, which the sentry unlocked with a huge key fastened about his waist with a chain.

Whatever they say of Cunningham, he had the courage of the devil—perhaps because something was missing in his brain. He walked straight into the jail and stood inside the hall, and the corporal's guard, closing in behind him, stood and knelt on either side of the doorway, their muskets leveled.

"Now then," we heard Cunningham shout, "there's been some talk here this morning about bad food, and too many prisoners being confined in these quarters, and similar complaints. Mr. Leighton, will you step forward, please?"

Evidently Soame Leighton strode out from among his fellow prisoners; for Cunningham went on: "So you don't find the food to your taste, Mr. Leighton?"

"That's putting it mildly, Captain," Soame said. "There's none of us here that'd recognize it as food if it wasn't served to us at meal-times."

Cunningham spoke almost regretfully. "I'm sorry indeed to hear it, Mr. Leighton! We've been busy the last few days, as you can well understand, and we can't inspect every mouthful of food the navy brings us."

"If the navy brought that food," Soame said, "that's probably the reason your ships didn't sail up to help the general. Probably the sailors were sick from the smell of it."

"Ah," Cunningham said, "but we were fighting rebels, who can be beat with no ships and only half an army! Any other complaints, Mr. Leighton?"

"Since you bring the matter up," Soame said, "we have. We'd like a chance to put our case before someone who has a faint conception of justice and mercy."

"Justice and mercy, eh?" Cunningham said. "Surely men who've been disloyal to their government shouldn't ask too loudly for justice! As for mercy, your people showed mighty little to their own countrymen in the Long Island swamps! But there, there, Mr. Leighton; you're a prisoner and I'm not, and it ill befits me to remind you of the many shortcomings of your fellow rebels. It's enough for me to know you're not satisfied. Since you don't appreciate this shelter we've provided for you, I'm going to take you out of it and send you to Gravesend, where there's more air and light, and where the food is fresh from the ships."

He turned to the corporal. "Corporal, send two of your men to Gravesend with Mr. Leighton. He's to speak with no one on the way —no one! I fear Mr. Leighton's ideas of justice aren't quite what they ought to be, and if he talks with anyone, he might misrepresent."

The corporal spoke to two of his men, who rose from their knees, went into the jail, and came out with Soame Leighton between them. In the early-morning light he looked ghastly, but he cocked his eye at me in that humorous way of his.

When I took a step towards him, Cunningham spoke to me peremptorily. "Mr. Wiswell, I need you and Mr. Stedman. You made a complaint about the overcrowding of these prisoners, and I'm going to leave it to you to put an end to it."

I looked helplessly after Soame as he went marching off between the two guards toward the wooded slopes that lay between us and Gravesend. In spite of his tattered breeches, his unshaved face and uncombed hair, his sweat-stained shirt, his wretched stockings, his broken shoes, there was something debonair and defiant about him still.

"Mr. Wiswell," Cunningham said again, and his voice was peremptory.

I went to the door of the jail.

"Now then," Cunningham said, "I want you and Mr. Stedman to escort all these prisoners to Flatbush. You say they're crowded. All right. I've just the house for 'em in Flatbush—just the house. You'll find it in the middle of the Hessian camp." The look he turned on me was triumphant. "You can start moving 'em this very minute, Mr. Wiswell. They'll not only be more comfortable in Flatbush, but there'll be less opportunity for 'em to stab us in the back."

He turned on his heel, beckoned to his black servant and abruptly left us. As he went I heard him laughing, and the sound was like the passage of a saw through ice.

CHAPTER XXXVIII

The transfer of the prisoners through the middle pass to Flatbush was a nightmare that so completely filled the next few days that I half forgot Soame Leighton.

Our prisoners would have tried the patience of saints. They hated Buell, Stedman and me with unrelenting bitterness, blaming us for all the evils suffered at Cunningham's hands. Encouraged by the almost miraculous escape of the army that everyone had regarded as lost, they made life hideous for us with jeers and recriminations, not only while we marched them across the wooded heights and down into the plains of Flatbush, but while we were trying to make their new quarters livable, and doing our best to locate for them the rations that Cunningham should have sent us but didn't.

The house to which Cunningham had ordered us was a farmhouse belonging to a celebrated rebel named Lefferts. This part of Long Island boasted as many Leffertses to the square mile as Boston did Adamses; but whereas all the Adamses were rebels, most of the Leffertses were Loyalists, so that a Lefferts who was a rebel was truly noteworthy.

I knew Cunningham must have chosen the Lefferts house for the prisoners because he wanted them to be tormented by the Hessians; and since I'd heard dreadful rumors of their cruelty to rebels, I feared the worst as we led our long line of unarmed, unshaven, half-clad prisoners between the tents that filled the fields on either side of the road.

The Hessians called gutturally to each other as we drew near, and came from their tents to see us go by. I didn't like their looks, al-

328

though there seemed to be nothing cruel about them. They looked heavy, slow-witted; their eyes were pale and cold. Yet they didn't look like men who would give no quarter, brutally pin defeated rebels to trees with their bayonets, or hack defenseless enemies with sabers for the mere fun of killing. Still, that's how the Hessians had behaved, according to what we'd heard from the rebels; and all three of us heaved a sigh of relief when we had herded the prisoners safely into the Lefferts house, even though it was smaller than the one they'd occupied in Bedford, and in worse condition.

The furniture, what there was of it, was smashed, doors were half off their hinges, windows broken, floors littered with broken crockery, broken bottles and all sorts of trash.

The prisoners grumbled at their filthy quarters; and Buell sided with them. "Hessians did this!" he cried. "What in God's name made King George get such pigs to help him? Look at the mess they've made! By God, if Cunningham had the decency of a catfish, he'd bring every Hessian into this house and make 'em clean the floors with their tongues!"

He was interrupted by a shout from the yard without. When I went to the door, I saw a pink-cheeked young Hessian officer, his eyes as blue as a china teacup, and his back so straight that he seemed about to topple backwards. At sight of me he spoke gutturally, as if in protest against everyone and everything.

"What's his trouble?" I asked Stedman.

"Nothing," Stedman said. "He says the rebels occupied this house before the battle—kept sharpshooters in it and made raids from it at night. He says that as soon as the rebels were driven out, a guard was stationed around the house so no further harm would be done. His men cleaned up the grounds and made 'em look decent, but the house is just as the rebels left it. He wants us to know his men weren't responsible for the damage."

The young officer saluted, turned sharply on his heel and marched away.

No provisions had been issued to the prisoners before we marched, nor were there any at the Lefferts house when we arrived; so Stedman and I scoured all of Flatbush for the provision wagon that I was sure Cunningham must have sent us. When we returned at dusk, empty-handed, the space between the road and the sentry fires outside the Lefferts house was packed with blue-coated Hessian soldiers, hundreds of them, all staring at the house as children stare at dangerous animals in a cage.

The sentries, pacing up and down behind the fires, shot uneasy glances over their shoulders at the rows of faces; and the prisoners, massed at the windows, were silent for the first time since they'd been imprisoned.

The sergeant in charge of the guard affected indifference when I questioned him about the Hessians. "They started coming here around sundown in twos and threes," he said. "They ain't done one damned thing but just stand. Stand and stare."

"Have they made any threats?"

"They ain't done a damned thing," the sergeant repeated, "except hang their jaws down so far a catbird could nest in their mouths, and stare up at those prisoners." He looked quickly over his own shoulder at the long pallid row of faces glimmering in the firelight, and added irascibly, "They ought to be taught some manners! There ain't anything so irritating as having a lot of people stare at you!"

"What did they want?" Stedman asked.

"I can't talk their lingo," the sergeant said. "Besides, they got me mad with all their staring. If they got anything to say, they ought to step up like honest men and ask permission to say it."

"They're pretty shy," Stedman said. "They're a lot like cows. I think we ought to find out what they want."

He went straight to the throng of Hessians and spoke to them sharply in their own tongue. Some of them gave him a muttered answer.

Stedman caught one of the blue-clad arms and held it up for me to see. In the man's hand was an apple. Stedman caught at two others. One held a hard biscuit, the other an apple.

"They want to feed the prisoners," Stedman said. "They want to go close up to the windows, so to see 'em better. They want to give 'em the food with their own hands."

We herded the Hessians into a double line that shuffled past the Lefferts house for two hours. Every man in that line had something that he freely gave. I marveled that men so miserably paid as the Hessians could bring themselves to part with possessions that must have seemed so important to them. I marveled, too, at the tiny scraps of food they had considered worth saving.

Soup bones, the half of a sausage, potatoes, a chicken wing, a calf's

foot, the quarter of a cabbage, apples, pears, a sheep's nose—such
were the offerings that blue-clad arm after blue-clad arm held up
toward the rebels that crowded the lower windows of the Lefferts
house; and from those open windows came reluctant laughter and
grumbling thanks.

Buell went back to the camp from which we'd started our march
across the hills to the battle of Brooklyn, got his four geese, his printing press and the rest of our belongings, and sacrificed his feathered
friends to make soup for the prisoners. He was bitter over the necessity of killing his pets to feed rebels, but he put the blame where
it belonged—on Cunningham. "I ain't going to forget this, Oliver," he
said. "Some day I'll get back at Cunningham for making me kill Old
Put, and I'll never overlook a chance to make his name a byword. I'll
try to fix it so that every man who writes on the wall of a privy will
write Cunningham's name before he writes anything else!"

God only knows to how many requisitions Buell forged Cunningham's name. I didn't ask, nor did I ask where he got the dried peas,
the turnips, the beans and the salt pork that he brought back. All I
knew was that he didn't bring enough.

The Hessians visited us daily with all the food they could spare,
but they weren't too well treated themselves; and when they'd
taken the edge off their own hunger, they hadn't much to give
away.

Only occasionally were we able to get army rations for our charges;
and all our protests to Cunningham were unavailing. His assistants
told us repeatedly and with every appearance of truthfulness that the
food had been ordered for us—had been sent, even—but must have
been waylaid by hungry enemies before it reached us.

On the second of September I started my hunt for Soame Leighton among the vessels and hulks that had been anchored in Gravesend
Bay to serve as prisons for captured sailors and for such soldier
prisoners as couldn't be accommodated on land.

Not until the thirteenth, however, did I find him, and even then I
only found out where he was; for Cunningham's vindictiveness had
almost hidden him from human sight.

I had visited the *Cantwell* hulk, the *Vigilant* hulk, the *Singapore*
hulk and the *Eagle* hulk without success; but when my boatman
rowed me under the quarter-deck of the *Canterbury* hulk, which was

nothing more than a brig whose best days had been spent in carrying rum from the West Indies, my luck changed.

The vessel was commanded, as were most of the hulks, by a gray-
haired lieutenant—one of those unfortunates without influence or
money, who would remain a lieutenant until he died of fever in
some African or West Indian port. Perhaps his trouble was over-
amiability; for when I shouted up to him that I was on the staff of
the commissary general and hunting Soame Leighton, a rebel captain,
he looked genuinely concerned.

"What was his particular sin that he should have been given the
Black Hole?"

"The Black Hole!" I said. "I think there must be some mistake.
With your permission, sir, I'll come aboard and speak with Mr.
Leighton."

The lieutenant looked even more concerned. "We've had strict
orders that no one's to speak to any prisoner who's given the Black
Hole. He hadn't the look of a desperate character when he came
aboard; but he must have been! Black Hole for the duration of the
war! Maybe the war'll be over in another month, as they say; but
if it isn't——" He raised his eyebrows and shook his head.

"May I come aboard, sir?" I asked.

"Certainly," the lieutenant said, "but there's no way I can let you
see Mr. Leighton. I'm sorry—I'm very sorry indeed; for he looked
to be a decent young man if ever I saw one."

I was sick when I had a nearer view of the *Canterbury,* for it told
me what Soame must be enduring. She was small and battered, and
she stank of bilge and rotten wood, bad food and sickness; even the
few marines and officers on her decks made her look crowded; and
I knew that if her exterior was miserable, her interior must be
purely horrible; her Black Hole a hell unspeakable.

"Sir," I said to the lieutenant, "I'm sure you'd never be a party
to unnecessary cruelty. Unless I'm greatly mistaken, that's what
this is. Won't you let me have five minutes with Mr. Leighton?"

"Unnecessary cruelty?" the lieutenant repeated. "On whose part,
may I ask?"

"Well, sir," I said, "you don't know me and I may be making a
great mistake, but the responsible person is Captain Cunningham."

The lieutenant eyed me doubtfully. "You're saying, I take it, that
Captain Cunningham is closing his eyes to the misbehavior of a subordinate."

"No, sir," I said, "I'm saying that Captain Cunningham is responsible. I'd prefer to say no more, but I give you my word of honor that your prisoner is guilty of no crime except that of irritating Captain Cunningham. Won't you let me talk to him for a few minutes, sir?"

The lieutenant stared hard at me. "A few minutes? What good would a few minutes do? You'd only sympathize with the prisoner, and he'd be more discontented with his lot. But that's neither here nor there, Mr. Wiswell. Orders are orders, and my orders are that when a man's sent to the Black Hole, no person shall hold communication with him."

"But if a prisoner's being unjustly treated——"

"Have no fear, Mr. Wiswell," the lieutenant said. "I'll look into that. I'll make inquiries at once."

"If you find I'm right," I said, "I assume you'd have no objections——"

"Objections!" the lieutenant cried. "If Leighton's been unfairly treated, you can spend all your days with him so far as I'm concerned! Come back here tomorrow, Mr. Wiswell. We'll have a glass of wine together, and perhaps your friend will join us."

Lieutenant Maynard's face, when I mounted the gangplank of the *Canterbury* on the following afternoon, told me without any words from him that Cunningham had been too much for us. He was angry, and he was regretful, too, and he voiced his thoughts as strongly as an old and timid naval lieutenant was able. "Devilish unfortunate! If I'd suspected this, you'd have seen Leighton yesterday, orders or no orders!" He put his hands beneath his coat tails and flapped them angrily.

"I might have known it," I said. "I believe there's no limit to what Cunningham will do when he hates someone."

"Oh, you're quite wrong, Mr. Wiswell," the lieutenant said. "Nobody could have been kinder than Captain Cunningham. He had nothing to do with moving Leighton from this vessel. Indeed, I've rarely seen a kinder man than Captain Cunningham."

I thought back to the days when I had first seen Cunningham calling affable greetings at us from the open door of Benjamin Thompson's office. I'd thought him kind then, too; and surely I couldn't blame a man who was still a lieutenant at the age of fifty if he too had failed to see beneath Cunningham's warm smile.

Maynard looked defiant. "I know what you're thinking," he said, "but I assure you you're wrong. I went in person to see Captain Cunningham. At first, when I mentioned Leighton's name, he didn't recall him."

"Nonsense," I said.

"No, no," Maynard said. "Not nonsense at all! You're prejudiced! He really looked quite blank at my mention of the name. He didn't remember Leighton till I reminded him that Leighton had been put in the Black Hole for the duration of the war. Then, all in a flash, it came back to him. Leighton had been guilty of insubordination and at inciting to riot—really a most serious charge in a rebel prisoner, my dear Mr. Wiswell."

"I think he was only protesting against unjust treatment," I said. "However, let that pass. Did Captain Cunningham know I'd come here to see Leighton?"

"Oh yes," Maynard said. "I told him at once that I saw no reason why you shouldn't be allowed to say a few words to Leighton if you wished." He shot a quick glance at me. "You'd assured me your desire to see him was prompted by nothing but personal friendship."

"Personal friendship only," I said. "Mr. Leighton has been my close friend and neighbor for many years. I know his brothers well. His father and mother were true friends of my own father. I know his sister. I've got to do everything in my power to make sure Soame Leighton is fairly treated."

"I see," Maynard said.

"I think I see something, too," I said. "I think perhaps Captain Cunningham gave you to understand that I was somehow plotting with Soame Leighton; that for me to see him would be somehow dangerous."

"He didn't exactly say so," Maynard admitted, "but I rather got that idea from the tone of his voice."

"Then it was Cunningham who had Soame moved from this ship," I said.

"But he gave no orders," Maynard protested. "He said nothing to me about having him moved. The orders came from headquarters. A sergeant brought them. We delivered Leighton to him for transfer."

"Do you have a copy of those orders?"

"They were verbal orders."

"What was the sergeant's regiment?"

Maynard looked unhappy. "Mr. Wiswell, a prison ship is something new for me and for all my men. In the future I'll accept no prisoners without orders, and release none without orders."

I had a gone feeling inside. "Yes," I said, "I understand. I suppose you have no way of knowing where the sergeant took Leighton?"

"No," Maynard said. "I don't know. I'm sorry, but I have no idea."

When I turned from him he put his hand upon my arm. "Won't you join me in a glass of wine, Mr. Wiswell?"

"No," I said. "Don't think I'm not grateful, but I've got to get to headquarters without loss of time."

CHAPTER XXXIX

I NEVER got to headquarters.

When I hurried back to our tent to shave and dress, Stedman and Buell were waiting for me. "Just in time," Buell said. "You'd better stay on duty if you don't want to spend the rest of your life on a prison ship yourself."

"I've laid out your things," Stedman said. "Loring wants us to go into New York."

"Into New York?" I said. "I'm not going into New York. Cunningham found out that I knew where Soame Leighton was, and he's moved him."

"Where to?" Buell asked.

"God knows," I said. "There's no record of who took him or where he was taken. I don't like it, and I'm going to headquarters to try and find out about it."

"You can't do that," Stedman said. "We're under orders. We're ordered into New York at once, and we can't go by day. If we do, the rebels'll capture us. We've got to go tonight, and that means we've got to go now."

"You don't understand," I said. "Cunningham's doing everything in his power to destroy Soame Leighton, and I've got to do what I can to stop it."

Buell took a firm grip on my coat lapel. "Don't do anything rash, Oliver. Orders are orders, and ain't to be disobeyed, even when they're senseless. You're worried about Soame Leighton; but I'd be more worried about you if you refused to carry out orders. Let *me* hunt for Soame Leighton. Maybe I'll have better luck than you would, because Cunningham won't be watching me the way he would you."

He broke off to stare at me glassily, and into his eyes came a far-away look. "Cunningham!" he whispered. "You say Cunningham found out you'd learned where Soame was. Now I wonder——"

"By God, Tom," I cried, "I believe you're right! When did these orders reach you—these orders for Stedman and me to go to New York?"

Stedman answered for him. "An hour and a half ago."

"Then Tom *is* right," I said. "It was an hour and a half ago that Soame Leighton was removed from the *Canterbury* prison ship on unwritten orders from headquarters."

"Now wait, Oliver," Buell said. "It's a coincidence. Anyway, you've got your orders, and you've got to obey 'em."

"I can see Loring and ask him to keep me on other duty, can't I? I've got to help Soame Leighton, haven't I?"

"You can't do anything for him that I can't do," Buell said. "Don't you do one damned thing to give Cunningham a hold on you! Obey your orders!"

I stared hard at Buell. He meant what he said. He was afraid of Cunningham; and that very fear of his would, I knew, bring all his ingenuity to the fore.

"I haven't even seen the orders," I said. "What are they?"

Stedman took a paper from his breast pocket. "We're to cross over to New York and make a report on warehouses, churches and public buildings that will hold all our supplies and ten thousand prisoners. Ten thousand prisoners means that Howe expects to capture nearly the whole rebel army."

"I don't like it," I said. "New York's full of Loyalists. Why doesn't the general get his information from somebody who lives in the city and knows more about it than we do?"

Buell was patient with me. "You've been around an army long enough to know generals can't do anything as easy as that. They got to have somebody to blame in case something goes wrong."

I wondered what Buell knew that I didn't. Clearly he knew something.

"I noticed one little thing about those orders," Buell said, "that maybe I wasn't supposed to notice." He took the paper from Stedman. "Listen to this: You're told what churches and what sugar houses to examine, and you're also told to go to Bushwick for a boat, and what boatman to hire, and where to land in New York, and what tavern to go to. How do you like that, Oliver?"

"I don't like it," I said. "I don't like it any better than I like the rest of the order."

"Why don't you like it?" Buell asked.

"You know very well why," I said. "The boatman might be a friend of Cunningham's. If we stay where we're told, the rebels might just possibly learn, in some mysterious way, where we're staying, and the tavern might burn down with us in it."

Buell looked relieved. "You're getting smarter every day, Oliver. Don't go near Bushwick; and when you get to New York, stay with somebody you can trust—somebody who can protect you from rebels, and get word to me if you need anything."

"How'll I find such a paragon?" I asked. "March up and down Broadway, shouting for someone who hates rebels?"

"I'm a printer, Oliver," Buell said. "Printers travel all over this country, sure of being helped wherever they go, provided there's a printer there. As far as getting help's concerned, I'd rather be a printer than a Mason. I'll send you to the printer that talked me into going to Dedham to print those broadsides that got me my coat of tar and feathers."

"What's his name?" I asked.

"Serle," Buell said. "Ambrose Serle. At the sign of the Bible and Crown in Hanover Square."

Our boatman put us ashore, late that same night, on the western side of the island near Coenties Slip. Late as it was, the streets were crowded, and we found ourselves wholly unremarked. Boston, as I had known it, was only a country town compared to New York, which was an overwhelming jumble of brick buildings, blacksmith shops, taverns, sugar houses, mansions, distilleries, churches, ship chandleries, clothing stores, jewelers, liquor dealers, goldsmiths, furriers, elegant homes and God knows what-all. The thing that struck me most about this strange city was the strange foreign names above the shop doors—Duyckinck, Bywanck, Van Dam, Brinckerhoff, Dyckman, Stuyvesant, Goelet.

We found our way to Hanover Square, but there were no lights at the address Buell had given us, so we rightly deduced that it was Serle's place of business and not his home.

We slept that night in the Province Arms on Broadway, representing ourselves to be shipbuilders from Massachusetts; and in the morning we went again to Hanover Square where, unwilling to ask questions that would show us to be strangers, we strolled around the town until the bars were removed from the door and windows of Serle's establishment.

Stedman and I were fascinated by the behavior of the people who passed through Hanover Square on their way to business. Every last one of them seemed to be in a hurry; most of them were shouting at each other: shouting about business. Their voices were harsher and louder than any I'd ever heard in Boston. They waved their hands in each other's faces, and seemed bent on outshoving each other. Many were Irish, and Stedman pointed out many others that he said were Jews—the first I'd ever seen.

Wandering among them, like louts at a fair, were rebel soldiers, recognizable as soldiers because they carried muskets, powder horns and cartridge boxes. Apart from their accouterments, they looked like the sweepings of gutters and farms. They were shambling, gangling, shifty-eyed, slovenly and, for the most part, pock-marked. Scarcely one of them, obviously, took pride in his personal appearance. Early as it was, many of these militiamen were already drunk, and went bellowing along the street, guffawing with the peculiar emptiness of brainless men.

Merchants hurrying to their work walked wide around the brawling militiamen, as they might have walked around a hog wallow; and the glances turned upon those sorry soldiers were worse than contemptuous. Not until we got in to see Serle, however, did we hear the thoughts that must have been in the heads of all those New Yorkers who had walked so warily around their defenders.

Serle was a pudgy man with a rosy face and blue eyes that stared expressionlessly at us through eight-sided spectacles. "Tom Buell sent you, did he?" he asked. "I wondered what had become of Buell. I'm surprised he's alive. He must have learned to control his tongue. I always told him he had nothing to fear if he'd only pretend to be dumb. Here in New York we've learned to talk politics as little as possible, and endure the rebels as best we can. If we did otherwise, there'd be scarcely a shop or a place of business open in the entire city. Anyone with any property would have been driven out long ago. Well, thank God we won't have to endure 'em much longer. Thanks to their pigheadedness, General Howe can take the city and the whole rebel army as soon as he makes up his mind to do it."

He looked at me speculatively. "How do you account for the general's slowness, Mr. Wiswell? Why doesn't he attack? Almost every printing press outside of New England is in this city, but we can't use 'em to get our case before the people until the rebels are driven out. Every rebel press in the country is pouring out lies at top speed, and we can't do anything about it. What's the matter with Howe?"

"I don't know, Mr. Serle," I said. "His own officers ask the same question, but there's no satisfactory answer."

Serle, his pudgy hands folded across his hard, round stomach, eyed us moodily. "Somebody'd better find an answer to it, or these damned rascals of Washington's won't let us live, much less carry on our trades. They're more like animals than men. A woman isn't safe on the street with these militiamen running loose. They steal, burn, rape, kill; and we can't lift a hand to protect ourselves! And now you and Mr. Stedman have been sent over here to hunt for our nicest jails and storehouses! That sounds to me as though General Howe expected the war to continue for some little time to come. What's he trying to do: turn this country over to the riffraff—to the most senseless, uneducated, intolerant good-for-nothings in the colonies?"

"Buell thinks your troubles'll be over in a week," I said. "Howe's a good general, and his men all say the rebels haven't a chance against him."

Serle's reply was irascible. "If he's so good, why in God's name doesn't he finish what he sets out to do? Good God, Mr. Wiswell, you wouldn't let the best barber in the world cut your hair if he left it half cut, would you?"

When Stedman and I were silent, Serle jumped from his chair, went to the paneled wall of the room in which we sat, and snapped a catch. The panels broke into small doors, and beyond them we saw the shining wheels and levers of a printing press.

"Look at that!" Serle said. "That's the finest press in New York, and it's got to stand idle when America needs it most! It's stood idle for two whole years, instead of running day and night to tell the people of this country all the silly reasons that are pushing us into war; to tell 'em who the lying politicians are that are keeping us there; to tell 'em how they're being ruined by a Congress that knows less about government than my cat; to tell 'em their chuckleheaded generals lack the ability to make a platoon of infantry order arms; to tell 'em their militia regiments run like rabbits whenever a gun goes off; to publish the facts about the thousands of decent Americans who've been mobbed and manhandled because they dared to stand up for what they knew to be right . . ."

Stedman interrupted him. "Mr. Serle, Mr. Wiswell and I are Americans and need help. Both of us were driven from our homes by the rebels. My father was a justice of the supreme court of Pennsylvania. He was driven to England. Mr. Wiswell's had to go to Halifax with Howe. He died on the way. Will you help us?"

Serle passed a shaking hand across his forehead. "Of course," he said. "You'll have to pardon my irritability. We find this waiting very disturbing. Now let me see: your commissary wants quarters for ten thousand prisoners, does he? Well, if I were you I'd look first at such buildings as King's College, the Brick Church, the North Dutch Church, the Scotch Church on Cedar Street, and the Friends' Meeting House on Liberty Street. And of course you mustn't overlook the sugar houses. They're the biggest, and I'd say they were the best, for your purposes—Van Cortlandt's, Rhinelander's and the Liberty Street Sugar House. You'd better start on Liberty Street. You can get damned near the whole American army in that Sugar House."

It was at the Liberty Street Sugar House that the rebels tried to catch us.

Probably I couldn't have proved in a court of law that Cunningham had lodged information about us with the rebels; but there's no question that Cunningham did it. He hated me, and he hated Stedman; and as I shall show, there was no limit to Cunningham's cruelty toward those he disliked.

The rebels had found out that there would be two of us looking at sugar houses; they had been told how we were dressed; how we looked; they had been instructed that of the two of us, I was the one whose capture was most essential—and from whom could they have got that information, if not from Cunningham?

Even now I can hear their voices bawling within a foot of my hiding place. "The other one," they called me. I was damned as a torturer of prisoners; as a "murdering Tory". Ah yes: their information came straight from Cunningham!

I never saw a gloomier building than the Liberty Street Sugar House. Its stone walls were a dirty gray, and the windows in all of its five stories were small and deep-set, with something of the look of cavernous, malevolent eyes. Its only entrance was an arched door large enough for a wagon loaded with sugar hogsheads to pass through it; and a high stockade of closely fitted hewn timbers enclosed every portion of this gaunt structure except the entrance.

We halted on the opposite side of the street and did our best to estimate the floor space of that unprepossessing place. There was a surprising amount of activity around it. The heads of two horses protruded from the entrance, and we knew that behind them a wagon was being loaded with sugar barrels. On either side of the arch stood an attendant, and in the street a dozen idlers watched the motionless horses with the vacant stares peculiar to city folk when they view the activities of others.

"Those walls are three feet thick," Stedman said, "and that building must be sixty by eighty. I'd say that ought to take care of fifty prisoners on each floor if they weren't overcrowded. That's a window for every three and a half men. In hot weather almost every prisoner could get close to a window if he wanted to."

"They'll sleep on the floor," I reminded him. "What do you suppose the floors are made of? How many partitions on each floor?"

"We've got to find out," Stedman said. "I'll find out about this place and you go on to the Friends' Meeting House."

"We'd better go together," I said.

"Nonsense," Stedman said. "We've got thirty places to see, and the sooner we do it, the sooner we can get away. I don't like the feel of the city or the looks of the people. You wait at the Meeting House for me, and I'll come there as soon as I look inside this cave."

I could see he was on edge, and I knew I was. I didn't like what we were doing, not only because I considered it unnecessary, but because I had a peculiar prickly feeling behind my ears, as though I were being watched and followed.

"Don't waste time," I told him, "and don't put anything down on paper."

I left Stedman and set off for the Friends' Meeting House. Its stumpy, brick spire was a hundred yards away; and as I approached it, I looked back at the idlers who stood before the Sugar House. Three of them had turned to look after me. In their faces I saw doubt and indecision, but no vacancy.

I stopped and faced them. As I did so, two more idlers turned to look at Stedman. Five of them were looking at him: looking from him to me and back to him again.

I tried to have orderly thoughts about those five staring faces, but a sort of numbness prevented me from thinking about anything. I found myself repeating again and again "Friends' Meeting House: Friends' Meeting House"—found myself, too, quickening my steps to reach the shelter of that squat brick spire—hurrying with tensed muscles; with ears strained for unusual sounds behind me.

I heard them all too soon, and from Stedman. He was shouting, and of course his shouts were intended for me. "There's some mistake!" he cried. "There's some mistake!"

I shot a quick glance over my shoulder. Stedman, his arms wildly flailing, was the center of a group of those who a moment before had been seemingly idle onlookers before the Sugar House. The other half-dozen of those onlookers were running toward me as fast as they could run, their faces no longer even doubtful, but angry and determined.

Stedman's case, I saw, was hopeless; and I feared that my own was nearly so. I ran as I had never run before; and as I ran I looked desperately about me for a sanctuary. From my pursuers then came shouts of "Spy! Spy!"

On my left was a narrow, curving street walled with narrow brick houses. I bolted into it and immediately turned again to dart into a passageway between two houses. What I'd find at the end, I didn't know. All I wanted to do was to keep clear of those six men behind me—those six men who were bound to be just such men as those who tarred and feathered Tom Buell; as those who slashed out the tongue of the mare so unfortunate as to belong to a man who opposed them politically; as those who drove the Loyalists of Long Island into the swamps; as those who had destroyed government, law and order in every province of America.

The alley, to my consternation, came to an abrupt end between eight-foot brick walls, above the tops of which rose the tips of weedy hawthorns. In each wall was a green gate. I tried the one on my left. It was locked. I turned desperately to the one on my right. It, too, was locked. When I threw my weight against it, it seemed as solid as the brick wall itself.

In the street at the mouth of the alley, a dozen voices bawled, "Spy! Spy!"

Desperation gave me an agility I didn't know I had. I leaped up, caught the coping of the wall, felt a finger gashed to the bone by broken glass, swung myself somehow to the top and somehow rolled across a coping studded with jagged fragments of bottles. With a crashing that to me seemed thunderous, I tumbled into thorny branches, and broke through them to the ground.

The shouts of, "Spy! Spy!" were loud in the alley. On hands and knees I crawled out from the hawthorns. Blood was running from a dozen cuts in my hands; my coat, waistcoat and breeches were slashed as by knives.

I was in a small yard with no outlets save the gate I had vainly tried to open, and a green door at the rear of the house.

With shouts of, "Spy! Spy! Spy! Spy!" echoing in my ears, I had no choice. I ran up the steps to the green door and wrenched at the latch with bloody fingers. The door moved spongily, and I knew it was being held against me.

"Spy! Spy!" the voices shouted. The loudest voice bellowed, "Over both walls! Climb 'em both! He's behind one of 'em!"

Heaven only knows from what source a man draws strength in the hour of dire need. All I know is that when I heard that harsh voice ordering men to scale the wall over which I had just climbed, I pushed back the door as easily as I'd open a cupboard in my own home and fell in a heap at the feet of the four persons who had tried to hold it shut.

CHAPTER XL

Whendsfin I got to my feet, I looked into the horrified faces of an enormously fat Negro woman and two plump ladies who were not, as we say in Milton, as young as they had once been. Beside them was a frail, pale young man, strikingly similar to the two ladies, except that he was concave where they were convex.

The hallway smelled faintly of old upholstery, dried rose leaves and burnt cloves; and the shouts of the angry men outside were a defilement.

The young man caught my wrist and turned my hand to look at the palm. "Euphrosyne," he said, "get a damp cloth. When I go out, wipe off the door handle on the outside. It'll be bloody. Wipe the carpet, too."

The black woman lumbered from the hallway, and almost immediately surged back like a dark storm cloud.

To his sisters the young man added, "If they come in, put him in the laundry chute."

With that he opened the door through which I had entered and stood in the middle of the small, brick-walled yard, his face a study in pure bewilderment and vacuity. The black woman, groaning faintly, wiped quickly at the latch on which my bloody hands had rested.

The ladies looked at each other. "Balsam of Peru," one of them said. "I'll get it, darling."

"Yes, dearest," the other said, "and clean rags. I'll take him to the laundry chute."

They both paused, listening, each with a hand upon my arm.

"What's all this?" the pale, frail man asked querulously. "Can't a man write letters in peace without people leaping in and out of his

345

back yard like confounded jumping jacks? By Gad, sir, I demand an explanation! Who was that man? What had he done?"

"Didn't he go in this house?" an angry voice asked. I knew its owner was staring down into the yard from the top of the brick wall.

"This house!" my host cried. "He most assuredly did *not!* He came over that wall into the yard and went out over the other wall. Could he have been a Tory?"

"A murdering Tory spy!" the voice shouted. "Open the gate and let us through your yard."

"I will indeed," I heard my benefactor say. There was the sound of a bolt being shot. "Come in, come in, and here's a ladder!"

I heard no more, for the two ladies hurried me to a narrow flight of stairs and pushed me up them into a room where the distant shouts of my pursuers reached me only dimly. Here the two kind ladies, whom I knew only as "Dearest" and "Darling", bandaged my hands and shook their heads over the gashes in my clothes.

When their brother came in, he fingered the slits in my breeches and waistcoat. "Where else are you hurt besides your hands?" he asked.

"Nowhere, much," I said. Then, as he seemed content to stand and watch his sisters rub ointment on me, I added, "What that man said wasn't true. I'm not a murderer and I'm not a spy."

The man raised his eyebrows. "He also called you a Tory."

My narrow escape had made me irritable. "Tory! What in God's name does it mean, anyway! Any man who runs contrary to the wishes of the mob is called a Tory! Anybody who wants to see this country at peace again instead of divided and wrecked by a civil war is called a Tory! Every man of property who doesn't talk publicly like a hypocrite and an idiot is called a Tory! What if he *did* call me a Tory?"

"Nothing," the man said. "Nothing at all. I knew as soon as you jumped over the wall that you weren't a rebel." He looked me up and down. "They had a perfect description of you. How'd that happen?"

"I'm not sure," I said. "Did they mention Stedman—the man who was with me—the man they caught?"

"Yes," the man said, "they spoke of him, but it was you they wanted most. They didn't know your name. They called you 'the other one'." He opened his lips to say more; then seemed to think better of it.

"Did they say what they'd do with Stedman?" I asked.

His eye wavered. "It wouldn't be for them to say, would it? That would be a matter for a court-martial, I fancy."

"Tell me the truth," I begged him.

He looked distressed. "Well, they said they were going to hang him. They said he'd be hanged as a rebel."

"So he is," I said. "A rebel against intolerance and brutality, just as any lawyer, any son of a supreme court judge, would have to be!"

"So it's *that* Stedman, is it?" he asked. "Alexander Stedman's son! I thought the name sounded familiar. My name is Vardill, of the faculty of King's College. Professor of jurisprudence."

"Then my name may be familiar to you too," I said. "It's Wiswell. I'm from Milton. My father——"

"Your father's Seaton Wiswell! Well, well!"

When I'd have told him more, my throat seemed suddenly constricted by bands of steel, and for the life of me I couldn't say a word.

"Well, well!" Vardill repeated hastily. "I'll take you to a room where you'll be safe, and we'll have off those clothes of yours. That glass must have cut you, Mr. Wiswell."

"I can't stay here," I said. "I've got to help Stedman. They can't hang him!"

"Yes, they can," Vardill said. "What's more, they'll hang you twice as quick! You're the one they're after. If you so much as make an attempt to get to Stedman, you're signing your own death warrant. You'd be as conspicuous with your bandaged hands as a militiaman in a satin coat. As long as they haven't caught you, they'll probably keep Stedman alive as bait."

"You're right," I said. "I won't try to see Stedman. I'll go back to Long Island and see Howe."

"You'll do nothing of the sort," Vardill said. "I'll arrange to have a message carried to Howe about your friend, but you'll stay here till you can go out on the street in safety—safety to you, and to us too. Nobody in this house can afford to take chances. It's true I took something of a chance when I helped you just now; but I knew I could hide you. But if you should go out and be captured, every man who chased you into my back yard would know I'd helped you. I've been skating on thin ice for a long time. If it gets much thinner, I don't like to think what'll happen to us."

One of Vardill's sisters placed her hand upon my arm. "They'll burn our house," she said. "They'll drive us into New Jersey; stone us, the way they did Mrs. Van Zandt and the Laidlaws!"

The other sister quietly added, "And the Hattons and Blakes and Pfeisters and Trents and Delanes."

"I can't let you send a message to Howe about me," I said.

"That's better," Vardill said. "All I want you to do is stay quietly here. You needn't worry about me. I know enough to do what every man ought to do in wartime when he's watched and threatened by bullies. I conceal my feelings; lie whenever necessary; pretend to admire the rascals who've ruined our city and our country; cheer dolts, bullies and knaves and damn all wise and temperate men!" He mincingly lifted his voice. "Hurrah for Sam Adams! Hurrah for General Lee! Hurrah, hurrah, hurrah for Liberty and Congress!"

He patted my shoulder and his voice became normal. "Don't worry, Mr. Wiswell. Two thirds of those in this city hate the rebels, and what they stand for, and the misery and fear and lawlessness they've brought upon us. Two thirds of 'em! We've all escaped by doing exactly the same things. Those who haven't done them—those who've been such fools as to speak their minds about the armed mobs that call themselves Patriots—are homeless wanderers like my cousin John."

One of his sisters fumbled for a handkerchief in the pocket of her bombazine skirt. The other turned and went quickly from the room.

"Well," Vardill said wearily, "it's the truth. John was a fool, in spite of all his brilliance. Mr. Wiswell, I hope you'll learn from John's experience. There was no more brilliant man in America than John Vardill. He was made rector of King's Chapel when he was twenty-one; and because he told the truth about the rebels, they'd kill him if he dared set foot in America. I hope we'll be rid of them before we're many days older; but if we aren't, never let one of 'em hear what you really think! This isn't a free country while they're at large in it; and there's nothing too horrible for them to do to you or me or any of us for daring to see 'em as they really are. That's why you mustn't try to help Stedman. It's a dreadful thing for a country to lose such men as my cousin, your father, Stedman's father and all the other thousands that have been driven into hiding by these fanatics who think they're patriots. There's nothing I won't do to keep more from being driven out. You'll stay in this house till your wounds are healed; and I hope by that time we'll have our country back again."

I wish Doctor Vardill might have been right; but never in his wildest imaginings could he have dreamed how wrong he was.

He put me to bed in a dark and quiet little room in the attic—a room to which I mounted by a ladder. Beside my bed he placed a suit that had belonged to his cousin, John Vardill; and when he left me, he made me pull up the ladder and close a trap door, so I'd run no risk of discovery.

I'd like to have known, as he bade me good night in his pleasant, weary voice, that I'd never again see him alive. I'd have tried to thank him for what he'd done for me and for Stedman. Like a fool—a New England fool—I hadn't instantly voiced my gratitude, but had planned to show my gratitude to him and his sisters when the war was over. Always, after that, I tried to voice my gratitude without delay whenever I had occasion to be grateful.

It was noon when Doctor Vardill left me. When I'd cleaned the slashes made on my stomach by the broken bottles, and eaten the cheese and pumpkin pie Doctor Vardill had left beside my cot, I felt as though I'd been without sleep for years. A pencil of sunlight stabbed like a golden blade into the gloom of my attic chamber, and even as I wondered how long it would be before the dust motes ceased their whirling in that shining beam, I fell asleep.

I woke sitting breathlessly upright. The golden ray stretched straight across the room, so I knew the sun was sinking; and in that ray the motes danced crazily.

I knew at once what had wakened me; for my bed shook, the dust motes jerked and the air in the attic beat against my face as on the day when my father, Andrew, Tom Buell and I had looked from our window on Sudbury Street, seen General Howe lead his men against the fort on Bunker Hill, and felt the concussion of the cannon in our ears.

The crash of distant guns swelled to a tumult that I knew to be the rolling boom of a ship's broadside. It was joined by another and another; and in between those thunderous volleys there were nearer, angrier crashings that must, I was sure, be the great guns in New York's forts.

I rolled stiffly from my narrow bed and pulled on John Vardill's clothes. I was slow and awkward at it, because my hands were swollen and painful.

I was fumbling with the buttons of the waistcoat when a deafening, snarling squeal burst into the attic chamber; and in the same instant the floor leaped beneath my feet. The wall fluttered like wind-blown bunting, and somewhere below there was a crash that wedged my heart into my throat. The air all about me was so filled with dust that the pencil of golden sunlight became a silvery shadow.

When the floor didn't fall from under me I groped for the trap door, raised it and listened.

The great guns still boomed; but after the shattering crash I had heard, they sounded harmless.

Somewhere outside the house I heard a child crying, dogs barking, the sound of running feet. The house itself was silent, except for a queer scraping sound, as though a clock's pendulum, in its swinging, dragged briefly against a gritty surface. There was something about it that made my knees weak.

I felt for the ladder, lowered it through the trap door, and scrambled down to the hallway below. Pictures had fallen from the walls; chairs and stair rail were covered with gray dust.

I shouted Doctor Vardill's name; then listened. All I heard was the banging of the guns, a distant hoarse shouting, and the noise of hurrying feet.

I ran down the stairs to the second floor. Clogging the stairway to the lowest floor was a heap of fallen timbers, dusted thick with powdered plaster. Jagged chunks of plaster lay among them; and splintered laths protruded from the tangled mass like broken bones.

When I crawled over the wreckage and reached the street floor, I seemed to be in a house no longer, but in the center of a rubbish heap, onto which had been dumped the shattered remains of a dozen houses.

I called Doctor Vardill's name softly, but heard nothing except the faint rustling of crumpled plaster slipping to another level.

I found them in the rear of the house, in what must have once been the dining room. The scraping sound I had heard before I left the attic had been made by the doctor's foot as he tried to free himself from the mass of sooty bricks and mortar that held him to the floor. His sisters had been swept from their seats by a single balk of timber. Like a giant flail, it had crushed them against the wall.

When I pried the timber away from the two women, they sank down together on the plaster-strewn floor as though they'd chosen that place to sleep.

I tried to move the bricks from Doctor Vardill, but couldn't. He was beyond human help, anyway; for his wide-open eyes were covered with plaster dust.

I went into the kitchen to look for the fat Negress, Euphrosyne. She was sitting on the floor, her face gray with powdered plaster. There was no mark upon her that I could see. I think she died of fright.

There was nothing I could do in that house, so I went into the back yard, opened the gate that I had found locked that very morning, and went out into the alley into which I had run to escape the six rebels. It was empty.

Far, far away the guns banged and banged.

I went to the mouth of the alley. A man and a woman ran past me. The man had a child under one arm, and over his shoulder a bundle tied in a sheet. The woman held another child. I ran after them into Liberty Street. In both directions I could see people running, and they were all running one way—north. Nobody paid any attention to me, so I started running myself, toward Hanover Square and Ambrose Serle's house.

CHAPTER XLI

NEW YORK, that night, was still guarded by rebel forts, and the rebel army continued to occupy it; but it was a city helpless and without a brain—a tumultuous, hysterical collection of people who stole, drank, fought, looted, fled for their lives, or hid themselves behind barred shutters and waited tremblingly or hopefully for what the morrow would bring.

Ambrose Serle was one of the latter. When I pounded on his door, the house was dark: not so much as a pinhead of light showed at any of the windows; but when, after I'd been scrutinized and questioned through a peephole and cautiously admitted, I found every room lighted as if for a wedding.

The main room was crowded with Serle's friends; the folding panels before the glistening printing press stood wide open, and bowls of flip decorated all the tables. The company into which I came was noisy and hilarious, but at my entrance the guests were suddenly silent.

Serle, who had been busy at his printing press, pushed his way through his guests and came to me, his face incredulous. "What happened?" He waved an oily hand to the others. "This gentleman's all right. He's one of us. He crossed from Long Island last night to look for places to store supplies and rebels—mostly rebels. Mr. Oliver Wiswell of Milton."

The men around us came closer. Someone handed me a glass of flip, and when I downed it, a dozen others were held toward me.

"What happened?" Serle asked again. "Where's Stedman?"

"I don't know," I said. "They were waiting for us, and they caught Stedman. Do you know what they'd do with him?"

Serle took my wrist and examined my bandaged hand. "Are you badly hurt?"

I shook my head. "Do you know where they'd put Stedman?"

"Probably in the New Prison," Serle said; "but they won't keep him there long. It's almost over now, my boy. The ships are past the forts. There's a fleet on both sides of the island. Howe intends to attack tomorrow, and when he does, we'll be rid of the rebels for good."

"Can't anything be done for Stedman?" I asked.

"There's no need," Serle said. "Sooner or later every rebel in this city will try to run for safety. Generals, colonels, captains, sentries and privates—they'll all run for dear life, and Stedman'll be as free as air."

He told the exact truth.

His friends, all men of substance and position, went back to their flip-drinking, hilarity and planning. Some of them, before the rebel army had poured into New York like a plague of human locusts, had been judges and city officials. Now they were planning to publish newspapers, re-open the courts, establish a police force and enlist the eager Loyalists of the city into American regiments, officered by Americans.

Their faces, moist with perspiration because of the stifling heat in that heavily shuttered room, shone with eagerness; but it was an eagerness that left me unmoved. The gabble of their voices seemed to surround me like a prickly and irritating shell of sound that scraped and scratched at my own unhappy thoughts.

I felt that nothing in this damnable war could ever be anything but hopeless discouragement, wasted effort, death and destruction, mismanagement and ruin. What did I care that Howe's frigates had sailed up the East River and penned the rebels in New York? I'd seen Howe pen up rebels before. Nothing, I knew, could ever go right for me again—nothing. I was doomed to go on and on, on and on, an unwilling participant in disaster after disaster until I went down myself beneath accumulated disasters, as Doctor Vardill and his sisters had gone down before the guns of those who, in trying to save them, had destroyed them.

My gorge rose at the miserable futility of this war and at the unbelievable stupidity of the fools who refused to let it end—at the five insignificant human beings who had sat together in a room on Staten

Island and blunderingly failed or stubbornly refused to find a way to put an end to all this misery and cruelty and waste and destruction.

If only those five human atoms who had sat together in a stuffy room could have been gifted with as much tolerance and understanding as there is in a hive of bees, this land of ours would have brought forth wealth and health and civilization instead of hatred, civil war and death.

I thought of all the wars of which I'd read, and clearly saw at last that not one of them—not one—had brought one solitary benefit that couldn't have been attained by peaceful means if only those who fought had been content to wait—had been wise enough to make the concessions that all human beings must make if they're to live in amity.

Every nerve in my body seemed to quiver at the thought of more delay and more uncertainty—of even waiting until tomorrow for Howe to bottle up the rebel army in New York, and end the war; at waiting until tomorrow to see Buell and find out what was happening to Soame Leighton; at waiting and waiting, perhaps forever, to see Sally Leighton; at waiting even one more hour to find out what the rebels had done with Stedman.

Thanks to the panic of the rebels, I didn't even have to wait that long to find out about Stedman. He pounded on Serle's door in half an hour, and I heard his voice impatiently asking, "What happened to Wiswell?"

When he came into the room and saw me, he coughed and pretended he knew no harm could have come to me; but I knew how he felt; for my own relief at seeing him safe again made me almost speechless.

He needed no coaxing to tell his experiences, for he still burned with resentment at the treatment he'd had from the rebels.

Soon after the British ships sailed up the river, Stedman said, the rebel guards and sentries at the New Prison had left their posts— probably to rejoin their regiments. When the prisoners had found themselves unguarded, they produced saws, ropes and iron bars from hiding places, opened every door in the prison, and left it almost as empty as the day it was built. The fleas and bedbugs, Stedman said, still remained, but every human made himself scarce. And every man who had been imprisoned there, he concluded, burned with a desire to get his fingers on a musket and let daylight into the rebels.

He turned to Serle. "How far up the East River did those warships go?"

Serle scratched his ear. "Kip's Bay, we heard."

Stedman's face reddened. "But that's only halfway up the island," he protested. Then he grew calmer. "Probably they stopped on account of darkness. No doubt they'll move on up at daybreak."

"How were you treated?" Serle asked.

"The same as all the rest!" Stedman said. "Bread once a day, made from clay and ground birdseed, with just a few sweepings from under a flour mill. The meat was horse that died of old age or worse. For amusements, a court-martial, the judges mostly unable to read or write, and the prisoners forbidden to speak in their own defense. I was found guilty of being a rebel."

"A rebel!" Serle cried. "You a rebel! A rebel against what?"

"Against Congress," Stedman said.

"Upon my word," Serle said, "that's amusing! Being rebels themselves, they bitterly resent being called rebels, and so apply that name to persons who are loyal! That's damned amusing!"

"I tried to see it that way," Stedman said, "but I wasn't overly successful. I was sentenced to be shot tomorrow."

Everyone in the room stared at him. Stedman looked thoughtfully at his hand, as if he'd never seen it before.

"Did it seem to you, Mr. Stedman," one of his hearers asked, "that your fellow prisoners would make capable soldiers?"

The man who spoke was tall, slender and a little stooped, and had what I can only describe as a good face—one which radiated benevolence and refinement. Even the careless richness of his clothes seemed to be a reflection of his inner self.

Stedman looked doubtful. "What's your reason for asking?"

Serle spoke up hastily. "This is Mr. John Harris Cruger. Mr. Cruger's father-in-law, Mr. Oliver DeLancey, is thinking of raising and leading a regiment of Loyalists, provided he's satisfied the men will fight."

"Mr. Cruger," Stedman said earnestly, "three of the men in that prison were Germans from near the Mohawk River. I speak German, and I was the only one they could talk to. I could raise two hundred of those Germans in two days, Mr. Cruger; and it wouldn't make any difference to them how fast rebel militia ran. They could catch up with the fastest of 'em and pull 'em to pieces with their bare hands."

"That's interesting," Cruger said. "Properly disciplined, such men could be extremely valuable." He turned to me. "What's been your experience with Loyalists, Mr. Wiswell? Do you think you'd have difficulty raising a regiment?"

I didn't know then that there was no man in America whose social standing was superior to that of John Harris Cruger, or that the resources of his family—including that of his father-in-law, Oliver DeLancey—were more extensive than that of many a European prince. I only knew that he was a man of extraordinary sympathy and understanding, that he poignantly reminded me of my father, and that I was instantly at ease with him, as eager to share my knowledge with him as though I'd known him all my life.

"You'd have no difficulty raising ten regiments among the men I've seen," I said. "I saw two companies of New York Volunteers come into Halifax. They'd been badly treated, Mr. Cruger. They'd been idle for five months, and the red tape of the British made it impossible for them to get clothes. They were nearly naked, and physically ill from insufficient food and exposure; but they fought like wildcats at the battle of Long Island. No rebel force twice their numbers could have stood against them."

Cruger seemed to find my enthusiasm pleasing. "I can readily understand their eagerness to come to grips with the rebels. It would be a gratifying experience to lead such men into battle and direct their energies."

"Yes, sir," I said, "and if you should take the men I saw hiding from the rebels in the Long Island swamps, and give them a chance to fight, you'd have your hands full directing their energies. Those men have lived through so much already—persecution, starvation, fever, disappointments—that they'll be hard to kill. I'm bound to tell you, though, that anyone who proposes to raise a regiment of Loyalists ought to make sure he can properly equip 'em before Howe orders 'em into battle."

I became conscious that Serle and his friends were staring at the floor, at the ceiling. They didn't believe me. They hadn't seen those New York Loyalists lined up naked on the dock at Halifax. They hadn't seen the incredible stupidity of Howe, or seethed with rage at the blind folly responsible for putting such a man in command of an army and leaving him there.

I would have said more, but Cruger's warm voice stopped me. "I'll remember what you say, Mr. Wiswell, and I'm grateful to you for speaking so frankly. It's possible, of course, that after tomorrow there'll be no need for Loyalist regiments. I have a farm in Bloomingdale, from which the rebels have been kind enough to banish me, and tomorrow I hope to see the rebels walk into a trap somewhere in that neighborhood. If you and Mr. Stedman would care to drive out that way with me, early tomorrow morning, I'd consider it a privilege."

I had the feeling, not uncommon at the beginning of those rare relationships known as friendships, that in a few short minutes an intangible and unbreakable bond had grown between Cruger and myself.

The next morning, the fifteenth of September—the day Howe's army crossed the East River from Long Island and landed at Kip's Bay near the foot of Murray Hill—is one of the dates that will live forever in my memory, as will the seventeenth of June, when Howe failed to follow up his victory at Bunker Hill, and the twenty-seventh of August, when he stayed his hand at a moment when he might have captured Washington and all the rebel leaders, and wholly destroyed the beaten rebel army.

Cruger came for us at six in the morning, in a spidery-looking carriage drawn by a beautiful dappled-gray mare and driven by a proud-looking white-haired Negro in gray smallclothes and a gray beaver hat. To the back of the carriage was tied another dappled-gray mare, evidently a saddle horse.

Cruger had the simple frankness so often found in men of great wealth, great power or great ability. I think he saw that the elegance of his equipage embarrassed us, for he explained that he wanted us to be comfortable as long as possible. "Let's enjoy it while we can," he said. "We may not have it long. Anyway, I want to talk to you, so we'll drive as far as we can; then I'll go ahead on the saddle horse and you can ride back in the carriage."

He had a map with him, and on it he showed us what he expected Howe to do. He had a mind that saw a military action in the smallest detail; and as he explained the trap into which the rebels, by their stupidity, had again got themselves, my confidence, that had sunk so low the night before, again rose high.

With warships anchored in the Hudson and the East River, on both sides of New York island, to prevent the rebels from escaping by water, Howe needed only to send his regiments in barges up the East River to Kingsbridge, where a creek separated New York island from the mainland. Once Howe's troops had landed at Kingsbridge, the rebels would be cooped up on the island. Howe's men could form an unbreakable cordon from the Hudson to the East River, move slowly southward toward the lower tip of the island, and capture every fort, gun, officer and regiment within that enormous trap.

All the people in New York seemed to be on the main road leading northward—the road on the high land, midway between the two rivers. Some, we were certain, were rebel sympathizers fleeing in carts and carryalls from the inevitable capture of the city by Howe's army; but by far the greater number were Loyalists, joyously traveling out to see the discomfiture of those who for years had threatened them with the loss of their homes, property and country.

Whatever their sympathies, every last one was adrip with perspiration; for the breeze, what there was of it, was fiery hot, and the sun like molten brass in a pallid sky.

To our right the waters of the East River were inviting; and if we could, we'd have moved down to the shore road to take advantage of the little breath of coolness that always rises from open water; but there were forts all along that shore road—forts around which distant small figures moved fumblingly, as bees grope upon the board at the entrance of a hive.

At all crossroads stood sentries, counterparts of the prisoners we had captured by hundreds at the battle of Long Island: shambling, dejected-looking, badly clothed, unkempt, unsoldierly. They blocked every attempt to move from the inland road down to the shore, and with peremptory head-jerkings and thumb-pointings motioned all of us to stay on the upper road.

At Murray Hill, less than an hour from Serle's house, Cruger called a halt. The place filled me with homesickness, for it was Milton Hill in miniature. The farmhouse on its highest point was high and square, with white columns like those on Governor Hutchinson's house; and the easterly slope of the hill was rolling land, set off with stone walls into orchards and cornfields, and bounded at the foot by the blue waters of the East River. From our own house in Milton we had looked across the Neponset River to Boston just as I now looked across the East River to the tip of Long Island—though I'm bound to say that those New York fields and shores looked dull and flat to one who had known the rolling meadows of Massachusetts.

Kip's Bay was like a symmetrical blue stage at the end of the long hillslope, and ranged across the mouth of the bay were five warships, almost as though a stage manager had placed them there to mark entrances for a drama.

Cruger seated himself in the shade of an apple tree, a little below the farmhouse and the upper road on which it stood. "We couldn't find a better place to stop," he said. "This hill's the highest land between the Bowery and Kingsbridge, so if Howe moves his men across from Long Island, we can see him almost as soon as he starts, and keep abreast of him wherever he goes."

Cruger, however, couldn't sit still. In spite of the sweltering heat he moved about the orchard, eyeing the bay unhappily. "Those warships shouldn't anchor here," he complained. "They ought to go twelve miles farther north, abreast of Kingsbridge."

"Perhaps they're more useful here," I said. "Suppose Howe's troops start up-river in boats. All these forts will fire at them; and if the forts aren't attacked in turn, they might destroy the boats."

"Not if the boats stay on the far side of the river," Cruger said. "There isn't a rebel gunner that could hit anything at such a distance. And what if the breeze should fail? Not one of those five warships could move an inch to help Howe, and he'd have to go all the way up-river without any support at all. It's strange, but these professional commanders seem incapable of using ordinary common sense! Look at all the rebel regiments left by rebel commanders on an island where they're bound to be caught! Look at all these warships, anchored where they oughtn't to be! I can't believe these commanders understand war! I think they're fighting as most men eat: without plan or foresight."

My dark forebodings of the previous night again possessed me. "Perhaps," I said, "Howe's going to land right here in this bay."

Stedman nodded. "I believe he is! I believe he's figured he needn't go all the way to the northern end of the island in order to capture the southern tip of it. Since he only wants the city, why shouldn't he land right here at Kip's Bay?"

Cruger looked amused. "You don't really think, Mr. Stedman, that Howe would rather take New York than destroy the rebel army!"

"That's exactly what I think," Stedman said. "Oliver and I have seen him fight before. Either he doesn't know what the true objective of a soldier is, or he thinks he can frighten the rebels into submission by taking America's largest city and making faces at them."

Cruger sighed. "Dear me, dear me! Soldiers ought to be forced by law to read Caesar. Then they'd know that no battle is really won unless the enemy force is destroyed or made wholly useless. They'd also know that it's essential, in war, to move fast."

"Howe wouldn't," Stedman said.

Cruger was silent. We watched people hurrying along the dusty road behind us—laughing people, apprehensive people, people who shouted and sang in gay anticipation of what the day would bring forth. Many of them came down from the road into the meadow in which we sat, until the fields were dotted thick with groups that stared and stared across the blue strip of water before us toward Long Island.

The morning was two-thirds gone when Cruger pointed across the river. The tip of a distant green point that jutted into that satiny blue water seemed to have bloomed into a rosy flower. The flower grew and grew, as if beneath a wizard's wand; magically turned into boats, laden with scarlet-coated soldiers—boats that came out and came out endlessly from behind a small headland, and flowed along that distant shore like a widening splotch of blood.

I was conscious of movement all around me among the other groups upon the hillslope; of faint, far cries from the forts along the shore road. They made a sort of frame for the silence that had shut down over the green hillslopes—a silence through which the monotonous shrill chirp of crickets struck painfully upon my ear.

There was no end to those scarlet-laden boats. We could see their oar blades shimmering in the hot sunlight. There seemed to be thousands of them.

"All those men!" Cruger said unhappily. "All those regiments, obliged to carry out orders that mean nothing! I wish——"

We never knew what he wished. Flame and smoke jetted from the sides of the five warships in the mouth of the little bay beneath us. The stillness of that Sunday morning ended in overwhelming thunder—a sustained and universal crashing that drove hot gusts of air against our eyeballs and set the flesh to crawling beneath our clothes.

Above the deafening roar of the guns I heard sharp and piercing wailings, unearthly squeals; recognized them, as I moved with

Cruger and Stedman to the shelter of a stone wall, as the sound of ricocheting cannon balls.

Spouts of foam and earth gushed from the edge of the bay beneath us. The whole bay and riverbank seemed to seethe and surge furiously; to rise up in a churning barrier of dust, spray, flying fragments.

Figures that I knew to be rebels ran out from that barrier, crouched behind the walls that bordered the shore road, rose again to dart into the fields and vanish in the corn. Men with muskets, sometimes singly and sometimes in groups, appeared surprisingly from nowhere, only to vanish, wraithlike. Magically, the shore road, empty when we came into the orchard, was suddenly thick with running rebels.

Then the boats came through the white smoke between the warships. The banging, thundering and squealing came to an abrupt stop, and the silence was as violent in its way as the sound of the guns had been.

As the smoke thinned, all the boats came into sight, acres of them, packed with men in scarlet. When they moved around the warships, they were like a field of crimson clover in full bloom—a field in which the ships were like five black cows, belly deep.

This scarlet field swept on past the warships, narrowed and lengthened into a sort of sickle shape, and ran onto the beach of the bay like a red wave. Men poured from the boats. We heard them shouting.

Cruger, Stedman, I and everyone else got up from behind our shelters to watch that long, curved, red line move up from the bay toward the shore road.

Beside me, Stedman groaned. "They'll never catch 'em," he said over and over. "They'll never catch 'em! They'll get away! They'll get away again!"

The rebels had run from their forts into the shore road, scurrying along it to the northward as the red line came up the slope from the beach. Then, as the red line came close, the rebels darted into the fields. Rabbitlike they raced from shelter to shelter, hid behind walls, dashed across openings in search of better cover, bumped into each other; they ran, dodged, tripped, fell and rose to dodge and run and stumble up and run again.

The whole slope of the hill was alive with running rebels. They flowed raggedly toward us; raced past us, a deaf, unseeing horde.

Their eyes were wild and staring; their faces chalk-white. When they fell, they seemed to feel neither pain nor distress. Their faces had a harried, wolfish look; they ran with animal-like stoopings and scuttlings; their mouths were open and they breathed gaspingly with tongues showing red and thick, a most distressing spectacle.

While still they pelted upward over the hillslope to go panting off to the northward, long lines of rebel companies came toward us on the upper road from the direction of the city. At the same time, from the opposite direction, a group of officers in plain blue uniforms spurred their horses along that same road and halted at the upper edge of the orchard, where the running men were tumbling over a stone wall into the road.

Stedman and I had eyes only for the advancing scarlet crescent of Howe's troops. Like a long, long scarlet harrow it moved across the shore road and up the hill, as if to scrape the world clean of the horde of rebels dodging through the cornfields and the orchards.

Cruger, however, was more concerned with the blue-clad officers at the upper edge of the orchard. "Watch this, gentlemen," he told us. "It might be important. Do you see, in the center of the group, an officer taller than the others—one with a tight look about his mouth?"

We said we did.

"That's Washington," he said. "I met him at dinner a year ago, when he was on his way to Cambridge to take command of the rebels. He made a speech—said the greatest calamity that could come to this country would be for it to be independent of England. Now he wants to be independent of England and to kill every Loyalist!"

We stared hard at Washington. He stood out from those around him like an eagle among crows. Something about him caught and held the eye. It seemed almost as though the others about him couldn't come too close: as though he rode always a little alone.

"He's supposed to have ability," Stedman said. "I hope he won't figure out a way to stop those troops of Howe's!"

Cruger looked regretful. "He couldn't think up a way of stopping Howe on Long Island, and this is worse than Long Island. The rebels are in a panic, and the best general in the world can't stop a panic. He can't turn rabbits into men, and up to now the rebels have behaved like rabbits!" He turned to me. "What do you think, Mr. Wiswell?"

I looked over my shoulder at the rebel regiments advancing along the upper road. By now they were so close I could make out their features. Their muskets were cocked every which way over their shoulders. Most of them were in shirt sleeves, their coats tied around their waists by the sleeves or fastened to their belts. Instead of facing to the front as they marched, every last one was peering white-eyed down the hill toward the scarlet regiments moving smoothly upward as if on parade.

Washington and the blue-clad officers with him were moving their horses back and forth across the upper road, so that the running rebels dodged to one side and then to the other, as hens scatter to elude a farmer's wife. We could see Washington leaning over to speak to the running men; but not one stopped to listen.

Stedman looked dubious. "Perhaps we ought to get out of here," he said. "What if Mr. Cruger's caught between Howe's troops and those rebel regiments?"

"I've got to stay," I told him. "If this is the end of the war, I couldn't ask for a better place to see it, and it'll be useful to me. You and Mr. Cruger go and leave me here."

Cruger only smiled; so there we stayed.

Washington and his officers, unable to halt the throng of men that poured upward from the lower road, gave up the attempt and cantered in a body to meet the advancing rebel regiments, and we found ourselves almost at the center of a singular tangle of movements. All around us, still, were wild-eyed, white-faced rebel soldiers running through the orchard toward the safety of the upper road. Halfway up the hillslope the long red line of Howe's regiments moved inexorably on. Just above us, on the upper road, the rebel regiments straggled north, while Washington and his staff hurried to meet them.

We heard Washington shouting in a flat, high-pitched voice that must have been audible to all those marching men, "Get behind the walls! Get behind the walls!"

In the very moment of his shouting we saw something we could hardly believe we were seeing, even though it was as clear to our eyes as though it happened on the palms of our hands. Those three marching rebel regiments seemed to explode, and, in the exploding, to dissolve. It was as though the long lines of marching men had turned to smoke; had gone swirling and drifting in tattered wisps into the groves and meadows on either side of the upper road. Almost they seemed to be driven and whirled by gusts that traveled

before the advancing scarlet columns, just as dust is driven by the
wind that goes before a thunderstorm.

In the twinkling of an eye those regiments ceased to be regiments
and became a mob without leaders, courage, wits or strength—a
rabble, willing to purchase safety at any cost, and at any man's expense.

They scurried along that upper road and through the fields on
either side like autumn leaves plucked from beneath a fence by a
November gale.

I felt Stedman shaking me; heard him shouting despairingly,
"They'll get away! God damn it, I *knew* they'd get away!"

I could only stand, shivering with excitement and with a sort of
shamed exultation, and watch a few officers and even Washington
himself wave their arms and hurl themselves from one side of the
road to the other in a fruitless effort to stem this unstemmable torrent.

If ever I saw a pitiable spectacle, it was Washington. He drew his
sword and used it as he might have used a goad on stampeding cows.
He leaned far out over his horse's neck, slapping and slashing with the
blade, first on one side, then on the other, trying to halt those running
men. His mouth was wide open from the violence of his shouting:
his face deathly pale and glistening with sweat. He shifted his sword
into his bridle hand, leaned from his saddle, caught man after man,
and threw them to the ground, only to have them slide from beneath
his horse like minnows, and like minnows wriggle and dart off to the
northward.

He swung himself back into the saddle, jumped his horse into the
orchard beside us to intercept a group of running men; but neither
shouting, cursing nor sword-striking affected them.

He looked sick and shattered. His sword hung slack beside him;
the bridle was loose in his fingers. When a few furtive figures scuttled
among the trees between him and the advancing scarlet column, he
sat staring at them and never moved.

Drums were beating along that quickly moving scarlet column. It
came onward and upward more rapidly, not more than a half-pistol-
shot away. I don't know whether Washington kicked his horse
toward it, or whether the horse moved instinctively toward the
sound of drums. Whatever the reason, he took a few steps forward,
his ears pricked up.

"Well, well," Cruger said coolly. "There's an opportunity! If I were in command of those redcoats, I'd take Washington prisoner or resign my commission."

I think he was right. What's more, I think Washington would never have raised a hand to help himself; for if ever a man was reduced by shame to overwhelming disgust and despair, that man was Washington. He just sat there, his face gray and sagging. When men shouted warningly, he paid no attention. Then two blue-coated officers galloped into the orchard and up to their commander. Without ceremony they snatched at his reins, wheeled his horse and with him between them galloped away to the north.

They were almost the last of the rebels that we could see. All the thousands who had been in the forts along Kip's Bay, all the hundreds who had marched so briskly out of the city to do battle with Howe's troops, every last one of those rebels who had so loudly called themselves Patriots, were already distant fleeing figures on the road to the north.

New York lay unprotected before Howe; all its defenders had run without firing a shot—and the worst of it was that they had been allowed to get away! Once more Howe had won, but the rebels had again escaped.

CHAPTER XLII

THE whole headquarters staff of the British Army moved up Murray Hill from Kip's Bay in the center of the long line of troops that had sent the rebels scurrying off to the north. They were all there, magnificent in brilliant uniforms—Howe, Percy, Clinton, Cornwallis, Vaughan, Leslie, the Hessian generals and all their aides and satellites.

"My God," Stedman said, "look at Howe! He's pleased! He's smiling! He thinks he's done well!"

There was no doubt about it. Howe's usually sulky face was genial; and in spite of the heat and their heavy uniforms, the officers around him looked cool and gay, as men always do when they think fortune has beamed upon them.

The long line of regiments, with Howe and his staff as an axis, began a turning movement that swung the line across the upper and lower roads at right angles. As the regiments came into position they stacked their muskets, lowered their heavy knapsacks to the ground; unbuttoned their scarlet jackets and mopped the sweatbands of their hats with wisps of grass.

"Dear me," Cruger said. "They're stopping here! They're not going on!"

"My God," Stedman whispered, "don't tell me he's going to make another mistake!"

"I fear he *will* make a mistake if he doesn't throw his troops all the way across the island," Cruger said.

"Can't you tell him so?" I asked.

"My dear Mr. Wiswell," Cruger protested. "A civilian tell a general —a British general—what to do?"

He stood beside us, his hands on his hips, staring bleakly at the group of laughing generals and the long lines of troops taking their ease on the sloping meadow. He seemed more of a leader to me than any of those scarlet-clad officers; and I was sure that he knew more about war than any of those great commanders before us.

Down from the Murray house on the top of the hill trotted a black boy servant on a fat gray pony. He was a gaudy thing in a brass-buttoned blue coat and pink-striped breeches, and when the troops shouted coarse pleasantries to him as he rode along their front, he only sat straighter in the saddle and lifted his nose higher.

When he came to the officers, we heard him say, "Personal letter from Mrs. Murray to Sir General Mr. Lord Howe, and an answer kindly requested!"

While the general read the letter, the little black boy sat goggling at him out of eyes the color of a duck's eggs. The general nodded. "Present my compliments to Mrs. Murray," he said, "and tell her we accept her invitation with the greatest pleasure. We'll be with her at once." He drew out a gold coin and tossed it up to the pop-eyed messenger, who caught it, stared at it incredulously, then went back toward the Murray house, bouncing precariously, like a sawdust doll, on his pony's broad back.

The general noted the positions of the regiments resting on the hillslope and spoke approvingly to Clinton. "That'll do for the present. Let 'em rest and eat, and have 'em be careful of the orchards and the corn. Keep 'em where they are, or they'll tear this lady's fields to pieces. Now then, gentlemen."

He turned on his heel and trudged up the slope toward the white-pillared portico of the Murray house, followed by his gaudy staff in scarlet, gold and white.

Cruger sighed. "Well, gentlemen, there's nothing for me to do but press on to Bloomingdale and see what the rebels have left of my home. If you're wishful of joining a Loyalist regiment and fighting under Loyalists more interested in destroying rebels than in accepting invitations to tea, I shall be happy indeed to have you call upon me in New York in a few days' time. Shall I ask my coachman to take you back?"

"No, sir," I said. "We'll stay here till we find the commissary of prisoners." I hated to see Cruger go. Even in this short time I had found something in him that gave me unbounded confidence in his judgment. If ever I should be caught more deeply in this war, I knew I'd be content to fight under Cruger's leadership.

It was around noon when Howe and his staff had vanished between the white columns of Mrs. Murray's house.

An hour later Buell galloped along the upper road from the city. When we shouted to him, he brought his horse to a plunging stop. The horse was black with sweat and streaked with lather.

Half climbing, half falling from his saddle, Buell pulled at the inner part of his breeches, wriggling himself within them as a woman frees herself from the pressure of her stays. Then he raised his foot, kicked an opening in the stone wall, and led his horse through it and toward us.

A young lieutenant instantly ran forward, shouting, "None of that! Let those walls alone! Let everything else alone around here! Get back outside that wall! I've a damned good mind to make you build it up again!"

"Well," Buell said, "I was wondering why you fellows came over here! You're just taking care of the walls!"

The lieutenant looked contemptuous. "You'll find out what we're doing when the general comes out and finds that wall broken down!"

"When he comes *out?*" Buell asked. "What's he inside of? Where is he?"

I caught at his shoulder to silence him; but he shook me off and again spoke to the lieutenant. "Where is he?" he asked again. "Why isn't he out here where he belongs? My God, man, what's he thinking of!"

The lieutenant took a step toward him.

Buell put a palm against his chest and pushed him back. "Listen," he said, "do you know what's on the other side of that ridge?"

He pointed past the Murray house, over the top of the hill and in the direction of the Hudson.

"There's another road over there—a road out of New York—a road that a regiment or a dozen regiments could march along as slick as a whistle."

The lieutenant just stared.

Buell tapped a finger against the lieutenant's gorget. "Listen, brother: I just came out from New York by way of that road. I hadn't gone more'n half a mile when I caught up with a whole damned division of rebel troops, headed by that old windbag, Putnam. There was three brigades—fifteen regiments. While I was passing 'em, they dodged off the road and went into the woods between the road and the Hudson. They're marching past you, hidden in those woods, right now—fifteen regiments! What are you going to do about it?"

The lieutenant goggled at Buell like a fish in a glass jar.

"Listen," Buell told him. "What in God's name are you waiting here for? There's no rebels on this side of the island. Get over on the other side, where you belong, and capture a few generals and colonels and brigades! Put an end to this war, for God's sake!"

"For everybody's sake," Stedman said harshly.

The lieutenant couldn't seem to understand. "Our orders are to stay here," he said. "The general issued those orders himself."

"They're all at that house on the hill," I told Buell. "They're drinking tea with Mrs. Murray, all of 'em: Howe, Clinton, Cornwallis, Percy, Leslie, Vaughan—every last one of 'em."

"Then for Christ's sake go there!" Buell shouted. "Take this damned horse of mine that's worn all the skin off my tail, and go to Mrs. Murray's and tell Howe that Putnam's running past him while he stuffs himself with cake. Oliver, you ride, and Stedman and I'll hang onto the stirrups and go with you!"

There was a sentry at the door of the Murray house, and he wouldn't let us past. He'd had his orders that the general wasn't to be disturbed, and he was one of those oft-encountered individuals who would rather see a nation ruined than risk five minutes' unpleasantness for himself. Yet he wasn't a dolt; for when he saw the glance that Buell turned on the windows, he summoned other sentries to keep us from doing what one of us surely would otherwise have done—thrust a fist through a pane and shouted the tidings so everybody in the house would hear.

We tried hard to change that sentry's mind. For his benefit Buell spoke of Howe's baronetcy. "They knighted him for letting all the rebels, including Washington, get away from Long Island," Buell said. "They'll have to make this sentry a duke for letting 'em get away here."

"Why should they?" Stedman asked.

"Because it's harder to let 'em get away here," Buell explained. "You've got to be a damneder fool. Over there, they got away at night, and in a rainstorm. Any incompetent officer might 'a' let 'em escape. But here a feller's got to be a plumb ass! They ought to make this sentry Earl Hindquarters for his day's work!"

We looked hopefully at the sentry, but he only stood there motionless, staring past us to the green hillslope running down to the shore of the East River and to the long lines of troops resting idly upon that slope while Putnam's division drifted unmolested through the woods behind us.

"I found Leighton," Buell told me, while we sat in the field across from the Murray house waiting for Howe and his officers to come out. "He'd been put on one of the little prison ships—one that had been a cattle ship. She hadn't been cleaned out—not in the part where they put Soame. He had to sleep on manure."

"On manure! Soame Leighton had to sleep on manure!"

Stedman moved his arms backward and forward in his coat as though something bound him unendurably. "Bunker Hill!" he exclaimed. "Halifax—Long Island—Kip's Bay—Cunningham—prisoners sleeping on manure! To hell with it! I'd rather get myself killed than stand on one side and watch idiots throw this country away. I'm going to see Cruger and raise those two hundred Germans." He meant it.

"Couldn't you do anything about Soame?" I asked Buell.

"Not much, Oliver. I tried, though. I got drunk with one of Cunningham's clerks, and sat up all night printing forty-dollar notes for him—gave him twenty thousand dollars, so's he'd let me know what was going on. Then I had a little talk with Cunningham and told him some things he didn't know about using cattle ships for prison ships, and having prisoners sleep on manure—told him how the manure kept 'em moist and cool in summer, and steamy and warm in winter."

He spat. "He didn't believe me, but I guess he'll move Soame. Yes, sir, I don't believe he'll let Soame stay in a place where he might possibly be comfortable under some conditions."

He gave me an uneasy glance. "I guess I was right. He doesn't like Soame and he doesn't like you. If he can, he'll put Soame where no human being can stay alive. If you want to help Soame Leighton, see Howe and see him quick!"

Not until three o'clock did Howe and his officers come out of the Murray house. They'd been in there three hours—three hours during which England's finest troops stood idly on a hillslope while their enemies ran to safety on the other side of the hill.

When they emerged on the porch of the Murray house, their empty laughter was muted by the heat waves that shimmered above the field; but the exasperation within us as we listened to those fools who were throwing away our homes for us, perhaps throwing away our country beneath our very eyes, was a constantly growing rending in our bowels.

In the cool of the afternoon, Howe's troops spread out in a long line across the island and moved down on the city—moved down onto it and into it without a shot being fired against them; but every ragged, thievish, timorous soldier in the whole rebel army, every shambling captain, ever bucolic colonel, every one of their blundering generals had run away to fight another day.

New York went wild at Howe's arrival. Its citizens thronged the streets, cheering, weeping with delight as his troops went by; and anything in the city was his for the asking. He was given a mansion for himself and a cozy little home for Mrs. Loring, and all the city hastened to pay its admiring respects to the man who had at last freed it from the hated rule of the rebels. He was dined and he was wined; he was praised and he was thanked.

Poor Byng, the British admiral court-martialed and hanged for showing insufficient activity! He should have lived twenty years later, commanded an army in America, and received the plaudits of his king and country!

I knew that if Howe did as he should, he'd immediately march in pursuit of the rebels, while still they were disheartened and in a panic; so Buell and I haunted his headquarters, fearful that he'd go galloping off to the north before we could interest him in Soame Leighton's case.

Yet four days passed before we were admitted to see him; and in those four days Howe had done little more than he had done after Bunker Hill or after Long Island. He had eaten and drunk and gambled with Mrs. Loring; he'd appointed a new government for the city and ceremoniously conferred with hundreds of Loyalists; he had taken steps to appraise all rebel property, so that it might be sold to those the rebels had so long intimidated.

Perhaps those things were necessary; but four days are four days. Much can happen in that length of time; and it seemed clear to Sted-

man, Buell and me that in those four days the rebels must surely
be mending their tattered clothes, filling their powder horns, getting
decent food into their bellies, and recovering at least a little of the
self-respect they had lost at Long Island and Kip's Bay.

We suspected, too, that in those four days Cunningham had been
to Howe and, in his soothing way, told Howe a pack of lies about
Soame Leighton.

Certainly when Buell and I were at last admitted to headquarters,
Howe's manner towards me, for the first time, was as sullen as his
face.

While I told him, as briefly as I could, about the persecution of
Soame Leighton, he stabbed with a quill pen at the pot of shot in
which the pen stood when not in use.

When I finished, he tossed the pen impatiently on his desk and
answered me in a long-suffering voice. "Aren't you making a great
to-do, Mr. Wiswell, about a rebel officer of no importance whatever?
If I understand the case correctly, his own unguarded tongue is responsible for most of his troubles. He's gone out of his way to make
himself offensive."

"I won't try to deny it, sir," I said, "but there are a few things I'd
like to mention, if you'll bear with me."

Howe grumbled a reluctant assent.

"Well, sir," I said, "this officer was my close and dear friend before the war started. He's still that, and I'm bound to do whatever
I can for him. In the second place, if Captain Leighton showed
resentment at his treatment, I'm forced to say that any man of spirit
would have done the same. Captain Cunningham——"

"Now see here, Mr. Wiswell," the general said, "if a commander
in chief attempted to busy himself with all the details of his army,
he'd go mad. I can't listen to fancied grievances against Captain
Cunningham. In this particular instance, the provost marshal is
answerable only to the Crown. His behavior and duties aren't my
province. My province is to suppress a rebellion and to defeat the
rebel army."

"It certainly is, General," Buell said heartily, "and we hope you'll
figure how to do it!"

Howe turned a hard eye on Buell, and his voice, when he went on,
was irascible. "This whole business of rebel prisoners, Mr. Wiswell,
is most annoying! You've seen them—ignorant, lousy, half starved;
riffraff! Now in any ordinary war we can get rid of our prisoners

by exchanging them for our own men who've been captured. But this isn't an ordinary war, Mr. Wiswell! The Congress that pretends to be governing the rebellious colonies refuses to do one damned thing for the rebels we capture! They won't exchange for them; they won't feed them; they won't write to them; they won't send them clothes or comforts. Nobody ever comes to see them— neither friends, relatives nor officers. Apparently nobody cares whether they live or die. It's a trying situation—one with which I wish to have as little as possible to do."

When Buell opened his mouth to speak, I kicked his ankle. I could see I was really annoying Howe by asking him to interest himself in a rebel prisoner. He may have felt that for him to inter- fere in such matters would be bad for discipline. Perhaps it would have been. I doubt that he was a party to Cunningham's sharp prac- tices, as Buell always insisted, or that he reaped any of the benefits of them. I knew for certain, however, that nothing I could say would induce him to interfere in Soame Leighton's case. That meant, of course, that whatever was done for Soame, I'd have to do myself.

"Well, sir," I said to Howe, "I'm grateful to you for listening. I'd like to ask one favor."

Howe spoke fretfully. "I've already told you, Mr. Wiswell, that I——"

I ventured to interrupt him. "I understand, sir, that you can't interfere in such matters; but I've been hoping you'd have no objec- tion if I did what I could. As I said before, this officer was my friend. I owe him much. If Buell and I could be relieved of duty and allowed to go where we wished, it's barely possible that I might be able to help my friend."

Howe looked doubtful. "Anything in reason, Mr. Wiswell," he said, "but if I gave you permission to go wherever you might wish to go in this city, I might readily offend——"

"Not in the city, General," I said hastily. "Outside the city. I want to go outside the city."

"Outside the city?" Howe asked. "Isn't that taking quite a risk for small results, Mr. Wiswell? I've had hopes—your feelings being what they are—that you might be of great value to the Loyalist cause in a way I haven't mentioned. I've had your case in mind, Mr. Wis- well, and I don't feel justified in encouraging you in a step that might—ah—render you valueless."

"There's no danger," I said. "I know what rebel militiamen look like and how they behave. They're deserting from the rebel army at the rate of five hundred a day. If they can run all over New England safely, so can Buell and I—provided we're dressed as they are."

"And smell the way they do," Buell added cheerfully. "That ain't easy, General, but it can be done."

Howe looked gloomy, but drew a piece of paper toward him and scratched upon it the order that gave me the privilege of trying to go back to Milton and to Sally.

CHAPTER XLIII

THE Boston Road, when we trudged out of New York, was an endless straggling procession of rebel militiamen, all putting as much distance between themselves and Washington's army as they could; and not one of them, so far as we could discover, was showing any trifling compunction at deserting the rebel cause when it was most in need.

They were so much alike that Buell said they all looked like twins. Their shoes, when they had any, were mere wrecks; their shirts and jackets were torn and filthy; the buckles were invariably missing from their kneebands, so that their leather breeches flapped around their calves; their hair hung lankly over their collars; their muskets, which some of them still retained, were rusty; and they turned defiant, hangdog stares on everyone they met, as if determined to resist all questioning.

Thus it was easy for Buell and me to look like rebels and by our demeanor to simulate these pseudo-soldiers scuttling back to the homes which in theory they were defending.

By exercising care, I think we might have gone all the way from White Plains to Milton without being challenged or exchanging a word with anyone; but both of us were agreed that the more openly we went, the safer we would be; and I think we were right. Certainly the property owners along the roads we traveled feared us as they might have feared Hessians. Whenever we stopped at a farmhouse in the hope of buying food, doors were locked, dogs were loosed, and sometimes farmers' wives threatened us with muskets.

At length Buell conceived the idea of approaching a farmhouse with a forty-dollar bill in the end of a cleft stick. He'd wave it in the air; go around to the back door and thrust the stick into the ground; then return to the front of the house to shout that he had left the forty dollars for bread and milk. Sometimes we got what we hoped for; more often we didn't; and once we embroiled ourselves in an affair that made clear why rebel militiamen were so despised by those for whom they were supposed to be fighting—an affair, too, that brought trouble upon us later.

Just at sunrise one morning, a few miles north of Hartford, we saw a snug farmhouse perched on a point above a curving river. Rising trout dimpled the brown water—a sight guaranteed to make a traveler ravenous. "Oliver," Buell said, "there ain't a soul in sight, and there's smoke coming out of that farmhouse chimney. I'm hungry enough to eat a pan of last week's sody biscuits, and I'm going to offer 'em two hundred dollars for a real good meal."

He drew five forty-dollar bills from his pocket, broke a switch from a near-by bush, wedged the money into its cleft tip, and went around to the back door. Then he returned to stand before the front door and shout, "One hundred dollars for a pitcher of milk and a squash pie! Another hundred for the hind quarter of any horned critter! Two hundred dollars for breakfast!"

Then we waited, but there wasn't a sign of life from the house, barring the wisp of smoke that drifted from the chimney to lie in a blue fog above the little river.

Buell scratched his head, puzzled. "That's mighty funny, Oliver! People who live in farmhouses always peek out of windows. There's people in that house, and they've peeked at us. Two hundred dollars is a lot of money in any currency, even rebel; and it ain't natural for 'em not to show interest!"

Again he shouted, "Two hundred dollars for anything I can eat!" The house was silent.

Buell shook his head. "That beats me." He walked toward the rear of the house once more, peering up at the windows. As he rounded the corner, he came to a sudden stop.

"Hey!" he shouted. He turned angrily to me. "They took it! They took my two hundred dollars and didn't leave any breakfast! By God, they can't do that to us! Come on, Oliver!"

He ran toward the back door; and I followed, though I did so reluctantly.

"Wait, Tom," I called. "We can't afford to have trouble with any. body. Wait!"

"Wait be damned," Buell cried. "I don't aim to have trouble with anybody. All I want's my two hundred dollars or some breakfast!" He banged the back door with his musket butt. "Open up!"

He cocked an ear at the door, as a dog might study a woodchuck hole. The house was still silent.

"Well," Buell said loudly, "somebody's asking for trouble, and two soldiers out of General Washington's army have plenty to spare. Oliver, fire your musket into that door and kick it open! I'll have some buckshot ready."

He cocked his musket. "Open up if you don't want to get hurt!"

A key turned slowly, and the door creaked open. Just inside stood three men dressed like ourselves. Each had a powder horn and water bottle over his shoulder, a cartridge box and bullet pouch at his belt, and each held a musket in his hand. They were unshaven, dirty all over, and without the confidence that being clean sometimes gives even a guilty man. They were furtive, apprehensive, and almost intrusively looked caught in the act—a most indecent act. I'd seen a dog look like that when he'd done something atrocious; and the very instant they opened the door I knew we'd have no trouble with them; for like conscience-stricken dogs they lost backbone, and visibly were in a condition to submit to anything. They were three born cowards; and if their faces hadn't so plainly shown that they knew themselves caught in a vileness, I could have laughed.

"Well, I'll be damned," Buell said. "Militia! No wonder I lost my two hundred dollars!" He swung the muzzle of his musket from one to another of the three men. "Militia," he repeated. "What you doing in here?"

"We live here," one of them said.

"Oh, so you live here!" The muzzle of Buell's musket came to rest, pointing at the stomach of the man who had spoken.

He spoke to me over his shoulder. "Go right on in, Oliver. Take these gentlemen's muskets and stand 'em in the corner, where we won't fall over 'em when we pay 'em a visit." He waved me past him.

To my relief, the three men relinquished their muskets without protest. As an extra precaution, I knocked out the flints, while Buell came softly in and locked the door behind him.

"Now then," Buell said, "let's see about this. Who took my two hundred dollars?"

"Not us," one of the men said.

Buell looked puzzled. "Not you, eh? My two hundred dollars was taken, and you live here, and you didn't take it! Well, well!" He seemed to change the subject.

"Just been in the army?"

The men nodded.

"Fought in the battle of Long Island, no doubt?"

Again they nodded.

"And at Kip's Bay?"

They made sounds of assent.

"Connecticut militia in the battle of Long Island and at Kip's Bay," Buell said thoughtfully. "Now let's see. What was it we heard about Connecticut militia? Did we hear they fought bravely, and preferred death to dishonor, and so on and so forth?"

He looked ruminative. "No, it wasn't that! Seems to me I remember hearing something about deserting and mutinous behavior. But there: that wasn't peculiar to Connecticut militia! It was something else: something peculiar to Connecticut."

He looked at me. "You don't happen to remember what it was, do you?"

"Was it anything like running away?"

Buell smote his thigh. "Running away! That's just exactly what it was! Running away! That and stealing!" He beamed upon the three militiamen.

"Looks like you gentlemen just can't get over the running-away habit! Here you are in your own home, but still wearing your powder horns and canteens, ready to start running again."

"You're running away yourself," one of the rebel militiamen pointed out.

"Not from you, we ain't," Buell said, "not till we've seen who else lives here. If you just got back from the army, the house must be full of people. To tell you the truth, I'm kind of surprised nobody's interested to learn what we're talking about." He made a move toward an inner door.

The leader of the three militiamen spoke up quickly and, I thought, desperately. "There ain't anything in there worth having! These people are Tories! They—they insulted us when we came in here. We had to protect ourselves. We'll divide—you can have——"

"Don't let 'em get away, Oliver," Buell warned me.

He kicked open the inner door of the entryway. Beyond was a kitchen, and the table was set for breakfast with a pitcher of cider, a loaf of new bread, an apple pie and a bowl of sour-milk cheese. There were five chairs.

"Well, well," Buell said again, "breakfast for five, and only three to eat it! I wonder why they couldn't have spared us a little of that cheese for our two hundred dollars."

He went to the kitchen table, picked up a knife, scooped up a generous portion of cheese, and filled his mouth as a mason fills a hole with mortar. His eyes darted about the kitchen and came to rest on a big bag of old canvas, unevenly bulky with what it contained.

Buell went over to it, loosened its drawstring and examined its contents. "Pewter," he said. "Just about all the pewter there was in the house, and a little silver, too. Canisters of tea. That's thoughtful! Dear me, dear me! Probably one of these three dutiful militiamen has a maiden aunt somewhere that he's thinking of taking some tea to! Too bad to interrupt him! Tory tea? The people that own the house are Tories, are they? Well, we'll see about it."

I lost sight of him; heard a door open. "Well, well," I heard him say for the third time, and he added, "Don't let 'em get away, Oliver."

Then he was silent, except for fumbling sounds and faint mutterings. When he came back into my line of vision once more, he held a dozen pieces of rope and swung them blithely against his leg.

"Bring in those boys of yours, Oliver," he said. "Come in, boys! Come right in!"

When I pushed the militiamen into the kitchen, I saw that five people stood near an open door at the far end—a father, a mother, a grown daughter and two half-grown boys. They were rubbing their wrists and ankles; feeling their jaws as though they'd been half dislocated.

"Just uncock your musket, Oliver," Buell told me. "This room's getting crowded and we don't want to hurt anybody. I'll tie up these gentlemen from Connecticut and roll 'em into a corner so they won't get underfoot while we're eating breakfast. If one of 'em undertakes to make any sort of protest, just tap him on the head—hard!"

He meant exactly what he said; and the three Connecticut militiamen made no objection nor uttered even a sound of protest except to swallow audibly. They were as helpless and as limp as three straw-stuffed scarecrows. Buell had stood them up side by side in the corner of the room to do his work upon them; and when it was finished and he had them tied hand and foot, he pushed them, almost

good-naturedly, and they collapsed, one after the other, and lay side
by side upon the floor, three unpleasant bundles.

"Now then," Buell said to the five who stood staring at him, "let's
have breakfast."

The mother and daughter stood behind us, anticipating our wants
and loading our plates with more and better food than we had seen
for months; and Buell, though loudly dubious of new bread and
apple pie as breakfast for a man of his internal sensitiveness, filled
himself so full that his belt squeaked.

"So you're Tories," he said, mopping his plate with a limp piece
of new bread. "I'm surprised they didn't treat you worse. How'd it
happen they didn't tar and feather you?"

"We ain't Tories!" the man said. "We ain't any different from what
we've always been. We're law-abiding citizens, trying to raise enough
for us and our children. I've worked hard, and so'd my father before
me. He got along all right, and so'd I till every grave-robber in Connecticut began to yell we were being made slaves of, and had to fight
for our liberty and our lives."

"Well, that was the truth, wasn't it?" Buell asked.

The farmer breathed heavily, put down his knife and fork, and
glared at Buell.

His wife placed a restraining hand upon his shoulder. "Now,
Simon!"

The farmer shook her off. "By God, I'll say it and I'll keep on
saying it, even if they kill me for it! We never had one hour's
trouble till those bug-eyed committeemen came out from Hartford,
telling us we'd got to swear to things we didn't believe, and threatening us with Simsbury Mines if we didn't swear to 'em. A lot of
sour-faced, law-twisting, sanctimonious skunks!"

"Dear me," Buell said. "That's no way to talk about Patriots!"

"Patriots be damned," the farmer said. With a shaking hand he
pointed his knife at the three militiamen in the corner. "Look at 'em!
Patriots! We never knew what trouble was till Patriots like that
began to march up and down the roads! They took our horses,
stripped our corn, ran off with our cows, stole every apple off our
trees, killed our chickens; and if you hadn't come along, these last
three would have cleaned us out of every damned thing we had
left!"

He shot a quick glance at his daughter, looked sidelong at Buell and lowered his eyes to his plate. The implication was clear and horrible.

"Patriots," he muttered. "Human lice! Good-for-nothing scoundrels and dregs!" He looked up at Buell defiantly. "That's what they are in *this* province, brother; and if saying so makes me a Tory, I'm a Tory!"

Buell looked puzzled. "That don't sound like being a Tory, does it, Oliver?"

Without waiting for me to answer, he embarked on a discourse. "No, brother: you ain't a Tory, but you're a damned fool! My friend, here, and I—we've had considerable experience. We've seen a lot of Patriots in our time, and our opinion of 'em ain't high. We don't think much of their best generals, and we don't think much of their best troops; and if I called Connecticut militia what I ought to call 'em, your little boys' ears would shrivel right off their heads, and they'd grow up without any, deef for life!

"We've watched these Patriots trying to fight, and we know their brains don't work like you'd expect brains to. They're all the time doing things backside-to; so if I was you, I wouldn't look for 'em to be reasonable when you tell 'em the truth. In fact, I wouldn't tell 'em the truth under any circumstances."

The farmer just stared at him.

"If I was you," Buell said, "I'd hang out a sign—Hurray for Sam Adams and to hell with King George, or something like that."

"To hell with both of 'em," the farmer growled.

"Have it your own way," Buell told him. "You're right, but don't expect the rebels to agree with you. Rebels don't agree with any-body—not even themselves! A year ago they didn't want inde-pendence, and now they do. A year ago they hated France; now they love her! If they lose a battle, they claim they won! The faster they run, the louder they talk about their masterly retreat. The more slaves they have, the more they yell about freedom. The more harm they do America, the more persistent they are in claiming they're preserving her. The more rebellious they are, the angrier they get when they're called rebels."

He let out his belt, helped himself to a final forkful of cheese, rose from the table and picked up his musket. "Well," he said, "we've got to move. We'll leave those three militiamen for you to dispose of. They'd make nice fertilizer. If you take my advice, you'll write General Washington and tell him you've got three of his militiamen

here, all corded up and ready to be called for—but you won't feed
'em or untie 'em till he sends for 'em. From all I hear, General Washington's got considerable sense. If it's true, he'll let 'em die on your
hands and no questions asked."

"We could put 'em in the smokehouse," the farmer's wife said.

Buell's voice was hearty. "Just the place for 'em! Give 'em a good
smoking and there's parts of 'em you might be able to eat. Before
you hang 'em up, though, go through their clothes. One of 'em's got
two hundred dollars of mine, and that'll pay for our breakfast."

In spite of Buell's confidence, I'd expected, when I undertook this
long journey through New England, to be perpetually on guard; to
feel like a fugitive; to be eternally conscious of enemies on every
side; to skulk behind hedges; to hide in holes and corners during
the day and to slink furtively through the outskirts of towns by
night.

For the most part my apprehensions were wasted. Connecticut,
as we saw it, wasn't enemy country, and the war seemed far away,
even though militiamen fleeing from Washington's army wandered
like homeless vagabonds on all the roads we traveled.

True, every farmer or villager we met looked upon us with suspicion—but that wasn't because we were thought to be Loyalists; it
was because we were supposed to have been with Washington's
army. As for the womenfolk, they refused to look at us at all.

Nobody halted us as we moved northeastward through Connecticut and into Massachusetts; nobody even questioned us—probably
because every citizen hoped we'd hie ourselves beyond the limits of
his town with all possible speed.

When we'd left Connecticut behind us, I own that my feelings
often became almost chokingly sentimental; and when we got into
the shaggy Massachusetts hills to the south of Worcester and worked
to the eastward through Uxbridge, Millis and Medfield, there seemed
to be a lump in my throat almost all the time. I was nearing home!

Then, on a fair afternoon, I saw far before me, like a dim cloud
above the forest ridges, the familiar bulk of Great Blue Hill. I had to
stop for a moment, to let my breathing grow regular again. We went
through a Norwood that seemed to me the houses and fields of a
dream, and I knew that I was laughing emptily when Buell spoke
to me; my eyes remained unchangingly upon the steadily growing
rampart of Great Blue Hill.

I knew every rock and every tree, every brook and every hillslope, between Ponkapog and Milton; and when we came to the ridge from which, eighteen months before, I had looked down through the gathering dusk at the splinter of fire licking at the corner of Henry Wade's barn, I glanced sidewise at Buell's face. A gray coldness had come upon him as he walked, and he was staring straight ahead.

"This is no place to be gaping about in, Oliver," he said. "Don't look as if you saw anything familiar in this neighborhood! I see a few things altogether too damned familiar, myself; but nobody could tell it on me, could they? We got to look like strangers here. We got to wear the expression of strangers, or somebody'll recognize us. Look like a stranger, can't you? This is damned familiar ground, but don't let yourself look as if you'd ever seen it before!"

It was indeed familiar ground! I knew every inch of it—every outcropping ledge, every bull pine, every little stream wriggling through its lush meadow, every twist and turn in the ascending road through those gray and green hills that I would always remember as blue.

We topped the shoulder of Great Blue Hill to see, far off, the gentle swell of Milton Hill outlined against a silver ribbon from which the three hills of Boston rose as from a mirror.

Milton Hill! Home and Sally!

CHAPTER XLIV

I LAY for four hours in a birch thicket bordering a brook on the east slope of Brush Hill while Buell went on to Milton Hill to get the lay of the land.

"They might not know you with all that stubble on your face," he told me, "but this is your home town, and a man's neighbors can recognize him by his ears or the way he uses his knees. Nobody in Milton knows me, so I'll carry a message to your young lady and be back here around dark with a thousand dollars' worth of food."

"If we're going to travel by night," I said, "I think I'll shave."

Buell looked disgusted. "Shave! You don't.have any confidence in your young lady! D'you think her affections depend on how much hair you have? According to history, women ain't like that, or else full-bearded men wouldn't 'a' got wives! Look at any engraving of King Henry the Eighth! History says *he* got married some, don't it? If he could marry six times without a shave, you don't need one just to talk to a loving maiden. Look at Henry the Eighth and look at me! And then after looking all you want to at us, look at Henrietta Dixon!"

With the pronouncing of this name, his eyes wandered and his face became vacant. "Did I have to wear a pretty neckcloth and powder my hair like you to be the one object of Henrietta Dixon's affection? Did she fight and make more fuss when I was beardlike than when I wasn't? Never! I could 'a' been a one-eyed hunchback with a beard wound round and round me to the knees, but would I 'a' been less dear? Nary jot or tittle, Oliver!"

I answered him coldly. "I'd feel cleaner if I shaved."

"You won't be, though," he said. "The truth is you'll only be easier to see, and that's what you want to avoid. Don't touch those whiskers! They look like good woodcock cover, yes; but that's your safety! They're your cloud by day and your pillar of fire by night. With 'em you may be painful to the eye, but without 'em you might get hanged any minute! Tell your young lady you decided to leave yourself as Nature made you, which is with hair on the face after puberty; and she'll like you all the better for your frankness. Oliver, don't shave!"

He set off down the road, bellowing "Yankee Doodle" and lurching a little. With his lank hair, his three-cornered hat with one side uncocked so that it flapped disgustingly against his ear, an enormous rip in the seat of his breeches, his stockingless legs, his broken shoes, his rusty musket, he was a perfect picture of a rebel militiaman.

For him, interested in his own play-acting, the next four hours may have passed rapidly; but to me they seemed endless.

For all I knew, Sally might not be in Milton. She might have changed her mind about me. She might be in love with someone else —and I could think of no good reason why the affections of anyone as sweet as Sally, and as beautiful and as good, should be permanently retained by a young man who had lost his property and his country; who had run from his enemies instead of fighting them; who couldn't believe as the girl he loved believed, and lacked the strength to persuade her to believe as he did.

All in all I think those four hours were the longest of the many interminable ones I'd endured since I last saw Sally.

Buell had a bag over his shoulder when he came back; and while he unpacked it, he discoursed.

"Well, Oliver, I got all the news of Milton. The rebels won the battle of Long Island, of course, just the way they won the battle of Bunker Hill. It was a moral victory. Some of 'em got away, so they won it.

"George Washington is the greatest general that ever lived, in spite of getting licked every time he fights a battle; and the second greatest is a toss-up between Nathaniel Greene and Henry Knox. Knox married a girl named Flucker over in Cambridge, so he don't have to do much to make Bostonians think he's the best general that ever lived.

"The next best are General Putnam and General Stirling and Gen-

eral Sullivan. Putnam was the one my goose was named after. Stirling
was the one that surrendered to the Hessians and then quick drank
up all their liquor. And you remember Sullivan. He was the one I
pulled out myself from under a hedge.

"Another thing, Oliver; God's fighting for the rebels, or so they
claim in Milton. As for the English generals, Oliver, you'd be surprised to hear how worthless they are. General Clinton, he ain't a general at all. He's just an assassin; and General Howe's a parricide.
They don't qualify as generals at all, not around Milton.

"The way Milton people figure, there's several Massachusetts generals crowding Washington on the list of great historical fighters.
Frederick the Great is about fifteenth on that list. Alexander the Great
is twenty-second. Oliver Cromwell and Julius Caesar haven't been
heard of at all—not in Boston! You'd be interested, too, in hearing
what——"

"Tom," I said, "I'm interested in just one thing."

"She's all right," Buell said hastily. "I saw her."

"You saw her! How did she—what did she—does she——"

"Yes, she is, and yes, she does," Buell said.

I drew a deep breath. "How did you—who did you——"

Buell waved me to silence. "Oliver, let me tell this my own way! I
know what you want to hear, and I'll tell you everything; but I can
do it quicker and neater if you don't keep interrupting me with your
'Does she's' and 'Is she's' and 'How did she's'. I've been kind of edgy
for the past four hours, and all these tongue-tied questions of yours
make me jumpy!"

He drew a squash pie from his bag, examined it solicitously and
shook his head. "I don't know about eating this whole pie. If we
had any running to do, it might slow us up."

I think I made a move toward him, for he handed me the pie and
moved to a safe distance.

"Well, Oliver," he said, "first off, I went right into Milton and
walked into Vose Leighton's store, just to find out where the old
groundhog was. He was there, and never took his eye off me all
the time I was in the place, and I'd almost 'a' thought he was expecting me to pretty near steal something. I didn't want to disappoint
him, so I gave him one of my forty-dollar bills and bought myself a
new belt, a jackknife, a horn cup, two papers of pins, a dozen buttons
and a box of fish hooks. Told him I was going up on the Kennebec
to settle, so I wouldn't have to be in the army any more. He said——"

I caught the front of his coat and shook him.

"I ain't doing it on purpose," he protested. "This is how it happened. Didn't I tell you she was all right and waiting to see you?"

"You've told me nothing," I said. "Exactly nothing! Where did you find her and what did she say?"

"Don't you want to hear about your own house? Don't you want to hear who's——"

I shook him again. "What did she say, Tom? How was she looking? Was she thinner? Do you think she's been unhappy? Did you tell her——"

Buell freed himself. "You're in too much of a hurry, Oliver! Now you listen quietly. I found out where she lived, and I went up there and knocked on the door. An old lady opened it and said her husband had told her not to give anything to soldiers. I asked her if she'd ever heard of Soame Leighton, and she turned the color of dough. Sat right down on the doorstep and began to wheeze like a horse with the colic.

"I said, 'Ma'am, you need water', and I stepped over her and went into the house and looked around. This young woman of yours was in the back parlor, darning thin spots in a sheet, and I'm bound to say, Oliver, that I never saw but one woman to touch her. I like 'em a little meatier myself—not so skinny. Still, for a skinny woman, she certainly had less corners on her than any I ever saw. I like 'em a little easier to handle, too, Oliver—no offense meant.

"When I walked in on her, she said, 'Who let you in here?'; and before I had a chance to make her a fair answer, she stepped over to the sideboard, pulled open a drawer and took out a pistol the size of an ax. She's nice to see, Oliver, but are you sure you want to go ahead? A lady that can get hold of a pistol that quick and look at me the way she did would make me think things over, I know, before I got led to the altar. I don't wish to intrude my advice; but if I was in your fix, so to call it, the thought of arguments toward the latter end of the honeymoon would——"

I took a firmer grip on his coat. "Get ahead with it! Go on!"

"All right, Oliver. Well, I said to her, 'I've got a message for you about your brother Soame.'

"She just cocked that pistol and said, 'Where is it?'

"I said, 'Well, I don't exactly have it. A friend of mine has it. He used to be a neighbor of yours, and he's waiting out on Brush Hill until it gets dark.'

"Well, Oliver, she turned a kind of cream color and let that blunder-buss of hers drop. I ain't had such a start since I saw the mob cut out that mare's tongue; but my luck must be getting better, because I caught the pistol before it hit the floor—caught it and her too."

"She fainted?"

"No, she didn't exactly faint," Buell said. "She just kind of lost her balance." He opened his eyes wide. "Weighed more'n I thought, too, for such a skinny little thing."

"For God's sake, Tom!"

"Made me homesick for Henrietta, the way she looked at me," Buell said. "She knew right away it was you I was talking about. She'll meet you tonight under Hutchinson's poplars, wherever those are."

The slope of Milton Hill was as familiar to me as the palm of my own hand, and familiar, too, were the scents, the sounds, the dim scenes that surrounded me as Buell and I came through the stubble of a cornfield and felt the loom of the governor's poplars above us.

I guided myself, as I had done a thousand, thousand times before, by the yellow pin points of light on the hills of Boston, below and to the left of the North Star. At the foot of the hill a dog barked, and the night breeze brought me the scent of wood smoke and marsh, of dust and distant horses, of autumn leaves and drying grass. Nowhere else in the world could sounds be as poignant or scents so sweet.

"My God, Oliver," Buell said, "there's more of these poplars than I thought there was! I never thought to ask her which one she'd be under."

"You stay here," I told him. "I know where she'll be."

"Not by a damned sight," Buell said. "I'm staying with you, in case we have to run."

"You can't," I said. "I haven't seen Sally for eighteen months and two days. I want to be alone with her."

To my profound annoyance, Buell wouldn't leave me. He went with me through the first line of poplars, crossed the road when I did, and scaled the banking on the far side.

Exasperation filled me. "Stay here," I said again.

"I won't do it," Buell said. "Maybe she won't come. Maybe you'll get lost hunting for her. Maybe—maybe she'll send somebody——"

"What are you trying to say?" I asked. "Are you hinting Sally might trap us? Don't you remember how she saved you from the mob?"

Buell was silent, but his very silence was stubborn, and when I crossed the wall into the darker shade of the second row of poplars, I heard him clambering after me and cursing beneath his breath as he knocked a stone from the wall.

"Tom," I said, "how'd you like to have me underfoot if you were seeing Henrietta Dixon for the first time in months—maybe seeing her for the last time?"

"I wouldn't care."

"You know better! How could you tell her what was in your heart if a third person was listening?"

"I don't talk that way with Henrietta," Buell said. "Henrietta's a sensible woman. We don't waste time talking. We don't ever talk much, anyhow."

"Let me put it another way," I said. "Suppose you——"

Behind me I felt something that might have been a faint warmth— a sort of tangible fragrance that seemed to crowd in beside my heart to hold it suspended and swollen against my ribs. I forgot Buell.

"Sally!" I whispered. "Sally!"

I felt her hands in mine. There was such a humming in my ears that I could scarcely speak or hear.

"I thought you'd never stop talking to your friend," she said. "My knees were like water, and I almost fell! You know what I thought, Oliver? I thought how terrible if he comes all this distance to see me and finds me—and finds me——"

She drew a quivering breath, whispered my name once more, and clung to me.

I could only say her name and say it, and somehow marvel, in spite of my dizziness and the pounding of my blood, that coherent speech and thought should so desert me when my imaginings, for a year of dreary, lonely nights, had dwelt upon this moment.

"You're well?" I asked stumblingly. "You've been well? I've thought so often—been afraid so often—afraid something might have happened and I not heard——"

"I know, Oliver," Sally said. "I have those very thoughts. They're worst before storms and in the early morning. That's when I've been most afraid—afraid you might be—afraid you might be hurt! So many things can happen to a man, Oliver! If only I could have known where you were, I—I mightn't have been so frightened. I imagine so many things, Oliver—so many terrible things about you and Soame——"

She clung to me. "Tell me now, Oliver. Your friend said you had a message for me—a message from Soame."

"Yes," I said. "That's why I came, Sally. About Soame."

"Soame's dead," she whispered.

"No, no," I said. "He's not dead. He's a prisoner. He was taken in the battle of Long Island and spoke his mind to the provost marshal, and now he isn't getting enough to eat."

"Not enough to eat!" Sally cried. "Not enough to eat! Couldn't the other prisoners give him food, Oliver?"

"None of them have enough, Sally; and if the provost marshal hates a man, he treats him accordingly. That's what I came to tell you, Sally. He's being badly treated. Bad things are happening to him, and worse may happen."

Sally caught my wrist in a grip that amazed me. "And you let such things happen!"

Buell spoke from behind us. "Oh my, yes! Oliver just sits around letting those things happen. Once or twice he went to the general about it; and in between his spells of sitting around, he thought we might run up here to see you. Things being dull, he thought it might be sort of interesting to see what the rebels would do to us in case they caught us."

"Yes, of course!" Sally said. "Thank you, Oliver! Thank you! Oh, why should they single out Soame? He's so gay—so kind!"

"Soame resented his capture, Sally. He resented being called a rebel, and it's a mistake for a prisoner to show resentment. It did him harm; and then, Sally, what I'm afraid was worse, I tried to help him. The provost marshal doesn't like me. He's a perverse man; and perhaps some of his persecution of Soame is due to his hatred of me. That's the unfortunate truth, Sally. I have to say it, even though it makes you hate me too. That's why I had to come to Milton myself to tell you about Soame. The prisoners aren't allowed to write to anyone, and something's got to be done about Soame, Sally."

"Something's got to be done," she whispered. "Do you mean Soame won't live unless he's released?"

I held her close.

"What can we do?" she whispered. "Oh, Oliver, what can I do? Should we write to General Washington and ask for Soame's exchange?"

"Don't write," I said. "Tell your father to go himself, and you go with him. Perhaps some of the rebel officers will listen to you; they're human beings."

"But Oliver," Sally said, "if he's in danger of dying they'll do what they can, won't they? They wouldn't do more just out of gallantry at the sight of a woman!"

"I don't know, Sally. The rebels aren't trying to help their own men who've been taken prisoner. If they exchanged captured British soldiers for them, the British would go to fighting again. I don't believe Soame would be exchanged unless you make a pretty strong appeal, Sally. If I were you—and your father—I'd appeal in every way I could!"

"I will," she said. "Oh, I will! Father and I'll go at once. We'll go tonight! Ah, but won't you tell me a little more about yourself—quickly? I've heard from you so seldom, Oliver!"

I took my journal from my pocket and put it in her hands. "It's all here," I said. "All I dared to write. You'll read between the lines, won't you, Sally? You'll understand, won't you, that I couldn't put down all the things I thought about you? There wouldn't have been room! Oh, Sally, Sally, when shall we——"

She thrust me suddenly from her. "You'll have to go," she said. "Don't tell me how you'll go, or where! I want to know, but I'd rather not! That's one of the horrible dreams I have; they're hunting you, and in spite of myself I'm just about to tell them where you are—and then I wake up, shivering! So just go, Oliver!"

"Wait, Sally," I said. "Give me another five minutes. I want to know so many things, and you've told me nothing."

She turned me from her and urged me toward the road. "Told you nothing!" she cried. "Do you *have* to be told? Do I need to say, in cold and meaningless words, that I'll never change, not even when I'm an old, old lady with a lace cap, sitting beside the fire and thinking of you? I'll never change; never! If I should reach heaven before you do, I'll find us a little pink cloud, and I'll be on it, waiting, when you come."

In the road she turned to face me. "Please, dearest Oliver," she said, "please go quickly! I'll keep the little book forever, and I'll be grateful always for what you've done for Soame. I—I——"

"I'll go when I have to," I said. "Not before." Then in spite of all she said to turn me away, I went with her up the hill toward her father's house, past the familiar half-seen landmarks on either side—the lane to our own home, the path to the Hutchinsons', the little rocky run I'd known as Jacob's Ladder because Sally used to run down it, like an angel in pink gingham, when she joined me to go sailing in the harbor.

Our footsteps lagged as we drew near the top of the steep path. "I can't bear to have it end, Sally," I said.

"Nothing's ended," Sally said. "I'll ask for you when my father and I come to New York to help Soame. I'm sure we'll be allowed——"

Buell's hand fell upon my shoulder and held me as in a vise. "There's men at the top of that path," he whispered. "They're waiting there!"

Sally gasped. "Men! At the top of the path! If they're at the top of the path, they're in our back yard. Oliver, they must be here for you! Oh, Oliver——"

I pressed my hand against her lips; and the three of us stood there listening.

From the top of the path came vague stirrings. I heard the peculiar dull click a bullet pouch makes when its cover is forced from the brass button that holds it shut; heard, too, the sharper click of metal against metal.

I felt, rather than saw, Buell look at me. "It's an ambush," he breathed. "Somebody must have told 'em!"

We stood silent, listening. From the darkness at the top of the hillslope came a muttering voice. "They claimed to be in the militia, but they called us rebels and dregs, and insulted us, attacked us and tied us hand and foot, and got us half smoked to death in a smokehouse before we kicked loose and got away! One of 'em was called Oliver."

Buell caught at my shoulder. "We made a mistake!" he whispered. "They weren't Connecticut militia! They were Massachusetts, were from around here, and must've been just behind us all the way. I *knew* we'd ought to done something serious to 'em!"

"Go to the eastward," Sally said softly. "I'll go back down the hill and keep talking till you've got away."

I was in a panic. "You can't! They'll know you've been talking to me. They'll make trouble for you!"

"They haven't seen you!" she whispered. "You could be anyone— you could be Steven!" She wrenched her hand from mine. Before I could speak she was gone, and I heard a half-sigh that seemed to make the words "Dearest Oliver, good-by."

Then her voice, louder, came from a little distance, seeming to move westward as she spoke. "How delightful, Steven! Do you think you'll be here all the week—a whole week!" She laughed and continued to laugh as she went on, prattling indistinguishably, seeming to talk to someone whose responses were too low to carry over the distance.

Buell tugged at my sleeve.

I drew him to the rail fence that divided the Leightons' fields from their neighbor's. "We'll go the opposite way," I said. "Over the fence with you, and be quiet!"

"Get over yourself," Buell said. "I want to leave a remembrance for that militiaman and his friends when they come down the hill to look for us." Silently he laid hands upon two ponderous boulders that lay among some weeds and rolled them into the path at a little distance from each other. "There," he added, "if they think they ought to hurry, I guess that'll let 'em exercise their unalienable right to make nuisances of themselves."

We set off across the fields, walking softly and bearing to the south, toward the shelter of the giant bulk of Great Blue Hill that blotted out the lower stars. We hadn't gone far when we heard, behind us, a sudden shouting and clatter.

"That's nice," Buell said, "I hope it was the one that did the talking!"

There was a second clatter and more shouting. "Found 'em both," Buell murmured. "I hope it was him again! It's encouraging what you can do with a little forethought, if you use the simplest means. From what my grandmother taught me, I judge he's sure to go to hell when he dies, on account of what he said when he hit the first one, let alone what he's saying now he's found out there were two. Terrible, ain't it, the way people can lose their tempers when they find they've made the same mistake twice!"

He was silent for a time; then spoke more thoughtfully. "To tell you the truth, Oliver, I'm sick of keeping my temper with these damned rebels! They've raised hell with us for a year and a half, and we've done nothing in return but borrow their food and cigars, counterfeit their money and trip 'em up with boulders. Well, Oliver, it's time we finished with childish things! If Howe ain't put an end to this war when we get back to New York, we better see what we can do to end it up ourselves!"

CHAPTER XLV

ALL our efforts, all our waking hours, when we came back to New York, were devoted to hunting Soame Leighton.

All we knew, when we set out on our search, was that the principal jail for military prisoners in New York was the Provost, that Cunningham made his headquarters in the Provost, and that Cunningham's persistent hatred of Soame Leighton would, in all likelihood, have led him to keep Soame close to him, where he could vent his spleen upon him whenever he wished.

My first inclination had been to go to Howe for an order to visit any prison; but second thoughts made me think again. If I had such an order, Cunningham would have to know of it; and so perverse was that man's cruelty that he would almost certainly add to Soame's misery out of sheer spite.

To be without orders in a military zone isn't pleasant. Up to the time I'd left New York, I had been—halfway, at least—attached to General Howe's army. Though I'd had neither rank nor uniform, I had always traveled on orders, and taken part in marches on orders; landed on Staten Island, on Long Island, on Manhattan Island on orders; been present at the battles of Brooklyn and Kip's Bay on orders; helped with prisoners after all those battles on orders. Yet I'd held no official position; and the footing I'd been on was, to put it mildly, indefinite.

Still, those orders—and orders are the very breath of life to any person who wishes to move in the shadow of an army—had always been in my pocket, ready to hand, whenever I needed them.

But now, since I'd gone off on my own devices after Howe's occupation of New York, I had no orders. My official position was more

nonexistent than ever, if that was possible. I had no right to enter
any building occupied by the army; no means of finding out, except
from civilians, what was happening in the army. I had no authority
to visit prisoners: in fact, I was no better than any drifting, impotent
private citizen—and there's nothing more helpless, more ineffective,
more sheeplike than a private citizen in time of war.

I knew I was a fool to go without orders; yet in addition to my
fear of what Cunningham might do to Soame if I had them, I had a
growing unwillingness to ask Howe for anything. Howe had used
me; and while I was willing to be used if that using would help
to end the rebellion, I had become more and more certain that
Howe had used his entire army and me too for some mysterious
private purpose of his own. I wanted none of that if I could avoid
it; so Buell and I tried our luck without the help of Howe or anyone
else.

It struck me, as Buell and I stood before the Provost, staring up at
its five dark tiers of barred and paneless windows, that there were
four unusual things about it.

The first was its smell. It stank as though all the decayed food, all
the soiled clothes, all the excrement, all the dirty animals and charred
refuse in New York had been piled within it.

The second was the unexpected number of church steeples that
rose from the triangular open space on which it fronted.

The third was the enormous number of guards and sentries who
paced up and down its long, forbidding front.

The fourth and most remarkable was the furtive and sightless
look of all the near-by private buildings. Their windows were shuttered, as if the occupants of all those dwellings had blinded themselves—or been forcibly blinded—to all that went on in the vicinity
of the Provost.

"Well," Buell said at length, "the first thing to do is to get inside
that prison the right way. People that stand outside prisons and
look at 'em most generally get inside the wrong way."

As if in answer to Buell's words, a sentry moved toward us. "Nah
then," he said, lowering his bayonet suggestively, "if you got no
business here, don't 'ang arahnd."

He followed us to the entrance and watched me pound upon the
iron door. "Sometimes they pounds 'ere 'alf an hour," he said, "but
most generally somebody comes in the end."

"'Alf an hour!" Buell cried. He kicked his heel against the iron door with an echoing crash.

The sentry looked horrified and left us hurriedly.

"'Alf an hour," Buell repeated angrily. Once more he raised his heel; but the iron door swung open. Framed within it we saw a dozen indignant guards in scarlet coats and black gaiters.

"What's all the bloody hurry?" one of them asked.

Buell looked embarrassed. "It ain't true," he said. "We heard it took 'alf an hour for you people to get the door open, but I couldn't have opened it much quicker myself. You got Soame Leighton in here?"

A sergeant of grenadiers moved out from the group and looked hard at Buell. "Who wants to know? What business is it of yours whether he is or not?"

I made my voice as conciliatory as I could. "We had charge of the prisoners' camp after the battle of Brooklyn. That's where Leighton was taken prisoner. He gave me something to keep for him, and I want to give it back."

"In charge of prisoners after the battle of Long Island," the sergeant said thoughtfully. "You want to see Captain Cunningham, don't you?"

"For sure we do," Buell said quickly, "but we heard he was always drunk at this time of night."

The guards exchanged glances. "You're Americans," their spokesman said. "Americans can't get in to see rebel prisoners without an order from Captain Cunningham."

"I'll get the order," I said. "I only wanted to be sure of Leighton's whereabouts."

The sergeant spoke irritably. "Don't put words in my mouth! I never said he was here! How can I keep track of three hundred and fifty good-for-nothing limbs of the devil, yelling for what they call their rights all day, and raising such hell all night you can't hardly think!"

"Don't you take their names when they come in?" I asked.

The sergeant gave me an impatient answer. "No, we do not! They move through here altogether too fast for us to keep records of 'em! Besides, you can't believe a bloody word they say! They lie about their bloody names, and they lie about the bloody places they come from—lie just for the sake of lying, most of the time! The way to deal with men like that is never to give 'em a chance to lie."

Buell looked baffled. "You don't keep records? I s'pose that's because the army can't spare anybody for guard duty unless he's no good anywhere else, and can't read or write."

"That's our business," the jailer said.

"Not exclusively it ain't," Buell said. "If we want to find Soame Leighton, that's our business, ain't it?"

"Maybe and maybe not," the jailer said, "but I'll tell you this much, right flat out. There ain't nobody named Soame Leighton here."

"Are you sure?" I asked.

"Certainly, I'm sure," the sergeant said brusquely.

"How can you be sure, when you can't keep track of the three hundred and fifty men you have here?"

The jailer looked contemptuous. "A little less insinuating, *hif* you please! I wouldn't have remembered him, only he happened to be transferred out of here and to somewhere else."

"When was that?" I asked. "When was he transferred, and where was he sent?"

The sergeant was suddenly and violently exasperated. "How'd I know where he was sent! Prisoners are moved out of here every few days, so to make room for others; and we've got enough on our hands without trying to play nursemaid to every dirty damned rebel! Why, two thousand of 'em were dumped on our hands when we captured Fort Washington! It takes nine jails to look out for 'em, in addition to all the prison ships in Wallabout Bay. We've got 'em in the old French Church, the old Dutch Church, the old Swedish Church, three sugar houses and two warehouses. Every time a platoon of our troops go out for exercise, another rebel militia regiment surrenders to 'em! You can't expect us to know what's happening to any such bloody big crowd as that!"

"Perhaps the other prisoners would know where Leighton was sent," I suggested. "Those things get around in prisons."

The red-coated guards stared at their spokesman. "Not in this prison, they don't," he said. "You'll never find a soul in this prison who'd know where Leighton went."

"His brothers might know," Buell said. "All we've got to do is find his brothers."

"It ain't as simple as that," the jailer said triumphantly. "Both his brothers are in this jail. They don't know a bloody bit more about him than you do."

"Well," Buell said. "They're in this jail, are they, and don't know where their own brother went! That shows Captain Cunningham probably didn't have anything to do with having him moved, because if Captain Cunningham had given an order, the order certainly would have leaked out. Yes, sir, they'd certainly have known what was in that order, and the Leightons would have known it first of all."

"Yes," I said, "I believe you're right—if it's really true that his brothers don't know where he was taken. Probably General Clinton or General Howe could have the brothers questioned for us, if the worst came to the worst."

To the jailer I added, "Of course, if you're sure the brothers don't know, I wouldn't need to bother the generals."

"They don't know one bloody thing," he said.

"You're sure?" I insisted. "I don't want to seem to doubt your word, but this particular case is important and——"

The jailer hastily interrupted me. "Not a damned soul in this jail knows where Soame Leighton was taken. I don't myself. If you want to talk to the Leightons, I'll get 'em down here. No, sir, any general that wasted time asking questions about Leighton, he'd just be wasting his time. Hawks, you go on up to the second floor and bring Leighton's brothers down here!"

Steven and Jeremiah Leighton were twins, who had always seemed to me as similar in some ways as two setter dogs from the same litter, but in other ways as dissimilar as though one were made of steel and the other of silk. Their height was the same; the clothes, hats and shoes of either fitted the other like gloves; they strikingly resembled each other in feature and gait; but Jeremiah was as rugged, forthright and loud-voiced as Steven was delicate, shy and soft-spoken.

They were two years younger than Sally; I had seen little of them after I went away to Yale, and had thought of them always as boys— boys I would recognize anywhere, and could infallibly tell apart.

But the two tatterdemalions who were ushered into the dingy, stone-floored lobby of the Provost didn't seem to me to be Sally's brothers. In eighteen short months they had somehow contrived to lose their distinguishing characteristics, and to become soiled, hard and bitter duplicates of each other. For the life of me I couldn't tell Steven from Jeremiah. In neither of them could I see a trace of that shyness, that quiet modesty, which had once been so strikingly apparent in Steven. They had beards an inch long. Their uncombed and untied hair hung to their shoulders; their hands were grimy. Through the rents in their stockings their legs were pallid, like dirty marble. Their buttonless uniform coats were fastened in front with buckskin thongs, and beneath those thongs was naked flesh. Their leather breeches were shiny from grease and hard wear; and through their broken shoes I could see their toes.

I looked from them to the red-faced, scarlet-coated jailers, with their black, thigh-length gaiters, their warm neckcloths, their stout boots with inch-thick soles.

"Can I see these men alone?" I asked the sergeant.

He looked pained. "What for? You want to find out where their brother went, don't you? You don't have to be alone with 'em to ask that. Go ahead and ask."

I turned back to Steven and Jeremiah. "I'm Oliver Wiswell," I said, "and I'm hunting for Soame. I've got a message for him from your father and your sister."

Steven and Jeremiah stared at the stone floor, almost as though they hadn't heard me.

"Your family's all well," I added. "They're anxious for your welfare: particularly anxious about Soame."

One of the brothers, whom I took to be Jeremiah because of the sullen hardness of his eyes, looked up at me. "Didn't they get our letters?"

"They've heard nothing from any of you," I said. "They don't even know you and Steven were captured."

"I'm Steven," he said. "How'd they find out about Soame?"

"A friend told them. When they heard he wasn't well, they made up their mind to appeal to General Washington to see if he couldn't be exchanged. We want to find him and tell him, so he won't be too discouraged."

The other brother looked up at me. "Discouraged? You couldn't discourage Soame!" His glance slid around to the silent red-coated jailers; then returned again to me. "Nothing discouraged Soame! Rotten meat, weevilly bread, no blankets, no water to wash in, lice, bedbugs—Soame stood 'em all! He couldn't stand your friend Cunningham, but you couldn't say he ever got discouraged. He just hated him, and he wasn't afraid to say so."

The sergeant made a contemptuous sound. "He most likely expected the captain to come in and put him to bed every night, and tuck him in, and hear him say his prayers. Well, this ain't a nursery!

It's a prison for rebels! Your brother got the same treatment as everybody else; and if prisoners were never treated any worse than those here are treated, they'd be lucky."

"Oh my," Buell said, "how true that is! Prisoners that have the luck to be in these prisons prob'ly wish they could spend the rest of their lives fighting wars and being took prisoner."

"Certainly," the sergeant said angrily. "Most of these rebels that complain about having no water to wash in—they never washed at all before they came here. And they're getting food, even if it *is* a little mite old—and that's more than our prisoners are getting from the rebels."

Jeremiah Leighton passed a trembling hand across his moist forehead. "Mr. Wiswell," he said, "that can't be true! Two hundred and seven men died in this prison during the last two weeks. Two hundred and seven is an awful lot of men, Mr. Wiswell. Some of 'em just shriveled away from not getting enough food, and some of 'em died of fevers and fluxes. The surest to die are those that complain about the food or the treatment here. The only one they couldn't kill was Soame. He just wouldn't die, Mr. Wiswell. I suppose I'll die myself for telling you this, but I might as well die one way as another."

"You bloody rebel!" the sergeant shouted. "Nobody asked you about food and dying! What's one man's testimony good for in a case like this? All this gentleman wanted to know was what had become of your brother. If you know, answer him. If you don't know, shut up!"

The two Leightons stared intently at the floor. I saw their throat muscles work.

"The sergeant's right, Jeremiah," I said. "He did me a kindness when he let me ask you about Soame. I've no business to listen to anything else."

"I haven't heard a word," Buell said. "So far as I know, all the rebels in this jail are getting lamb stew and dumplings and mince pie and hot bread three times a day."

Both the Leighton boys drew deep, quivering breaths.

"Can you tell me anything about Soame?" I asked again. "Anything about where he went when he left here? When was he taken away?"

"Eleven days ago," Jeremiah said. "It was late at night. Somebody came to the door and called his name, along with five others, and they marched out. They hated Cunningham."

"You *all* hate him," the sergeant said. "He's a warmhearted, good officer, but he's goaded almost beyond endurance by these bloody ungrateful rebels! Who wouldn't be!"

I spoke up hastily. "Arguments won't help me find Soame Leighton. They won't help anybody. Can't you tell me anything else about Soame? Can't any of the other prisoners guess where he was taken?"

Steven Leighton answered wildly. "He was taken out and shot! Cunningham couldn't kill him by starvation and mistreatment and exposure, so he had him killed! He was taken out at midnight. Why? Why didn't we ever hear from him again? Why is it that all those who're taken out at midnight never come back? Why do they always take men who hate Cunningham? Why do they always take men that dare to talk about his cruelty?" He shivered, and beads of sweat stood out on his forehead. His quick and angry gestures seemed to release from him an acrid odor of sour perspiration.

"Look at that!" the sergeant complained. "That's the way they make mountains out of molehills! This prison's the clearinghouse for all the prisons. All prisoners pass through the Provost first; and as a matter of course they have to pass on to the other prisons."

"Seems kind of a shame not to keep records of 'em, if you make 'em come here first," Buell said.

"Who says they don't keep records?" Jeremiah Leighton asked. "I was logged when I came in here, and so was Steven. So was everybody."

"That's right," the sergeant said heartily, "we keep a man's record until he leaves here. Then we send the record to where he's going when he leaves."

"Oh," Buell said, "you send the record where he's going! Well, that's better than nothing! Where'd you send Leighton's record?"

The sergeant looked exasperated. "Good God, man! That was weeks ago! Do you think we can remember one man out of hundreds? I've clean forgot where we sent that record."

Buell looked at him admiringly. "Now that's what I call clever! Who do you suppose invented it?"

"Pah!" the sergeant growled. "We spend months working up a fine system, and then it's criticized by somebody who never even heard of it till the minute before! I s'pose that's human nature! Anyway, this rebel Leighton you're looking for was taken out at midnight, because midnight's the handiest time to transport prisoners through the streets. As for not hearing from him again, what did you expect him to do? Hire a chaise and drive up here every day to pay a call on all his old friends? And you bet they never come back! They stay where we send them, or they go on to another prison. No, gentlemen; you told me these prisoners'd know where their brother'd be taken. I said they wouldn't, and I was right. They've heard a lot of idle rumors, based on prison gossip—and that's no good! Hawks, take these two men back to the second floor."

"Wait," I said. "Give me another minute or two with them, won't you, sergeant?"

"Not another bloody minute! You wanted to find out about Soame Leighton, and you haven't done it! If you want to talk to anybody else in this prison, get an order from Captain Cunningham! That's final!"

There wasn't much to choose between the prisons for rebels in New York. They were all crowded; they were all bad; all the prisoners in them were cold, dirty, hungry, sick.

The prisoners invited many of their troubles, for they were fretful and contentious by nature, insistent on what they believed to be their rights; narrow-minded, suspicious, jealous, parsimonious, like so many of the so-called Puritans; intolerant of any sort of restraint or discipline.

More than that, they felt themselves ignored, forgotten, unrewarded, for they were never visited by their own officers; their situation was never investigated by the army of which they had been a part; they were avoided as much as possible by their guards because of their rude and uncouth behavior.

The prison ships in Wallabout Bay, that shallow indentation in the Brooklyn shore just across from the lower tip of New York, were the worst of all the prisons because of their perpetual dampness, and their hopeless remoteness from the surroundings which their occupants had known before they were taken prisoners. I thought it likely that Cunningham might have sent Soame to one of the worst of these; so it was to the prison ships—those dark and noisome hulks anchored in forlorn disarray beneath the Heights of Brooklyn—that I went first.

I went alone, for Buell, in spite of his hatred for rebels, seemed to have an almost equal hatred for prison guards. "They wouldn't be jailers, Oliver," he argued, "unless there was something wrong with 'em; and when there's something wrong with a man, I'm apt to speak my mind to him. It wouldn't do you or Soame Leighton any good if I went around speaking my mind, so I'll stay here and make myself a little more counterfeit money and find out what I can in my own way."

The *Jersey* was the receiving ship for that fleet of eleven miserable vessels; every prisoner sent to the hulks went first to the *Jersey*, where his name was entered on the books.

The officers of the *Jersey*, in spite of the many harsh things I have since heard said of them, were kind enough to me, and gave me free access to their damp and musty ledgers, on which appeared the names of men from Pennsylvania to Maine; but nowhere among them could I find Soame's.

They were even helpful. Perhaps, they said, the name had been wrongly entered. New Englanders, they told me, had a strange and drawling manner of speech, so that "Towne" sometimes became "Towan"; "Perkins" became "Pukkins"; "Wilde" became "Wyall".

We looked under "Layton"; under "Lane"; under "Late"; and even under "Some" and "Sowam": but there wasn't a name that even faintly resembled the one I sought.

One of the officers from the *Jersey*, a pleasant young lieutenant named Barrett, rowed with me to all the other hulks, on the chance that Soame's name might somehow have been dropped from the *Jersey's* books. His name was read out from the quarter-deck of every vessel; but he was on none of them; and not a man came forward with information concerning him.

From the prison ships I turned to the sugar houses, warehouses and churches in which rebels were imprisoned; but each night I came back to our lodgings, half sick from the stenches of those foul and crowded tombs, and never a bit the wiser as to Soame's whereabouts.

What was worse, Buell had taken to drinking. He stayed out half the night, and came staggering home to lie morosely on his bed, muttering and grumbling to himself, and without a cheerful word for me or anyone else.

I'd been to every prison but one—the Beekman Street Sugar House —before I learned what had become of Soame; and it was Buell who found out.

CHAPTER XLVI

THAT night he came home a little before twelve, cold sober, walked into the room as softly as a cat, shielded his eyes from the lighted candle that stood on the table, and peered hard at my bed. Then, without a sound, he pulled off his coat and began to loosen his neckcloth. His eye sockets were dark caverns.

"Tom," I said, "he wasn't in the Dutch Church. If he isn't in the Beekman Street Sugar House, I'm stumped."

Buell rolled his stock carefully around his fingers. "I hoped you'd be asleep, Oliver," he said.

I sat up in bed. "You found out something. He's dead, isn't he?"

"Yes," Tom said, "he's dead." He cleared his throat; then came over and sat on my bed, looking tired and old.

"Was it Cunningham?" I asked.

"I guess so, Oliver. You know as well as I do that he's got to be at the bottom of it."

He stared contemplatively at his shoes. "This damned war must be weakening me, Oliver. I've figured and figured how to get back at Cunningham, but I just can't seem to think of anything—except things that would get me into too much trouble. I think about him so much, Oliver, that I don't believe I can stay around where he is any longer. If only he was in the army, I'd be willing to join it myself, just for the sake of getting a shot at him during a battle; but of course I wouldn't want to take a shot at him if I wasn't in uniform, because then it would be murder.

"Whatever we do, Oliver, I think we ought to do legally and in order—particularly when it comes to murder. That's the trouble with all the schemes I think of. They ain't quite legal enough, and——"

404

"What happened to Soame, Tom?"

"Yes," Buell said, "yes." He scratched his head. "I'll think of something in time. This damned war makes me slow. Since I've been connected with it, I've lost half the brains I had in the beginning; and if I stay in it much longer, I'll be like half the officers on both sides. I won't have any brains left at all."

"What happened?" I asked again.

Buell sighed. "Well, Oliver, it stood to reason that those who moved Soame out of the Provost would be the ones who'd know what had become of him; so I found out who was on duty the night he was taken away. It was the same Provost guard that's been on duty ever since Cunningham took over the prison. Regan, a sergeant, commanded it. Regan was a friend of Cunningham's brother. Cunningham's brother was the sergeant we talked to the night we went to the Provost. That makes it plain that Regan could be trusted to carry out Cunningham's orders, doesn't it?

"Well, Oliver, Regan's had money ever since he's been on guard at this prison—more money than any sergeant ought to have. I found out where he gets it. He gets it two ways. He gets it for taking letters from prisoners to their families, and then he sells their belongings after they're dead. Most generally he tears up the letters that he promises to deliver for 'em. He had one for you from Soame Leighton."

I threw off the blanket. "What was Regan's regiment? I'll see about Regan."

Buell pressed me back on the mattress. "Lay still," he said. "You can't do anything about Regan. I saw about him myself."

"Did he tear up my letter?"

"Yes," Buell said. "He read it and then tore it up. I'm glad you weren't with me, Oliver. You certainly wouldn't have liked Regan, but you might not have fixed him as well as I did."

He looked almost contented. "Yes, sir, I certainly fixed him! He was kind of interesting, too, in a way. I'm mighty glad I got to know Regan. He was telling me about a young feller you probably know, because he went to Yale. Name of Nathan Hale."

"Why, yes," I said. "I know Nathan Hale. He was a class behind me. What happened to him?"

"He was a rebel," Buell said. "He was sent over to Long Island to do a little spying, the way we were; and Colonel Rogers—the one we crossed the Sound with—caught him and turned him over to

Cunningham. He wrote a lot of letters home just before they hanged him, and Regan tore 'em all up."

I felt suffocated, so got out of bed and pulled on my clothes.

"Well," Buell said, "Regan and his men took Soame Leighton and five other prisoners out of the Provost at half past twelve on the night of the fifth of November. Told 'em they were going to the hospital. That's what Regan always told 'em. It struck him funny, always, because everybody in the Provost is always sick, and can't get to the hospital fast enough. Regan's had a lot of fun out of this war —or did, up till tonight. He told me he'd never had a better time. Plenty to drink; plenty to eat; lots of women, good clothes and a tight roof over his head. He'd been let out of prison to join the army, he told me, and he certainly appreciated his opportunities."

"How'd you learn all this, Tom?"

"With liquor," Buell said. "I drank so much with Regan that I practically ain't got any stomach left. I spent twelve hundred and fifty dollars buying rum for him"—he looked thoughtful—"and I'm still out of pocket, because I only got nine hundred of it back tonight. Nine hundred dollars and a chronometer. He had a real nice chronometer. I'll make a new case for it, and it'll be worth maybe five hundred dollars hard money."

He darted a quick look at me. "I thought he'd never talk, Oliver. I got him drunk ten times before he opened his mouth. He was a purple-faced feller with red hair in his ears and a big stomach, and I don't like purple faces or bushy ears when they go with a big stomach. Nobody ought to have all three; it's repulsive. Well, what happened was that when anybody in the Provost got to making too much trouble, Regan and his men took 'em out at midnight and——"

"On whose orders?" I asked.

"Cunningham's," Buell said. "I can't prove it; but it's *got* to be Cunningham. Howe's a damned fool, but he wouldn't kill prisoners in cold blood. Neither would any of the other officers we've come across. Regan wouldn't waste the time on it unless ordered to, and his orders *had* to come from Cunningham. Anyway, Regan took 'em out of the Provost and marched 'em around the corner into the field. All the windows in the houses along that street have wooden shutters on them. That's supposed to be so nobody can signal to the prisoners and maybe help 'em get away, but actually it's so nobody can see what happens to those that Regan takes out at midnight.

"When he got 'em to the field, Oliver, he shot 'em in the back with buckshot. Then he went through their pockets and took whatever they had; then put 'em into a pit with quicklime in it. It's all for prison insubordination, but kept quiet for the good of the service. You'll never see Soame Leighton again, and nobody'll ever even find his bones."

I felt tired and old. How could I ever tell Sally Leighton what I had just heard! I couldn't tell her! I could never, never tell her!

"This Regan," Buell went on, "kind of fell into a stupor after he'd told me all this. Before he fell into it, he was doing a good deal of laughing over something Soame said just before he died. Soame asked Regan to tell somebody named Oliver that if he hadn't died like a soldier, it wasn't because he hadn't tried to. Regan thought that was pretty funny, and he thought there was something funny about your name, too, Oliver. Seems like he thought it was sort of girlish."

"I see," I said.

"Yes," Buell said, "then he fell into that coma I was speaking about. We were in a nice warm room, Oliver—one that I'd hired special to get Regan drunk in. It had a nice fire in it, and a nice loggerhead in the fire for mulling ale. I never saw a nicer loggerhead. It was big enough to mull a pitcherful at a time. When Regan fell into his coma, I happened to be looking at the loggerhead, and it fell down across Regan's throat. The smell of flesh burning must have scared me, sort of, because I knocked over a table, and it fell on the loggerhead and pressed it down so it burned into his windpipe. It made such a whistling noise that I ran out to get some help, but as soon as I got out, I realized there wasn't anything anybody could do. Of course I didn't want to make any more trouble than I had to, so I came right back here."

He looked at me expectantly.

"That's good," I said. "You did just right! I'll go to see General Howe in the morning. We can't stand this stuff any longer!"

Not until midafternoon of the next day could I gain admission to General Howe's office, and I found Howe as sullen, but no more sullen, than he had been when I first met him in Boston; as disgruntled-looking, but no more so, than he had been after he was driven from Boston; as richly dressed and as studiously careless about his garb as though the winning of battles and the suppression of a rebellion were the least of his troubles—and I'm not so sure they weren't.

"Ah, Mr. Wiswell," the general said, "I've had you in mind for the past two days. You needn't worry about your friend any longer. The rebels seem to want him back. They've offered to exchange for him, and for his brothers, too. Very generous terms, I'm bound to say. They offer us a colonel for a captain and two ensigns. Your friend'll be back with his adoring family in another week."

"Back with his family," I said. "Soame Leighton! Back with his family!"

"Yes," the general said. "We're accepting the rebel proposals for him and his two brothers."

"But he's dead!"

Howe's lip hung slack. "The devil you say! How do you know? Who told you so? Where'd he die?"

"He died in the field behind the Provost Prison," I said. "He was taken there and shot. I can't tell you who told me."

"Bosh!" Howe cried. "Shot! You've been listening to rebels, Wiswell! According to them, we shoot prisoners every night in every prison in New York! That's poppycock! If your friend's dead, he probably died of the fever." He looked up at me from under heavy lids. "In all probability he isn't dead at all! You've no proof of it, have you?"

"He was a prisoner when I left New York, General, but he's not in any prison now. There isn't a jailer in New York or aboard the prison ships that admits to knowing anything about him."

"Admits?" Howe asked slowly. "Not a jailer that *admits* to knowing? Are you suggesting, Mr. Wiswell, that they're hiding some dark secret about this rebel officer?"

"That's precisely what I'm suggesting, sir," I said. "I'm also suggesting that the provost marshal is a disgrace to your army. I'm suggesting that his brutality toward rebel prisoners is bound to enrage the rebel forces, and make them more difficult to destroy. I'm suggesting that every rebel prisoner who dares to protest against Cunningham's cruelty is taken out on Captain Cunningham's orders and shot down in cold blood. I'm suggesting that Cunningham's a thief, a liar, a bully and a murderer—that he's——"

Howe interrupted me. "Aren't you getting above yourself, Mr. Wiswell?"

"No, sir. I threw in my lot with you because my family and my friends hadn't been fairly treated by the mobs who called themselves Patriots. I wanted my father and his friends to be treated fairly. I wanted every American to be treated fairly, and that's what I still want. I want fair treatment for myself! I won't stand by and see——"

"Come, come, Mr. Wiswell," the general broke in. "You're speaking wildly!"

"Wildly?" I asked. "Wildly? What have I said that's wild, General? When one political party tries to destroy another, war's inevitable! There can't be peace anywhere so long as conquered people are mistreated; and while Cunningham's in charge of prisoners, he'll mistreat 'em! He hates 'em all the time! He won't let 'em ask friends or families for help! He won't feed 'em properly! He won't let 'em have proper medical attention! Good God, General, those rebel prisoners are dying at the rate of a hundred a week, most of 'em starved or frozen to death!

"He destroys their records, so they can't be traced! There's firing every night in the field behind the Provost. Prisoners are taken there every night, and nobody ever sees 'em again! You don't think they evaporate, do you, General? They're killed, and England's responsible! England takes the blame!

"The provost marshal has charge of all prisoners, hasn't he, General? If they're killed, he knows about it, doesn't he? If you think I'm talking wildly, get him in here! Question him! Cunningham's hands may not have held the gun that fired buckshot into Soame Leighton's back, but Cunningham's the murderer! I'll stake my life on it! You can't allow such things, General! You can't—not unless you want to make a gift of these American colonies to men not fit to have 'em! For God's sake, General, get rid of Cunningham!"

Howe jumped up and strode about the room, muttering, "wild Irishmen", "damned stupidity", "no self-control". Then he turned on me. "Have you, by any chance, openly aired these views of yours?"

"I've made no secret of my feelings for Captain Cunningham. If he came into this room now, I'd say to him exactly what I've said to you."

"Listen to me," Howe said. "An army's a delicate and dangerous monster! Its business is to kill ruthlessly; its duty to be killed, if need be, without protest. It's hard, brutal, unfeeling; yet the merest pin prick can make it quiver with anguish from nose to tail. One word, injudiciously spoken, can send it into paroxysms! I can't have this army endangered!"

I laughed.

"No laughing matter," Howe said. "I won't have squabbling or fighting, violence or gossip, in my army. I mean, Mr. Wiswell, that I'm taking considerable pains to explain to you that we can't have a scandal. A scandal's peculiar in that it's full-fledged the moment it comes to life. In general, Captain Cunningham is considered a useful, able officer in the King's service. He's well liked, and I think I've just made it plain to you why I can't have all my officers thrown in a turmoil over charges that for all I know may be groundless."

"Groundless!" I cried. "Do you think I'd——"

"They may not be groundless," Howe broke in, "but unfortunately, a court-martial must decide whether they are or not. If a court-martial is held and our dirty linen washed in public, our enemies will benefit. They'll damn us, lie about us, send back word to England that may ruin scores of us. In an army, Mr. Wiswell, the first thing to be considered is the good of the service. Always the good of the service!"

"Sir," I said, "you don't mean you'll let a vindictive murderer go free—you don't mean that because of something somebody *might* say, you won't lift a finger to halt an assassin!"

Howe looked at me gloomily. "I fear the progress of affairs in America has been too much for you. You have the American failing, let us say, of being too impatient. When things don't go rapidly enough to suit you, you become overcritical. You've been of great service to our cause and to your own country; but I'm forced to say that in your present frame of mind, your worth is considerably impaired."

High army officers know from long experience that their very rank almost always intimidates and silences inferior officers; and I think Howe expected me to be intimidated—as I probably would have been if I'd worn a uniform.

"Sir," I said, "I'm not overcritical! I resent the implication that my value's impaired for telling you that Cunningham murdered Soame Leighton!"

"You misunderstand me, Mr. Wiswell," Howe said. "Perhaps I didn't make my meaning clear. I still need your help; and God knows America needs it, too. She needs all she can get if she's not to be governed by the worst incompetents I've ever seen. No, no, Mr. Wiswell! Under no circumstances would I want to lose you, but the place for you is England."

A year ago I would have looked at Howe and seen England's greatest general—a gigantic figure with power of life and death over

thousands of men; a colossus, entrusted with the preservation of the
British Empire. Now I saw a sulky, fat, aging, sensuous politician—a
weak-willed man who again and again had sacrificed victory because his spirit had weakened at the crucial moment. He wasn't a
big man at all, but a small man, hampered by every mossy tradition
of England's army, England's politics, England's governing class.
Never, so long as I stayed in America and tried under Howe to
work for a peaceful solution of America's troubles, would I ever
be sure of justice, ever be sure that I wasn't being uselessly sacrificed
to the stubbornness of inept politicians and incompetent soldiers.

"If you'd consent to go to England," Howe said again, "I'd send you
to Lord Germaine. You're a New Englander, and you'd be extremely
valuable in obtaining information concerning the rebel privateer
captains who're interfering with my supply ships. They sail from
French ports, but their intelligence comes from England. Somebody's
got to find out how they get it and from whom, and I think you're
the one to do it."

"Could I take Buell?" I asked.

"I think it would be advisable," Howe said. "I was going to suggest that you take him. In fact, I was going to *insist* that you take
him. Knowing your peculiar regard for him, I was even about to
tell you to act with some precipitation in the matter. Buell is often a
useful man, but I fear he's sometimes—ah—impulsive."

He looked at me oddly. I saw that he knew about Buell and Regan.
I saw more: I saw that others knew how Regan had died.

"We'll go, sir," I said.

"Very good," Howe said. "The *Holyhead* frigate sails for England
day after tomorrow; but you'll go aboard her today. Today, do you
understand? Find Buell and get him aboard with no loss of time,
and don't let him out of your sight until you're at sea."

BOOK III

☆

Paris

CHAPTER XLVII

So HEARTILY did we detest the frigate that carried us to England that the sight of the chalk cliffs of Dover showing white above the lead-colored channel on a January morning in 1777 was a welcome one; and the rattle of the cable, as our frigate rounded into the wind before the enormous Admiralty pier in Dover Harbor, was music in our ears.

The captain and the officers of the frigate had been kind enough to us; our quarters had been as comfortable as could be expected on a King's ship, aboard which one lives about as spaciously and privately as in an open coffin; but both Buell and I had found the ship almost unendurable.

Day after day we had been forced to listen to the opinions of Englishmen concerning America and Americans; night after night, in the wardroom, we sat silent while reedy-voiced lieutenants spoke insufferably of *"our* American colonies", *"our* American plantations", as if the property and persons of all Americans were absolutely theirs. We had to hear them assure each other that no Yankee—which was how they referred to all Americans—was anything but contemptible, a coward, cruel beyond belief, and utterly depraved.

Buell and I, God knows, had reason enough to hate the rebels and everything for which they stood; and yet the insufferable conceit, the ignorant assurance of these condescending Britons filled us with a perverse desire to rush to the support of any American they attacked.

I must admit that many of their beliefs were strikingly similar to our own; yet there was a difference—sometimes only the difference of a word; sometimes, even, only the difference of an inflection—that made our opinions as far apart as the poles.

When they damned *all* Americans for poltroons, I remembered that brown regiment of Maryland rebels returning again and again and again to the attack at the battle of Long Island, doing its utmost to hold back what must have seemed to them like Howe's entire army.

I thought of Soame Leighton, defying Cunningham with his last breath. The rebel ranks, I knew, were full of men like Soame Leighton; full of men like those brown-uniformed Marylanders; full of men who believed passionately—just as Buell and I believed, just as all men in all armies have always believed—in the righteousness of their cause; who only needed proper training in the ways of war to be the equal of any men who ever bore arms.

I wanted to tell those thick-headed naval officers that there was hardly one of the rebels they despised who couldn't, if he wished, lie all night on an icy ledge to kill ducks as they swam across the moonpath; who hadn't walked for miles through tangled shrubs and across rocky hillslopes after deer or bear. The rebels were enemies, mine and Buell's even more than England's, but they were no poltroons; they were no more cruel or depraved than any similar group of ignorant fanatics would be. They were just men like all the rest of us—misguided, certainly, and ingrates, but as valuable to the world, if wisely governed, as spindle-shanked English naval lieutenants with a fondness for whipping seamen.

Again and again, and with increasing irritation, I found myself impelled to quarrel with these insufferable Englishmen, to defend the rebels who had killed my father and driven me from my home; and so, even, was Buell.

"Oliver," Buell said to me repeatedly, "ain't there something we can do to educate these British? Ain't there any way we can persuade 'em that there's quite a number of Americans able to think almost as fast and straight as Englishmen? I wouldn't trust Sam Adams with the management of a dog fight, but damned if he ain't smarter than King George and General Howe put together. Why, I'll bet that old General Putnam, even, is twice as smart as King George, and three times smarter than these squirty little naval officers."

"There's nothing to be done about it," I said. "Keep your mouth shut and let others do the talking."

"Look, Oliver," Buell said, "what's the objection to telling 'em a thing or two? If they keep on damning all Americans, it won't be long before all Loyalists get as sick of 'em as the rebels are. God knows I'm sick of 'em, and I'm a lot sweeter-tempered than most."

I had hard work to keep him quiet. "It's no use, Tom. All we can do is keep our mouths shut till we get ashore; then try to talk to someone with influence. These officers are too small to bother with, and we'd get nothing for our pains but trouble. Let 'em think as they please about America and Americans. They're English; they'll do it anyway."

That was one reason I was so glad to go ashore at Dover. Another was that we were almost penniless. Our joint resources were a five-pound note and fourteen shillings, seven pennies and three farthings; but somewhere in England, we knew, were Mrs. Byles and Henrietta Dixon with the prize money we had entrusted to them in Halifax; and as soon as we could find them, we were certain of obtaining from them enough at least to keep us from beggary.

Still another, and by no means the least, reason was the belief that somewhere and somehow, in England, I would hear from Sally Leighton—and Sally, now that my home had been taken from me, had come to be my greatest reason for being: my one anchor in an unstable world that seemed to be staggering and reeling like a rudderless ship in a storm.

So we were as glad to back down the companion ladder of the *Holyhead* frigate and drop into the jollyboat below as the *Holyhead's* officers must have been to see us go; and we were gladder still when we climbed the slippery stone stairway of the enormous Admiralty dock and saw the crew of the jollyboat rowing briskly away from us, already oblivious of our existence.

Being short of funds, we could waste nothing on stagecoaches; so we shouldered our scanty belongings and set off through the streets of Dover, hoping to stumble on the London Road. "Don't ask questions," Buell insisted. "This is England, and the worst thing about England is that it's full of Englishmen. If you speak to one of 'em, he'll recognize you as an American, and tell a naval lieutenant. Then we'll be pressed into their damned navy, sure as shooting! I'm willing to help 'em win the war. If they don't, I can't ever go back and live in Newport without being tarred and feathered in case I want to speak my mind about a rebel general that cobbles shoes and milks cows when he ain't in the army. I'll do all I can, but I'll be damned if I'll join their navy and let English naval officers have me licked just because they hate everyone but themselves."

There was something in what he said; so we took the nearest road out of the Admiralty grounds, and laid our course along the tavern-studded promenade toward the white cliffs into which Dover is driven like a gigantic wedge.

We didn't get far on foot, however; for as we passed a tavern, its door opened and a tall, roughly dressed man backed with dignified rapidity from the doorway and came to a stop immediately before us.

He was dark, thin, gangling, awkward. His eyebrows were bushy; his eyes jet black. Beneath the cloth of his breeches his knees seemed made of laths; and his wrists and knuckles were huge and wooden in appearance, as though carved by someone who intended to return later and finish the job.

He stood there frowning at the door which had been closed in his face, and spoke his mind in language that marked him not only as an American, but as a seaman whose associations and upbringing had not been of the best. It indicated, too, that he had been forcibly ejected.

"You and your fast brigs," he shouted. "You limeys don't know the meaning of the word 'fast'! A ship's fast to you if it outsails a lame goose! Why, by God, I could sail rings around any of your slave brigs in a Poughkeepsie stoneboat! Damned if I understand how the British Navy got where it is!"

He seemed to get angrier, shaking his fist at the closed door as if it listened attentively. He even made kicking motions toward it. "What say?" he shouted, seeming to think his monologue was in reality a dialogue. When no reply was forthcoming, he made as if to turn and walk away, but wheeled suddenly, as though the door had given him an insulting answer. "You're a liar," he shouted, "a dirty liar! You got all the money in the world, you can build all the ships you want, but the ships ain't worth a damn, and you ain't got a sailor that knows how to sail 'em! Show me an English-built cutter that can sail thirteen knots, and I'll buy her and give you fifty pounds bounty for finding her! By God, I will, and I got the money to do it, by God!"

He decided finally that he was through with the door and turned away in such haste that he bumped into Buell. He looked surprised; then wagged an enormous forefinger at us. "You heard me! Go spread the word! Go tell 'em Captain Joe Hynson of Maryland, by

God, can prove there ain't a thirteen-knot brig in all England! Fifty pounds to anyone who can prove different, and here it is!"

He fumbled in a breeches pocket, clumsily dragged out a wad of paper money, and shook it in my face. "There! Fifty pounds! Find me a vessel that can do thirteen knots and it's yours!"

His breath in my face was like the exudation from a distillery. "Well, what you got to say? You're a sailor, from your looks. Cat got your tongue? Bet you ten pounds you never even saw a vessel that could better ten knots! Come on! Ten pounds to a knot! Ain't that a fair offer?"

Buell gave him an answer. "You're too damned noisy! What you want to do? Get us pressed into the British Navy?"

Hynson clung to me. "For God's sake!" he cried. "Americans! This country's overrun with 'em! They ought to wear red hats, so you can tell 'em from the English! Come on, gentlemen, let's have a drink." He looked haughtily at the closed door beside us. "Not in there, though! Never set foot in the place again. What's more, they won't let me. We'll go some place else."

"To tell you the truth," I said, "we're uneasy while we're in sight of the Admiralty. We can't afford to be pressed, so if you'll excuse us, we'll be on our way."

"On your way where?" Hynson asked. "London? If it's London, what's your hurry? Wait for Uncle Joe Hynson and he'll keep company with you." He drew out a huge chronometer, examined it carefully; then added, "Stagecoach goes in half an hour. We'll ride in the back seat, 'n' sing good old American songs. 'Nut-Brown Maiden', 'n' all that! Meanwhile, let's have that little drink! Nobody's going to touch you while Uncle Joe Hynson's got you under his wing. You'll be protected—courtesy of the ocean 'n' so on."

"Courtesy of the ocean?" Buell asked. "Never heard of it! Come on, Oliver; let's be off for London."

"No, you don't," Hynson bellowed. "None of that, now! You've had a friendly invitation to take a glass of gin with Joe Hynson, and Uncle Joe Hynson don't take no for an answer! We'll have a little drink; then we'll ride up to London together, just as happy and contented as a lot of—a lot of—a lot of——"

A thought seemed to strike him. "I'll show you my nut-brown maiden! 'Nut-brown maiden, thou hast a slender waist to clasp! Nut brown'—— By God, gentlemen, you never saw nothing like London! To hear Ben Franklin talk, you'd think every woman in

France wasn't no better'n she should be; but take the word of Uncle Joe Hynson, gentlemen! French ladies ain't nothing but a lot of sticks compared to those nut-brown maidens up in London! We'll put in a few evenings with Mrs. Jump's nut-brown maidens that'll make you boys think you ain't never seen nothing! Yes, sir, we'll drink a bottle of gin right now, and we'll drink another bottle on the way, and then——"

"I'm afraid that's impossible, Captain Hynson," I said. "We're walking to London."

"Walking?" Hynson said. "What in God's name you walking for?"

Buell coughed the dry cough that heralded a suddenly invented lie. "We're walking because we're on a secret mission," he said. "We're examining the country."

Hynson looked baffled. "Secret mission? Secret mission for who?"

"If we told you, it wouldn't be secret," Buell said.

Hynson nodded profoundly. "There's something in that. But no walking! Gentlemen on secret missions can't be undignified. Can't consort with riffraff! You come along with me, and we'll see all there is along the road, and get good and drunk doing it. People are nicer when you're drunk. All the girls look pretty till you're sick, and then you got your eyes shut and can't see 'em anyway."

"We'll see you in London," Buell said. "We can't ride because we just got here, and the only money we've got is a few thousand dollars in Continental currency. From what we hear, that's no good in England."

"It certainly ain't," Hynson said, "but what's wrong with giving it to Uncle Joe to use when he goes back to America? If that's all that's troubling you, give your currency to Uncle Joe, and he'll see you ride up to London in style! Yes, and have your pick of nut-brown maidens, too!"

"This Uncle Joe's a rebel," Buell insisted when the captain left us to get his luggage. "He's a rebel sea captain from New England, and he's got plenty of money, and that's something New England sea captains don't have unless they've been up to no good. If Uncle Joe's nursing ill-gotten gains, it's our duty to find out where he got 'em, ain't it? You know it is, Oliver! I'd say Providence was taking a personal interest in our affairs, Oliver. If she wasn't, we'd never 'a' found any way to use up that last two hundred thousand dollars I struck off just before we left New York."

I had to admit that there was something in what he said.

Buell eyed me thoughtfully. "You don't have to stay with me and Hynson if you don't want to, Oliver. Howe sent you over here to do certain things, and you got to do 'em. I'm different. I'm free to do my duty as I see it, even if it obliges me to drink a lot of rum I don't want to drink, and suffer with hiccups something terrible."

"I was counting on you to find Mrs. Byles and Henrietta Dixon," I said. "How'll we contrive to live if we don't find 'em?"

"Oliver," Buell said, "I know what's in your mind, and I resent it. I ain't got the least bit of interest in those nut-brown maidens of Uncle Joe's, except as a means to an end; but I'm going to find out where Uncle Joe gets all that English money, even if I have to get drunk with every nut-brown maiden east of Greenwich."

CHAPTER XLVIII

Americans in London should wear red hats, Hynson had said, implying that they were so numerous that Englishmen were lost among them; and when I climbed from our coach in Piccadilly Circus, leaving the already drunken Hynson to depart with Buell for Mrs. Jump's establishment, I soon realized that Hynson hadn't exaggerated as much as I'd thought.

My first thought was to report to Benjamin Thompson, as Howe had told me to do; but while I stood on the sidewalk, looking for someone who might advise me, and trying to seem oblivious to the hoarse and drunken directions as to how to find Mrs. Jump's that Hynson bawled at me from the departing coach, I saw, among the hurrying throng about me, a man and woman I had often seen in Halifax; and while I watched them, trying to remember who they were, the man greeted a passing acquaintance. The acquaintance was Colonel Saltonstall, whom I knew slightly, and he was deep in conversation with a man I couldn't place, though I'd seen him a score of times on Tremont Street. In the space of two minutes I saw Colonel Saltonstall speak to half a dozen friends, all of them Bostonians. The last one was Ward Chipman, that brilliant lawyer and Harvard graduate in whose home I had overheard the revealing conversation between General Howe and Mrs. Loring.

"For God's sake," Chipman cried, when I hailed him, "you got here at last, did you? Where've you been all these months?"

When I said I'd been with Howe's army, he took me by the elbow and turned me into a side street, away from the clattering and banging of Piccadilly Circus.

"You're just in time," he told me. "Just in time to take dinner with

422

us at the Crown and Anchor." He glanced at my hat and neckcloth, and quickly added, "As my guest, Oliver."

Almost in the same breath he said, "Are you in funds, Oliver?"

"I'm all right," I said. "Buell and I turned over some property to friends before we left Halifax. I think they're here, and if we can find 'em, we'll have nothing to worry about."

Chipman looked at me oddly. "Nothing to worry about, eh? Well, you're lucky! I near starved before I got on the government pay roll. Lived five and a half weeks on a Cheshire cheese, a keg of small beer and a dinner a week at Governor Hutchinson's. A good many of us wouldn't be alive if it weren't for the governor. If you run out of funds, Oliver, keep away from Cheshire cheese. I can't look at a piece without wanting to throw up. The beer wasn't bad, even when it went stale; but I give you my word the Cheshire cheese damned near finished me."

He stood back and glanced at my stockings and shoes. "Gad, Oliver! You're well shod! Where'd you get those?"

"From a man named Vardill."

He raised his eyebrows. "Vardill? How long have you been in London?"

"Less than half an hour. I landed in Dover this morning and came up by coach. You're the first person I've spoken to."

He looked baffled. "I thought you said you got your shoes from Vardill."

I didn't know what he was driving at. "I did. He was professor of law at King's College, and helped me escape from the rebels in New York. He was killed the same day by a shell when Howe's ships went up the river."

"Ah," Chipman said. "I thought you meant another Vardill." He changed the subject. "Sometimes I shudder at myself, Oliver, when I find myself asking mere acquaintances the most personal questions about their financial affairs. There's no such thing as reticence any more—and a good thing, too! Sometimes our people go so long without food that they're beyond help when someone finds it out."

He put his arm in mine. "You're telling me the truth, aren't you, Oliver, about giving funds to friends?"

"Certainly," I said. "I'm not sure where they are; but before the day's over my pockets should be well lined."

"Good," Chipman said, "good! There's too much of the other thing. It mighty near breaks your heart to see people like the Olivers

and Judge Pallon and Mrs. Hatton and her daughters living in rooms
the size of dog kennels and hoping to God the government'll allow
'em just enough so they won't freeze to death. Ah—who are the
friends to whom you gave the funds, if you don't mind my asking?"

"Mrs. Byles," I said. "Mrs. Belcher Byles and Henrietta Dixon."

Chipman stopped short. "Mrs. Byles! Damnation, Oliver!"

My heart sank at the implication in his words. After all, Mrs.
Byles was an old woman, and life in Halifax had been hard enough
for people younger than Mrs. Byles.

"Did she have *all* your money?" Chipman asked. "Haven't you
anything except what you turned over to her?"

"Never mind that," I said. "What happened to her?"

"Nothing happened to her," Chipman said, "except that she
opened a coffee house here in London and nearly lost everything. If
she hadn't gone to France, she would have lost everything."

I couldn't believe my ears. "Nearly lost everything! How could
that have been? If *anyone* in England can run a coffee house, Mrs.
Byles and Henrietta Dixon can do it too."

"You're quite right about that, Oliver. They did so well with their
coffee house that all the Loyalists came to London to try it. You've
no idea how many there are in England, and how little they have
to live on. Some of 'em haven't a penny—literally not a penny.
They go out on the streets and walk until they meet another
American, and then they stand and talk, each hoping the other'll
ask him to dinner. Too often, when you see two Americans talking
and talking to each other on the street, both are penniless, and each
hopes the other has been fortunate."

"If they're penniless," I asked, "how do they live?"

Chipman shrugged his shoulders. "God only knows! Everyone's
after a government allowance. They're entitled to it; for all their
losses, all their misfortunes, are the result of their loyalty to the
government. Occasionally one of 'em's successful. He gets his allowance. When he does, he loans a few pounds to the unsuccessful
ones."

He shook his head. "To be honest with you, nobody understands
how they live. I think each one of us has a private hope that keeps
him alive! Every little town and village in England is full of
Americans who've gone there hoping to find living cheaper than in
London. You'd think you were on Sudbury Street if you walked

down the main street of Exeter tomorrow—or of Plymouth or Bristol or Portsmouth or Hythe."

He made a sweeping gesture, indicating that England, north, south, east and west, was aswarm with Americans; and I saw the seam at his armpit was held together with coarse twine. Through the opening I saw naked flesh. He must have felt my eye upon that gaping seam, for he dropped his arm and held it close against his side.

"I've been in Bristol myself," he said hurriedly. "Very pleasant—a little like Salem. Judge Curwen's there; Judge Sewall and his family, Peter Faneuil, Francis Waldo, Nathaniel Coffin and his family, the Richard Lechmeres, the John Vassals, the Robert Hallowells, Colonel Oliver and his six daughters—— Ah yes, we're fortunate, most fortunate."

There was a singularly apprehensive look in his eye, and I knew why. He hadn't been fortunate, and neither had his friends. He was afraid I'd know how poor he was, and how bitter the poverty that stalked all those New Englanders in Bristol.

I had been conscious of something odd about Chipman, and I suddenly realized what it was. It was the color of his face, which had a peculiar greenish sallowness. That sallowness, I knew, came from insufficient food.

"You were speaking of Mrs. Byles," I reminded him. "It's a subject in which I'm deeply interested."

"Of course," he said. "Well, Oliver, what happened was inevitable. When all these poor people found there was food and drink to be had at Mrs. Byles', they renewed their acquaintance with her. That was the end of her successful coffee house."

"I see," I said, "I see."

What I saw was that the brusque and outspoken Mrs. Byles, as is often the case, had been soft as putty in the hands of her needy countrymen; that the timid and tenderhearted Henrietta Dixon, threatened with the loss of the money that Buell had given her for safekeeping, must have made a firm stand against impending ruin.

What I also saw was that Buell and I were in a strange country without means of livelihood. True, I expected to report to Benjamin Thompson; and since Howe had sent me to England, I hoped eventually to be put on pay. But I wasn't on pay yet; and if I'd learned anything about the English, I'd learned that they never did anything on time. They were always late, and usually too late.

I didn't like the prospect; for Buell and I had only five pounds, fourteen shillings, seven pennies and three farthings between us and destitution; between us and starvation; between us and beggary.

The Crown and Anchor Tavern in the lower Strand seemed more like a coffee house in Boston's King Street than like the one-time haunt of Boswell and Doctor Johnson; for the rooms were thronged with Americans, many of them Bostonians known to me by sight or reputation. The moment I entered the room I saw Sir William Pepperell, Benjamin Pickman, Daniel Leonard, the Boston artist John Singleton Copley and his father-in-law Isaac Rich; Dr. Sylvester Gardiner, who owned most of the land on the Kennebec River; a dozen of my father's lawyer friends, among them Sampson Salter Blowers, who defended Captain Preston after the riot that the rebels always called the Boston Massacre; Joseph Galloway and Judge Auchmuty; Colonel Edward Winslow and young Adino Paddock, son of the Colonel Paddock who planted the elms on Tremont Street. Most welcome sight of all to me was the slender, graceful figure and sensitive face of that dear friend and neighbor Governor Hutchinson.

When I hurried toward the governor, a hand clutched my sleeve and an apologetic voice said, "Your shilling, sir, for the punch."

Chipman pushed me onward, and I heard him explaining that I was his guest; but the waiter's demand lingered distressingly in my mind. All these men, who had been generous hosts in beautiful homes, had been dunned for a shilling so that they might drink punch before their dinner; and most of them, doubtless, had been hard put to it to find the shilling!

Hutchinson's smile was vague when I went to him, and I saw he didn't recognize me.

"Sir," I said, "I'm Oliver Wiswell of Milton."

He caught my elbow. "Wiswell? Of course! Oliver! Why, bless me, my boy, you're older—I mean—yes, yes!—I heard about your great loss—a great loss to me—a great loss to America—I hope——"

"He seemed quite easy in his mind," I said. "We buried him at sea."

Hutchinson held tight to my arm and turned to his companions, who were eyeing me covertly.

"This is my friend Seaton Wiswell's son, gentlemen," he said. "I don't need to tell you about Seaton Wiswell. His son Oliver, here, was my respected neighbor on Milton Hill. I know he'll have news for us, because I had word from Halifax that he went with General Howe's forces to Long Island and New York."

He turned back to me. "You *were* with General Howe, weren't you, Oliver?"

I nodded; but before I could open my mouth I was the center of a storm of questions, exasperated questions, furious questions. Why had Howe delayed? Was it true the rebels had run like rabbits before Howe's troops? Was it true Howe could have captured the entire rebel army? How long would it be—how long—how long—how many months—how many years—before they could go home again?

Governor Hutchinson raised his hands protestingly. "Gentlemen, gentlemen!"

To me he said, "Oliver, we're never sure, over here, when we're being told the truth about what's going on in America. Everything that happens is supposed to be printed in the *National Register.* Unfortunately Mr. Burke edits the *National Register,* and Mr. Burke's a Whig. Consequently there's nothing in the *National Register* that isn't colored. Every line in it is calculated to further the interests of the Whig party. The Whigs will lie, steal, destroy the British Empire to get back into power. We've all of us been deafened with the shouting of the Whigs, and we're pretty sure we've heard a lot that isn't so. That's why these gentlemen were pelting you with questions."

He turned to those behind him. "Suppose I question Mr. Wiswell for you? Then he won't be confused by unnecessary shouting."

All those shabby, sallow-faced countrymen of mine looked helpless and hungry.

"Oliver," the governor said, "there's one question that's foremost in the minds of all of us. I doubt that any man can answer it, but it does no harm to ask. When do you think the war'll be over? When do you think we can go back to New England without being mobbed—without being treated like criminals?"

"I don't know," I said. "Four months ago I thought surely the war'd be over by now—as it would have been if Howe had behaved as he should. Now I've stopped trying to guess what'll happen. If Howe stays on as commander in chief, the war'll never be over. If Howe's called home, the one who replaces him might do no better. Something happens to British generals in America."

"Something happens to British generals everywhere," a voice said.

"Some of our members," the governor said, "think they'll be able to go home in August. Have you heard anything that leads you to think so?"

"No, sir," I said. "I haven't. No British general has gained a military advantage in America without instantly throwing it away. I see no reason why this or any other custom should suddenly come to an end. I hope with all my heart the rebels'll be beaten in next summer's campaign, but I'm not confident."

"Why aren't you confident?" a man shouted. "Aren't all Americans cowards?"

The room was a babel of angry shouting; and to make himself heard, Governor Hutchinson had to come close. "Being newly arrived in England, Oliver," he said, "you probably don't understand that allusion. Not a day passes that we don't hear Englishmen telling each other that all Americans are cowards. Americans, they say, won't fight as Englishmen fight: Americans are traitors and hypocrites! We don't quite know what to make of it, Oliver. We've no use for rebels; but after all, rebels are Americans, just as we are. Is it true that all the rebel troops were in a panic at the battle of Long Island? That they ran like rabbits?"

The room was so silent that the governor and I might have been alone, instead of ringed by scores of sallow-faced men in threadbare garments.

"Yes, sir," I said, "it's true. They certainly ran, and they hid under hedges and in wheat stacks. The Hessians caught one rebel general under a pile of brush. They found another lying in a ditch and prodded him out with bayonets. Later, when Howe captured Fort Washington, the rebels ran so fast that the British gave fox-hunting calls."

The circle of listeners moved uneasily.

Governor Hutchinson cleared his throat. "You know, Oliver, we're in a peculiar situation, here in London. Probably you won't understand it. All of us hate the rebels. They've exiled us and ruined us. Yet there's something mighty upsetting in hearing Englishmen say all Americans are cowards."

"Yes, sir," I said. "I feel the same way."

"Yet you admit the rebels always run," the governor said. "If that's so, why should you resent hearing them called cowards?"

"Well, sir," I said, "troops that aren't properly trained can't be controlled when conditions aren't to their liking. You can't expect regiments of untrained men, commanded by ignorant, untrained officers, to march into a position that looks and sounds like certain death. There was a regiment of Marylanders at the battle of Long Island that did its best to stand off the whole British Army. No British regiment ever fought better. If I were a soldier, I believe I could raise a regiment of Loyalists that would outfight any regiment the British could bring against it."

"If you were a soldier?" Hutchinson repeated. "So you weren't a soldier, even though you were with General Howe's army. I trust you won't take it personally, Oliver, but why weren't you a soldier?"

"Because I'd have been subject to the whims of a British commanding officer. I couldn't fight the rebels the British way. If I had men under me, I'd feel responsible for them. I couldn't order them to do some of the insane things that I've seen British soldiers ordered to do."

"That's your only reason for not wanting to take up arms against the men who drove you from your home?" the governor asked. "You'd have no feeling about killing your own countrymen?"

"Why should I? If a trespasser picked the lock of my house and tried to drive me from it, I'd fight him if I could. He might argue that his behavior was virtuous; that I was a traitor and an unprincipled scoundrel to resist him; but it wouldn't be true, and I'd shoot him fast enough, no matter what country he belonged to, provided I had a chance for my life."

The governor gave me a friendly pat upon the shoulder. "Don't think I ask these questions out of impertinence. Every American in London is asked them, far too often; and it makes us all feel better when we hear the answers of someone we can trust."

He shook a warning finger at our audience. "And now no more questions, gentlemen, till we've had dinner. Mr. Wiswell only landed in England today, and he's hungry and tired."

As he turned me toward the dinner tables he whispered, for my ear alone, "Be guarded in your speech, Oliver. An English Whig can be as murderous as an American rebel."

CHAPTER XLIX

IF GOVERNOR HUTCHINSON hadn't rescued me, I think I might have answered questions all the rest of that day. All those Loyalists who had gathered at the Crown and Anchor were men of ability in their chosen professions; and like all such people, they were eager for all the details about the things that interested them most.

They wanted to know how the rebel army was constituted; how many commissaries it had and how they functioned; how the soldiers looked, dressed, ate, marched; how they talked; how they obeyed their officers; how they were punished for infractions of discipline.

They probed into every detail of the battle of Long Island, of the landing at Kip's Bay, of Howe's march northward against the rebels.

They were particularly eager to know whether the average Americans—the farmers, the laborers, the servants—had a genuine understanding of the principles that had involved their country in a long and costly war.

I answered as fully as I could, and from the manner in which my hearers' eyes turned oftener and oftener to their neighbors, I knew they were making deductions. They were jumping to the conclusion that the rebels could never win, and that the war would be over in a few months' time. They were refusing to take into account the singular lethargy of British generals in America; and I, realizing this, was suddenly overcome with unwillingness to discuss war with persons who hadn't been a part of it.

Governor Hutchinson, seeing how matters stood, smilingly insisted that I had an engagement with him—one that must be kept. On that he almost dragged me from the Crown and Anchor, and firmly repulsed those who wished to go with us.

"That's one of the evils of New England, Oliver," he said. "An educated New Englander shuns action and thrives on argument. I'm afraid your education hasn't been a success according to New England lights; for unless I'm mistaken, you prefer activity to argument."

"Well, sir," I said, "I must admit that I find it difficult to sit still with a war going on around me; but I can sit still long enough to help you with anything you may be writing on the war in America."

"My boy," Hutchinson said, "I'm an old man. As a man grows older, he becomes restrained in his speech. He's more temperate, less indignant, than when he was younger. I'd like your help, but I'm not in actual need of it. What I'd rather do, Oliver, is make it possible for you to see and understand as much of this war as you can, and to write the truth about it—write the truth about the stupidity of those who started it; write the truth about the criminal way in which it has been fought; write the truth about how at any moment it could have been peacefully ended by either side, but wasn't; write the truth about the manner in which America is looked upon as nothing but a means by which European politicians can attain their miserable ends!"

His voice became brittle. "Politicians! There's a great chance for you, Oliver! If only you could write a history of this war that would show our people how easily they'd been used by scheming politicians —how needlessly they'd ruined themselves, killed themselves, brought misery, destruction, hatred to their country just to further the schemes of reckless men—you might be doing something for future generations."

He gave me a sidelong glance. "What are they saying about France in America? Do they know what the French are up to?"

"No, sir," I said. "I've heard a little talk that the rebels are trying to get help from France, but nobody knows more than that."

"I suppose not," Hutchinson said. "You don't know; neither do I; neither does anyone else; but we *ought* to know. We've *got* to know! They're up to something! They always have been, and they always will be! If I were twenty years younger, I'd rather find that out and write it, than win ten battles and kill ten thousand men!"

He piloted me across the turmoil of Piccadilly Circus and into quiet little streets that put me in mind of Boston.

When I spoke of the similarity, Hutchinson pressed thumb and forefinger to his forehead in a well-remembered gesture. "Ah yes! Now I know why your arrival in London wasn't more of a surprise to me. A week ago my daughter had a letter from Milton, and in it was a letter for you."

There was something about a letter from Sally—about the certainty of hearing from her once more—that stirred me almost as deeply as if it were a prospect of seeing her.

My fingers were like thumbs as I fumbled with the seal, and even my heart thumped clumsily. Truth to tell, I was afraid of that letter —afraid of what I'd see when I opened it. I remembered that Soame Leighton might have been alive today if I'd acted more quickly to save him; that the war might have been over if Buell and I had been allowed to reach Howe and tell him how to bottle up the rebels by moving his troops across New York island instead of spending the best part of the day at dinner with Mrs. Murray.

I was conscious, as is every man who takes part in a war, that all my efforts had helped nobody: that all my time had been wasted in bafflements. I seemed so useless to myself that ridiculously enough I had a fear that even Sally might have discovered at last how useless I was. I was so low in mind, indeed, that I feared this letter might tell me that Sally had tired of the long, long waiting for so useless a man. This was my unhappy mood—until, finally, I opened the letter.

"Dearest, dearest Oliver [it read]:

"The moment I had the message you sent me by another of your dear dust-colored men, I knew beyond a doubt you were leaving America because you had been disappointed or hurt. I knew, too, what you meant when you sent me word you couldn't tell me anything about Soame. I knew you meant you'd had no good news of him, and I feared—and how bitterly true that premonition proved to be—that you'd had news of him, and that it had been bad.

"I think I know everything now. My father and I went to see General Washington at White Plains, and when Father told him we'd learned Soame was being badly treated by that beast Cunningham, I was frightened at his anger. There's something magnificent and breath-taking about him, even when he's calm; and when he's angry, he's terrible! I was so frightened at him that I almost forgot Soame.

"Oh, Oliver, how anybody can so much as see General Washington and not fight for him to the last gasp is beyond my understanding! If I were a man, I'd follow him across ice and through hot coals on my bare feet! I don't care if it's blasphemous to say so: I don't believe

*there has ever been but one man like him! He looked ten feet tall
when my father told him about Soame, and his eyes were like blue ice.*

*"He sent a flag to General Howe; and when it came back, Steven
and Jeremiah were with it. They gave us Mr. Buell's letter.*

*"We knew then what had happened to Soame, and I thought my
heart would break!*

*"It was foolhardy of Mr. Buell to do what he did; but I shall thank
God always that at least one of the creatures who helped kill Soame
was made to suffer for his cruelty.*

*"No matter what anyone else may think, I know you did every-
thing you could; and of course, dearest Oliver, I know you left New
York because you couldn't stay any longer with those who murdered
Soame.*

*"Steven and Jeremiah came home with us, but already they've gone
back into the war. I know you're doing what you think is right, and
of course I know you're not alone in feeling as you do. I'm not blind;
all around us I can see hundreds and hundreds of people who feel
in their hearts as you feel, but haven't the courage to say so openly.
There are times when I think I hate everyone who's against our
Cause; and then I remember you're against us; I remember you're
doing what you think is right; and I know I shall never hate you!*

*"It seems to me that everyone in this whole great country is per-
petually unhappy or bitter or angry or in want. I can hardly remember when it was that I wasn't unhappy, except for those few short
moments when you were last in Milton.*

*"I seem to have no heart to write; but I still have the heart to pray
that nothing more insurmountable than an ocean will ever come between us. I don't need to count the number of nights I've prayed for
you since you took your father down Milton Hill and into Boston.
It's been every night since then, Oliver, and it'll be every night as long
as I live.*
                                        "Sally."

☆   ☆   ☆

I suppose most people think of war as an unending angry conflict
between two armies, one made up of soldiers nobly fighting for the
right; the other of brutal, venal wretches deliberately battling to uphold something they know to be wrong.

In reality war is mostly waste, idleness, dirt, discomfort, fright,
blundering and uncertainty; and well-nigh everyone on both sides
spends his waking hours wishing with all his heart he had never let

himself be drawn into it. He comes to know that the war that has him by the heels can accomplish nothing that couldn't be equally well accomplished by honest discussion between reasonable men—accomplished without loss of freedom, loss of life, loss of property, loss of all the things men value. He forgets, if he ever knew, the principles for which he's fighting, and they seldom enter his mind except when he hears them mouthed by politicians who have never under any circumstances faced enemy bullets and would never endure the daily discomforts of a soldier.

As I folded Sally's letter and placed it with the thin packet resting like a frail shield above my heart, I wished myself wholly and forever out of this war; and even while I wished it, I knew that I couldn't be. Sally loved me still; but I wasn't a rebel, and that was the end of me so far as her father was concerned, and her brothers, and General Washington, and every man in the entire rebel army, and all those who gave lip service to the rebel cause, and enriched themselves from it by gobbling up the property from which their neighbors had been driven.

I was caught, as every man is caught when he lets himself be made a part of an army. I didn't want to go on, but I couldn't stop; and since I couldn't stop, I desperately knew I must do everything in my power, puny though my efforts must be, to help bring this war to an end—do every last thing I could, spend every last ounce of strength, in making America a place where such worthy patriots as Hutchinson and Oliver, Chipman and Saltonstall, Curwen and Judge Sewall, Faneuil and Waldo, would be suffered to live and work for its welfare, instead of being persecuted, beaten and banished if they dared to speak one warning word against demagogues and time-servers, or if they tried to save the land they loved from falling into the hands of men who would stop at nothing in order to stay in office.

CHAPTER L

I F CAPTAIN HYNSON's information was correct, Mrs. Jump in her earlier days had been a cook in the household of a Royal Personage—a cook so pleasing to the Personage, in more ways than one, that on his death he was found to have left her a commodious house at 13 Stepney Causeway.

It was dark when I reached Mrs. Jump's—the thick, sooty dark of a London afternoon in winter; but not a ray of light was visible at the door or windows of Mrs. Jump's establishment. I thought I must have the wrong address, but I knocked upon the door as a matter of form and was rewarded by seeing the door open an inch. An eye studied me through the opening; then suddenly vanished and the door was opened by Buell, who hiccuped violently at sight of me, so that I knew he'd been free with the bottle.

"I thought it was you," he said, speaking slowly and carefully. " 'Bout time, too, Oliver." He caught me by the arm and drew me into a candlelighted lobby smelling strongly of cabbage, coal smoke and musk. In an adjacent room, that I took to be the parlor, a female voice declaimed thickly.

Buell pushed me toward the open door of that room and gestured largely toward a woman who stood alone before a small coal fire, clinging to the mantel and talking to herself in a grand manner. At our entrance, she screwed up her eyes at me. Clearly they weren't focusing properly.

She was tall, a little stooped, and everything she wore seemed about to become unfastened. Her yellowish hair—probably it was a wig—gave the impression of being looped precariously over invisible hooks. Her bodice was not only askew, but had been fastened so that one

435

side was two inches lower than the other. Her skirt, seemingly, had been attached at random to her waist, so that it hung upon her as a sail hangs in brails. She looked like a woman whose stockings would always be wrinkled; and though I couldn't see them, I was sure hers were down around her ankles.

In her free hand she held a glass of wine; though she swayed from side to side as she peered at us, not a drop of wine was spilled, which seemed to me almost a miracle.

"Meet Mrs. Jump, Oliver," Buell said. "She says she used to be the best cook in the world. Maybe she's right; but if you use your nose, you'll see she never invented a way to cook cabbage so it wouldn't smell up the whole house."

Mrs. Jump made a simpering gesture of despair. "Never been so talked to in my life! The creature's an original! Says things so droll I can't answer him for laughing."

She released her hold on the mantel to pass a hand reflectively over her mouth; then instantly caught at the mantel again and gave me a haughty glance. "I've a reputation myself for saying unexpected things, Mr. Oliver. That's the name, ain't it? I tell you, Mr. Oliver, I've demolished men for saying a quarter of the things this creature has—positively demolished them!"

"I don't wonder," I said. "Mr. Buell always speaks out of turn. At heart he's a jewel, but it's seldom apparent to women unless they're wise like yourself."

"Blarney," Mrs. Jump cried. "Don't blarney me! I can smell blarney a mile off; but I'm a woman and I won't hold it against you. Have some champagne, Mr. Oliver. That's all we ever drink in this house— if I'm in possession of my senses."

"Thanks," I said, "I will."

"Thank God for that!" Mrs. Jump cried. "This Buell creature's for-ever thinking up 'scuses for not drinking and not giving us a pair of those Perkins' Metallic Tractors of his! I'm s'picious of men that always have a 'scuse for staying sober! Either they ain't well, or they're trying to take advantage of you!" She stared accusingly at Buell. "Says he's got a weak stomach! Tell that to the marines, Buell! You're juss one of those damned American hypocrites, thass what you are!"

"It ain't so," Buell said sullenly. "I'd drink as much as the next man, if it didn't fix me so I couldn't hear on account of hiccuping so much. What's the use of drinking to have a good time, and then getting deaf just when you're ready to start enjoying yourself?"

Mrs. Jump looked at him owlishly. "That by no means accounts for your coldness to my charming friends Miss"—she seemed on the verge of an internal convulsion, which she conquered by drawing a deep breath—"my charming friends Miss Cotton and Miss Pinto."

"No, it don't," Buell admitted. "I ain't Hynson. Hynson can sit for hours and say 'Whose ducky is oo' to that nut-brown Cleghorn, and be satisfied when she keeps saying 'I's oor ducky'. Well, that ain't enough for me! I got to talk about something except whose ducky I is."

"What for?" Mrs. Jump asked.

Buell scratched his head. "What for? What for? Well, there you seem to have me."

"I wouldn't," Mrs. Jump said.

"Wouldn't what?" Buell asked.

"Wouldn't have you," Mrs. Jump said. "Besides, that's no answer to what I was saying."

"What were you saying?" Buell asked.

"What about?"

"I don't know," Buell told her. "Do you?"

"When?" Mrs. Jump inquired.

I thought I'd better interrupt this conversation, as it didn't seem to be getting forward with anything. "Where's Captain Hynson?" I asked.

"He's where any sensible man would be," Mrs. Jump said. "He's up-stairs engaged in polite frolic with my charming friends Miss Cleg-horn, Miss Cotton and Miss Pinto. I s'pose, Mr. Oliver, you've got one of those American stomachs, too. I s'pose you ain't able to indulge in fashionable chatter with poor mortals like I and my friends unless partially sober."

"No," I said, "my stomach's all right. I'll be happy to try your wine, delighted to see Captain Hynson again, and honored to make the acquaintance of your charming friends."

Mrs. Jump tossed her head at Buell. "I'm glad indeed to learn that there's at least one American who's a gentleman and a man of birth."

She lurched from the room.

Instantly Buell gave me his news.

"Oliver," he whispered, "either Hynson's damned dangerous, or a damned liar! After I'd had a few drinks with him and those charm-ing friends Mrs. Jump talks about, he began to tell me so many things that I got scared! I wanted a witness, Oliver."

I thought he was exaggerating, and said so.

"It's the truth, Oliver," Buell said earnestly. "I don't claim to be entirely not in my cups, but there's a part of my head that's clear as a bell, and if I were to repeat all that Hynson says, you'd think I was raving. Well, I propose to find out a whole lot more from Hynson; and when I repeat it, I propose to be listened to! I'm going to have a witness to bear me out."

Mrs. Jump returned, reeling dangerously, and with three bottles of wine clutched to her bosom drove us before her up the stairs, thrusting herself between us to kick at a door from behind which came the tinkle of a harpsichord and a gay chorus.

The voices were mostly female, but were submerged beneath a bellowing baritone, unmistakably Captain Hynson's, that roared out the familiar chorus:

> *"Nut-brown maiden*
> *Thou hast a slender waist to clasp;*
> *Nut-brown maiden*
> *Thou hast a slender waist!*
> *A slender waist is thine, love,*
> *The arm around it's mine, love;*
> *Nut-brown maiden*
> *Thou hast a slender waist to clasp;*
> *Nut-brown may-hay-den*
> *Thou hast a slender waist!"*

When no attention was paid to Mrs. Jump's kicks, she opened the door and walked in.

At the far end of the room I saw Captain Hynson with a girl in his lap and a glass in his hand. Beside him, before a harpsichord, sat two other young women. One of them, a sulky-looking girl with narrow shoulders and broad hips, evoked tinny music from the ancient instrument with an air of disdain. The other, garbed in lacy garments, and chalky white of face, sang throatily and with upward-rolling eyes.

As the chorus ended, Hynson leaned forward and resoundingly whacked the sulky-looking player on her generous buttocks.

"Play it again, Cotton," he shouted. "Don't stop till I tell you to!"

Miss Cotton screamed and slapped at Hynson, and in the act of slapping caught sight of Buell. When she would have risen, Hynson whacked her again, so that she stayed where she was and screamed again, more from irritation than pain.

The girl in Hynson's lap, a small, brown thing with a mop of reddish curls, struggled to her feet.

"Come back here, Isabella Cleghorn!" Hynson bawled. "If you get a pair of those damned metallic what-you-call-'ems, you'll get 'em because I buy 'em for you!"

He hooked a sausagelike finger over the edge of her bodice and pulled her back to his lap. I heard the bodice rip, and Miss Cleghorn squealed angrily.

Hynson's face darkened. "Look at that!" he cried to Mrs. Jump. "Gets a sour face just because I tore off a button! If Cleghorn and Cotton and Pinto want to go to Paris with me, they got to learn to keep smiling, even if I tear *everything* off 'em! French women keep smiling, no matter what you do to 'em! S'pose Frenchmen saw Cotton looking sour, just because someone cut her stay laces. They'd know she was English! Like as not they'd throw her out for fear she was spying on 'em!"

"What you need," Buell said, "is a pair of Perkins' Metallic Tractors for each one of 'em. There ain't hardly a woman alive that ain't subject to the vapors at one time or another, and Perkins' Metallic Tractors put an instant end to the vapors and all gross, corrupt and putrid humors."

"They're too damned expensive," Hynson said.

"On the con—," Buell said, "on the conterary, the expense of not having 'em would be greater than buying 'em. Ain't it a economy to save yourself from violent and tormenting pain that might keep you from your labors for days on end?"

"He said it was good for teeth," Miss Cleghorn shouted. "You ought to have a pair for yourself, and I can use yours." She appealed to Buell. "Didn't you say they cured teeth?"

"They cure all the teeth a person's got left to him," Buell said. "They cure everything except the best kinds of drunkenness. There's some things like that nobody wants to get cured up after they spend their money to get it. They won't cure the afterpains of drunkenness either, because that's a punishment intented—I mean intended —to teach you not to do it again, but who heeds it? Proper use of Perkins' Metallic Tractors will make the foulest teeth most beautifully white even if they're twisted. They'll assuredly fasten those that are loose and infallibly preserve 'em from decay. They perfectly cure the scurvy in the gums, encourage 'em to grow up to the teeth again before you can say 'Scat!', and fix an ill-scented breath as well as a thing like that *can* be fixed. Their use is as natural as the act of breathing, for their size and sharp points make 'em marvelous for removing food from between said teeth."

"Fifteen guineas for three pairs of toothpicks!" Hynson growled.

"Listen," Buell said, "they got precious metals in 'em. I'm not talking about teeth now: I'm talking about Perkins' Metallic Tractors! If the French are fighting a war, as you claim, they'll be awful touchy about foreign women that ain't up to snuff. You let these girls use Perkins' Metallic Tractors regular and as directed, and any disagreeable rednesses, roughnesses, morphew or the heats are cured at once. They smooth, clean, plump, nourish and whiten the skin to the last degree; they make persons who before looked haggard and old into visions of youth, beauty and fairness. They kill worms in the face, take away freckles, spots, wrinkles, pits or marks of the smallpox, and give a charming luster and fine air to the features. They also open all obstructions in the stomach, lungs, liver and bladder. You'll need Metallic Tractors in France! No man can say what I've just been saying and be accused of the slightest drunkenness."

"Yes, but I'll thank you not to use indelicate words even if sober," Mrs. Jump told him.

"What indelicate words?" Buell asked.

She shook a roguish forefinger at him. "Go all over it again and I'll pick 'em out."

"You say the French are fighting a war," I interrupted. "What war is that, Captain Hynson?"

"What war!" Hynson repeated. "Why, the war with England, of course! Didn't you know about that?"

"No, I didn't," I said. "France and England weren't at war when we sailed from America. When did it start?"

"Oh," Hynson said carelessly, "it's only going on under cover so far; but it'll start in earnest as soon as we get to Paris, and that'll be the end of England!"

He took a newly opened bottle from Buell and poured our glasses full. "Here we are," he said brusquely. "Le's drink to ole England while there's some of her left to drink to! Here today and gone tomorrow: that's England! Here's to her! Here's to ole England—

never sees nothing, not even when it's happening right under her nose! Here's to her, sending all her men and ships to fight America over somep'n that ain't worth fighting about, and so giving France the chance she's wanted for a million years! Here's to England, gentlemen and ladies! Great admirer of her, I am! Great admirer of anybody that's better'n anybody else at doing something! Tha's what England is: better'n anybody else at being a damned idiot 'bout what's going on around her!"

He poured the tumblerful of wine down his throat, wiped his lips with a hairy hand, and reached for the second of Mrs. Jump's three bottles. As he fumbled with the cork, he continued his discourse.

"Mark my words, ladies, you'll be grateful to Uncle Joe Hynson for getting you out of this country when you get news how the French fleet and the Spanish fleet sailed right up the Thames and blew the whole damned city of London into the middle of next week with their great guns! Yes, sir; damned if I know how England makes out as well as she does, considerin' she's always gettin' a damned fool for a prime minister 'n' an idiot for a king!"

"Oh, indeed," Mrs. Jump said. "Kindly be a li'l more esplill—explicit! S'pose you give us details juss how the King shows his idiocy, if you know so much!"

Hynson flapped a bearlike hand. "There's an Englishwoman for you! Starts getting nasty just because I let drop a few plain facts! All right: I'll tell you! Everybody in America says the King's a plumb idiot! Where there's smoke, there's always fire! I'm a sensible man, I am, and if everybody says the King's an idiot, I know he *is* one. It ain't necessary for me to be any more esplillits."

The cork broke in his thick fingers, and he cursed as he picked at it with a blackened fingernail.

"Listen, Uncle Joe," Buell said. "You ought to be more restrained. S'pose it got around that you knew France was going to start a war with England, but never said nothing to the King so he could take steps to stop it. You'd get put in jail for criminal negligence."

"That shows how much you know," Hynson said. "I could go right out in the middle of Piccadilly and say the things I've been saying to you at the top of my lungs, and nobody'd so much as listen to me. I'm an American, ain't I? You don't suppose an Englishman'd believe an American, do you? No, sir, Englishmen never, never, never do the things they ought to do! Why, all they'd have to do to stave off this war with France is to agree to what every patriotic American wants; but that would be too simple for 'em. They can't do it! Their natures won't let 'em! They think they know what's good for us better'n we do ourselves, and they'll keep right on thinking so till they wake up with a bang 'n' find they ain't got nothing whatever to say about our affairs no more."

At the words "every patriotic American" Buell opened his mouth like a hungry trout, but closed it without speaking.

Mrs. Jump poured herself a drink and eyed Hynson over the rim of her glass. "My, my," she said, "I don't know 's I ever heard anybody talk so loud 'n' important, not even the lord mayor of London."

"You're jealous," Hynson said. "You ain't got nothing important to talk about, so you don't like to hear nobody else talk that way."

"Oh, indeed," Mrs. Jump said. "And why should I be jealous, if I may ask, of the idle statements of an idle sailor? Here you are, sitting in my boardinghouse with nothing to do so far as I can see but squeeze my friends' knees and drink my wine. Seems to me an important man could find more to do than paw a lady's knees."

"You're jealous because I ain't made no effort to get at your knees," Hynson said. "If you want to start getting personal, I can tell you——"

Buell spoke quickly. "Now, Joe, don't take offense! All Mrs. Jump meant was that you're so simple and unassuming she'd never dream you were a captain, let alone think you were familiar with the plans of the French government. Wasn't that what you meant, Mrs. Jump?"

Mrs. Jump breathed heavily.

"It don't matter a damn to me what she thinks," Hynson said. "The English don't give a damn what Americans think, 'n' I don't give a damn what *they* think. That don't alter the fact that she'll go a long way before she finds anybody who knows as much as I do."

"My, my," Mrs. Jump said elegantly. "I'm surprised you ain't traveling with a blackamoor to fan you and a couple of valets and a red carpet to roll out whenever you cross a sidewalk."

Buell spoke soothingly. "Now, ma'am, Captain Hynson's entitled to fair play. You ain't being fair to him. You keep hinting he ain't important, instead of giving him a chance to prove he is."

"I doubt that he could," Mrs. Jump said loftily. "I do indeed! He's a great hand to drink wine and wrestle with my girls, but I should be very, very much surprised if he were able to do anything else. That's what I think I think, if you desire to know!"

"I don't," Hynson said. "It's only what you think you think you think, so I don't desire. If you'd ever visited the eastern shore of Maryland, where I come from, you'd know all about me. You'd know Lambert Wickes was my stepbrother. I bet you never even heard of Lambert Wickes! A person's got to be damned ignorant not to have heard of Lambert Wickes."

"Lambert Wickes?" Mrs. Jump said. "That ain't a person! That's part of a lamp—or else it's a place. I think it's around the docks somewhere."

"It is not," Hynson said. "Lambert Wickes took Ben Franklin to France. He's the best damned sea captain in the whole damned world, pretty near. Truth is, Lambert's a lucky sailor. Leave luck out of it, and I can beat him. Them that knows us say you can't hardly tell the difference in the way we sail. I guess he's a little cautiouser than me. Prob'ly that's why I get along with the ladies better'n he does."

"Do you?" Mrs. Jump asked interestedly. "How many's been sent to jail for trying to murder him?"

"Not one," Captain Hynson said. "He don't get along with 'em as well as I do, but they like him. If you want to know the truth, they like him better'n I do. Please remember I know enough to be a gentleman, don't I?"

"When?" Mrs. Jump asked.

Buell spoke up quickly. "Well, well! So you're Lambert Wickes' stepbrother! I guess Mrs. Jump made a mistake when she thought you didn't know what you were talking about! It wouldn't surprise me any if you'd been to France your own self."

He turned to Mrs. Jump. "You don't want to be too hard on Uncle Joe, ma'am. If his stepbrother took Ben Franklin to France, Joe might have gone, too. He might even have seen some pretty important people, because they say Franklin gets around a lot."

Hynson gave us a contemptuous snort. "*Might* have gone to France! *Might* have seen important people! All I'll say is, you'd be surprised if you knew who I saw!"

"When did your stepbrother land in France, Captain?" Buell asked.

Hynson laughed scornfully. "He landed there long enough back so that Franklin could do whatever he intended to do. Yes, sir! You never heard of Franklin failing to get anything he set out to get, did you?"

He examined the backs of his hairy hands and seemed puzzled by them. "I wouldn't say this except among friends—friends of the good cause——"

"What good cause?" Mrs. Jump demanded.

Hynson stared at her. "The cause of making England mind her own business," he said thickly. "The cause of making England stop thinking everybody in the world ought to fall down and lick her boots juss because England happens to want her boots licked! If that don't strike you as a good cause, wait till the French sail up the Thames and knock your house about your ears! Then you'll remember Uncle Joe and wish you hadn't been so damned skittish when confrontled—confronted by the simple truth!"

How reliable Captain Hynson's information about the projected attack on England might be, I didn't know; but there was no doubt in my mind that if it *were* true, the American war might continue for unnumbered years. I was also certain of another thing: Hynson's information had so much the ring of truth that all my instincts told me it should immediately be lodged with somebody capable of acting upon it.

When I looked desperately at Buell, he came at once to my rescue with a shout of, "Three cheers for bes' cause in the world! Mind your own business!"

He picked up the last of Mrs. Jump's bottles and filled our glasses with an unsteady hand. "Here's to Captain Hynson and the Cause," he cried. "Good ole Captain Hynson, 'n' mind your own business! Tell you what I'll do, Captain Hynson and ladies! I'll make all of you a present of a pair of Perkins' Metallic Tractors the day we get to France!" He gulped his drink; then slowly collapsed and lay full length upon the floor.

Mrs. Jump and her friends looked annoyed, and Hynson said solicitously, "He don't look well. He muss 'a' eaten somep'n."

I hoisted Buell to my back and, guided by Miss Cotton, carried him to a room that she said Hynson had rented for Buell and me. It seemed to be true, because our portmanteaus were already there.

When Miss Cotton had left us, I dropped Buell on the bed and went to my portmanteau.

Buell sat up to watch me. "Did you ever hear the beat of it!" he asked. "France fighting on the side of the rebels to keep Americans out of America! That certainly knocked every hiccup out of me! Who you going to see?"

"Thompson," I said. "He's Lord Germaine's secretary. If he won't help me I'll figure out something else to do."

"If he won't help you," Buell said, "come back and get me. We might be able to break a window in the palace and tell the King—though he probably wouldn't believe us."

CHAPTER LI

Thompson wouldn't, I knew, be in his office; but I was bound to see him if I had to sit on his doorstep until midnight. I found his house in Pall Mall; and from the servant who answered my poundings, I learned that he was supping with Lord Germaine and that Germaine's house was also in Pall Mall, only five doors from Thompson's.

Under ordinary circumstances, I'd never have dared to pursue the matter farther; but this concerned my country, and might readily concern it deeply; so I had no hesitation in going to Germaine's imposing residence and letting the brass knocker fall with a disconcerting crash upon the glistening dark green front door. As I did so, I marveled at the amazing turn in the fortunes of Benjamin Thompson, who had been, only two years before, a penniless Concord schoolteacher married to a rich old widow, and now was secretary to England's Minister for Colonial Affairs and able to afford a fine house on the same street with his wealthy patron.

When I had said my say to the footman who admitted me, and he had silently scrutinized my shoes, waistcoat, neckcloth, and unwigged and unpowdered head, I had a dreadful feeling of futility. The tale I had to tell, I suddenly saw, was thin, unreal, fantastic. It could have no possible interest for the great man who dwelt securely and aloof amid all these brilliant portraits, all this gleaming furniture and silver.

Yet the footman had scarcely left me to go silently up a stairway, when Thompson himself, beautiful in a scarlet coat, white waistcoat and scarlet smallclothes, came to the head of the stairs and looked down at me.

"For God's sake!" he cried. "Oliver Wiswell!" He ran down the

446

stairs and clapped his hands upon my shoulders. "What in God's name brings you here?"

"Lord Germaine," I said. "I've got information for him."

"My dear boy," Thompson protested. "Surely tomorrow'll do as well. I'm his secretary: I'll take you to see him as soon as he reaches Downing Street."

"I want to see him now," I said. "This information is important. It ought to be acted on at once."

Thompson patted my hand—a gesture that brought back to me a forgotten discomfort. "You're in England, Oliver. In England there's nothing that can't wait until next week or perhaps until next year."

"So I've heard," I said. "A gentleman brought up in that school of thought gave me a letter of introduction to Lord Germaine. It's a theory that hasn't worked well in America."

I took General Howe's letter from my pocket and gave it to Thompson, who immediately broke the seal.

"Very interesting," he said, when he'd read it. "He thinks you can be useful."

He eyed me dubiously. "For your sake, Oliver, I hope your information will prove interesting to Lord Germaine. *I* won't be damaged if your message is unimportant; but *you* will; so be sure of your ground."

"I'm sure," I said.

Thompson turned me toward the stairs. "Don't mind, Oliver," he said as we mounted to the second floor, "if I monopolize the conversation. I know his peculiarities. One of them is an aversion to the unexpected introduction of a strange subject."

He opened a door and ushered me into a dusky dining room hung with dim portraits. In the center of the room a round table made a gleaming dark pool in which were reflected four tall silver candlesticks and the powdery blue coat of a sheep-faced gentleman who sat staring palely at me over the rim of a glass of port. Even in the faint golden light of the candles he was the whitest-looking man I had ever seen. Everything about him—hair, hands, face, garments, the lace at his throat and wrists, and even the surface of his eyes—seemed to have been dusted with flour.

"My lord," Thompson said, "this is Oliver Wiswell. You may recall my mention of him in connection with Governor Hutchinson, and of his father's high reputation as a lawyer."

Germaine put down his glass, and I almost had the feeling that flour had in fact caked upon his face. His lips hardly moved when he spoke, and his voice was faded, as if he found enunciation painful.

"Wiswell, yes, yes," he said. "Happy to welcome a friend of Thompson's. Glass of port, Mr. Wiswell?" He motioned me toward a chair at his left with the faintest movement of an eyebrow.

Thompson took the chair across from me, so that he sat at Germaine's right instead of across the table from him, and so close that Germaine could place his hand upon Thompson's knee—which he did as soon as Thompson had sat down, though all he had to say was, "Let the port come around to your friend, Benjamin."

"Mr. Wiswell's just arrived in England with a letter of introduction to your lordship from General Howe," Thompson said. "This is his first visit to England and our customs are strange to him. I'll warrant he never even heard of passing port to the left."

"Fancy," Lord Germaine said.

"It doesn't seem possible," Thompson went on, "that the world can be so happy in its ignorance of things vastly important and unchangeable to Englishmen."

He turned to me. "You know, Oliver, England's a great country, but she's as strange as she is great. On top of this house there's scores of smoking chimney pots; and on top of every other house in London there's scores of other chimney pots, all belching soot. The soot, being heavier than air, must, of course, come down. When it comes down, everybody and everything in London is covered with it. You know what soot is, Oliver? Indians paint themselves with it because it doesn't come off easily. You'd think the English would be glad to get along without soot, wouldn't you?"

Without waiting for an answer he continued hastily, "Well, you'd be wrong! I've figured out a way to stop fireplaces from smoking, but the English'll have none of it. They have more chimneys than any people in the world, and suffer more from 'em; but being cursed with 'em, they're content to do nothing to remedy their misfortunes."

He turned deferentially toward Lord Germaine. "Pray correct me, my lord, if I exaggerate."

Germaine looked noncommittal. "Not at all sure but what you're right, Benjamin. Wouldn't give a farthing, myself, for a fireplace that didn't smoke. Smoke in the chimney keeps heat in the fireplace, where it belongs. Do away with smoke, and all the heat rushes up the chimney, where it's no dashed good to anyone!"

Thompson beamed upon me. "You see, Oliver, you have to live here to understand the English point of view. Take their ships, for example. England has more ships than any other nation in the world; but when she's built 'em, she seems to feel she's done her full duty."

He turned to Germaine, who stared down his pale nose with the most vacant expression I ever saw upon a human face. "I venture to say, my lord, I could find you a thousand men in America—men who have nothing whatever to do except sit on rail fences or in tavern corners—confidently competent to tell the British how to improve their fleet, great though it is."

"I've no doubt of it, Benjamin," Germaine said.

Thompson turned to me. "You'd scarcely believe it, Oliver, but when a British admiral takes a fleet of a hundred warcraft to sea, those warcraft are almost cut off from each other from the moment they set sail. They can't talk back and forth. They're deaf, dumb, half blind! Yet all of 'em have flags, and masts to hoist 'em on. They know the English language. I've told 'em how to hoist flags so to spell out words—so an admiral can tell all his captains where to go and what to do when they get there; but again they'll have none of it! They want to sail as they've always sailed—deaf, dumb, damned near blind! They've got more colonies than any nation on earth, and they run 'em the same way they run ships, chimneys, fireplaces and damned near everything else—damned badly!"

"Pass the port," Germaine said.

Thompson passed it. "Perhaps," he said to me, "you noticed a certain imperviousness to new ideas during your association with General Howe."

"Since you bring the matter up," I said, "I did."

Germaine sighed.

"Perhaps I shouldn't be frank," I said. "Perhaps not wanting to hear the truth is an English custom, like passing port to the left."

Germaine gave me a frosty look. "We don't mind the truth, if it *is* the truth, and told with proper spirit."

"Well, sir," I said, "I hope you'll find nothing offensive in what I believe to be fact. I mean no offense when I say General Howe seems to me to have behaved like those Englishmen who want their chimneys to smoke, and those admirals who want to sail blind."

Lord Germaine made a singular bleating sound, which I took to mean that he wished me to go on.

"It's common knowledge in America, sir," I said, "that General Howe has won all his battles, but refused every opportunity to win the war. After each battle he's been on the verge of victory, but never once would he let his troops move forward and take that victory. Nobody in America understands why he behaves as he does; but the rebels thank God for General Howe and drink a toast to him whenever they have anything to drink."

Thompson looked faintly amused. "Perhaps it's just as well that nobody in America understands English politics. If the rebels should understand General Howe's behavior, they might actually win a war that so often looks hopeless to them."

He raised an eyebrow at Lord Germaine. "Have I your lordship's permission to explain matters to my ignorant young friend here?"

Germaine moved a languid hand. "Tell him all, Benjamin. Don't spare us! And by all means let him know how you yourself have suffered in this land of tyranny and oppression."

Thompson looked reproachful. "I hope my lord knows that I'm deeply grateful for what he's——"

"Tchah!" Germaine interrupted. "Pass the port and tell your young friend anything that comes into your head. It'll always be too close to the truth for comfort. Damned if I understand how you pick up all your information, Benjamin!"

Thompson spoke to me, but I knew his words were directed even more to Germaine. "You'll never understand Howe's behavior, Oliver, until you understand English politics. If you intend to write a history of this war, you'll have to learn them from top to bottom. Are you at all familiar with them?"

When I said I wasn't, Thompson looked satirical. "Then why shouldn't you find Howe's behavior unfathomable! For years, in this country, the Whigs were in power and had things their own way. All good Whigs had splendid government positions, and received splendid salaries for doing nothing. Then, not long ago, the Tories ousted the Whigs, and took the splendid government positions and the splendid salaries for themselves. The Whigs are out in the cold, Oliver, and they don't like it! They'd been in power so long that they regarded all those fine positions, all those highly paid sinecures, as theirs by divine right. They're doing everything on earth to get back into power again. They're attacking the Tory party in every possible way, and stopping at nothing. The Tory party is the government, Oliver; so every Whig is against the government. The rebels in

America are against the government; therefore the Whigs support the rebels. That's the only reason Pitt and Burke make speeches in favor of the rebels, Oliver—to embarrass the government. If the rebels should be defeated, the Tory government would have been successful: the Tories would remain in power. That would mean the Whigs would be out of power for another term of years—would be left pining fruitlessly for those high positions and those enormous salaries that used to be theirs.

"I'll tell you the horrible truth, Oliver. The English don't like to admit it, but you can corroborate it in a thousand ways—if you work hard enough. The Whigs, in their attempt to get back into power, aren't even hesitating to wreck the British Empire. That's a peculiarity of politicians in this country, just as in our own."

"It sounds fantastic," I said.

"I admit it," Thompson said, "but it's the simple truth. It only sounds fantastic to you because you're hearing it for the first time. Here's another simple truth: Nearly every member of the Whig party in Parliament, for purely political reasons, has seized every opportunity to give aid and comfort to the enemies of his country. Never in any nation has anything been seen like the malignant and daringly outspoken treason of the English Whigs."

I didn't believe him, and Thompson knew I didn't.

"Don't take my word for it," he said. "Investigate for yourself. You'll find my statements painfully conservative! You'll find that General Howe is a Whig. You'll find that if he should put down the rebellion in America, he'd have won a great victory for the government, which is Tory. On the strength of such a victory, the Tories would stay in power for the next two generations. For two generations they'd keep their splendid government positions and their splendid salaries. For two miserable generations the Whigs would be out in the cold! They'd starve in the midst of plenty, and all the blame would fall on Howe! Single-handed, he'd have defeated his own friends, his own party! He'd have undone all the Whig trickery, all the Whig treason, all the Whig plotting and planning to destroy the Tories and get the Whigs back into power."

"Well," I said, "I'm afraid General Howe, in failing to destroy the rebels when he had the chance, has done more than help the Whigs. I'm afraid he's given France the opportunity to make war on England and perhaps destroy her. That's why I ventured to come here to find you. I figured Lord Germaine should know at once."

I told him briefly how we had met Captain Hynson and found our way to Mrs. Jump's. "Hynson claims to be a close friend of Silas Deane's," I said. "If he's telling the truth, Deane hasn't dared send Congress his reports on what he's done in France. He's afraid the ship that carries 'em will be captured by the English. If Hynson can find a fast vessel, he'll carry Deane's reports to America. Those reports will make sad reading for everyone who doesn't want America to fall into rebel hands and perhaps, in the end, into the hands of France."

"Nonsense," Germaine said.

"I think not, sir. Hynson wasn't talking nonsense. He believed what he said, if ever a man did."

"Then he's an idiot," Germaine said coldly. "Benjamin, give me that port! Now see here, Wiswell! This Captain Hynson of yours, according to your own statements, is a boor, a drunkard, loose-mouthed. He has other grave faults. Do you seriously believe Deane would confide in such a creature? No, no, Mr. Wiswell! He'd be a gullible fool if he did, and not even the rebels would send a gullible fool to represent them in France. You don't send a gullible fool to get help for you! Come now, Mr. Wiswell, admit you may have misjudged this Hynson fellow."

"I'll admit nothing of the sort, sir! Hynson's exactly the sort of boor that the rebels have put in positions of authority. Their army, their Congress, their committees are packed with them. You see, sir, there are mighty few men of property and education who think as the rebels do, and fewer still whom the rebels trust."

Germaine darted a quick glance from me to Thompson. "Damned if I don't think you've cooked up a story between you! Thompson's forever harping on the stupidity of those rebel fellows; and here you are, Mr. Wiswell, saying the selfsame thing in the selfsame way. Can't expect me to believe anything so obvious, by Gad!"

Thompson raised his eyebrows. "Your lordship's entitled to believe what he pleases. Mr. Wiswell and I have told you the truth as we see it. We know the rebels and you don't, but your knowledge of statecraft may give you a better understanding of them than we have. Up to now the rebels have been stupid through ignorance, whereas your lordship's advisers and soldiers have been stupid because of politics and bad leadership. I can assure your lordship that the rebels won't always be stupid. Children learn, and so will the rebels. They won't always put their trust in boors and yokels. Whether your leaders will learn, I can't say."

Germaine gave Thompson a soothing pat. "Now you're angry, Benjamin! I can always tell when you're angry, even when you smile! To be quite frank, I have no doubt you and Mr. Wiswell are telling me the truth; but after all, what can I do about it?"

"I'll tell you one thing you can do, my lord," Thompson said. "Mr. Wiswell's my friend. He's reliable. He's been recommended to you by General Howe, so you've every reason to treat him kindly. He's come to us with information of vital importance. It seems to me you're almost bound to place the matter before Sir William Eden, and instruct Sir William to include Mr. Wiswell among his—ah— assistants."

"Damnably easy to say, my dear Benjamin," Germaine said, "but Sir William doesn't know where to turn for money! He says the £80,000 we allowed him last year isn't nearly enough. How can I order him to put an expensive young man to work, and at the same time fail to obtain for him the money that he needs? Answer me that, by Gad, and pass the port."

Thompson looked fatigued. "I can only say, my lord, that you should find some way to get Sir William what he needs. Ten times £80,000 wouldn't be an unreasonable expenditure to prevent America from falling into the hands of France."

"Tchah," Germaine said. "France!"

"From falling into the hands of France," Thompson repeated.

"Bah," Germaine said. "Bah, my dear Benjamin!" He sipped at his port; then added, "It's not true; and if it were, the King wouldn't sanction the expenditure."

"You've told me that before, my lord," Thompson said, "and I make you the same answer I've always made: the matter hasn't been properly explained to His Majesty. His Majesty's behaving like a nobleman who keeps a handsome equipage but insists—for economy's sake—on employing chimney sweeps as footmen and postilions. If your lordship would let me talk to His Majesty——"

"Oh, by Gad and blast it," Germaine cried, "don't go into that again! Haven't I explained everything to His Majesty? Let's have no more talk about it! Since you make such a point of it, I'll send Mr. Wiswell to Sir William. God knows where we'll get the money! I suppose I can beg, borrow or steal it somewhere! You're a damnable nuisance, Benjamin, you and your confounded Loyalists!"

Thompson turned to me. "There's a start for you, Oliver! Sir William Eden's Under-secretary of State. It's his business to know every-thing that goes on in this world. He'll make it possible for you to find out whether Hynson's telling the truth; and perhaps he'll make it possible for you to get the information that'll put an end to the war in America."

CHAPTER LII

Sir william eden, when he received us at 10 Downing Street on the following morning, had that air, peculiar to Englishmen of birth and breeding, of being completely uninterested in everything except the business on which we'd called, and only remotely interested in that.

He was the most elegant and languid gentleman I had ever seen. His profile was that of a Greek god who had perhaps been an oversedulous thumb-sucker in his infancy; and his own hair came so far down on his forehead that his wig had the look of shading his eyes. His coat and breeches fitted him as perfectly as if glued on him; the lace at his wrists and throat was almost like a waterfall after a storm, for its foaminess was yellowed with age. A handkerchief, edged with a similar yellow lace, lay before him on the table; and from time to time, as he spoke, he daintily picked up the cambric and swung it idly before him, as if to waft away stray thoughts that hovered near.

"Mr. Wiswell," he said, "I've had a letter from Mr. Thompson about you this morning. Most interesting; most interesting." His eye wandered to Buell and passed vacantly on, as if Buell didn't exist.

"Didn't Mr. Thompson mention my friend, Tom Buell?" I asked.

Eden fumbled in the lace that foamed from his waistcoat, and drew out a single eyeglass on a cord. He thrust it in his eye and stared at me. "Mr. Thompson said nothing about a Mr. Buell."

"Well, sir," I said, "he's been my constant companion since early 1775. He was of great service to me in Boston when we'd been driven from our homes; and later, on Long Island, he was of material assistance to me and General Howe."

"You might as well tell Sir William," Buell said, "that General Howe most generally was too busy to take advantage of what I did for him."

Eden's face had what I might call a frostbitten look. His eyeglass fell from his eye like a chip of ice and vanished amid the folds of yellow lace.

"It was Buell," I added, "who got Hynson's story from him by adroit questioning."

Buell corrected me. "You mean adroit drinking! My digestion ain't what it ought to be, Sir William, and liquor doesn't help it any; but if you want to know what a man's up to, you've got to drink with him, hiccups or no hiccups!"

"Drinking," Eden said coldly, "is not exactly a recommendation for the sort of confidential work on which a government depends for its plans of action."

Buell stared moodily at the floor.

"Sir," I said to Eden, "we have only one object in view: to do everything we can for our country. That's why I went to Mr. Thompson last night. That's why I brought Buell with me this morning. For a year and a half, in America, we made every effort to help put down rebellion. I regret to say most of our efforts were rewarded with doubts and suspicion. It was Mr. Thompson's suggestion that we come to you. If we can be of service, we'll be well content. But if we're to encounter the same suspicion here, I fear we'll be wasting our time."

"Yes," Buell said, "and I'd be wasting something that's more valuable to me than time. I'd be wasting my stomach. That Hynson, he can hold as much liquor as a British general! No, sir, if I got to keep up with Captain Hynson, I want to be sure my efforts are appreciated."

Eden looked disconcerted. "I seem to have given you the wrong impression, Mr. Wiswell. You may be quite sure your efforts will be highly appreciated; highly. Our best and most dependable men are Americans! I assure you, you completely misunderstood me! Now about Captain Hynson: there's no doubt in your mind that he's dangerous—that he ought to be watched?"

"Well, sir," I said, "he's close to Silas Deane, and he obviously has ways of finding out whatever he wants to know about the movements of your transports and supply ships. What's more, he has the funds to buy a fast vessel in this country. If he finds it, he'll use it against you.

Perhaps you should be the one to say whether or not he's dangerous: whether or not he should be watched."

Eden turned to his desk and picked up one of the papers on it. "Dear me," he said. "By a singular coincidence, your information is corroborated. Why, yes: I believe this Hynson of yours should be watched. You've done very well, Mr. Wiswell: very well indeed."

"Corroborated!" I said. "May I ask how?"

Eden pretended he hadn't heard.

A light dawned upon me. "Oh, I see," I said. "Mrs. Jump!"

Buell laughed. "By God, Oliver, I'll bet it was! I'll bet she told him about us, too, and got it all wrong."

Eden had the grace to blush. He tweaked a bell-pull; and while he waited for his ring to be answered, he said: "What anyone may have said is none of your affair." To the boy who answered the bell he said, "Ask Doctor Vardill to be kind enough to come in for a moment." Then he ignored us, and unfortunately gave the impression of despising us, though I was certain he was merely embarrassed.

When the door opened again to admit a slender, pleasant-faced young man, I think I'd have known, even if Eden hadn't mentioned it, that his name was Vardill; for he was the image of the kind professor who had succored me in New York—the kind professor I had last seen crushed to death beneath a tangle of beams and laths.

If ever a young man looked both gullible and guileless, it was the Rev. John Vardill.

His cheeks were smooth as a girl's; his slender eyebrows were arched and the eyes beneath them round, so that he seemed perpetually lost in trusting admiration. Candor, inexperience, credulity were so stamped upon his boyish features that I wondered of what earthly use this young man could be in the office of Sir William Eden, Under-secretary of State.

There was, too, a fumbling ineffectiveness in his manner and speech that put me in mind of an amiable puppy, indiscriminately fawning upon anyone who took the trouble to throw him a kind word.

When Eden presented me to him and mentioned that I had been recommended by Benjamin Thompson, a friend of long standing, Vardill nodded and smiled, smiled and nodded, voicing half-inarticulate gratification and wonderment. "Indeed, indeed! Thompson, Thompson! Well, well!"

What, I wondered, was the matter with these British, that they should so often employ persons of little talent in ventures of tremendous moment. In the midst of Vardill's sugary murmurings, his roving blue eye fastened suddenly upon Buell. There was a sharpness about his darting glance that made me think of a hawk's pounce.

I looked more carefully at him; and since Sir William showed no signs of introducing Buell, I took it upon myself. "This is my friend Tom Buell, Mr. Vardill," I said. "He's——"

Buell stopped me. "I'll tell him myself, Oliver. Otherwise he might trust to Mrs. Jump for some of his information about me, and I'd find myself in jail, suspected of God knows what! I'm Thomas Buell, Mr. Vardill: printer; repairer of military arms; maker of fashionable ornaments for military caps and cartridge boxes; painter and gilder of escutcheons; copier of handwriting and maps on copper plates; engraver of silver plate with elegant ciphers and arms; cutter of blocks and ornaments for printers; maker of models for canal locks, paint-grinding mills, machines for cutting and polishing crystals and precious stones; and European agent for Perkins' Metallic Tractors, guaranteed to cure all pains and restore youthful vigor."

At Buell's mention of copying maps and handwriting, Vardill's eyes went swiftly to Sir William's, and I knew there was no more candor and innocence to the Rev. John Vardill than to a steel trap.

When Buell had finished, Vardill made cooing sounds of admiration. "Useful," he said, "useful. Unusual and useful, oh vastly! Do you copy signatures, Mr. Buell?"

"I copy anything," Buell said.

Vardill tittered. "Vastly interesting and entertaining! Would it be possible, do you think, for you to copy that letter of Mr. Thompson's"—he motioned toward Sir William's desk, though I hadn't been conscious that he'd previously looked in that direction—"in such a way that the sense was wholly changed?"

"That's something I never tried," Buell said.

Sir William cleared his throat. "Mr. Wiswell brings us a singular story, Doctor Vardill," he said. "It concerns a Captain Hynson—Captain Joseph Hynson. If it's true, I think I've reason to protest that somebody has been remiss in his duties."

Doctor Vardill looked worried. "Oh dear! That would be unfortunate—vastly so! Captain Hynson is related by marriage to an American mariner of some ability—Captain Lambert Wickes; but Hynson, Sir William, is a gentleman of another kidney. He's a braggart, Sir William, and not at all the sort of person in whom one could repose confidence—or so we've been told——"

"Who told us?" Sir William demanded.

"One of our friends in Paris."

"Had we also been told," Eden asked, "that Captain Hynson was in England? That he's here on a mission for Silas Deane? That his mission is to purchase a fast vessel in an English port for our further discomfiture? That he has even come to London on this singular business of his? I think not, Doctor Vardill."

Vardill seemed deeply distressed. "Dear, dear! I fear somebody underrated Captain Hynson!" He looked helplessly from Buell to me. "You've seen Captain Hynson? You've spoken with him?"

"We have," Buell said. "We've seen him, heard him, smelled him, got drunk with him and been invited to go back to France with him and a few of his female friends."

"Indeed," Vardill said disapprovingly. "And in spite of these short-comings you mention, do I understand that you consider him a person in whom one could repose confidence?"

"Up to a certain point," Buell said. "He ain't what I'd call inventive, and when he's got a dozen drinks inside him and a couple of nut-brown maidens draped across each shoulder, he don't have the time or the ingenuity to tell lies. Whatever he tells you, under circumstances like that, you can believe. But I shouldn't wonder if there was other things about him that ain't worthy of so much confidence."

"Such as?" Sir William asked.

"Such as his loyalty," Buell said. "If I was a betting man, I'd bet he couldn't be loyal to anything very long. I was kind of watching him with those nut-brown maidens at Mrs. Jump's. Cleghorn was his, but he'd have made free with either of the other two at the drop of a hat. You give me a free hand, and I'll bet I can take him away from Silas Deane just as easy as any pretty girl could take him away from the lady he's supposed to be attached to."

Vardill made a series of rapid sucking sounds, as if shocked; but his eye was eager. "A rash statement, Mr. Buell," he said, "considering Hynson was recommended to Mr. Deane because of his fidelity."

"Who recommended him?" Buell asked.

Vardill glanced at Sir William Eden. So far as I could see, Eden made no sign; but I knew he must have done so, for Vardill answered Buell frankly. "Edward Carmichael, Deane's secretary."

Buell stared thoughtfully at the ceiling. "Carmichael," he said, "Carmichael. Now let's see: would Carmichael maybe be from Maryland? Would he be a handsome young squirt from Baltimore who thought he could sail rings around any clipper captain that ever lived?"

"That description, so far as I know," Vardill said, "applies accurately to Edward Carmichael. Are you acquainted with him?"

"Only by hearing about him from Hynson," Buell said. "I guess maybe Carmichael must have done something to Hynson. Maybe he took a nut-brown maiden away from him, most likely."

For the first time since we had entered the office, Sir William Eden looked interested. "Indeed," he said, "indeed!"

"Well," Buell said cautiously, "that's how I'd figure it. It was somewhere around the fifth or sixth bottle that Hynson began to bring up the subject of Carmichael. He had a nut-brown maiden wrapped around him, and sometimes I couldn't quite catch all he said, partly on account of his words being muffled, and partly because I had a lady clinging to me, too."

He shook his head, as if recalling a danger narrowly escaped.

"Do I understand," Sir William asked, "that Captain Hynson cast aspersions on Mr. Carmichael's ability?"

"Yes and no," Buell said. "It seems Carmichael knows a lot of gossip about the Empress of Russia. Carmichael figures that if she's distributing her favors with a lavish hand, as you might say, he's in line for 'em in case he wants to go to Russia. The way it looks to Hynson, Carmichael figures on taking a trip to Russia and getting to be Grand Duke Carmichael. Pretty wrought up about it, Hynson is, too. Not because Carmichael has so much confidence in himself, the way I figured it, but because Hynson's afraid Carmichael may get to be Emperor of Russia before Hynson can get to be that way himself."

"The Empress of Russia!" Eden exclaimed.

"Fantastic, ain't it?" Buell said. "Any man that would plan to get himself led astray by the Empress of Russia, he can be bought. Any man he recommends can be bought! He recommended Hynson, and Hynson's such a damned fool that he's willing to buy three pairs of my Metallic Tractors. You give me the money and I'll buy Hynson as easy as buying a quart of gin."

Again Vardill made a series of slight sucking sounds; but they were perfunctory. "Truly," he said, "the Lord has delivered the Egyptians into our hands! He's given us a handle with which to open the door to all that Deane and Franklin are doing in Paris—if only Lord North and the King will trust us to open that door."

I think Vardill's greatest asset was his innocent, guileless face, and the odor of sanctity that seemed to cling about his every utterance. Nobody could suspect so ingenuous and simple a young man of harboring involved and tortuous plots, nor would anyone hesitate to trust their innermost thoughts to such a sympathetic churchman.

Yet the Rev. John Vardill had a brain that dodged and squirmed as elusively as a frightened squirrel in a lofty pine. When he worked with Colonel Edward Smith, his chosen companion in the British Secret Service, the two of them could think of more schemes to outwit a victim than could all the adventurers in Newgate Prison.

Sir William Eden was the avowed head of all the secret agents who ferreted out for England the peculiar activities of the American rebels in France; but it was Vardill who provided Sir William with ideas that might—save for the stubbornness of a willful king—have changed the history of America and the world.

"It's like a kaleidoscope," Vardill told Eden exultantly. "All the broken pieces fall into a pattern! We can make sure of Hynson through the Cleghorn woman. We'll get a double hold on him by paying both of them: then he can't betray us without losing her. We'll find him a likely ship, and have it delivered to him in France at the suitable moment. We'll have a dozen bully boys under hatches, and when the vessel sails, they'll off hatches, seize the ship and the papers and——"

Eden interrupted him. "I don't like it, Vardill! Too many men in it! One of 'em's bound to talk! You'll have to do better than that! Where's Smith? Send for Colonel Smith. Let's see what he has to say!"

Behind the curtains near Eden's desk were several bell-pulls, and when Eden tweaked one of them, Colonel Smith appeared at the door almost simultaneously, so that his arrival seemed a coincidence rather than the response to a summons.

There was nothing impressive about Colonel Smith. He seemed kindly in appearance, loud of speech, slow of understanding, watery of eye—the epitome of the bluff old soldier who had always done his duty honestly and fairly, but without much imagination. One look at his frank, open countenance was an assurance that his word was as good as his bond; that he would never take unfair advantage of anyone. One who jumped to such conclusions, however, would have been wholly wrong; for Colonel Smith could tell the most monumental lies with a candid and level eye, and had so wide an acquaintance among the lower elements of society, both in England and in France, that if given one day's warning, he could arrange to have anyone beaten, spirited away or murdered.

Eden introduced Buell and me to the foggy-eyed colonel as the persons who had brought the information about Hynson, and outlined the singular circumstances concerning Hynson, Mrs. Jump's establishment, and the part Hynson was to play in carrying Deane's and Franklin's reports to Congress. "Now then," Eden said, "how'll we make sure of obtaining those dispatches?"

Smith made puffing sounds. "Most interesting, eh? Fortuitous! Sure he can be bought?"

"I wish I was as sure of going back to Newport to live," Buell said.

"Good!" Smith said. "Buy him; then get him his fast vessel. Make him a present of it, but have it look like a genuine sale! Most important transaction! Must be bona fide or French might smell a rat! Have the money change hands publicly, eh? Get him a cutter. I know just the one! French prize! The *Rochefort!* Sell it to him and let him take it to France and stuff it with a rich cargo—the very richest: brandy, laces, silk, eh? Arouse the avarice of the woman and Hynson too. Offer 'em part of profits."

"By Jove!" Eden said thoughtfully.

"You'd use our own men as crew?" Vardill urged.

"No, no, no!" Smith cried. "Never! Very suspicious! We'll go to Paris, establish contacts, get Hynson's sailing date. Mr. Vardill and these friends of Hynson's remain in Paris: I arrange matters in Calais, Havre, Boulogne—back and forth, eh? Lord Sandwich should be seen at once—five ships detached to lie in wait. Let's see—captains such bloody damned fools nowadays—see nothing, know nothing, brains all addled, must be the brand of port they drink! Let's see now: five vessels on station, watching for Hynson—*Speedwell, Courageous, Royal Oak, Ranger, Hector*—three of those captains have brains—a few. Well, there you are: see Lord Sandwich; have him station *Speedwell* off Cape Barfleur, *Courageous* between Barfleur and la Hague, *Royal Oak* off la Hague, *Ranger* between la Hague and Gaskets of Jersey, and *Hector* north of Ushant. We'll nab him, by Gad!"

"Splendid," Vardill cried. "He'll throw his dispatches overboard when he's chased, but they'll be the wrong dispatches!"

"Certainly," the colonel said, looking almost painfully honest. "We find the true dispatches in his cabin but never admit it. Hynson's taken aboard vessel that captures him, and treated roughly, so no suspicion attaches. French never know we have dispatches. Congress never knows. A most interesting and worthy undertaking, and of great value if successful."

Vardill looked hopefully at Eden, and so did I.

"That's not unreasonable," Eden said. "That might give us the proof the King's always demanding—proof that the French are secretly supporting the rebels. It might even help to end the war."

Help to end the war! To end the war, I'd have grasped at any straw and plotted with anyone to corrupt a dozen Hynsons.

CHAPTER LIII

Wars are senseless things, frequently lost because of the strangest of reasons—because, for example, a king likes to gamble with lives, but doesn't approve of gambling in stocks; because politicians are more concerned with their own desire for power than with the needs of their country; because a general puts politics and a mistress ahead of his duty; because a king and his ministers won't believe the men from whom they sought advice and information— men of great ability, like Edward Bancroft, Paul Wentworth and John Vardill.

Edward Bancroft, Paul Wentworth and John Vardill were Americans working as diligently for the welfare of America as any statesman or soldier that America has ever known. They were spies. I suppose that for a time I was a spy myself. I thought then, and I think still, that we were working in the worthiest of causes and for the best of purposes; and I know that if the results of our work had received proper consideration, America would have been saved untold misery, and spared the loss of thousands of her bravest and ablest sons.

The Hôtel DeBailles on the Rue des Sts. Pères had a dark and narrow front, like most of the buildings on that steep and narrow thoroughfare. So narrow was it that the whole ground floor was a carriage entrance; and when our coach turned into that dark passage, the street seemed to explode in a bedlam of scraping wheels, clattering hoofs, shrill neighings, whip-crackings, angry shouts of passers-by, and a chorus of squeals from inside the coach.

So this was France! How different were its people, its buildings, its smells from anything American! Then my eye lit upon an evil-

464

looking dark gray cat, perched on a window ledge. In the very moment that I saw it a boy's hand shot from the partly open window and snatched at it. The cat vanished like a wisp of smoke, and the boy's voice said something emphatic in a foreign tongue.

The cat alone would have meant nothing to me; but the combination of the animal and the boy's voice brought into my brain the picture of a harried yellow-faced dog patiently enduring the loving but painful attentions of little Nathan Dixon.

I thought to drop a hint of my suspicions to Tom Buell; but when I glanced at him over the heads of shouting porters who wrangled over our luggage, I found warnings unnecessary.

"That's Nathan Dixon, Oliver," he said. "I'd know his voice if I heard it in the middle of the Sahara Desert."

When Vardill led us up two steps, past a glass door on which "Joyeux Noël" had been inscribed long since with soap, and into the long foyer of the Hôtel DeBailles, we found ourselves face to face with Henrietta Dixon, but a Henrietta Dixon far removed from the one we had known on the *Osprey* and in Halifax.

She stood behind a tall, raised desk, at the foot of a narrow flight of stairs, and there was none of that clinging softness to her, none of that fluffy, fumbling indecision that had so distressed me when she had forced herself upon us on the day we sailed from Boston. Her dress was black and stylishly severe; her elaborately coiffured hair was an imposing bank of curls and braids. One swelling hip was thrust daringly outward; and her fist rested upon that rounded shelf in alluring defiance.

"Zut alors!" she cried. "You never expect us to accommodate this gathering at one small minute's notice!" Her accent was distinctly Gallic.

Mr. Vardill abased himself. "Under the circumstances, dear lady, I'm sure you'll find a way."

Henrietta looked condescendingly at all of us, with no glance of recognition for Buell or me. "Enfin," she said grudgingly, "is possible Madame DeBailles might find the means. I go ask."

"An excellent idea," Mr. Vardill said. "I'll go with you, if I may, to explain the circumstances."

"You will not," Henrietta Dixon said sharply. "Madame DeBailles does not wish gentlemen walking into her boudoir at all times.

Madame DeBailles is sympathique, and understand all circumstances without explanations." She emerged from behind her desk in a cloud of penetrating perfume and with undulating hips mounted the narrow staircase to the upper regions.

"My, my," Buell said, watching her go, "that lady's mighty independent! Mighty independent! Who is she and how's it happen, Mr. Vardill, you let her take that tone with you?"

"Sometimes I wonder myself," Vardill said, "but in the end I control my resentment. She's the protectress of Madame DeBailles, with all the stubbornness of an inherently weak nature. Yet she can be trusted, Mr. Buell—trusted not to repeat anything she overhears: trusted not to pry into pockets and valises when backs are turned. Such women are not easy for an American to find in France. Others may exist, but I doubt it. French women are born with an instinct to make trouble for Americans and Englishmen. She is known as Dijon—Henriette Dijon—from her place of birth, I believe."

From the dimness above him Henrietta Dixon's voice sounded shrilly. "M'sieu, m'sieu! Madame DeBailles will speak to you! Please to come up at once and bring the American gentleman aussi."

We mounted to a narrow hallway and found ourselves before a partly open door through which I saw a veritable tangle of ornate tables and settees.

When Vardill tapped upon the door and swung it farther open, a wave of homesickness washed over my heart; for one corner of the little room was cleared of gilded chairs, and in that corner stood Belcher Byles' wigstand, Belcher Byles' tall clock with the faces of the sun and moon upon its dial, and a dozen other pieces of furniture that my father and I had learned to know well during that cold winter we had spent on Sudbury Street in Boston.

In the midst of all those well-remembered things, looking at us imperturbably, sat Mrs. Belcher Byles herself, her hands clasped over the ivory head of her cane. Henrietta stood behind her, and since neither of them seemed to know me, I stared at my shoes and tried to show no emotion at seeing those two old friends together.

"Friend of yours, Vardill?" I heard Mrs. Byles say.

"A friend indeed," Vardill said. "He's acting with us—a new recruit to our little army of Americans in France."

"A new recruit?" Mrs. Byles asked. "What's his name and where's he from?"

"Mr. Oliver Wiswell of Milton," Vardill said.

"That's right," Mrs. Byles said heartily. "I never quite know, Vardill, when you're going to forget to tell me something I ought to know."

She got up with a groan, dropped her cane, caught my shoulders and pressed them hard. As suddenly as she had risen, she sat down again, and if I hadn't felt the pressure of her hands, I'd have thought our meeting had left her wholly unmoved. For my part, I couldn't say a word, and could only pick up her cane and give it to her.

"Look here, Vardill," Mrs. Byles said, "I know Oliver Wiswell, and I knew his father. His father was a great lawyer; and if Oliver isn't ruined by this nonsensical war, he'll be a great historian. Don't try any of your tricks on him, Vardill! Understand? Don't get him into trouble! You play fair with Oliver, or you'll end as vicar of Lower Weevil Super Chutney instead of rector of King's College!"

She narrowed her eyes and poked his knee with the ferrule of her stick. "What's the game this time, Vardill? Let's hear it—all of it!"

Vardill looked horrified. "Game? There's no game, dear lady! We've merely come over here to be with Captain Hynson. Captain Hynson's a sea captain who's been closely associated with Mr. Franklin and Mr. Deane."

He coughed delicately behind his hand and lowered his voice to a whisper. "He's going to carry their dispatches to the American Congress—unless they fall into our hands first."

"Hynson's a rebel, eh?" Mrs. Byles said. "Then you're not sure of him, Vardill!"

"Oh, but we've bought him," Vardill said. "He's taken our money!"

"You're still not sure," Mrs. Byles cried. "The only ones you can be sure of are those who've been driven out of America by the rebels and who can't go back until the rebels are beaten. I'll find a way of putting you up, Vardill—you and Oliver and Buell, and that old wall-eyed bloodhound Smith. But I won't have Hynson! I can't have people nosing through my papers and bursting open trunks and bureaus in this house, and rummaging in lodgers' luggage with dirty hands. That's what the French'll do if Hynson stays here."

"We can't afford to let him out of our sight," Vardill protested. "Didn't you hear me say we've got to get our hands on the dispatches he's supposed to carry to America?"

"Certainly I heard you," Mrs. Byles said, "but you've got three ladies with you. I know Downing Street methods, so one of those ladies must be Captain Hynson's personal property. She is, isn't she?"

Vardill looked shocked. "My dear lady! I know nothing about Captain Hynson's private life."

Mrs. Byles swelled visibly. "I've warned you, Vardill! I've told you a hundred times not to try your little trickeries on me! You don't know anything about Hynson's private life, indeed! If there's anything about him you don't know, it's because he doesn't know it himself! I'll help in every possible way to put an end to rebellion in America, and to keep the French from stealing everything we've got; but I'll work with no one that doesn't tell me the truth! What's more, if I know Oliver Wiswell, he won't either! Don't lie to me, and don't lie to him! One of those women belongs to Hynson, doesn't she?"

Vardill squirmed. "I suppose you might say that Miss Cleghorn——"

"You suppose," Mrs. Byles cried. "Don't forget, Vardill, that Belcher Byles told me about the world before you were born! Thanks to Belcher's frankness, I suspect you and Eden of supplying Cleghorn with spending money. I suspect you and Eden of buying new dresses for her, to make sure Hynson'll stay bought."

"I believe something of the sort may have been done," Vardill admitted.

Mrs. Byles sighed. "Vardill, you bring out all the Barrell in me! If I asked you whether you were born on your birthday, you might say you believed so! We're helping to fight a war, Vardill: not giving a tea party." She turned to me. "Who are the three women, Oliver?"

"Cleghorn belongs to Hynson," I told her. "Eden gave her £200 before we left Paris. She'll get £30 a month as long as she stays on good terms with Hynson, and she'll get another £200 when the papers are safely delivered to us. The other two, Miss Cotton and Miss Pinto, are for Silas Deane's secretary, Mr. Edward Carmichael. Eden authorized Mr. Vardill to provide them with a wardrobe, their lodgings and £30 a month in return for letting us know the more interesting details about Deane and Franklin that their male associates might overlook."

Mrs. Byles poked Vardill's waistcoat with the ferrule of her stick. "There you are," she said. "That's the way we Americans like our information. Take my advice, Vardill, and see the King gets his in the same way."

Vardill looked virtuous. "Nothing's more dangerous than arbitrary statements."

"Pah," Mrs. Byles said. "Here's an arbitrary statement for you. Hynson can't stay in this house, but the three girls must. I'm going to keep my eye on 'em! They'll stay in one room and they'll receive guests in the parlor and nowhere else. I'll force 'em to be honest women for at least part of the time, and that'll make Hynson all the more eager to see his little Cleghorn. I well remember Belcher telling me one night, after we'd gone to bed, that a fool never makes a complete fool of himself except over a wench pretending to be an angel."

"If Hynson's not where we can watch him all the time," Vardill protested, "we can't be sure what he's doing."

Mrs. Byles eyed him pityingly. "You can never be sure what he's *thinking,* Vardill, even if you hold him in your lap all day and all night. The trouble with you, Vardill, is you're young!"

Vardill was offended. "My age, dear lady, has nothing to do with the situation."

"Yes, it has," Mrs. Byles said. "You're twenty-two years old. You and Eden and Smith and North have tried to tell the King what's going on, and he hasn't believed any of you! Why not? My guess is, he thinks these bright Americans over here are too young to know what they're talking about. If so, he's right. It's time for you to do what some of us older Americans think you ought to do!"

"If the rebels win," Vardill protested, "you'll be to blame!"

"That's nonsense, and you know it," Mrs. Byles said. "The rebels can't win, if the English listen to good advice. Take Hynson out and find him a place to live. If he doesn't like it, send him to see me. I'll put him in his place! My father was a Barrell from Salem, Vardill, and Barrells have a way with sea captains. Whenever a sea captain tried to stand up to my father, Salem people used to say a Barrell rolled over him. You leave Hynson to me, Vardill! I'll roll a Barrell over him for you!"

Henrietta Dixon lived in a peculiar cavern sunk beneath the level of the lobby of the Hôtel DeBailles in such a way that those within the room saw the lobby through a window at the level of the ceiling, so that they had a constant foreshortened view of everyone within the lobby.

There, after Vardill, Smith, Isabella Cleghorn, Miss Cotton and Miss Pinto had been safely ensconced in their respective rooms, Buell and I were at last alone with Mrs. Byles and Henrietta.

"Épatant, eh, this room," Henrietta said coyly. "Épatant et pas chère, comme on dit à Paris! I sit here freely, not recognized by anyone who looks in the window. You know why, mes amis? Because we nevaire see people from above!"

Mrs. Byles sighed. "Stop it, Henrietta! Oliver and Tom Buell don't want to hear your imitation accent or your philosophy."

Henrietta tossed her head. "So you think they'd prefer to hear about rebels and war and spies and Beaumarchais and guns and privateers and American commissioners and Silas Deane and General Howe and Lord Howe and King George and confiscated estates and how nobody on God's earth can do anything without doing it wrong! I say such talk'll hurt their ears, as it does mine!"

Mrs. Byles sighed. "Henrietta may be right," she told us. "It's the everlasting uncertainty—always hoping the war'll be over next month, but having it go on and on, on and on; finding worse and worse people mixed up in it; feeling more and more helpless!"

"It never occurred to us you'd feel that way," I said. "We thought things would be different in France."

"Different!" Mrs. Byles cried. "War's always the same! Children starve, women suffer, men lose their fortunes or turn into beasts! I say about all wars what Belcher used to say about the Old French War —though he never said it till after we'd got to bed, for fear he'd be mobbed by his friends at Harvard who liked wars. 'Damn wars and those that can't find ways of escaping 'em till it's too late,' Belcher used to say."

She leaned forward and patted my knee. "I'm glad you're here, Oliver—glad and sorry; glad because it's a joy to have another person near me that I can trust: sorry because of the company you're in."

"I was sent here," I reminded her. "I didn't choose my company. I only chose to do something that might help to end the war."

"I know, Oliver," Mrs. Byles said. "I apologize! We all have to do what we can; but drat these tricky, underhanded ways of doing things! Damn these spies that spy on everybody, including each other, until sometimes you wonder which side you're on yourself!"

She hastily explained how she and Henrietta had got to France. Swamped by Loyalists in London, she had conceived the idea of moving to Paris.

"It was easy," she said. "I spoke a little French, because Belcher taught it at Harvard. Sometimes, after we'd gone to bed, he used to tell me about France—about the snails and frogs and powerful cheeses the French eat, and I always wanted to see the place. To tell you the truth, I always thought Belcher was drawing the long bow about France."

She sighed. "Well, Oliver, I went to Sir William Eden and his cronies and pointed out that England was spending £50,000 a year to send investigators to France. The investigators stayed in French taverns, and naturally got themselves well investigated by the French. Thus the French were benefiting more than the English, and at England's expense. I told 'em that was all nonsense, and that I'd operate a tavern in Paris where English investigators could investigate without being investigated. In wartime, a government always says yes to any proposal that costs money, so Eden loaned me £10,000 to start this Anglo-American tavern, and guaranteed to send all his investigators to me and be responsible for all bills incurred."

"I still don't quite understand," I said. "Do the French know your sympathies? Is this supposed to be a tavern for rebels or a tavern for Loyalists?"

"My dear Oliver, I'm a truthful woman, and I came here in my true colors—those of a Bostonian driven from her home by the unrelenting vindictiveness of men in rebellion against their sovereign; then driven from England by the rapacity and hunger of her own countrymen."

"Why don't the French make things uncomfortable for you?" I asked. "I hear talk of a war between France and England."

"You know, Oliver," Mrs. Byles said, "war's a peculiar thing. It makes people think oddly. If you're in enemy country in wartime, and tell the exact truth, you're never believed. Everyone's suspicious of you. You're investigated—most unpleasantly investigated, as a rule."

She looked as bland as though butter wouldn't melt in her mouth. "Well, Oliver, I consider it my duty to be prepared for anybody who intrudes on my privacy. When Henrietta and I first came here, we hired French servants. You'd never dream how many interesting papers they stumbled on while they were putting our rooms to rights. They found papers proving we were agents of certain wealthy Americans who wished to buy privateers capable of destroying English merchantmen. They found other papers proving we were keeping an eye on the American commissioners at the behest of certain patriotic Bostonian rebels."

She eyed me sleepily. "At the end of a week, Oliver, I discharged all the French servants, and replaced them with Loyalists I brought over from England. But the French don't bother me any more. They know I'm harmless, and they can tell from Henrietta's accent that she's French at heart."

"Zut alors!" Henrietta said.

CHAPTER LIV

In all likelihood Volume I of *Civil War in America* would never have been written if it hadn't been for the insistence of Mrs. Belcher Byles.

"I want you to have a reason for being in Paris," she told me, when we were alone, "and it's got to be a reason that'll give you an excuse for meeting any one of the queer human midgets responsible for keeping this war alive. From now on your brain'll be a jumble of benevolent old rebels who look like clergymen and have mistresses up a dozen alleys, poets masquerading as War Gods, schoolmasters turned diplomats, novelists who've learned how to be on both sides of the fence at the same time, and the smartest man in Europe, who can't get anybody to believe the important things he says because he's too successful as a speculator.

"What you'll have to do, Oliver, is start writing your book. You've always wanted to write history, and the way to write history is to write history. Once you've started, we can arrange to have spies examine your papers, and satisfy themselves that you're a perfectly harmless young gentleman. You'll have to write letters to important personages, demanding that your great historical work be translated into French as soon as you write it. We'll see that those letters reach the Quai d'Orsay. As soon as that's done, Oliver, you can meet the people you ought to meet."

The next morning found me seated before a rickety table, cudgeling my brains as to where to start, and hopelessly telling myself, as would-be authors always do, that I didn't know enough about anything to write a book. Only too clearly I saw I had been a fool ever to have thought of such a thing.

But when I came out from my room and told Mrs. Byles I couldn't do it, she went at me like a Fury.

"You've been working less than four hours," she cried. "It's taken you only four hours to decide to abandon that history you've been talking about for over two years! Well, let me tell you this, Oliver Wiswell: a book's nothing but a lot of sentences on paper! You need an idea behind the sentences, a determination to make the sentences clear and readable, and a moderate amount of good taste in your selection of words. That's all!

"The way to write a book is to write one sentence and then write another, and keep on doing it every day, rain or shine, sick or well!

"One of the things Belcher liked to talk about, after we'd gone to bed, was the number of people who thought they could write books if they only had the time. The trouble with 'em, he said, was that most of 'em lacked the brains, even, to understand that the way to write a book is to write a book!

"Don't let me hear any more about how you can't write a book, Oliver Wiswell! Just you step right back upstairs and put something on paper. It won't be what you want to say, of course. No writer ever writes a thing decently the first time. When Belcher was in bed, he always told the truth; and many's the time he told me, in bed, that even Shakespeare had to tinker with his sentences, just like every other author. Belcher said the way to get a sentence written properly was to write something, and then keep changing it. You can be mighty sure of one thing, Oliver: if you don't write anything, you won't have anything to change."

I told her I couldn't make up my mind where to start.

"Start anywhere," she cried. "Start with your own father! Tell how he was against the Stamp Tax, along with every other American! Tell how all of us, rebels and Loyalists, wise and foolish alike, were against bad government and silly measures. Then tell how the fools began to advocate silly measures of their own: how they raised mobs to destroy those who disagreed with them, and to tear down everything they didn't like, no matter whether it was good or bad. Tell how the wise men couldn't stand it and so refused to have dealings with the fools! Tell all the things that happened in the very beginning—all the things we've already forgotten, but should never be allowed to forget. That's easy enough, isn't it?"

"Yes, I suppose so," I said.

"Listen, Oliver," Mrs. Byles said, "when my father was nineteen, he was told to sail a brig to Cadiz for salt. He didn't say he *supposed* he could do it! He went and did it! You do what I tell you! You have a hundred pages of manuscript on your desk by the end of this week, so I can arrange for French spies to drop in and go through it."

Our work in Paris was divided.

Vardill, the center of our little spider web, hardly left the shelter of the Hôtel DeBailles. It was important, he said, that he should always be where he could be found when needed, and perhaps this was truly the reason that led him to stay so constantly indoors.

Buell, too, was no better off than he would have been in jail; for Vardill insisted that day and night he must remain within call, in case a document or a letter had to be forged in a hurry.

Colonel Smith, Vardill felt, would be most valuable in Havre, keeping watch on the movements of the American privateer captains who made that port their headquarters.

Thus I, the only remaining male of our little group, was entrusted with the task of visiting Paul Wentworth, that most singular and able man whose name will be forgotten in his own country when the names of many lesser men will be long remembered.

"Personally," Mrs. Byles told me, "I don't like Paul Wentworth— probably for the same reasons I don't like your friend Benjamin Thompson. They're both great men, with the complex brains of all great men. I can't tell what they're thinking, and that makes me un-comfortable. Wentworth projects his mind into the future so far that he gives me the shivers, and *that* makes me uncomfortable, too."

"What's Wentworth's business in France?" I asked.

"Nothing but money, you'd think," Mrs. Byles said, "but you'd be far from right. Yet he can't get wind of anything—shipwreck, storm, war, drought—without wanting to make a profit from it. He seems to think in terms of money, Oliver. If a hurricane spoils the sugar crop in the Indies, or the Spaniards build more frigates than usual, or we have too much rain, or the King of Sweden dies or the British lose an extra dozen merchant ships, Paul Wentworth knows how to make a fortune out of it."

"He's from Portsmouth?"

"He was," Mrs. Byles said, "but that was long ago. Now he's from anywhere and everywhere—Paris, London, Surinam. He has agents in Amsterdam, Hamburg, Brussels, Copenhagen, Lisbon. Through 'em he speculates in British funds, French funds, Dutch funds. He still owns land in New Hampshire. He has a plantation in Surinam. Before the war he was agent for New Hampshire in London; and he still"—she eyed me with a basilisk stare—"has the interests of New Hampshire and all the other colonies very much at heart. He loves Dartmouth College. That's how you're to make his acquaintance: because he's interested in colleges and college men, and because the president of Yale wrote a letter to President Wheelock at Dartmouth about you, and because the president of Dartmouth wrote Paul Wentworth in your behalf."

She took a package from the table beside her. "Here, Oliver."

I slipped the string from the package and opened the topmost letter. Its creases were dark, as though it had been carried in a pocket for weeks. It was signed Eleazar Wheelock, spoke glowingly of my abilities as a historian, and urged Paul Wentworth to let me have access to his large library and voluminous records.

I didn't like it, and I asked Mrs. Byles whether she'd thought what might happen if the letter should fall into the hands of someone who had access to Wheelock's signature. Probably, I reminded her, Benjamin Franklin and Silas Deane had corresponded with Wheelock.

Mrs. Byles was unmoved. "Oliver," she said, "if Eleazar Wheelock himself got hold of that letter, he'd never be able to make himself believe he didn't write it."

I asked her where she got the original.

"Borrowed it from Wentworth," Mrs. Byles said. "Now listen, Oliver: Tie those letters up and hide 'em in your room. Hide 'em carefully, but leave your manuscript scattered around everywhere. Tomorrow you're going sight-seeing. While you're gone, spies'll go through your room. The next day you can call on Wentworth."

"How'll the spies know enough to come to my room?" I asked.

"I thought you'd understand," Mrs. Byles said. "Wentworth's so close to the French that he's bound to warn them that he suspects you of being dangerous. They'll have to find out for themselves that you aren't."

Paul Wentworth lived at the home of his mistress, Mlle. Desmaillis, on the Rue St. Roch; and when I presented myself at the door and gave my name to a Negro page boy in a red turban and green velvet trousers, it was Mlle. Desmaillis who received me in a small reception room, all gold furniture and mirrors.

I'd never before seen a woman who openly admitted to being the mistress of a man, and I expected her to be a bold and shameless creature, bedizened, painted and overdressed. Instead of that she was a small brown girl with round brown eyes which gave her the look of being vaguely puzzled by everything that was said to her.

She spoke English easily but a little peculiarly, as though each word, as it came from her lips, were prettily twisted out of shape.

"You ask for Mr. Wentworth," she said. "I am unhappy to tell you he is at his desk. We do not disturb him unless the matter is of great importance. You are a friend of his?"

I told her I hadn't the honor.

"Then you tell your business," she said. "At the proper time I inform Mr. Wentworth."

"To tell you the truth," I said, "my business is so unimportant I hesitate to mention it. I'm writing a book on the war in America. I have a letter from a gentleman in America, introducing me to Mr. Wentworth."

She held out her hand. "May I see that letter?"

When I gave it to her, she examined it carefully, and even went to her desk for a magnifying glass so she could better see the seal. Then she lifted admiring eyes to mine. "But this is beautiful! I've never seen a letter written more beautifully. You wait, and I show it to Mr. Wentworth. He will be much interested—much. I, too, am much interested. The gentleman who wrote this—you know him?"

"No, I don't. It was written by President Wheelock of Dartmouth College at the request of the president of the college I attended myself."

Mlle. Desmaillis looked at me thoughtfully. "Of course! How I am stupid! I read that very thing in the letter." She stared at me and I stared back at her; then she went quickly from the room.

When she returned she seemed more friendly. "You come with me," she said. "Mr. Wentworth is most happy to see so close a friend of his great friend Doctor Wheelock." Again she looked at me wide-eyed. I had a feeling she was mocking me, so I made her a little bow and said nothing, which, under most circumstances, is as good a form of repartee as any.

She led me to a high-ceilinged room, at the end of which two tall windows looked down on a courtyard almost filled by two enormous thorn trees. Between the windows was a desk, and behind it a ruddy, smiling man who might have been anything at all—a painter, a butcher, a clergyman, a country gentleman, a sea captain. He had a merry blue eye and an air of carelessness, as if his mind almost never dwelt upon serious things. Even his clothes seemed thrown upon him carelessly, though with a pleasing sort of carelessness.

He jumped up as I entered, and held out his hand. "A great pleasure, Mr. Wiswell! And a most interesting letter from President Wheelock! Please be seated."

He retreated behind his desk, sank into his chair and moved everything before him—pens, inkwell, sand box, paper cutter, sealing wax, lamp, papers, books—a quarter-inch to the left. When he spoke, he did so with a slight intake of the breath—a sort of stammer that was a little like a gasp. "Let me see, Mr. Wiswell; you're a resident of Milton, Massachusetts, and for the year just past you've fought with General Howe's army against the rebels. Is that correct?"

"Not quite," I said, "but it's close enough."

Wentworth looked annoyed. "I hope, Mr. Wiswell, you won't permit inaccuracies to creep into any reports you make to me. 'Near enough' isn't sufficiently accurate. We must know exactly. Exactly, Mr. Wiswell."

"Yes, sir," I said. "I didn't bear arms against the rebels. I acted as an assistant commissary of prisoners, and I was able to be of some help to General Howe in gathering information."

Wentworth cleared his throat in a peculiarly surreptitious manner —a habit of his, I soon found. "That's better. Now I've been told, on what seems good authority, that I can rely implicitly upon you. My sources of information, I may as well tell you, are Mrs. Byles and Benjamin Thompson. If they should have been so unfortunate as to make a mistake, I fear the results might be unpleasant for both of them."

"I'll do my best," I said.

"Oh, I was quite sure of that, my dear Wiswell," Wentworth said. "Now let's see exactly where we stand. This business of getting information can be somewhat precarious under the best of circumstances. When we deal with the French, we must be unusually careful, because the French are both tricky and cruel when antagonized." He adjusted a wristband and added "dreadfully cruel" in a mild voice.

"Perhaps, Mr. Wiswell," he went on, "that will explain to you why I make it a rule not to appear in any of these matters. I cannot know your friend Mrs. Byles or Mr. Vardill. Do I make myself clear?"

"Perfectly," I said.

"Each time you see me," Wentworth went on, "you'll take home for use in your history, certain documents concerning New Hampshire provincial affairs. These were written to me when I was agent for New Hampshire. These you'll copy at your own lodgings, leaving both copies and originals displayed conspicuously on your desk. But never must you write down anything else that you have from me. Make no notes of places, of dates; never mention the names of gentlemen you meet at this house. If you should—as you probably will—meet a Mr. Edward Bancroft, you must know nothing about him except that he is in the confidence of Silas Deane, Benjamin Franklin and Arthur Lee, the American commissioners. Can I depend upon you, Mr. Wiswell?"

"Yes, sir."

Wentworth seemed to cogitate. "I knew your father, Mr. Wiswell," he said. "He was a lawyer of remarkable abilities. Whenever we found ourselves threatened with legal difficulties in New Hampshire, we were eager, always, to have your father's opinion, or Daniel Dulaney's. We knew they'd give us sound law, unswerving honesty, absolute secrecy."

I told him I saw what he was getting at, and added, "The fewer secrets I'm required to conceal, the better pleased I'll be. I'm here for just one purpose: to find out when Joseph Hynson is handed dispatches to Congress, and to get hold of those dispatches. I'm certain they'll prove what the King doesn't believe—that France intends to help the American rebellion with ships, troops and supplies; then strike England in the back while she's busy in America."

"I can help you keep an eye on Hynson," Wentworth said, "but the information you're after isn't new. We've told Eden again and again that the French government is already helping the rebels secretly, and publicly denying it. We've told Eden that in all likelihood the day isn't far distant when the French will help the rebels openly. We've urged him to treat with the rebels before this happens. We know the rebels are still willing to listen to reason. We know they still fear they can't get the official French help that they must have in order to have a chance to be independent. We've told Eden that the rebels will still listen to reason, but that they'll never listen to reason if the King and his ministers don't act without delay."

"That's why I'm here," I said. "They won't act at all unless they're frightened into acting. Eden says the King doesn't feel he's had sufficient proof that France intends to help the rebels. I want the proof."

Wentworth shook his head. "The English are mighty queer people, Mr. Wiswell. When they don't want to do something that ought to be done, they think up a thousand reasons for not doing it. The King and his ministers don't want to admit they're being damned fools about America, so they say they haven't had sufficient proof that France is cutting England's throat by helping the rebels. What nonsense! We've told Eden repeatedly that arms and supplies are being shipped to America by the French firm of Hortalez and Company. We've proved conclusively that Hortalez and Company is an invention of a playwright—Beaumarchais—who certainly hasn't sufficient means to finance the shipments of arms he's sending to the rebels. We've proved that Beaumarchais gets all his funds from Vergennes, the French Minister of Foreign Affairs. Vergennes isn't taking the money out of his own pocket! He's getting it from the royal treasury. Consequently, Mr. Wiswell, we've proved that the arms and supplies that are going to America are going with the full knowledge of His Majesty Louis the XVI and his ministers. I don't see how we can provide Eden or the King with more convincing proof."

Wentworth made minute adjustments in his desk set. "Sometimes, Mr. Wiswell, the world is stricken with mass sickness, mass blindness, mass madness. We're subject to it in America, as was shown when the freest people in the world began to scream, in 1773, that they were enslaved. We were subject to it in 1692, when the leading citizens of Massachusetts unhesitatingly took the word of a few vicious servants, and hanged hundreds of innocent men and women for witchcraft.

"They're subject to it in England, where thousands of stouthearted Britons are overcome with panic, and run breathlessly from Devon and Cornwall at the mere rumor that the French are about to attack them.

"When such madnesses sweep over the world, nations lose their judgment. They put boobies in the highest places. They forget everything men have learned by experiment and experience. Nations as well as individuals know that the way to save is to save; but in times of mass madness, you hear them insisting that the way to save is to spend. It's so in England, in France! Thousands of seemingly intelligent people fanatically take up the cudgels for this great new doctrine. The way to save is to spend! The way to be at peace is to make war! The way to create is to destroy! The way to swim is to sink!

"There's such mass madness all over the world today, Mr. Wiswell, that nations' policies are based on half-truths and the half-formed theories of crackbrained statesmen. Your father was a lawyer, so you doubtless have a high respect for the value of evidence. It should be accepted and acted upon; and in normal times it is. But at the present moment, evidence is worthless. No matter what evidence we give the King and his ministers, they'll neither accept it nor act upon it."

"Well, sir," I said, "that's no reason why they shouldn't be given additional evidence. They can't ignore evidence forever."

"I hope not," Wentworth said. "If they do, they'll force America into the hands of shoemakers, horse traders, storekeepers, fishermen; and what's worse, they'll make a French colony of it! At all events, Mr. Wiswell, I'll do everything I can for you. We'll try to stuff the King so full of evidence that he'll have no room for pigheadedness."

He changed the subject as quickly as a pickerel darting at a baited hook. "What's your opinion of Captain Hynson? Can he be trusted?"

"Not under ordinary conditions, sir. Under the present circumstances, I think he's safe. Before we left London, Mr. Eden gave him £200, and he's to receive a more substantial amount if he's successful in getting Deane's papers for us. Sir William Eden has an additional hold on him through the Cleghorn girl, who'll receive £30 a month as long as she keeps Vardill informed of everything Hynson does. Hynson's in love with Cleghorn, and his idea of heaven is to get enough money out of the British government so he can settle in some pleasant English port like Bristol or Plymouth, and raise chickens."

"That won't be difficult," Wentworth said. He looked thoughtfully at the ceiling. "I seem to recall reading somewhere—perhaps in a letter from Mrs. Byles—that you are interested in a young lady whose political opinions are quite different from yours."

"I scarcely see why that needs to be brought up," I said.

Wentworth raised the lid of his inkstand and seemed embarrassed to find it filled with ink. "Quite right, Mr. Wiswell! Quite right! I have no doubt, too, that it's unnecessary to warn you that we must exercise the greatest care in selecting our acquaintances among the fair sex."

He cleared his throat almost secretly. "Fortunately for us, Benjamin Franklin has been peculiarly susceptible. So has Silas Deane's secretary, Mr. Carmichael. We must guard against being indiscreet in the same way. If you should feel the need of such—ah—relaxation, I suggest you put yourself in my hands."

"You're very kind," I said.

"Not at all," Wentworth said hurriedly. "Now go back to your lodgings, Mr. Wiswell, and wait for word from me. At five o'clock each evening, rain or shine, walk in the Tuileries gardens. Just inside the northernmost gate is a plane tree, and at the bottom of its lowest crotch is a small hole. Look in the hole each evening. If you find a spill of yellow paper in it, take it out, destroy it, and come to my house at midnight. If you find a spill of white paper, come immediately."

CHAPTER LV

I MIGHT, Mrs. Byles had hinted, meet benevolent old rebels who looked like clergymen; poets masquerading as War Gods; schoolmasters turned diplomat; the smartest man in Europe, so successful as a speculator that nobody could believe him. . . .

I met them all, and more. Paul Wentworth, formerly of Portsmouth, New Hampshire, was the one she meant when she spoke of the smartest man in Europe. I believe he was known by twenty different names in as many cities, and had an equal number of addresses, to which secret agents all over the world sent information. He was Sir William Eden's mainstay on the Continent, and certainly no government was ever supplied with more accurate and more valuable information than the King and his ministers received from Paul Wentworth. If the King had acted on this information, as he should have acted, both England and America would have benefited beyond all telling.

By the benevolent old rebel with mistresses up alleys she had meant Benjamin Franklin, who, with Silas Deane, was engaged in creating sympathy and getting help for the rebels in France.

Never, I do believe, has there ever been a more adroit and unscrupulous government agent than Benjamin Franklin, or a more harmless-seeming one. He delighted in forging letters, full of barefaced lies and foul hints, that destroyed the character and reputation of anyone antagonistic to the rebel cause. His greatest fault, and Deane's, too, was his inability to gauge the true worth of those who worked for him, as was evidenced by the fact that the greatest part of our information concerning rebel dealings with France came from Deane's and Franklin's closest friends—the astounding and audacious

Dr. Edward Bancroft, novelist, chemist, botanist, spy, of Surinam, London, Paris and Westfield, Massachusetts; Jacobus VanZandt of New York, known to Franklin and Deane as George Lupton; the immeasurably vain and undeniably handsome Edward Carmichael of Baltimore, Deane's secretary—as honorable a young man as ever lived, according to his own lights, but unable to resist telling everything he knew as soon as he had drunk a bottle of the champagne that VanZandt was always ready to buy for him at Sir William Eden's expense.

When Mrs. Byles mentioned a schoolmaster turned diplomat, she meant Bancroft, for by a singular freak of chance, Bancroft, when younger, had taught in a school attended by Silas Deane, who was now the agent in France of the rebel Congress.

Mrs. Byles' reference to a poet masquerading as a War God had been to that amazing liar, ladies' man, watchmaker, fire-eater, dramatist and revolutionary, Pierre Caron de Beaumarchais, author of those two great comedies, *The Barber of Seville* and *The Marriage of Figaro*.

I wish I had the space to set down here the singular things we discovered, during the long months we reluctantly spent in France, concerning the peculiar persons with whom and against whom we worked.

Our work, I think I ought to explain, was divided. At the head of our organization was Vardill, who never moved from the hotel.

Next to him was Colonel Smith, who went—or so we were led to believe—back and forth between France and England, carrying Vardill's messages to Eden, and Eden's instructions back to Vardill.

My duties consisted of seeing Wentworth whenever he was able to see me, and of taking reports from Wentworth, Cleghorn, Buell, VanZandt, Hynson, Cotton and Pinto and boiling them down for Vardill into a coherent whole.

Buell, posing as an American inventor, had a free hand to work on the outside with Hynson and in any other way that seemed valuable.

Hynson himself, infatuated with Cleghorn, ran daily to her with interminable tales of the rebel sea captains who were hoping for commissions as rebel privateersmen; of Benjamin Franklin's tricky conniving; of lecherous Edward Carmichael. As Buell had predicted, Hynson stayed bought.

VanZandt, who had been a student of medicine in New York, had come to Paris as an assistant to Benjamin Franklin, and had secretly been won over to Vardill's way of thinking, was in constant attendance at rebel headquarters, and as constantly lodged information with Vardill concerning the names of rebel sympathizers in England from whom Deane and Franklin received information, and to whom they sent news that would be of value to the Whigs in Parliament who were sparing no efforts to oust the Tory government. Vardill was inordinately proud of VanZandt's work, for all letters from or to the persons on VanZandt's lists were secretly opened and copied by the British post-office authorities, and enormous amounts of valuable information obtained from them.

In the beginning, all the driblets of information that came to the Hôtel DeBailles seemed confused and useless. I put them together for Vardill as best I could, and longed for the day when Hynson would be entrusted with the letters to Congress from the rebel committeemen. Then, suddenly, the different confused reports flowed together to make scenes in a drama.

I had a picture in my mind of the clever Beaumarchais, unscrupulous secret agent of the King of France, sitting at the center of an enormous web, and tweaking each thread of the web as he'd have tweaked the characters in one of his own comedies.

I saw Beaumarchais roaring with laughter as he plotted the comedy of his imaginary firm of Hortalez and Company, which bought arms from French government arsenals with money advanced from the French treasury, and shipped them to the rebels in vessels supplied by the French Ministry of Marine.

I saw scores of American sea captains, rebels all, lurking in half a dozen French ports with their privateers, ready to dash out at British shipping whenever Beaumarchais gave the word.

I saw forty French merchantmen, loaded with ammunition, guns, cannon and uniforms destined for the rebel army, waiting in other French ports to get their sailing orders from Beaumarchais.

I saw the French King, hidden in his palace with his ministers, pretending to know nothing of Beaumarchais or of the assistance he was sending to the rebels, but hoping for news of a great rebel victory won with French arms—a victory so great that France could come out from behind her mask of seeming ignorance, and safely and openly attack those small islands that for centuries had stood between her and world dominion.

I saw the Count de Vergennes, French Minister of Foreign Affairs, secretly supplying Beaumarchais with unlimited funds, carefully arranging that the royal cipher should be chiseled from the French muskets and French cannon he was sending to America, blandly denying all knowledge of Beaumarchais, of Hortalez and Company, unctuously professing profound affection for England.

And most revealing of all, I saw the rebel commissioners, Franklin, Deane and Lee, hooted and booed in the streets of Paris by the common people, those miserable, helpless human atoms like Buell and myself, who had no desire to fight for American rebels or anyone else —who wanted to be left in peace—who wanted with all their hearts to escape a war that could mean nothing for them but misery and, in all likelihood, death.

It was Buell who became friendly with Beaumarchais and enthusiastically recounted to us the strange details of that man's life.

Never before had I known Buell to become excited over any personage in high position. The rebel leaders in Boston had filled him with contempt; the highest British generals and admirals had sickened him; the British statesmen who fumbled with the destinies of England and America had pained him almost beyond words. But over Beaumarchais he became lyrical.

He had come to know Beaumarchais because Paul Wentworth arranged to have him taken there by Dr. Edward Bancroft, so that Buell could display his drawings of the breech-loading rifle that had been so useful to us in the past.

It's almost impossible to speak adequately of any person of ability in the secret service of any country without dragging in a score of others. Paul Wentworth was a great man, whose advice, if taken, would have saved thousands from ruin, banishment and death, and spared his country untold misery; but mention of Wentworth requires mention, too, of his most reliable confederate, Dr. Edward Bancroft.

The same thing is true of Beaumarchais. He was an astounding and fantastic figure, but some of his greatest schemes came to nothing because of this same Dr. Edward Bancroft, who, on the surface, was a harmless, kindly, helpful, educated friend of Franklin and Deane, but underneath as astute, calculating and audacious a worker in the Loyalist cause as America produced.

Bancroft, we learned, had been a doctor on a Surinam plantation, had studied tropical plants and dyes while there, and had later gone to London to obtain a monopoly on certain vegetable dyes. In London he had written a book on the natural history of Guiana, many scientific papers and a novel, and had been made a member of the Royal Society and the Royal College of Physicians.

When Silas Deane was sent to Paris by the rebel Congress, he at once corresponded with Bancroft, who joined him in Paris. Finding Deane wholly ignorant of European politics and diplomatic usage, Bancroft resumed his role of schoolteacher and gave him good advice as to how to act. At the same time he delivered to Vardill and Eden a copy of the instructions which Franklin and Deane had received from Congress.

Later, in order to convince Franklin and Deane of his eagerness in the rebel cause, Bancroft let himself be arrested in London and expelled from England on the charge of being somehow involved in one of Silas Deane's more pretentious plans: that of destroying the great arsenal at Portsmouth. He then went to Paris, where he was enthusiastically received by Deane and Franklin, and lived in the same house with them until Miss Cotton came from England to join him, at which time he set up an establishment with her.

Bancroft, so far as I know, retained the friendship of Franklin, Deane, Vergennes, Beaumarchais until their deaths, but he sent daily reports of their activities to Wentworth, who sent them to Vardill, who sent them to Eden, who sent them to Lord North and the King. The King, unfortunately, knew Bancroft to be a speculator, and so distrusted him. Because of that distrust, the King insisted that he be watched, and so Miss Cotton reported daily to Vardill about everything that Bancroft did, and everyone he saw. He was, in short, honored by those he most harmed, and despised by those he most helped.

The more I learned of Bancroft, and the deeper I saw into the confused tangle of suspicion in which a nation's secret agents are perpetually enmeshed, the more I longed to include, in the pages of *Civil War in America,* an account of the secret agents in that struggle. It would, it seemed to me, provide incontrovertible proof of the fundamental idiocy of war.

At all events, Buell was introduced to Beaumarchais by Bancroft; and Buell, by the simple expedient of telling the truth about the reception accorded his breech-loading rifle in America, had immediately enlisted Beaumarchais' sympathy and even been admitted to his confidence.

"There's no use talking, Oliver," Buell told me. "These Frenchmen know how to fight a war. I'd hate to be tied up with 'em, because they're harder than nails and tougher than fish hawks, and I'd certainly feel mighty bad to see 'em take over America and run it to suit themselves, which is what they figure on doing if they can contrive to give England a licking.

"But that don't alter the fact that they've learned how to fight—when they *do* fight—with everything they've got. They ain't like the English. The English idea of helping us Loyalists against the rebels is to call us 'My good man', and to send us generals and admirals who've been trained how to act and think like generals and admirals ever since they outgrew diapers.

"Well, Oliver, there ain't a general or admiral alive that can fight a battle or go anywhere or do anything without drawing up a lot of plans. You know what that means, Oliver! By the time the plans are drew up, it's most generally too late.

"Well, Oliver, the French know that, and when they set out to help the rebels, they went and got this Beaumarchais to take charge of everything. Being a playwright, he ain't ever been trained to do anything but tell lies, and think up new ways to get himself out of difficulties without expecting help from anybody."

He wagged his head admiringly. "Gosh, Oliver, if the English only had an author half as smart as Beaumarchais, and if they'd trust him a tenth as much as the French do Beaumarchais, and if they'd put him in charge of the American war, we'd have peace in six months!"

When I urged him to restrain his enthusiasm, Buell was indignant. "Why should I!" he cried. "Look at the records! The French ain't even fighting for the rebels yet, not officially! Everything that's being done is being done by Beaumarchais! You read that last report of Van-Zandt's! What happened when Deane made a request to Beaumarchais for eighty thousand stands of arms, and a corresponding number of pistols, swords and uniforms? In three days' time eighty thousand stands of arms were cleared from Nantes for Martinique in one of Hortalez and Company's vessels. They never went to Martinique, though: they went right straight to the rebel army in America! That's where they went!

"And now let me ask you another. Do you know what would

happen if Loyalists in America made an urgent request to General Howe for eighty thousand stands of arms?"

I said I feared I did.

"You know damned well you do! When Howe got around to it, he'd send the request to England in a frigate with eighty thousand pounds of barnacles on her bottom. When the request eventually reached England, Lord Germaine would accidentally push it under last month's *Gentleman's Magazine,* and go down to a watering place for a couple of weeks, and after a month or two somebody might dig it out and ask a question about it in Parliament. Then Lord North would clear his throat and talk about the needs of our worthy friends the Loyalists; and eighteen months later a clerk in the Ministry for War would authorize the shipment to the Loyalists of twenty-five hundred muskets captured from the Spanish Armada. Meanwhile the Loyalists who needed the eighty thousand muskets would be dead, in jail, or expelled from America."

I reminded him that the English were the English, and that we must do as well as we could with the means at our disposal.

"Oh, I know it, Oliver," Buell said, "but I wish to God I could work with people that were smart-crooked and inventive-crooked, like Beaumarchais, instead of stupid-crooked like Howe and those damned fools on Downing Street. I wish I could work under people that trusted us, instead of treating us like criminals! Maybe you won't believe it, Oliver, but the King of France trusts Beaumarchais! Yes, sir! Gives him a free hand! A few years ago a French author wrote a book attacking Madame Du Barry, and started to publish it in England. Damned if the King didn't call on Beaumarchais to go to London and destroy the book! Another French author wrote a book attacking Marie Antoinette, and the King sent Beaumarchais to run him down. He did it, too—ran him through England, Holland and Germany, and got the manuscript back!"

That was what Buell resented most: the trust reposed in Beaumarchais by the French King, as opposed to the seeming lack of faith that the King of England had in the information supplied to him by those of us who were working so hard, under Eden and Vardill, to end the war. In this resentment, Buell wasn't alone.

We had come to France with Hynson for one purpose and one only: to obtain from Hynson the reports that Silas Deane proposed to send to Congress by Hynson.

We had emphasized to Thompson, to Germaine, to Eden, our belief, based on what Hynson had told us, that French intervention might be near at hand. We had convinced them, certainly, that if the King couldn't be persuaded to make peace with the rebels before the French openly came in on their side, the rebels would in all likelihood refuse to listen to peace proposals of any sort. We had urged the necessity of acting quickly if the war was to be brought to an end.

And now, of a sudden, Vardill received from Eden a message that clearly showed Downing Street either had forgotten our urgings, or had never trusted them.

Vardill, when he gave us the news, did so without comment. "I had word from Eden today," he said. "He thinks it's more important to have Hynson supply us with information about rebel privateers, just at the moment, than to get the Deane Papers. He wants Hynson to make excuses to Deane—keep Deane waiting a few months."

"Good God," Buell shouted. "He started stalking a turkey, and now he's going to stop to shoot dicky birds!"

"Downing Street always has its reasons," Vardill said.

"Yes, and the British Navy always has food," Buell said, "but half the time it's rotten."

"Buell's right," I told Vardill. "Eden's chasing his tail like a puppy. If Hynson stays in France, he can't carry Deane's dispatches to America. If he doesn't carry them, we can't get them. We're here for proof of what the French are doing, and that proof can only be found in Deane's letters and other papers. The only way we can get them is from Hynson when he sails, and now Eden says he mustn't sail! Eden's being ridiculous!"

"Those rebel privateers can do great harm if not circumvented," Vardill said weakly. "It's important to know about them."

"Nothing's as important as putting an end to the war," I said. "If we can get Deane's dispatches, we can show the King he's *got* to end the war."

Mrs. Byles tapped her stick against a table leg. "Look here, Vardill: Why don't you go back to London and see Eden? Why don't you tell him what Oliver just told you? Tell him he's delaying the discovery of the truth! Remind him what delay has cost already! Show him, in pounds and shillings, how much England would have saved if she hadn't delayed, delayed, delayed!

"If General Howe hadn't delayed at Bunker Hill, the war'd have ended then, and English taxes would only have been a shilling in the pound! If Howe hadn't delayed in seizing Dorchester Heights, the war'd have been finished in the spring of 1776, and they'd only be taxed two shillings in the pound! If Howe hadn't delayed when he was winning the battle of Long Island, the rebel army'd have been destroyed and the rebellion ended! If General Howe hadn't delayed at Kip's Bay to have dinner with Mrs. Murray, he'd have bottled up the rebels, and they'd never have escaped! But they *did* escape, and now every Englishman's paying *five* shillings in the pound.

"Another delay, and it'll be six in the pound, then seven; and first thing England knows, she'll have another revolution right in her front parlor!"

Vardill looked uncomfortable. "Why don't you go to England yourself and tell him, ma'am?"

"For an excellent reason," Mrs. Byles said. "If I did, I'd have fifty French secret agents fingering my petticoats and ripping the lining out of my bonnets. I'd be under suspicion, and then where would your safe retreat in Paris be? That's the truth: let's have the same from you, Vardill: why don't you go yourself?"

Vardill looked acutely unhappy, and said nothing.

"I'll tell you why, Vardill," Mrs. Byles said. "You know nothing upsets the King so much as news he doesn't want to hear. If the King should be upset at you, you're afraid he'd never appoint you to the royal chair of divinity in New York."

And until the end of time men will suffer, agonize, die in every war because little human peacocks fear to lose a ribbon, a promotion, or an appointment as worthless as that of Dr. John Vardill to the royal chair of divinity in King's College, New York.

When, inwardly raging, I obeyed Vardill's orders and carried word of the change in plans to Paul Wentworth, he listened attentively to what I had to say. When I'd finished, he made careful readjustments in all his desk ornaments. "That's very interesting, Mr. Wiswell. What's your opinion of those orders?"

"Well, sir," I said, "Hynson isn't the only person in the world who can get information about privateers. Mr. Bancroft could do it, I think."

"In all likelihood," Wentworth agreed.

"Yet Hynson," I reminded him, "is the only one that Deane trusts to carry his reports to Congress. You ask me what I think of Vardill's orders, so I'll tell you honestly: I think the man responsible for them is doing everything he can to throw America away. If it was his to throw away, I wouldn't mind; but it's not his! It's ours—yours, Bancroft's, Mrs. Byles', Tom Buell's, mine!"

Wentworth seemed puzzled. "His? To what 'his'—what 'he'—are you referring, Mr. Wiswell?"

"You know as well as I do," I said. "I mean the madman who puts a Whig in command of his forces in America; who leaves Cunningham as provost marshal of New York; who shilly-shallied for ten years before putting down sedition and mob rule!"

"Mr. Wiswell," Wentworth said slowly, "nobody except a few professional soldiers, a few politicians and a few speculators are ever satisfied with the progress of any war. The rest of us work at war as we'd work at building a house of cards. We spend all our time and all our energies erecting handsome structures that are almost certain to tumble down before they're half finished.

"Bancroft and I have been building houses of cards ever since this war started. Whenever, after infinite labor, we complete one, a dolt of a general or a numskull of a statesman knocks it down, either deliberately or unwittingly.

"Then we start building another, because we think we're the only persons qualified to do it. We try to keep our minds centered on our own little card house; try to forget that if this one doesn't stand up, another thousand men will be condemned to death; another thousand mothers and wives made miserable, another million pounds wasted. Don't think, Mr. Wiswell, that you're the only one who's exasperated by a war. Everyone's exasperated, except the generals and admirals and commissaries and merchants who make money from it."

"Then why don't they stop fighting?"

"They can't," Wentworth said. "They're ordinary human beings, and ordinary human beings never do what they should. They're gamblers, gambling with human lives. Only a mighty smart gambler knows enough to stop when he should. Ordinary gamblers go right ahead risking all their resources—risking ruin, even—when they haven't a chance to win.

"Downing Street's full of gamblers who can't stop because they don't know how. For months Bancroft and I have told Downing Street that there's only one sure way of keeping America's trade and friendship, and that's to give in to the rebels before they take to murdering everybody who's against 'em, as the Irish do. Do you think they'll act on our advice? Never! And yet we can't abandon all our efforts just because Downing Street won't listen! If we don't keep on advising, nobody else will—and there's just a chance that our advice might be taken before it's too late. You'll have to be patient, Mr. Wiswell. Wait, watch Hynson, and hope for the best."

He was silent and so was I. There isn't much that a man can say when he's caught in a war to which there seems to be no end, in the conduct of which there seems to be no humanity or intelligence, and from which there seems to be no escape.

All he knows is that if he escapes from this war, nothing and nobody can ever get him into another.

That spring of 1777, and the long hot summer that followed, was pure hell. Everything went wrong.

The first blow was the unexpected decision of Deane and Franklin to seize the cutter which Colonel Smith had got in Dover for Hynson.

From this blow came our discovery of the plot of Franklin and Silas Deane to force the French into a war with England before France was ready, but even this discovery failed to awaken Eden, Lord North and the King to the need of putting an end to the war before disaster overtook all of us.

Our discovery came about because Mrs. Byles and I, as an excuse for passing through the Tuileries gardens and keeping an eye on the plane tree in which Wentworth had told me to look each evening, had made it a habit to go daily to the Hôtel d'Hambourg, which was the meeting place of all the rebels in Paris.

Night after night the two of us sat at a table on the sidewalk before that dark little hostelry, which smelled so powerfully of mold, ammonia and sour soil. We pretended to be engrossed in our light beer and on the pages at which I constantly scribbled; but in reality we were watching, fascinated, the three rebel commissioners—pussy-faced Benjamin Franklin; haughty Arthur Lee, who put Mrs. Byles in mind of the disagreeable and tiresome Mrs. Kirby of Tremont Street, from whose house Buell had taken the gold patch box with the picture of Howe in the lid; worried, stringy-haired Silas Deane; the handsome Edward Carmichael, Deane's secretary, always studying himself in mirrors and windows.

Nightly these busy commissioners held levees and purchased vast

quantities of liquors for French officers who came to whisper earnestly
in their ears. They were a hard-bitten lot, most of those French
soldiers: pouch-eyed, hollow-cheeked, soiled-looking and very much
the worse for wear. One exception was the young Marquis de Lafayette, a slender, dandified boy who looked too young to shave. He was
the politest young man imaginable, and was forever smiling, kissing
his finger tips to denote enthusiasm, or jumping from his chair to
bow with his hand on his heart.

I always knew when the little marquis arrived, because of Mrs.
Byles' muffled artificial exclamations of "Oh mercy me!" and "Heavens
to Betsy!"

Most of these French officers, we saw, were in desperate financial
straits, and it was painfully apparent that Franklin and Deane were
promising them inordinate amounts of fame, fortune and glory in
return for their services.

In addition to the French officers, there was always a group of
Americans on whom Carmichael danced attendance. They invariably
drank rum, and they particularly fascinated Mrs. Byles because she
recognized them for sea captains.

"You can't fool a Barrell on sea captains, Oliver," she told me again
and again, "and what's more, a Barrell is born with a sort of sense of
what sea captains are up to. Those captains aren't just ordinary
privateer captains, waiting for simple orders to take their vessels out
on a cruise. They're planning something. They've got a scheme and
it's a tricky one, and Carmichael knows what it is! Look at 'em,
Oliver! Look at 'em try to act innocent! Don't they almost reek of
sanctimoniousness! And what are they doing in Paris, Oliver, when
they ought to be aboard vessels, or hunting for them? Find out
from Hynson right away, Oliver!"

Hynson made light of the query. "Why," he said, "those captains
ain't anything to worry about. One of 'em's Lambert Wickes, my
stepbrother. They're in Paris because they're waiting for commissions as privateersmen. Nobody but Congress can give out those
commissions, and if a privateersman don't have his commission all
in order, he can't sail from a French port. The French won't let him.
Like I told you, the French'll fight England when they're ready, but
they ain't ready yet. If they fought before they were ready, they'd
get licked, and they don't want that. That's why they're so all-fired
careful."

When Hynson had gone, Mrs. Byles brooded over his reply. "That doesn't account for their sanctimonious look, Oliver. They must have some scheme or other, and they haven't told Hynson what it is. Wickes is his stepbrother, and he knows Hynson talks too much; so of course he wouldn't tell Hynson anything. Now I wonder——"

She ceased to wonder, two days later, when Hynson, grief-stricken, came to tell us that the privateer commissions had arrived from Congress, and that every last one of the sea captains we'd seen so often at the Hôtel d'Hambourg had gone to sea. "And they've taken the *Rochefort*," he said bitterly, "to cruise in the Channel, along with half a dozen other privateers. They say they've got to destroy British shipping—that nothing else is so important."

"That's nonsense," Mrs. Byles said briskly. "The amount of shipping they'll destroy won't be a drop in the bucket! There's something going on here, and we've got to find out what it is! We'll put Cotton and Pinto to work on Carmichael."

Perkins' Metallic Tractors was the bait that Mrs. Byles told Buell and the two girls to dangle before Carmichael, and Henrietta Dixon gave the girls private instructions while Mrs. Byles told Buell what to do.

"You keep harping on what happened to Perkins," I heard Henrietta tell Miss Cotton and Miss Pinto. "Tell Carmichael that Perkins was an old man when he discovered the tractors, with one son twenty-two years old; but after using the tractors on himself, his wife had triplets. The way to catch that young rip Carmichael is to keep hinting to him that if he uses Perkins' Metallic Tractors steady for six months, the Empress of Russia'll make a personal trip to Paris to get him to accept a private palace in Moscow."

Mrs. Byles had prepared for every eventuality. "If anyone questions you," she told Buell, "say you're here to study Doctor Mesmer's methods, and propose a business combination of Mesmerism and Tractoration, on account of Tractoration being simpler, cheaper and more effective. Tell Carmichael he won't be able to take Mesmer's Temple to Russia; but he can carry ten pairs of tractors in his weskit pocket, and get better results."

Doctor Mesmer was vastly popular in Paris that year. He claimed to have originated, in his native Vienna, a method of curing ailments by something he called "animal magnetism", or Mesmerism. He had a Temple of Animal Magnetism on the Rue de Rivoli, all incense, stained glass, dark draperies, hushed voices and dim lights; and its holy of holies was a tub filled with bottles of water standing on powdered glass and iron filings. Cords and rods were attached to the tub; and when sick people congregated in the Temple, Doctor Mesmer cured them by stroking the rods over their afflicted parts. Cripples rose and walked; and so many women fell into ecstatic convulsions at Mesmer's powers that he was obliged to install *salles des crises* in the Temple, in which ladies could have fits over him.

As a result of these instructions, Miss Cotton brought word from Carmichael that he would be most happy to see Buell and a pair of his tractors.

Not for another three days did we catch a glimpse of Buell; and when he next stumbled up the stairs of the Hôtel DeBailles, he brought with him a powerful odor of stale rum, onions and coach interiors, and he also brought a packet of letters which he wagged triumphantly at us.

"God knows what's in these," he said. "I ain't had time to look! Nobody ever kept me as busy as that Carmichael! After I'd given him two pairs of tractors, he kept wanting to see how effacious— effafacious—well, he had to find out how they worked. He'd roam through the city like an alley cat, dropping in here and there for a bottle of wine. I had to go along and drink with him and wait for him and show him how to use the tractors. Seems he didn't quite have the knack of applying 'em to himself so to get as much benefit out of 'em as the Empress of Russia'd be expecting. Funny, ain't it, how everybody that has anything to do with running a war is most generally a skunk?"

He yawned profoundly, and when Mrs. Byles took the letters from him, he lowered himself to a couch and was instantly asleep.

Carmichael's letters were mostly to young women in America, protesting his undying love for all of them, and speaking freely of his vast importance in European affairs. Mrs. Byles, reading them, moaned as if in pain; but in the end she crowed in triumph.

"Here it is, Oliver! Carmichael writes to Mr. Brigham in Martinico, and tells all! Listen!

"'The French Court [she read] *is bound there shall be no open violation of the treaties with England, but it's our business to force on a war, in spite of their inclinations to the contrary. We believe the best way to do this is to fit out privateers from the ports and islands of France. The natural antipathy of the two countries is such that if we can excite their passions, they will embark on acts of reprisal and mutual violence. These acts will cause clamor and altercation that no soft word can palliate.'"*

Mrs. Byles slapped the letter. "There's the rebel mentality for you, Oliver, spread right out on paper! These rebel privateers haven't sailed to destroy English commerce: they've sailed to force the French into a war they don't want to fight! That's what these rebel commissioners are here for, damn 'em! To make England think France is conniving at sending out privateers! To get the whole world into a war! No wonder the French people hiss Franklin and Deane and Lee when they see 'em on the street!"

The obtaining of Deane's dispatches to Congress became an obsession with all of us during the remainder of that summer.

Vardill went back to London to tell Eden of our discovery, but Eden refused to believe it. There was, he said, no proof. Carmichael, he insisted, was an irresponsible fool, writing bragging letters to friends in the hope of impressing them with his own importance.

Vardill and Colonel Smith planned a new campaign, amazingly intricate. Miss Cotton and Miss Pinto were provided with speeches for frequent delivery to Carmichael—speeches that dwelt upon Carmichael's nobility and loyalty in continuing to spend time urging the use of Hynson as a carrier of dispatches.

Since Carmichael was vain beyond belief, he became more than ever insistent that Hynson should carry the dispatches when they were ready.

Bancroft was assigned to inform Deane that a remarkably fast French packet boat could be obtained at staggeringly low cost at Havre.

Hynson, at Carmichael's suggestion—a suggestion put in his head by Bancroft—was sent to Havre to inspect it and oversee its refitting, and with him as a guardian went Colonel Smith, keeper of the money bags. Isabella Cleghorn was sent back to England, not only to keep Hynson from running constantly to Paris to see her, but to give Vardill the opportunity of having Hynson's letters to her opened and scrutinized for faintheartedness or double-dealing.

Buell remained constantly in communication with Carmichael; and at night, when not engaged in accompanying Carmichael on his tractor-testing ventures, he worked with his engraving tools, imitating the commissioners' seals that the broad-buttocked Miss Cotton brought him, one by one, from Carmichael's rooms.

Wentworth learned from Bancroft what was going on in Deane's head, and then told me; and at the same time Pinto and Cotton found out what Carmichael knew about Deane's thoughts, and told Mrs. Byles. Then the two of us compared notes and drew our own deductions.

As autumn approached, our depression lifted and our hopes again rose high; for Hynson's hopeful reports from Havre concerning the speed of the new packet, his repeated assurances—sometimes tampered with and added to by Buell—of the scarcity of British men-o'-war near Havre, had again filled Deane and Franklin with the desire to send an account of their schemes and successes to Congress.

Then, in a moment's time, our whole venture was in jeopardy, and our months in Paris were on the verge of being wasted.

The only warning I had was a spill of white paper in the plane tree in the Tuileries gardens. It was the first white spill that had been put there, and it sent me to Wentworth's home on the Rue St. Roch as fast as my legs would carry me.

I knew from the manner in which the little black page boy stood to one side when he opened the door and saw me, and from the way Mlle. Desmaillis peered out at me from Wentworth's study, that I'd done well to hurry.

Wentworth's air of careless merriment was gone, and his stammer was pronounced. "Duh-devil to pay, Wuh-wuh-Wiswell!" he said. "Bancroft brought news this afternoon! Couldn't have waited much longer—planned to suh-suh-send Mademoiselle Desmaillis to tell you. Look here, Wuh-Wiswell! All dispatches and letters between March twelfth and October seventh—today—are guh-going to Huh-huh-Havre before you can say Jack Robinson! And by special messenger! You've got to get there first!"

"I think I can," I said.

"No thinking about it," Wentworth said. "You've *got* to. You'll have to take Buell and Vardill, too, in case you need help! All of you'll *have* to get there! If that messenger reaches Havre before you do, you'll never get the dispatches. All our work'll be lost!"

"Hynson's in Havre," I reminded him. "So's Colonel Smith."

"Hell and duh-duh-damnation!" Wentworth cried. "Hynson's been superseded; and Smith, just when we need him most, has gone to London to see Eden! Listen! Not long ago a sea-captain relative of Benjamin Franklin's, John Folger, came over here to make some easy money. Folger's no fighter, but he's a rebel and a good sailor; so Franklin's arranged with Deane to let Folger have that sloop of Hynson's and carry the dispatches to Congress. Hynson, being more of a braggart, strikes both Deane and Franklin as a good fighter; so they're going to make up to him for his loss of the sloop by giving him command of a privateer. There you are! If the dispatches reach Havre before you do, Hynson'll have to hand 'em over to Folger and you'll never so much as see 'em! All Smith's arrangements to have the sloop taken when she sails will be useless, because Folger'll toss the dispatches overboard if he's captured."

"When do the dispatches leave Paris?" I asked.

"At dawn tomorrow," Wentworth said.

Those were the last words I ever heard from Paul Wentworth; for I turned and ran for the front door without even waiting to say good-by.

The road from Paris to Havre follows the Seine to the sea, and the Seine winds like a snake through little towns whose odors on chill autumn nights are exasperating to travelers in a hurry. The scents of manure, of apple mash left over from cider-making, of stagnant meadows and decay, cling in the nose. St. Germain en Laye, Poissy, Vernon, St. Pierre—all those towns were little more than bad smells in the dark, and always the same bad smells. We seemed to stand still, as though the horses of our light coach galloped fruitlessly on a treadmill.

We clattered through Rouen in the early morning, stopping long enough to snatch a breakfast of hard bread and hot cider—a mixture that set Buell's insides to rumbling like far-off drums.

At midmorning I had a pang of homesickness, for through the coach windows came the same faint smell of the sea that every east wind brings to Boston.

At noon the Seine broadened into a wide bay on which we saw the little brown lugsails of fishermen, the stumpy masts of coasters, and the tangle of spars that marked the heart of Havre, and by early afternoon our horses were struggling to keep their footing on the slimy cobblestones before the main pier of the town, and the three of us were running for the door of the address from which Hynson had always written us—Madame Moreau's lodginghouse.

I can laugh now, when I think back to the strange conversation between the three of us and those two rebel sea captains, one of them eager to give us every help and the other ignorant of everything. But at the time it took place, none of us laughed. We were deadly serious, for we were playing a game for high stakes. If we won, we knew we'd have the means of stopping a war and putting an end to all the misery in which our country was embroiled. If we lost, our own fate and our country's might be dark indeed.

During our long coach ride we had planned the parts we were to play.

I was to be the spokesman; Buell had to be an invalid; Vardill was to be a learned clergyman. It was well we'd planned in such detail; for at Madame Moreau's we found Hynson and Folger together, writing letters in the narrow, glass-fronted dining room. At their elbows stood small glasses of cognac—a sign their funds were too low to allow them to purchase refreshment by the bottle.

Hynson's jaw dropped when he saw the three of us coming through the door; and when I hurried to him and grasped his hand, he looked wholly witless.

"Captain Hynson," I said, "you probably don't remember me. I'm Perkins, who makes Perkins' Metallic Tractors. I met you in New York before the war, when I was struggling so hard to confer the benefits of my tractors on an unhappy world. I remember you well, Captain, because you wouldn't buy a pair of my tractors."

"Oh yes," Hynson said vacantly.

"You can help me, Captain," I said earnestly. "I'm greatly in need of help. I've got to get to England, Captain, to replenish my supply of platinum so I can continue to make tractors. The demand for tractors has been so great in Paris, Captain, that I've only one pair left—the pair this poor gentleman"—I pointed to Buell—"uses."

Hynson, I feared, wasn't following me. "Don't say you can't help me, Captain," I urged. "This gentleman"—again I pointed to Buell—"can't live a week unless I can increase the platinum content of his tractors. He has the King's Evil—the only ailment that won't yield to the tractors as I invented them. The King of France himself needs a pair with an added platinum content. Great things depend on my getting platinum immediately, Captain, and I'm sure you can help me!

Let me get this poor gentleman to bed, Captain, and then I'll ask you to let me explain further over a bottle or two of cognac. Perhaps you —or your friend—will help us get a satisfactory room near your own for this unhappy sufferer and his spiritual adviser. He takes little nourishment except cognac; and since his spiritual adviser doesn't drink, it's always a boon to him to have other acquaintances near by to share his supply."

Hynson looked more interested. "This here's Captain Folger," he said. "He'll help your friend find a room and I'll help you get the cognac. Madame Moreau's got some real good stuff in her cellar, but if you don't watch her, she'll give it to you out of a keg that's half burnt sugar and Seine water."

When Folger and Vardill had left the room, solicitously supporting Buell between them, I first made sure the commissioners' messenger hadn't arrived; then told Hynson the reason for our visit, and how the dispatches were to be turned over to Folger.

"By God!" Hynson cried bitterly. "Those damned commissioners ain't got the least little sense of honor! First they take away the cutter that I got cheap for 'em, and now they fix it so I can't hand over the dispatches I've wasted the best part of my life waiting for! They can't play fast and loose with Joe Hynson like that, by God! I'll show 'em!"

When Folger came back, he came alone, and he was filled with a consuming interest in Perkins' Metallic Tractors. Even while I was telling him of their almost magic curative powers, the commissioners' messenger arrived, carrying under his arm a bundle wrapped with linen and twine, and sealed in a dozen places with daubs of red wax. If we had been an hour longer on the road, we'd have been too late.

Hynson signed a receipt for the letters and dispatches; then picked up the bottle of cognac and motioned us toward the stairway.

As we mounted to his room, I continued to expatiate to Folger on the virtues of the tractors, as Buell had told me to do. "There ain't a man on earth," Buell had said, "who don't think he's got something the matter with him. If he's as stupid as all these rebels are, you can make him believe he's got anything, and that there's only one thing that'll cure it. Look at me! I'm a sensible feller, but I'll try pretty near anything to make my food sit easier in me!"

In the hall outside the room occupied by Hynson and Folger, there was a powerful odor of burning candles and sealing wax—an odor which Buell, I was sure, had intentionally caused as a cloak for what might happen later.

In the little bedroom Folger and I sat on the bed, the cognac propped against a pillow, while Hynson read his letter.

When he'd finished it, he snorted and tossed it to Folger. "Some people have all the luck!" he said. "You'll spend Christmas at home, Captain! I guess your uncle Ben Franklin don't like my kind of sailing, because you're the one that's got to carry the dispatches. What's more, you've got to start this evening with the turn of the tide."

"Start to sea?" I asked, and I tried to put shocked incredulity into my voice. "Captain Folger's expected to sail for America tonight?"

Captain Folger looked up from the letter. "What's wrong with that?"

"Let me ask you a few questions, Captain," I said. "Do you frequently wake at night when the moon shines in at your window?"

"Pretty generally I do," Folger said.

I tried to look distressed. "And on combing your hair," I said, "do you sometimes notice that strands detach themselves from your head and become caught in the comb?"

"I certainly do," Folger admitted.

"There's something even more important," I said. "Do you have to get up out of bed, early in the morning—usually around five o'clock— to make water?"

Folger nodded apprehensively. "What if I do?"

"Does your tongue sometimes feel hard and dry when you wake up?" I persisted.

Folger looked genuinely anxious. "What's that a sign of?"

"Look here," I said, "why don't you put off sailing for a week, until I can get more platinum and make more tractors? If I'm right about you, Captain, you should never undertake another long sea voyage without a pair of my Metallic Tractors beside your bed! Never!"

"What's the matter with me?" Folger asked. "Sometimes, when I have an extra helping of pork and beans at noontime, I feel sort of dizzy. Does that mean anything?"

"I fear it does," I said, "but I can't tell for sure unless you'll come out in the open air and do some exercising for me."

"What sort of exercising?" Folger asked.

"Merely running and walking," I said. "You'd run a hundred yards, taking deep breaths; then walk the same distance as slowly as possible, still taking deep breaths. I want to see if you'd get dizzy."

"And what if I did?" Folger asked.

"I'll tell you when I'm certain," I said evasively, "but I can assure you of one thing, Captain: if you're in need, I'll find a way to help you, even if I have to give you my last pair of tractors."

I have no doubt the stolid-faced fishermen and mariners of Havre thought us insane when they saw us first galloping and then crawling through their streets. When, however, we returned to Madame Moreau's lodginghouse, where the odor of sealing wax had penetrated even to the lower floor, Folger had my last pair of Metallic Tractors, and the assurance that there was nothing wrong with him that the tractors wouldn't cure.

Buell, of course, was still in bed, and Hynson had locked the package of dispatches in his trunk for safekeeping.

In return for our kindness to Folger, Hynson went with us to find a smuggler who would take us to England. Later that evening Hynson stood with me on a wharf, watching Folger's sloop ghost out to sea; and an hour later Buell, Vardill, Hynson and I sat in the cuddy of a Dieppe lugger, examining the package of dispatches that Buell had replaced with sheets of blank paper, all neatly sealed with the commissioners' own seals.

"Those dispatches would 'a' been wasted on Congress, anyhow, the way they were," Buell said. "Folger's carrying the only kind of reading matter that Congress has the brain to understand: blank paper!"

CHAPTER LVI

W<small>E HAD</small> hoped to obtain incontrovertible proof that the French government was actively engaged in helping the American rebels, with the intention of attacking England when she was so occupied in America that she would be unable to resist the attacks of France; and as we went through Deane's and Franklin's dispatches by the dim light of the lugger's whale-oil lamp, we knew we had that proof beyond question.

Never, I think, had I felt so much elation as when I saw the countless implications in those papers. They were full of evidences of French duplicity; they involved the King himself, as well as all his ministers; they showed how France was using the rebels as a cat's-paw; they gave complete assurance that France had promised her official assistance to the rebels as soon as the rebels should win one important victory; and certainly they left no doubt in my mind, or in Vardill's or Buell's, what would happen if the rebels, assisted by France, could draw enough of England's army and navy to America. France would attack England; and if England was defeated, France would have all of America, all of Canada. She would be mistress of the western hemisphere.

We were a happy company when we landed in England and set off for London. Not only had we done what we set out to do; but our work, we were certain, couldn't help but bring peace to America. When we reached London, therefore, Vardill, Buell and I wasted no time making ourselves presentable, but hurried at once to Downing Street and Eden's office.

When Vardill silently handed the package to Eden, Eden seemed almost indifferent. "So this is the mouse that your mountain of a Hynson brought forth, is it? You're quite sure it's worth my trouble to read them?"

"It is indeed, Sir William," Vardill said. "When I saw what was in them, I had no hesitation in giving Hynson £200, and in your name promising him £200 a year for the rest of his life."

"Good God, Vardill!" Eden cried.

He pulled a letter from the package and opened it.

"Ah!" he said.

He picked up another. "Well, well!" he whispered. "You were right, Vardill! I'll take these to the King at once. While I'm putting them in order, I'll ask you to wait here. I may need you in the anteroom to explain doubtful points to His Majesty."

We never saw the King. We waited in an anteroom furnished with rickety chairs and tables that might have belonged, long ago, to His Majesty's poor relations. After two hours Eden came back to us, as curt as only a disappointed Englishman can be. With a jerk of his head he motioned us to follow him, and back we went to Downing Street without a word being spoken.

When we were again in Eden's office, he sat at his desk and examined a pile of papers as though he'd forgotten us.

"Well," Buell said, "I see something's gone wrong, but it looks to me as though we'd never find out what unless someone asks. Did you see the King?"

Sir William was distant with him. "I laid the papers before him, but I regret to say that they didn't seem convincing."

"They didn't seem convincing!" Vardill repeated incredulously. "Then all our work was——" He stopped, stared wildly at Eden; then went quickly from the room.

Buell looked puzzled. "That's strange," he said. "I never heard of any other human being who wouldn't admit there was a thunderstorm till he got hit by lightning!"

"What was there about the papers," I asked, "that wasn't convincing? He could see, couldn't he, that the French will soon be fighting for the rebels?"

"His Majesty," Eden said inconsequentially, "is greatly annoyed at Mr. Wentworth and Mr. Bancroft. They are inveterate gamblers on the stock market, and they've persisted in their contention that France intends to give open assistance to the rebels. It seems apparent to His

Majesty that their determination to have this news made public is
due to their desire to depress British funds. They'd be the first to
benefit, and he has no doubt they'd make a fortune as the funds fall."

"What's Wentworth and Bancroft got to do with the dispatches
we stole?" Buell demanded. "Didn't you see 'em? There was a list of
supplies furnished to America by the French Minister of War!
There was a document from the French admiralty, promising fifteen
more privateers for the use of the rebels! There was a letter from
Deane to Congress guaranteeing a French fleet would be sent to act
with the rebel army as soon as the rebels won just one battle! There
was——"

Eden stopped him with an uplifted hand. "I know what was in
those documents as well as you, Mr. Buell."

"Good," Buell said. "What's going to be done about 'em?"

"At the moment, nothing."

"Nothing!" Buell cried. "Oliver and I risked our lives a hundred
times to get that bag of letters! We did it so you could take steps
that should 'a' been taken two years ago! We did it so you could put
an end to this rebellion, and give Oliver and me and about ten thousand other Americans in England a chance to go home! We certainly
didn't do it so a lot of putty-wits could have the pleasure of making
another mistake."

"Your language, Mr. Buell," Eden said coldly, "would be highly
offensive under any circumstance. When applied to your sovereign it
becomes inexcusable."

"We're mighty glad you can get upset about offensive language that
don't harm anybody," Buell said. "We're even more interested in
learning how you feel about stubbornness that kills thousands of
men, robs thousands of families of their homes, and drives more
thousands of helpless people from their country."

I trod on Buell's foot to silence him.

"Sir," I said to Eden, "if Buell speaks in heat, he shouldn't be held
accountable. We know those papers mean French intervention on the
rebel side unless the King does something without delay. For him
to do nothing is more than disheartening: it's sickening!

"We thought we'd done effective work for the future of America
and the future of every Loyalist; but if what you say is true, we've
only wasted our time. Can't the King recognize evidence when he
sees it? Doesn't he believe anything unless he hears it from somebody
he's pleased with?"

"His Majesty," Sir William said, "knows strange things happen when men are unscrupulous. Knowing that Mr. Wentworth and Mr. Bancroft were deeply interested in proving their case, he feels he can't be positive who wrote the papers you brought. After all, anybody *might* have done so, I think you'll agree."

"Anybody?" I asked. "Anybody?"

"Why, yes," Sir William said. "Anybody capable of copying handwriting. It's happened before, you know. Mr. Buell is able to copy letters very well indeed, as His Majesty already has observed. After all, Mr. Buell has been in Paris for the past few months."

"Did he say that to you, in so many words?" I asked.

Eden didn't answer.

He didn't need to. I was sure I knew what had happened. The King, hating all Americans, had arbitrarily and angrily delivered himself of a stupid and unjust opinion. He hated the documents our months of planning had got for him, because they proved he'd been wrong all the time—proved Wentworth and Bancroft had always been right. He'd behaved like an angry child, and Eden had lacked the courage and ability to make him see reason.

"Look here, sir," I said, "among the letters were several from M. de Sartine, French Minister of Marine, to Franklin and Deane. Those letters, in particular, cast great discredit on the French Court. They prove conclusively that the French King has been guilty of lying and double-dealing. In all likelihood, the publication of those letters would so deeply embarrass the King that M. de Sartine would be forced to resign, and the King would have to order Beaumarchais to stop helping the rebels. Those letters couldn't possibly have been forgeries. Did you show them to the King?"

"He saw them all," Eden said.

"Did you specifically call the King's attention to the Sartine letters?" I persisted. "Did you tell him what they'd mean if made public?"

"Certainly not," Eden said. "His Majesty's a statesman. His perception is acute. For me to explain what must be apparent to him would be a gratuitous insult."

"Look here, sir," I said, "it seems to me there's a possibility that His Majesty's dislike of speculators might result in the loss of the American colonies. Take me to see the King, sir. Let me try to show him what a mistake he's making."

"Let me go too," Buell said. "I'd certainly like to tell him what a damned fool he's being."

Eden's stare was icy.

"Well," Buell said, "he *is* being a damned fool, isn't he?"

I spoke up hastily. "Sir William, I swear to you that not one of those dispatches was forged! Those letters from M. de Sartine to Deane are positive proof that if the rebels *do* win a victory, France intends to declare war on England. If the King can force the French openly to deny they'll help the rebels—as he easily can with all this material in his possession—he only needs to make a generous offer to America to put an end to the war. A generous offer, with French help out of the question, would inevitably divide American opinion. It would most certainly halt the colonies in their wish for independence. Let me see the King, sir! Let me tell him so!"

"Impossible, Mr. Wiswell," Eden said.

"What's impossible about it?" Buell asked.

"It seems to me," I said, "that nothing should be impossible when His Majesty's colonies are at stake."

"You don't understand our procedure, Mr. Wiswell."

"I don't care what your procedure is! Once the French openly ally themselves with the rebels, nothing on earth can ever make the rebels listen to any terms except complete independence! Complete independence will not only mean that England will have lost forever the colonies on which she has lavished blood and treasure for a hundred and fifty years: it'll mean that every American who's been loyal to his government will be hounded, maltreated and refused justice in his own country! Don't for God's sake let this happen because of some stupid little formality called 'procedure'."

Sir William looked bored. "You alarm yourself unnecessarily, Mr. Wiswell. Your fears for your personal safety are quite groundless. England never deserts those who stand by her, and England will see you come to no harm from the rebels."

I thought it best to ignore his insinuation. "Sir," I said, "England'll be able to protect nobody in America—nobody—if the rebels are given a free hand. What can England do, once she acknowledges that America belongs only to rebellious Americans? What can she do if she admits that the rest of us—the equal number of Americans who've been loyal—have no rights in our own country?"

Sir William brushed my words aside. "Really, Mr. Wiswell, your imagination is something to marvel at. You'll find, when the proper

moment arrives, that the rebels will listen to reason. Every man has
his price, Mr. Wiswell. You'll find the rebel leaders no different from
everyone else."

I stared at him, puzzled, and Sir William enlightened me further.
"Come, come, Mr. Wiswell! There's one thing nobody can resist,
and that's a title. You're on friendly terms with enough rebels to
know we'd have their wholehearted support if we were generous with
our titles—if their leaders were made peers."

I'm afraid I snorted. "You'll have to revise some of your ideas of
America, sir," I told him. "God knows I'm not on friendly terms with
rebels, as you suggest, but I don't have to be on friendly terms with
them to assure you the last thing to tempt them will be titles. Any
American who called himself the Duke of Sebasticook or Lord Tren-
ton would be inviting broken windows and worse."

"Earl Putnam of Brooklyn," Buell said dreamily. "Sir Thomas
Buell, Baron of South Boston. Oliver Wiswell, Duke of Neponset.
Sam Adams, Lord Bunker Hill. Sounds nice, don't it?"

"You don't understand America or the Americans, Sir William,"
I said. "I mean no offense, but your ignorance of them is almost
criminal. Won't you let me talk to the King, sir?"

Eden fingered his neckcloth and looked faintly amused. "My dear
Wiswell," he said, "I hope you won't think me rude, but I've a score
of things to attend to. I must ask you to excuse me. I'm not, as you
know, an idle man."

CHAPTER LVII

W<small>E WERE</small> inexpressibly discouraged when we set off from Downing Street for Mrs. Jump's.

"Damn these Englishmen," Buell said. "It ain't as if they didn't have the brains to understand about America. They just won't! Damned if they don't deserve to lose it, and damned if I wouldn't be in favor of it, if only they could lose it to anybody except the rebels and the French. They could hunt all over the world and not find a worse combination!"

As for myself, I was so dejected by the King's lack of appreciation that I couldn't bring myself to say a word.

All I wanted to do was to get back to Mrs. Jump's and take Sally's letters from their hiding place: to throw myself upon the bed and again read and reread the sentences that I'd long since learned by heart. I knew them by heart; but never, by repeating them to myself, could I obtain from them the pulse-quickening feeling that I had when I held the very sheets on which Sally's hand had rested, and with my own eyes saw the words her pen had formed.

We were admitted by a young woman I had never seen before, but Mrs. Jump herself stood in the doorway between the hall and the sitting room, exactly as I had first seen her, a glass of wine poised unsteadily in her hand.

At sight of us, she seemed to wag her glass, though never a drop of its contents was lost; and a racking hiccup burst from her.

"My long-lost boys," she cried. "My wandering Americans! Home at last from perilous adventures." She drained her glass and swayed forward to lean against Buell's chest. "It's been dull since you been gone. No merry laughter! Not a soul in the house except"—she hiccuped—"except a few sailors. Le's see: three admirals of the blue, two admirals of the red, twelve captains, sixteen post captains, and some lieutenants, but all of 'em damned dull! Thank God you're back!"

I didn't like the way she pawed at Buell. "We're only here to pick up our luggage that you were so kind as to keep for us," I said.

"No, no!" she protested. "Won't hear of you leaving! Consider this house your own! We're sick of sailors! They're all alike. They talk hoarse about places they've been; always telling about somebody falling down Valetta Steps in Malta; or how they cut out a privateer, or saw the sea serpent; or how young Cavendish was bit by a sea snake and died of convulsions all stiffened out like made of marble inside of three minutes; or how the currents flow around the Wager in Hudson's Bay. If there's anything I care less about than the currents in Hudson's Bay, it's sea snakes or their getting rigor mortis from eating young Cavendish off Fernando Po. That kind of talk just dries up the blood in my veins! I want to hear about the bright candle-lights of Paris, and international intrigue."

So smartly did she hiccup that her head jerked backward. "Come 'n' have a few bottles with me and tell me everything."

"I'm sorry," I said. "If you'll show us where you stored our luggage . . ."

"Now listen," she said. "Stay here 'n' be comfortable. They know this is your address, and——"

"They?" I asked. "What 'they' are you talking about?"

She looked slightly disconcerted. "The post office," she said. "The Postmaster General sent a letter here for you, so he knows you live here."

As we'd had reason to learn in France, the Postmaster General could be trusted to examine every letter that came into his hands and use it in any way that suited his purpose; but I felt sure he'd never examine a letter of mine. "Where is the letter?" I asked sharply.

"They put it in your bag," she said.

Realizing too late what she'd revealed, she tried to hide her words beneath a fit of coughing.

"They!" I said. "What 'they'? And how'd they ever get into my bag when I've got the only key! Take us to our luggage at once!"

Mrs. Jump looked defiant, but led us upstairs to a locked closet in a bedroom. When she opened it, all our familiar battered luggage was there.

Buell and I hauled our bags to the light like two dogs worrying bones. Mine was still locked, and when I took a key from my watch chain and unlocked it, I saw, on top of everything, a letter from Sally, addressed in care of Governor Hutchinson's daughter, as was the last one I'd had. Like the last one, it was sealed with a blob of green wax, and in the wax was the print of a small thumb.

The clothes beneath the letter looked rumpled and disarranged, but I had no time to think about that. I stroked that small thumb-print in the wax of my letter, and worked to free it unbroken from the paper.

Buell stopped me. "Wait a minute, Oliver. Let me see it before you break the seal. I've examined so many of 'em, the last six months, that I feel guilty if I miss one."

He reached past me, took the letter, held it almost against his nose and moved it from side to side.

"Nonsense, Tom!" I said. "They wouldn't dare!"

"I don't know why not," Buell said. "They suspect Wentworth, don't they? They paid Bancroft's mistress to keep an eye on him, didn't they? I ain't heard 'em say anything that indicates they're oversatisfied with you and me."

He whipped out his knife and pried the seal from the letter with the skill of long practice. "Yes," he said, "I thought so! That wax was taken off and stuck back on again. Nice clean work, too!"

He gave me the letter and went back to his own luggage.

I stared hard at the green seal Buell had so neatly detached. "Who do you suppose made that thumbprint?" I asked. "Could it be Sally's?"

"I wouldn't think so," Buell said. "They had to soften the wax when they loosened it to read the letter. They'd 'a' borrowed a thumb for the occasion."

I had a mental vision of a sly postal clerk working at Sally's letter with knife blades, sponges, blotters; of sweaty faces bent over it; of a dozen common little Englishmen prying into what Sally had written for me alone; of one of Postmaster General Todd's forgers pressing a dirty thumb against the same wax that Sally's thumb had pressed.

My upper arms, my eyelids, the pulse in my wrists, seemed to flutter, my fingers ached as though they'd been clenched rigidly for too long; and I somehow knew that if I could have got my fingers on any man who had dared to read the words Sally had written for me, I'd have throttled him.

I sat down at the desk, opened the letter and held it flat with hands that trembled.

"*Dearest Oliver* [I read]. *Whenever I write you, I'm frightened; because everyone here wants to kill those who write to or hear from anyone not on our side in this terrible war. I can't believe they'd dare do anything to me, but still I'm frightened, even though I'm sure my father and brothers would try to save me from being punished.*

"*I'm frightened when I write; but oh, Oliver, I'm even more frightened when I don't. It's frightening never to hear from you, dearest Oliver, but still you mustn't write me. Sometimes I can safely send you a letter; but if you sent me one, someone would be sure to find out, and then my whole family would be under suspicion.*

"*I think, Oliver, that most of us get nothing out of war but fear. We're frightened of something all the time: frightened about the things we eat; about the things we do and say and even think.*

"*We're afraid to read the newspapers and afraid not to; afraid to build houses for fear of using material we shouldn't; afraid not to for fear that if we don't, our money'll become worthless and we'll have nothing at all.*

"*I feel somehow wicked, saying that our money may become valueless; yet everyone knows it. At the same time, even though everyone knows it, it's supposed to be shameful to mention it.*

"*War is terrible and confusing. I hope and hope it'll soon be over, and I truly believe that perhaps it will; for the rage over the things Burgoyne and his men are threatening and doing is like a fire in the woods.*

"*There was a time, not long ago, when nobody seemed interested in fighting. Everyone wanted to stay at home and raise enough food to see him through next winter; but the stories of what Burgoyne's Indians and Hessians are doing to the poor people near Lake Champlain have made everyone angry and determined that they must be defeated.*

"*Now, Oliver, it's my unhappy task to tell you that a law has been passed in Massachusetts, forbidding the return of anyone who left here after the nineteenth of April, 1775. Your father's home in Milton has been sold. A man from Boston bought it. He was a ship's carpenter before the war broke out, but now he's a privateer captain and doing well. Because of being an ardent patriot, he was allowed to buy your house for a very small amount.*

"It's terrible and confusing, Oliver, and only one thing is certain: everywhere men are pouring out like hornets against Burgoyne. 'Agin Burgine' is New England's battle cry. Albion, Steven, Jeremiah, Richard, Timothy and John have all gone 'Agin Burgine'. If anyone anywhere hopes Burgoyne will win, he's silent as the tomb. I feel in my heart, dearest Oliver, that all these determined men will swallow Burgoyne, Hessians, Indians and all, and that we shall at last be free of war.

"Oh, Oliver, where are you! I'm frightened and oh so lonely! If I could see you for even just one instant—but now—I'd never be lonely or frightened again! How long since I've seen one of your dear dust-colored men!

"Don't forget me, Oliver!

"Always your
"Sally."

I sat and stared at that confused and troubled letter, and despair was in my heart because of what this miserable war had done and was doing to Sally and to me—this war that could have been so easily avoided if Sam Adams hadn't been so persistently bitter and vindictive; that might have been immediately ended if the King had been blessed with understanding; if his ministers had been wise and courageous; if General Howe's politics had been different.

To think of fears preying day and night upon Sally made me hot. I sweated at the thought that Sally's letter had been read by Sir William Eden and his men. I boiled to think that after all I'd sacrificed for the government under which I'd been born and reared, that very government should reward me by spying upon me and thrusting dirty fingers into my most sacred possessions.

For the first time I understood that an integral part of statesmanship is ingratitude for past favors; that statesmen always betray those who do most to save them from disaster.

I put Sally's letter on the table and looked at my hands. They trembled and were damp with perspiration. I saw Buell at my elbow.

"Oliver," he said, "somebody's been through everything we've got. They even busted a couple of pieces of my type. I can stand a lot, Oliver, but I can't stand anybody being careless with my type."

"Yes," I said, "I know how you feel! We'll make another call on Benjamin Thompson. I've had all I can stand."

CHAPTER LVIII

W<small>E TOOK</small> a little room in Museum Street, so that I could be near that wonderful library whose treasures were as difficult to locate as the gold in a mine; and on the next day I saw Benjamin Thompson.

Even before I opened my mouth, I knew he knew why I had called. He had never been more amiable; he spoke fulsomely of the work we'd done in France, and plans for the future poured from him—to let me see, I suppose, that he'd had no hand in what had happened.

When I rudely interrupted to tell him my mail had been opened, he dropped his eyes and listened with the half-smile of a man who knows what's coming.

"All our time, all our work, in France was wasted," I said. "The King thinks we forged the letters we brought him."

He did his best to look distressed. "I wish there were something I could do about it."

"There is," I said. "I can't work for Eden any more. I can't work with the English. I want to go home."

"But my dear Oliver," he said urbanely, "none of us can go home, can we, as long as the rebels hold our homes and our property?"

I looked at him hard. "I suspect you saw a copy of that letter Sally wrote me," I said.

"A letter from Sally?" he said. "I?"

"I think so," I said. "While we were in France, somebody went through the luggage we'd left at Mrs. Jump's. My letters were opened, which means they must have been copied, too. If they were copied, Eden had to see them, and since one of them contained rather important military information, Eden would have had to show it to Germaine. You see everything Germaine sees, don't you?"

Thompson threw himself back in his chair and made play with the lace at his wrists. "Since you raise the question, Oliver," he said, "I must admit that one of Eden's men made a routine examination of your effects. I had no hand in it, and if I'd known about it beforehand, I'd have stopped it. At the same time you should remember that your own father, being a great jurist, unquestionably investigated his witnesses."

"Perhaps he did," I admitted, "but the witnesses gave testimony before able and honest judges, and my father protected them. He wouldn't allow intimate details of their lives to be pawed over by court loafers."

"I hope you're not changing sides because you're squeamish about methods used in warfare," Thompson said. "You'll find Eden no worse than anyone else—rebels, French or Spaniards. Don't forget that Franklin, the old scoundrel, stole Hutchinson's letters and published them. He doesn't hesitate to sign anybody's name to his own clever forgeries. Don't forget Deane wanted to burn the Portsmouth Arsenal and start an insurrection in Ireland."

"I know that," I said, "and I'm not changing sides. It's just that I've had enough of British generals and British cabinet ministers. I still believe the rebels are doing their utmost to destroy America. I still want to do what I can to put an end to intolerance and bigotry in my own country, so I've made up my mind to go home and take my chances in a Loyalist regiment. I want your help."

Thompson looked interested. "A Loyalist regiment! That might not be a bad idea, provided you could accomplish anything by doing it."

"I can't accomplish anything here," I said. "I've just wasted six months."

"It's most unfortunate," Thompson admitted. "Devilish unfortunate for all of us, and I hope things'll change. I'm not supposed to tell you, and I think you're the only man I *would* tell, but Lord North has a scheme that should put an end to rebel plotting in France. He has a plan to kidnap Franklin and Silas Deane, and spirit them away where the rebels'll never find 'em. If you had charge of such an enterprise, Oliver, and were successful, your future'd be assured."

I shook my head.

"Don't refuse too hastily," Thompson urged. "Vardill's already been given £200 a year and the post of rector of King's College for his part in your venture. You'd be rich and famous if you captured Deane and Franklin."

"I'd be nothing of the sort," I said. "The edges of a war are the dirtiest places in the world, and anybody who lets himself be drawn into them is bound to regret it as long as he lives."

Thompson's lips curved in that queer half-frown, half-smile of his. "That gives me an idea," he said. "You know, Oliver——"

"I want to go back to America," I said. "If you won't help me, I'll be forced to fall back on my own resources."

Thompson waved aside my persistence. "Don't be so impetuous, Oliver."

"Why shouldn't I be? You read that letter of Sally's! Every rebel in New England is arming against Burgoyne, and every Loyalist that dares open his mouth will be shot like a woodchuck! You read Deane's letters. The French are pouring money and supplies into rebel hands, and before long they'll pour a fleet and an army across the Atlantic. If ever any situation called for impetuousness, this one does!"

"Now listen, Oliver," Thompson said, "I know what's going on better than you do. You want to fight in a Loyalist regiment, but you don't want to fight under British officers. Well, there are fifteen regular regiments of Loyalists in the northern part of America right now—DeLancey's Refugees—three battalions of 'em; the New Jersey Volunteers—seven battalions; the King's Rangers, the Queen's Rangers, the New York Volunteers, the King's American Regiment, the Prince of Wales' American Volunteers, the Second American Regiment, the Loyal Americans, the Guides and Pioneers, the Orange Rangers, the Royal Fencible Americans, the Bucks County Light Dragoons, the American Legion, the Pennsylvania Loyalists. That's not counting Loyalist militia regiments, or Loyalist cavalry regiments in the south. Do you know where all those northern Loyalist regiments are stationed?"

I said I didn't.

"It's important you should know," Thompson said. "They're all on Long Island and Staten Island—every last one of 'em! The only fighting they're doing is against cows, horses and hayricks. That's what the general's using 'em for: collecting forage for the British Army!" He snorted contemptuously.

"On Long Island? He's put the regiments who'd fight hardest for him to collecting forage?"

"Exactly," Thompson said. "Which form of activity would you prefer: taking out a squad of men twice a week to round up cows, or commanding a detail of four carts and gathering hay for the general's horses?"

"Are you sure?" I asked.

He reached into a drawer of his desk and drew out a sheet of foolscap. "Here's the last return. Look for yourself."

I had only to glance at the sheet to see he'd told the exact truth.

Thompson leaned over and patted my knee. "Even if you wanted to spend all your time collecting corn husks and stealing hens, I wouldn't connive at it, Oliver. If they ever use Loyalist regiments as they should be used, I'll see you receive a commission in one of the best. What's more, if Loyalist regiments are ever used as they should be, and put wholly in command of American officers, I'll go back to America myself. There's a promise for you. Wait a little and we'll go back together!"

Thompson squeezed my knee. "Look, Oliver: I said you'd given me an idea, and this is it: the only easily accessible records of this war, unless we do something about it, will be Whig records. The records of this war are supposed to be published in the *National Register,* but they're being written by Edmund Burke, and Burke's a Whig. Nowhere in those beautifully assembled records of Burke's can you find one word in favor of our side of the argument. When you read the *National Register,* you never find a sentence to tell you what happened to the Americans who couldn't stomach mob rule. Never a line do you find in support of those who were loyal. Nowhere do you find a true account of Bunker Hill, of the battle of Long Island, of the capture of New York. Every account of everything is a Whig account, colored and one-sided. You're the man to offset the millions of half-lies in the *National Register.* You're the man to give our side of the case. I'll arrange it for you, Oliver! I'll arrange for you to have access to all the papers in the Colonial Office. I'll get you an allowance from the government."

I weighed his words. My first inclination had been to refuse his offer; and I was forced to admit that my only reason for wishing to do so was the vague hope that if I returned to America to join a Loyalist regiment, I might somehow find an opportunity to see Sally. A little contemplation, however, showed me that I'd be as badly off in America as in England. I'd be nearer Sally, it's true, but that very nearness would be an added aggravation. I could never see her, and in all likelihood—if I were in a Loyalist regiment—I'd never let her endanger herself by writing to me. To be cooped up on Long Island, prowling for cattle over those flat plains, cold and damp in winter, hot and muggy in summer, seemed, now that I thought of it, to be worse than futile.

"Well," I said slowly, "there might be something in what you suggest. I couldn't take an allowance from the government, or I'd be obligated to write what the government wanted me to write. Of course I wouldn't want to do that. I'd want to live on my own resources, but I'd still have to be given access to Colonial Office documents."

"I think that can be arranged," Thompson said.

"You'll have to do better than think," I said. "I won't start unless I'm sure I'll be unhampered—unless I'm certain I can tell the truth, no matter how much it offends the government. Can you guarantee that? Will you go so far as to put your guarantee in writing?"

Thompson said he would.

"There's one more thing," I said. "Even if I undertake this work, you'll have to promise that as soon as there's an opportunity for me to be of real use in America, you'll arrange to have me go."

That was the bargain Thompson made with me, and three long years were to pass before he kept it.

No author deserving of the name can work alone and unassisted. Many a writer's fame and fortune have been built upon the unseen sympathy and efforts of one whose very existence sometimes remains forever unknown; and many a man who might have been a writer of note has gone unproductive to his grave because he lacked the encouragement, the protection or the help of understanding friends or of a woman.

Whether I could have written *Civil War in America* without the help of friends, I cannot say. What I can say is that those friends gave me the inner warmth that keeps a writer's pen from freezing, and spurred me to my dreary task on those oft-recurring occasions when I feared and freely said I'd never write another line.

How well I remember that dreary, smoky, foggy autumn day in 1777 when Buell toiled up the stairs to our top-floor room in Museum Street to throw upon our bedroom floor the bags of documents and letters he'd got from Thompson at the Colonial Office.

I feel again the cottony dryness of my tongue, the hotness of my eyeballs, the hopeless confusion that gripped me when I'd read a small fraction of those documents. Even that small fraction littered the entire bed, all the floor space and every chair.

"There's too much of it, Tom," I said desperately. "Too much! I don't know how to use it, or how to start." The palms of my hands were damp with nervousness, and I felt in my temples, like stabbing knives, the penetrating noises of London—the unending clopping of horses' hoofs; the shouting of apprentices on the street without; the eternal squirplings of the countless sparrows that dwelt behind the blinds.

"Pshaw, Oliver," Buell said cheerfully. "The way to use stuff like that is to use one piece of it. Then every other piece goes before it or after it. I've been a printer, Oliver. I'll boil these things down for you, and then you won't have to keep going through 'em over and over."

I looked desperately around the room. There was something else I needed to do, but I couldn't think what.

I might have prayed for guidance and received a direct answer. Far away a door slammed, and I was conscious of one of those strange feminine clamors made by women talking all at once, each hopeful that her voice is rising triumphant above all others. One of the voices was partly distinguishable. "My late husband," it said, "knew the English well. He often told me the real truth about them late at night, after we'd gone to bed. He always said they had a knack for building uncomfortable houses. He said they always made 'em either too large or too small, and that they had a positive genius for locating 'em in damp spots. Sometimes I thought Belcher exaggerated a little, but from what I've seen of English houses, he didn't tell me the half of it."

"For God's sake!" Buell whispered.

I went out into the hall; and there, rising above the level of the stair-treads, was the white lace cap and the beady brown eyes of Mrs. Belcher Byles of Cambridge, born Barrell of Salem. Behind her was Henrietta Dixon, peering about like an inquisitive duck, obviously in search of Buell. Behind Mrs. Dixon was Mrs. Jump, discoursing thickly.

"I begged 'em to remain with me," Mrs. Jump said, "but they were naughty, stubborn boys! Wouldn't have cost 'em a cent! They could 'a' met nice people at my house; but no: they had to come to this den where nobody'll so much as look at 'em! At my place they'd 'a' met admirals."

"Full admirals, I'll warrant," Mrs. Byles said lightly. She gave me a cold nod. "Pack up, Oliver. You're moving out of here to an address unknown to this lady—who has been kind enough to tell us where to find you."

"Well, I declare!" Mrs. Jump cried. "I like that!"

"Pack up, Oliver," Mrs. Byles said again. "I've seen Sir William Eden. I want you where you can't be used by any of his sucking doves."

Mrs. Jump swayed forward. "Just what, if I may ask, is the reason for all these innuendoes and insults?"

Mrs. Byles ignored her. "When I learned from friends in London that Mrs. Jump had taken an interest in you, Oliver, I knew our days in Paris were numbered." She seemed willing to turn the conversation to safer channels. "We were glad of the excuse, Oliver. Neither of us liked the French."

"Deary, deary me," Mrs. Jump said in a mincing voice. "How unhappy the French will be if ever they learn of that."

"Yes, Oliver," Mrs. Byles went on, as if Mrs. Jump didn't exist, "we couldn't go 'em! We found 'em dirty, tricky, dishonest, dishonorable."

"And I suppose you lived among 'em so long," Mrs. Jump said, "that you found yourself getting just like 'em, only much worse, you having been that way to start with."

Mrs. Byles faced her. "My good woman, I don't like your tone and I don't like you. I wouldn't like you in the natural course of events, but I like you even less because of what I know about you. It just happens that I know some of the things that happen in Sir William Eden's office. I know you have an unfortunate, though sometimes useful, habit of opening the letters of every foreigner who stays in your house, on the chance that the information in them may be of value to Sir William. I know your house has a loose reputation and was financed in the beginning by money obtained from Sir William Eden. I know your young ladies are experienced pilferers of the written word, and adept at other occupations that won't bear discussion. Your house, Mrs. Jump, is noisy, disreputable, dirty, dangerous, and so are you! I don't intend to allow Mr. Buell or Mr. Wiswell to remain at an address where you or your young ladies can have access to them or to their papers whenever you desire."

"Is that so!" Mrs. Jump said. "Is that so! I deny it!"

"Naturally," Mrs. Byles said. "Ladies of your profession always deny everything when it's not to their advantage to tell everything."

I heard Henrietta Dixon, in a voice of deadly calm, say to Mrs. Jump: "Just what do you deny about Mr. Buell?"

Acutely conscious that we hovered on the brink of impending disaster, Buell and I pushed Mrs. Jump from the room, locked the door, and saved ourselves by letting Henrietta help us pack.

CHAPTER LIX

I REALIZED, when I saw the quiet lodgings that Mrs. Byles and Henrietta had already succeeded in finding in Chelsea, across the river from the imposing buildings of Whitehall, what it was that I had needed to help me write my book.

I had needed peace and privacy, the opportunity to work without interruption; and in this house I had all those things, in spite of the penniless Loyalists who daily asked for help, in spite of perpetually disappointing news of the war that reached us with unfailing regularity; for around me I had sympathetic friends to spur me on during those hours of black discouragement that fall to the lot of every writer, and to protect me from the niggling details of living that have ruined more authors than starvation and alcohol put together.

There was no excitement in the life we led, if play-going, roistering, and attending dull routs and dinners with half-known idlers be excitement; for the four of us lived—not with discomfort, it's true, but without a wasted penny—on the funds Buell and I had turned over to Mrs. Byles and Henrietta in Halifax.

Yet there was something profoundly exciting in emerging, each day, from my workroom with a dozen or so pages of manuscript, and hearing my friends read and discuss them in the quiet hours after supper.

There was a deal of satisfaction in hearing Nathan—far from little now, and at an age when his voice broke constantly from a girlish treble to an uncertain bass—reading aloud to Mrs. Byles from the books we'd chosen for him.

Henrietta had thought to spend a portion of her savings in giving Nathan what she called "an English gentleman's education" by sending him to an English school; but she'd been overridden by the rest of us.

"English gentlemen," Mrs. Byles told her, "get their educations in their fathers' libraries. Most of what they get out of schools isn't fit for innocent ears like yours to hear, Henrietta! I can tell you this, though: if you send Nathan to an English school, he'll in all likelihood turn out a snob, a toady or a rake."

When Henrietta protested, Buell and I upheld Mrs. Byles. "If it's really education you want for Nathan," Buell said, "have him read the papers, so he'll know what's going on in the world, and why. Teach him to be interested in everything he doesn't understand— interested enough to find out about it from books or people that aren't afraid to tell the truth."

"But Oliver had to go to school and to Yale College to be educated," Henrietta complained, "and if it's all the same to you, I want Nathan educated like Oliver."

"What little education I have," I told her, "isn't what I learned at Yale, but what I learned how to learn there, on top of what I learned from my father and what I've learned since. My father, in the short time I knew him, taught me more than any college could, because he knew more than most college professors. And don't think Tom Buell isn't educated. He knows more than most college graduates, because he's kept his eyes open, read widely and has an inquiring mind. Let *us* educate Nathan, Henrietta. We'll do as well as we can by him, and I don't think he'll lose by it."

Henrietta, somewhat dubiously, agreed; and as a result each of us had his day's work cut out for him, with no time for idleness and no wish to see idle people.

Thanks to Buell's knowledge of printing and his native inventiveness, he worked out a system of shorthand that made it possible for him to copy Colonial Office papers and so save me long hours of drudgery.

Mrs. Byles rewrote my interlined, scratched-up manuscript pages in her spidery hand, or knitted stockings for the lot of us while Nathan read to her from Fielding, Smollett, Swift and Defoe in that voice of his which alternately piped and bumbled.

Henrietta bought our provisions, saw to the cooking of them and busied herself at a score of tasks, each one designed to further our comfort and convenience.

If only it hadn't been for the war, I think I'd have been as completely happy as I could have been in a strange land—and with Sally three thousand miles away. But that cursed war kept us perpetually on edge. Some dreadful thing was forever happening—some horrible miscarriage of military plans, some unexplainable and unjustifiable fiasco.

The first and worst of these was the defeat and capture of Burgoyne's army at Saratoga; and little did I dream, when Buell returned one evening with the painful news, how sharply the later events of my own life were to be altered by the results of that defeat and capture.

When Buell told us of Burgoyne's downfall, he could hardly contain himself, as the saying goes.

"Why, by God," he cried, "you just can't believe anybody could make as many mistakes as Burgoyne, until you hear how many the rebels made! What frets me most is that we told Eden what was going to happen, and the King called us forgers for proving it. We told him the French would join the rebels openly as soon as the rebels won a battle! We told Eden he'd either have to recognize American independence or keep on sending regiments to America and losing 'em for the next fifty years! We said——"

Mrs. Byles rapped his knee with her cane. "If Burgoyne made mistakes, and you know what they are, let's hear 'em."

"I know so many," Buell said, "that you'd sit here all night if I told all of 'em. In the first place, Burgoyne was supposed to go from the St. Lawrence to the Hudson by way of Lake Champlain, and Howe was supposed to come up the Hudson and join him, so that the two forces together could divide New Englanders from the rest of the country and push 'em into the Atlantic Ocean."

"What's wrong with that?" Mrs. Byles asked.

"Not a thing," Buell said, "except that nobody told Howe what he was supposed to do."

"How do you mean that?" Mrs. Byles asked.

"I tried to say it in plain English, ma'am," Buell told her. "I said nobody told Howe, and what I meant was that nobody told Howe. He was supposed to get his orders from Germaine. The orders were all written out for Germaine to send, but Germaine had an engagement with a couple of nut-brown maidens at Brighton. Naturally he was in a hurry to get away from the office, and in the rush Howe's orders got pushed underneath a pile of papers and there they stayed."

"Such a thing couldn't happen," I said.

"You'll find it *did* happen," Buell said. "When you get around to writing about Burgoyne in your book, you'll see that Howe never received orders to join him."

Mrs. Byles' skirts rustled as she stirred restlessly in her chair.

Buell coughed apologetically. "Another interesting little mistake that you might think couldn't happen was how Burgoyne followed the rebels when they ran away from Ticonderoga as a result of their own mistakes. If he'd followed 'em by water, he could have caught 'em, wiped 'em out and marched right down the Hudson into New York City. Instead of that, he followed 'em by land. That took ten times as long as by water, so the rebels got away. What do you think of that?"

"What made him do it?" I asked.

"Nobody knows for sure," Buell said, "but I got a feeling it was because Burgoyne's a fox hunter. You know how they kill foxes over here. They never shoot one! Oh my, no! Thirty men and women on horseback go out with fifty hounds and chase the fox ten miles through cornfields and potato patches, breaking down fences, frightening cattle and destroying flower beds. When the hounds catch up with the fox and begin to tear him to pieces, a hired man in a red coat gives all the dogs a licking and takes the fox away. What I figure, Oliver, is that Burgoyne wanted to be sporting when he chased the rebels, and it ain't sporting to do things easy."

"How much of Burgoyne's army was captured?" Mrs. Byles asked.

"The whole kit and caboodle," Buell said. "Lock, stock and barrel. Generals, colonels, sutlers, officers' wives, private soldiers, Hessians, camp followers, bad girls and everybody. They'll all be marched to Boston and sent back here to England, where they can't take part in the war any more."

The effect of this unhappy news on the thousands of American Loyalists in England was truly pitiful.

Up to that time, I think, every Loyalist had felt certain that the rebels, with their incompetent generals, their badly disciplined, badly drilled troops and their insufficiency of supplies, could never prevail against the flower of the British Army.

Now they didn't know what to think, and for the first time they realized that there was a possibility that America might forever be denied to them.

No words of mine can describe the dejection, the despair, of all those banished Americans when, two months after the news of Burgoyne's surrender had reached England, every dismal prophecy contained in Deane's dispatches came true.

France, seeing England crippled in America by Burgoyne's defeat, threw off her pretense of neutrality, and openly allied herself with the rebels. Automatically, as it were, England found herself not only at war with the American rebels, but with France and France's ally, Spain.

On the day the news reached London, Buell came back from the Colonial Office in a rage that made all his other memorable rages seem pale and harmless. His hands shook as he told me what he'd heard and seen, and his voice trembled and faded as though he were half frozen.

"By God, Oliver," he said, "it must have been an English cabinet minister, and a damned smart one, who thought up that motto you see all over England—'Evil be to him who evil thinks'! It as much as says: 'You're a skunk if you dare to think evil about what we're doing, even when we're doing it wrong'. That's mighty clever, Oliver! They know they're going to be wrong, so they attack everybody who so much as dares to think they're wrong! I wish to God I could be appointed Motto-Maker to His Majesty the King, God bless him, for about five minutes, and to His Majesty's ministers! I'd chisel a motto on every building in England, embroider it on the garters of Her Royal Highness' ladies-in-waiting, stitch it on every regimental flag, and hammer it into the breastplates of those brass soldiers down in Whitehall. I'd put it where all Englishmen, particularly the King and his ministers, could see it every day of their lives. 'Too late.' That's the motto England ought to have instead of 'Evil be to him who evil thinks'! They captured Bunker Hill too late! They made up their minds to take Dorchester Heights—too late! They could have wiped out the rebels after the battle of Long Island—if they hadn't waited till too late! They could 'a' got 'em at Kip's Bay if the general had followed up his victory instead of waiting till too late! They didn't believe those letters of Deane's till too late! Now that France has joined the rebels, the King's willing to make terms, but he's too damned late."

I'd known, when I started to write my book, that there had been glaring stupidities on both sides, but I hadn't dreamed that the be- havior of British and American commanding officers, if truthfully presented and the proper deductions drawn, would destroy so many military reputations.

Night after night Mrs. Byles read aloud what I'd written during the day, and night after night Buell muttered approval at the things she read: at the idiocy of both the rebel and the British leaders in Boston in 1775; at the blundering incompetence of the rebel leaders at Long Island in 1776, and the bewildering stupidity of Howe immediately afterward; at the perpetual unreliability of the rebel militia, who vanished in thousands, like dust-wraiths, at any hint of successful opposition; at the ghastly fiasco of Saratoga in 1777, with St. Clair, Gates and Putnam blundering miserably for the rebels, with Howe and Sir Henry Clinton insanely wasting opportunities for the British; at the French Alliance with the rebels in 1778, the pigheaded incapacity of the French admiral d'Estaing, the rage and helplessness of the rebel generals when they found that the French had come to America to injure Great Britain first and help the rebels last; at that deathless remark of Washington's—that it is a maxim founded on the universal experience of mankind that no nation is to be trusted further than it is bound by its own interest.

I had planned in the beginning that no matter what happened I would carry my book only to the end of 1778; for I felt sure that by then, in the face of the French Alliance, the King would have taken the advice of those who urged making peace with the rebels at any cost.

I had accumulated all my notes for that year and was ready to start writing, when it occurred to me that I'd heard nothing of the return of Burgoyne's army to England.

The thought was so distracting that I went to Thompson about it. "How does it happen," I asked him, "that Burgoyne's troops haven't reached England yet? They were captured over a year ago."

Thompson seemed surprised. "Didn't I tell you about that? I thought everybody knew about the Convention Army. The rebels won't let it come home."

"But I read the Convention that Gates and Burgoyne signed," I said. "I've put it into my book. It agreed that the entire Convention Army, officers, men and camp followers, were to be marched immediately to Boston, embarked as soon as General Howe could send ships, and carried to England."

"I know," Thompson said, "but the rebel Congress refused to ratify the Convention."

"On what grounds?"

"They've trumped up several reasons," Thompson said. "They said Burgoyne's men, if allowed to embark on transports, would themselves break the Convention that Burgoyne signed, and join Howe's army.

"They said the Convention was dissolved when Burgoyne complained to Congress that his officers and men were being barbarously and cruelly treated.

"They said Burgoyne's men had retained cross-belts and cartridge boxes, and consequently hadn't fulfilled the Convention clause requiring them to give up all arms. . . ."

"But cross-belts and cartridge boxes aren't regarded as arms," I protested. "They're private property, purchased by the colonel of the regiment."

"It makes no difference," Thompson said. "Congress is determined not to live up to the Convention. According to the information we've received, Congress is convinced that if Burgoyne's men are allowed to go back to England, they'll be sent to India, say, and troops from India will thus be released for service in America. They say that to observe the terms of the Convention would be conniving at putting enemy troops in the field."

"That argument would have pleased my father," I said. "He always held that men who behaved as the rebels behaved at the beginning of this war could be depended on for only one thing—to sacrifice faith and reputation to expediency. He argued that no dependence could ever be placed upon the promises and public faith of intolerant men who persisted in forcibly taking the law into their own hands."

Thompson shrugged his shoulders.

"What's being done about it?" I asked.

"What *can* be done about it?" Thompson said. "Nothing! What would you do about it yourself? Nothing! Burgoyne and other officers have protested repeatedly to Congress and to General Washington, but they get no satisfaction."

"What's become of the Convention Army?" I asked. "What happened to them? Where are they now?"

"They were in Cambridge for nearly a year," Thompson said. "I hardly need to tell you the sort of treatment they've been getting. The rebel officer who had charge of them has just been court-martialed. He was charged with indecent, violent, vindictive severity against Burgoyne's men as a whole, and the intentional murder of one of them. He was acquitted—by a court composed of rebel officers, of course—and ordered to resume his command."

A sudden icy rage swept over me. Often before in this war I'd resented the brutality of the rebels. I'd despised them for their severity toward my father at a moment when harshness was an almost certain death sentence. I'd hated them for their unrelenting persecution of all who opposed war and believed in orderly government. I'd detested them for their malignant ferocity toward the refugees in the Long Island swamps, for their ignorant aversion to wealth and education; for their grim determination to pull all men down to their own level; for their blatant insistence that only Americans of their own confused and ever-changing political beliefs were patriotic, and that all other Americans were traitors.

Yet my hatred of these strange Americans—these Americans who had rebelled against a government that for years had fought their battles and protected them against the French and Indians when they couldn't protect themselves—had been, it seemed to me, as nothing up to now.

Hitherto my hatred of them had been aversion rather than true hatred. The things they'd done, I'd often told myself, were done at the urgings of leaders as ignorant, as cruel, as inconsiderate as angry children.

But this breaking of a treaty, this refusal to keep faith with uniformed enemies who'd fought honorably, who'd laid down their arms, trusting to the promises of brother soldiers—this deliberate dishonoring of a solemn covenant—tightened the muscles in my stomach until they ached.

In time, I think, I could have forgiven the rebels' treatment of my father; forgotten those scenes I'd witnessed in the swamp at Hempstead; pardoned the seizing of our home in Milton and its sale for next to nothing to professional patriots. The men responsible for those outrages, after all, were products of mobs; and the riffraff, in every age and in every civilization, are no better than brutes when for a moment they rise to power. But never until the last day of my life would I forget the stamp of dishonor put upon the whole body of rebels by their representatives, their spokesmen in Congress. They were branded now as men who would break their promises just to win; as men who would oppress the weak and helpless just to win; as men who would descend to any knavery, and count it honorable if by that knavery they could win.

I was completely obsessed by the fate of the Convention Army—those men of Burgoyne's who had surrendered at Saratoga over a year ago, and ever since had been kept prisoners by the determined bad faith of the rebel Congress.

I sent Buell to the Colonial Office to copy every available document and letter about the Convention Army; and as I read those documents and letters, my indignation steadily rose. The more it increased, the more my interest in the history on which I had worked so hard and so long began to flag. My book grew less and less important to me, and the fate of that army filled my mind to the exclusion of all else.

Then, one day, I discovered that Congress, not content with keeping Burgoyne's officers and men in Cambridge, half fed, half clothed, and constantly subject to the brutalities of their guards, had ordered that they be marched hundreds of miles to a prison camp in the interior of the country. At the end of that day I came from my workroom without a line written; and when Mrs. Byles and Buell looked at me expectantly, I had to tell them the truth about the unfortunate situation in which I found myself.

"It's that Convention Army," I said. "It clings in my brain like a barbed hook! If I'm going to go on writing, I've got to write about that, because I can't think about anything else. It dwarfs everything else in the war, so far as I'm concerned."

I didn't know it at the time, but I'd been caught by war, as every author is caught when exposed to the strange, destructive miasma that hangs like a poisoned fog over warring nations. Some men come whole out of a war, but no author ever does. He may seem unhurt: he may even write books; but literature dies within him, strangled by war.

Buell looked puzzled. "I don't see why it should. What's happening to the Convention Army ain't any worse than what Cunningham did to rebel prisoners on Long Island and in New York."

"Yes, it is," I said. "What happened on Long Island and in New York was the work of one man—a sick man, who took a dreadful sort of pleasure in the sufferings of his enemies. What's happening to the Convention Army is the fault of the heads of the rebel government. They've gone back on the word of honor of their generals. Since none of their generals have resigned in protest, they're conniving at faithlessness. Such people are a disgrace to America! They've sacrificed national honor to immediate convenience! They're the people who boast of being American patriots, and brand you and me as traitors to our country. We're loyal, and so we're traitors. They break their words, dishonor their treaties, make war on women, oppress the weak and helpless, practise the worst sort of political oppression, and so they're patriots! It rips me to pieces inside, Tom, to see such men take our country from us!"

"The way you put it," Buell said, "I begin to see why you're having difficulty with your writing."

"That's the trouble with us Loyalists," I told him. "We're just beginning to see what's happening to us. I've thought in my heart, the last year or two, that in the end we'd lose nothing if we accepted rebel rule in America—if we left it to them to do as well as they could, and trusted to them to let bygones be bygones when the war's over. Well, I've been wrong! Men who'd do what Congress has done to Burgoyne's men could never be honest with themselves or anyone else. They'd break faith with anyone if it suited 'em to do so. If we tried to live in America under their rule, we couldn't call our souls our own without being stoned, chased, tarred and feathered, and driven from the country again."

"It might be different some day," Mrs. Byles said. "Belcher often spoke, after we'd gone to bed, about the way people change. He'd fuss and fume over the wildness of all those little Harvard Casanovas, but he'd always say 'Give 'em another ten years, damn 'em, and they'll be twice as tame as I am.' I hate rebels as much as you do, Oliver, but I shouldn't wonder if they'd feel kinder toward us when they're living in our houses and wearing clothes that don't smell of fried fish. They'll be old Boston families then. They'll change!"

"They'll never change," I told her. "Not the ones that count: not the ones that'll drive us out for daring to think unlike 'em! They're opportunists, cheap politicians, and nothing else, just as my father always insisted. Statesmen change; opportunists and cheap politicians never change—never! Those men started the war with a lie—started it by swearing the last thing they wanted was independence. When they got a sufficiently large following, they changed entirely around. Then all their followers were caught. Thousands among 'em were against independence with their whole hearts, but they couldn't withdraw without being called traitors and parricides—without being beaten by mobs and hunted into swamps."

It was Mrs. Byles who broke the silence. "What's to be done with the Convention Army, Oliver?"

"God only knows! Congress ordered 'em imprisoned in a safe

place. I suppose that means they'll be marched inland during the worst cold spell of the year and put into a mountain camp where they'll all freeze to death together. How the devil can I or any other man sit over a desk, trying to finish a piddling thing like a book, while those men, thousands of 'em, are being driven off into the mountains, half starved and half frozen!"

Henrietta Dixon raised her shoulders in a Gallic shrug. "Mais, mon ami," she said, "ees eet not feeneeshed up to where you stopped writing?"

"Finished?" I asked. "Of course it isn't finished until I've got it the way I want it—until I tell everything that's happened."

Henrietta abandoned her accent. "But you *have* told everything that happened up to the end of 1778! The first four years *are* finished."

"Henrietta," Buell said coldly, "I don't know any woman that can make a nicer pumpkin pie or stitch a prettier shirt than you, but you better stick to shirts and pies, and leave books to Oliver."

"Mate Buell," Henrietta said, "I may not know much about books, but I know this about 'em: if they're not worth reading, they can be ended any place with no loss to anyone. If they *are* worth reading, it don't much matter where they end."

Mrs. Byles whacked her stick against the floor. "She's right! Henrietta's right! Of *course* Oliver's book's finished, as far as he's gone. *Civil War in America—The First Four Years.* What better title could you have! It gives people a hint of what we've been through—helps 'em to understand how long we've been homeless! We'll see a book printer tomorrow, Oliver, and by the time your book's published, the Convention Army'll probably be back in England, and you'll be free to start writing again."

CHAPTER LX

I<small>N</small> <small>MY</small> ignorance I'd thought, like many another author before me, that when a book has been written, no further work upon it is needed.

I soon discovered my mistake, though even now I find it impossible to decide which of the after-labors of writing a book is most discouraging.

At times the interminable waiting seemed the worst. Apparently those who publish books cannot read as easily as those who buy them, and authors must wait weary weeks for a printer to read a manuscript that could easily be digested in ten hours.

At other times I was sure nothing was so shattering to an author's nerves and his peace of mind as hearing a publisher deliver weighty opinions concerning matters of which he was wholly ignorant. The drudgery of writing was far less tiring than the arduous task of listening to suggestions as to how my book could be made safer and more salable by eliminating certain parts and rewriting others.

Every printer I saw—and it seemed to me I saw them all before I acknowledged myself defeated—was willing to publish my history if only I'd change it. No two wanted the same things changed, but all of them wanted something changed and too many wanted everything changed. For a while I argued with them; but soon I understood that for a fledgling author to uphold his views only makes a publisher more determined to have things his own way, and to let the author have his way in nothing.

All printers, it seemed to me, lived in dark caves smelling of dust, glue, soft-coal smoke and mice, and under no circumstances did one of them ever keep an appointment at the stipulated hour. Why those who print England's books should make appointments at all, when they never kept them, was and still is a mystery to me.

After a two-day wait, I was finally admitted to the presence of Dilly, most successful of London printers, and found him a mousy-looking little man with lips perpetually pursed. He glanced up at me out of beady black eyes; and while his clawlike hands fingered my manuscript as a mouse paws a piece of cheese, he complained about it. "Your history, Mr. Wiswell, is most interesting and commendable: agreeably and directly composed, sir; something of Defoe in it, I venture to say; but it's not for us, Mr. Wiswell! No, no, no! And every other publisher in London would say the same thing, I'm shaw!" He was addicted to the word "shaw", which was his English way of saying "sure".

"I don't understand, sir," I said. "If it's commendable and like Defoe, why not print it? Why refuse it?"

Mr. Dilly held up a protesting hand. "I assure you, Mr. Wiswell, the word 'refuse' hasn't passed my lips. That word, sir, will be used only by you, if at all. Your history, I said, is not for us; but that, sir, is only if you persist in certain small errors that may readily be altered."

"Errors?" I asked. "If there are errors in my book, sir, the evidence is in error. Will you show me where I've been wrong?"

"Perhaps not wrong in the strict sense of the word," Dilly said. "It's your attitude of—ah—of disrespect that impairs the value of your history." He laughed lightly. "Dear me, Mr. Wiswell, surely you realize your history is full of libels."

"I've libeled no one," I said. "I've told what people did, and in some cases I've told what they didn't do, but I haven't libeled them."

Mr. Dilly's glance was indulgent. "Whether you know it or not, Mr. Wiswell, your book libels some of the most respectable characters in the British Army and Navy. It libels Sir William Howe, Admiral Lord Howe, General Sir Henry Clinton, General Thomas Gage and a number of others. You've said dreadful things about our admirals! I might almost say that it libels every high British officer."

"But Mr. Dilly," I said, "I've written nothing that isn't the truth! I can prove everything I wrote! I can produce letters and documents to establish the accuracy of every statement in the book."

Dilly's voice sharpened. "As a printer, Mr. Wiswell, it's my business to know English law. I repeat again that your statements are libelous. If I were to publish this book of yours as you've written it, you might be wealthier than the Duke of Bedford and still be unable to pay the damages that might be recovered against you if your book were published as it stands."

"But I've told only the truth," I said again.

"English law," Mr. Dilly said, "doesn't permit such truth to be produced in evidence." He seemed to take a grim satisfaction in this astounding statement. Then he frowned and said, "Another thing, Mr. Wiswell: your book is too favorable to the Americans to have a sale in England."

"Favorable!" I cried. "Favorable to Americans! Why, I've tried to be favorable to no one! I've just tried to be fair. I've only tried to show that if English generals hadn't more than matched the stupidities of the rebels, England would have won the war a score of times."

Dilly spoke testily. "Pure libel, Mr. Wiswell! Now see here: if your book weren't so full of libel, so one-sided, I'm shaw we could do something with it. Why not be sensible, Mr. Wiswell? Let me show you how to touch it up a little, and I think—I can't guarantee it, of course: I can't perform miracles—but I think I can make you an enviable reputation and a tidy sum to boot."

He leaned forward persuasively, his lips pursed as if to kiss me. "All you need do, Mr. Wiswell, is take out those libelous references to General Howe's failure to follow up his victories. Just let them go as victories, my dear Wiswell. They *were* victories: why muddy them by references to greater victories he *might* have had! Who are we to say what might have been? Oh, by all means take out scurrilous and libelous sentences that sully the deeds of a great soldier!"

"Show me one sentence that's scurrilous!" I said. "And Howe isn't a great soldier. He's a cheap politician; and what's more——"

"Some passages," Dilly interrupted, "you'll have to delete in toto. Those bits about Clinton's failure to co-operate with Burgoyne, for example; those repeated references to Howe's inertia and what you call his refusal to capture Washington and his army; your remarks about the sacrifice of America on the altar of British politics; your defamatory statements about the willingness of the Whigs to sacrifice the British Empire to their personal ambitions——"

"But all those things are true," I said. "If they're taken out, those who read the book won't understand what England's throwing away, or why! They won't understand that half the population of America is loyal to a government that's too ignorant or too impotent to support them. If I do what you suggest, I won't be telling the truth!"

"My dear Wiswell," Dilly protested. "Of course you'll be telling the truth! You'll merely be refraining from irritating English readers with gratuitous insults."

I thought I'd make one more try. "Mr. Dilly, no true history of this war's going to be published in America for many a long year, for the rebels'll kill any man who tries to tell the truth about 'em. I doubt that any Englishman will write a true history of the war, because I don't believe there's an Englishman who understands America or Americans sufficiently well. In other words, I think you've got, in this book, the only honest history of the war you're likely to find. What's more, I'm certain that not one of the generals who are, according to your ideas, libeled in it, will dare show his face in court to defend his behavior in America."

Dilly shook a playful finger at me. "A dangerous manner of thought, Wiswell—oh, very!"

"Well, sir," I said, "it all comes down to this: my name's going to be on this book, and I won't let it appear on something that isn't true. If I do as you suggest, my name'll be on a lie. I won't do it."

"Sheer stubbornness, Wiswell!" Dilly cried. "If you persist, I'll have to step aside in favor of another publisher. I thought you Yankees had too much common sense to be guilty of such stubbornness."

"In this particular instance," I told him, "I think I resent having such words as 'guilty' and 'stubbornness' applied to me."

"Nonsense," Dilly said briskly. "Of course you're guilty of stubbornness! If you persist in caviling at a few small changes, you'll sacrifice fortune and reputation. Come now: isn't it reasonable to say that a man who deliberately sacrifices fortune and reputation is gravely at fault? I'm shaw it is!"

"Was I gravely at fault," I asked, "when my conscience wouldn't let me join the mobs in America—wouldn't let me fight against the government under which I'd always lived?"

"That's a wholly different matter," Dilly said.

"No, it's not, Mr. Dilly. My father refused to join the mobs, and so he lost his home, his country and his life. If he were alive today, he'd do the same thing over again. So would all the thousands of Americans now living in England. All of us sacrificed our immediate fortunes and what the mob called our reputations rather than agree to what we considered wrong."

Dilly raised a protesting hand. "My dear Wiswell, you and I were discussing business! Why inject war and politics into the conversation? I must ask you to spare me! Men at war are guilty of indiscretions and stupidities that wouldn't for a moment be tolerated in business. Pray don't be hasty in your judgment, Mr. Wiswell. Give my words more careful consideration. Sleep on them a night or two, eh? Then come to see me again next week. You'll view my proposal in a different light, I'm shaw."

"I'd view it for what it is if I slept on it for a thousand nights," I said; and so eager was I to get my hands on my manuscript and remove myself from Dilly's presence that I can't remember another word he said.

Yet when my manuscript had gone to other publishers, and all of them had said their say to me about the faults of my book, I realized that Dilly was no worse than all the others. Their desire for the half-truth, which to an honest author is a downright lie, was maddening; and as I repeatedly refused to make their despicable changes, I came bitterly to realize that if my work were not utterly in vain, it might not see the light of day in England within my lifetime.

The failure of my book—this apparently utter waste of the three long years I'd spent in London since our fruitless capture of the Deane Papers—seemed like one more step on the road to despair; and yet it was my book that served me, that set a term to my stay in England, that took me back to America, that brought me one step nearer Sally.

Mrs. Byles went with me on a foggy morning in the autumn of 1780, when I went to see Benjamin Thompson for the last time—or for what I thought was the last time. He lolled in his chair, half bored and half amused, while Mrs. Byles told him of my experiences with English publishers, and what they wanted me to do to my book.

When she'd finished, he got up from his desk without a word and went from the room.

"Hoity-toity!" Mrs. Byles cried. "That young man's above himself from associating with King's ministers and lord privies! I knew Benjamin Thompson when he didn't have a piece of satin to his name except what Sarah Rolfe bought for him, and now he turns his back if we tell him something he doesn't consider interesting!"

Mrs. Byles, however, did him an injustice.

When he came back and slid in behind his desk with that catlike grace of his, he consulted a slip of paper.

"In more ways than one," he told Mrs. Byles, "I feel responsible for Oliver's literary efforts. I hadn't correctly gauged the timidity of publishers, so I've made special representations to Lord Germaine, who has been so gracious as to agree with me. In fact, he authorizes me to furnish transportation to New York for Mrs. Belcher Byles, Mrs. Henrietta Dixon, Nathan Dixon, Second Lieutenant Thomas Buell and Captain Oliver Wiswell."

"Captain," Mrs. Byles whispered. "Second Lieutenant! New York! Am I dreaming?"

"Wait," I said. "I don't understand this! Me a captain? What do I know about being a captain? What in God's name will Henrietta and Mrs. Byles do in New York? And I thought you knew it was the Convention Army that I——"

"Quite so, Oliver," Thompson broke in. "Give me credit for remembering details! His lordship gratefully recalls the services rendered by Mrs. Byles and Mrs. Dixon in Paris. In his opinion, they'd be equally valuable in New York if they were to go there and operate a tavern similar to the one they operated so successfully in Paris."

Mrs. Byles shook her head. "I'm afraid not. There's nothing so hungry as a hungry American. The British Army may hold New York, but its population is American. Those Americans are Loyalists, and something tells me half of 'em will come to our back door every night and claim they knew Belcher. Then I'll have to feed 'em!"

"I can persuade his lordship to make allowances for such a contingency," Thompson said. "We'll commandeer any house you want, and we'll allow you £2,000 to get it started."

Mrs. Byles looked as all her seafaring ancestors must have looked when they made quick decisions. "I'm not dreaming! Put that £2,000 in writing, Benjamin, and I'll accept your offer—provided, of course, that Oliver wishes to leave England too."

Thompson turned to me. "I've never told you, Oliver, but I hold His Majesty's commission as colonel of the King's American Dragoons. That regiment doesn't exist yet, but some day it will. Every man in it will be an American, a Loyalist, and it'll be the finest cavalry regiment in the world. Your commission—Buell's too—is in that regiment, Oliver, and for the duration of this war. You're a good horseman, because Buell told me how you picked him up and carried him back to Milton the night he was tarred and feathered. You know tactics, because you've studied all the battles of this war, and recognized all the mistakes made in them. So you *do* know something about being a captain."

When I began to protest that I knew nothing about drill, he shut me up. "Listen, Oliver: you may never see active service; but take my word for it: if you're in the vicinity of a war, you're bound to find a commission mighty helpful. It's like a key to a sanctuary. If you're in trouble, there'll always be some small part of an army to which you can turn for help."

"If you're giving us these commissions just to get us out of trouble," Buell said, "perhaps we ought to have higher rank. From what I've seen of armies, there's only one thing that would get me out of trouble with generals, and that's being a general myself."

"As a second lieutenant, Mr. Buell," Thompson said pleasantly, "you won't get to see a general once in a dog's age, so don't worry about that!"

He turned to me. "Here's the situation, Oliver. You hold army rank, but you're under special orders, and they're mighty important ones. We can learn nothing definite about the Convention Army, except that it's been sent somewhere in the southern provinces—probably into the mountains of North Carolina. We want you to find it and determine whether it's possible or advisable for an armed force, by swift marches, to rescue it and bring it out to the seacoast. In addition to that you've got to find out for me some of the things that I can't find out from anyone—probably because nobody knows them. I've got to know them, though, and from someone on whose honesty and good judgment I can absolutely rely. You can easily understand how important it is that I should have this information. Lord Germaine is placing more and more reliance on what I tell him about American affairs. If I give him my word about something, he takes it for gospel. He's head of the Colonial Office; and it won't be long, Oliver, before the Colonial Office needs all the accurate information it can get about the southern provinces."

He opened a map case and spread out on his desk a map of the southern colonies—Virginia, North Carolina and South Carolina. The three of them together looked like a huge rough triangle, with Savannah and Charleston at the lower point.

"It's just been decided," he said, "that the war's to move into the south. General Clinton's going to lead a force against Charleston and Savannah; and with those two cities as a base, it's believed we can control the entire south. According to what we hear there's no revolutionary movement anywhere in the south except on the seacoast. We've been told that the people in the interior have no use for the rebel governments on the coast; and unless we've been misinformed, all we need to do is send a force into the interior of North and South

Carolina. If we do that, we'll find thousands of Scotch refugees from Culloden, every last one of them loyal. We'll find thousands of others who hate the rebels. We can set up a loyal government in the interior of the south, raise half a dozen regiments, march up through Virginia into the north and wholly destroy the rebels with an army of Americans. If the south is ours, and New England cut off from all supplies from that section, the rebellion will probably die of starvation."

He put the point of his pencil on the city of Charleston, ran it up toward the tangle of mountains that stretched across the entire upper and inland portions of the three colonies, and tapped its point against a place that bore the peculiar and vaguely familiar name of Ninety Six. Then I remembered: Ninety Six was the post about which Colonel Rogers had spoken so feelingly on that hot night when he'd traveled with us to Long Island to start recruiting his Queen's Rangers.

"This fort of Ninety Six," Thompson said, "is the citadel, as you might say, of a section that's solidly loyal. According to what I hear there's an enormous belt of Loyalists extending from Ninety Six across South Carolina and North Carolina into Virginia. It's our understanding that they greatly outnumber the rebels, and are eager to take up arms against them.

"Well, I want definite information. Have they taken up arms or haven't they? What kind of soldiers do they make? How many are there? I've heard a lot of talk from people who pretend to know; but the truth is, Oliver, they don't know one damned thing that's definite and accurate. Seemingly the people from the coastal sections of those southern states are wholly unlike those from the mountain regions. I'm forced to conclude that they hate each other so heartily that neither'll admit the other exists. I can't even be definite about that. But we're going to conduct a campaign in that part of the world, and we've got to know. It's life and death for us, perhaps. You see that, don't you?"

"Certainly," I said.

"Then that's all that's necessary," he said. "Good luck to you, Oliver, and to all the rest of you. I'll be in America myself if this war goes on much longer, so I won't even say good-by." He made it clear the interview was over.

When I tried to thank him for getting commissions for us, he wouldn't listen. "Pure selfishness on my part, Oliver! When I join the King's American Dragoons, which I shall certainly do some day, I must know there's somebody in it on whom I can depend; and if I

come to New York, as I have every intention of doing, I want to be
sure of a soft bed and food that won't choke me."

I didn't believe him, which should have proved to me that Thompson was a great man. Great men tell the truth and are never believed.
Lesser men are always believed, but seldom have the brains or the
courage to tell the truth.

BOOK IV

☆

The Wilderness Trail

CHAPTER LXI

W HEN Buell and I sailed past the familiar coves and wooded ridges of Long Island in November, 1780, we'd been away from our native land four years to a day.

During those four years much had happened and yet little had changed. The rebel army, badly officered, half starved, wretchedly clad, poorly armed, had somehow contrived to stay beyond the reach of British commanders who backed them into corners again and again, only to be struck motionless and seemingly brainless at moments when overwhelming victory was within their grasp.

Never had there been a stranger army than that rebel army. At times its numbers had been even larger than those of the Loyalist regiments who fought under British leadership. At other times, disheartened by defeat or overcome with homesickness, it had dwindled to the mere ragged ghost of an army.

In battle after battle rebel militia regiments had run farther and faster than soldiers had ever run before; and yet that rebel army, sometimes mutinous, often cowardly, never reliable, still remained in existence, an object of scorn to friend and foe alike, and less of a terror to those against whom it marched than to the unhappy Americans past whose homes and fields it pursued its unsoldierly way.

The rebel Congress, only source of authority in the rebellious states, was without authority, honor or ability. Made fearful by its own weakness and ineptitude, it behaved shamefully to the troops that kept it in existence; it ordered the printing of money that constantly grew more worthless; it was so busy with jealous bickerings that it found no time to provide food or money for its army. These were the people who were ruling America, and as a result America no longer seemed a home or a refuge to me or to Tom Buell: it seemed a lost province: a sinister country, dangerous because of its pitfalls and the treachery of its inhabitants.

It's true I was happy to see those low Long Island shores again, but not because I thought of it as my native land. It had ceased to seem like that to me, and it stirred emotions in me only because Sally lived somewhere to the northward of that long, low coastline. That was all America meant to me now: the land where Sally lived.

It seemed worse than ironic that the only thoughts we uttered, as our vessel closed with that blue Long Island shore, were not of home and those we loved. Our homes were gone. We spoke only of the violent scenes those shores recalled to us—scenes that would live more vividly in my mind than my happier, dimmer memories of Milton Hill: those dark unhappy hours in the swamps of Hempstead with Judge Hendon and his persecuted Loyalists; that cautious march across the wooded heights of Brooklyn, where we had taken the rebels in the rear; the scuttling insectlike figures of rebel militia trapped in the cornfields, hiding in ditches, floundering and drowning in the mud.

Except for the uniforms that thronged the principal streets of New York—the green uniforms of the regiments of Loyalists that guarded every ferry and every approach to the city, the scarlet and gold of British officers, the blue and white of German troops—we might have come home to the America we had known before that April night, five long years ago, when the mobs had driven us into Boston.

There was no need to guard our speech, for all New York—soldier, sailor, civilian, master and servant, poor and rich alike—was against the rebels and everything for which they stood. It was a loyal city.

By the time I had made the rounds that a newcomer to the British Army was obliged to make unless he wished to be regarded as criminally negligent or treasonably secretive—to the commandant of the city, Colonel Patterson, on Wall Street, to leave a record of Mrs. Byles, Mrs. Dixon, Buell and myself in the city, to the adjutant general's office on Broad Street to file my orders from Germaine, and to the office of General Clinton's secretary at No. 1 Broadway to leave the letter which Thompson had told me to give him—Buell had somehow contrived to soak up information like a sponge.

I truly believe that if Buell had stood in the middle of the Sahara Desert, Bedouins and Djinns would have burst from the sand to deluge him with personal and general information of the most intimate nature.

Mrs. Byles and Henrietta, he told me, when I joined him at the Sign of the Happy Man near Brownjohn's Wharf, needed no help from us. Holding New York to be a wicked city, they proposed to take their time locating the house that seemed best adapted for a tavern.

He looked at me significantly. "I guess they're right, Oliver. Sam Adams had kicked this country quite a way along the road to hell when we left it four years ago, but it's been kicked considerably farther along right now. I don't suppose you've happened to walk through Canvas Town."

He didn't wait for me to say No, but poured out a flood of information.

"There's thirty thousand Loyalists in this town, Oliver! That doesn't take into account the Negroes in Canvas Town."

He looked sardonic. "Eight thousand Negroes in Canvas Town, Oliver; all of 'em refugees from liberty-loving rebels! I can't understand why such tyrants as us don't make a nice little profit out of those slaves, selling 'em back to the Sons of Liberty. All we'd have to do is cut off a Negro's head and send it back to his master. We'd get more for his head than if we took him back alive. A head brings £25; and if there's life in 'em they're only worth £5."

He clucked an admiring tongue. "Looks like the rebels were getting prosperous, Oliver—barring those that do the fighting. Half the rebels in Jersey and Connecticut are selling food to us Loyalists for three times what it's worth. According to what I hear, all the British admirals and generals are holding back supplies from those that ought to have 'em, so to sell 'em to whoever's got enough money to pay for 'em. If you want to know what I think, Oliver, I think everyone on both sides in this war, barring those that carry guns and fire at each other from behind fences, are a misbegotten pack of——"

"Nonsense," I said.

Buell became argumentative. "All right, Oliver! Name one that ain't misbegotten! Name just one! How about Sam Adams? How about John Hancock? How about Sir William Eden? How about Germaine? How about North? How about the——"

I stopped him before he could shout out the name of the King; but I admitted to myself what I'd never have admitted at the beginning of the war—that every war is brought about by mediocrities who always insist they're right, and seldom are; that all wars are prolonged because rulers and cabinet ministers are stupid, stubborn, vindictive, shortsighted and timid.

On the very next day, to my gratification, I was summoned to General Sir Henry Clinton's headquarters at No. 1 Broadway, and in due course admitted to the presence of the same kindly, pudgy, big-nosed little man I had first seen by lanternlight on a Long Island knoll four years before, directing that great march that resulted in the defeat of the entire rebel army, and should have resulted in its complete destruction.

Up to a certain point I remember next to nothing of my conversation with Clinton, barring the fact that he was anxious to have all the latest London gossip, which I wasn't able to give him, and that he was polite to me, which was something unusual in a high British officer. General Philips and General Riedesel, he told me, had been with the Convention Army until recently, but had now been exchanged and were in New York, so that if I wished to save myself a long and arduous trip, I might get my information from them.

When I thanked him and said I could only follow my orders by seeing for myself, he looked mildly amused and said he'd be happy to send me to the south with an expedition soon to leave for the James River.

"I'll send you with Colonel Simcoe's Rangers," he said. "They're all Loyalists, and they'll get as far inland as anybody."

I remember only the bare outline of what had been said up to that point; but I remember as if it were yesterday the conversation that followed.

Clinton darted a quick look at me when he had said he'd send me with Simcoe. "That doesn't please you, Captain?"

"Yes, sir," I said. "I'm grateful for your courtesy."

He puffed out his chest, and somehow his hooked nose, his scarlet coat and his bright dark eye put me in mind of a suspicious parrot. "What's wrong, Captain?"

I said nothing was wrong.

"Then why," Clinton asked, "did your face change when I spoke of sending you with Colonel Simcoe?"

"I wasn't conscious of it, sir," I said. "It was wholly unintentional."

Clinton clasped his hands behind him and tipped himself forward and back, forward and back. "Unintentional, perhaps, Captain, but none the less noticeable. When I said I'd send you to the James River, I felt a withdrawal. Something gave you an unpleasant shock. You can't object to Colonel Simcoe. Any man would consider it a privilege to accompany Colonel Simcoe. Perhaps you have enemies on the James River—or friends." He came closer and stared at me. "Perhaps friends?" he asked.

"No, sir," I said, "you misunderstood me entirely. I feel nothing but gratitude for your kindness. Why, once I'm on the James River, sir, I'll be only a short distance from the Convention Army."

"Come, come, Captain Wiswell," Clinton said, "I'm not accustomed to being evaded in this way. I know I was right. Perhaps your changed attitude was due to something you hesitate to tell me because I'm a staff officer. Is that it?"

"Well, sir," I said, "I'll have to admit that's the reason. Occasionally, in England, I advanced opinions to superior officers and was usually laughed at or ignored. Sometimes I thought an American should never suggest a course of action to Englishmen unless he wished them to do the opposite."

Clinton looked as haughty as only a small, fat man can look. "Oh, come now, Captain! You had one or two unfortunate experiences, or presented your ideas to Englishmen who knew nothing about America. My father was governor of New York for many years. I have no instinctive distrust of an American—unless he happens to be a rebel. Now then, Captain: what brought that look into your face when I mentioned the James River?"

"Well, sir," I said, "it's a matter I had many an argument about during my stay in England. An expedition to the James River must be to seize territory and destroy property. As an American who wants to see this war brought to a successful conclusion, I think such expeditions are worse than useless, General."

General Clinton's already round face seemed to grow puffier. "Do you, indeed, Captain! In what army did you learn strategy?"

"I've never been a soldier, sir. I've spent the last three years writing a history of the war. But I know that all the campaigns against the rebels have been calculated to increase their resistance rather than to help and encourage the loyal Americans whom the rebels are destroying."

Clinton frowned. "If this were an ordinary war, Captain, you'd no doubt be right; but this is no ordinary war. There's no way of making the rebels fight: consequently the only way to remind them there's a war is to make them feel the burden of it. The only way to do that is by destroying their stores and supplies—by driving them from sections that are suffering from their misrule. That's why I'm taking over the south, Captain Wiswell. Perhaps you haven't heard about my capture of Charleston?"

I rubbed my knuckles, feeling within myself that hopeless emptiness, not far removed from nausea, that always swept me when I tried and failed to explain to an Englishman my views about my own country.

"Thousands upon thousands of Loyalists were freed of rebel misrule by that capture, Captain," Clinton said, and he puffed out his breast like a duck in the mating season. "It was no hollow victory, like some we've won in this country. It cost me less than three hundred killed and wounded; and when the city fell, I took six thousand prisoners, four hundred guns, and all the rebel supplies. The residents wept with joy at being delivered from the rebels!

"As a result of that victory we hold Charleston, Savannah, Beaufort, Norfolk. When General Arnold takes this expedition into the James River, we'll hold Petersburg and Richmond as well. General Cornwallis, with his army, is marching into the interior parts of North and South Carolina. In a short time the whole south will be ours. Then the south will no longer be able to send supplies and troops to the New England agitators, smugglers and disappointed politicians who keep this rebellion alive. The Loyalists themselves can march north and end the war."

"Yes, sir," I said.

Clinton snorted. "What's wrong with that strategy, Captain?"

"I hope it'll be successful, sir," I said. "A great many thousands hope so, General. It's been a heartbreaking experience for 'em—to be kept from their own country by the unreasoning and unaccommodating temper of the government they've tried to support."

Clinton's face darkened. "Unreasoning! Unaccommodating! Scarcely the words to apply to a government dealing with a rebellion instigated and carried on by men whose motives are selfish, partisan and ignoble."

"That's not quite accurate, sir," I said. "The men who instigated this rebellion aren't those who're now carrying it on. So far as we're concerned, Samuel Adams, John Hancock, Patrick Henry, Isaac Sears and the other rabble-rousers are dead. Those you're dealing with now are John Jay, Alexander Hamilton, John Adams, John Marshall,

George Washington, Philip Schuyler, Benjamin Franklin, Thomas Jefferson. I think you'll find there's nobody in the British government whose foresight and ability is equal to theirs."

"Indeed," Clinton said.

"Yes, sir," I said. "And as I see it, a policy of continually irritating one region after another, instead of striking at the heart of resistance, is bound to exasperate more and more Americans, and bring more and more of them to the rebel side. The pages of history prove repeatedly that there's no way of cowing high-spirited people by noise and destruction and a display of force. Whenever it's been tried, the result has been the exact opposite of what was intended. You asked for my opinion, sir. It's my opinion that a continued policy of raiding would eventually array the whole American continent against us, even though more than half of its inhabitants believe as we believe at the present moment. You wanted me to be frank. Well, sir, if raids are continually launched, the temper of America will change. Where you now find friendship, I fear you may soon find something very different."

Clinton cleared his throat, and into the sound he somehow contrived to put disbelief and condescension. "You've been a long time away from America, Captain Wiswell. I think you don't realize how destitute the rebel army is. It's worse this year than last—worse than anything you can imagine. The rebel cause is bankrupt, and in another year France will own the rebel government, body and soul. Naturally, you aren't aware of that, whereas I am." His voice became overly solicitous. "Don't think too harshly of us, Captain, if we carry on this war in a way that soldiers think will be successful, even though historians disapprove."

My insides quaked, as they had at the determined ignorance of the British admiral in Halifax; at Howe when he recalled the troops who were straining forward to put an end to the rebel forces at Brooklyn; at Eden and the King and the rest of the British cabinet when they refused to believe our unimpeachable proof that France was coming in on the side of the rebels; as it would always quake, no doubt, when I attempted to discuss the insanities of war with persons who could have no conception of them, or when I tried to explain this strange young giant of a country of ours to men who couldn't comprehend a strange young giant when they saw one.

"Do you think, Captain Wiswell," Clinton persisted, "that your own temper will alter? Will your loyalty be changed to something different?"

"No, sir," I said, "I'll never change. I can't hold with people who say I must think their way or not at all."

"Of course you can't," Clinton said heartily. "Write your histories, Captain: write your histories, carry out your orders and leave the planning of wars to professional soldiers."

CHAPTER LXII

Less than a month after we had arrived in New York, Buell and I, as Clinton had promised, were on our way to Virginia with Arnold's expedition; and if any soothsayer had prophesied to me where we'd eventually find ourselves because of that expedition, I'd have called him mad.

Clinton's orders had attached us to Colonel John Graves Simcoe, commanding officer of the cavalry branch of Arnold's expedition—the Queen's Rangers that Colonel Rogers had gone with us to Long Island to raise.

Arnold himself, up to three months ago, had been the most brilliant officer in the rebel ranks. He'd led a mere fragment of an army to Quebec through five hundred miles of trackless forest, and done all that any man could have done to separate Canada by force from its allegiance to the King.

In three months' time, on Lake Champlain, he built a fleet with which he delayed England's best soldiers and sailors—a delay that contributed more than any one thing to the blunders that had cumulated in the capture of Burgoyne at Saratoga.

Like so many other rebel leaders, Arnold had entered the war with the understanding that the colonies weren't seeking their independence, but would fight for the right to choose their own governing bodies, make their own laws and levy their own taxes. Like all other Americans who had fought with England in the Old French War to drive France from America, he profoundly distrusted the Catholic French; and one of his and all other rebels' chief sources of dissatisfaction with England was the passage by England of the Quebec Act, which gave to the French in Canada the liberty to profess the Roman Catholic religion. This hatred of French Catholicism was so deep and bitter among New Englanders that they held an alliance with France to be as bad as an alliance with the devil himself.

When Arnold, in addition to being treated outrageously by the rebel Congress, saw Congress conclude a French alliance, he refused to fight the battles of a governing body that to his way of thinking proved itself incompetent, treacherous, futile and childish.

He offered his services to Sir Henry Clinton, and Clinton, instead of accepting them immediately, had urged him to wait until he could strike a more effective blow against the rebel cause. The blow on which Clinton finally settled was the surrender of West Point, controlling fortress of the Hudson, to the British. Before the scheme was carried through, it was discovered, and Arnold had barely escaped to New York with his life.

Since this expedition to Virginia was made up almost wholly of Loyalists, Arnold had been put in command of it.

Arnold, Simcoe and the Queen's Rangers! Many's the tale I've heard about them from many a rebel who never saw any one of them. Arnold, I heard them say, was a monster; Simcoe no better than a bandit, stabbing in the dark; the Queen's Rangers a cowardly horde of renegade Americans who pillaged, raped and barbarously destroyed, or fled in terror before the brave attacks of patriot troops.

I find there's no arguing with those who hold such views; for noncombatants, to their dying day, continue to believe the lies they heard from demagogues who spurred them into war.

But for many a long year, Arnold, Simcoe and the Queen's Rangers have been symbols to me. The Rangers have epitomized all the many, many thousands of Americans who hated the rebels and everything for which they stood; for the Rangers fought the rebels from the beginning of the war to the very end with indomitable courage and ingenuity, and so despised them that they went together as a regiment into exile rather than endure the rule of men they knew to be intolerant and disloyal.

Simcoe will always symbolize to me the pitiful ignorance, the useless delusions, that follow in the wake of war. Simcoe was a scholar, a gentleman, a student of history and military campaigns. He was tireless, beloved by his men, honorable, just and able. So capable a cavalry leader was he that his Rangers were never once routed in their many battles with the rebels. So ably did he comport himself as governor of Upper Canada that lakes and rivers, mountains and townships will forever bear his name.

But Simcoe, in the land where he fought gallantly at the head of gallant Americans fighting to regain the homes from which they had been unjustly driven, will always be unknown or scorned or reviled because he fought on the wrong side—the side that didn't win.

Nothing, I know, is more fruitless than to speculate on what might have been; but I'm as sure as I am of anything that if all the Loyalist regiments could have fought as an army under Arnold and Simcoe, there never would have been a Yorktown.

When Buell and I found ourselves aboard the transport that was to carry us to Virginia, we agreed that war could hold no greater discomfort for us.

Half of Simcoe's Rangers were cavalry; the other half light infantry who would be mounted if ever horses were available. Since Simcoe took boundless pride in his regiment of Rangers, and since it acted as the eyes and the ears as well as the flashing spearhead of every army it accompanied, he insisted, always, that his men and horses be separated as seldom as possible.

"It won't be for long, boys," we heard him telling his men, as we stood on the dock in New York and watched a seemingly endless procession of green-clad Rangers, each man leading his horse, pass thunderously across the gangplank and onto the echoing deck of our transport. "It won't be for long. Pack 'em in and make 'em fast, front and rear."

Those horses were packed into the hold of the transport like herring into a barrel. They were guyed head and tail to keep them from falling when the vessel rolled; guyed under the belly and made fast to hooks overhead so they wouldn't break loose in a storm. Their hoofs were hobbled, and their legs padded with trusses of straw so they'd be damaged as little as possible in case anything hit them.

They stretched the whole length of the hold in a double line, tail to tail, with passageway between. Their heads faced the sides of the ship and the deep, coffinlike shelves in which their masters slept.

Buell's insatiable curiosity took him into the hold to see how the horses were being stowed; and I, realizing that I knew less about the transport of an army than a historian should, went with him.

Already the air was heavy with the breath-taking stench of ammonia peculiar to stables. Even though the hatches were open, the hold was a cave of dark shadows; and the candles, in their pierced tin lanterns, were dim pin points in the choking reek of ammonia.

Buell, scanning the lashings on the horses already jammed into this noisome dungeon, shook his head. "I don't like horses, Oliver," he bawled, to make himself heard above the thunderous thudding of hoofs upon the deck, "but if I was taking one on this trip, I'll be damned if I'd hitch him this way—not if I wanted to use him when I got where I was going! I'd put him in a sling instead of hitching him fore and aft. Why, those critters'll have their legs pulled out if this vessel hits the wrong breeze."

A green-clad officer wearing a dragoon hat shaped like a pewter water pitcher came suddenly from nowhere and thrust his face close to Buell's. "You're not taking a horse?" he asked sharply.

"If I was," Buell said, "I'd be tending to him: not standing here watching other people fix him so his legs would be busted."

"Would you indeed!" the officer said. "Might I ask what you're doing on this vessel if you haven't a horse?"

He looked from Buell to me, seemed puzzled, then turned back to Buell. "If you haven't a horse, you don't belong on this ship. What's your regiment?"

"King's American Dragoons."

"There's no such regiment," the officer said promptly. He raised his voice. "Blake! Sergeant Blake! Bring a lantern." He stared hard at Buell. "King's American Dragoons, eh? We'll see about that."

"I think I can explain," I said. "If there's still doubt, Colonel Simcoe can clear it up. The King's American Dragoons haven't been raised yet, and won't be till Colonel Thompson comes here from England and does it."

A sergeant ran up to us with a tin lantern. The officer seized it and held it to my face. "I guess you'd better see the colonel with me. What's your name?"

When I told him, he said, "Wiswell, eh? I think I may have had a bowing acquaintance with your younger brother at Yale. His name was Oliver Wiswell."

"I'm Oliver Wiswell," I said. "What might your name be?"

"Phillips. Frederick Phillips of New Haven."

I recognized him. He'd been one of the best-liked men in the class ahead of mine—the son of one of Connecticut's oldest and wealthiest families—but he bore only the faintest resemblance to the boy I'd known at Yale. His face was hard, suspicious, old; and it suddenly dawned upon me that he was finding in me exactly what I was seeing in him. I rubbed my face and looked at Buell. Yes, it was true of Buell, too. He'd been hard and bitter when the rebels had covered him with tar and feathers, five long years ago; but he was immeasurably harder and bitterer now. Phillips, at twenty-eight, looked forty-eight. I didn't like to think how I looked to Phillips.

"Don't take offense," Phillips said, "but we have to watch everyone who comes near us or our horses. I take it you're loyal, and your friend, too?"

I said we were; that Colonel Simcoe would vouch for us.

"That's all right," Phillips said. "I'll take your word for it. I want to know what your friend meant when he said he'd put those horses in slings. If he's in a dragoon regiment that doesn't exist, maybe his knowledge of horses is like that too."

"I use horses when I have to," Buell said. "Other times I stay away from 'em. I don't think they've got any brains. I never saw one yet that acted as if he knew what he was doing. I'd rather have a good mule any day. A good mule's got ten times the brains that a horse has. Why, I've seen horses——"

"A horse is a noble animal," Phillips said. "How do you know how to sling 'em if you don't know any more than that about 'em?"

"Because I think about 'em," Buell said. "When you don't like a thing, you're bound to think about it. Being an inventor is part of my trade, and I don't have to think about these horses more than three minutes to invent a better way of tying 'em than you've got here."

"Where you from?" Phillips asked.

"I lived in Newport, Rhode Island, before the riffraff got up from the gutters and started being rebels."

Phillips raised his voice. "Sergeant Blake! Bring four Rhode Islanders." He kicked wet straw from beneath his feet so to have a dry place on which to stand.

"I hope you know what you're talking about," he said to Buell. "I hate to admit it, but horses are the only things in this war that give us trouble. We've won every skirmish we've been in. We've seen almost every rebel regiment between here and Philadelphia run from us. But as soon as we get our horses aboard transports, we're licked! Whenever we put to sea, they get tangled up in knots, break their legs, kick each other to pieces, and die faster than we can throw 'em overboard."

Four Rangers, led by Sergeant Blake, came to attention close behind Phillips. The sergeant saluted smartly and Phillips turned and eyed them as if hopeful of finding something wrong with their dress or appearance. If that was what he expected to find, he was disappointed, for I never saw neater-looking soldiers. They must, I thought, have been drilled by English officers.

"Now listen," Phillips said, "you probably know what happened to General Clinton and Colonel Tarleton when they went down to attack Charleston last spring. They ran into a storm and couldn't handle their horses. You heard about that, didn't you?"

The men silently shifted their feet in the wet straw.

"You must have," Phillips went on. "They had twelve hundred horses to begin with, and they landed with forty-nine. All the way to Charleston they pulled screaming horses from the hold, smashed all to hell, and pitched 'em overboard, still screaming. When Tarleton's Legion got ashore, with the whole army depending on 'em, they couldn't move for a week."

"We heard about it," the sergeant said.

"Yes," Phillips said, "I guess everybody did. Well, we don't want it to happen to us. Now Lieutenant Buell, here, is in the King's American Dragoons. Maybe you haven't heard much about 'em yet, but you will. He's figured out a way to fasten horses so they won't break their legs. He's a native of Rhode Island, like a good part of this troop, and you can trust him. Do whatever he tells you. We'll find out whether his scheme's a good one."

I hoped, as I watched Buell and the five Rangers move toward the tangle of whinnying, snorting, kicking horses wedged into the ammonia-scented gloom at the end of the hold, that his ingenuity wouldn't fail him; for I knew that Phillips' judgment of both of us would be based on Buell's results.

Phillips eyed me thoughtfully. "I thought I'd kept track of all the Yale men who'd joined the Loyalists," he said. "Now and again some of us have dinner together. Both my brothers are captains in Colonel Fanning's regiment—the King's American Regiment. The colonel went to Yale too, and I thought between us we knew every Yale man who'd stayed loyal. If I'd known you were in the army, I'd have tried to get you in the Rangers. It's strange none of us knew."

"I wasn't in the army," I said. "I've been in England. We went to Halifax with General Howe, and when we came back to Long Island, the general had some special work that he wanted me to do. When that was over I went to England and I didn't get home until three weeks ago."

"Special work, eh?" Phillips said. "I see. I see." He didn't see, for he gave me another puzzled look and said, "Well, let's find out what your friend's up to."

Buell's work had been as successful as it had been rapid. He was sitting in a cavalryman's coffinlike bunk, a group of green-clad troopers before him. They had snugly adjusted around a horse's belly a piece of canvas that I took to be half an infantryman's tent. The canvas cradle was suspended by stout rope from two blocks in such a way that as the ship rolled, the rope slipped through the blocks and kept the horse on an approximately level keel.

"Hm," Phillips said, "that doesn't look like much to me. It's too simple."

Buell said nothing, but all the cavalrymen turned to the captain as one man and told him he was wrong. When I first glimpsed the smartness of these green-clad Rangers, I thought they might perhaps be Englishmen recently arrived in America, or long trained under British officers; but this outbreak showed they were Americans, trained by American officers.

When the men stopped shouting, Phillips walked around the horse, pulling dubiously at his fastenings.

"All right," he said, "if you say so, I'll recommend to the general that all Ranger horses be fastened this way. Do you think well enough of it for that?"

They assured him profanely that they did.

Phillips beckoned to Buell. "You and Captain Wiswell come on up with me and see the colonel. I'm going to get him to put you in charge of all horses on this expedition."

Buell groaned. "I always knew that would happen to me as soon as I got in an army! I knew damned well I'd be put to doing something I didn't want to do, and that anybody else ought to be able to do better!"

CHAPTER LXIII

Aɴʏʙᴏᴅʏ who sees war as a romantic adventure would be cured by travel on a horse transport.

Everybody in every war, barring the hermaphrodite soldier who wears a uniform but doesn't fight, lives in a sort of hell. He is perpetually uncomfortable: perpetually too hot or too cold; almost dead from overwork or half mad from inaction; badly fed and worse housed.

But those who live aboard a horse transport live in a true hell. Even in calm weather, a horse transport can be the very devil, rolling insanely from the restless surging of the horses. In rough weather it becomes the seventh or ultimate inferno.

If I had my way, I'd use horse transports as prison ships, and on them I'd incarcerate those human vermin who dare to play with helpless people's lives and happiness—politicians who start wars for simpler, honester men to finish; statesmen who won't end wars because their miserable pride won't let them; statesmen who impose vindictive terms on conquered enemies; all those who profit by wars and talk drivel that passes for patriotism.

We boarded our transport on the eleventh of December. On that day we moved out into midstream and anchored; and there we lay ten days, with a cruel wind from the north howling through our shrouds and kicking up a chop that made the ship stagger and groan, even when at anchor.

The horses were sick; their ammonia-drenched straw froze nightly and had to be chopped from beneath their hoofs each morning. It was the coldest winter New York had known in many a long year; and to keep from freezing aboard that icy ship was a labor in itself.

I saw Buell only at night, when he came to our little cubbyhole off the great cabin, smelling indescribably.

"By God, Oliver," he said, "I knew this was the way it would be! War ain't what you think it's going to be, not once in ten times! In Boston it was eating cats and dodging smelly old rebel grandfathers. In Halifax it was selling secondhand furniture. On Long Island it was parboiling ourselves in a swamp. In New York it was getting drunk to find out how Cunningham murdered prisoners. In London it was feeling guilty for being Americans. In Paris it was stealing papers that didn't do us any good after they were stolen. Here it's horses and horse manure.

"Oliver, I feel as if I'd been aged in frozen horse manure for ten years. Even if I could get myself a bath, which I can't, and splash myself with Henrietta Dixon's French perfumery, I'd still think I had horse manure in my hair and ears and boots. Everything I pick up smells of horse manure. Sometimes I suspect the cook puts it in the soup!"

For me those cold, cold days of waiting had only one advantage. They let me become acquainted with Colonel Simcoe and the officers of his Rangers.

Simcoe was the only Englishman in the regiment. Every other officer and man was an American from Connecticut, Rhode Island or New York. For three years they'd scouted and skirmished in the forefront of every expedition, every battle that Howe and Clinton had fought; and so often had the rebel ranks broken before their charges that they were supremely contemptuous of the rebels: supremely confident of their own ability to outmaneuver and outfight any force that the rebels could bring against them.

A map of Virginia and the Carolinas had been pinned at one end of the great cabin, and Simcoe and his officers stood before it for hours at a time. On it, with colored chalks, was drawn the route followed by Clinton's army, headed by General Cornwallis, when it had struck inland from Charleston, seven months earlier, on its campaign to drive all the rebels out of the south and to release the enormous Loyalist population of the south from rebel persecution.

I had learned a little about that march before I left London—enough to know that it had been a great achievement; but not until I saw Simcoe's map with its long snakelike line of Cornwallis' route wavering up from Charleston into the interior of South Carolina, across into North Carolina and almost to Virginia, did I realize what a tremendous thing he had done.

Cornwallis' long line of light and heavy infantry, artillery, baggage wagons and supply train, with Colonel Tarleton's Loyal Legion ranging ahead as his eyes and ears, had gone almost due north from Charleston. With him had gone officers whose names were to be perpetually on my tongue in the months to come, but now were only names, uttered respectfully in connection with exploits that seemed unreal, like passages from mythology—Lord Rawdon, Colonel Cruger, Colonel O'Hara, and scores of others. Two of the names, Cruger and Rawdon, seemed to be mentioned together, always, like tongues and cheeks, eggs and bacon. Rawdon and Cruger; Cruger and Rawdon; Rawdon had sent for Cruger and marched forty miles in a day; Cruger had marched a hundred miles in three days; Cruger had routed a thousand rebels with one battalion of DeLancey's. The two names, Cruger and DeLancey's, recalled the flight of the rebels from New York, and John Harris Cruger, son-in-law of Oliver DeLancey, who had driven with Stedman and me to Kip's Bay.

Those regiments of Cornwallis' had marched one hundred miles up the Santee River, another thirty miles up the Wateree River to Camden, where they had defeated General Gates and a much larger rebel army so decisively that the rebel militia ran all the way back to Virginia, while Gates himself ran eighty miles between sunrise and dark.

From Camden Cornwallis had marched another sixty miles north to Charlotte; then made a two-hundred-mile swing back to South Carolina and around to Salisbury in North Carolina in order to rally the cowed Loyalists in that region.

His army had last been heard from in Salem, North Carolina, midway of an arc drawn from Charleston to Richmond, Virginia; and it was the country between Salem and Richmond that Simcoe and his officers were studying on the big map.

They were memorizing every river, creek, swamp, fork, run, bridge, falls, ford and ferry in that whole stretch of country. There were few towns to remember; but all crossroads and ordinaries were marked on the map, and they knew the location of every one of them.

After they'd studied the map for an hour, Simcoe would question them. Their answers seemed to me little short of marvelous.

"Captain Phillips," he asked, "where's Hatton's Ordinary?"

"Hatton's?" Phillips said. "Hatton's? Let me see!"

He covered his eyes with his hand, and I thought he was at a loss. but he wasn't.

"Hatton's," he said slowly, "is twelve miles south of Petersburg. It's on a road that touches Indian Swamp at that point. Four miles south of Hatton's is Hall's house. Three miles south of Hall's there's a crossroad that crosses two creeks on the north side of the Nottoway River."

"Exactly right, Captain Phillips," Colonel Simcoe said. "Captain Hallet, are you familiar with that section?"

"Yes, sir."

"All right," Simcoe said. "Suppose you're moving south on a scout from Petersburg. When you've passed Hatton's Ordinary, you find yourself cut off by a greatly superior force. What road will you take back to Petersburg?"

"I won't take that crossroads over the two creeks," Hallet said. "I'll keep on twenty miles south, to Bick's Ordinary on the Meherrin. There's a road to the westward at the Meherrin. I'll go west eight miles to Brunswick Four Corners, west another eight miles to Westward Ford. From Westward Ford there's a road to Petersburg."

Never a word of advice did Simcoe give me during those first days aboard the transport, but again and again I caught him studying me.

"What's the matter with him?" I asked Phillips. "He acts as if he didn't trust me."

"He doesn't," Phillips said. "He doesn't trust any Americans who aren't Loyalists; and he says he's never quite sure they're genuine Loyalists till he's seen 'em fight. He thinks most Americans are hypocrites, and never realize it. He says they start a rebellion against constituted authority, but resent being called rebels; that they talk at the top of their lungs about freedom and liberty and being made slaves of, and all the time they're killing and beating Loyalists, and treating Negro slaves a hundred times worse than any other country would ever treat 'em. He says their gods are Intolerance, Bigotry and Prejudice."

"My, my!" Buell said. "He sounds kind of prejudiced."

"He is," Phillips agreed. "He says they find excuses for doing any unfair thing, and all the time insist they're not doing it. He says all the New England rebels swore to God they didn't want to be independent, but planned to be as soon as they'd coaxed the rest of the country into the revolution.

"He says Connecticut and Rhode Island's full of rebels who howl

at the top of their lungs against Tories and England during the daytime; then row over to Long Island at night in whaleboats and sell us
everything they own.

"He says Philadelphia's full of Quakers who talk mighty impressive
about being neutral and not doing anything to help war; then sell
supplies to the British provided they're paid in gold.

"No: Simcoe doesn't like rebels, and he's got to make up his mind
about you before he likes you."

Fortunately for us, Simcoe made up his mind the day before we
sailed, and for no reason except that he heard me say the merest
fragment of what was in my mind about the British ministry.

Phillips and I were standing alone—or so we thought—before the
great map, familiarizing ourselves with the mountain chain that
separates Virginia and the Carolinas from the interior of America, and
Phillips was confidently predicting how easily the vast stretch of
country between the mountains and the sea could be cleared of rebels

"They can't cope with the way we fight. They particularly can't
cope with our cavalry. They don't understand anything about it.
Mostly they run as soon as they see cavalry. When they don't run,
they try waiting till they can see the whites of our eyes, the way they
did at Bunker Hill. It never seems to occur to 'em that such waiting
can't stop cavalry. We're on top of 'em when they fire, and then it's
all over because they don't have time to reload. They haven't got a
chance against us!"

I told him that I hoped he was right, but that I'd never feel wholly
confident until we were relieved of the necessity of depending on
British ministries for supplies and assistance.

The words had scarcely left my mouth, when I found Simcoe at
my elbow and heard him ask in a coldly brittle voice exactly what I
meant.

"I didn't know you were there, sir," I said. "I'm sorry I spoke as I
did."

Simcoe spoke frostily. "May I ask why you're sorry?"

"Because I learned long ago that an American can't discuss British
politics with an Englishman without antagonizing him."

"I don't want to discuss politics, Captain Wiswell," Simcoe said.
"I'm a soldier. A soldier should be above politics."

"Yes, sir," I said, "I've heard so."

Simcoe cleared his throat. "I mean what I say, Captain Wiswell.

I'm neither Whig nor Tory. I welcome information, no matter where I find it. You seem to have formed some definite opinions about the British ministry. I'd like to know what they are. They might help me form an opinion some day, if I ever found myself in a tight corner."

"Well, sir," I said, "my experience has been that the ministry will never do what it should about America when it should—never! They were told they'd have to send forty thousand men over here this year if they wanted to see the war settled favorably. They didn't even send half that number. They've been told again and again the amount of supplies that would be needed in America at stated times. Never once have they sent the amount they were supposed to send! Never once!"

Simcoe looked me up and down, then turned to the map and thrust his face close to that long mountain range that extended like a barrier along the western ends of Virginia and the Carolinas. "Not a good map," he complained.

He turned back to me. "Tell you what you do, Captain. General Arnold's coming aboard the flagship this afternoon. I think you'd better meet him. From what I hear, he knows more than most about the back parts of America. I'll get him to tell you what he knows before the expedition gets under way. You'll find it helpful."

He seemed startled at his own loquacity, turned on his heel and left the cabin.

Phillips looked surprised. "Now don't that beat hell!" he said. "I had to lead a cavalry charge to make him stop looking over my head when he spoke to me, and here he's cottoned to you before you've even taken part in a skirmish."

I don't know what sort of commanding general I expected to see when I rowed with Colonel Simcoe and half a dozen of his officers— Captain Phillips, Captain Murray, Captain Shank, Lieutenant Spencer, Captain Althause of the York Volunteers, Captain Thomas of the Bucks County Volunteers—to General Arnold's transport.

Arnold had led troops hundreds of miles through the wilderness. He had inflicted defeat after defeat on English armies. Even rebel militia, who had earned the reputation of being the worst soldiers ever to take the field, had willingly followed him into battle. He had built a fleet out of nothing and fought as brave a fight with it as any admiral could have fought.

I had a picture of what he must be: a nebulous outline of a giant of a man—rough, hearty, violent, hail-fellow-well-met.

I could see that all the other officers in our boat were a little doubtful about Arnold. I was a little doubtful myself, but I wasn't sure why. He had fought long and ably for the rebels, in behalf of a cause that I despised with all my heart. Perhaps I was doubtful whether, so soon, he could fight as ably on the side I hoped would win. Truth to tell, I had no clear thoughts about him except a sort of vague antagonism—though why I should have felt antagonism for a man who had abandoned a cause I hated to take up arms for the one to which I was attached is more than I can say.

There were forty officers crowded into the great cabin of the *Pendrith* when we entered it, and from the way they leaped to their feet when Simcoe came down the companionway, I knew General Arnold wasn't there.

The cabin was bitter cold, a knifelike wind blew through the stern gun ports, and all forty officers were glum and silent—perhaps from cold; perhaps from uncertainty; perhaps because of that vague antagonism toward General Arnold that seemed to fill us all. For my own part, I had no desire to speak, and depression weighed upon me like a pall.

CHAPTER LXIV

WHILE we stood there staring dourly at each other or at our own half-frozen feet, a door in the bulkhead swung open with a crash. Beyond the door we saw a small, candlelighted cabin. There was a table in it, and at the table sat two officers with papers before them. A third officer—the one who had thrown open the door—stood over them. He was a short man in a green coat and white breeches, and he stood balanced on his toes, springy and alert.

"Send five copies to every transport before nightfall," he said. "Commanding officer of troops, captain of the transport, three copies tacked up where all can see." His voice had a peculiar harsh shrillness, as though he forced it out by main strength; and the sound of it drove from me all depression and uncertainty.

He clapped a three-cornered hat on his head, whirled and came out among us. He was swarthy and not tall; yet there was something about the way in which he threw back his head, something about his manner of balancing lightly on the balls of his feet, that made him seem large. If I hadn't known he was a fighter, I might have taken him for a fop, for he wore white lace at throat and wrists, and under his beautifully fitting green coat was a waistcoat of pale fur that I took to be winter weasel.

He looked up at Simcoe, as cocky as a bantam. "My sincere apologies, Colonel and gentlemen," he said. "The delay wasn't intentional, I assure you. Where's that punch? I ordered hot punch to take the curse off this damnable cold."

As if he'd made a silent signal, a waiter came into the cabin bearing an enormous bowl of steaming punch, and another waiter followed with glasses.

567

"Hah!" Arnold said. "Have a tot with me, gentlemen, to success and warmer weather!"

He handed a steaming glass to Simcoe, took one himself and waited till the rest of us had been served.

"Here you are, gentlemen," he said. "A quick trip and a victorious campaign: confusion to all rebels and success to every loyal American!"

When we'd downed our second glass, we felt better. There was something about Arnold's quick movements, his brisk utterances, his harsh voice, that sent the blood more rapidly through my veins; and from the look of those about me, they felt as I did.

He wasted no time on small talk. "The tide serves at sunrise tomorrow, and we're sailing then, no matter what the wind is. We've waited too long already, but we'll make up for lost time when we get where we're going. After we've started, we won't see much of each other until we're ready to land; and you can take my word for it that there'll be no delays in landing. That being so, I've called you here to wish you all a good voyage and to give you one order in person."

He clasped his hands behind him, thrust out his underlip, balanced himself upon his toes and rounded his eyes at us. It was almost as if he strained to catch from somewhere among us a murmur of disaffection or criticism. He made me think of a hawk making ready to stoop on his prey.

There wasn't a sound in that cold cabin except those from outside —distant shouts from other transports, the tap of sentries' heels on the quarter-deck above, the whinnying of horses from below, the squalling of the sea gulls that soared endlessly across the openings of the gun ports.

Arnold seemed to relax. "This expedition," he said, "has only one objective. Too many supplies are reaching the rebel army from Virginia. Our business is to stop it—to destroy all supplies we can reach. This is a part of an even greater objective, gentlemen—that of putting an end to this war in the shortest possible time.

"Now all of you, barring Colonel Simcoe, are Americans. All the men you command are Americans. The entire rank and file of the Queen's Rangers, the American Legion, Captain Althause's York Volunteers and the Bucks County Volunteers are Americans. Their desires, I'm certain, are no different from my own, and no different from those of the commander in chief.

"Some of you've said openly that you consider the execution of the unfortunate Major André a barbarous and ungenerous act. You've held yourselves personally injured and insulted by his hanging. I'm familiar with Colonel Simcoe's orders in which he said that the Queen's Rangers will never sully their glory in the field by any undue severity—that they'll always consider everyone in captured towns and districts, Loyalists and rebels alike, as under their protection—that they'll strike at their misguided fellow countrymen only with the greatest reluctance."

He made Colonel Simcoe a quick little bow. "Those orders, Colonel, are a credit to you and your corps of loyal Americans. I hope they'll be taken to heart by every member of this expedition. Unfortunately this is a civil war, marked by the bitter hatreds that go with all civil wars; and many and many a time the whole lot of you will find yourselves close to forgetting those orders."

He balanced himself on his toes in that peculiar way of his, thrust out his underlip and stared at us speculatively from round eyes that were startlingly blue against his swarthy skin.

"You've seen bitter hatreds in your fighting around New York, gentlemen," he went on. "You've seen Loyalists treated as you thought no human beings could ever be treated by men who call themselves civilized. You've seen 'em beaten, kicked, driven as though they'd committed crimes."

He tapped his forefinger against his palm. "That's what you've seen, so far; but what you've seen in the north isn't a scratch to what you're going to see in the south. Down there they hate! They're bitter and they're cruel! They kill with axes, in the dark! The Loyalists are mostly Scots, and when they're badly treated—and they have been!— they repay with interest. The rebels are even worse. If any of you fall into the hands of southern rebels, it'll go hard with you, so stay out of their reach!"

His already swarthy face seemed to broaden and grow darker. "You'll find yourselves close to forgetting your orders," he said again, "but you mustn't do it. You must not forget! Let none of your men try to avenge themselves for real or fancied injuries to themselves, their officers or their country. It's our sacred duty to overthrow the rebel Congress that has brought misery and ruin to America, and is now doing its utmost to turn it over to the French; but if any member of this expedition is guilty of unnecessary violence—if any member of this expedition commits depredations against private citizens or private property, he will be increasing the bitterness of the rebels against the Loyalist cause. He'll be encouraging rebels to take even more violent action against Loyalist neighbors than they have already taken. If this should happen, we'll be deprived of the services of southern Loyalists just when we need 'em most.

"So it's the order of the commander in chief, and it's my fixed intention, that any man taken in misdemeanors shall suffer death!"

He seemed to swell and grow taller. I could have sworn a sort of warmth came out from him and struck against our faces.

"This is our country!" he said, and his voice made me shiver. "It's our country, and we want it back. If any man is so willful, so short-sighted, as to hinder us in getting it back, I'll kill him myself!"

He turned abruptly to the punch bowl and picked up a glass.

"That's all, gentlemen! Now we can drink to the day when hypocrisy and misrule in America goes back to the gutter, where it belongs."

I was impressed, when Simcoe presented his younger officers to Arnold, by the alertness of Arnold's mind. He was genuinely interested in them, and seemed to know something about nearly every man Simcoe brought to him. Those protruding dark eyes of his pried into those to whom he talked. He placed men's homes from the mere inflection of their voices.

"Captain Carlyle, eh?" he said to one. "What's your first name, Captain?"

The green-jacketed officer stared over the general's head. "Meredith, sir."

"Pennsylvania," Arnold said. "There was an Abraham Carlyle in Philadelphia. You're a relation?"

"Yes, sir."

"Indeed! What relation was Abraham Carlyle to you?"

"Uncle, sir."

"Good," Arnold said, "good! Glad to have you with us. You'll do well, Captain: I'm sure of that. I knew Abraham Carlyle. One of his ancestors founded Philadelphia. He was respected and loved—even after the rebels accused him of treason. He was loved and respected even more when Joseph Reed and Judge McKean had him hanged. He was guilty of nothing but telling the truth! We'll try to see your distinguished uncle is some day properly honored for his stand against disloyalty and oppression."

He turned his round-eyed stare on me. There was wariness in it, and defiance, and a sort of inflexible determination.

"This is Captain Wiswell, General," Simcoe said. "He's the one I told you about."

"Yes," Arnold said, "Wiswell, I know. Wiswell. I've got a few questions I want to ask you, Captain—questions about France and England."

"I ventured to tell Captain Wiswell," Simcoe said, "that you might give him some information about the south that he won't find on the maps."

"No time like the present," Arnold said. He turned on his heel and went at what I might almost describe as a limping run toward the door of the room in which I'd first seen him. When he threw the door open, his aide and his secretary still sat at the table, writing letters.

"Here, here," Arnold told them, "I can't have this! Get out, both of you! Get yourselves some hot punch! Make yourselves known to all these officers here, and get acquainted with them."

As the two young men rose to their feet, Arnold added, "Get my map of the Virginias and Carolinas, Sims."

The table at which the young men had been sitting was stacked with books, letters and papers of various sorts. When the aide brought the map, Arnold flipped it open, tentlike, over the piles of papers and books. He kicked a stool before the table, swung a leg stiffly before him, let himself down on the stool with a thump and gave me a quick stare out of those eyes that seemed so strangely blue in a face so swarthy. "You were in France a few months, General Clinton tells me, Captain Wiswell. See much of the French?"

"A little, sir."

"Enough to form an opinion on the officers the French were sending to the rebels?"

"Yes, sir," I said. "They were a bad lot. Most of the titles they boasted weren't theirs at all. Half of 'em traveled under assumed names."

"Why, in your opinion," Arnold went on, "are the French so enthusiastic in the rebel cause?"

"They aren't, sir. French people don't care two snaps for the rebels or their war. The rebel commissioners, Franklin, Silas Deane and Arthur Lee, couldn't go out on the streets in Paris without being jeered."

Arnold thumped the table. "Yes, by God! Isn't the French govern‑ment helping the rebels for the sole purpose of embarrassing Eng‑land?"

"Certainly, sir."

Arnold turned pop-eyes on Simcoe. "There you are, Colonel! You'll come around to my way of thinking some day. Send your regulars home and let us fight this war with American troops, and you couldn't keep a Frenchman within three thousand miles of America."

Simcoe made no answer.

Arnold laughed sardonically, and turned to his map. "I know why you're going south, Captain Wiswell. The idea's not bad, but look out for yourself. You'll have to be mighty careful. Had reports of the battle of King's Mountain reached England before you sailed?"

"No, sir."

Arnold grunted. "Well, that'll give you the general idea. The battle was fought by Major Patrick Ferguson of the British regular estab‑lishment, and eight hundred North Carolina Loyalists. He was march‑ing to join Cornwallis when fifteen hundred North and South Caro‑lina rebels contrived to catch up with him. He made a stand on the top of King's Mountain. Ferguson was an able leader, but like many other British officers"—he half rose to make a quick bow to Simcoe —"of whom you, Colonel, are not one, he couldn't forget lessons learned on European battlefields.

"His post on the mountain exposed him to fire from every side. The rebels, as any woodsman would have anticipated, crept up on Ferguson's men behind the shelter of the trees, surrounded them, and shot them to pieces at their leisure.

"When Ferguson was killed, his force surrendered, but the rebels kept right on killing. You'll find the southern rebels a pretty hard lot, Captain. They're backwoodsmen; savages! Over a hundred Loyalists were killed after the white flag was raised. Ten Loyalist officers were hanged without trial—presumably for fighting too persistently against overwhelming odds. Major Ferguson's body was stripped and slashed with knives."

Simcoe muttered under his breath.

Arnold slowly turned his head, owl-like, to stare at him. "Too many expensive old retainers in that army of yours, Colonel! Some day it'll bankrupt you!"

Seemingly banishing King's Mountain from his mind, he pulled the map to him and put a finger on the diagonal dark line of mountains across its upper corner. "When you've gone as far as you can with me, Captain," he said, "you'll probably be somewhere near Richmond, and you'll in all likelihood have to travel about a hundred miles due north, through Virginia, to find the Convention Army. I'm not sure, but I think you'll find it near Winchester or Frederick.

"When you've got the information you need about the Convention Army, there'll be several courses for you to follow in order to make that information available to your superiors. You can try to get back to my expedition on the James River. That's a hundred miles. Or you can keep on to the northward and try to reach New York. That's about five hundred miles. Or if you find yourself intercepted, you can strike inland to the mountains and skirt around to the south until you're able to strike off for one of Cornwallis' bases, like Camden or Ninety Six in the interior, say, or Charleston or Savannah on the coast. That's a long, long way.

"If you choose either of the first two courses you can depend on your maps, but you can't depend on the people. That is, you can't be wholly sure anybody's a Loyalist unless you actually see him fighting rebels. God knows how many messengers Ferguson sent to Cornwallis. He sent plenty, but none of 'em got through. All shot on the way. Every last one of 'em!"

He rubbed his finger along that diagonal dark line of mountains. "If you decide to skirt around to the south, don't ask anybody any questions, and don't expect any map to help you. You'll be hunting for just one thing: Boone's Wilderness Road, and it isn't on any map."

He jabbed his finger against the town of Winchester, high up in Virginia; then drew it diagonally southward, through the heart of the shadowed mountains.

"There's a road through those mountains, Captain," he said. "Boone's Wilderness Road to Kentucky! I know it goes through Salem and Roanoke, but beyond Roanoke there aren't any towns, and I can only tell you that it goes on and on till it slips through a big gap in the mountains and vanishes into Kentucky. Somewhere south of that gap there's a place called Ninety Six. If you ever get within striking distance of Ninety Six, you'll be in the heart of a section that's almost solidly loyal—more so, even, than New York or Long Island or Philadelphia. They say there isn't a house within a hundred miles of Ninety Six that hasn't at least one Loyalist in it.

"But how near Boone's Wilderness Road runs to Ninety Six, I can't tell you. I wish I could. You couldn't bring us more valuable information than a full description of that road—where it goes, who travels on it, who's in Kentucky. I'd like to know all about it. The information's bound to come in handy one of these days.

"I know this, though: anybody in Virginia or North Carolina will strike Boone's Road if he keeps moving northwest."

He pushed back his stool and fixed an appraising eye upon me. In that pale glance of his there was a cold calculation that once more put me in mind of a hawk. Simcoe had the same look. Clinton had it, Howe had it, and so, I think, do all professional soldiers whose business it has been to send men to their death.

"You're going alone, Captain?" he asked.

"No, sir," I said. "I'm taking a good friend. He's resourceful, and I figured that if I didn't get through, he might."

Arnold looked doubtful. "Two's a lot."

"I don't think so," I said. "Buell and I figured we needed two."

"In what way?" Arnold asked.

"Well, sir," I said, "if this expedition attacks towns along the James River, we figure it'll be the most natural thing in the world if a lot of the people get scared and run away. We figure nobody'd ever think of stopping a doctor and his assistant who were making their escape, particularly if the doctor had a full supply of Perkins' Metallic Tractors and made a point of giving a pair of 'em to anyone who started to be unpleasant."

"Perkins' Metallic Tractors," Arnold cried. "Why, I know all about Perkins and his tractors! He came from Norwich and so did I! Those tractors of his wouldn't cure anyone but old women who claim to be sick because they can't think of anything else to talk about! You'll have to be careful how you make claims for those tractors."

"That's what Buell thinks," I told him. "He says their chief advantage is their power of distracting rebels. He says the rebel mind is discontented with everything and everybody, and so constituted that it accepts any remedy for what ails it. He says a rebel can't resist buying Perkins' Metallic Tractors—that he turns toward bad leaders and worthless remedies just as a flower turns toward the sun."

Arnold smacked his hand on the table. "By God, it's the truth!" He opened his mouth wide in a silent laugh. "Worthless remedies and bad leaders! Paper currency, Committees of Information, General Putnam, Ethan Allen, Congress and Perkins' Metallic Tractors! It's perfect!"

He tapped a finger on the table to emphasize his words. "You'll get through all right, Captain; and I have only one suggestion to make: When you make up your mind to go somewhere, go quick! I mention this because you've been in England, and might just possibly have picked up some English ideas."

I saw he was talking as much for Simcoe's benefit as for my own. "The English like to make up their minds to do something, and then take their time about it. This fleet has been lying here ten days. It could have sailed eight days ago. Eight days' delay is damned nonsense, Captain! If every British army that needs help has to wait eight days for it, there'll be many a time when the help won't do anybody any good."

He looked at Simcoe. "Maybe you remember, Colonel: help could have been got to Burgoyne eight days before he surrendered. If he'd got it, he needn't have surrendered."

Simcoe didn't answer. Arnold looked satirical, and I caught in his eye the merest faint hint of a wink.

"You understand, Captain," he went on, "that these observations of mine probably wouldn't be welcome in some quarters, where the need of rapid movement hasn't yet been grasped. I must confess I don't understand why it isn't welcome; but it certainly isn't! Not long ago I had occasion to observe a march made by General Tryon and Sir William Erskine into Connecticut. They barely escaped. Yet if they'd marched two hours sooner, as they easily could, they'd have met no opposition whatever. And if they'd delayed another hour, they'd have been utterly destroyed. So when you decide to move, move fast. If you move as fast as possible, you'll nearly always be successful."

He jumped up, clapped me on the back, and wished me luck. When I'd have voiced my gratitude, he waved my thanks aside, opened the door and pushed us out into the great cabin.

What he had told me, I knew, was the simple truth, and yet I sensed that Simcoe didn't quite approve of him or of anything he'd said.

I have thought often of Arnold—of his astuteness, his great ability as a soldier, his kindness to me, the ingratitude with which the British repaid the sacrifices he made for them. I think many high British officers, though they sought Arnold's help and welcomed it, were always illogically resentful of him for being a turncoat. I know Simcoe admired him as a soldier, and never thought of him as a traitor and therefore objectionable or untrustworthy. I think Simcoe's attitude toward Arnold was at bottom what Eden's and Germaine's and the King's had been toward Buell and me, toward Wentworth and Bancroft. I think he was bound by the peculiar class distinctions of England, which make it impossible for any Englishman to take criticism from an Englishman of a lower class, and make all Englishmen regard every foreigner, every colonial, every American, as an inferior from whom criticism cannot be accepted.

CHAPTER LXV

Never, I think, has any soldier been as misrepresented as
has Arnold.

Why this should have been so, I can only surmise. He spoke the
truth, which is offensive to many at any time, and usually a downright crime during a war. He was quick to show contempt for stupidity
and carelessness—which infuriates most soldiers, who are by nature
both careless and stupid. He aroused jealousy and fear in lesser men
and lesser soldiers, which accounts for the bitter enmity shown toward
him by Congress and by his most inveterate enemy Joseph Reed, the
Philadelphia Quaker-Killer.

He was a great soldier, doing his utmost, singlehanded—which is
in itself held to be a crime—to save America from self-ruin and
French domination. I suspected this even before our transports had
been sheathed in ice and blown on their beam ends by the miserable
northwest wind that yowled through our rigging as loudly, almost, as
the horses squealed and whinnied in our holds. I was sure of it nine
days later, when two thirds of our little fleet lay at anchor in the
shelter of Point Comfort at the mouth of the James River.

In a few short miles we had passed from frigid winter to the balmy
light airs of spring; from frozen misery into a bearable existence;
and if any Britisher had been in command of that expedition, we'd
have lain there at anchor, shooting our hurt horses, throwing over
the dead ones, ridding decks and holds of filth and stench, recovering from our own seasickness, and waiting—waiting weeks,
perhaps—to be rejoined by ships that might, for all we knew,
have either been blown five hundred miles to sea, or gone to the
bottom.

But Arnold was different. When he set out to do a thing, nothing on earth, seemingly, could stop him. He was like a tireless demon, driving himself and everyone with him to endeavors and accomplishments beyond the abilities of mere humans.

Scarcely, it seemed to me, had our anchor cable rumbled through the hawsehole when we saw a boat from the *Pendrith* rowing from ship to ship. The general's aide, Captain Sims, stood in the stern, and when he reached our own vessel, he gave his message without bothering to come over the side.

From our little cubbyhole of a sleeping box, off the great cabin, where we were cleaning the traces of sleepless nights and stormy days from us as best we could, we heard him repeating his orders to the officer of the deck:

"All cavalry officers from and including the rank of captain to General Arnold's vessel for a council of war. All other officers clean and repair ship. All vessels will move up-river in exactly one hour."

Buell, shirtless, his face covered with lather and an open razor in his hand, leaped from his seat on the edge of his bedplace and thrust his head from an open port.

"Hey, Sims," he bawled, "tell 'em not to cut down the horses! Tell 'em to leave the horses trussed up. Don't let 'em take off the slings!" He withdrew his head from the port, reached for his soiled shirt and hurriedly wiped the lather from his face.

"Jesus, Oliver," he said, "this feller Arnold ain't like the others! When he sets out to fight, Oliver, it looks to me as if he didn't propose to waste time on anything but fighting."

He dashed shirtless from the cabin, and I heard him on deck, bawling: "Let those horses alone! Don't cut down one damned horse!"

True to Captain Sims' word, we were on our way up the river in another hour almost to the minute; and if ever any expedition showed more energy and alacrity than this one showed, I never heard of it. On every vessel the troops, dissatisfied at the slowness of the sailors, did duty as sailors themselves. They hauled around the yards to take advantage of bends in the river and shifts in the breeze. Whenever the breeze slackened, they manned the boats and towed the ships.

I've heard it said that Arnold's motives in leading that expedition up the James River were purely vindictive: that he ordered troops to

destroy public and private property out of a vicious desire to injure
the country which he had already foully wronged.

Nothing could be farther from the truth. He was fighting, just as
thousands of us were fighting, to save his country from misery and
ruin. His sole object was to destroy military stores; no depredations
of any sort were committed; and rebel militia who mistook a body of
the Queen's Rangers for their own people and stumbled into Simcoe's
lines were treated both by Simcoe and by Arnold with more consideration than any body of Loyalists in a similar situation ever received at the hands of rebels.

On the morning of January fourth our fleet of thirty vessels rounded
a bend in the river and came into a basin on the far side of which
stood a grand mansion of pink brick. This was Westover, the home
of Colonel Byrd, whose wife was Arnold's cousin; and it was from
Westover that we would set out on our forty-mile march to Richmond.

What we needed to screen our departure from Arnold's army, Buell
and I agreed, was some sort of battle between Arnold's troops and
rebel forces. Only under cover of the excitement and tumult of an
engagement, it seemed to us, could we leave the expedition in circumstances that would seem wholly natural.

For a time we thought the opportunity would never come; for
whenever we saw rebels, either mounted or on foot, they scuttled
off down side lanes or into the forests like human rabbits. What
was more, from every plantation we passed, from every side road
and every little cabin, came a trickle of Negroes, who fell in on both
sides of our long mounted column, so that we rode, as it were, in a
sort of torrent of black men and women and children, all staring open-
mouthed as they trotted beside us.

We had the feeling that if we left the column for a moment, we'd
be surrounded and followed by these friendly black people, and so be
unable to conceal our movements from anyone.

God only knows what harsh treatment brought these Negroes in
such numbers to the protection of our green-clad squadrons; but
their eagerness to cling to our stirrup leathers didn't speak highly
for the brand of liberty and equality of which the rebels claimed to
be the sole exponents.

We were two days marching from Westover to Richmond; and
they were days of recurring pictures—fine big houses with brick

walls and tall pillars, from behind whose hedges Negroes rose up grinning, then came out into the road to patter along with all the other blacks who ran beside us; miserable windowless shanties and tumble-down stands of buildings at bleak crossroads; distant hilltops from which groups of mounted rebels watched us, only to vanish like smoke when Simcoe's advance guards trotted toward them; Arnold, swarthy, high-chested, sardonic, cantering back the length of the column, urging us on, urging us on; the unending stumbling of our horses, weak from the pitching and rolling of the transports; Arnold spurring up to regain the head of the column, his black mare miraculously tireless, as if fed by some inexhaustible reservoir of her master's; the strange formation in which Arnold made us march, strung out in a long, long single file so that rebels, looking at us from far away, would think us twice as numerous as we were.

"They won't fight," Arnold kept saying. "They won't fight! Push on fast, boys. They won't fight!"

He was right. The rebels wouldn't fight. Not a trench, not a militia company opposed us as we rode up a steep bank onto the high land where Richmond stood; and when we clattered with the green-coated Rangers into the central square of the little town, nobody could have been friendlier than the crowds who watched from the windows of houses and shops.

We didn't stay there long—only long enough for Arnold to unroll his maps and point out to his officers the location of the property he wanted destroyed. In ten minutes' time the square was half empty, and in fifteen minutes the Rangers were on their way toward Westham, six miles above Richmond.

Westham was a grimy, desolate-looking settlement beside the river, centered around a sprawling foundry from which tall brick chimneys strained upward like the dead fingers of a stricken giant. So quickly did Simcoe lead his men into the little town that the inhabitants had no warning, and went scuttling off into the brush in panic terror, leaving behind them household belongings, poultry, horses, cows. In five minutes a third of the Rangers stood guard on the outskirts of the town, while the others, dismounted, destroyed the contents of the foundry.

The noise and the turmoil of that destruction was like something out of an inferno. Rather than run the risk of unnecessarily hurting one of his own men, Colonel Simcoe refused to fire the buildings until the powder in the main magazine had been destroyed. Accordingly the Rangers worked like slaves, carrying powder barrels down the steep cliff and emptying them into the river. The other half, with tools from the forges, knocked trunnions from cannon, destroyed thousands of muskets, and finally set fire to the main building and the warehouses.

To the tune of clanging steel on steel, crackling flames, thunderous explosions and hoarse shouts of officers spurring their men to greater activity, Buell and I set about turning ourselves into refugees.

Two hours later our work was done. Our belongings, augmented by a pen of chickens and various odds and ends which Buell found in deserted houses, were stowed in a commodious wagon which we had constructed from three farm carts.

When we left Westham in the early afternoon of January fifth, 1781, a boiling curtain of black smoke was pouring upward from the whole long line of warehouses, shanties, foundry and sheds that together made up the rebels' most important munitions works. The smoke lay over the countryside like a sulphurous fog, and as our cart bumped and rattled out from the shelter of that fog, we made a perfect picture of panic-stricken refugees fleeing from barbarous invaders.

Nobody, Buell said, is so trusted by frightened, sick or ignorant people as an unscrupulous doctor, willing to promise anything an audience wants to hear.

I think he was right; for whenever travelers approached us, on that long trip to the northward, Buell's bombastic utterances in behalf of Perkins' Metallic Tractors either held them spellbound and oblivious of everything except their desire for a pair of the miraculous implements, or filled them with a desire to be off on other business before they could be talked into purchasing such expensive luxuries.

On the approach of any person or group of persons, Buell would stop the horse, hand me the reins, and lean eagerly from the wagon.

"Opportunity," he'd say, "knocks but once on every man's door; and here, sir, is your opportunity—the last remaining set of the celebrated Doctor Elisha Perkins' Metallic Tractors."

In trembling tones he'd tell how the arrival of the British in Richmond had cut off his supplies by sea, and how he had been forced to flee before the tyrants and set off for the home of the celebrated Doctor Perkins, in order to replenish his stock of tractors.

"With these tractors," he'd say, holding up two from the bagful he carried under the wagon seat, "sufferers can draw from the body diseases of the most obstinate nature, which have hitherto baffled medical art. Only one human ailment sometimes resists the potent power of Perkins' Metallic Tractors. Occasionally the headache that arises from drinking to excess refuses to yield immediately to them. All others, if the tractors be used properly, intelligently and diligently, flow outward from the limbs in the wake of the tractors, and vanish away like snow before the spring rain. In the city of Philadelphia, sirs, a lady of quality was so affected by chronic rheumatism that for three years she had been unable to rock her baby's cradle. Then Perkins' Metallic Tractors drew the crippling pain from her and I myself saw her swim across the Schuylkill River with one arm tied to her side. The itching of insect bites, the burning of poison ivy, sore teats in cattle, offensive catarrh, black eyes, all are expeditiously vanquished by the use of Perkins' Metallic Tractors. Heart trouble, tender bowels, sprained ankles, gallstones, pimples, weak kidneys, torpid liver, acid stomach, consumption of the lungs, warts, toothache and piles may be cured once and for all by Perkins' Metallic Tractors. If used daily while the user thinks persistently of love, business success or money, the user will inevitably be rewarded by the thing of which he thinks. It draws the carbon from the inner recesses of the body, relieves men and women of gas on the stomach, and restores virility to the aged. It extracts pin and stomach worms, stops dizziness and belching, makes childbirth easy, cures boils, palpitating heart, ulcers, shortsightedness and cross-eyes, and is unrivaled for pricking powder from the touchhole of a musket.

"Merely draw the tractors downward from the seat of trouble . . . as a great sacrifice I am parting with this invaluable tool and weapon for five guineas. . . ."

Sometimes his audiences shared their suppers with us, and on such occasions Buell would give them his "last" pair of tractors and urge them not to expect a complete cure for a month.

It was a miserable country through which we passed—a country harried, deadened, frightened, strangled by civil war. Men hid in patches of woodland to watch us go by. A dozen times a day groups of surly armed men halted us, listened to Buell, bought his "last" pair of tractors, and let us go on.

The plantations we passed looked unkempt and deserted, as if their owners had long since moved away. The small houses were miserable beyond words, dirty, unglazed, unpainted—the homes of people idle and lazy beyond the conception of New Englanders in similar walks of life.

All through that long trip, we slept wherever night overtook us; and when it rained or snowed we turned the cart on its side, propped it with poles, and slumbered beneath it as comfortably as if we'd been in a tent.

That flatlands and scrub growth of the coastal plain gave way to rolling valleys and towering tulip trees; then to oaks and rolling hills that put me sharply in mind of Milton's five blue peaks.

The farther north we went, and the nearer we came to that blue ridge of mountains to the westward, the oftener we had news of the Convention Army, and the more fantastic were the tales we heard about it.

I truly believe that no people anywhere have ever been so misinformed as were the American rebels concerning those who held opposite political views. "Deluded people", the rebels were called—and rightly. Certainly they were deluded at the beginning of the war when they mobbed Governor Hutchinson, my father and so many other good Americans for counseling moderation. They were deluded when they believed everything Sam Adams and John Hancock told them. Now, six years later, in Virginia and the Carolinas, they were still deluded about the Convention Army; still so deluded as to follow leaders more violent and far more ignorant than Sam Adams.

They seemed instinctively to shun the truth. They would listen to nothing but grotesque falsehoods about the Loyalists, about the British, about anybody at all who opposed them or was even suspected of opposing them.

We were less than half way on our cold, dreary journey to Winchester and Frederick when we received unexpected proof of the frenzy into which southern rebels had fallen—a frenzy that led the unbelievably cruel and bitter residents of remote settlements to regard education and religion as hallmarks of the English and therefore, also, as the stamp of those who at heart were loyal to British rule.

According to my map we were in Spotsylvania County, and we were keeping to narrow, frozen country roads, so to skirt safely to the westward of the towns along the Potomac. We were hunting Stevens' Ordinary, which the map showed to be at the junction of two roads, one leading north toward Frederick; the other west toward Harrisonburg and the Blue Ridge Mountains that had loomed at our left for days.

"We must be near some kind of a tavern," Buell said. "I can hear people singing, and they don't sing in these parts unless they're drunk."

Hopefully he added, "If there's a lot of people drunk at Stevens', he must make an extra special kind of that white licker they drink down here. If it was ordinary white licker, they'd 'a' lost control of their vocal cords right after their first drink. We better look into it, Oliver. We'll need something corrosive like that to help us digest this southern pig meat we're living on."

We turned a corner and came suddenly on the crossroads. Sure enough, a tavern stood there—one of those unpainted, disreputable southern taverns with porch askew, chimneys all cock-a-hoop, and a few scraggly bushes growing miserably in the frozen, grassless land around it.

No gay company, making merry at that tavern, accounted for the singing we'd heard. Between us and the tavern, on the road that crossed the one on which we traveled, was a straggling long line of men, women and children plodding to the westward. A few men were on horseback, and the horses were hitched to loaded carts or to long poles to which bundles were tied. Other men drew light carts, and alongside the carts walked women leading cows and pigs. The children, too, carried bundles or led animals—hound dogs, pigs, sheep, goats.

One of the mounted men looked up and saw us. He turned in his saddle and raised his arm. Instantly the long line of people broke into song. When I first heard it, the song seemed to be only a repetition of the words "Oh promised land!"; but there was something so pleasing about those words, something so hopeful and gay about the simplicity of the tune, that it stuck in my mind like a burr.

I got to know it better, later, and never got it out of my mind. I find myself whistling it unconsciously at odd times—usually when things have been dark and are growing brighter—always when I'm finishing a difficult chapter:

> "Oh promised land, Oh promised land!
> Lead, lead me to that promised land!
> Guide, guide me with thy loving hand!
> Oh promised land, Kentucky land!"

We stopped at the crossroads, and the line of singers went past us without giving us so much as a glance.

Buell, ready with a pair of Perkins' Metallic Tractors, pointed out that nobody except the man on horseback had looked at us.

"They're afraid," Buell said. "They ain't looking at us for fear of what we might say to 'em. What's more, they're running away from something or somebody! I'll bet you a million dollars—Congress money, of course—that those people are Loyalists."

The man on horseback came back toward us, scanning the marchers as a captain might examine his company. He was a youngish man with a strawberry mark on one side of his face. The mark extended from his ear to the corner of his mouth, and lifted his lips, at that side, in a half-smile that gave him the look of being indulgently amused by everyone and everything.

I knew I had to find out about that long, laden line of marchers, and why they avoided us. Buell, I was sure, was near to the truth. I called to the man on horseback, and he kicked his horse a little closer to us.

Buell held up his tractors and commenced his explanation of their virtues, but the man on horseback gathered up his reins. "That's blasphemy," he said. "Only God could effect such cures."

Buell put the tractors away. "He's no rebel," he told me. "He's an honest man."

The man, I could see, was suspicious of us. "I want to ask you a question," I said. "I want to ask if you'd have any objection to us going along with you—if we happened to be going your way."

He looked faintly amused, but only because of the red mark on his face. "If you were members of my church," he said, "we'd be glad for your help. You're Baptists?"

"Your church?" I repeated. "You're a minister?"

His eyes darted over the two of us, and came to rest on Buell's feet. "I'm Lewis Craig," he said. He swung his arm toward the marchers, who still sang that gay chorus as they straggled past. "This is my congregation—the congregation of Upper Spotsylvania. Some call it Craig's Church. We aim to find ourselves a new location in Kentucky."

I could hardly believe him. "You're moving a whole congregation— your whole church—to Kentucky? Kentucky's five hundred miles away! Do you mean to say these women, these children, can walk five hundred miles?"

"Those who walk with God," Craig said, "walk in the furnace and come out unharmed." He lowered his voice. "Are you truly in need?"

"No," I said, "we're not: not yet; but we might be. We might need to go to Kentucky ourselves. We're not Baptists. I'm an Episcopalian. If you wouldn't be willing to let us go along with you, would you be willing to tell us how to reach Kentucky?"

Craig pointed to the Blue Ridge Mountains. "The road's there, on the other side—Boone's Wilderness Road. Nobody'll try to stop you if you head west, for the Wilderness Road. That'll mean you've abandoned your property to anyone—or any committee—that wants it."

The last of his congregation—a thin, sick-looking man, with a wife seemingly clothed in nothing but shawls—puttered past, coaxing and pushing a white-faced black heifer. Craig looked at them uneasily and picked up his reins.

"Just a minute," I said. "Evidently you've abandoned your property to the rebels. Men don't do that unless they've been badly treated. They don't go five hundred miles on foot into the wilderness to found new homes and practise their religion unless their lives have become unendurable. I'd find it helpful if you'll tell me why the rebels treated you and your congregation badly. I've been badly treated by them myself."

Craig studied me and seemed satisfied. "A tumultuous and discontented generation is abroad in the land," he said. "They scoff at religion and the holy word, and scorn everything but ignorance. They've heard it said we believe 'Do good to them that hate you.' They stoned our church. They tore the door from the hinges. They desecrated the altar and threatened our congregation. Their threats grew louder with each passing year; their behavior more violent. If we stayed and suffered their tyranny, we would have neither congregation nor religion."

He looked after the thin man, the shawl-clad woman and the heifer; then kicked his heel against his horse's ribs. "God be with you, brothers," he said. "You'll be free of ignorance and rebellion in Kentucky."

The song that came back to us was faint, but we could distinguish the words:

"Oh promised land, Kentucky land!"

Rebel information concerning the Convention Army was of a piece with all their information. The mere mention of those unhappy men of Burgoyne's seemed to kindle in all rebels a sort of perverse flame that so scorched and warped their brains that they lost the power of thinking clearly.

If a man had spoken reasonably about that army—had reminded his hearers that promises made to it by the rebel government had been deliberately and repeatedly broken—he would have been instantly charged with Toryism, with treachery. He'd have been insulted, assaulted, dragged before a rebel committee for trial.

If he'd dared to call them average human beings, unfortunate victims of circumstances wholly beyond their control, but no better and no worse than a similar number of soldiers from the rebel army, he'd have been tarred and feathered and his property confiscated.

If we'd credited what we heard, we'd have believed that the officers and men of that Convention Army, before coming to America, were slaves, hirelings, criminals; that all of them were without decency or honor; that no woman's virtue was safe when they were near; that they were ogres, monsters of iniquity and degradation, fouling whatever they touched.

That they were allowed to live at all was thought to demonstrate the nobility and magnanimity of Americans. Rebels everywhere said openly that such magnanimity was a mistake—that every man in the Convention Army was like a mad dog, dangerous, worthless, and should be incontinently destroyed.

That's one reason why a civil war is worse than any other sort. When two parties in a given country resort to arms to settle political differences, every man is a potential enemy to every other man, and the distinction between legalized killing and murder is not clearly drawn in the minds of average men, who are incapable of sustained thought. Death is held to be a fitting reward for those who dare hold contrary views, and a nation involved in a civil war is a breeding ground for children reared to look with tolerance on next to nothing but violence.

CHAPTER LXVI

THE town of Frederick, sprawled at the bottom of a cup-like circle of bleak Maryland hills, was frowsy and unkempt when we came into it under leaden January skies; but the dreariness of the town itself was nothing by comparison with that of the barracks where the Convention troops were held prisoners.

The barracks, on the outskirts of the town, stood on a treeless, wind-swept plain dotted with frozen puddles. The fields in which they stood looked as if a giant had scraped them clean of grass, then sprinkled them with cold plums of skull-shaped gray rock.

There was a tumble-down fence around the barrack field; and the gates, a half-pistol-shot apart, were guarded by rebel sentries only recognizable as sentries because they carried bayoneted muskets and wore crossed belts around the nondescript coats with which their upper bodies were padded.

As we drove past the barracks, we saw, just inside the main gate, a man lying face down on the rocky, frozen ground. I knew he was a British soldier; for though his breeches were of calfskin with the hair outside, and his shoes, what was left of them, bound in muddy cloth to keep the soles from coming off, his jacket showed streaks and squares of scarlet beneath the patches that almost hid the original cloth.

Our horse stopped of his own accord, as if to let us view that prostrate figure at our leisure. The sentry walked out to us and peered into the cart. ·

Buell, a pair of Perkins' Metallic Tractors in his hand, was ready for him. "Brother," he said earnestly, "are you troubled with carbuncles, pimples, cutaneous eruptions, cracking of the lips or venereal diseases? If so, look well at this pair of Perkins' Metallic Tractors. Persistent applications of these little instruments will infallibly effect a cure."

"I ain't got a venereal disease," the sentry said quickly.

"Do you never," Buell persisted, "suffer from paleness in the face, itching of the nose, hollowness of the eyes, grating of the teeth when asleep, dullness and painful heaviness in the head, a dry cough, itching of the backsides, unquiet sleep, lost appetite, swelled belly, frightful dreams, extreme thirsts, stinking breath, and so on?"

The sentry looked more interested. "Yes, I do," he said. "Leastways, I suffer from most of 'em. The other night I dreamed——"

Buell broke in upon him. "Then you got worms! You draw these tractors over the abdomen and toward the extremities, in the way I prescribe, and the knots of worms in the duodenum or gut are busted, and they thereupon pass through the smallest passages of the body, relieving you of those ropy and slimy humors which prevent the juice of food from being conveyed to the liver and turned into blood."

The sentry was fascinated. "Is that so!" he said. "What does a pair of 'em cost?"

"Five guineas," Buell said.

The sentry shook his head. "There ain't five guineas in this whole prison."

"That's a pity," Buell said. "You wouldn't believe what these things'll do! They've been known to bring the dead back to life. I never tried 'em on a dead man myself, but we could try 'em on that one in the field yonder."

"He ain't dead," the sentry said. "He's drunk."

"That's too bad," Buell said. "The only thing these tractors aren't any good for are drunkenness and headaches following drunkenness."

He grew suddenly indignant. "You say that man's drunk, and he an Englishman—one of them that struck the dagger into our back? He's a tyrant—a parricide! He hadn't ought to be allowed to have any pleasure like getting himself unconscious on drink!"

"Well," the sentry said, "I know that's how people feel about 'em, most places; but around here they feel different. This here town of Frederick's a poor town, and it figures it ought to make some use of all these Ministerial tools. It aims to sell 'em stuff. Everybody in town makes white licker, so they're allowed to work in the fields and earn money enough to buy it. They drink it hot out of the still, and it hits 'em hard."

Buell sounded horrified. "You mean they'r≥ treated like human beings?"

"Well," the sentry said, "not exactly. They have to work twice as long as people generally do, and only get paid half as much. The way Frederick people figure, it's flying in the face of Providence not to sell to 'em."

Buell stared at him doubtfully. "Could we sell to 'em our own selves if we had something to sell?"

"You certainly could," the sentry said heartily. "Sunday's market day, and you can sell to 'em all day Sunday. They'll buy anything—kittens to chase rats in their barracks—anything that's eatable or drinkable or alive."

"Brother," Buell said, "I never had a chance to see Englishmen before, and I got to make a medical study of 'em. I'll come here Sunday and sell 'em something, and if you'll be here that morning and guide us around, I'll give you this pair of Perkins' Metallic Tractors free gratis for nothing."

As our cart moved onward, I knew from the exalted look on the sentry's face that there was at least one man in the rebel army who would make no trouble for us.

By the time I had spent an hour in the barrack field on Sunday morning, I had all the information I needed about the private soldiers of the remnants of Burgoyne's once-splendid army. The rest of my information would have to come from the officers of that army and from those among whom they lived as prisoners.

I think that in the beginning many of Burgoyne's soldiers were recruited from jails, or allowed to choose between penal servitude and fighting in America; for most of those who wandered from farm cart to farm cart in the rocky barrack yard had the resentful sullenness—the hard-eyed wariness—peculiar to men who prey upon their fellows. What impressed me most about them was not, I think, their whipped look; not their scowling resignation; not their appearance of being discarded, unusable, unwanted members of society; not the strange rags and ravelings with which their clothes were patched and darned, making them appear like masqueraders in fuzzy caricatures of uniforms. What struck me most forcibly was their noisy and pretended merriment; sudden gusts of mirthless laughter over nothing, almost as if four years of captivity had warped their wits. I thought perhaps this strange cackling was a form of armor against the bitter antagonism, the determined spite, of the men and women who took their money, and—if I was any judge of looks—would have gladly taken their lives when no more money was to be had from them. It may have given them courage to resist the vindictive enmity with which they had been surrounded since that long-gone day when they laid down their arms at Saratoga.

Our excuse for being in the barrack yard was a basketful of kittens which Buell had discovered and acquired, and they brought the prisoners flocking around our cart like flies around a syrup barrel.

"Keep your hands off those kittens," Buell told them. "I can't sell 'em unless I get the proper price for 'em. They're six-toed, and a full-grown six-toed cat can lick three five-toed cats! A six-toed cat'll walk right down a badger hole and scare a badger half to death! You get a six-toed cat mad, and he'd tackle a bloodhound!"

"How much is one of 'em—the littlest one?" a man asked.

"I told you before," Buell said. "I'll sell these kittens when I get what they're worth."

"What *are* they worth?" the man persisted.

"How much you got?" Buell asked.

"I'll give you five hundred dollars Congress money."

Buell laughed scornfully. "Five hundred dollars! I already *got* five hundred dollars! There ain't one of you that wouldn't pay five hundred dollars for a quart of white licker. If you pay five hundred dollars for something that only lasts long enough to give you a stomach-ache and a headache, you can afford ten times as much for something you'll have all the rest of your life. These kittens are five thousand dollars apiece. More if I got to keep on telling you so!"

The men whispered among themselves. One of them ran off and soon returned leading a towheaded man dressed in flour sacking through which short bits of wool from old stockings had been stitched for warmth. His feet were bare and knobby from chilblains. When he saw the basketful of kittens on Buell's knee, he clasped his hands like a woman and murmured in German.

A man with a scraggly mustache and protruding front teeth spoke to me angrily. "Why don't he put a price on 'em? We had a thousand cats at Charlottesville to take care of the rats in our huts, but when we moved up here, we had to leave 'em behind. That German, he's homesick for the one he had to leave. He cries all night. Tell your friend to put a real price on one of 'em, for God's sake!"

"Suppose I got you a kitten for nothing," I said. "Could you give me some information in return?"

The man looked over each shoulder; then spoke without moving his lips, as prisoners do. "All you want, sir."

I took one of the kittens from Buell's basket and handed it to the man with the protruding teeth, who instantly put it into the German's arms. The German, openly weeping, instantly hurried away, his huge red face bent over the kitten in his cupped hands.

The man with the protruding teeth looked relieved. "Thank God for that! Maybe he won't cry himself to sleep every night now. What is it you want to know, sir?"

"I'm a friend," I said. "Where can I find one of your officers?"

He looked incredibly stupid. "What you want to know for?"

"I want to find out where this army's been and how it's been treated."

"You don't need to see an officer for that! Ask us! The officer don't know the half of it! They live in decent houses! They sleep in beds with roofs over their heads! The rats don't eat *their* clothes and *their* fingers when they're asleep! They got boots, and money to buy food with. They don't have to listen to these bloody damned rebels calling 'em murderers and thieves and baby-killing bastards all day and all night, year after year." He uttered an ejaculation of despairing contempt, made as if to leave me, then turned back.

"All right! Go ahead and see 'em! You'll find 'em getting drunk and fighting duels pretty near every night. Fighting duels, for Christ's sake!"

"You were drunk yourself last night, weren't you?"

He clasped his head with a chapped hand. "Yes, I was, and so would you 'a' been if you saw as much of these bloody rebels as we do! They don't treat prisoners right! They never keep promises! Their dollars aren't worth a damn today, and tomorrow they'll be worth considerably less than half of that! They're always setting out to do something, and changing their minds in midstream. Their women can't even make up their minds to go to bed! They keep their clothes on and call it 'bundling'. And look at their licker! It's supposed to be for drinking, but it'll eat lead out of a dirty rifle! Three drinks of it and you think you've got a wildcat in your stomach. Certainly I was drunk last night!"

"See here," I said, "I must see one of your officers—one who can get drunk and still keep from being angry at everyone and everything, including himself. Maybe you didn't have any like that."

The man looked defiant. "We had a lieutenant as good as any general that ever lived, and a damned sight better than most. If the lieutenants in this army could 'a' been generals for about——"

"In what way was he better than a general?"

"Because he was human! He acted as if we was as good as he was! He'd give us a shilling every time we'd find him a flower or animal or bird he hadn't seen before. He drew pictures in a notebook, and sat up half the night writing in it. When the rebels tried to starve us and freeze us, he wouldn't waste time sending 'em letters. He'd walk right up to the highest rebel officer he could find and call him a bloody beast for not seeing we got better treatment."

"He's the one I want," I said. "What's his name and where'll I find him?"

The man seemed astounded to have his opinion asked and accepted. "His name's Anburey. Lieutenant Thomas Anburey. He lives in a rebel colonel's house—Jones."

He frowned. "Where you been these last four years? Don't you know anybody seen speaking to one of our officers gets himself watched day and night? If you go looking for Lieutenant Anburey, somebody'll inform on you and the rebels'll be after you in five minutes! First thing you know, they'll press you into their militia, seize your horse and cart, and drive both of you into the woods."

He turned to look at Buell, who was disposing of his last kitten. The sight seemed to reassure him.

"I'll tell you what you do," he said. "You and the doctor drive over to Harpers Ferry tomorrow. When you come back, along about five o'clock, you'll find me on the road about two miles out. By that time I'll be able to tell you where you can see the lieutenant without getting yourself in trouble."

CHAPTER LXVII

The Dustin plantation, a mile outside Frederick on the
Harpers Ferry road, had the same unkempt look peculiar to so many
of the houses we had seen on our travels through Virginia. The
foundations seemed insecure; the chimneys too fragile. There was too
little paint on the walls and doors; the trees bordering the avenue
leading to the front door were straggly and untrimmed; the avenue
itself was rutted, rocky, a hoorah's nest of fallen branches.

When I rapped on the door, as instructed, it rattled open a meager
two inches, and was held there by a stout chain. Beyond the crack
I saw an old, old Negro who chittered and peered out at me like an
ancient, wizened monkey.

He was pushed aside by a girl whose appearance, in the first quick
glance I had of her in the dim light of the darkened hallway, struck
me as almost repulsive. All I could see of her, through the narrow
opening, was dead black and deader white. Her dress was dull black;
her hair, brushed severely back from her face, was like a snug coif
of dusky velvet; so dark were her arching eyebrows and the enormous eyes beneath that they seemed like holes in the blank whiteness of her face.

"I'm Major Dustin's daughter," she said. "You wished to see him?"

"Yes, ma'am. I was given to understand your father might be
interested in disposing of a horse."

She unbolted the door; then turned to shoo the ancient Negro
toward the rear of the house. "Heavenly land alive, Theodrick," she
cried. "How many times you going to make Papa tell you to let the
little boy answer the doorbell? You know Papa! He'll sell you to
a South Ca'lina gentleman, sure's you're bawn!"

She rolled up her eyes at me with a martyred look. "Good grief an' gracious, I dunno anything more exasperating than not bein' paid attention to! When they're old like Theodrick, they just won't pay attention! I declare to goodness, sometimes I'm tempted to take a whip to him."

She led me to a front room off the hallway and with a pretty hand airily waved me to a chair. "You just try 'em all an' take the one that fits you best! I'll go for Papa."

As she turned away, she raised her eyes and shot a quick look at me, and to my surprise I was conscious of a sudden sensation of warmth—a warmth that was almost heat. Major Dustin's daughter, I saw, was no study in flat white and dull black, but a tremulous pale flame like the invisible blaze above coals beneath a summer sun.

As I waited, I found myself wondering about this white-faced girl —wondering how a woman who could dart at anyone a look such as she had given me could endure the dreariness of a farm in Maryland. The burning intensity of that look clung in my mind, and, strangely, brought to me dim memories of Sally Leighton—as I had once seen her, brown-faced, wind-blown, at the tiller of her little sloop, working out of Dorchester Bay and into the deep channel in the lee of Castle William; of her flushed cheeks as she knelt before the oven to test the progress of a cake.

Why this pale-faced girl should have turned my mind so acutely to Sally; why those well-remembered scenes should seem so dark, so dim, as if reflected from a polished table top, was beyond my understanding. Something, I knew not what, about the smoldering flash of those sooty eyes, gleaming at me from the dazzling whiteness of her face, had made me uncomfortable. Again I wondered what she found to do in a place like this: how she kept herself amused—and with whom. I felt a need to have these questions answered—and then I heard her footsteps again. She was running lightly down the stairs.

I got up, swallowing hard, fearful of making a fool of myself in her eyes; but instead of coming to me, she stopped at the door of the hall, unchained it and threw it open.

To my disappointment, a tall young man came quickly in, caught her hand and raised it to his lips. Now, I told myself, with a feeling of inexplicable disappointment, I couldn't ask her the questions that I'd hoped to have answered. I damned this unwanted stranger —this intruder—this uninvited interloper. . . .

He turned and looked at me. He was stooped, and his face thin, so that he constantly seemed to be peering and listening. It didn't seem to be an inquisitive peering, but an anxious one, rather, as though he feared something might escape him.

"You're the one?" he asked. "You sent word by one of my men?"

His eyes made a quick appraisal of my countryman's garb. I expected him to be coldly contemptuous of my appearance, but he wasn't.

"My name's Oliver," I said. "I was told I might buy horses here." I glanced at the young lady.

"There's no occasion for suspicion," the young man said. "I'm Lieutenant Thomas Anburey of His Majesty's Forty-seventh Foot, and this is our very kind and good friend, Julia Bishop. Mrs. Bishop's father, Major Dustin, has been extremely hospitable, and the mere thought of having a secret either from the major or Mrs. Bishop would be distasteful. So far as anybody else is concerned, you and I are here to buy horses—you for your purposes, I for mine."

"You said nothing about Mrs. Bishop's husband," I said. "Am I to take it he's as trustworthy as the lady?"

Mrs. Bishop made a small adjustment to her smooth black helmet of hair, and gave me a cheerful smile. "You'll just tumble right over in a swoon when you heah about my husband, Mr. Oliver. He'll never say one word about anything to anybody. He's dead."

Anburey looked regretful, as men do when a woman openly admits to being a widow. I muttered an apology, but I was conscious of a feeling of relief. For the first time since Buell and I had started north from Westover, I felt safe. Anburey and Mrs. Bishop, I instinctively knew, were wholly dependable.

"Well, Mr. Anburey," I said, "I hope it'll be enough to say my name's Oliver, and I'm here to learn the truth about the Convention Army—if I can. I've got to make up my mind whether at this late date there's anything to be done about it. There isn't much known either in New York or in England about what happened to this army, Mr. Anburey."

Anburey gave me a blank stare. "In England, eh? You're in a dangerous part of America, Mr. Oliver. I take it you wouldn't mention—that is to say—might I ask what you're *supposed* to be doing here, as well as what you *are* doing?"

"Why, sir," I said, "let's say I'm hunting a place to settle. Let's say I was living as peaceful as you please on the James River, when along came that black scoundrel Benedict Arnold and that contemptible assassin Simcoe and drove us from our home."

Anburey looked incredulous. "They drove you from your home! When was this, Mr. Oliver?"

"January fifth," I said. "Arnold sailed from New York December twenty-first with fifteen hundred men. His ships were scattered by a storm, but he sailed up the James with eight hundred and struck at Richmond like lightning."

"Fifteen hundred men!" Anburey whispered. "Simcoe! Arnold and Simcoe!" Behind his blank gray eyes I could almost see his mind racing, racing.

Mrs. Bishop laughed gaily. "My land alive, Mr. Oliver!" she cried, her speech becoming exaggeratedly southern, "how on uth could you 'a' lived on the James River and kep' that James River talk off your tongue! I declare to goodness, Mr. Oliver, I jes' wouldn't have one little teeny-weeny thing to do with a James River gentleman that talked so kinda frosty."

"Ma'am," I said, doing my best to sound equally southern, "Ah cain't help mah speech."

"Oh deary me!" Mrs. Bishop said, "it ain't your speech, Mr. Oliver! It's your manner! You don' *ack* James Rivery!"

"Well," I said; and then, completely at a loss, I stopped.

Mrs. Bishop rolled her eyes despairingly. "Listen at that, now!" she cried. "Landy, landy! Those James River boys, they cain't be in a room with a lady more'n half a minute without bustin' out tellin' her all about how her hair's like a raven's wing, an' her cheek like moonlight on a magnolia."

Her tinkling laughter put me in mind of the sound of far-off sleigh bells on a winter's evening in Milton.

"Sit way across the room from you, those James River boys do," Mrs. Bishop ran on gaily, "an' say things northern people couldn't say except in the middle of a real dark swamp at midnight."

She looked provocative. "You're making a big mistake, Mr. Oliver. Nobody'd come all the way up here from the James River to buy horses. How long do you suppose he'd keep his horses, Mr. Oliver, with rebels stealing 'em whenever they got a chance—or requisition-ing 'em, if you like that word better!

"Lawsy me, Mr. Oliver! You better forget all about the James River! You better be from Kentucky, where Papa's starting for to-morrow. There's people going to Kentucky from all over, so they don't have to talk any particular way, and in Kentucky there's no need for armies, and no fighting, and nobody to seize your horses or steal your slaves!" She spoke gaily, so that I thought she wasn't serious.

Anburey, however, was serious enough. "You'll never have better advice, Mr. Oliver. If, as Mrs. Bishop says, your manner of speech is such as to arouse suspicion, you'll be in trouble with the rebels before you know it. That's something one should put himself to some inconvenience to avoid. Have you committed yourself? Have you told many people hereabouts that you're from the James River?"

"No," I said. "Fortunately we've been sleeping under our cart. Nobody's asked us anything."

"Then be a Kentuckian," Anburey urged. "Be a Kentuckian!" He lowered his voice. "If the rebels really suspect you're working openly against them—if they even dream you're actively working for the Loyalists—you won't have a chance! I've seen ruthless enemies, Mr. Oliver, but none to equal these rebels. There's a relentless cruelty to 'em that isn't human! If you're newly arrived in this country, you may not know what we've learned in the years we've had to stay here. You can't depend on the rebels behaving like civilized people at all! They're barbarians—savages! Most of 'em have lived all their lives in the woods, or in houses no better than dens. They wolf their food like animals—talk in growls!"

I must have looked incredulous, for Anburey made his words even more emphatic. "Make no mistake about it, Mr. Oliver! The rebels in this part of the country are bad—bad! I think I'm a fair-minded man, but I can't find one redeeming trait about 'em. Here and there you find an officer with some of the instincts of a gentleman, but not often! The English language hasn't words strong enough to convey their hatred of us. They only let us stay alive because they hope to use us. They think they can starve us or freeze us or broil us into joining their own miserable army, or into agreeing to act as slaves to rebel farmers for three years. Some of our men have done one or the other rather than endure this living death—rather than keep on facing those bitter, hating faces. Most of 'em'll die before they'll do either."

"What had you done to make them so bitter?" I asked.

Anburey groaned despairingly. "Done? We'd done nothing! From first to last our men have had strict orders not to resent insults. In Cambridge, when a few of our men got out of hand and defended themselves against the brutality of Henley, a rebel colonel, they were shot and bayoneted! General Burgoyne made official protest, and Henley was court-martialed; but he was acquitted. No rebel sees anything wrong in bayoneting or shooting one of us!"

He rose from his chair to pace the room. "You can't be too careful! Those of us who're part of the Convention Army are prisoners of war, so we can't be murdered outright. We can only be killed by degrees. But you're defenseless! The rebels'll stop at nothing where you're concerned! Nothing!"

"Have you found the rebels the same everywhere? In Charlottesville, for example?"

Anburey looked disgusted. "Try to understand, Mr. Oliver! They're *all* alike! Four years ago—no, five years ago—no, it was four . . . I get confused about time: it seems an eternity we've been at the mercy of these people. . . . Four years ago, when we marched through Philadelphia and then down through Winchester and along those beautiful damned mountains to Charlottesville, there wasn't a town, a village, a crossroads settlement, not even a log tavern, where rebel men and women didn't gather to spit on us when we passed! We'd been told we'd occupy barracks in Charlottesville. The barracks we found were nothing but the bare foundations of log huts in forest clearings, where the stumps stuck up through the slashings! Those damned skeletons of huts were full of snow. We dug it out with our hands; slept in it! I've heard a lot of talk down here, Mr. Oliver, about how the noble rebels suffered at Valley Forge. Bah! It makes me sick! The rebels chose their lot. My own men endured far more than those at Valley Forge, and because of other men's unnecessary brutality! Nobody gave my men any sympathy! All they got was hatred for refusing to die! You've got to see a close friend suffer— really suffer—at the hands of the rebels before you can understand!"

Mrs. Bishop looked at me curiously and spoke to Anburey. "I guess Mr. Oliver knows what you're talking about. I guess you can go right ahead and tell him whatever you want to without puzzling him much. He can, can't he, Mr. Oliver?"

"Yes, he can," I said. "The rebels drove us out of Boston when my father was sick, and he died."

Mrs. Bishop's eyes seemed enormous, and she laid her fingers against her cheek in a strange, hesitant gesture that oddly brought memories of my father flooding into my mind.

She turned suddenly to Anburey. "Mr. Oliver asked about Charlottesville. Now you do as I say, this very minute! You tell him all about those barracks down there! My land, Mr. Anburey, I just never did hear you so silent before in all my whole life, I do declare!"

Anburey looked uncomfortable. "Most thoughtless of me," he said. "So easy to get the idea that one's experiences are unique! Extremely stupid!"

"Please don't think of it again," I said. "If you could tell me about Charlottesville——"

"A beastly hole," Anburey said hurriedly. "I'll never forget it! Never! We were there three damnable years. We finished those barracks ourselves, without help of any sort from the rebels. We felled our own trees, sawed out our own boards, split our own shakes."

His voice grew stronger. "When we'd finished the cabins we grubbed out the stumps around 'em, and then we cleared the land on all sides of us. We cleared a piece six square miles, Mr. Oliver. Hacked it right out of the forest. We levered out the rocks and spaded up the land with our hands—turned up every inch of those six square miles. We planted vegetables so we'd have something to live on. We traded our labor for cats to keep down the rats that came over to us from the filthy damned rebel huts! We worked harder than slaves, Mr. Oliver, and in all that section there wasn't a piece of land to compare with ours! And when we'd finished everything, those damnable rebels moved us out on the ground that Clinton and Cornwallis had landed in Charleston and might march north to rescue us.

"They took the barracks we'd built; they took those fields we'd cleared; they took our crops; they even took our cats. They drove us out on the road again—cattle to be spit at; animals to be stoned!"

"Well," I said, "it *is* true that Cornwallis might have freed you, isn't it?"

"God knows," Anburey said. "All I know is, you can't expect anything better from a rebel. The rebel leaders in this part of the country are fighting so they won't have to pay their just debts to England. These southern states have repudiated their debts by law—a course I'm told is without precedent among civilized nations. The Confiscation Act so highly approved by all southern rebels is a disgrace to every state that approves it, and to the entire country.

"What the rebels have done to us is of a piece with what they've done to everyone. They aren't civilized. I never hated an enemy before, Mr. Oliver, and I don't think soldiers do, as a rule; but I'll tell you this much: the cruelties, the injustices we've endured for four long years have made me hate American rebels as I've never hated anyone before! I know what to expect from 'em at all times and under every circumstance; and as long as I live I'll never forget or forgive our treatment in America!"

Anburey, making a queer gasping sound, sat suddenly on the edge of a chair. Embarrassed by his emotion, I dropped my eyes from his face and saw with painful clarity the distressing details of his appearance. I'd already noticed that his eyes were red and swollen, his lips pale—signs of far too little food. But now I observed that his coat had been so often darned that the original cloth showed as little patches of clear scarlet against a muddier overlay of scarlet darnings. His boots, black and shiny at first sight, were bulky masterpieces of repair, effected by placing patches of tarred canvas over the broken leather, and covering the patches with a wash of tar.

Mrs. Bishop went quickly to a cellarette in a corner and took from it a bottle and a glass. She filled the glass, gave it to Anburey and stood beside him, her hand on his shoulder. "Don't you dare talk like that when I ain't here," she whispered. "It's got to end some time soon, and if you go letting out like this, you won't be good for nothing at all! What'll Mr. Oliver think of you!"

Anburey nodded, drank off the glass of wine, drew a deep breath, and raised his eyes to mine. "If you're doing what I think you are, Mr. Oliver, go back to those who sent you and tell 'em it's a waste of time to bother their heads about us. We've got along somehow up to now. Sometimes we've been desperate at the thought of being forgotten by our own people. Sometimes, when they kicked us and spit on us, we wanted to die. But we'll get along. Even if the rebels should seem to listen to reason, they'd break their promises. Their words are no good!

"Here's the truth, Mr. Oliver. If we had enough gumption—if all our officers gave the proper thought and attention to their men, instead of wasting their days acting as they think gentlemen ought to act—all of us could probably escape and get back to New York! Over five hundred have tried it, at one time and another. Nearly three hundred have succeeded, and so could the rest of us if we'd dress in rags, slouch when we walk, talk through our noses, intrude on the privacy of everyone we met, boast about our honor and bravery, speak contemptuously of everything beautiful and decent, rant at the top of our lungs about liberty and at the same time tear the land inside out to catch runaway slaves——"

Mrs. Bishop jumped to her feet, drowning Anburey's words in a burst of prolonged and affected laughter. "My merciful stars, I never heard anything so absolutely foolish! It just ain't possible to breed running horses in Maryland like what my papa'll breed in Kentucky! Sure as you're bawn, my papa'll breed the fastest horses this old world ever saw! I dare you, Mr. Oliver! I absolutely dare and double-dare you! When you get ready to come back to Kentucky, Mr. Oliver, you fetch along the fastest horse you can find anywhere in Maryland, and I'll wager anything at all one of my papa's yearlings'll beat him over any distance you choose to name! You just wait, Mr. Oliver, until we get to Kentucky! You know it's the truth, Mr. Oliver, be-cause you've been there!"

She broke off to run to the door and open it, and I realized that her noisy gaiety had been for the benefit of someone else; for when she threw open the door I saw, in the dark hall beyond, two men in the remnants of uniforms I hadn't seen since Buell and I, in the dress of rebel militiamen, had made our way from New York to Milton to tell Sally Leighton about her brother Soame. The plain blue coats, the crossed belts, the black leather neckbands, the greasy leather breeches were those of the Massachusetts Line.

Mrs. Bishop swept them an exaggerated curtsy. "I declare," she cried, "I'd given you gentlemen up for lost! I told Papa Captain Hitchcock and Lieutenant Leighton must 'a' either gone back to New York to tell Mr. Washington how to carry on his war, or gone chasing slaves up the Potomac! I told Papa you'd never on this earth be back here before we started for Kentucky, and we'd never again see the brave Captain Hitchcock and the brave Lieutenant Leighton unless they could both requisition themselves real fast little running horses, so's they could come out to Kentucky and try to win Papa's stable away from him!"

She threw back her head and laughed a long and tinkling laugh, at which the two rebel officers grinned vapidly, after the universal manner of young men rallied by a pretty woman.

I tried to laugh too, but I think I did badly at it; for the lieutenant was Sally Leighton's brother, Steven, who as a child had spied upon Sally and me when we walked together on the slopes of Milton Hill; whom I had last seen, grim, unshaven, unbelievably dirty, angry, defiant in New York's Provost, asking me for information about that other brother of his whom Cunningham had murdered.

CHAPTER LXVIII

I SHUDDERED, as I tried to look unconscious of Steven Leighton, to think what my fate must certainly have been if I had refused to let Buell alter my appearance; and even now, changed as I was, I feared the change was insufficient. I twisted up an eyebrow and let my jaw go slack, hoping to add to the effect of my disguise—and still feared that it was too little.

Lieutenant Anburey clicked his heels together, inclined his head and contented himself with saying politely, "Gentlemen."

The nods of the two rebel officers were even briefer than Anburey's, and the gaze which they immediately turned upon me was stony.

"Lawsy me," Mrs. Bishop cried. "Don't it beat all how we know a thing ourselves, and think of course everybody else knows it too! I don't believe you gentlemen have met Mr. Oliver after all. He's buying horses from Papa—if Papa can find any that haven't been requisitioned by that old army of yours! He's Mr. Oliver from Kentucky."

Both officers stared hard at me, and their glances brought back something I had almost forgotten—the deadly, dour, dull, unsmiling earnestness of every rebel I had ever seen.

"Kentucky?" Captain Hitchcock asked. "You arrived here recently from Kentucky?"

"Three days ago," I said. "There's a great dearth of horses in Kentucky, Captain. I never saw a place that needed 'em more."

Hitchcock nodded and took no further notice of me, but Leighton seemed to wish to be friendly—or at least, I tried to assure myself that this was why he questioned me further. Certainly there wasn't a flicker of recognition in his glance: no hint of enmity or suspicion. His eyes were as candid as Sally's; and the sound of his voice brought

603

back to me images that had slowly grown dimmer and dimmer in my mind. "Many people on the road, Mr. Oliver?" Leighton asked.

"Mighty few coming this way," I said, "but a whole kit and caboodle of 'em moving to the southwest. You have to watch yourself, or you're trampled by 'em."

"They're bound to be disappointed," Captain Hitchcock said sourly. "There's too many going! No room for 'em! You're making a great mistake, Mrs. Bishop—going all that distance across the mountains."

Mrs. Bishop laughed long and gaily. "Why, for the land's sake, I never heard such talk! Mr. Oliver, you come to my help! You just tell Captain Hitchcock it ain't so, Mr. Oliver."

"Oh, it's not at all so, Captain," I said. "There's meadows out there waist-deep in grass—meadows that roll across the hills as far as your eye can see. There's streams running through 'em with water sweet as honey and cold as ice. The fish in 'em beat anything you ever tasted. It's the prettiest country in the world!"

A little man with an angry blue eye, a clay-gray face and oddly dark hair stepped quietly into the room and looked from one to the other of us. He must have been nearly seventy years old; yet his spine was so straight that he seemed almost to curve backward.

"Now what!" he shouted. "Somebody passed a law we can't go to Kentucky?"

"My goodness me, Papa," Mrs. Bishop cried. "These gentlemen ain't doing a thing except make a social call, so you needn't go flying at 'em as if they was Indians, after our scalps!"

She patted her black hair and eyed me encouragingly. "This here's Mr. Oliver, Papa. He's from Kentucky and he wants some horses. He's the only one that ain't purely social."

Major Dustin gave me a quick glance. I saw that the strange appearance of his hair was due to a dye that had left it a bright brown on the surface and a greenish brown at the roots. "Happy to know you, Mr. Oliver. Happy to know any man who's interested in something sensible, instead of in this damned war." He glared at Captain Hitchcock and Sally's brother, who stared glumly at their feet.

"I was listening at the door before I came in here," the major went on. He gave me a defiant look. "A man's got to do it nowadays, as you probably know, Mr. Oliver." To the rebel officers he went on, "I was listening, and I heard one of you tell Julia she's making a mistake to go to Kentucky. Mistake! If you're going to continue to

make social calls in this house, I'll thank you to restrict your conversation to social topics. Otherwise there ain't one of us can give you an
honest answer without being in danger of persecution."

"Not from us, Major," Hitchcock said.

"I'll run no risks," Dustin said. "Every last one of you rebels is
bound to have his way in spite of hell and high water. What happens
to me if you tell me I'm making a mistake to go to Kentucky, and I
dare to deny it? It's all over town tomorrow that I'm a friend of
England and want to make slaves of all of you!"

He shook his fist at Hitchcock. "If you want to talk about the war
and advise me or my daughter what to do, stay away from my house,
Captain Hitchcock. I'm no Englishman and I'm no Tory, and I'm no
rebel either! I don't want one damned thing out of this world except
to be let alone, me and my horses—yes, and my family too—and to
live at peace with my neighbors, and to be governed by somebody
who's got a little common sense! That's all I want, by God, but it's
what I can't have—not here, anyway! For a government, I'm supposed to put up with that feather-wit Congress of yours, that ain't
got the brains God gave catfish! Half my neighbors yap about liberty,
and want to kill me if I tell 'em not to talk liberty to me till they've
freed their slaves. We're ruled by committees, and they're just like
rebel committees everywhere else: fellers that always made a mess of
what they made, raised or ran! The only thing they're a success at is
hating anyone who dresses better'n they do, or owns more land, or
reads books and doesn't spit on the parlor floor."

"My goodness, Papa," Mrs. Bishop said, "I certainly wish you
wouldn't always talk politics to my gentlemen social callers."

"I ain't!" the major shouted. "Talking politics is just what I ain't
doing! Captain Hitchcock and Lieutenant Leighton came in here
and started advising you not to go to Kentucky, and I'm just hinting
to 'em not to talk that way! No, by God! Talking politics is the last
thing I want to do, and that's one of the big reasons I'm going to
Kentucky: so I won't have to!"

Captain Hitchcock, ill at ease, got to his feet as if to go.

"Lawsy heavens!" Mrs. Bishop cried. "You've made 'em feel uncomfortable, Papa, and I ain't just barely had enough time to say
'Howdy do'! First thing you know, folks'll be saying we ain't
hospitable!"

"I won't allow nobody to say no such thing," Dustin said. "If they're
uncomfortable, it's on account of the way they feel inside them-

selves—not on account of anything I'm tellin' 'em! What I've said is just the ordinary simple truth: nothing to get uncomfortable over! Of course, if I was in Taylor's place, I'd say a few things that might make 'em feel uncomfortable."

He frowned at Hitchcock. "You heard about Taylor yet?"

Without waiting for an answer he went on: "Course you have! You've had to keep an eye on his house, on account Captain Wedderburn of the Convention Army lives there. Everybody knows Taylor! He's a Quaker—as quiet and mild a man as you'll ever see. Well, that damned committee had a tax bill against him of forty-eight shillings. Said he'd got to pay it in hard money. He didn't have hard money, so the committee seized a mare in payment of the tax. I know the mare they seized, because I bred her. She's worth thirty guineas hard money if she's worth a cent. They took her for a forty-eight-shilling tax! There's a fine committee for you! In another year Taylor won't have anything left at all—no house, no land, no horses. The committee'll have 'em all. Why, let me tell you——"

I felt a touch upon my shoulder. It was Lieutenant Leighton. "I've got a map in my saddlebag, Mr. Oliver," he murmured. "I'd like to get a little information about that road to Kentucky, and I don't think these gentlemen would miss us if we left 'em for a few moments."

My heart was like a lump of lead. I looked desperately at Julia Bishop, at Anburey; but they were intent upon Major Dustin and Major Dustin was wholly absorbed in what he was saying. Pretending to more confidence than I felt, I went with Sally's brother to the door. As we passed through it the major's voice was shrill: "Every damned bit of Taylor's hay, too—£40 worth of it seized in payment for a tax bill of £5, and not a committeeman would listen to his protests! Those same committeemen used to yell bloody murder when asked to pay a tax of three pennies on a pound of tea. I tell you, gentlemen——"

The door closed behind us. "Tiresome things, political arguments," Leighton said. "Always a waste of time—unless one of the arguers kills the other. I'd rather busy myself at something more useful."

He went to the corner of the portico, where the horses were tied to a long rail, and took a map from his saddlebags. The hard knot that had come into my stomach when he tapped me on the shoulder seemed to have untied. Leighton's interest in me, probably, was purely accidental—but I blessed Benedict Arnold, his map and his amazing knowledge of America; blessed, too, Colonel Simcoe for insisting that we memorize every detail of the country in which we might find ourselves.

Leighton unrolled the map and held it before me. It was like the one we'd seen in Arnold's cabin—not a good one, that is to say, and with lots of blank space on which to write. Leighton handed me a pencil. "Start at the point nearest Frederick. Where would that be?"

"Winchester," I said. "I thought everybody knew that." I ran the pencil along the southern side of the Blue Ridge Mountains, making little crosses as I progressed. "From Winchester you go to the Shenandoah River," I told him, "then to the North Branch; then to Staunton; then to the North Fork of the James; then to Botetourt Court House, Catawba River, Roanoke River, Alleghany Mountains, New River, the Head of Holston, then Cumberland Mountain. When you're at Cumberland Mountain you can see the pass into Kentucky."

"You make it sound easy, Mr. Oliver," Leighton said. "Where's your home, by the way?"

"Long Island," I said. "Don't get the idea it's easy, though. It's four hundred and twenty miles of as hard going as you'll ever have in your life. Every time it rains, the path washes out. The trail's full of boulders, some the size of a house. The laurels are so thick that you couldn't run ten feet through 'em if your life depended on it."

Leighton took the map from me. "When do you figure on starting back to Kentucky, Mr. Oliver?"

"I haven't decided," I said. "I've got horses to buy."

"How many horses?" he asked.

Again my heart sank. I'd been right in the first place. He knew who I was. Yet when he spoke his voice was neither friendly nor unfriendly. "Kentucky's an odd place for a Long Islander to go to, Mr. Oliver."

I thought as rapidly as I could. For some reason he seemed to want to beat about the bush; and I, God knows, was willing enough to play at that game. "Odd?" I asked. "Why?"

"Oh," he said, "it's as far as you can get from the home you lived in and your relatives and your friends."

"I never think of it that way," I said. "Nowadays, back where I came from, a friend might turn to an enemy overnight. Besides, it was getting harder and harder to earn a living honestly. Half the world seemed to be trying to make money out of the misfortunes of the other half. I'd rather buy horses here from anybody who wants to sell 'em, and sell 'em in Kentucky to anybody who wants to buy 'em."

Leighton's eyes wandered from my face to my shoes and back to my face again. "I see," he said. "I see. Well, I'll tell you how it is, Mr. Oliver. I'm pretty much attached to my family and my friends. I'd never leave 'em unless I had to. Probably I feel more strongly that way than some, on account of losing a brother that I—that I looked up to." Manifestly uncomfortable, he rubbed his chin and stared up at the gray January sky as if in search of weather.

"I'm sorry to hear it," I said, and I meant it.

"Yes," he said uncomfortably. "We all felt bad. Friends did what they could to help him, but they couldn't do anything. All of us were grateful, of course."

The portico seemed painfully silent. From beyond the two closed doors behind me I could hear the rumble of Major Dustin's voice, still holding forth.

By making an effort, I contrived to speak casually. "Your friends must have felt as badly as you did, Lieutenant. You speak as if your family was a large one. I had only my father, and he died some years ago."

Leighton said nothing.

"You were fortunate," I said, hoping desperately that he would speak of Sally, "fortunate to have had the brothers and sisters! A sister must make a home gayer."

He stared at the barren rim of hills. "I suppose so," he said. "A brother gets to looking at a sister as a nuisance when he's pretty young, and it takes him quite a time to appreciate her. If she gets married, or gets sick, he wakes up to a lot of things he never noticed before."

My heart came into my throat. "Your sister's married?" I whispered.

Leighton shook his head. "No. Sometimes I wish she were. I'd rather have her married, even to someone she doesn't love, than to see her growing thinner and thinner because she can't forget a man who doesn't love her enough to think as she thinks."

I could only repeat the words, "See her growing thinner and thinner!"

"Look here, Mr. Oliver," Leighton said suddenly, "I don't know why I should discuss my family with a stranger I've never seen before and certainly won't see again. I have my duties and you have yours, and we mustn't keep each other from them. I have time to tell you just one thing, and this is it: We have no quarrel with those who want to go to Kentucky. We don't care why they go. We don't care what they do when they get there. We *do* care, though, if a man says he's going to Kentucky, and abandons his property, as Major Dustin's doing—then changes his mind and comes back to make trouble. We won't allow that. We can't. Is that clear?"

I nodded.

"There's too much trouble farther south, as you may or may not know," he went on. "That army of Cornwallis' seems to be in a dozen places at once, and for all we know Cornwallis may be sending messengers to the northward for reinforcements. We don't want it to happen. We're guarding against it. We've blocked all roads to the north, Mr. Oliver—blocked 'em tight. My advice to you is to keep off all roads to the north. What's more, you're bound to get into trouble if you stay in Frederick. Strangers aren't welcome. So you've got to get out of here, and get out right away! You've got to go back to Kentucky, Mr. Oliver, whether or not you get your horses. Understand?"

"Yes," I said. "I understand. I'll say good-by to Mrs. Bishop, and then——"

"Not at all necessary," Leighton said. "Mrs. Bishop's leaving for Kentucky herself. You can see her on the road, if you think it's necessary."

He untied my horse from the hitching pole, handed me the reins, and added: "If I find you in Frederick again, I'll know you're here on business so important that you're willing to run the risk of being shot as a spy."

I have no doubt that Steven Leighton thought he was preventing me from finding out what I'd been sent to find out, but he wasn't; and as I rode off in search of Buell, there was elation mixed with the fears for Sally that had come upon me. I'd learned what I needed to know about the Convention Army. In our journey from Richmond, I'd found out what was happening to Loyalists everywhere; and beyond any question I knew what would happen if an attempt were made to rescue that Convention Army.

The outlook wasn't good, but neither was it hopeless. That's one of the few good things about war: it teaches a man that if he isn't dead, there's still hope.

CHAPTER LXIX

THERE MAY HAVE BEEN a way in which Buell and I could have got safely past the ragged rebel militiamen who, in wretched twos and threes, seemed to have taken up a permanent residence by the side of every path to the north and the fords across every creek and river. If there was such a way, we never found it.

As soon as we were safely out of sight of Frederick and on our way toward Winchester, we camped in the brush so that I could go over in my mind the report I'd make to Thompson—when I dared—on what I had seen and learned.

I didn't want to commit such a report to paper for fear it might be found on me, but I was satisfied that my report must say that the mere existence of the Convention Army was a poison in the minds of the rebels, but that its rescue by force would be a perpetual searing flame, spurring on every rebel in America to even greater vindictiveness and cruelty toward Loyalists than they were now showing.

Another thing I'd have to say was that if soldiers from the Convention Army should ever serve again against the rebels, they would certainly try to revenge themselves for their sufferings; and the moment they did, all chances for a reconciliation between rebels and Loyalists, or between England and the rebels, would be forever lost.

What seemed most important of all to me was that I must get word to Thompson that the war in the south, in my judgment, was bound to be wholly useless—a waste of time, a waste of money, a waste of life, and worst of all, a source of steadily increasing rancor and hatred.

When I told Buell what I'd been thinking, he sat staring bleakly across the rocky Shenandoah.

"Well," I said, "where have I gone wrong?"

"Nowhere," Buell admitted. "That's the trouble! It's the exact truth. Haven't you always said that the exact truth is what nobody at the head of a war wants to hear? Haven't you always claimed that it's only little fellers like us who're willing to tell the truth about a war, or to admit there's no use fighting?"

"Yes," I said, "I have, but this is different. This is so clearly the truth that they'll have to believe it."

"They will?" Buell asked. "What makes you think they will? Did Eden believe us when we told him the truth before? He did not! Did Germaine believe us? He did not! Did the King believe us? He did not! Did Howe ever listen to the truth before Bunker Hill? He did not!

"If Sam Adams and Thomas Jefferson had told the people of Massachusetts the truth, do you suppose there'd ever have been a war? There would not! Nobody on either side, so far as we know, has ever told the truth or believed the truth. They're all alike, every damned one of them—Eden, Clinton, Franklin, Silas Deane, Vergennes, Sam Adams, old Putnam, Arthur Lee, Germaine. What do they want of the truth! If they spoke the truth and admitted it and accepted it, nobody'd fight in their damned wars! There wouldn't be anything to fight about!"

He eyed me sullenly. I had a sudden horrible fear that he meant what he said. "You think it's useless for us to make this report, Tom?"

"I certainly do," he said, "but we got to do it! If we can get it into Thompson's hands, he *might* believe it! He might even make Lord North and the King believe it! They might get word back to Clinton and Cornwallis, and make 'em either start fighting the war the way it ought to be fought, or stop fighting entirely."

He groaned. "I knew this would happen, Oliver! I knew that if I ever let 'em get me into the army I'd be just as much of a damned fool as all the rest of 'em!"

In spite of Leighton's warning, we felt in duty bound to try the roads to the northward; but on every path, every road, at every bridge and ferry we found rebel militiamen, lank-haired, unshaven, half clothed, living like vagabonds in little huts and dealing insolently and inquisitively with everyone who tried to go north past them.

Again and again we watched men and women being searched by those vagabonds, who constituted themselves a court of last appeal on the truth or falsity of the statements they heard. With bleak laughter they searched women down to the skin, making great play with their hands beneath the skirts of their frightened victims; often discharging their muskets as if by accident between the feet of men who looked as though they might protest. Again and again we saw men marched off, cocked muskets pressed to the smalls of their backs.

At night the campfires of those shambling, pock-marked ragamuffins burned in a wavering line across the countryside; and long before we gave up our attempt to break through that ugly cordon, we knew that if we tried it, we'd soon afterward find ourselves confronting Steven Leighton; and I, for one, knew that Steven, in warning me, had done even more than I had a right to expect. He could do no more.

"We've got just one chance," I told Buell, after two days of these futile attempts. "Arnold's suggestion was the right one. We'll have to take the Wilderness Trail to the southwest. Then, when we can, we'll have to cut back southeast and reach the coast. There'll be Loyalist regiments at Savannah and Beaufort and Charleston, and all along Cornwallis' line of march. All we've got to do is reach 'em."

I suppose Buell and I should have been filled with unhappiness and despair as we set out for Winchester and the beginning of that long trail into the unknown; but one of the oddities of war is that it numbs the brain of those caught by it. If it lasts long enough, he becomes insensible to weariness, to his own appearance, to suffering. His grasp on honesty and honor is often weak and at times nonexistent. If the conditions are right, he finds himself not only willing but eager to lie, steal, murder, while his conscience sleeps quietly within him, stifled by war.

So the Wilderness Trail had no terrors for us. We went toward it as we'd have gone toward any road, confident in our ability to conquer it and emerge unscathed.

CHAPTER LXX

Wilderness trail—miserable, rocky, crowded, danger-strewn path from civilization into the unknown!

How often and how often I've thought back to that twisting, turning, foot-bruising, back-breaking road on which men, women and little children pressed on and on, farther and farther from the scenes and the people they had always known, deliberately beggaring themselves to escape misgovernment and the threat of war, deliberately undergoing every hardship and every uncertainty in order to find a land where they could again be free. God grant to all peoples a Wilderness Trail at whose end they can find surcease from demagogues, interference, greed, intolerance, and politicians who bring war upon their countries because they lack the courage to insist upon a peaceful solution of their nation's troubles.

Winchester, because of the endless stream of people moving to the southwestward, toward Kentucky, was like a never-ending fair, but a fair viewed sidelong by a fearful and suspicious audience.

While Buell shopped for hatchets and flints, needle and thread, fishhooks and lines, pans, kettles, bacon, rope, meal—all the countless things we needed for our long trip—I questioned those who passed, hoping to find someone who knew Massachusetts—someone, perhaps, who had lived in the shadow of Great Blue Hill and could give me news of Milton; but every last one to whom I spoke looked sour and made short and reluctant answers—and I knew why.

They were Loyalists, neutrals, people sick of war, and so afraid to talk—afraid of what would almost certainly happen to them if they let slip one unguarded word to any man of rebel sympathies.

They'd had too much war, too much Congress, too much talk of Liberty from men who didn't know the meaning of the word.

From daylight to dark they plodded past; single families and groups of families, every family carrying with it the material for a new home in a new world—chickens, ducks and roosters packed into coops; cows fastened to tailboards of carts; plows lashed out of harm's way along the sides; cats suspended in bags from seat tops; dogs of every size and color perched beside drivers, barking importantly from the shelter of carts; every cart a crammed storehouse of mattresses, chairs, frying pans, farm utensils.

Buell returned from his shopping trip with nothing but a short-handled wooden maul, a purchase that seemed to me useless since I knew it was too light for anything except driving tent pegs.

"For God's sake," I said, "what's the reason for this? You spend five hours hunting supplies to take us to Kentucky; then come back with a bung starter! If we waste time here or anywhere else, we may be responsible for people's deaths."

"Oliver," Buell said, "if you think I want to stay in this place longer than I must, you're mistaken. The town's lousy with rebels, itching for a chance to find a Loyalist and take everything away from him. And that ain't the worst of it! Winchester's overrun with Frenchmen, just like all those towns in Virginia. There must be French storekeepers in every town in America! You can't buy a damned thing without having to dicker with one of 'em, and you know what happens when you try to outdicker a Frenchman! Give 'em two years more, and they'll own the whole country!"

He spat copiously. "You just can't handle 'em, Oliver! They know everybody going through here is on his way to Kentucky, and they know nobody's going to turn back if he can help it. They know pretty near everybody traveling this road is doing his damnedest to get shut of war and Congress and rebels, and I never heard of a Frenchman that could help taking advantage of a situation like that! They won't sell you ten flints: you got to buy the whole bag at ten times what it's worth. You can't buy a little piece of cloth: you got to take the whole bolt at robbers' prices. Same with rope. Same with everything they've got in their shops! I tried to buy two sheets of note paper, so you and I could write a letter if we wanted to, and he wouldn't sell it to me unless I took the whole quire at five hundred dollars."

He tossed up his bung starter and caught it neatly. "Well, Oliver, if I've got to buy a whole quire on a Frenchman's terms, I'll buy it;

but he'll have to take some of it back on *my* terms. That's fair enough, ain't it? Why should the French have it all their own way? They figure on helping the rebels take this country away from us, and then taking it away from the rebels. I don't like 'em, Oliver, and they certainly don't like Americans. You ought to hear what they call us! They don't have a good word for anyone. Look you right in the face and call you names like the ones we learned in Paris. Blue camel—species of decayed filth—son of an old pig and a female canal boat! That's what one of 'em just called me, thinking I didn't know what he was saying! That's a Frenchman's idea of being funny, Oliver. Well, to hell with 'em!"

From his waistcoat he drew a piece of rebel currency, regarded it scornfully and handed it to me. It was a hundred-dollar bill, bearing a crude likeness of a beaver gnawing a tree and the word *Perseverando.*

"Look at that beaver," Buell said. "Nothing but a woodchuck with a gouty tail! I could grave a better beaver than that with a cold-chisel! And look what they call that beaver! A Perseverando! Dirty, like the French!

"Well, Oliver, before I leave this town I'm going to grave a Perseverando of my own. We'll buy out half the Frenchmen in Winchester with hundred-dollar Perseverandos!"

We left Winchester on a bright March morning that smelled of moist earth and growing things; and to our northern eyes the buzzards that hung far, far overhead, describing slow circles against a pale blue sky, seemed to guarantee that spring and fair weather lay before us.

The numbers of people I had seen at Winchester, bound for Kentucky, had impressed me; but not until we were on the road ourselves did we have the feeling that the whole world was Kentucky-bound.

As we moved along the fertile Shenandoah Valley—that enormous cradle of rich soil, snug between guardian ranges to left and right—we found the road congested with those migrating families, each one a self-supporting, self-sufficient entity complete with horses, cow, dogs, chickens, father, mother, sons, daughters, sons-in-law, daughters-in-law, gloomy aunts, helpless grandfathers.

So crowded was the road that to travel on it was almost like traveling with an army in which everyone marches always in an allotted place. We couldn't hurry, for while we could pass one family with little difficulty, we had to pass fifty in order to make genuine progress, and to attempt such a thing would have caused broken carts, hard feelings, angry words.

Buell didn't seem to mind our slow advance, but to me it was galling. For one thing, I was uneasy because my report to Benjamin Thompson was still unsent.

For another thing, I had a singular half-formed desire, only partly admitted to myself, to see and speak with Julia Bishop.

If I was to see her at all, I knew, I must see her soon; for at the first opportunity I planned to branch off from the Wilderness Trail, cross the Blue Ridge Mountains on our left, and strike toward a seaport.

Buell was sure that when we reached Staunton, a hundred miles from Winchester and the last real town on the road to Kentucky, we'd find a pass through the mountains that would lead us to a river that eventually flowed into the James. All we'd need to do, he said, was to get ourselves a boat and travel by water down through Richmond and beyond. Eventually, he said, we'd come across Simcoe's Rangers, or some other of Arnold's men, and our troubles would be over.

I was dubious about this plan because I knew that Arnold's attack on Richmond would have stirred up the rebels for miles around, and that for us to go there would be like walking into a hornets' nest.

"I think we shouldn't leave this trail," I told him, "until we have reliable intelligence of what's happening on the other side of those mountains. When we find out for certain where Cornwallis' army is, and Arnold's army, and what sort of troops the rebels are using against 'em, we can decide what to do. Until then we ought to stay on this road and keep our eyes open for friends."

What I said to Buell was the exact truth; but I also knew in my heart that I'd be disappointed indeed if we learned of a safe road to the seacoast before I'd had the chance to speak with Julia Bishop.

If I'd been put to it to explain why Mrs. Bishop's pale face and enormous dark eyes recurred so often to me, I might have said it was because she so poignantly brought back to me all my memories of Sally Leighton—the memories that, with the passage of the years and the repeated dashing of my hopes, had become dimmed and at times unreal.

I might have said it was because there had been things I had wanted to say to her, and that she had wanted to say to me—things we had been prevented from saying by circumstances beyond our control.

I might have explained, no doubt, in a dozen different ways; but the real truth was that her pale gaiety had held out to me a promise of something mighty strange and mighty pleasant—something piercingly sweet and exotic—something like an embodiment of all the intangible delights of a summer moon over still waters; of the night scent of honeysuckle flowing of its own weight down to the sea.

I was young and I wanted to see her for the excellent reason that I was lonesome and wanted to see her. I'd been long away from a sympathetic woman, and from two or three words that Julia had let drop and the way she'd looked at me, I knew she was sympathetic.

Buell smelled a rat as soon as I refused to travel at night, when all those slow-moving families had gone into camp by the roadside, and their fires twinkled in a long line, like a jeweled snake, across the meadows of the flatlands and through the laurel thickets where mountain spurs came down into the valley.

"Might miss somebody," he cried. "Miss who! Who is there for us to miss? You must 'a' been looking at the people in Craig's Church a good deal harder than I was if you saw somebody I didn't." He was puzzled and suspicious; and I was puzzled too—puzzled at myself and my unwillingness to discuss Julia Bishop with my dearest friend.

So many things, so many, many things had gone wrong for us in the past six years that I think I expected none of my hopes to be fulfilled; so it seemed to me like a dream when, as we topped the rise that looks down upon the crossroads settlement of Staunton, I heard a voice say, "My landy land! It's Mr. Oliver!", and looked up to see Mrs. Bishop's pale face and dark eyes beneath a wagon hood.

There was a little stream between us and the wagon, and I never remember how I got across it. Buell said I transferred myself as a magician might. "One minute you were walking alongside our cart," he told me, "and the next second you were standing beside that wagon looking up into it like a hound dog looking up a tree at a raccoon, hoping he'll fall out!"

Our meeting with Mrs. Bishop and her father was a fortunate thing for us.

"We've been here four days, hoping you'd come along," Mrs. Bishop said. "I told Papa we *had* to wait, in case you'd feel tempted to turn off here."

"I'm glad you did," I said. "The road was so packed with people I thought we'd never catch up with you. What made you think we'd take this road?"

She laughed lightly. "My land, Mr. Oliver, didn't I tell you I was coming this way myself? Surely a gentleman couldn't have done anything else when a lady drops a hint like that!"

She leaned forward and spoke earnestly. "Don't you s'pose Papa and I and Mr. Anburey could put two and two together? Don't you s'pose we knew the roads to the north were guarded? If you went north, you'd 'a' been killed! You couldn't go back to the south the way you must have come up—not without walking straight into a rebel army. My goodness lawsy, Mr. Oliver, don't you s'pose I knew you'd had trouble with the rebels, and been obliged to go somewhere, and in a hurry? Don't you s'pose I knew you'd have come back to say good-by to me if you hadn't been driven off? My land o' land, Mr. Oliver: I knew!"

"My name isn't just Oliver," I said. "It's Oliver Wiswell."

She fluffed out her skirts and sat upright. "That's a real nice name, Mr. Wiswell! I'm kinda used to Oliver, though, so I'll just call you Oliver. You wouldn't dream how tore to pieces I was because you'd been so northern-formal, and forgot to tell me your first name before you went away! My land, Oliver, I've had to put up with a deal of hasty language from my papa on account of wanting to wait for a gentleman when I didn't even know his whole name, so I'd be obliged if you'd look around this camp till you find Papa. When we're on the road again, I'd like to have you clear up quite a number of things for me, but right now you go see Papa!"

Julia Bishop had so engrossed me that I had been scarcely conscious of my surroundings. Now I saw that her father's wagons, five of them, were drawn roughly into the form of a crescent, with a picket line of horses, mules and cows running straight across the open end, like a bowstring. An open fire, covered with a heavy iron gridiron on four legs, burned in a hole midway between the sides of the crescent; and over the fire, stirring something in a pot, was a fat and gaudy Negress. Her dress was brown with irregular yellow splotches on it, interspersed with occasional splashes of crimson; and her eyes, as she tasted what she had been stirring in the pot, rolled wildly and seemed to be the size of the brass buttons on a seaman's coat. Around the horses puttered six or eight Negro men, most of them white-headed.

"Where'll I find your father?" I asked Mrs. Bishop.

She peered around the hood of the wagon, and screamed at the fat Negress. "You, Primula! Where's the major?"

The Negress, looking defiant, hurriedly attempted to replace the spoon in the kettle, dropped it on the ground, snatched it up and wiped it on one enormous buttock; then pointed with it to the end wagon. "In there with that sick man, Miss Julia."

Mrs. Bishop glanced upward despairingly, as if asking Heaven to witness her trials. Then she screamed at the Negress again. "How many times I got to tell you not to point with a spoon! You go tell the major I want him! Tell him Mr. Oliver's come!"

The side curtains of the end wagon were suddenly and violently agitated, and the head of Major Dustin appeared between them. "Cato," he shouted, "Hasdrubal! Romulus! Hitch up those horses!" To his daughter he bawled: "Send him over here in a hurry! We got to get back on the road quick!"

As I went toward the wagon, Major Dustin continued to shout at me. His words were abusive, but I knew his irascibility was assumed. "Hell and damnation, Mr. Oliver! What you been doing with yourself all these days? Seems like we'd been here a year, letting all the riffraff in the world walk by us, just so we could give you some advice you prob'ly won't take! I tell you, young feller, any man who tries to give advice these days is just a plumb damn fool!"

"I'll be mighty grateful for all you can spare," I said.

"By God, sir, if you are, you're one in a million," Major Dustin cried. "Come up into this wagon!"

I climbed to the seat and saw, on a mattress in the body of the cart, a half-naked youth with such a singularly sandy-red coloring that he was like a giant carrot. His hair was sandy red, his body mottled with clusters of rust-colored freckles, the flesh of his upper chest swollen in ridges, as a carrot is swollen. Beside him was a bucket of water and a heap of bloody bandages.

The major climbed down beside him, picked up one of the bandages, soused it in the water, wrung it out, and carefully placed it against the boy's head, where until recently an ear must have grown.

The major looked up at me. "This is Ian MacFreel from Deep River. I know him well. His father bought two horses from me four years ago. The father's all right and so's this boy. Take a good look at him."

He lifted up the bandage, to let me see the spot where the ear had been. A patch the size of a saucer had been carved from the side of his head. His whole upper body, seemingly, had been pounded with something that had broken the skin in places, and left welts and bruises tinged with pale green and dirty yellow.

The major laid the bandage over the earless spot and bound it lightly in place with what I took to be a woman's stocking.

"How you feel, Ian?" he asked.

"Good," the boy said. "I've got kind of a stuffed feeling, like as if I'd been drinking new licker."

The major was obviously pleased. "Look at that," he told me. "Ian was out of his head and crazy as a dipper duck when we picked him up five days ago. Now all he's got is a headache, and tomorrow he'll be fit to ride a horse same as any of us." He tapped my shoulder. "You got here just in time, young feller! I told Julia I'd wait till Ian was fit to travel, and not one minute longer. To tell you the truth, I wouldn't 'a' waited this long if Julia hadn't raised so much hell! I thought they'd prob'ly killed you long ago, but she said she knew a damned sight different. She said she dreamed you'd try to cut across to the James River or down the Roanoke, and she said you'd got to be warned not to."

He looked down at MacFreel. "You feel like telling about Alta mahaw Ford again, Ian?"

"Yes, sir," the boy said. "I'd like real well to! I'll tell it and tell it till everyone knows what kind of bastards those rebels are, God damn 'em to hell!"

"I told you not to cuss," the major said irritably. "People like to do their own cussing. You tell the story, and let the other feller cuss to suit himself!"

To me he said, "Maybe I can save Ian some trouble by telling you what's been goin' on for the past two or three months. I guess you know how Cornwallis came into Charleston with an army a year and a half ago and started north, so to clear the rebels out of North and South Carolina."

"Yes, sir," I said. "General Arnold told me about that."

The major slapped his leg and spat copiously from the wagon. "He did, did he? Did he tell you how Gates got licked at Camden and ran eighty miles in one day?"

"Yes, Major."

"Ain't war the damnedest?" the major asked. "Arnold beat Burgoyne's army and Gates got all the credit. Gates signed the Convention with 'em, and then nobody paid any attention to it. Arnold couldn't stomach the rebels any more, so he took an army of Loyalists up to Richmond and knocked hell out of the rebels; and Gates, who used to be an English officer, brought an army of rebels down to fight the British and got worse licked than Burgoyne was."

He shook his head and spat again, as if to say that the folly of the human race exasperated him beyond expression.

"Well," he went on, "here's a few things Arnold *didn't* tell you. Cornwallis marched his men three hundred miles straight up through South Carolina and into North Carolina—a great march! A couple of months ago he turned northeast and went after General Greene, who'd come down to try to stop him with an army of rebel militia and a thousand or two Continentals. He made another great march with that army of his, half of 'em Loyalists and half British, and a month ago he chased every last man of Greene's army out of North Carolina and across the Dan River into Virginia. That army of Cornwallis' is about a hundred miles due south of us."

"That's good news," I said. "If it's that close, I can join it."

"That's what Julia thought you'd try to do," Dustin said. "You can't do it! Listen: the rebel militia that was with Greene, especially the North Carolina militia, were skunks! Every time Loyalist troops or the regulars went for 'em, they broke and ran. All along the route Cornwallis followed, the country's full of North Carolina militia that ran away. They're all armed, and they're hiding in every ditch and under every pile of brush. Every night they break into barns, rob henhouses, kill sheep, steal cows, scare all the womenfolk within an inch of their lives. They murder anybody that tries to stop 'em, and if they come across a man they suspect of being a Loyalist, they stab him in the back or cut his throat. Julia says you've got some information you want to get out safely. If that's so, don't try to head south from here. You'll never get through."

"Buell thinks we can," I said. "He's inventive, and he's got a knack for disguising himself. He thinks——"

"Who's Buell?" the major asked.

I told him about Buell's skill at printing and inventing, and of what a help he'd been to me in Halifax, England, France and on the trip from Westover to Frederick.

"If he thinks he can get through to the southward," the major said, "he ain't half as smart as you think! He just don't know rebels."

"They tarred and feathered him in Boston, Major."

"That don't mean a thing," the major said. "Those Boston rebels were nothing but playful little children compared to these fellers down here. Go get Buell. He needs to hear what Ian has to say."

Two minutes later Buell was huddled beside me on the wagon seat, staring down at Ian MacFreel and the major.

CHAPTER LXXI

WHEN my eyes were accustomed to the dimness of the wagon, I could see that the welts on MacFreel's breast, stomach, ribs, shoulders and upper arms had raised lines along their centers, like miniature ridgepoles.

"Tell Mr. Oliver about the Loyalists down your way, Ian," the major said helpfully. "How many are there?"

"Not as many as there was," MacFreel said. "Not nearly as many as there was. There used to be a lot of us. Everybody up and down Deep River was a Loyalist."

He twisted a sandy eyebrow in my direction. "The Deep River and the Haw River are about thirty miles apart," he explained. "They run together to make the Cape Fear River that comes out at Wilmington. Pretty near every family on those two rivers and in between 'em was Loyalist. There used to be more Loyalists in North Carolina, my father said, than in any of the other twelve colonies. Those that weren't Loyalists were trash."

He made a groaning sound. "Stinking cattle! Damned worthless loafers out of the gutter. Lousy, sneaking——"

"Now, Ian," the major said severely. "Abuse don't help. Just stick to the truth, and any man worth his salt'll get madder'n you could make him with any amount of language."

"Yes, sir," the boy said dutifully. "Well, us folks between those two rivers, we're all Scots. We kept our land cultivated, and worked hard. When this rebellion started, none of us felt any need of rebelling, so we didn't rebel. Those that turned rebel never worked much. Most of 'em started being rebels just because they were tired of doing nothing. If they owned land, they'd never cleared it, so when the rebels offered 'em bounties to go in their militia, they could get richer taking bounties than they could staying home on their land."

"Patriots!" the major said.

MacFreel laughed. "Yes, and when they started marching around in crowds and calling themselves Patriots, we couldn't stand 'em off. First they seized all our arms—all we didn't keep buried. Then they stole our farms. If one or two Loyalist families tried to resist, five hundred rebel militia'd chase 'em into the woods. The only chance we had of getting at 'em was to have Cornwallis' army come close, so we could join it and have officers to lead us. We knew if we could do that, we could fight off all the rebels in the world."

He seemed to lose interest in what he was saying. Major Dustin prompted him. "So when Cornwallis reached your section, I suppose you-all were pretty excited?"

"We certainly were," MacFreel said. "That army of Cornwallis' would 'a' excited anyone! You never saw anything so pretty! It made you want to cry, the way they marched, all their flags flying and drums rolling, and a Scots regiment with kilts swinging, and dragoons like pictures in a book. The whole lot of 'em went right close to the headwaters of Deep River and the Haw River, chasing rebels. We got word Greene's whole army was being chased out of the state, and some of us went up to see what was happening."

He quirked that sandy eyebrow at me. "You never saw such a sight! Those rebel troops were running, tight as they could run, to reach the Dan River and cross it into Virginia. Cornwallis' light troops—regulars and Loyalists—were treading on their heels."

With an effort he sat up. "I never saw such nice-looking men! Tarleton's Legion was out in front, every last one of 'em a Loyalist. I'd 'a' given a heap to 'a' been in that legion, chasing those chicken thieves of Greene's! The last twenty-four hours, when they were trying to catch Greene before he got across the Dan, they marched forty miles! Forty miles in twenty-four hours! That's marching, that is!"

Major Dustin fussed at him. "Now, Ian! Just lay yourself down before you get excited!"

The boy propped himself on his hands to face us. I was fascinated by the greenish color of the freckles on his welts. "The rebels got away, God damn 'em! That meant there wasn't any rebel army left in either of the Carolinas, so that was our chance. I spoke to one of Tarleton's officers and asked him if we could join the army.

" 'You go home,' he told us, 'and get as many more as you can.'

"We had to be mighty careful, I told him, because there was still a lot of rebels left in our section, and if they got wind of what we were doing, they'd kill us separately before we got together. What was more, they'd kill our womenfolk too.

"So he planned it for us. We were to go home and spread the word. Ten days later we were to come to Altamahaw Ford on the Haw River—sort of straggle there. We'd find some of Tarleton's Legion waiting, and they'd escort us to camp, where we'd be made part of the army."

MacFreel stopped and with cautious fingers explored a purple spot on his ribs. "I ain't bleeding there, am I?" he asked the major.

"No," the major said, "but you will if you don't lie down!"

MacFreel lowered himself to his mattress.

"Well," he said, "when we got home and told what had happened, pretty near every white man on those two rivers wanted to go to Altamahaw Ford with us. We got Colonel Pyle to lead us, and we could 'a' raised a thousand Loyalists right in that one section! You never saw men so anxious to fight! The rebels had robbed 'em and beaten 'em and treated 'em like nigras for six years!"

He stopped, seemed to cogitate, and made a sound that might have been faint amusement or faint despair.

"Well, we took the best shots—three hundred and seventy-two of us there was. We traveled in twos and threes, so not to be noticed. Most of us didn't have guns, because the rebels long ago rounded up all they could find.

"We got to Trapper's crossroads, a mile to the eastward of Alta-mahaw Ford, on the twenty-fourth of February and lay there till morning, without building fires or making a noise. You couldn't take a step through the brush, hardly, without stumbling over one of our boys from Alamance and Randolph.

"In the morning Colonel Pyle blew his whistle, the way we'd agreed, and we came out and started for the ford. Halfway to it we saw dragoons in green coats walking their horses toward us, and we felt mighty good, I want you to know! The noise we made, hollering to those men of Tarleton's, was as loud as though there'd been a thou-sand of us instead of only three hundred and seventy-two."

Young MacFreel sighed, a long quivering sigh that made my heart sink.

"The hell of it was," he said, "they weren't Tarleton's men. They were Lee's rebel dragoons. Seems Greene, after he'd crossed the Dan, got word about us wanting to join Cornwallis. He knew if we did, there wouldn't be a rebel left in the south after the way we'd been treated, so he sent Lee's cavalry to try to stop us. I guess somebody must have told Lee where we proposed to meet.

"Well, we marched right up to 'em, hurrahing and waving our hats, and they took off their hats and waved back. When we came close, they opened up and let us pass between."

He was silent, and so were we—so silent that we clearly heard the faint sound he made as he plucked at his blanket.

"I didn't see it start," he went on in a low voice. "Someone shouted, and then all those dragoons had their sabers out, slashing with 'em. I guess what saved me was Hal MacLaren having his head split in two and falling on me. When I got my ear cut off, it didn't hurt much. I'd 'a' got up again, I guess, if it hadn't been for MacLaren. When he fell on me, the blood ran out of him like out of a pail. I never heard screams like that before. I didn't know men had enough wind in 'em to scream so long. In between the screaming you'd hear 'em shouting for quarter. I don't suppose the whole thing took five minutes." He yawned profoundly.

Buell cleared his throat. "How many got away?"

MacFreel yawned again—the sort of yawn that precedes seasickness. "I ain't sure. I got away. The major heard four others crawled out and got to Cornwallis' army. I didn't see any of 'em. I thought everybody was killed but me. After that first five minutes, they rode up and down slashing the bodies, just to make sure. I didn't feel much of anything, but I suppose that's how I got most of these." He gestured toward the welts that covered his upper body.

I heard Buell licking dry lips, and my own mouth was coppery.

"Didn't any of 'em fight back?" Buell asked.

"Not that I know of," MacFreel said. "If they did, they fought barehanded. There wasn't even time to get out a knife."

He raised his head from the blanket. "Come to think of it, they couldn't 'a' fought back, because they laid there in a long line, just the way we were when we marched between the dragoons. They hit us so quick we didn't have a chance to fight."

He shook his head. "That was a long line of dead men! A long line! You'd never think men could look so twisted when they died so quick."

I remembered the boatloads of dead officers and men that had been rowed back to Long Wharf from Bunker Hill, hacked and mangled by rebel musket balls; remembered the strange angles at which their legs had protruded from their bodies, the boneless contortions into which those bodies had been stiffened by death.

It occurred to me with something of a shock that the MacFreel boy had lived six years in the midst of civil war. He was a mere child when it had begun. He'd known war's indignities; and yet he knew mighty little about war, since the death agonies of his friends had come as a surprise to him a short ten days ago.

"How did you get away?" I asked.

"Same as a wounded buck. At night I crawled into the brush. In the daytime I laid up, waiting for a nigra to come along. Seems like all this talking about Liberty has made the rebels harder and harder on the nigras for fear the nigras'll want some of it themselves, so I knew if I could find a nigra I'd be all right. Well, I found one, and he brought me up here to the Wilderness Trail, where Major Dustin's nigras came across me and told the major."

Major Dustin snorted. "Don't it beat hell? The rebels kill nigras for being so ignorant as to believe all their tarradiddle about Liberty, and they kill white men who're educated enough to question the damn fool things they say."

He gave me a meaning glance; then said to MacFreel, "Let's see, Ian: I suppose you're figuring on going back to Deep River when you get healed up."

"Going back?" MacFreel cried. "Not by a damned sight! Those British didn't protect us, like they promised they would! Loyalists can't go back if they're known or suspected! Somebody'd tell on me, sure! They'd run me down with hounds, like a runaway nigra, and if I was such a damn fool as to ask someone for food, they'd most likely kill the people I asked!"

The major seemed surprised. "But supposing, Ian, that these gentlemen wanted to strike over to the coast from here—over to Norfolk or Beaufort or Savannah or Charleston. You'd be willing to go along with 'em to show 'em the way, wouldn't you?"

"I would not," MacFreel said. "A hundred miles south of here every road's full of troops. You can't dodge 'em. If you don't run foul of Lee's rebel dragoons, you'll strike Tarleton's Legion, or North Carolina militia regiments running away, or Loyalist regiments that shoot first and ask questions afterwards, or Greene's Continentals living off friends and enemies alike, or Cornwallis' regulars, who'll stick you with a bayonet before you can say knife! They're all moving up and down those roads like tide rivers, Major—a hundred miles up the road today and a hundred miles down the road tomorrow! They're always popping up where you think they ain't.

"No, sir, Major! I'm through with fighting! I don't want any more of it! All the rebels know is they want to kill all the Loyalists, and all the Loyalists know is that they can't never have peace till they drive out all the rebels!

"Well, Major, it ain't possible to do either of those things. If it ain't possible, what's the use getting killed over it? You ought to have a damned good reason for getting shot or hacked to pieces! You bet I ain't going back to North Carolina!"

There was no adequate answer to MacFreel's remarks, and the three of us attempted none. I sat and stared at his bandaged head and the long saber bruises on his freckled body, and thought about that long windrow of distorted bodies, transformed in a moment's time from cheering Americans to disemboweled corpses. I was satisfied that MacFreel was right.

"Well, sir," I told the major, "we're mighty grateful to you for taking the trouble to wait for us. We'd be fools if we ran contrary to your advice. We'll keep on toward Kentucky with you for a piece, but if you see any way for me to reach the coast with my information, I'll count on you to find it for me."

CHAPTER LXXII

As we went on and on, into the southwest, we left settlements and stores, homes and farms, peach orchards and meadows, far behind, so far behind that those familiar marks of civilization might have been wiped from the earth. It was as though we ventured farther and farther into an ocean of a wilderness that grew constantly more turbulent.

The mountains rolled toward us in longer and longer waves out of the southwest.

Each morning, as we pressed on toward the northward-rushing spring, those mountain waves were lustrous in the rising sun, all softness and pearl and misty blues—beautiful ramparts of a land of hope and plenty.

Each evening those waves were an ever-deepening threatening purple against the crimson sky—a barrier to the unknown.

Our only milestones were creeks and the tributaries of far-distant great rivers; fords and rude ferries; log trading cabins, hot springs, bridges of insecure logs over roaring torrents, rude roadside taverns, mountain meadows. The names along that trail became as familiar to me as those of Tremont Street, Piccadilly, the Rue St. Honoré, the Rue des St. Pères—North Branch of the James, Woods on Catawba River, New River, Inglis' Ferry, the Forks of the Road, Mac's Meadows, the Head of Holston, Atkins' Ordinary, Seven-Mile Ford, the Block House, Clinch River, Powell Mountain, Martin's Cabin, Big Spring.

Week after week we stumbled, creaked, bumped onward, scorched by the sun, frozen by icy dews, drenched by sudden showers, parboiled to a crinkled pallor by deluges from the northeast that howled down the valleys.

Day after day, whenever we topped a rise, we saw our fellow travelers behind us and before us, stretching off into infinity. Everywhere, beside that rough road, men labored with rope and rawhide to repair the wagons wrenched apart by the cruel ruts and boulders, the mud holes and gullies of that endless road.

I remember well the broken axles, the broken wheels, the broken spokes, the broken harnesses of that journey; the rattling, rumbling, thumping, screaming, whip-cracking and cursing with which we crossed the rocky fords; the endless miles of dark laurel thickets that crouched upon the mountainsides, as if waiting to sweep down upon that endless line of travelers and engulf them; the daily search along creeks and up side valleys for deer and turkey, for geese and bear, for any edible thing that would eke out the johnnycake and salt pork, the crackling-bread, beans and catfish that were the staples of our smoky meals; the moaning songs of the major's Negroes late at night.

All these things come back to me as clearly as though they'd happened yesterday. Clearest of all my memories of that long journey are those of Julia Bishop's disembodied, pale face beside me in the scented spring darkness of the wild, wide valleys; the rough gray dress she daily wore, pinned at the throat with a brooch shaped like a daisy with petals of pink glass; the glossy black of her hair that, in the sun, showed unexpected gleams of underlying brown; her interest in every least thing; her readiness to have a hand in any labor or in any play; her wide and candid glance, never so candid as when she hung on Buell's words with simulated admiration; never more sweet than when she led me to tell her of Sally, as she almost daily did, and spoke with pretended wonderment of the miracle of Sally's enduring love for me.

I never rode out in the early morning to look for deer or turkey that I didn't find her dressed and ready to go; at night, when we crowded around the fires, she sat beside me, knitting away at a woolen stocking, or sewing on something of her father's; and always she contrived to bring the talk around to Sally and her rebel leanings.

"Don't you think, Oliver lamb," she'd say, "don't you think that when a woman's in love with a man, her interests should become his? Don't you think that if she truly loved him, she'd find it impossible to cling to her own ideas—if she had any—provided the ideas might hurt her man's feelings, or harm him?"

If I tried to point out that a woman might honestly and rightly consider it her duty to persuade a man to other ways of thinking, she laughed lightly.

"My merciful gracious heavenly goodness!" she'd cry. "Why on *uth* should a little snippety snoop of a girl, who cain't even coax her brain to figure out when to butter a cake tin, consider herself a fit person to persuade *any* man to change his mind about war or politics or business? My kindly shinin' stars! A little jellyhead like that, she wouldn't hesitate a teeny minute to tell Mr. William Shakespeare he wasn't writing interestin' plays, an' why didn't he do something more worth while, like figurin' out charades for the Queen to act in?"

"But Sally's not like that," I said. "She always encouraged me."

Julia wouldn't let me go on. "She did *not,* Mr. Stubborn Ice-Water Boston! How could she encourage you if she let you go away? You couldn't do any sort of writing if your head was all worried up by a little mash-brained female all the time, could you? Certainly you couldn't! *She* encouraged you, indeed! My lawsy land o' love! Don't you dare to talk to Julia as if she was a little twitty bird too, with chinaberries for brains!"

In the course of her arguings with me, she was free with information about herself, her dead husband, and her father's fortunes.

Her father had somehow acquired title to twenty thousand acres of land on the Kentucky River—land unbelievably fertile and rich in game.

Her husband, she said—when she spoke formally—had been mortally injured on the hunting field. In her franker moments she told me, with a lack of reserve she often displayed when we were alone, that he had been a morning drinker; that his breakfast, on the morning of his death, had been a full bottle of whisky; that he had soon thereafter fallen while opening a gate, and had his head ruinously stepped on by his horse.

"But my deary me," said Julia, with appalling frankness, "it was a mercy all round! He'd 'a' busted a blood vessel before long, and got awful tired of himself! Papa never liked him much, and it didn't take me long to find out he had too much truck with nigra women." She spoke casually, as though saying her husband had a minor affliction, like a sprained ankle.

She was a great hand to say outrageous things with such wide-eyed innocence, such sweet friendliness, that I couldn't be as angry with her as I sometimes thought I should.

"I'm sure that Miss Sally of yours must be one of the sweetest ladies in the whole wide world," Julia might say at such a time. "I just *know* you're going to have a happy, happy life with her, because you're so devoted to argument yourself; and from what you tell me about her, she can argue even you down any day. Does she ever kind of squeak and squeal when she argues? And does that get you to walking up and down the floor and cussin'? No, I s'pose not, because you ain't married to her yet! Ah yes, Oliver lamb; I always *did* hear those New England ladies were mighty sweet. They tell me sometimes the neighbors had to take 'em out an' dip 'em in the river in a ducking stool, they hollered so much at their husbands."

Julia'd finish such a bit of humor with a burst of musical laughter, lean her cheek against my shoulder for just an instant, leap up lightly and run away laughing, mocking me.

She lost no opportunity to convince me, both by hints and by direct statements, that I could never get to the seacoast from the Wilderness Trail; that I was a fool to go back to the insanities of war when the peace and security of Kentucky lay before me.

There were times when she half-seriously seemed to be trying to arouse my cupidity.

"You want to know what kind of a house me and my papa going to have in Kentucky, Oliver duck?" she'd ask. "Right smack in the middle of twenty thousand acres we're going to have a house as big as one o' those ancient old palaces of King George's, and a big silver punch bowl always filled on the hall table. We'll have a whole mountain range of woods that gentlemen can go hunting in, and horses for fox huntin' and racin', and lashin's and lashin's of nigras to wait on us. We'll have Maryland cookin', like there ain't any anywhere else, and Papa's going to start a bank. Yes, there'll be plenty of everything for anybody Papa and I like, but they'd pretty soon have to begin being mighty sweet to us if we're going to like 'em much!

"You're a right pleasant gentleman some ways, Oliver pet, but you don't often come right out and be sweet. What's the matter? Swallered a prickly porcupine or something? Or maybe just thinking of that little prickly, seven-year rebel that got herself frozen to that old frozen hill up in that frozen-up old New England of yours!"

Usually she waited for nightfall to sing the praises of Kentucky to me. There was a soft smokiness to the night air in those long valleys to the eastward of the Blue Ridge; and the moon, when there was one, was a glowing scarlet, like a flame seen through crimson silk.

What with Julia's coquetries, the red moon, the sweet smokiness of the air, and that persistent habit of hers of leaning close, I didn't always find it the easiest thing in the world to seem as frostbitten as she made me out to be.

It was at Fort Chissel that we had the news of Cornwallis' great fight at Guildford Court House—a great victory, but gained at such a cost that it was almost as bad as a defeat.

I had known, when we sailed to Virginia with General Arnold, that his expedition up the James River was only a minor matter—only a divertissement, so to speak, to confuse the rebels and lead them to divide their forces while Cornwallis, with his larger army and his famous officers, swept everything before him in South and North Carolina.

How unimportant Arnold's expedition had been by comparison with Cornwallis' tremendous effort—how unimpressive Arnold's dash to Richmond by comparison with Cornwallis' magnificent march— I hadn't fully understood until I heard how the battle of Guildford Court House was fought, and at Fort Chissel saw some of the results with my own eyes.

Fort Chissel was a rude trading post of logs, built many years before by that tireless hunter and explorer, Colonel Byrd of Virginia. Beyond Fort Chissel lay the worst part of the Wilderness Road, the highest mountains, the terrible long valleys of the turbulent Holston and Clinch rivers—and everybody who got as far as Fort Chissel on the road to Kentucky was urgently in need of supplies of all sorts, both to replace losses and breakages, and to guard against running short along the Holston and Clinch.

For days before we reached Fort Chissel, every one of our own little flock of travelers had talked of what he'd buy there. The major hoped for whisky. Julia Bishop wanted green broadcloth for skirts to replace the ones torn to tatters by her passage through the laurel thickets.

MacFreel, who had escaped from Altamahaw Ford with literally nothing to his name, expected to become a man of property at Fort Chissel. Buell and I out of gratitude for his information, Major Dustin out of friendship for his father, Julia out of the kindness of her heart, had promised him a rifle, a bag of bullets, a blanket, a hunting shirt, leather breeches, moccasins.

Even the major's Negroes knew that the white man's Providence would attend to their needs at Fort Chissel, and supply them with an iron spoon for stirring stews, a jew's-harp, checked calico for shirts. . . .

Every last one of us needed something; and so too, I think, did everyone in the straggling long line that stretched unbroken from Fort Chissel back to Maryland and Pennsylvania.

Fort Chissel was nothing but a group of log buildings on a mound. There was a stockade around them, and from under the stockade ran a stream of clear spring water. It was an excellent place for a trading post; but its mere situation didn't account for the unexpected number of carts, wagons, tents, tethered horses and mules that were crowded against the stockade.

When we reached the first of those tents and carts and wagons, we knew something was wrong; for nobody among them was properly equipped for travel. The carts and wagons were makeshift. Their owners' clothes seemed to have been snatched up in a hurry.

The men, for the most part, were freckled like MacFreel, with a look of rawness—almost of savagery. The women, the young girls and boys, seemed half wild. Their over-shoulder glances made me think of nervous colts, ready to kick and run.

Major Dustin groaned when he saw them. "Those folks are North Carolinians," he said. "Sure as you're born, there's been some other kind of hell down to the southward! These folks are running from somep'n, drat 'em! I'll bet you anything they've drunk up every drop of whisky in the place!"

The major's worst fears were realized.

We found a group of men sitting on the sunny platform before the store and idly staring across to the misty slopes of the Blue Ridge. A road ran straight from the platform across that hazy valley toward a notch in the far-off mountains; and upon the road two distant wagons crawled, mere dust specks on the valley floor.

"Well, gentlemen," the major said heartily, "here's a little business for you. Major Dustin and party, bound for Kentucky, and wishful to buy. We'll even trade what we've got for what we need most."

A tall, straggly-mustached man in a checkered shirt and buckskin trousers yawned cavernously and stretched until his shoulders cracked. "I hate to have to say it, Major, but we're out of stock."

"You can't be out of stock!" the major cried. "I'm Major Dustin from Maryland, suh, an' I won't listen to no such talk! I got to have whisky! You ain't out of whisky!"

The straggly-mustached man looked concerned. "Major, I can find you some whisky that won't kill you, maybe, if you can hold on till tomorrow morning. Right now everything's gone. We had unexpected guests from the Dan River a week ago. They took it all."

MacFreel pushed his horse past the major and sat looking down at the half-dozen silent men on the platform. "What happened on the Dan River? I'm Ian MacFreel. I'm from Deep River my own self."

The men pondered this statement. One of them asked, "Ain't you kin to Robbie Clymer?"

"He's my uncle. What happened on the Dan?"

"Robbie Clymer had a nevvy at Altamahaw Ford," the man said.

"That was me," MacFreel said. "What happened on the Dan?"

The man stared across the valley. "We heard nobody got away from Altamahaw Ford."

"Well, I got away," MacFreel said.

"How?" the man asked.

MacFreel looked at him. "Maybe because I had better cover than some—Hal MacLaren's brains spattered all over me and Lauder's insides twisted around my legs. What happened on the Dan?"

The men seemed to relax. "There was a battle, son," the flat-voiced man said. "Cornwallis won, but it cost him so much he had to move toward the coast. You can figure how that affected folks around your section."

"Did you hear anything about my people?" MacFreel asked. "Did you hear what happened to 'em?"

"No, I ain't," the man said. "News is skeerce. If we're looking for somebody, we sit here and wait till they come through the gap at the Meadows of Dan, the way we did. I wouldn't worry, if I was you."

MacFreel nodded. "I'd like to hear about that battle. What's the reason one of you Dan River men can't scare up some whisky for Major Dustin? He took care of me after Altamahaw Ford. Besides, he's been counting on it."

The straggly-mustached man got to his feet, spat copiously over the edge of the platform and wrung brown moisture from his ragged mustache with a gnarled knuckle. "Light, son," he said abruptly. "Seems to me I saw a jug of white whisky cooling in the spring, last time I came past it. It ain't for sale, but Major Dustin's welcome to it."

How the flat-voiced man knew so much about it, I couldn't say, but I think he may have been an officer in the North Carolina rebel militia, and when his troops ran away during the battle, he doubtless decided he was a fool to be killing men against whom he had nothing. His name, he said, was Bent. Whether it was or not, I didn't care, nor did any of the others who sat on that platform of hewn logs, staring across the valley to the far-off notch beyond which lay the tumbling highlands and enormous coastal plains of North and South Carolina—those thousands upon thousands of square miles of forests and fertile fields wherein, as we knew, lines of antlike human creatures crept along the trails, seeking the lives of others—who similarly were seeking theirs.

"I guess you remember how Cornwallis chased Greene across the Dan," Bent said to MacFreel, "and how he called for Loyalists to come in and help him."

MacFreel just spat.

"Well," Bent said, "Cornwallis had fifteen hundred men when he chased Greene across the Dan. He'd destroyed his own baggage and stores, so to move faster, and he had to have food and lots of it. He couldn't get enough supplies up around the Dan, so he fell back to Hillsborough, where cattle were easier to get, and camped there, waiting for Loyalists to join him.

"Greene got word that pretty near the whole province was ready to come out in the open and give the rebels their come-uppance, so back he marched across the Dan, bound to stop the Loyalists from assembling.

"He'd got himself a lot of reinforcements, Greene had: a detachment of Continental troops, a brigade of Virginia militia and two brigades of North Carolina militia, so he must have had seven thousand men to Cornwallis' fifteen hundred. Even so he wouldn't take chances. Every night, pretty near, he moved his whole army, to keep Cornwallis from surprising him.

"Three weeks after that trouble at Altamahaw Ford, some rebel light troops picked a bad camping ground, and Cornwallis got wind of it in about five minutes. That Cornwallis is as good a soldier as you'd want to see, and he didn't waste time. He set right out to beat up those light troops, figuring either that Greene would be obliged to come to their assistance and risk a general engagement—which was what Cornwallis wanted—or that the rebel light troops would be wiped out.

"Well, Greene wouldn't risk coming to their assistance, so Cornwallis caught the light troops and chopped 'em up. That made Greene mad. He began to figure that if Cornwallis was so eager to fight, he might be coaxed to fight on a battleground that Greene picked himself.

"So Greene moved over to Guildford Court House, hunted up the nicest piece of high land anywhere around, and fixed his troops just the way he wanted 'em—North Carolina militia in front as a first line; Virginia militia three hundred yards to the rear as a second line; Continental troops four hundred yards back of them as a third line.

"On the right flank he had Colonel William Washington with his dragoons, light infantry and riflemen; on his left flank Colonel Henry Lee with cavalry, light infantry and riflemen.

"He'd sent away his baggage, so he had no encumbrances; all his troops had eaten well and had a good rest, and he was sure he could lick anyone that dared to attack him, even if the attacker had twice as many men.

"Well, sir, Cornwallis with his fifteen hundred men didn't give a damn for Greene's superiority in numbers or position. He and all his officers said they could outthink, outguess and outfight any rebel army that ever was. The morning Cornwallis found out where Greene was, he and his men marched twelve miles without food. Not a man in the army had a mouthful all that day, or till sundown the next day.

"They marched twelve miles to Guildford Court House, and when they got there they went right into action. Didn't wait a minute. The rebels were so sure of winning that even the militia held onto their positions till the last second before they ran.

"I don't believe there ever was a battle fought better or harder than Cornwallis' troops fought that one on an empty stomach. They walked up to that first line of North Carolina militiamen as if they never even noticed the way their men were dropping. They bayoneted the North Carolina militia the way you'd pitchfork hay. When Cornwallis' troops moved on to the Virginians in the second line, the whole place looked covered with dead, and with wounded just able to heave themselves around. You'd never have thought, even then, that Cornwallis had men enough left to fight anyone, but there was enough of 'em to rush at the Virginians with bayonets and drive 'em into the woods. Then it seemed as though Cornwallis' dead got up from the ground and began to run toward the third line, the Continentals."

Bent leaned forward, and with a stick sketched rapidly for us in the dust how Cornwallis' artillery had been dragged up that long hill to face the last line of rebel troops; how guards, grenadier and infantry regiments, in spite of empty stomachs, a twelve-mile march and violent labors on the lower slopes of the hill, had moved with the regularity of machines from one part to another of that thunderous hilltop, bayoneting Continental troops from impregnable positions, and crushing detachments that were trying to re-form.

"When it was over," Bent said, "the only rebels left on the hill were dead or wounded, but there was enough of those for ten battlefields. A third of Cornwallis' troops had been killed or wounded, but there was twice as many rebels. God only knows how many the rebels lost, because they never tell the truth, but from the screaming and groaning that night, you'd have thought half Greene's army was bleeding to death in the rain and the dark. It was worse than a thousand pigs being butchered—made you want to plug your ears! I never heard no such sounds!" He hesitated, then added, "And I don't propose to hear 'em again!"

He looked defiantly from one to another of us, but nobody spoke.

In a low voice he said, "You never saw a blacker night or heard a harder rain. It was like a waterfall, and the screaming was terrible. Those away, away off sounded like hurt cats fighting—big cats, hurt bad. Some screamed like mountain lions. It made your ears ring and your insides shake."

He frowned. "What beat me was how clear the far-off ones sounded. They made you feel hot in the shoulders and cold in the stomach at the same time."

A listener cleared his throat. The others stared toward the two far-off dots that were wagons crawling down from the Meadows of Dan. Beyond them I could see another pin point—a third wagon.

"Three days after the fight," Bent said, "Cornwallis started for the coast. He'd lost so many he couldn't chase the rebels any further. If he could 'a' chased 'em, there wouldn't 'a' been any more rebellion in the south, because the rebels were more licked than Cornwallis."

"Do you mean to say," MacFreel asked, "that Cornwallis walked away and left *all* the Loyalists without anybody to protect 'em—without no place to go to?"

"That's what, son," Bent said. "That's what he *had* to do, or starve.

That's the big difference between Cornwallis' troops and the rebels. Cornwallis' men don't know how to get along on nothing; but most of the rebels ain't had anything but nothing all their lives. So far as I know, there's only one place in the whole south, barring the seaports, where the Loyalists are still safe, and that's around Ninety Six where the fort's garrisoned by Loyalists, without any British officers to think for 'em or treat 'em haughty."

For an instant I had a feeling that I was hovering near the solution of a mystery. When Robert Rogers, five years before, had spoken of Ninety Six, my mind had seized upon his words and retained them long after I had forgotten things told me more impressively by greater men. When Arnold in turn had spoken of Ninety Six, I had been stirred, as by the name of an old friend. And now, hearing of Ninety Six for the third time, I felt that Ninety Six had always, mysteriously, been a part of my destiny; and I knew that I must try to reach the coast by way of Ninety Six.

CHAPTER LXXIII

T<small>HERE</small> were times when I feared that none of the thousands who moved so painfully along the Wilderness Trail would ever reach their destination.

All our troubles, up to Fort Chissel, had been as nothing by comparison with the difficulties that lay beyond. Beyond the fort, the road ceased to be a road in the accepted sense of the word. It was a scar—a gash through the laurel thickets, over mountains, along valleys, that might have been torn through this untouched wilderness by a knifelike cataract that cut the earth to its bone and marrow.

Such was the narrowness of the gash that carts, horses, travelers were backed up at Fort Chissel, as a stream is backed up in a narrow valley during a spring freshet. A thousand families were camped around the fort, restoring their depleted strength, repairing carts, mending ripped garments, patching broken shoes, killing deer and drying meat to tide them over the evil days to come.

Even as Major Dustin hunted a camping place after our talk with the men on the platform of the fort, Buell was at me like a gadfly.

"You're figuring on trying to get to Ninety Six, aren't you, Oliver?"

"Yes," I said, "I am. I'm satisfied we can get out that way."

"I thought you might think that," Buell said, "and I believe I've got a better plan. If we went on to Kentucky with these people, we could keep on to the Mississippi and work down it to the sea."

I looked at him hard, and saw his eyes waver. His plan had come from Julia Bishop.

"No," I said. "My mind's made up. I'm going by way of Ninety Six —if I can get there."

Buell was grieved. "Don't say No before you've given it some thought, Oliver! Think it over while we're here, getting ourselves rested up."

Ahead of us I heard singing. I kicked my horse in the ribs and moved toward the sound, for the tune was one that had run through my head for many a long week. I made out the words—

> "Oh promised land, Oh promised land!
> Lead, lead me to that promised land!
> Guide, guide me with thy loving hand!
> Oh promised land, Kentucky land!"

It was Craig's Congregation, whom we'd seen passing us at the crossroads near Spotsylvania, and they were a ragged and hungry-looking crew. Craig himself, who'd been a sturdy specimen when he'd become suspicious of Buell, back in Virginia, was gaunt and wasted almost to a shadow.

His congregation were grouped around him in a half-circle, singing. The faces of the children were so pinched that they looked like the skulls of birds. Two women, I saw, were nursing babies who couldn't have been more than a month old.

When I kicked my horse around the semicircle and to Craig's side, I saw Julia had followed me.

"You've come quite a piece since I saw you in Spotsylvania," I said to Craig. "I wanted to let you know that song of yours has stayed in my head ever since. How've you made out?"

"Good," Craig said. His eyes went to Julia, passed on and found Buell, then returned to me. "Three were taken from us, but the Lord gave us two in their place. Those taken were women: those given were men. The Lord will provide!"

"Your people look hungry to me," I told him. "Haven't you any hunters with you?"

"Yes," Craig said, "but when the children were born, we waited, and were forced to eat our horses. We find hunting difficult without horses. The Lord will provide!"

I looked at the women of his congregation. They were staring wild-eyed at Julia.

"How long before you set off again?" I asked.

"Today," Craig said. "The Lord is my shepherd, I shall not want." I shook hands with him and said I'd see him later.

"Oliver lamb," Julia said, as we moved away, "did Buell speak to you about Natchez?"

"Yes," I said. "I've got to go on today. I'm going by way of Ninety Six."

"That's impossible, Oliver," Julia said.

"Our horses ought to be rested," Buell protested.

"Papa'll never be willing to leave here inside a week," Julia said, "and you can't go alone, Oliver pet."

"I won't go alone," I said. "I'll go with Craig's people. Somebody's got to kill food for 'em, or they'll never reach Kentucky."

I didn't dare look at Julia. After a little she moved up ahead to ride beside her father.

We moved out of Fort Chissel that same afternoon, just ahead of Craig's Church.

I look back at our journey down those remaining valleys—the valleys of the Holston and the Clinch—as at a dark and troubled dream.

They were narrow and gloomy, rimmed by higher mountains than any through which we had passed.

Laurel thickets lay upon the mountain slopes like funeral palls.

The road, what there was of it, crossed and recrossed streams that swelled thunderously from a trickle to a cataract at the merest faint hint of rain. It writhed snakelike over ridges that rose from the valley floor as though the jealous gods of Kentucky had tossed them there to hold us back. It staggered back and forth across the valleys as if made by men at the limit of their strength, unable to see but stumbling blindly on.

There was no one to whom that road wasn't a nightmare. Daily we passed exhausted families, families whose determination had been drained from them by fatigue. They were too tired to light a fire, too tired to eat, too tired and discouraged to unharness their emaciated horses.

I knew how they felt. I had a horse, but I was seldom on his back. Most of the time, it seemed to me, I was pulling him over bad spots by main strength, or holding exhausted women from Craig's Congregation in the saddle. Like everyone else, I had footscald; such was the pain that I shrank from each step as from thrusting my hand in fire. My muscles ached and trembled from hoisting wagons over fords; my blistered hands burned from helping to unload and reload the wagons unnumbered times a day.

I could always escape from Buell by taking to the laurel thickets after game, but I couldn't so easily avoid Julia when she came to sit close beside me, and brought to bear upon me not only a score of softly whispered arguments, but many an unspoken one, as to why I should follow her through the mountains into the Great Meadows beyond the Gap. Truth to tell, I didn't always wish to evade her.

"Listen, Mr. Cavalier Gentleman Honey," she might say, detaining me without much difficulty. "You put that gun right back in the wagon where it belongs and sit here on this nice warm stone with poor Julia awhile! No; don't act like I'm a centipede! I'm not going to bite, and there's plenty room for two. Look down with Julia at that pretty valley there."

Then most likely, as she pointed, her soft arm would touch my cheek, not briefly. "Just across three or four more of those pretty valleys and we'll be in Kentucky, you and Julia. My goodness, I have seen gentlemen that liked Julia better'n they would a war. Honest, sometimes I believe you want to make me cry, Oliver lamb!"

"No, Julia; that's the last thing I want to do!"

"I wish I thought it, Oliver! Look, lamb: ain't you making me feel you love an old war better'n me? Ain't I entitled to think you almost can't stand me, if rather than sit by me, all cozy, you wish you were sticking a dirty old bayonet up under some other gentleman's waist-coat, and having him slosh your ears off with his great big saber while you're cutting his stomach out!

"Look, petty pie: look at all these miles and miles of people up and down this road, getting away from all such vile doings! When they're in Kentucky, they aren't going to have any quickfoot little Julia playing around to wait on 'em and make 'em comfortable! All they'll have is Kentucky itself, but they'd rather have that than all the fighting and tearing out people's stomachs!

"But you, you old Mr. Granite-face Boston Frost, you'd rather have your ears sloshed off than have Kentucky and Julia too, with your slippers warming by the fire. Now you let me alone, Oliver Wiswell! I have *not* got tears in my eyes! I am *not* crying! I wouldn't cry for any ice-cake, ear-sloshing gentleman on this whole big round uth!"

Then she'd lean closer, so that I could feel the warmth of her shoulder through my leather jacket, and speak more seriously.

"Papa knows everybody, Oliver lambkin! He knew everybody in Virginia; and when we get to Kentucky, he'll know everybody there! That's how Papa is: he gets to know everybody and can say anything he wants without being killed, even by rebels. Papa's got a way with him, Oliver, so't not even rebels dare touch him. Folks just can't deny Papa nothin'. If you go to Kentucky with us, Papa'll take a lot of interest in you. He'll never rest till you're a part of the government—judge of the Supreme Court, maybe, or governor, or any-thing he likes the looks of better."

It was my tedious habit to give her the same answer that I'd given Buell: I was an officer in an army; it was my duty to rejoin that army as soon as I possibly could.

"I'm tired of hearing that, Oliver Wiswell!" she cried. "You'll find a thousand men on this road who'd still be in an army if they thought the way you do! The truth is you've still got your mind on that lady you haven't seen for five years! You can't be happy living with that lady, Oliver duck, any more'n you could living with a hitch-ing post—one of those black iron ones with a horse's head on top!"

She caught my arm and shook me. "Why don't you wake up, Oliver goose? I declare, you New Englanders must sleep in brine barrels so's not to warm up to anyone! Do you think there's any woman on uth, Oliver Wiswell, that'll wait and wait for somebody she'll prob-ably never see again?"

"It's been known to happen," I said.

Julia was furious. "Been known to happen! I'll warrant you don't know of a case! If you do, you read it in a book! Name me just one case, Oliver Wiswell!"

"It happens all the time in New England," I said. "Salem and Bos-ton and Newburyport are full of girls waiting for sea captains."

"Sea captains!" Julia exclaimed contemptuously. "Pah! Maybe they do wait for sea captains, but not for sea captains whose ships disap-pear for five years! And let me tell you this, Oliver Wiswell: it isn't natural for women to wait and wait and wait! Did you ever hear of a widow that didn't get married again—generally to the first man that asks her—unless she's so old and wizzled that everybody under fifty calls her Grandma?"

"You haven't married again," I said, "and unless I'm mistaken, it's not because you haven't had chances."

She followed the workings of my mind with the speed of a vixen.

"No, it's not, Mr. Mistaken Sea Captain! *Course* I've had chances! Didn't I tell you I'd never marry a man I couldn't agree with? Do you think I'd marry a rebel like Lieutenant Steven Leighton, no matter how often he begged? Never! Do you think I'd marry a man who'd want a girl to wait for him forever? I wouldn't want a man around me who'd be willing to wait and wait! Life's too short, Oliver silly! I believe, on my soul, you think I talk to you this way for somep'n beside your own good! I'll bet you think I've taken a fancy to you, Captain Oliver Snow-man! Don't you believe it! I wouldn't marry any man in this world that didn't drag around on his knees after me for years and years! The only reason I give you advice is because you're an orphan and ain't got a mother to talk sense to you! I do believe I'm wasting my time talking to you at all, Captain Oliver Slowpoke! I'd be better off talking to our old fat nigra cook. She's got lots more to say than you have! Good-by!"

We came in sight of Cumberland Mountain a week before we saw the Gap. First it hung straight ahead of us, a long dark mass tipped with white when the early-morning sun shone on it; and we marveled that snow could exist beneath a sun so hot.

As we moved closer to that lofty barrier, it took on the look of a gigantic wave, foam-crested, curling above us. What we had taken for snow was white rock, impenetrable and cruel.

The last valley—Powell Valley—before we reached Cumberland Gap was a hellhole.

Mountains boxed us in—on the right that threatening, oppressive, towering, wavelike mass of rock whose white crest seemed perpetually to surge and undulate, as a rushing breaker lurches in the moment of its fall: to the left the long dark mass of the Clinch Mountains.

Spring had come to all the other valleys through which we had labored; but in Powell Valley there was frost at night, so that we froze and ached from dark to dawn. When the sun rose over the rim of that gigantic dark cup, the rocks gave off a shimmering heat; steam drifted above the foaming waters of the Clinch and from the cold black earth; and in a moment's time the icebox of a valley was an oven.

In Powell Valley the faces of the women and the children took on a singular pallor. The faces of the men were corpselike.

How all those women and the little girls got safely across the last ferrying place in Powell's River—the one between Martin's Station and Cumberland Gap—is more than I can say. The river was a thundering torrent: its shores a churned soup of slimy clay. The men, black and white, stood on the far bank and hauled women across with ropes, as they'd have pulled in fish.

Buell and I, working with Craig and his menfolk, Major Dustin and his slaves, dragged the women of Craig's Church through that roaring quick water for half the morning. All up and down the river, women lay sprawled in the mud, retching. When they'd coughed up all the water in them, they wrung it from their hair and clothes and went reeling on, green-faced, pale-lipped, smudgy-eyed, draggle-haired.

When I went on myself, I overtook Julia. Even she, though she'd swum her horse across the torrent, looked green. One of the little girls from Craig's Congregation rode behind her, eyes closed, pale hair plastered to her head, the image of a drowned chicken.

When Julia looked around and saw me behind her, she forced her horse to the side of the path and busied herself with the little girl.

I pulled up beside her to ask how she was, but for the first time since I'd known her I couldn't get a word out of her. She just sat there, her head bent over the little girl and her fingers at work braiding the draggled pale hair, until people behind shouted for me to get on—to save my love-making for Kentucky—to make up my mind what I wanted to do.

The Gap appeared in the towering breaker of a mountain as surprisingly as though the barrier were truly a wave, and had been suddenly cloven by an invisible obstruction. At one moment the wall was solid: the next moment there was a diagonal cleft in it.

At the foot of the Gap, where a winding path went upward into the tangled laurel thickets toward the dark gash in the hills, it seemed to me that all the hopeless, helpless people in the world had gathered to stare at that gateway to the promised land.

There were hundreds of ragged women in calicoes, hundreds of dirty children clothed in sacking and mud; there were Negroes, old and young; there were traders of every description, and a thousand campfires. Yet the sounds of that crowded place were those made by horses, cattle, dogs. Humans whispered when they spoke. For the most part they were silent, lost in contemplation of that diagonal crevice in the wall above them.

The whole end of that dark valley made me think of a half-remembered passage from Virgil—something about sailors being washed disjecta membra on a rocky shore. The place looked like a sculch-heap where lost souls were abandoning all the unnecessary things with which their lives had been burdened.

Never since the beginning of time, I truly believe, had so many carts and wagons been gathered in one spot. They lay in heaps. They were scattered far and wide, as if a hurricane had dropped them there. Everywhere men were stripping carts of pins and bolts, canvas tops and seat braces, hub caps and axle sockets, even the nails and rope with which these sorry conveyances had been bound together.

Major Dustin led us through wrecked and useless vehicles until he found a space where we could draw our own small caravan into a circle. The ground was scarred with the black remnants of former campfires, littered with odds and ends left by other travelers who'd camped upon that spot to stare up at Cumberland Gap.

As we made camp, we couldn't keep our eyes off the Gap. Strung along it like jewels were points of light.

Major Dustin shook his head. "First time ever I saw people camping in a gap! I'd hate to be in their place if a storm comes up! Shows how anxious they are to get away from a Congress and a war! Well, we all know how they feel! Unload the wagons and break 'em up! We've got to be on our way through that Gap ourselves by sunrise tomorrow."

He turned suddenly to me. "You haven't told me your plans, Oliver, but I can't get through the Gap without that horse of yours. You'll have to see us across the mountains, anyway, and I hope you're going to Kentucky with us."

I think every man will understand why I hadn't told the major I intended to leave him at the Gap, and why I was glad for even one more day with Julia. She'd avoided me for several days, and she did the same that night. By the light of our campfires we worked till midnight, sorting the contents of the major's wagons into piles and making them into packs, and for once Julia didn't come near us. I watched for her and hoped for her as I worked, and yet I was conscious of a great relief. I didn't know what to say to her, now that the time had come for us to part. The truth was that I was filled with an oppressive discomfort, a distressing feeling of guilt, at leaving her; and it still persisted even when I assured myself that I had no reason for feeling so.

When, dog-tired, I rolled myself in my blanket beside Buell, I told him what I'd decided.

"I'll be back here in three days, Tom," I said. "There's no need for

you to come through the Gap with us, and in three days you can find
out exactly how to get to Ninety Six and Charleston. Pick up all the
information you can—how long it'll take us: where we can find friends
if we need 'em. We don't want to make any mistakes at this late day."

Buell was silent so long that I thought he'd fallen asleep.

"Did you hear me, Tom?" I asked.

"Yes, I heard you, Oliver. I was thinking about what you said—
about not making mistakes at this late day. There's no chance you're
making a mistake not to go to Kentucky, is there?"

"No," I said. "There isn't."

Buell cleared his throat. "No offense meant, Oliver."

"No offense taken."

"Well," Buell said, "don't you think you ought to consider whether
anybody's going to pay any attention to that information you're so
anxious to get out?"

"We were sent to get it," I reminded him.

"I know it," Buell said, "but when you said you'd go, you didn't
know what things were going to be like when you got over here.
You didn't know the English were going to walk away from all the
Loyalists, just when the Loyalists needed 'em most. You didn't
know——"

"That's enough, Tom," I said. "I came to get the information, and
that's——"

Buell coughed, squirmed in his blanket, and began again. "Look
at it another way, Oliver. Take this Julia Bishop, Oliver. You like
her some, don't you?"

"I don't want to discuss it, Tom."

"Just as you say, Oliver. Just as you say. I only want to be sure
nobody makes a mistake. Seven years is seven years, and that's what
you'll have waited for that girl in Milton. I remember another feller
waited seven years for a girl. Jacob, his name was. Waited seven
years and then got the wrong one."

"Not through any fault of his own," I reminded him. "And you're
to wait for me right here if you have to wait seven years yourself."

CHAPTER LXXIV

CRAIG's Congregation came past us before sun-up the next morning, while we were loading the last of Major Dustin's possessions on the pack saddles we'd made from tree crotches on Wallen's Ridge.

Most of them were limping from footscald, and were bent over with the weight of their packs, but they were singing that song of theirs.

> *"Oh promised land, Oh promised land!*
> *Lead, lead me to that promised land!*
> *Guide, guide me with thy loving hand!*
> *Oh promised land, Kentucky land!"*

As we kicked our horses onto the trail behind them, I caught a glimpse of Julia, but only a glimpse; and after that glimpse I was too busy keeping my horse on his feet to think of anything else.

The Gap was a villainous trace through that chaos of heaped-up rock. It seemed, almost, to have been gashed by mountain torrents that for untold centuries had raged over the same snakelike course; and for hours we scrambled around boulders the size of farmhouses, through a tortuous maze of other boulders, conscious of nothing but keeping our feet, of staying ahead of those pressing behind us, of climbing on and on, up and up through that narrow rocky gap, amid an unending chorus of rattling hoofs on rock, shouting men, blarting cows and calves.

I thought the Gap and the struggle to get through it would last forever, and so firmly fixed was this thought in my head that I wasn't conscious of passing the crest of the Gap and starting downward; couldn't have told when the cold and damp wind of the dark mountains gave way to a warm breeze smelling of meadows and spring; was surprised to find that the men around me had stopped shouting and cursing at their horses and that I could again hear Craig's Congregation singing.

Then I shouldered my horse around a bend and caught my first glimpse of Kentucky, small and far-off, framed darkly between walls of rock and interlaced gray fingers of laurel—a sunny plain, all blue and gold, dotted with groves of trees. There seemed to be no end to that golden plain. It stretched off and off into a soft warm haze—a milky infinity.

Craig's Congregation were sprawled in the first meadow on the Kentucky side of the Gap. I saw Julia's horse hobbled among them; then Julia herself on her knees beside one of the women. I knew, as soon as I saw her, that this was as far as I could go.

I moved off the rocky path until Major Dustin came up with me; then led my horse to Julia's and put the hobbles on him. Julia was rewinding the bandage on a girl's foot. The foot was so swollen that the toes seemed grotesquely like cloves stuck in a ham.

"Julia," I said, "I reckon I can't go any farther. I'll have to get back."

She looked up at me and I suddenly remembered how repulsively white and expressionless her face had seemed to me when I'd first seen her in Frederick.

"I'm surprised you got as far as this," she said. "I really am! I figured you'd leave in the night, back on the other side of the Gap, so to save yourself the trouble of being polite."

"Julia," I said, "I'm mighty grateful for all your kindnesses. I'll always remember how kind you've been."

She tucked in the end of the bandage, gave the girl's leg a pat, and got to her feet. "My land, Mr. Wiswell," she said lightly, "you northern men don't have enough feelings to remember anything or anybody very long! If you ain't going any further, you better run along. All this talk about nothin', I don't mind sayin', is extremely fatiguin'."

"Well," I said, "if you feel that way about it——"

"Oh my goodness!" Julia said. "That ain't half the way I feel about it, but I don't reckon you'd care to have me say what I feel, right out in public."

At the look in her black and level eyes, my spine crawled. For the first time I thought about her dead husband and his habit of drinking heavily in the morning.

I turned to my horse and began to loosen the knot that held the pack in place. On the instant Major Dustin shouted at me. "God-amighty, Oliver! What you doing?"

"Why," I said, "I've got to go back through the Gap, Major! That was understood, wasn't it? You asked for the loan of my horse to get your goods across the Gap, and we're through the Gap."

"Hell and damnation!" the major shouted. "We're through the Gap, yes, but we ain't where we're going to—not by two hundred miles! I got to have that horse, Oliver!"

"But Major," I protested, "two hundred miles for you means four hundred miles for me! I've got work to do, Major! I'm under orders!"

"Son," Dustin said slowly, "on this side of the mountains I don't recognize nobody's orders but my own! I've got to have that horse of yours, and that's all there is to it! Let that knot alone until we camp for the night."

"Look here, Major," I said, "you've got half a dozen Negroes fit to carry loads. You've got one horse that hasn't any load at all—except a rider."

"He's referrin' to me, Papa," Julia said. "I ain't a lady any more: I'm just a common ordinary rider, like all the other riders on this trail! No doubt Mr. Wiswell, being from the north, wouldn't feel sorry if I walked all the rest of the way on foot, like the Craig's Church women, and maybe carried a pack to boot! I don't doubt he'd take my own mare and ride away on it his own self, if you gave him the chance!"

"Well, he ain't goin' to have the chance, honey pet," the major said. "He's going to come along with us, starting right now, or he's going to go back through the Gap on foot, same as a nigra or white trash."

I looked from the major to Julia and found the same cold hostility in their black eyes.

Suddenly something important seemed to be finished—finished in a way I couldn't have expected. Perhaps other travelers who have come a long road and found their companions abruptly changed in the moment of parting might understand how bemused I was. For some reason the alteration in Major Dustin didn't trouble me; it was simple enough—the mere selfishness of an adventurer bent solely on his own ends—but I seemed to be aware that Julia had a lump in her throat, as I had in mine. Mine hurt and so did hers; I knew it—and yet there didn't seem to be anything that I could do about it, and there wasn't. After so much borne together, after so much kindness, this was a poor parting, I thought, but knew no way to make it a better one.

I took off my hat. "Take the horse," I said, and then quoted, "God bless you and bring you good fortune in Kentucky."

Then I turned from them and set off into the cold, damp Gap, back the way I'd come: back against the never-ending stream of men and horses, cows and women, calves, children, dogs, ponies, Negroes pressing through that boulder-strewn notch into Kentucky; and strangely enough I could think of nothing but Sally Leighton.

BOOK V

☆

Ninety Six

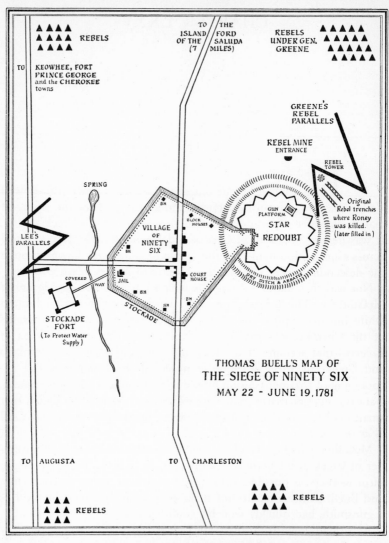

Ninety Six received its name because of being 96 miles from
Fort Prince George which was built at Old Keowhee in 1753.

CHAPTER LXXV

Buell, when I came out of the Gap and down into Powell Valley again, was furbishing and mending the guns of the strangest man I ever met—Alexander McGillivray, head of the Creek nation. It was he and his party of Creeks and Cherokees who led us safely across Clinch Mountain and the Great Smokies and down through the descending shelves of South Carolina to Ninety Six.

Nor was that the only thing for which I'm indebted to Alexander McGillivray. The information with which that wise and educated white Indian supplied me during our journey across the mountains of the Cherokee country gave me the groundwork for *Victims of Liberty*—that account of the ferocious persecution of the Cherokees and Creeks by the avaricious whites, and the condoning and encouraging of that persecution by the rebel Congress and government. I always thought that without the widespread recognition which that small book received in Europe, I might never have published *Civil War in America*.

McGillivray had come all the way to Cumberland Gap with a number of Creek and Cherokee landowners, in order to purchase Negro farm workers, if possible, from those who were going to Kentucky; and Buell, with his facility for making acquaintances and his skill as a gunsmith, had quickly won his confidence.

As I came down from the Gap, I passed McGillivray and his party camped beside the path. Their peculiar dress and their magnificence caught my attention, and I couldn't believe my eyes when Buell jumped up from among them and hailed me.

McGillivray, who got up and stood staring at me, as if I were a horse and he a prospective purchaser, was about forty years old and extremely handsome. His face was brown with a faint bluish cast, and his hair a glossy blue-black. On the right side of his forehead were two blemishes, copper-colored, the size of half-pennies, and below his eye, on the same side, was a larger copper-colored mark. They looked as though an Indian had placed a thumb and two fingers against his face, and lost the copper color from his finger tips. His dress was almost startling, for he wore pantaloons of bright red flannel, a tunic of white-striped pale blue calico bound at the waist with a red-and-yellow sash, and a turban of thin red cloth so tied that an end hung down over one ear.

When Buell asked me what I'd done with my horse, and I'd told him that Major Dustin had needed it and so refused to give it back to me, McGillivray winked portentously at Buell. "You see, my friend," he said, "even those who go to Kentucky to escape the rebels are too often rebels at heart."

To me he said: *"Dulce et decorum est pro patria ambulare!* Fortunately we aren't rebels, and you're welcome to one of our horses."

The quoting of Latin, I soon found, was a habit of McGillivray's. Another was to give strangers, at the first opportunity, and with seeming humility, a brief résumé of the reasons that had made him the head of the Creek nation. I think he did it with good reason, for it was both disconcerting and disarming to hear perfect English, quotations from Horace and Seneca, and abstract speculations falling from the lips of an apparent savage.

"To one like yourself," he told me—and Buell said that he used almost the identical speech on everyone—"our ways will seem peculiar and perhaps unpleasant. They are the ways of the Creeks and the Cherokees, and we are, of course, savages, lacking the many blessings enjoyed by the white man. Our farms, in the mountains, will doubtless seem pitifully inadequate to you. My own small holding, from which I take no great quantity of corn, indigo and a modicum of necessities, has a certain rugged beauty that you might find pleasing."

I found later that he had thirty-seven slaves, a twenty-room white-clay house filled with furniture and silver purchased in Savannah, and a herd of nearly sixteen hundred shaggy-haired horses running loose on the plateaus of the Georgia mountains.

"It's a privilege," he said, that first day we met, "to encounter a gentleman like yourself, who has known the advantages of a college. My poor father, I think, had hoped that I might have something of the sort, perhaps in his native Edinburgh; but my mother, who preceded me as head of the Creek nation, preferred that I pursue my studies under the care of my uncle, Mr. Farquhar McGillivray, of Charleston. I cannot blame my mother, Mr. Wiswell, but there are times when I deeply regret my comparatively untutored state. Ah well, Mr. Wiswell, as my father so often said: 'Wisdom is the principal thing; therefore get wisdom; and with all thy getting get understanding.' "

Why McGillivray and all the Creeks and Cherokees with him despised the rebels so profoundly, I have told at length in the pages of *Victims of Liberty*. I shall never forget the prophecy he made to me on our travels through the mountains: "If those who call themselves Sons of Liberty should, by some mischance, win the war, we shall be despoiled of our private possessions, the indefeasible property of individuals. We shall be stripped of every attribute of freedom and eligibility for legal self-defense. Our property will be plundered before our eyes. Violence will be committed on our persons. Even our lives will be taken away, and there will be none to regard our complaints. We will have neither land nor home nor resting place that can be called our own!"

McGillivray loved to speechify to us like this, and would do so for an hour at a time—by which I don't mean to imply that he didn't mean what he said.

Those mountains to the south of Cumberland Gap, once we'd crossed the valley of the Clinch, might have been formed by some tremendous explosion beneath the earth's crust—an explosion that had heaved rocks and earth into an exaggerated likeness of a storm-tossed ocean.

They rose up in sharp pinnacles, like monstrous inverted stone icicles; in massive hogbacks, like enormous tilted millstones broken jaggedly across; in massive domes; in long serpentine ridges; in saw-edged peaks.

The valleys were hardly valleys at all, but tremendous gashes, pot-holes, traps, sinks, none of them running far enough in any one direction, seemingly, to be worth following.

There was a singular smokiness to all these mountains when rain clouds didn't obscure them; and so far did they extend that there were days when it seemed to us we would never escape from among the bald domes, the needle-pointed rocks that stabbed the smoky sky, the hogbacks that bared rocky teeth at us, no matter in which direction the twisting valleys led.

And then, one morning, we came out of a cañon into a true valley, a grassy valley rimmed on the far side with hazy, abrupt knobs that were only half mountains. The pines of the mountains gave way to misty forests of oak and tulip trees, of gum and magnolias; and among the knobs and forests the streams ran clear through green shelves that widened and narrowed and widened again, and were suddenly a broad savannah in which stood twoscore Indian houses, white as snow and roofed with brown bark.

"New Keowhee," McGillivray told us. "To the Cherokees, this is Boston. All distances are measured from it. That's how Ninety Six got its name, because of being ninety-six miles from Keowhee."

There were peach orchards, tobacco fields, cornfields around the rim of the savannah, with Negroes working in them. On the river two dugouts were fastened together, and four men, sprawled in their bottoms, were lazily fishing. It was another world from that which we had known in the years that lay behind us. I had the feeling that it was a world in which there were no wars, no rebels seeking the lives of Loyalists, no Loyalists living in perpetual fear of rebel attacks; no stupid kings, no idiotic kings' ministers. I wondered whether it was possible that the nightmare of the past six years had come to an end; that we could forget about the war, and just go to living again without bothering about anything except our own affairs.

The inhabitants of Keowhee couldn't have made more to-do over McGillivray if he'd been the King of England himself, and in a few minutes he had the information that I'd asked him to get.

"Perhaps you'd better not go down to Ninety Six just yet," he said. "Things aren't good. The young men here think bad times are coming for everyone in Ninety Six."

On the ground before him McGillivray, with his forefinger, traced a fat triangle, point downward, explaining that its left side was the Savannah River and the right side the ocean. He made dots at the left for Ninety Six and Augusta, poked a hole at the right and called it Charleston, and in the middle made another dot which he called Camden.

"I suspect," McGillivray went on, "that these young men have more information than you'll like to hear. After Cornwallis fought that battle at Guildford, he moved two hundred miles down the Cape Fear River to Wilmington, and the rebel general Greene came down into South Carolina to try to drive out all the Loyalists and all the King's troops. He's been successful, except at Ninety Six. The young men say that now he's going to Ninety Six."

"Where's Cornwallis?" I asked.

"After he'd reached Wilmington," McGillivray said, "he turned around and marched back north into Virginia, three hundred miles, hoping to coax Greene to come and chase him. The young men think Greene won't do it. The young men think Greene will stay in the Carolinas until he has killed everyone at Ninety Six. The young men think Cornwallis has made a mistake not to come back to Charleston, where he could defend himself against all the rebels and all the Frenchmen in the world. They think he should never have gone to Virginia. They say that if Greene conquers Ninety Six, the rebels will come up here and seize our land, our crops, our horses, and drive us away if they can."

"Do the young men know who's at Ninety Six?" I asked.

McGillivray consulted his friends; then nodded. "They know all. Three days ago they carried corn to Ninety Six. The entire garrison of Ninety Six is taken from Loyalist regiments—DeLancey's, New Jersey Volunteers and South Carolina mounted militia."

"Do they know who's in command?" I asked.

McGillivray looked surprised. "I took it for granted you knew! Everybody in the south knows who commands at Ninety Six. It's Colonel Cruger. Haven't you heard of Cruger? John Harris Cruger of New York?"

"I met him long ago," I said. "I didn't know he'd become a soldier."

"I have always said that wars are fought by the wrong men," McGillivray said. "Cruger is a great soldier. The Creeks and Cherokees say he's better than any two generals on either side. He moves like the wind in the night; and whenever he's struck, he strikes back harder."

"That sounds good," Buell said. "I've seen so many of the other kind that I'd go a long way to see the right kind."

"I warn you," McGillivray said. "The rebels in the south are merciless to Loyalists and Indians."

"We can't turn back now," I told him. "You've been kind to us, and we'd like to have you do us just one more good turn. You say some of these young men carried corn to Ninety Six three days ago.

Would you be willing to persuade two or three of those same young men to get us safely to Ninety Six?"

"I would and I will," McGillivray said. "I have a liking for you, and more for the cause you represent. Unless that cause is triumphant, I foresee as pharisaical an upheaval as the world has known!" Thereupon he made us another speech, but he gave us the young men.

CHAPTER LXXVI

IF EVER a country reflected the fears and bitter hatreds of those who dwelt within it, it was that part of South Carolina through which Buell and I traveled to Ninety Six.

The river down which we floated was bordered by dark groves of gums and cypresses; by silent savannahs. The few houses were unpainted, unglazed, withdrawn, despondent.

As we approached them every sign of life and occupancy hastily whisked from sight. At one moment children played before them; a moment later the children were gone. Cows and horses flung up their heads and ran for cover. Masked raccoons grinned and washed furtive hands as we went by. Deer leaped in the swamps; logs came startlingly to life in the shallows along the bank to swim swiftly out of sight. There was a sticky heat over everything, a depression that distressed the mind more than the body.

On the twentieth of May our guides turned into a swampy creek, rapping their paddles against cypress knees to dislodge the cottonmouths. We had come to the Island Ford of the Saluda, three miles from Ninety Six.

Under no circumstances, our guides explained before we left them, should we show ourselves to anybody until we knew him to be a friend, or harmless.

We came out of thick woods into open fields and saw Ninety Six a mile perhaps before us. It was upon a little hill, and around it was a circular stockade with bastions jutting out at regular intervals, so that the stockade had the appearance of a gigantic circular saw. To one end of the stockade—the end nearest us—a little star-

661

shaped redoubt was stuck perkily, like a bustle on a woman's skirt.

From inside the stockade rose the roofs of the town, a squat belfry among them, and the Island Ford road led us straight to the town gate. The gate was flanked by two small cannon, and our way barred by two sentries. They wore baggy green hunting shirts patched front and back with enormous pockets.

An officer came from a guardhouse and turned a hard eye on Buell and me. "Where you from and where you going?"

"From Cumberland Gap," I said, "by way of the Cherokee towns. We're bound to Charleston."

He laughed, and I thought he didn't believe me.

"It's the truth," I said. "Alexander McGillivray, chief of the Creeks, gave us an escort down here from Keowhee."

"I'll take your word for it," he said. "First time I saw you, you were telling Judge Hendon about the Declaration of Independence. Next time I saw you, you were with Cunningham when he brought us word that Howe had landed and that we could come out of the swamp. I'm John Roney. The rebels drove me out of Metuchen, New Jersey. I'm a lieutenant in the New Jersey Volunteers, Third Battalion. You'll find pretty near everybody from that Long Island swamp right here at Ninety Six. Come on: let's go see the colonel."

Roney led us straight to the little star-shaped redoubt, which was busy as an anthill. Half-naked whites and Negroes were carrying heavy balks of timber and digging holes in earth as red as a New England schoolhouse.

I hardly recognized as officers the five men before whom we stood, for their green shirts might have been cut from the same piece of cloth as were those of the two sentries who'd stopped us. I'd have known them for men of quality, however, even if they'd been clothed in rags. They were tall, lean, tanned, straight as arrows, and their eyes were hard and humorous. The central one of the five was the same John Harris Cruger who'd talked to Stedman and me at the home of Ambrose Serle on that hot September night, five years before, when the rebels had fled from New York City.

"God bless my soul," Cruger cried. "Seaton Wiswell's son! You rode out to Kip's Bay with me from Ambrose Serle's."

"Yes, sir," I said. "Stedman and I. I hope you found your house undisturbed."

A queer glint seemed to flicker in Cruger's eyes, and then for a moment to fix itself as if for that moment it froze. "You didn't hear about my family? Haven't you seen Stedman?"

"No, sir."

"Stedman's commissary general of Cornwallis' army," Cruger said. "The rebels raided my home in Bloomingdale, burned the house, killed the children of two servants and drove my mother-in-law, my wife and all her sisters into the brush in their night clothes on a cold winter night." He spoke without much emotion, as he might have discussed a long stretch of bad weather, but I understood why his fighting had stirred the admiration of McGillivray and his Creeks and Cherokees.

I explained the reason for our lack of knowledge by telling him how Buell and I had gone to England and France, how Germaine had sent us to report on the Convention Army, and how we'd had to go to Cumberland Gap by the Wilderness Road in order to get away from the rebels.

"Good!" Cruger said. "I've wanted information about that road for a long time. Were the rebels fighting as far inland as that?"

"No, sir, but we had news of fighting south of the mountains."

"Did you pick up any news on the Wilderness Road?"

"We picked up a boy that escaped from Lee's dragoons at Altamahaw Ford, and we heard about Guildford Court House."

"Altamahaw Ford? Just what was that?"

"That was three months ago, sir. Three hundred and seventy Loyalists got together to join Cornwallis. They mistook Lee's rebel dragoons for an escort from Tarleton's cavalry; and before they knew what had happened, Lee's men had killed all but four of 'em."

"Can't afford to make mistakes like that," Cruger said. "Who else was traveling on the Road?"

"Loyalists, sir. It's fairly crawling with Loyalists, all heading for Kentucky. Some are going because Cornwallis deserted 'em; some because they can't stand Congress any more."

"What's happening between here and the Gap?" Cruger asked.

"We came across the Great Smokies with Alexander McGillivray and some Cherokees," I told him. "We saw nobody but Cherokees. They hate the rebels. They told us no messengers had got through to you from Charleston up to a week ago. Everybody on the Saluda was acting mighty scared, and it looked to us as if Greene's army might be getting pretty close."

Cruger pressed a contemplative knuckle against his lips. "Scared, eh?" He turned to one of the four officers who stood silently beside him. "Get your South Carolina militia together, Colonel Deveaux, and tell 'em that in my judgment Greene'll be crossing the Saluda tonight. All your men have horses, haven't they?"

"Yes, sir."

"Well," Cruger said, "tell 'em I've decided to let 'em go. They can make for Charleston, or they can head for Savannah, whichever seems most feasible."

He turned back to me; the other three officers stared at Deveaux.

"Is that an order, Colonel?" Deveaux asked.

"You don't need to be so military," Cruger said. "I wasn't ordering: I was just telling you what I've decided. Greene's got Virginia and North Carolina militia with him, and you know what southern rebels do to southern Loyalists—if they get a chance. We'll try to hold Greene off until help reaches us, and I think we can; but if we shouldn't, I don't care to be responsible for your men."

Deveaux turned on his heel and marched away. It seemed to me I'd never seen more stubborn resentment in any back.

"I'd like to continue this talk, Mr. Wiswell," Cruger said, "but time's getting short. I think you could reach Charleston or Savannah safely by riding out with those Carolina militiamen when they leave. It's a mounted regiment, and they're first-rate men. I'm sure they'll get you safely to the coast."

"If it's all the same to you," I said, "I'll stay here. I'm a captain in a Provincial regiment that hasn't yet been raised—the King's American Dragoons."

"Well," Cruger said, "I won't deny we can use everybody who's willing to stay. Captain Barbarie, take Captain Wiswell and his friend to the barracks, find quarters for 'em, and see they get what they need. If we have time to eat, I want the pleasure of Captain Wiswell's company."

Colonel Deveaux came briskly back. "Sir," he said to Cruger, "I gave your message to two of my officers. They said our South Carolina men had already talked the matter over and decided they wouldn't go. They turned their horses into the woods this morning. We'll stay."

"Colonel Deveaux," Cruger said, "do you think they understand that if we should be so unfortunate as to have to sign a capitulation with the rebels, they couldn't possibly be protected?"

"Yes, sir," Deveaux said. "I think they understand everything."

Cruger made an elaborate pretense of being unconcerned. "That's very kind of 'em, Colonel Deveaux. Very kind indeed! I'll do the best I can for 'em." He seemed to have trouble with his throat, for he was seized with a fit of coughing and left us hurriedly.

There are no monuments to Lieutenant Colonel Andrew Deveaux in South Carolina, where he fought so gallantly for the loyal residents of that state. There's not even one to him in the Bahamas, which became, solely because of his leadership and daring, a refuge for thousands of persecuted Loyalists from the Carolinas, Georgia and Florida. Deveaux's reward was that of most brave soldiers who fight in lost causes—ingratitude and oblivion.

The captain whom Cruger had told to take us to barracks shook my hand. "You wouldn't remember me, I guess. John Barbarie, De-Lancey's Third Battalion. I was mighty glad to see you once before, when you let us know that we could get out of the swamps and be supplied with boots and rum and a gun and a chance to fight rebels. We're just as glad to see you now, and so's the Old Man. We've licked hell out of the rebels every time we've fought 'em; but five hundred of us never tackled four thousand rebels before. Come on up to headquarters and I'll introduce you to a lot of other officers you saw at Demott's Mill five years ago."

It was a mighty strange thing, I thought, that for six years the only places that had seemed like home to me were the miserable holes where I was surrounded by persons who thought as I did and were willing to fight for the same things. I was happier at being in the wretched town of Ninety Six, with Cruger and Buell, Roney and Barbarie, than I'd have been in New York or London.

When we crossed the main street of Ninety Six, I understood why a fort had been built in such a Godforsaken part of the country.

Roughly speaking, a plan of Ninety Six looked like the cat a schoolboy draws upon the pages of his books—a large circle for a body, a smaller circle above it for a head, and below it a protuberance representing the cat's tail.

In the case of Ninety Six, the large circle was the stockade around the town itself. The small circle was the Star Redoubt in which we'd stood with Cruger and watched the Negroes dig in the red soil. The tail was a covered way that joined the town to its water supply and a little stockaded fort that guarded the gully through which a stream trickled.

Through the center of the stockaded town ran a road which led from the high mountains in the north to Charleston on the seacoast. Just beyond the fort on the hill was another parallel road which led from the high mountains in the northwest down to Savannah. At Ninety Six these parallel roads were less than a quarter mile apart, so that the fort commanded both.

"Tom," I said, "I'm not sure, even now, that it wouldn't be a good thing for you to make a try to reach Charleston or Savannah. You're resourceful, and you might be able to get through. You don't have to stay here just because I do."

"What makes *you* stay?" Buell asked.

"Well," I said, "this section is heavily settled. If the fort doesn't hold out, there'll be a Loyalist massacre. Those witchcraft killings up in Salem won't look like anything beside it, and Altamahaw Ford'll seem just like a little visit between neighbors. I don't believe I'd feel quite right if I didn't stay."

"I s'pose not," Buell said carelessly. "Well, we been together quite a while now, so I might as well stay with you a little longer, same as you did with me once. Maybe someone in this place knows how to make potlicker."

I could think of no adequate reply; so I made none.

CHAPTER LXXVII

To THE eye of a New Englander, accustomed to the lushness of meadows around his town, the rich and swelling curves of
groves and orchards, the gleaming white of the houses fronting on
the village green, there was something pathetic about that barren,
dusty main street of Ninety Six.

The church was brick, with a squatty square steeple. On one side of
the church was a square brick courthouse; on the other side a
tavern—a rough affair of squared logs, with slave quarters and a
summer kitchen spreading out crescent-shaped behind it.

Across the road from the courthouse was a brick jail, and on both
sides of the jail were arched tie-ups for horses. At the far end of the
street were two brick barracks; and between the courthouse and the
barracks, surrounded by baked red earth in which weeds grew
sparsely, were the run-down, unpainted houses of those whose lots
were cast in this frontier outpost.

Colonel Cruger had taken the tavern for his headquarters; for
since Ninety Six was a courthouse town, the tavern had a big downstairs barroom in which, during peacetimes, all the members of the
bar slept when court was in session.

We found the colonel in the barroom, staring at two maps upon
the wall while he chewed on cold lamb that a Negro servant was
deftly slicing from two huge haunches on a near-by table. One of the
maps was of Ninety Six; the other of the Carolinas and Virginia.

He nodded to us and jerked his head toward the table. "Have
some lamb, gentlemen. Then I'd like to have you look at this map.
Some of my most helpful suggestions come from men who stare
at a map five hours before saying a word."

He and Roney introduced us to officers who, in the next month, I was to come to know better than anyone I'd known in my life, with the exception of Sally Leighton, my father, Tom Buell and Mrs. Belcher Byles. What was more, I was to come to admire them more profoundly than I can say.

There was the young man who'd helped carry Judge Hendon's chair in the swamp at Hempstead—Captain Stephen DeLancey of the New Jersey Volunteers, nephew and aide to Colonel Cruger, later chief justice of the Bahamas; Lieutenant Colonel Andrew Deveaux of the South Carolina Loyal Militia, who in a few months was to lead his Loyalists against Nassau in as daring an attack as was ever made, and capture the Bahamas from the Spaniards; Captain Thomas French of DeLancey's First Battalion—the Long Islander who arrived in the swamp at Hempstead the night Buell and I got there and told how he'd escaped from Simsbury Mines; Captain John Barbarie of the New Jersey Volunteers, who always contrived to stop a bullet in every battle, but eventually became one of the founders of St. John; Lieutenant Edward Stelle of the New Jersey Volunteers, later a founder of Fredericton and a distinguished judge; Captain Peter Campbell, attainted of treason by the Executive Council of Pennsylvania because he couldn't agree politically with them, but as true and brave a soldier as ever lived.

Such was the quality of these men, heroes of the Siege of Ninety Six—now all of them old and dear friends of mine, without whose unshakable loyalty and resourceful courage I wouldn't be alive to write these words.

I see those tanned officers now, their green shirts open at the throat, sweat-stained beneath the arms in black crescents, between the shoulder blades in triangular patches shaped singularly like the green-tinted province of South Carolina on the big map before which they stood.

When we'd helped ourselves and moved up to the map, Cruger pointed to the little Star Redoubt at the bottom of the map of Ninety Six. "That's where I was when Roney brought you in, Captain Wiswell, and in my opinion that's where Greene will attack. It's the only spot that commands the whole town, and it's the place where Greene's men can best raise a tower, as they did at Augusta. If he raises one here, it's our duty to make him wish he hadn't. We've got the holes dug to raise one ourselves, and with riflemen on it we ought to be able to hold our own."

"You could more than hold your own," Buell said, "if you mounted guns on it—those sparrow guns you've got at the north gate."

Two of the officers snorted.

Colonel Cruger, his mouth full of lamb, stared at Buell. "That platform would be thirty feet tall, Mr. Buell! If you fired just one gun from it, the recoil would probably tear down the whole tower. If it didn't, the gun-loader would have two dozen buckshot in him the second he leaned out with his rammer."

"No, he wouldn't," Buell said. "I watched the guns being exercised on the frigate that brought us to America. The way their power was wasted was terrible. The recoil wasn't used for one damned thing except pulling ringbolts out of a deck. When I showed 'em how they could use it, they almost threw me overboard."

"They didn't try it?" Cruger asked.

Buell looked pained. "Try it? An Englishman try something nobody'd ever tried before? An Englishman try something an *American* thought up? Good God, Colonel!"

Cruger looked from Buell to me. "Do you know anything about this scheme of your friend's?"

"No, sir," I said, "but if he says it'll work, I'm willing to bet on it."

"Well," Cruger said, "there's no harm trying it. We wouldn't want to overlook anything." To Buell he said, "How would you figure on handling those guns so they wouldn't wreck the tower?"

"Well, Colonel," Buell said, "there's two ends to every gun, but it ain't ever occurred to anybody to use but one end. Damned if I don't think everybody in a war wastes twice as much as he uses! Now look, Colonel: suppose you put two guns side by side, rigged blocks and tackles before and behind 'em, and hitched up their breechings. You fire one: it kicks back, jerks the breechings through the front tackles and yanks the other up to the front of the platform. You load the first gun without anybody seeing the gun crew. When you fire the second gun, it kicks back and pulls the first gun forward. See? Pretty as a picture! You use up all the gun's kick, so there ain't any left to damage the platform."

"Suppose the breechings broke," Cruger said. "In all likelihood you'd lose guns, platform and men."

"They won't break," Buell said. "We had a lot of trouble over in England, Colonel, because the English never gave us credit for thinking. We'd work months on a plan, Oliver and I would, and then we'd hunt up a general or a king's minister or somebody, and we'd say: 'If you do thus and so, you'll be all right.'

"Well, Colonel, we might have spent maybe three months on our plan, and they wouldn't have spent three minutes, but they'd always know more about it than we did."

"I see your point," Cruger said. "What was it you've figured out to keep the breechings from breaking?"

"Simplest thing in the world," Buell said. "I'll raise the rear end of the platform a few inches, and lay a little roof over it at an angle. Then the gun carriage'll always kick back into a slot and wedge there."

The young officers around Cruger looked at each other in the peculiar bland way with which men of action show appreciation and approval.

"Build your platform," Cruger said. "Mount your guns on it according to your ideas, and you'll have to rig your sights on 'em and lay 'em, too, yourself. I don't know how many men your platform'll hold when you begin to work your guns, so I'll leave it to you and Roney to pick the men you want to have helping you."

He was interrupted by the abrupt entrance of a sentry, who kicked the door shut behind him, dropped his musket butt smartly against the floor, and stood to attention.

"What is it?" Cruger asked.

"Families coming out of the woods, sir. They're pouring out, ten times as fast as this morning, some of 'em running! They say Greene's army's at the Saluda. They say he'll be here in another hour."

Clearest of my memories of South Carolina is that of the wilting heat. It was sticky, dead, breathless. It made leaves hang limply on the dusty trees, and seemed to hold in indefinite suspension the red dust that rose from beneath our feet. Even the rolling of the drums, as we walked back to the Star Redoubt, sounded flabby; and the Negroes carrying rock to the platform holes droopingly turned their heads to watch the soldiers hurry toward that throbbing.

When I followed Cruger to the fire step of the Redoubt to look across the fields and ravine toward the far-off woods through which we'd come on our way from the Saluda, the whole landscape seemed withered in that sick heat. Circling buzzards, high overhead, wheeled slowly, as if oppressed with weariness. Distant figures on the road we had traveled three hours earlier were mere crawling insects in the dust cloud through which they moved. The wall of gums and live oaks that stood between us and the Saluda quivered in the heat like rippling water.

Against that far pale green wall of trees a white dot came suddenly into view. It was a mounted man in a white coat, and so motionless was he that he might have been a statue.

At sight of that solitary far white figure, all the officers looked around at Cruger.

"Yes," Cruger said. "That's one of Colonel William Washington's rebel dragoons. If *they're* here, the rest of the army ought to be along in half an hour."

The far white figure moved along the foot of the wall, toward the right. Behind it another white dot appeared and slipped along in the wake of the first. Another and another and another trickled from those pale woods and drifted off in a long line, like a string of white beads.

Behind me, in the dusty little town of Ninety Six, the drums were silent and I could hear the lonely sound of officers' voices calling orders.

"Well," Cruger said, "they can't attack for an hour, but I'll talk to everyone in town right now. They might as well know all there is to know before the trouble starts."

The dusty rectangle between the courthouse and the jail of Ninety Six was like a New England fair on a hot September day. The green-clad garrison was formed in thick regular lines along three sides of the square in front of the tavern.

Outside those silent green lines a throng of blacks and whites, men, women and children, milled and muttered.

On the far side of the rectangle there was a constant flow of people, who might have been late arrivals to the fair, except that everyone among the newcomers, young and old, blacks and whites, carried burdens—bundles, kettles, farm implements, carpetbags; and beyond, between the shabby buildings, we could see a jam of farm wagons.

At sight of the crowd, Cruger groaned. "They'll have to be told again about water," he said. "Captain Wiswell, you tell 'em. I think I'll put you in charge of these South Carolina civilians, Captain. Make friends with 'em. Tell the newcomers to get down to the spring at once. Tell each family it'll have to take care of its own water supply. Tell 'em while I'm talking to the troops."

He pushed his way through the restless rim of people, who were gawking at the green uniforms; and as I skirted the audience to deliver my message, officers called raggedly for attention, the green lines stiffened, and Cruger went to talking.

Cruger didn't look like a soldier to me. He didn't have the hawk-nosed look I'd noticed in Howe and Clinton, in Arnold and Simcoe. He was more like a kindly teacher, more like a thoughtful, amiable scholar who had worked too hard over his books. Like an earnest student, he peered owlishly at the throng, seeming to scrutinize all the officers and men in those green-clad ranks, all the perspiring men and women who stared open-mouthed from behind the rigid lines of troops, every window in courthouse, tavern and jail: even the buzzards floating in weary circles overhead.

"Try to forget nothing I tell you," I heard him say. "Any man who forgets may be endangering not only his own life, but the lives of all.

"I expect hard work from every man, every woman, every child. The enemy'll take this town if he can, and we can only prevent him by fighting harder than he fights, working harder than he works, thinking faster than he thinks, studying harder and longer than he studies."

I looked back and saw him make a quick turn, head bent, hands clasped behind his back, just as my father used to pace his study when working on a case. Then, caught in the crowd, but more by the man, I paused and listened further.

"We're all in the same box," he went on. "You know what happens to Loyalist families when the rebels learn they're loyal. You've seen with your own eyes that no male Loyalist can have a home in any part of South Carolina. You've seen 'em shot, sometimes just on suspicion of being loyal. You've seen 'em driven beyond the mountains, or to New Providence, or to the Sugar Islands. You've seen their wives and children, if allowed to live at all, living on what they could beg or steal."

He pounded his fist into his open palm. "No man or woman in this town must ever lose heart! I could hunt the world over for soldiers to defend this post without finding as good ones as mine! This very day I gave permission to the South Carolina militia to leave camp. Their answer was to drive their horses into the woods. They stand here on my left. Their names are familiar to every resident of this province. They'd rather die than turn South Carolina over to rebels!"

That whole crowded square seemed caught in a silent spell, through which the squealing of a wagon wheel in the distance was an irritation in my ear.

"The rest of these troops of mine," Cruger said, "are all countrymen of yours. They're from New Jersey and New York, but they think exactly as you think. In the early part of this war they made Long Island safe for thousands of Loyalists who took refuge there. More recently they helped capture Savannah—a great feat—and successfully defended it against the combined attacks of the French and the rebels. They gained great honor in the capture of Charleston and received high praise for the part they played in the rout of Gates and the rebels at Camden. There are no better troops in the world than these of mine. Do as you're told, and they'll take care of you."

Among the onlookers who barred my way I spotted two tall South Carolinians. They were watching Cruger intently and shivering like hunting dogs making game. They looked exactly alike. Even the curly-maple stocks and grips of their long squirrel rifles were inlaid with the same number of stars and crescents.

"That's about all," I heard Cruger saying. "The rebels' light troops are here already. By sundown the whole rebel army will be outside this stockade, camped for a siege. In all likelihood they'll make four camps, one astride each of the four roads into town. Obey the orders you're given. Stay quietly where you're ordered to stay, so I can find you promptly when I need you. Treasure your water as if it were gold; hoard your provisions as if they were rubies. If you have complaints to make, make them to me. Remember it's not only ourselves we're fighting for. If we're unsuccessful, other thousands of Americans will be ruined."

I spoke to the two Carolinians. "Colonel Cruger wants help," I said. "He wants to be sure every bucket and dish in this town is filled with water before the attack starts. He's sent me to do all I can to see everything's looked after. Will you help spread the word?"

"What's your name, Bud?" one of them said. "Wheah you f'om an' what's your pappy do?"

"My name's Oliver Wiswell," I said. "Captain, King's American Dragoons. I was driven out of Boston by the rebels. My father was a lawyer. The rebels killed him."

"You don't say," the questioner said. "Our pappy was killed, too. Some o' Marion's men shot him in the back while he was eating supper. We'll help tell 'em to get the water for you. Smallwood, you go no'th an' I'll skin around this way."

"What's your name?" I asked.

"Pshaw!" the boy said. "We're Kirklands. We're related to half the folks in the Ninety Six District. I'm Lonnie, and this here's my twin, Smallwood. We'd like real well to help you and the colonel, whenever you need anything."

He and his brother departed, bawling in slurred voices, "Git your empties, evybody. Evybody's got to git water!"

CHAPTER LXXVIII

WE COULDN'T look over the stockade, the next morning, without seeing rebels. Half a mile to the north, and half a mile to the south, their tent towns straddled each of the roads to the outer world; and all around us the smoke of hundreds of rebel campfires was hazy blue against the pale greens of the forest.

How many thousands there were, we couldn't tell; but they moved in and out of the shelter of the far forest like ants fumbling in the grass around an anthill.

What Greene's men had done in one short, hot night was astonishing. On the afternoon of May twenty-first, when we first saw Colonel Washington's white-coated rebel cavalry come out from the forest, there wasn't a mark upon the surrounding fields, barring the ditch dug for defense close under the walls of the Star Redoubt.

Now, seventy paces from the stockade over which we peered, two long parapets of red earth stretched across the fields. So close were the red embankments that we could hear men talking in the trenches behind them; hear the gritting and tapping of shovels; see gouts of dirt fly up out of the two long ditches; hear rocks and dirt trickle down the face of the red slopes when shovelfuls were tossed upon them.

Buell had begun his work on the gun tower before daylight; and with Roney's approval he'd called upon me to assist him.

"I want you to pick five South Carolina hunters who can shoot. I don't mean men that can shoot fieldpieces: I mean men that can shoot off a squirrel's tail with a rifle at two hundred yards. I want them to be one of the gun crews and I want you to lay one of the guns. You learned how to sight a gun from a platform while we were on the frigate, and I want one of those guns worked by men who aren't trained artillerymen, all full of drill and rules. Either you or I've got to stay there on that tower and work those guns as long as we aren't shot off of it. That's our job, Oliver: to take charge of those guns till we've taught the regular crews how I want 'em handled. Go get me those squirrel-murderers and have 'em in the Star Redoubt just after first daylight."

I immediately went to look for the two Kirklands, Lonnie and Smallwood, found them, took their advice in selecting the other three from among their neighbors, and at the first hint of sunrise the six of us were on our way, crossing the town to the Redoubt. In the pale dawn light the circular enclosure seemed overcrowded with restlessly moving figures, and the fire step inside the stockade was packed with watchers.

Roney, who'd come with us, went to the fire step and grasped an ankle. "Can you see 'em?"

"See 'em!" the man whispered. "You can damned near spit on 'em!"

"Where's the colonel?" Roney asked.

"How do I know?" the man asked irritably. "He's jumping around like a flea on a hot iron."

Roney walked along the base of the fire step, staring up at the heads outlined against the pale sky until he found the right one.

"Who's that?" Cruger asked. "Is that you, Roney? Where's Buell?"

"Here," Roney said. "We're ready."

"How long'll it take you to raise your tower, Lieutenant?"

"Buell figures we can have the platform in place in eight minutes, Colonel. We can't work many men on the platform, so it'll take longer to make the parapet, sway up guns and rig blocks and tackles."

"How much longer?" Cruger asked.

"Half an hour, Colonel."

Cruger pondered. "Half an hour, eh? That's good time."

He rose to his feet to peer over the stockade once more, and I climbed to the fire step to look over his shoulder. Colonel King was with him, I saw, and Colonel Deveaux, Captain French, Captain Campbell, Captain DeLancey, Lieutenant Hatton.

The east was brighter and tinged with pink; and in the abatis that protected our ditch, mockingbirds and cardinals had begun to sing. Beyond the abatis I could dimly make out two long ridges, as if a gigantic plow had made parallel furrows. From behind those furrows came faint clankings and the gritting of shovels in gravel.

"Seen any more men come into those works, Colonel?" Cruger asked.

"Not a man, Colonel," Deveaux said. "If you look hard, you can see the shovels when they toss out the dirt. Both those trenches are so full of men, I don't believe you could get ten more into 'em."

"Can you see reserves anywhere?" Cruger asked.

"There aren't any," Deveaux said. "I can't understand what they're thinking of! They must think we're deaf and blind—or lack powder."

Cruger rose on tiptoe, as if that slight advantage might help him see more clearly what the rebels were doing. "Yes," he said, "there's something mighty queer about it, but I think it's the queerness of stupidity."

He turned to Roney. "All right, Lieutenant. Raise that platform. When it's up, screen the front so they can't see the guns swayed into place. Don't waste time, once you've started. We've got to wipe out those trenches before they have a chance to stop us. We can't attack till we get the guns into action."

"Sir," Roney said, "Buell ought to be in charge of the platform and the guns. If you're going to clean out those trenches, sir, I'd like the privilege of going with the party."

"Hell and damnation, Lieutenant," Cruger said testily. "Get that platform started and I'll let you lead the party!"

Roney pulled me from the fire step; and as we hurried toward the pile of timbers, Negroes rose from it as crows rise from a cornfield at the approach of danger.

When the sun came up like a disk of white-hot steel from behind the far-off hills of Georgia, Buell had arranged timbers, planks, guns, carriages, Negroes to his liking.

A heavy timber pointed outward, like a compass direction on a map, from each of the four holes dug the day before. Planks to brace them lay in piles between the holes, and beside each pile was coiled rope for lashings. At the timber ends were the three guns, as if to mark north, east and south on that huge compass; and to the carriage and trunnions of each were fastened other coiled ropes.

Crews of Negroes were gathered alongside each of the timbers that extended outward from the platform holes; and all of them, despite the back-breaking labors they had undergone, despite Buell's seeming despair because of their slowness, were immensely pleased with Buell and themselves. They rolled white eyes at each other with furtive delight; burst into stifled laughter; seemed to look upon all this violent toil as a sort of game.

Buell, in the center of his geometric arrangement of men, timbers, ropes and guns, spoke warningly.

"When I say go, go; but don't go too far! The first black boy that does anything wrong, I'll throw him over the stockade with my own hands!

"Those that do as I've told 'em, they'll get meat to eat! Yes, sir: they'll have the best horse meat in this garrison! Those that do best'll get the best horse meat, naturally!"

He drew his sleeve across his eyes to free them of sweat, cast a final glance at the material around him, and carelessly added, "Those trenches are seventy yards away. If you don't raise this platform quick, you'll stop a million buckshot."

The Negroes exchanged admiring glances.

"Well," Buell said. He hitched at his breeches and glanced quickly around the inside of the stockade. I knew it to be an instinctive glance, and it brought back to me scenes at which I'd cast similar desperate looks—our comfortable kitchen in Milton on that unhappy far-off night when I'd refused to admit the mob; the sunny back yard of Demott's Mill when the pig-faced colonel had peered down at me; that golden Long Island cornfield into which we had ridden when the guns signaled that we had cut off all of Washington's army from their base; the dark lane on Milton Hill in which Buell and I had stood, listening to the rebels planning our capture; Julia Bishop's front room, and Steven Leighton staring at me over Julia's shining black hair.

Yes, I knew too well why Buell's eyes had made the circuit of the crowded Star Redoubt: and my own eyes followed his around that hot kettle of a place, with its sharply angled bastions, its stockaded wall, solidly lined with green-clad troops.

Colonel Cruger and his other officers were staring thoughtfully down upon us—wondering, no doubt, whether this strange gun platform, this peculiar invention of Buell's, would work, or whether it would collapse when half finished.

"Up," Buell shouted. "Lift 'em! Up with 'em! Get 'em up!"

The whole interior of that bowl-like Redoubt seemed to boil and swirl. Men grunted and groaned, shouted and cursed. The four timbers rose slowly, like the wings of the windmills we had seen on Long Island. Their butt ends slipped into the rock-filled holes. Half-naked Negroes ran with long crotched poles; and suddenly, miraculously, the four timbers were upright, inclined a little toward each other and neatly held in place by those crotched poles. Men, glistening with sweat, lashed planks and poles from timber to timber.

"Go on up," I told the five Carolinians who waited behind me for orders.

The four-legged structure swarmed with crawling humans.

On the ground the four timbers had been unimpressive enough. Raised, they were enormous. The platform at the top looked mountain-high. From it the men on the fire steps below were mere dots; the ditch and abatis outside the Redoubt walls seemed almost beneath us; and the two rebel trenches looked close enough for a man to jump into. I could see rebels crowded in them, working with pickaxes and shovels, see their faces turn toward us; but their picks continued to rise and plunge downward into the red earth. Shovels flashed, machinelike, and gouts of earth fell from them.

The encircling forest at the far edge of the fields seemed closer to us. In that one quick glance for which I had time while my five men were swaying up their gun, I could see figures moving quickly at the edge of the forest; see mounted men scurrying from far-off groups of tents.

The sun's rays were like the blast from the door of a furnace; the boards beneath us were so hot that pitch bubbled from them; at times, on Buell's order, a part of us lay flat on our faces so that others could walk over us. I heard the rattle of musket shots, heard faint poppings and snappings close at hand, and knew them to be passing bullets. As we sweated to settle the trunnions of our gun into its carriage, a parapet of sandbags appeared from nowhere and concealed us from the dusty fields and the red trenches below.

My feeling of insecurity began to fade. When the gun at last was mounted, I was at ease upon that small square platform. It seemed safe, a coign of vantage from which I couldn't fall or be dislodged. I was in that peculiar state that comes only to men at war—a state of concentration so intense that nothing exists beyond the little space around them. All I knew was that that gun of mine must be placed in the exact center of the platform; and when at last it stood there, and I thought to straighten up and look around, Buell pushed a rope into my hand.

"Here," he said, "keep this rope taut! Don't let it go slack!"

I found Stephen DeLancey, Colonel Cruger's aide, next to me, crouched beside the carriage of his gun, and similarly holding a rope's end.

Beyond DeLancey, Captain Barbarie and his gun crew were pushing the third gun into place. One of Barbarie's hands was covered with caked blood.

"What happened to the captain?" I asked DeLancey.

"I don't know," DeLancey said. "He gets mad when you ask him. He's all right."

Buell crawled to me with another rope. "Hold this, too," he said. "Tell your men to lay out rammers and sponges. Tell 'em for God's sake not to kick over the water bucket!"

He crawled away. I heard him say to Roney, "All right, Johnny! Get the spare men off this platform. Tell the colonel these guns'll be working in fifteen minutes."

"Don't you make a mistake," Roney said. "I'm starting for those trenches in fifteen minutes, and if the guns *shouldn't* be working, I wouldn't like it!"

"Don't talk so much," Buell said. "Go ahead down!"

CHAPTER LXXIX

Across the front of each gun carriage was a bridle, and before each gun, ready to be attached to the bridle, lay a heavy cable with a hook spliced to the end. At the front edge of the platform, in line with each gun, a pulley was fastened to the planking with spikes and blocks.

Buell moved from pulley to pulley on hands and knees, like a spaniel in a rabbit warren; and when he turned to us, still hunkered in the shelter of the sandbags, his eyes were sunken, his hands claw-like and bloody from the ropes, his lips dirt-caked, his bare shoulders streaked with red mud.

"Load all three guns," he said. "Run Number One gun—Captain Wiswell's—up to the sandbags. Hook the rope from Number One to Number Three gun—Captain Barbarie's. Captain Wiswell and Captain Barbarie'll do the hooking when I give the order. Then Number One'll fire. Got that straight?"

We made sounds of assent.

"All right," Buell said. "When Number One fires, it kicks back and jerks Number Three forward. When Number Three fires, it kicks back and pulls up Number Two. When Number Two fires, it pulls Number One into position again."

On hands and knees he scrambled to the rear edge of the platform and looked over, then crawled back to the sandbags again.

"Roney's ready," he told us. "The sally port's open. He's going out. He's got thirty men with him. When I give the order, hook up. When I give the order to fire, fire. Keep out of the way of the guns, or they'll kick you to pieces! Lie on your bellies! Don't raise your heads to see what's happening, or you won't have heads! All right; load those guns!"

On that hot and crowded platform the three gun crews moved with hushed and hurried scuffling. The men of my own crew slid past one another like dancers to push in the powder bag and ram it home, to toss a bag of grape after the powder, to press the tube down the breech.

"Quick, Oliver," Buell said. There was something in his voice that raised goose flesh between my shoulder blades. "Run your gun to the bags! Hook on the rope!"

I had time for just one flashing look through the opening in the bags before I jerked the hook over the bridle and crawled back to lay the gun on the far-off woods. In that one flash I saw white faces raised in the rebel trenches—white faces with open mouths and saucer-eyes.

I saw, too, running from the shelter of the stockade beneath us, a line of men in green, led by Roney. I knew it was Roney because the right sleeve of his green shirt was almost torn off.

As I squinted along the gun I could see rebel troops forming in long ragged lines on the edge of the forest. I kicked at the carriage and threw my shoulder against the breech, to line that pitted brown barrel with the thickest of those distant lines. I knew it was useless: knew I hadn't the necessary time to lay the gun properly.

"Fire!" Buell shouted.

I picked up the match and pressed it against the tube. The gun crews went down on their bellies. For a moment I had the illusion that I was alone upon a spacious, silent tower—that all around me lay a land as peaceful as it was shimmering and fertile; as secure as the brooding, changeless bulks of those misty mountains to the north and west. For just that one fleeting moment, it seemed to me, the whole earth was friendly and smiling, majestic and beautiful.

Then the planks beneath me jerked like living things. The gun leaped backward past me with deafening thunder. The platform seemed to flutter and surge above a choppy sea of musketry fire.

"Sponge and load," I told the men. I picked up the burning match from beside me and saw it had rested against my arm, though I'd felt nothing.

I crawled back to the gun and freed the hook from the bridle. I caught another glimpse of Roney and his men. They had come out through the abatis, and were running across the open field toward the rebel trenches. They seemed to be running slowly and I had the vague thought that Roney was fortunate: could take his time, whereas we couldn't. We had to load again, dodge the recoil of the other guns; fire, sponge, load, dodge, cough thick smoke from our throats so we could breathe; fire, sponge, load, dodge, fire, sponge, load, fire, dodge, dodge, sponge, fire. . . .

Buell caught my arm. "Wait," he said, and shook me. He raised his voice. "Let the guns cool. Swab 'em out! Let 'em stand a minute!"

He was splashed from head to foot with the black water from the gun swabs that had sprayed the platform. The men around me were black as Negroes from that same sooty water, and seemingly I hadn't been aware of them until, all at once, it was as if I found myself surrounded by blackly grotesque figures in some swirl of a crowd at a masquerade. Something like a fever must have been consuming me; my hands shook, my eyeballs stung, my face burned beneath the caked soot upon it.

The Kirklands were on their feet, peering over the sandbags and shouting.

I looked down at the field and saw Roney standing on the lip of the first trench. His men were already in the trench or just about to jump in. I could even distinguish Roney's voice. "Get in here! For God's sake get in here!"

He jumped in himself. All along the whole length of the trench, musket butts rose and fell, shovel blades glittered, pickaxes flashed. From the trench came reedy cries, thin human howlings.

A rebel rolled out of the back of the trench and got to one knee. A bayonet darted upward from the trench and vanished in his back, but he got to his other knee and crawled toward the second trench, the affixed musket dragging along behind him like a tail.

A green-shirted figure scrambled after him, reached for the musket, missed it and fell down, got to his feet and leaped forward, this time successfully. The rebel sprawled on his face, the bayonet pulled loose, the green-shirted figure stabbed twice at the fallen man; then stopped and looked around.

Two more rebels popped from the trench; then others. A dozen were running toward the second trench, with Roney's men after them, prodding and stabbing like farmers hurriedly pitchforking hay before a storm.

Then, surprisingly, rebels were climbing from the second trench, too—climbing out and running away before Roney's men could reach them.

Roney and his raiders went into that second trench like rabbits scuttling for shelter. Again we saw musket butts rise and fall; heard shrill squealings.

"Hah!" Buell said. "They bayoneted the whole lot of 'em! Roney must 'a' killed every damned man that didn't run away!"

He was right; for when Roney's men climbed out of that second trench, they stood unmolested on the embankment. Some fired at the few rebels running for the shelter of the far-off forest. Others cleaned their bayonets, plunging them into the red parapet.

More green-shirted figures clambered from the trench. They were kneeling and tugging at something. When that something came into view, it wore a green shirt. I caught a flash of white at its shoulder, where the shirt was torn.

"That's Roney," I told Buell. "Something happened to Roney!"

Buell ran to the edge of the platform. "Roney's hurt," he shouted. "They got Roney! I can't fire these guns while they're bringing him back."

A confused shouting came up to us from the Redoubt.

Half of Roney's detachment had started back. Roney sat between two of them, on their clasped hands. His head drooped, as if his neck were rags and sawdust. The rest of Roney's men stayed at the second trench, lying behind the newly turned red earth as a rear guard.

The little knot of returning men was so near that we could see their looks of concern. One of the men broke from the group and ran toward us. At the edge of the abatis he stopped and shouted, "The lieutenant says to send out some blacks to pick up the tools and fill in the trenches. He says send riflemen with 'em!"

Buell looked across the fields. At the edge of the woods a rebel regiment was in motion.

"Oliver," Buell said, "go down and tell Cruger those fellers have started. It's over a mile to those woods, and unless I'm mistaken they'll be close enough to fire into the trenches in fifteen minutes. Ask him if he wants us to start firing now, or wait till they get closer."

When I reached the ground, Roney's men were crowding in at the sally port. Roney, his arms around the shoulders of two of them, seemed to have no bones in his body. His face was ashen.

I thought he tried to hold up his head when his dull, half-opened eyes fell on Cruger, but he couldn't. He spoke thickly. "Send 'em right out, Colonel! Get those trenches filled up!"

"Put him on the stretcher," Cruger said.

One of the New Jersey men who carried him looked helplessly at Cruger. "Take hold of him! My hands are slippery. Put him face down."

Cruger nodded to an officer of South Carolina militia, who in turn addressed his men in a drawly, lackadaisical voice. "Go on out, now! Half of you stay in front of these nigras; half behind. Don't let none of 'em get hurt."

The militiamen started out through the sally port, and their leader's voice rose a little as he harangued the Negroes.

"Lift up your feet, you black scoundrels! Move along there! Don't you pay no attention to nothing except'n those tools! Get your black hands on those tools and fill up those trenches, or first thing you know, by God, those rebels'll toss you into 'em and cover you up! You know how those northern folks treat nigras!"

He herded the Negroes and the last of the riflemen through the sally port, and we heard no more.

A dozen eager hands took Roney from the Jerseymen, lowered him to the stretcher, and turned him on his face.

The men who had carried him were drenched with blood.

"How'd it happen, Sergeant?" Cruger asked.

"A rebel played dead," the sergeant said. "Got up on his knees when the lieutenant's back was turned and slashed him with a shovel. The blade cut his ribs away from his backbone. I saw the ends when we picked him up."

The colonel got down on one knee beside Roney. "You did well, Lieutenant," he said. "There isn't a man in this or any other regiment that could have led that attack any better."

There was so much confusion all around—gabbling from the fire step; persistent shouting from the top of our gun tower; the slow spitting of squirrel rifles from the far side of the stockade—that I had difficulty hearing Roney's reply.

"Tell my father, Colonel. Rebels burned our house same as they did yours. He don't like 'em."

"I'll let you tell him yourself," Cruger said heartily. "We'll stitch up that back of yours and you'll be all right."

"You write him," Roney said thickly.

"I certainly will, my boy," Cruger said. "I'll do better! I'll read it out before the whole battalion. What's more, I'll make you a captain for this day's work."

Roney didn't say anything.

Cruger nodded to the stretcher bearers and pointed toward the town. When he turned away, I gave him Buell's message.

Cruger heard me; then looked up at the platform where Buell, his head thrust over the edge, was watching us.

"Are they filling the trenches?" Cruger asked.

"They certainly are," Buell shouted. "They'll be full and level in ten minutes, and the rebels haven't covered a third of the distance yet. Shall I give 'em a few shots?"

"Oh, dear me, no!" Cruger said. "Oh, by no means!"

"For Christ's sake, why not?" Buell bellowed.

Cruger looked pained. "Because, Mr. Buell, the rebel leaders were both injudicious and insulting when they dug trenches so close to this Redoubt. Rashness and impudence should be treated with contempt whenever possible. If we can contrive to fill their trenches without firing another shot, we'd be treating their efforts in a way that would rankle for years in every rebel breast."

Cruger was right. When the South Carolina militiamen came back to the Redoubt, not another shot had been fired; not another man lost. The blacks who had gone with them were laden with shovels, pickaxes and crowbars. Where the trenches had been there were only two red scars across the fields to mark the graves of a hundred rebels.

Beyond those red scars the long lines of Greene's rebel infantry, drawn up in the field, wavered uncertainly. Not a shot was fired at them. After a time they wheeled into columns of fours and marched back toward the woods, while from the stockade rose shouts of mocking, ironic laughter.

CHAPTER LXXX

On the next night the rebel army, cured of its rashness by Roney's unexpected and daring attack, opened a long trench at a respectful distance—five or six times as far from us as were the two red scars that marked their first attempt.

Half an hour after the sentries had reported the opening of the new trench, every officer in the garrison, from colonel down to cornet, was crowded into the stuffy, fly-infested barroom of the tavern. When Buell and I came in, Cruger, with young Stephen DeLancey at his elbow, worked with a little brush on a map of the town and the Star Redoubt, neatly tracing in dark blue water-color the trench the rebels had just opened.

"Now, gentlemen," Cruger said, turning to face us, "I've got you here for three reasons. I want to explain our situation, so you can pass it on to your non-commissioned officers and let them tell the men. Then I want to hear any suggestions you care to make. Finally I want to dispose of the rumors about Lord Rawdon that have been flying around this camp."

He turned to his map and with his little brush tapped the open space between the dark blue line of rebel trench and the saw-toothed circle of the Star Redoubt. "That's where they dug their first trenches —the ones Lieutenant Roney destroyed," he said. "I didn't put in those original trenches, because I'm going to need that space later."

He twirled the brush in his fingers and added, seemingly as an afterthought, "I'm sorry to say Lieutenant Roney died last night."

Nobody said anything.

"Well," Cruger went on, "I want to tell you what I think the rebels intend to do. The trench they dug last night is four hundred yards

687

from the Star Redoubt. When that's finished, they'll mount light guns in it—three-pounders, perhaps—for protection; then run a second trench out toward the Redoubt on a long slant. When that's done, they'll probably move their guns into it and dig a third trench parallel to the first. That third one's going to be too close for comfort. If they dig that third trench, and we let 'em stay in it unmolested, they can do us considerable harm."

"Such as?" asked a voice in the rear of the room.

"Such as running a tunnel to the wall of the Redoubt and laying a mine," the colonel said. "If they set off a mine under that wall, they'd have a hole big enough to drive a hayrick through. Now then, gentlemen, let's have suggestions. I'll hear the younger men first. Lieutenant Barbarie, what do you think we ought to do about this rebel trench?"

"Raid it," Barbarie said.

All the green-shirted officers laughed, as men do at the sudden expression of a unanimous opinion.

"Yes," Cruger said, "I think Lieutenant Roney showed us the way. You'll have to remember, though, that we'll have to do our raiding at night, and that we won't be able to raid often enough to stop their work entirely. They'll always gain on us. You'll have to point that out to your men. They'll have to see those trenches coming closer and closer, day after day; but you can tell 'em that in the end—provided they do their duty—the rebels'll find a hedge of steel they'll never be able to pass."

He turned to his map. "Here's another thing, gentlemen: I don't know how many men General Greene's got; but I do know that if he had enough, he'd move some of 'em around to the north and start operating against the upper fort and our water supply. He'll probably get reinforcements before anybody comes to our help. That means we've got to do some digging ourselves. Look here——"

He tapped his brush against the blue line representing the trench dug by the rebels the night before; then moved the brush a third of the way around the stockade, to a point looking down into the ravine between the upper fort and the town.

"Suppose," he said, "the rebels put guns at the head of this ravine as well as in that trench they just dug. We'd be enfiladed, and our water supply cut off. There's nothing as disturbing to a civilian population as a cross fire. It makes 'em jumpy.

"Well, gentlemen, we've got to prepare for that. We've got to dig trenches in the town—trenches large enough to hold every noncombatant. What's more, we've got to dig a well. Everybody not needed for defense has got to dig—everybody! If we dig hard enough, no rebel force can ever take this town!"

He opened his mouth as if to say something more; then closed it again, and I was sure he'd been about to remind us of what would happen to the loyal residents of those rich Carolina valleys if we didn't dig hard enough.

"There's just one more thing," he said. "A lot of our men think Lord Rawdon has deserted us. They're whispering it in every corner. I want you to make it plain that this isn't possible. There've been a lot of hard things said about British officers, some of 'em justified. Every officer in these battalions, I dare say, has had cavalier treatment from one or two British officers. But nobody ever got such treatment from Lord Rawdon! There's no better soldier, no more courageous officer, no greater gentleman, no better friend than Lord Rawdon. Tell your men I say so.

"Tell 'em, too, that something's gone wrong. I don't know where he is, and I haven't heard from him for a month, but I think I know what's happened. I think the messengers he's sent to me have been captured. I think that in all likelihood the messengers I've sent him have been captured, too. If that's the case, it's mighty unfortunate, but that's all it is. It doesn't alter the fact that Rawdon's an able soldier and a good friend. If we hold out long enough, he'll be here."

It had been on May twenty-second that Greene and his army of four thousand crossed the Saluda and showed themselves at the edge of the woods. It had been on May twenty-third that they dug the trenches that Roney's men filled in. It was on the twenty-fourth that Greene opened that first long parallel, four hundred yards in front of the Star Redoubt.

The next ten days were bad. They were phantasmagorias of blinding heat, shot through with foul smells, incessant labor, unslakable thirst, greasy food that stank, clouds of flies and stinging insects, daily thunderstorms that came down into the very trenches with us and exploded in blasts of lightning that tore our shovels and pickaxes from our hands.

From sun-up to dark we dug and dug on those endless trenches that cut through the baked earth of the town like a giant cross. All through the nights there was a constantly recurring spatter and sputter of rifle shots as raiding parties crawled through the fields on their bellies to stab like wasps at the ever-growing, ever-nearing rebel trenches.

All through the day, long lines of women and children moved in and out of the ravine between the high fort and the town, filling buckets with spring water and plodding back to the trenches with them; but no spring could have flowed fast enough to quench our thirst, or to drown the searing flame that the Carolina sun kindled within us.

Buell, at first regarded dubiously by Cruger's officers because of the freedom with which he damned everyone in England, from the King and Germaine down to Mrs. Jump, quickly won their hearts because of his inventiveness and his willingness to work day and night at anything that would help to defeat the rebels.

He arranged three mirrors on a stick in such a way that the top mirror, elevated above the stockade, would reflect into the lowest mirror all that was happening beyond the stockade—a convenient contrivance when rebel riflemen were sending bullets uncomfortably close to every head that showed itself.

He made a small shield out of iron that could be fastened above the breech of a gun to protect the gunner when he sighted it.

He made a singular contraption out of a drum and a lance, fastening the butt end of the lance to the drumhead with a thong, and driving the lancehead into the earth beyond the stockade. One who pressed his ear against the opposite drumhead could hear with singular clarity the sound of enemy picks in the soil, and gauge almost exactly where they were digging.

His best discovery was his simplest, and saved the lives of many a member of the garrison. He held that a man whose face, arms and body were blackened with soot was next to invisible on a dark night, and in proof of it he covered himself with soot, slipped from the Redoubt one night, and returned an hour later with a rebel sword made from a scythe blade.

"If you have your men cover themselves with soot," he told Cruger, "they can kill so many rebels in those trenches that they'll have to waste half their nights carrying out their dead. Why, I laid right on the edge of that parapet, and I could have laid there all night if a rebel officer hadn't mistaken my head for a rock and started to pick it up and throw it out into the field."

"Did you have a chance to notice regimental marks on him?" Cruger asked.

"Yes," Buell said. "I had a chance. I went over him mighty careful, but the only thing on him was his sword. I guess he was a militia officer, wearing clothes that would let him look like a simple bare-footed farmer in case he had to run away."

We dug incessantly, like moles, from the twenty-third of May, when the rebels started their first parallel, to the third of June, when they completed their second parallel; but that work was nothing by comparison to what we did, beginning with the third of June.

It was on the third of June that we heard drums rolling in the rebel trenches. Then our own drums rolled and Captain DeLancey went from the Star Redoubt to the stockade, and from the stockade to the little fort, shouting: "All officers to headquarters for a council of war! Come as you are!"

We were a sorry-looking crew when we crowded into the tavern, most of us naked above the waist and streaked with red dust that had changed to black beneath our eyes, under our chins, on our breasts—wherever that red dust had drifted into the channels along which sweat had trickled.

Cruger was changed. He didn't seem to be the same man Buell and I had seen on the day when we came to Ninety Six. His face, tanned when we first saw him, had a peculiar greenish cast, and the circles beneath his eyes were the color of cooked liver.

As we trooped into the big room, the colonel, who was sitting at a desk writing, repeated, over and over: "Sit down on the floor, gentlemen. Sit right down on the floor, gentlemen."

When he rose to speak to us, he picked up a paper between his thumb and forefinger, looked at it as he might have looked at something disgusting, and dropped it again.

"Half an hour ago, gentlemen," he said, "the adjutant general of the rebel army came to our lines under a flag of truce and demanded my presence. Lieutenant Stelle of the New Jersey Volunteers was officer of the day, and rightly informed the rebel adjutant that it was unusual for commanding officers to receive and answer flags of truce in person."

Again he picked up the letter between his thumb and forefinger. "I might add," he said, "that this peculiar document, although addressed to the commanding officer of this garrison, is not signed by the rebel general, but by the general's adjutant—by way of hinting to us, I assume, that the general considers us unworthy of his personal attention. This is what he said:

"'To the commandant of the fort at Ninety Six: Your post, maintained contrary to the interests of the Government of the United States of America and to the welfare of the people of South Carolina, has been surrounded beyond all hope of rescue or relief by the courageous and indefatigable Southern Army.

"'In all probability the commandant and the garrison of Ninety Six, because of the impenetrable barrier thrown about them by the tireless bravery of the Patriot Army, know nothing of the magnificent successes which, with God's unfailing support, that army has won.

"'It has swept from the banks of the Congaree, the Wateree and the Santee all the armed invaders sent by your royal master to harry and enslave our suffering people. With invincible gallantry it has driven Rawdon's troops from Camden and from Orangeburg, and forced him to retreat to the seacoast, whence he will never return. The brave Pickens, Lee and Sumter are even now demolishing the forts at Augusta; and when they have fallen, nothing can protect you from complete destruction.

"'If you persist in your opposition to our arms, you will bring disaster upon your deluded men and death to unfortunate residents of this district. You have everything to hope from our generosity if you bow to the justice of our cause and cease your opposition to the will of Divine Providence. If you do not, you have everything to fear from our resentment.

"'We are generous in victory, and terrible to the wicked. Unless you immediately and unconditionally surrender to the Army of the United States of America, you yourself, as commandant of the post of Ninety Six, will be held personally responsible for a fruitless resistance, and for the death of those who will die from sword, bullet and starvation in a vain attempt to defend an undefendable position.

"'This summons will not be repeated, nor will any flag of truce be received from your garrison for any purpose except instantaneous capitulation.'"

Cruger dropped the paper on his desk and cast a deprecatory glance at the half-naked officers who sat staring up at him, round-eyed and slack-lipped. "How does that strike you, gentlemen?"

An angry murmur, in which no one voice was distinguishable, rose from the men before him.

"Now, gentlemen," Cruger said, "remember what I've always told you! Don't lose your temper. Let me hear from one or two singly. Colonel Deveaux, what's your opinion of this letter?"

"It's an insult, sir," Deveaux said. "General Greene knows who's in command here as well as I do; yet he pretends he doesn't. What's worse, he lets a subordinate sign it! That letter doesn't come from a generous enemy!"

"It doesn't exactly inspire confidence," Cruger said. "Perhaps one of you younger gentlemen would care to say a word in behalf of the rebel argument."

The room was a tumult of shouting. "No! No! No surrender! To hell with 'em!"

Cruger held up his hand. "As I understand it, gentlemen," he said, when the room was quiet, "you prefer to fight rather than to surrender."

He waited until the roar of assent had died away, then went on. "I suspected you'd feel that way, because that was my own immediate sentiment. I wrote an answer to General Greene's adjutant, but instead of sending him the written paper, I'm going to let Lieutenant Barbarie deliver it to him by word of mouth. I think that'll impress him more.

"Lieutenant Barbarie, go to the Redoubt and report to the rebel officer you'll find just outside. Tell him Colonel Cruger directs you to say to General Greene that Ninety Six was committed to his care; that Colonel Cruger's duty and inclination make it necessary for him to defend the post to the last extremity; that Colonel Cruger, his officers and his men, all of them loyal Americans, are indifferent to the promises as well as to the threats of General Greene, and for the same reason."

CHAPTER LXXXI

.

Tʜᴀᴛ day the rebels brought artillery along into the newly finished second parallel and opened fire on the Star Redoubt, Buell's tower and the town.

In the sun's scorching heat the baked earth, the wooden surfaces of buildings, the logs of the stockades were like coals. I had the feeling of being coopered up in a colossal tub on which insane squealing giants beat thunderously with flails. The squealing was the sound of cannon balls passing overhead. It was like a thousand files biting into a thousand saws, and it made the muscles flutter and the eyelids twitch.

Under cover of this cannonading, the rebels started the construction, out of baskets filled with earth, of a tower of their own, a mere thirty-five yards from our abatis; and such was the violence of their fire that Cruger ordered everyone to shelter. Men, women and children crawled down into the trenches and went to living in holes like woodchucks, or lay huddled against the inside of the stockades. The town, just now an anthill of industry, suddenly seemed deserted, and lay scorched and motionless in the quivering heat like a dying town in which there was neither strength nor resistance.

Yet there was enduring strength, and certainly there was resistance that has never been exceeded.

When the rebel batteries first opened on us, Colonel Cruger took for his headquarters a little fox hole of a dugout in the side of a trench halfway between the courthouse and the Star Redoubt. He chose the spot because it was equidistant from the town gates, the entrance to the Star, and the covered way to the little fort that guarded the water supply.

In that stuffy hole, lighted with a candle stuck in a bayonet socket, the colonel was supposed to be found at any hour of the day or night. As a matter of fact, he was there when he had to be, which was seldom. Most of the time he was hurrying all over town and keeping an eye on everything. And I had to go with him, along with his aide and nephew Stephen DeLancey. He wanted me with him, he said, to keep him in touch with the South Carolinians. In reality, I think, he only wanted us for messengers and for an audience. "I like to talk to Stephen DeLancey," he told me once. "He never says anything that interferes with my thoughts."

He seemed to use me as he'd have used an encyclopedia—a faulty one. Hopefully he'd demand information on past battles, and seem only mildly disappointed when he failed to get it.

When he learned the rebels were starting a tower of their own, he scuttled into the Star Redoubt like a rabbit.

When he climbed on the fire step and saw what the rebels had done, he made muted sounds of exasperated surprise and called loudly for Colonel Deveaux.

"Right here, Colonel," Deveaux said from behind us.

Cruger jerked a protesting thumb toward the rebel trenches. "We can't have this, Colonel! How'll we stop it?"

"Blest if I know, Colonel," Deveaux said. "Those gabions of theirs are so thick that three-pounders don't harm 'em. It's a waste of powder, and we haven't any to waste."

"Where's that Buell?" Cruger asked.

"He's making spears——"

"Well, get him," Cruger said. "They'll run that damned thing forty feet in the air if we don't find a way to stop 'em."

I borrowed a loophole from a South Carolina rifleman. Almost under my nose, a mere thirty-five yards away, the rebels had pushed up a circular wall of the earth-filled baskets that military men call gabions. Before my eyes a fresh basket came into place, as if magically materialized out of thin air. I saw two shovels toss earth into it, though the men who wielded the shovels were hidden.

Buell, when he appeared, looked as if he'd been smoked and oiled from forehead to belt. Perspiration, trickling down his face and naked chest, had washed white channels on his sooty skin.

Cruger looked at him hopefully. "You seem to have an answer to everything, Buell. Have you one for that structure?"

"I don't know the answer to a lot of things," Buell said, "and that's one of 'em. If I was you, Colonel, I wouldn't waste time on it."

"How about hot shot?" the colonel asked. "If we could get hot shot into those gabions, they might burn."

"They might," Buell said, "but you got to have a furnace to heat shot red-hot. Unless it's red-hot, it's no good."

"Couldn't you build a furnace?"

"Yes, sir," Buell said, "I could build one, but we'll have to stop making spears if I do. Colonel Deveaux figures that if the rebels break through the stockade, we'll need three spears for every man in this garrison. Which would you rather have, Colonel: spears or a furnace?"

"I'd rather have the spears," Cruger said. "What are you making the spearheads from?"

"I took all the tires off the wagons and cut 'em into short lengths," Buell said. "I wish you'd figure out a way to get spear-shafts, Colonel. If you can't, I'll have to use wheel spokes for most of 'em."

Cruger sat on the fire step and rested his chin on his hand. He looked no more like a soldier than did Nehemiah Strong, who taught me mathematics and natural philosophy at Yale. "All right," he said. "We can't destroy their tower, so we'll raise our own stockade three feet. The riflemen'll have shelter when the tower gets higher. We'll raise it with sandbags. We'll need three hundred. We'll cut up our tents and put the women to sewing."

"Colonel," Buell said, "did you ever see the drawers the South Carolina women wear? They weave 'em out of linen. They'll turn buckshot, those I've seen; but they'd be easier to stitch than tent canvas."

Cruger looked interested. "That's a useful piece of intelligence, Buell! How'd you pick it up? Well, never mind! Captain DeLancey, run up to the town and see what you can do about getting those appurtenances of the ladies away from 'em. They may be reluctant. I suggest you explain our necessities first to their husbands; and be diplomatic about it, Captain! Arrange to have each lady make her own appurtenances into sandbags, and fill 'em herself. We'll pick 'em up tonight as soon as it's dark."

As Cruger had feared, that tower of gabions mounted twenty feet higher than Buell's artillery platform. On its top, behind sandbags, lay riflemen, who looked almost directly down into the Star, so that no man in the Star was safe unless he was crouched close to the wall, or concealed in one of the deep trenches at which Cruger's Jerseymen and New Yorkers worked all through the night of the fifth.

Bullets weren't the only things they fired from the top of that damnable tower. In the gray dawn of June sixth a sergeant of De-Lancey's, gasping and sweating, burst into our dugout carrying a smoking object that filled our little fox hole with an acrid, eye-watering stench.

Cruger, yawning cavernously, took the smoking thing from the sergeant. "That's an African arrow," he said. "Where'd it come from?"

"The rebels shot it in, sir," the sergeant said. "That stuff on the end is flax dipped in melted pitch. It came in blazing, and stuck in the courthouse roof. If we hadn't seen it, the courthouse would have burned, sure, and all the rest of the town with it!"

"Beat the assembly," Cruger said. "I'll put an end to that! We'll take the roof off every building in town."

We ripped off shingles with the entrenching tools captured from the rebels by Roney's men. From our posts on the roofs we could see across the surrounding fields to the blue folds of the mountains to the northeast and northwest, and to the far flat horizon to the south—that enormous expanse of Low Country, land of sand, of rice fields, of steamy creeks and winding sluggish rivers flowing blackly through swamps festooned with gray moss.

Somewhere in that Low Country Rawdon was camped; and as I sweated and grunted to drive the shovel under the shingles, I wondered helplessly whether Rawdon knew of our plight, and whether, if he did know, he'd move the way I'd seen Clinton and Howe and British admirals move—when they got ready: when it was too late!

All day black men and women stood beside us on the roofs as we worked, watching for burning arrows.

At sundown on the sixth of June, the jail, the courthouse, the tavern, the barracks and every other building in the town were roofless and safe. Piles of shingles, heaps of boards, lay where they could harm nothing if rebel arrows set them afire.

All through that night every man in the town, black and white, carried water from the spring to replenish the receptacles that had been emptied to get us through that one day.

CHAPTER LXXXII

THE sixth of June was bad, but the eighth was worse. It was so packed with bitterness and disappointments that for many a long day thereafter I thought such youthful emotions as hope and anticipation had died within me.

Early on the morning of the eighth we heard jubilant shouts from the sentries on the south side of town—the side toward the Low Country.

At the first shout, Cruger reached for his clothes. "It must be Rawdon," he told us. "I *knew* he'd get here if we held out long enough! I'll shave! I'll put on a wig so Rawdon won't think we've been getting careless!"

When we went out into the trench, we found the town in a turmoil. Officers and soldiers, militia and Negroes, men, women, children, dogs had poured from the trenches and were running toward the south stockade. Their feet raised red dust, on which the early sun projected their capering shadows, grotesque and huge.

An ensign from DeLancey's saluted the colonel. "Sir," he said, "there's cavalry and light infantry moving out of the woods on the Augusta road. We figure it's Lord Rawdon!"

The colonel did his best to look cool and dignified, but he was excited and exultant. If anyone had a right to be pleased, it was Cruger; for he'd worked as hard as any soldier or Negro in the garrison, and successfully held off a force eight times the size of his own.

When we went to the south stockade and climbed to the firing platform of the blockhouse, there seemed to be thousands of exultant people below us, beside themselves with excitement.

We found Colonel Deveaux of the South Carolina militia on the platform, with two of his officers, and a handful of riflemen. A pink glow shone upon them from the newly risen sun, but their faces were dejected. There was nothing jubilant about any of them.

My heart sank. At the far end of the road to the south, where it entered the forest, I saw a black mass of troops and above them a gleam of white.

Cruger looked sick. "That's unfortunate," he said. "If I'm not mistaken, those men have white coats!"

DeLancey, at my shoulder, breathed hard. "That's not Rawdon!" he whispered. "Nobody in these parts wears white except rebel cavalry! Colonel Washington's already here, so that must be Lee's rebel dragoons."

Cruger leaned over the edge of the firing platform and spoke to the green-clad sentries at the gate. "Keep that gate closed! Let nobody out!"

I could almost see silence sweep, wavelike, across the crowd.

The white-coated figures had formed in a thin line and were coming toward us. I could make out dark horses beneath them and a cloud of dust billowing out on either side of the riders. At the front of the column a flag fluttered.

The sentries' faces, turned upward to stare at Cruger, were troubled.

A woman's voice, shrill and cracked, asked querulously, "Ain't it Rawdon, Colonel?"

Cruger's voice, in the hot silence of that June morning, seemed to scratch my eardrums. "I'm sorry," he said, "very sorry. We've been mistaken. That isn't Lord Rawdon. It's rebel cavalry."

Somewhere on the edge of the silent crowd a child began to cry.

"We'll just keep on as we were," Cruger went on. "We'll be as safe in our trenches as we've ever been, and I'll see to it you come to no harm. You can trust us. You'll be protected."

Colonel Deveaux cleared his throat. "Shall I send 'em back to the trenches, Colonel?"

Cruger shook his head. "No. Let 'em watch Lee go into camp. He won't dare come within gunshot, and those white coats make his men look harmless, for once."

Cruger was wrong. Lee's cavalry *did* come within gunshot. They marched straight up the road from Augusta, the road that skirted the western side of the town—the side opposite the point where Greene had dug his trenches. At first we couldn't understand why they should approach in such a way; for to reach Greene's main camp, they'd have to make a complete circuit of the town.

We couldn't understand how they dared to march to the tune of four fifes and four drums, that rattled and squealed a gay tune over and over, louder and louder as they drew nearer.

As they came abreast of us, however, we understood. They were so close we could hear them talking, hear sabers clanking against stirrup irons; but as they went by, the whole garrison of Ninety Six stood and looked on without firing a gun, almost speechless from rage.

Marching close beside those rebel troopers, against their stirrup irons, as servants might march, was a body of men, some in green uniforms, some with naked brown upper bodies, and here and there a few in scarlet. All were unarmed; many had bloody bandages on heads, arms, legs. Several were bound, and their cords made fast to the stirrups of white-coated dragoons.

I could hear the rebels making merry at the expense of their captives; see them waving triumphantly toward us, gesturing derisively at their unhappy charges. They seemed to be saying that we, too, would receive the same treatment.

All around me officers muttered to themselves, made faint hissing sounds such as men make at the sight of someone in distress—someone they can't help. I heard DeLancey, at my elbow, cursing. French, Campbell, Barbarie, Buell, Colonel Deveaux, Colonel Cruger, stared rigidly at that passing column of dusty prisoners. On Cruger's face there was a contemplative wry smile; he continually wiped perspiration from his cheeks with a hand that trembled.

Colonel Deveaux spoke hesitantly. "I figure that would be the Augusta garrison, Colonel."

"Augusta, yes," Cruger said. "Browne had Cherokees in his garrison, and I see about fifty of 'em yonder. So far as I can tell, the rest are Loyalist troops—King's Rangers and Loyalist Georgia Militia."

"That's right," Deveaux said. "I can make out Captain Traill and Captain Clay. They're both Georgia Militia under Grierson." He coughed. "I don't see Grierson."

"No," Cruger said, "and I don't see Browne, either. There's a lot of Augusta officers I don't see—a whole lot."

The white-coated dragoons and the dust-coated prisoners passed behind and beyond the little stockaded fort that guarded our water supply. They left the road and marched across the fields, drums thumping and fifes shrilling. We could hear Lee's dragoons laughing and shouting as they made their triumphal circuit of Ninety Six, armored from attack by that line of captured Loyalists.

Cruger, as silent as though fascinated by the spectacle, kept abreast, within the stockade, of the slowly moving column; and we went with him, equally silent. When the white-coated horsemen approached the rebel trenches, the fields were filled with jubilant rebels running from the far-off tents, climbing out of the batteries, clambering down from the tower to form a jeering, cheering lane through which Lee's men and their prisoners marched toward Greene's camp.

"Well, gentlemen," Cruger said, "I can't say I'm sorry the rebels saw fit to let us see how free they are with insults. If anybody ever had any doubt about the need of defending this garrison to the last, I hope this exhibition has changed his mind."

Those next days were like the hot distortions of a fever—endless, full of unending discomfort, shot through with flashings that stabbed the eyeballs, roarings that pressed upon the eardrums until they almost burst, flitting blackened faces grotesquely like those of friends, insupportable heat that scorched the lips and throat, an overwhelming, searing thirst.

With the arrival in the rebel camp of Lee's cavalry the reinforced rebels set out to deprive us of our already scanty water.

We saw troops moving to the high land between the spring from which our water supply came and the stockaded fort that guarded it. On the morning of the ninth a yellow scar, the parapet of a new-dug trench, stretched along that high ground. Thus trenches flanked the town on opposite sides.

When, early on the ninth, we looked across at that trench from the windows of the old brick jail, there seemed to be no life in it; but at the bottom of the ravine through which ran the overflow from the spring where we got our water, four dead men sprawled in singularly froglike attitudes. All along the inside of the stockade, timorously peering down into the ravine, were men, women and children with empty buckets.

From both the trench and the stockaded fort that faced each other on the far side of the ravine came a slow, irregular popping, as harmless-seeming as the white wisps of smoke that drifted down into the ravine and clung around the four sprawled bodies as though ghostly emanations were rising from them to drink at the rivulet.

Cruger knelt at the window, between two riflemen whose rifles were leveled at the trench. "When were those men killed?" he asked.

" 'Round about false dawn," the rifleman said. "There must 'a' been thirty of our people down there when the rebels let go at 'em from the rebel trench. It's God's wonder all thirty of 'em weren't hit."

Cruger went down to stand among the people who stared over the stockade at the spring and the four dead bodies. "How much of a water reserve do you have?" he asked.

Some owned to a pailful. Others said they had none. I didn't like the sound of their voices.

"Now look," Cruger said. "Some of you'll be tempted to go down into that ravine today, when you're thirstier. You're not to do it. If you go down, you'll be shot, and there's no real need of it. When night comes, I'll get water for you, but you'll have to divide it evenly. I'm going to give Captain Wiswell complete authority over your water. He'll have the final say in disputes, and he'll enforce obedience even if has to call out the troops."

He looked distressed. "I don't like to take these steps, and wouldn't if I didn't have to. But this garrison has *got* to hold out till Lord Rawdon gets here. It's *got* to! We've got to find a way to do it.

"The first thing to be done is for each of you to pick up pebbles and put 'em in your mouth. Hold 'em there all day. You won't get thirsty so quick. Go back to their trenches with 'em, Captain Wiswell, and see my orders about water are carried out. Bring 'em back here when it's dark with their buckets. Line 'em up in front of the water gate, and don't let 'em make a sound."

The distress that goes with hunger is nothing by comparison with the agony of thirst. It's possible to forget hunger for minutes and hours on end, but thirst is a perpetual and almost insupportable craving.

Yet in spite of this most violent of all desires that gnawed at their vitals, and in spite of their own violence—for never had I encountered people as violent as these South Carolinians in their likes and dislikes—they made no effort to resist an equal division of their water.

I divided the trenches into two sections and set Lonnie and Smallwood Kirkland over them as lieutenants. Until I did this, I was regarded doubtfully by the menfolk; but after I'd done it, they became both affable and insatiably curious. Where had I been born, they wanted to know; what did my father do; did I have book learning;

how had I acquired it; what was Yale College like; how many King's men were there in Boston; how had I happened to become a King's man myself; what brought me to South Carolina; was the town of Boston as big as Charleston; were Bostonians as bastardly as Charleston folk?

Those back-countrymen hated, with a bitterness almost beyond expression, the rich planters who lived in Charleston and worked their Negroes like cattle in the rice fields and indigo plantations.

When I rebelled against their unlimited inquisitiveness and questioned them myself, I got a picture of a civil war more bitter, more useless, more stupid than any war of which I'd ever read.

If I had never encountered those unhappy people, I couldn't have heard the stories of the butcheries inflicted on helpless civilians, rebels and Loyalists alike, by freebooting bands of raiders. These raiders, the unhappy Carolinians told me, had two purposes in life: the extermination of their enemies and loot—loot from anybody, friend or enemy. Without the notes I took from the information I gathered from the South Carolinians on this and other points, I doubt that the third volume of *Civil War in America* would have aroused the interest it did.

If I had left South Carolina without spending long days and longer nights with those long-suffering people, I'd never have known what the rebels refused to admit and the British never grasped: that the British, by persistently regarding all non-Episcopalians in South Carolina as rebels, and treating them as dangerous suspects, alienated thousands who at heart were loyal; that there were more Loyalists in South Carolina than in any other colony, and that the British lost their support through sheer stupidity.

I mightn't have known that if Yorktown hadn't been chosen by Cornwallis—contrary to Arnold's judgment—as the spot in which to defend himself, Cornwallis could have held out forever. I wouldn't have known that if Clinton, through inertia, hadn't delayed in sending Cornwallis the reinforcements for which he'd asked, Cornwallis could never have been defeated. I wouldn't have known that if Cornwallis had only marched back through the Carolinas to Charleston, he would have been safe from any attacking force, and the entire south would have stayed loyal. I wouldn't have known that the war in the south was a nine-year man hunt, crafty, unscrupulous and merciless, between the ragged forces of Marion and Sumter, Pickens and Lee, Tarleton, Cunningham and Fanning. Nor could I have sensed the miseries and futilities of a war that left a greater percentage of widows between the Broad and Saluda rivers than had ever been recorded in a similar space in any war between supposedly civilized peoples.

Certainly I would never have understood why the Loyalists uncomplainingly held out in Ninety Six, eating carrion and enduring such thirst that their lips cracked open and their tongues were like dry sponges, rather than surrender to rebels.

CHAPTER LXXXIII

THE WATER GATE in the north stockade, when I led my long line of South Carolinians up to it in the gray June darkness, seemed deserted except for two sentries.

As I came close, a shadow rose from between the sentries. "I'm Captain French," he whispered. "The colonel's down at the Star. I'm in charge here. Station these people of yours so the head of the line'll always be at the water gate, holding out an empty bucket to be filled. I'll keep a line of full buckets moving up to the gate. We can't afford to have 'em delayed."

He whistled. Another dark figure got up, almost from under my feet. He seemed a part of the night, for his face and body were mere blotches, without beginning or end. He smelled like a damp fireplace. He was naked above the waist, and his face and upper body were darkened with soot.

"Anchor your people to this man," French said, "and make 'em keep quiet. Don't let 'em talk or knock those buckets around, even if they have to wait here all night."

"Pass the word along," I told the South Carolinian next to me. "Not a sound out of any of you, if you want water."

I heard the whispered word passing back along the line. My eyes, more accustomed to my surroundings, made out figures on the ground near the gate and at the foot of the stockade on either side. At first I thought there were a dozen thick shadows; then I saw more and more, more and more, sprawled full length, waiting.

"Any other orders?" I asked French.

"No," he said. "Just lie down here, where I can find you if I want you." He moved away.

One of the dark figures, breathing heavily, flopped itself over beside me. It was Buell. I felt the movement of his lips against my ear. "I hadn't meant to go out with these fellers, Oliver; but when the colonel said he'd let 'em drink at the spring before they raided the rebels, I told him he could pay me for the gun platform and the spears by letting me go too."

He moved convulsively. "There ain't *anything* I wouldn't do for water, Oliver! If we reach the spring, I'd stay there the rest of the night if it wasn't for missing the rebels."

I could hear his tongue, gummy like mine, trying to moisten his dry lips.

"Whose plan is this?" I asked.

"It ain't a bad one, is it?" Buell asked smugly. "It's simple, and there ain't any reason it won't work, if we don't suck water like cows when we get to the spring. That's all I'm afraid of."

"Is it yours?" I asked.

"Mine and Cruger's," Buell whispered. "Ain't it a godsend to have Cruger in command? Instead of getting insulted when you give him an idea, the way an Englishman would, he takes your idea and puts frills on it. When I told him we could rub soot on ourselves and not be seen at night, he said, 'That's a good idea, Buell! Round up all the light-colored Negroes in town and set 'em to digging the well. I'll use the black ones at night, without any clothes on, and you won't be able to tell 'em from old stumps.' "

From the far side of the ravine, high up, came stabs of flame and the sharp crackling of rifle fire. At the same moment, from the Star Redoubt on the other side of the town, we heard the roaring of our own three-pounders.

"That's the signal," Buell said. He reached for my hand and shook it. "We're going out first, and then the Negroes. The way I figure, the water buckets ought to get back here eight minutes after the first Negro goes out."

He got to his feet and walked to the gate.

I crawled a little way after him. Against the velvety starlit sky, I saw dark figures moving through the gateway. When they were no longer outlined against the stars, they were wholly gone.

I was conscious of Negroes rising to their feet all around me, dozens of Negroes, scores on scores of them, naked. French herded them from the water gate in a double line. Each man carried a bucket.

The two Negroes who brought up the rear of that long double line were left standing in the gateway, the last links in a double line of black men extending all the way from the stockade to the spring.

"Go ahead," French said. "Start the buckets!"

I could see them, but not the black hands that held them. The buckets seemed to float of their own accord toward the ravine.

Far away I heard a faint splashing. French darted forward. "Good!" he whispered. "That's good!" His cupped hand, dripping with water, slapped against my lips.

To let those buckets go past, to let their precious contents be emptied into other containers and go from us, was a sort of agony.

For what seemed an eternity, I urged Carolinians away with their filled pails, urged them to see that their women and children had water before they drank themselves, reminded them not to stumble, not to spill a drop; reminded them that if they fell, they must contrive to fall so that their clothes would soak up the water.

Now and again I dipped my fingers in that beautiful, cool water and licked them; but it must have been midnight before I had my first real swallow—a swallow that seemed to hiss as it passed down my hot and sticky throat.

For hours those water buckets came slowly up the hill to us, splashed their contents into the insatiable receptacles held out by half-seen hands; then passed down again, empty, into the darkness.

I could have sworn that I had stood at the gate for an aeon—though the gray of dawn had just come into the sky—when I heard scufflings and muffled shouts on the far side of the ravine.

Captain French ran from the gate. "That's enough," he called. "Everybody in, quick! Pass the word! Tell 'em to come in!"

The Negro water-passers were exhausted. As soon as they were safely inside the gate, they dropped to the ground and slept, groaning.

Behind them was the raiding party, soot-covered, sweaty, but swaggering and gay with smothered laughter. With them walked a dozen prisoners, all of them lank-haired, pock-marked, sullen. They were being prodded along at the point of hunting knives.

Buell reached out, caught my arm and drew me along with him. He had a prisoner of his own. "Well," Buell said expansively, "I got me so much water I'll never run out of sweat again."

He coughed dryly, a signal that he was talking for effect. "We had a real pleasant time, Oliver. I could 'a' killed a score of these fellers if I'd wanted to, but pshaw! What would 'a' been the use! I want him to talk to us: that's all I want."

"Has he talked yet?" I asked.

"No," Buell said. "I ain't asked him anything. I hope he does, though, because if he don't, I'll have to keep that promise I made you."

"You will?"

"Oh, there ain't any doubt about it," Buell said. "When Old Reliable Tom Buell promises to do a thing, it's as good as done! You remember what the promise was, don't you?—that if I took a prisoner who wouldn't talk, I'd kill and scalp every other rebel I came across on one of these raids. Well, Oliver, you never knew me to go back on a promise yet, so if this feller won't talk——"

He made a horrible yawping noise, which I knew to be his conception of the sound that comes from a severed windpipe.

Before sun-up every officer in the garrison was summoned to a council of war to hear the news. It was a strange council. Half the men packed into the trench outside Cruger's dugout were naked above their waists, and covered with soot. Except for their hair, which looked unreal above their blackened foreheads, they might have been Negroes.

Cruger's officers had changed beyond belief. A few days ago they had been tanned, lean-looking, wire-strong from years of hard marching and hard fighting.

Now there was a greenish-yellow tinge to the faces of those who hadn't blacked themselves; their skin was like old parchment. Their noses had become beaklike. Their lips had shrunk and their teeth protruded like false ones badly made. Buell looked the same. I suppose I did too, for my face felt drawn, as though tightened at the ears with drum braces.

"Now then," Cruger said, "I've called this council because I've got information from the prisoners, and I want everybody in the garrison to know exactly what to expect.

"As you know, enough water was brought in last night to give each one of us a pint. We've struck no water in the well yet, but we hope to find it soon. Keep telling your men: we hope to find it soon. We've gone down sixty feet through stiff clay. Nobody on earth could have dug faster or harder than those black men have. There must be water somewhere, so tell everybody we're close to it."

He rubbed his eyes, which looked red and tired. "We found out from the prisoners what happened at Augusta. I want that news passed around. Most of you remember Colonel Grierson, who commanded the Loyalist Militia there. Well, after the Augusta garrison had been guaranteed all the honors of war by the rebels, and had surrendered, Colonel Grierson was shot down in cold blood. Colonel Browne, who commanded the garrison, would have been murdered by Georgia rebel militia if the rebel commanding officer hadn't hurried him to Savannah under a strong escort. There's no question in my mind that the rebels besieging this town would unhesitatingly massacre all Loyalist officers and troops if given half a chance."

The colonel peered at the pallid South Carolina sky from which heat seemed to pour down upon us as from a polished sheet of hot metal. "There's no use trying to dodge facts, gentlemen," he continued, "and these, as I see them, are the facts:

"Our prisoners will tell us nothing about Lord Rawdon; and to be honest with you, I think they're as ignorant of his whereabouts as we are. There's no way of knowing where he is, or how long it may be before he gets here. Meanwhile, our orders are to hold this garrison.

"Now it's quite possible there are no Loyal troops, no King's troops, between here and the coast. On us, gentlemen, in other words, rests the defense of the thousands of Loyalists along the Saluda River, along the Broad River, everywhere in the western part of this province. Nothing stands between those people and complete disaster but the First Battalion of DeLancey's Loyal Refugees, the Second Battalion of New Jersey Volunteers and Colonel Deveaux's Loyal South Carolina Militiamen. If we fail in our duty—if we lay down our arms before brute force and superior numbers—the militiamen who murdered Colonel Grierson will turn upon the inhabitants of these valleys, who have supplied us with food, forage and information. They'll be murdered, driven into swamps, tortured, beaten, robbed. That's my greatest concern, gentlemen: that some of us may forget what must happen if we give in."

In the restricted space before his dugout—no larger than the cockpit of Sally Leighton's little sloop—Cruger took two hasty turns. "I'm not going to ask for your opinions," he said. "We've been together five years. In that time the rebels have never made a successful stand before Loyalist troops. Perhaps it's because we have more at stake than they, and perhaps it's because of the lesson we learned together years ago, when we repeatedly defeated all the regiments that Washington sent to Staten Island to wipe us out. Whatever the reason, they've never once beaten us.

"Now there may be times, while we're waiting here, when it seems to you that we're caught in a box. Well, gentlemen, we aren't—not unless you let yourself forget everything you know: that men determined to kill can't be stopped except by overwhelming numbers, and often can't be stopped even then; that opponents can't stand the charge of such men, and will always run—always; that well-conducted surprises are invariably successful in war, because the first instinctive thought of a surprised man is escape, not resistance.

"Just remember those things until Lord Rawdon gets here, gentlemen, and the rebels will never, never, never take Ninety Six!"

CHAPTER LXXXIV

I DOUBT, when we fought the rebels at Ninety Six, that I ever thought of the place as a sort of hell.

The reason I didn't, probably, was because the most miserable conditions of life, to the person enduring them, come so gradually upon him that the worst moments seem little worse than those that went before.

As I look back to the place, and to our endless thirsty striving, I know we dwelt in a worse hell than Dante ever visited. I have heard clergymen threaten their congregations with hell fire; but the hells they picture are pale and unimpressive beside those of Ninety Six.

It was on June tenth that Cruger told us what he'd learned from the captured rebels. For two days, in retaliation for our raids, rebel cannon thundered from opposite sides of the town, plowed the baked parade as with scores of giant rakes, smashed ragged holes in the roofless walls of the jail, the barracks, the church.

Those days were hot as fire—so hot that the few garments we wore for decency's sake seemed clamped against our bodies by invisible hot hands. The air was full of red dust thrown up by exploding shells, and heavy with the fumes of gunpowder.

On the twelfth a storm rolled up in the west, and we thought we'd get relief from that awful heat; for it looked to be one of those sudden, ripping, tearing, bellowing Carolina thunderstorms that burst out of the west to empty cooling reservoirs of water on the land.

But instead of much-needed rain, we got something very different.

The rebel leaders, I think, must have thought Cruger would never look for an attack during a storm. If that was what they thought, they

711

were wrong; for when that black wall came surging up from the western mountains, with a ragged fringe of yellow clouds racing in advance, Cruger sent warning messages to every part of town.

"Take all your men to the stockades," Captain DeLancey shouted to me. "Colonel Cruger says to watch like hawks until this storm is over. He wants everyone out in the rain, too, so to get good and wet. Have the women put out all buckets and cloths, so to catch water. Have 'em make holes where water'll run into 'em."

Our station looked down upon the spring in the ravine and across to the rebel works on the high land beyond. In spite of the nightly raids upon those works, they had grown and grown. The single long trench which we had first seen had now become a zigzag—a sort of enormous reversed Z.

From the left end of the original trench, another trench had been extended at a sharp angle in the direction of the rivulet at the bottom of the ravine; then had turned sharply again, parallel with the first one. The angle at the turning point was a mere twenty-five yards from the rivulet: a mere fifty yards from the stockade through whose gun ports I peered across the ravine at that enormous Z-shaped scar.

Not a head showed above the red-earth ramparts of the trenches. There certainly were men in them; but for all the signs of life they gave, they might have been cowering before the inky black wall of clouds that rose higher and higher above us—a wall from which came the unending roar of approaching thunder, and the continual flickering of green lightning.

A greenish twilight descended on us as the storm came close. Lightning leaped at us with a whirl of red dust and a yowling of wind as though innumerable wildcats fought in the upper air. On the wings of that wind there were scattered drops of rain the size of musket balls. We could see them land and burst like miniature bombshells, and while we waited for the drops to become a drenching downpour, the crashing of the thunder was like hammers in our ears.

The rain never came. Black clouds boiled overhead; the thunder almost stunned us; the glare of the lightning seared our eyeballs; but after those first few drops, the wind was a hot and dry blast, in which our baked flesh shriveled and crawled.

Then the storm passed over. The greenish blackness slowly turned to gray. The thunder became sonorous. In the west there was a golden glow, and in that strange half-light I could see every pebble in the ravine, and even the movements, at its bottom, of the trickle of water that meant life to us.

As I studied the rough meadow between the stockaded fort and the rebel parapets, my eye was caught by something strange about the slope of the ground. The ground, I thought, moved. When I looked hard at the spot, I thought I must have been mistaken. Then I wondered whether I had indeed been mistaken, for there was a dark bulge to the earth, and the bulge bothered me, just as a squirrel's nest in the crotch of a tree repeatedly draws a hunter's eye.

I called Lonnie and Smallwood Kirkland to me and showed them the dark spot. "I want that hit," I said. "It may be nothing, but I don't like it."

Without comment they dropped pinches of powder into their rifle pans, and ran the long barrels out through ports.

Lonnie counted "One, two, three" in a far-away voice. The two rifles cracked together, almost feebly. On the ridge across the ravine the dark spot moved.

"That's a man," Smallwood said, pressing his ramrod into his rifle barrel.

There was a far-off shouting. At the base of the abatis I saw figures get to their knees. They had buckets, and from among them smoke rose in a sudden white puff.

"Those are rebels," I told the Kirklands. "They're trying to fire the abatis! Get your men shooting and hurry up about it!"

On both sides of me men crouched over, picking at the pans of their guns, pounding them with their fists to make sure the powder was loose, dumping powder from flasks.

I've heard a deal of talk about why the rebel colonel, Lee, should have sent out that squad of men at midday and in a storm to set fire to the abatis outside the little stockaded fort. I've heard it said that he did it in a paroxysm of temerity and folly; that there was no explaining the rashness of his act; that he was no better than a murderer to send those men out at such a time.

It seemed to me, however, that his intention was clear. I think he thought that if he could set fire to the abatis of that little fort, Colonel Cruger would be obliged to open a gate and make a sally in order to put out the fire; and I think he planned, if that had happened, to attack us with his light troops, compelling Cruger to send us reinforcements from every part of the stockade and giving General

Greene the opportunity to launch a successful attack against the Star Redoubt, on the opposite side of town.

Bullets whacked the upright logs before us, passed above us with the sound of cracking whips. Everybody, everywhere, was shooting, and the roaring of the departing storm seemed speckled and dotted with incessant rifle fire.

Against the distant abatis one of the rebels straightened, threw his bucket high in the air, and fell full length.

Another crawled from the abatis and set off toward the rebel trenches. His legs gave way and he sprawled flat. He got to his hands and knees again; then flattened out and lay still.

Still another, from whose bucket white smoke was gushing, worked a little longer at the abatis, then slumped to one side. His bucket overturned on him, and the white smoke became thick and gray, like the smoke of a mosquito smudge.

There was no more movement among the figures at the abatis. Every last one lay motionless. They were dead.

CHAPTER LXXXV

O<small>N THE AFTERNOON</small> of the fourteenth hope unexpectedly arrived to bolster our determination.

That afternoon we were all of us, perhaps, even more dazed with heat and thirst than we'd been at any time since the siege began. Wherever there was shade outside the trenches—at the foot of the western stockade, in the rear of the roofless houses along the town's main street, on the eastern side of all the blockhouses—men and women sprawled as if they were dead. The slow banging of Lee's cannon from the trenches above the spring, the measured roaring of General Greene's artillery from outside the Star Redoubt, no longer provoked either fear or interest in them. They'd heard that monotonous booming so long that it wasn't noticeable to them unless it stopped, or unless it became more intense.

Yet when someone shouted near the south gate, all those sprawling figures rolled over and sat up. Some of them rose and started for the gate, their bare feet raising clouds of red dust.

A wild hope stirred within me, and I ran for the south gate too.

When I got there, the whole garrison was converging on that one spot. Half a dozen New Jersey Volunteers were working at the bars across the inside of the gate. Riflemen in the blockhouses and along the inside of the stockade were firing at the far-off rebel lines, from which jetted the little white clouds of cannon fire.

Pelting up the road that led to the south was a man on horseback, riding hard. Far, far behind him rebels were running and letting off guns.

As the rider came closer to the gate, I saw he had a paper in one hand. His mare was caked with dust and foam, and must have been

715

well-nigh spent; for she wheezed horribly as she clattered through the gate, then stumbled, stopped, spread her legs and hung her head.

The rider groaned, took off his hat and swabbed his dirt-streaked face with his arm. When he stood in his stirrups, easing his legs where his breeches cut him, I saw he was black with sweat from ankle to crotch.

"Where's Colonel Cruger?" he asked hoarsely. He leaned over and spat, and his spittle was cottony white. "Rawdon's coming," he said. "He left Orangeburg this morning." He raised his right hand with the paper in it. "This here's a letter to Colonel Cruger from Rawdon."

Those half-naked men from DeLancey's and the New Jersey Volunteers, those haggard South Carolina militiamen, all those drawn-faced, crack-lipped South Carolina farmers and their wives, just stood staring numbly up at him as if they hadn't comprehended.

My mind was clogged with questions I wanted to ask; it moved slowly, like a sick man's.

"Who is it?" people were asking, as they ran up. "What's he want? Where's he from?"

When they heard that he was from Rawdon, that Rawdon was coming, that Rawdon had already passed Orangeburg, they, too, were silent, and like the rest of us just stood and stared.

The messenger looked disgusted, and kicked his tired horse in the ribs. Before he could move on, I caught his bridle. "These people haven't had much to eat or drink," I told him. "The reason they don't say much, I guess, is because they don't want to make a show of themselves."

There was a commotion near us. A woman among the silent onlookers, her head thrown back and her eyes tight closed, made a peculiar croaking sound, and I took it that she was crying. The messenger looked mollified.

"Did you ride all the way from Orangeburg today?" I asked.

"Yes," he said. "Not with this horse, though: I took this one off a rebel. I guess I better take Rawdon's message to the colonel."

"Yes," I said. "How far is Orangeburg?"

He gathered up his reins. "A hundred and twelve miles."

"Just one more question," I said. "How big is Rawdon's force?"

"Big enough," the messenger said. "He's got a lot of cavalry, and you needn't worry about him getting here. The only trouble is, his infantry's wearing heavy clothes, thick enough for the Upper Country in the winter." He stared at me defiantly and his saddle squeaked as he eased himself in it. "Where'll I find the colonel?"

I showed him where to go, and tried to remember only that Rawdon was coming; tried to forget the hundred and twelve miles between Orangeburg and Ninety Six; tried to forget the size and slowness of Rawdon's supply train; the heavily garbed infantry regiments that must cover that hundred and twelve miles in heat that made even Negroes sick.

All around me men spoke in thick voices.

"If he betters thirty miles a day he'll have to throw away his carts."

"Hell, he *can't* throw away his carts—not and do *us* any good!"

"What good would it do him to throw away his carts if he still has to drag his guns?"

"He can't throw away his guns: the rebels'd get 'em!"

"I say he can't beat fifteen miles a day."

"I say he can do nineteen; but if he tries to do twenty he'll bust a gut!"

They spoke in flat voices, as if discussing the building of a shed.

Twenty miles a day! Six more days! Six more waterless days!

I turned and looked at Buell. There were black ridges on his lips, and his eyes seemed to have been pushed deep into his head with a charred stick.

At my glance he licked his blackened lips. "Don't worry about me, Oliver! Six days ain't nothing! I'd wait six years to see those rebels get their come-uppance! I'll be here waiting when Rawdon comes, even if I'm dried up to a harness strap!"

Thanks to the mysterious beneficence of an all-wise Providence, the worst interludes in our lives—our most dreadful mistakes, our severest agonies—are oftenest soonest forgotten; but I'd be glad to forget forever the things that happened in Ninety Six on the fifteenth, sixteenth, seventeenth and eighteenth of June.

We lived, during those four days, at the center of a storm of cannon fire, dust, heat, sweat, wounded men, constant labor, eternal vigilance.

Cruger seemed to have mastered the art of being in a dozen places at the same moment. His endless peregrinations around the stockade put me in mind of a weary rabbit hound, impelled by instinct to struggle on and on through an alder swamp. Day and night were alike to him. If he slept, nobody ever caught him at it. He drifted from point to point, during the night, as silent as a questing owl; and if, from any part of the rebel trenches, the musketry fire slack-

ened or increased, Cruger instantly appeared as though he'd popped
from the ground.

From lack of sleep he looked like a walking mummy, but his voice
was patient and kindly, as on the day when I had first seen him. He
looked less like a soldier than ever, but he was the best soldier I ever
knew—far and away better than Clinton or Howe or Gage, and only
approached, as a leader, by Arnold, Simcoe and the rebel general
Greene, against whom we fought at Ninety Six.

When he peered over the stockade, he made me think of a sea
captain soaking up the feel of the weather by smelling it, feeling it,
tasting it. He'd cock his head, listening; snuff up the night scents;
breathe deep of that hot, still air; and when he gave up his peering,
sniffing and head-cocking, and sat himself down on the fire step to
talk to us, we knew we weren't in any immediate danger of a rebel
attack at that particular point.

He repeated the same things, like a father hammering truths into a
child's brain. "Keep your eyes open every second," he told us.
"They've got no option. If they want to take this town, they've got to
attack, and that means they'll have to attack before Rawdon gets
here. That's how we'll know Rawdon's close. A general attack'll be
the best news we could have, remember. That being so, their attack's bound to fail!"

When he left us, he walked lopsided, and held a hand against his
stomach. I think he had hunger cramps. I know I did.

They attacked at noon the next day, June the eighteenth, the
twenty-eighth day of the siege. There wasn't a soul in the garrison
that didn't know what was coming; for every piece of artillery in the
rebel trenches started firing on us at dawn, and kept it up all through
the morning. We were the center of deafening booming, smashing,
crashing; shrill squealings of solid shot, yowlings of shells, the nerve-
racking clattering whistling of grape.

It seemed to me, now that the end of our interminable labors, of
our endless suspense, was drawing near, that grimness suddenly gave
way to gaiety; that care and anxiety had wholly vanished from the
minds of Cruger's men.

Thirst, heat, hunger had become minor incidents in their lives.
They were living to hear Rawdon's drums: to see Rawdon's troops
come cutting their way through the lines of rebels that encircled and
tortured Ninety Six.

When, at nine o'clock, a messenger slid into the trench to give me a message from the colonel the South Carolinians crowded around to watch me read it.

"*Captain Wiswell* [the message read]: *When firing ceases, enlist services of ten women and bring to Star Redoubt. Each should have shears, tourniquets, cords and if possible bandages. Can promise they will be in no more danger here than where they are, as rebel artillery must cease firing during attack. Can also use ten sharpshooters. John Harris Cruger.*"

When I looked up, the eyes of men and women alike were fierce, hawklike. "There's nothing in this about Lord Rawdon," I said. "It's from Colonel Cruger. He wants more sharpshooters in the Star Redoubt. He'd like ten women, too, in case some of our people get wounded."

Men and women alike darted apprehensive looks at each other.

"You'll be as safe as you are in these trenches," I protested.

They ignored me. Then they began to shout at each other, and to squabble.

Buell and I were a good quarter-hour calming them and picking the best ones for Cruger's purpose; for every last one was determined to be of those who went.

The rebel trenches were so close to the ditch around the Star Redoubt that we could hear the clicking of the accouterments of the men who waited to attack us.

We could hear the occasional husky orders of officers; hear ramrods tamping, flints being chipped, musket balls rattling in shot pouches.

We could hear, but we couldn't see; for the rebels had raised a tower twenty feet higher than the one we'd raised on the first day. Thus anyone who showed his head was more than likely to take no interest in anything that followed.

To offset the raking fire of the sharpshooters on the rebel tower, Cruger had piled sandbags above the stockade of the Star Redoubt. There were slots between the sandbags through which our men could fire, and at each slot were two riflemen: one to fire, and the other to take the first man's place while he reloaded. The rest of us crouched in the shelter of the sandbags, listening to the sounds from the rebel trenches and waiting the attack.

When the rebel cannon ceased their continuous thundering at half

past eleven, the silence weighed upon us like a hot and thick blanket.
There was a pattering of rifle shots still, but in the cavernous silence
that came with the stopping of cannon fire, they seemed as feeble
as children's popguns.

Against the stockade walls, in the shelter of the sandbags, men
swarmed like flies. They had the look of being in a sort of arbor; for
all around the stockade, leaning against the shelf on which the sandbags rested, were spears—hundreds of them—enough, it seemed to
me, to impale the whole rebel army.

Near the neck of the Star, where it opened into the stockaded
town, were two shieldlike fences made of logs, and behind those
shields were squads from DeLancey's Battalion and the New Jersey
Volunteers. They seemed to have no interest in the battle, but just
squatted there, arguing and laying down the law as we used to do at
New Haven, when we sat in the lee of a fence, waiting to have the use
of a football.

Almost above me, in the outermost salient of the Star, Colonel
Cruger and Colonel Deveaux had made themselves a sort of headquarters—a little corner cupboard on stilts jammed into the peak of
the salient.

Huddled under the cupboard were Buell and myself with Captain
DeLancey, Lieutenant John Hatton of the New Jersey Volunteers,
three of Cruger's messengers from DeLancey's regiment, Captain
Campbell of the New Jersey Volunteers, and Captain French of
DeLancey's First Battalion—the two last being the commanders of
the two squads of men behind the log shields.

Cruger's little cupboard had a roof of logs, and up through the logs
was thrust the reflecting machine that Buell had made for the colonel
out of a few pieces of looking-glass and one of the giant thirty-foot
canes that had so amazed us when we came down from the Great
Smokies into South Carolina. Through it the colonel could see the
ditch immediately in front of our stockade, the rebel trenches just
beyond the ditch, and the screened laterals which the rebels had dug
only that morning—the laterals that would let them run under our
abatis and into our ditch at the moment of attack.

From time to time Cruger turned from his reflecting machine to
give an order or tell what he saw. It seemed to me that he and Colonel
Deveaux together had thought of everything.

I was told to post my Carolinian sharpshooters all together in one
salient. "You're to stay with them," Cruger said, "and keep your eye

on Captain DeLancey for signals. Don't let your men expose themselves unless DeLancey gives you the word; but if he does, make your men keep up a steady fire. Don't let 'em get excited, because they've got to hit what they shoot at. What they're to do is stop rebels from pulling down our sandbags. That's their job."

I heard him sending word to sharpshooters in other salients to concentrate their fire on the mouth of the two lateral trenches. "Tell 'em to pile up the rebels there. It may make 'em panicky."

In the rebel trenches a cannon went off with a roar that set the sweat crawling on me.

The crowded Star Redoubt, the swarm of men pressed close against the inside of the stockade, the whole ruined town beyond, with its roofless buildings, its trench-scarred fields, was breathless and motionless, like a crudely colored chromo of devastation.

A second cannon shot blasted hot air against us, and the world became a tumult of shouting and rifle fire. Below us, in the ditch outside the stockade, I heard rushing feet, heavy breathing, strangled cries.

A steel hook, like a giant fishhook, flew into sight above our heads. Its point sank into a sandbag on the upper edge of the parapet, and the sandbag surged slowly.

I leaned down to catch DeLancey's eye, but when he saw me he shook his head.

"They've got hooks," I told him. "They're trying to pull down the parapet!"

Smallwood Kirkland jumped high, caught the hook, freed it from the bag and threw it back into the ditch; then pawed at the side of his head and stared at me with an expression of ludicrous surprise, as well he might, for a rebel bullet had torn his ear into a frayed and bloody fragment.

When I was sharp with him, he looked hurt. "Hell, Captain," he protested, "they cain't have those sandbags! My ma used up all her underclothes makin' 'em. If we lose these, we cain't get no more."

The rifle and musket fire was continuous, and there was a quality to the shouting from the ditch outside that set my muscles to twitching.

I didn't dare take my eyes off DeLancey, but I could feel sandbags tumbling from the parapet above me. I saw DeLancey wave, and then, all around the inside of the stockade, men rose above the parapet to fire into the ditch. The Carolinians were up. I was up. Everyone was up.

For the first time I saw the ditch entire. It was packed with rebels. They were clinging against the face of the stockade by scores, some clawing at the sandbags with hooks, some hacking with axes and mattocks at the logs of the stockade.

The musketry fire was so rapid that I seemed to float on a sea of explosions. White smoke rolled toward us from the rebel trenches, and so near were those trenches that I saw the powder-horn stoppers between the rebels' teeth as they reloaded; saw the rivulets washed by sweat on their contorted faces; saw rebels falling from the face of the stockade like scorched caterpillars.

The stir and movement, the chaos of shooting and shouting, of frantic straining and hot discomfort, seemed to me like the anguish of a fever, in which vast occurrences are over in a flash and small events hang in suspense for endless ages.

I tried to make the Carolinians keep their heads below the level of the stockade while they reloaded; but they were like hunters, unwilling to take their eyes from their quarry. I felt only exasperation when Smallwood Kirkland seemed to stumble, so that his chin was caught between two of the posts. When he let his rifle fall, I knew he was hurt. I got him under the arms and lifted him free of the logs. His brother gave me a quick glance.

"It hit him in the haid," he said. "I heard it." He ran his rifle between the sandbags and fired, said, "There, by God", and immediately fumbled with his powder horn. "Keep his rifle and powder horn for me, Captain," he added. "They might come in awful handy."

When I examined Smallwood, I saw that Lonnie was right. A rifle bullet had drilled a neat hole an inch in front of his torn ear, and he'd no longer have to puzzle his head over thirst, heat, marauding rebels, or the fate of Ninety Six.

I took off his powder horn and bullet pouch, hung them over my own shoulder, rolled him to the edge of the platform, and let him fall to the ground. I could hear, above the shouting and firing, the deadman's grunt he made when he landed. When I looked down at him, I saw he had company. A semicircle of bodies lay at queer angles at the foot of the stockade, as if washed there by a flood. I saw, too, that Captain French, Captain Campbell and their detachments were crowded against the sally ports. They were going out into the ditch— out to put an end to the rebel attack if they could.

I picked up Smallwood Kirkland's rifle. The ramrod was halfway down the barrel, and as I finished loading, the vague thought passed through my mind that all of us, probably, would die like that: unexpectedly, in the middle of something we wanted to do, instead of at the end of our endeavors, as we always fondly believe.

"Fire faster," I told the men. "Watch the traverses. Cruger's sending Campbell and French into the ditch. If anybody moves in the traverses, let him have it."

In spite of all the rebels who had been shot from the face of our stockade, there seemed to me to be more than ever of them clawing with hooks at the sandbags, hacking at the posts with axes, sawing at logs with narrow saws.

I cast a quick look over my shoulder. The two sally ports were open, and out through them were running the two detachments of DeLancey's and the New Jersey Volunteers that had been sheltered behind the screens of logs.

Almost on the instant the ditch beneath us was filled with struggling men. French and Campbell came in sight, stabbing and pitchforking with their bayonets at men who stumbled, tried to run and screamed sickeningly.

I saw French slapping his men on the back and pushing them forward. He looked up over his shoulder at the rebels clinging against the face of the stockade and hauling with hooks at the sandbags. He ran to one of them, caught his ankle and pulled. The man came down in a heap, and two of French's men leaped at him and stabbed him with their bayonets. Then they waited like crouched cats for French to pull down two more men from the stockade.

Rebels, escaping by crawling into the traverses, seemed to strike invisible walls against which they crumpled and lay in heaps.

There was something unbearably exciting in the advance of French and Campbell, something shockingly gratifying about the way in which the dodging, scrambling rebels between them grew fewer and fewer, fell beneath the feet of the onrushing Loyalists, raised their hands in surrender and were spewed out into quiet backwaters to stand motionless and dazed.

The men around me howled and cursed, and I screamed too—screamed at French to look out—a rebel had a knife. It seemed to me I couldn't stand where I was and do nothing when the knife drove upward and disappeared in French's back. French reeled to one side.

A dozen bullets must have hit that rebel, for he crumpled as he fell, as if broken at every joint.

Then, miraculously, there was an end of screaming, scuttling and scurrying in the ditch. There were rebels there still, but they were dead, or standing disarmed and helpless.

Captain Campbell ran to French, whose hand, covered with glittering blood, was pressed to the small of his back.

Taking him beneath the arms, Campbell turned him toward the sally ports and signaled to the men to go back the way they'd come.

We stood roaring at those men from DeLancey's and the New Jersey Volunteers as they went quietly back around the bend in the ditch and out of sight. My gratitude to them was so profound that I wanted to cry.

We stood there waiting for the rebels to come out of their traverses and attack again, but they didn't come back, not even to pick up their dead. They'd had enough. Five hundred of us had beaten Greene and four thousand men. After all, we didn't have to use those spears; nobody'd got over.

CHAPTER LXXXVI

Late on the afternoon of the day we stopped the rebels, they retreated from their advanced lines. We watched them falling back across the fields, straggling out of the trenches to their camps at the edge of the woods.

That night the entire population of Ninety Six went down into the ravine unhindered; and there, by the light of torches, they drank their fill, poured water on themselves, lay on the wet ground soaking up moisture. Officers and men, farmers and their wives and children, Negroes and rebel prisoners were drunk with water. All night long they gabbled and shouted, screamed and squealed, like children in a delirium of excitement.

The next day, June nineteenth, the rebels struck their tents. All day long their infantry, artillery and cavalry regiments, their baggage wagons and supply trains, converged on the Island Ford road—the same one on which Buell and I had come up from the Saluda to Ninety Six.

All afternoon those rebel troops moved slowly off through a haze of red dust; and when the morning of the twentieth came, the fields were empty of men and tents, horses, artillery and wagons. Nothing remained of the rebel army save the tall tower just outside the stockade, and the gashed trenches in the sun-baked earth.

Patrols, sent by Cruger to Island Ford, came back to report that the rebel army had crossed the Saluda without even leaving a rear guard on the far bank. When this word reached the South Carolinians, they'd have gone back to their farms if Cruger hadn't stopped them.

"You're safe here," he told them, "so here you'll stay till Rawdon comes and tells us what's to become of this garrison."

725

By the grace of God, the patrolling parties found a few cows and pigs that the rebels had overlooked; so although we spent the night of the twentieth in that stinking, roofless town, we had fresh meat to eat, all the water we needed, and were happy.

Early on the twenty-first, a month from our arrival at Ninety Six, we heard guns to the south; and at midmorning there was a flickering of scarlet against the dark forest that screened us from the Low Country. It was Rawdon's column; and as the long line flowed out across the fields, it seemed to flow into my own veins and set my blood afire.

To the troops Cruger had massed on the parade ground, the deliberation with which that column moved, and the slowness of its arrival, was beyond belief.

Cruger had drawn up his three battalions in a long line, and behind it were the civilians and Negroes; and I'm bound to say that there was something mighty impressive about the silent rigidity of those ranks in faded green—about the long line of wounded men propped up against the ruined wall of one of the barracks to see Rawdon come in—about the scores of white bandages with which the long lines were speckled—about the silence and stillness of that throng of men, women and Negroes packed solidly behind the troops.

We heard Rawdon's drums long before we saw them; heard the reedy shrilling of the fifes; and when the bright flags came through the gateway, I heard officers all along the ranks mutter "Steady! Steady there! Eyes front!" but I think they did it to steady themselves as much as their men.

Captain DeLancey dropped back beside me. "That's Rawdon on the black horse," he said, and there was pride in his voice. "He's the only man in the army who's as good as Cruger!"

Rawdon was tall and thin, and there was an eager, friendly smile on his face as he came through the gate, a troop of cavalry close behind him. He cast a quick glance around the whole parade—at the silent green ranks of Cruger's men; at the roofless buildings beyond; at the crisscrossed trenches, the observation towers, the mountain of clay around the well; at the sandbagged observation posts above the stockade.

He half turned in his saddle to call out something to the column behind him. I think perhaps he may have told his officers not to be too strict.

Then he did a handsome thing. He brought the hilt of his saber to his chin, saluted Cruger with a sweep of the glittering blade; then dropped the saber so that it dangled by the cord from his wrist, clasped his hands together and shook them in a gesture that seemed to be not only for Cruger, but for all of us.

DeLancey laughed queerly. "They don't come any better than Rawdon," he said. "He's never lost a battle in this country, and he never will. I wish to God he and Cruger were fighting this war for us!"

The cavalrymen, as they came through the gate, whooped exultantly. Close on their heels were two regiments wearing green cotton. They marched abreast, four pieces of artillery between them. I thought they were poorly disciplined, for they crowded through the gate to get a look at us, and their shouting, to say the least, was uncontrolled.

"Why," I said, "I believe I know those officers! They're DePeyster and Coffin! They're New York Volunteers, aren't they, those troops in green?"

"They certainly are," DeLancey said. "They haven't missed a fight in the south, barring this siege, and they'll feel bad about missing this. They're the ones that broke Gates' center at Camden and started him on his eighty-mile run."

It seemed mighty strange to think I'd first seen these men in Halifax five years before, shoeless, ammunitionless, in rags; that I'd fruitlessly attempted to persuade Howe to help them, and that they should be here in South Carolina, coming eagerly to our relief.

"I guess they're glad to see us," DeLancey said, with a boyish embarrassment. "We've been in a lot of engagements together. Probably that's why they're making so much noise. I guess they're glad the rebels couldn't hurt us."

Treading close on their heels was a British regiment. Their scarlet coats, through that hot red dust, looked like flames. On their backs were packs that must have weighed a hundred pounds; yet they marched with beautiful precision. They were shouting, too, and grinning at us with a sort of wildness. I saw then that all these men —Lord Rawdon, Loyalists, British, officers, rank and file—were telling us, as well as they could, that we'd done well.

I looked uneasily at DeLancey, and saw his throat move convulsively, as if he'd tried to swallow, but couldn't. I knew how he felt. If I'd tried to speak, if I'd even tried to look anyone in the eye, I'd have had trouble myself.

An hour after Rawdon's cavalry clattered through the south gate, his supply wagons were drawn up in a square near the old brick jail and we were drawing the first real food we'd seen in many a long day—winter-killed beef, sweet potatoes, corn meal, chocolate, rum. Two hours afterwards, I was waiting outside the door of the barroom in the roofless tavern while Captain DeLancey, who had brought me there, went in to tell Cruger I was waiting.

When DeLancey beckoned me in, I had the impression of entering a sort of countinghouse; for dining tables stood along two sides of the room, and at the table a score of officers and clerks were busy with letters and papers. At the far end of the room Rawdon and Cruger, coatless, their shirts open at the throat, were bent over a map on a table, their chins on their hands like schoolboys.

Rawdon straightened up as I came to attention before him and said, "Oh, there you are. Don't bother about formality, Captain." He shook hands and added, "I've been most interested in what Colonel Cruger tells me about your travels. Would you mind tracing for me on this map the route you followed from Virginia to Ninety Six? I think I'll have you mark it lightly, if you'll be so kind."

He gave me a little silver pencil; and as I stooped over the map and lightly scratched upon it the enormous semicircle that Buell and I had described in going from Richmond to Frederick, over to Winchester, down the Wilderness Road through Staunton to Fort Chissel, through the dark laurel thickets of the valleys of the Holston and the Clinch to Cumberland Gap, and thence south between the towering sharp pinnacles of the Great Smokies to the white towns of the Cherokees, I felt Rawdon studying me.

When I'd finished and returned his pencil, he retraced my route with care; then gave me a quick smile. "Remarkable piece of luck, Captain, to be forced into such a journey. Plenty of game, I dare say."

"More than I ever dreamed existed."

"Wish I could see it," Rawdon said. "Blasted nuisance, spending your life killing people when you might be seeing such things—Kentucky and all that. See here, Captain: the colonel tells me you found no end of people going to Kentucky. I'd like your first-hand impressions of them. These people that you saw going to Kentucky—why were they going?"

"They were getting away from the rebels," I said. "They'd had more than enough of Congress and committees and rebel militia: of Congress troops, Congress money, Congress taxes. They were afraid of injustice and stupidity and intolerance. They were running away from a war that was bringing nothing but misery to everyone connected with it."

"You're sure?" Rawdon asked.

"I was never surer of anything in my life."

"You're certain they came from every province, eh?"

"Yes, sir. Virginia, North Carolina, South Carolina, Maryland."

"They're not going from this part of South Carolina," Rawdon said quickly. "They're staying right here. Why's that?"

"Because of the Cherokee country, sir. Some of the Cherokees can't distinguish between rebels and Loyalists, and don't stop to ask questions. After the way the Cherokees have been treated by the rebels, they figure they can't afford to take chances."

"No doubt," Rawdon said. "Now look here, Captain: to be quite frank about it, I need your help. As soon as my men are rested, I'm going after Greene. I'm leaving every ounce of baggage and equipment right here. If it's humanly possible to catch Greene, I'll do it. But whether I do or don't, I can't afford to spread my men all over the whole blasted continent in the future. You can understand, of course, that I must hold Charleston at all cost, what? Can't run any risks with a post Cornwallis might come back to at any moment! Well, there you are, Captain. Properly garrisoned, Charleston can be held against any force, military or naval, that the rebels and France together can bring against it. If, on the other hand, I try to garrison the whole confounded frontier, I'll make Charleston so weak that a handful of these damned rebel molasses-eaters could take it with two rolling pins and a popgun, what?"

He mopped his face with a handkerchief the size of a pillow slip, and shook his head in silent protest at the stifling heat.

"So I'm going to give up Ninety Six," he went on. "Colonel Cruger agrees there's nothing else to be done. At the same time I don't propose to abandon the Loyalist population of this section as they've been abandoned in other parts of America—unless they want to be abandoned. I'm going to do one of two things: either I'll leave a skeleton force here at Ninety Six to instruct the inhabitants in the use of this fort as a citadel for the entire district, or I'll move out the Loyalists lock, stock and barrel and send 'em to Charleston. There's no other alternative that I can see. I propose to leave the choice to them; and that's where I need you, Captain. They trust you, and so do I. I want you to find out for me what their sentiments are. Will you take the leaders among those South Carolinians of yours and ride out into the country with them? Find out how the settlers feel?"

"I can tell you now how they feel, sir," I said. "They'll give up everything they've got rather than stay here and be robbed, whipped, raped and murdered by rebel salvage troops."

"I hope so," Rawdon said. "I hope so, but they've got to decide their own fate, I won't have it claimed that I forced 'em out of their homes. Go out and talk to 'em. If they want to leave, tell 'em to assemble at Ninety Six tomorrow night. Tell 'em Colonel Cruger'll escort 'em to Charleston so they can take whatever they please without fear of being robbed. Is that all clear?"

"Yes, sir."

Rawdon seemed fascinated by the manner in which his damp shirt clung to his thin shoulders, and he plucked at its moist folds until I thought he'd forgotten me.

"If that's all, sir," I said, "I'd like to start now. About horses——"

"Look here, Wiswell," Rawdon said, "Cruger tells me you've a report to make to Germaine. What were your plans?"

"I haven't any, sir, except to get to New York as soon as possible. I thought I'd see the commanding officer in Charleston and ask for transportation to New York."

"Yes, yes, of course. By the way, Captain, would you mind if I offered you a bit of advice?"

"I'd be extremely grateful for it," I said.

"Good," Rawdon said heartily, "good! Delicate matter, offering suggestions, especially to Americans or British. Makes 'em angry, somehow. Don't know the French or the Russians, but fancy they're not much different. Great relief to find a chap like Cruger here: you might think you'd done him a favor when you offer him a suggestion."

"The same to you, my lord," Cruger said.

"Nonsense," Rawdon said. "Now look here, Captain: there's only one way for you to go to New York. That's by whaleboat. There's a whaleboat express from Charleston to the Chesapeake three times a week. As soon as it reaches the Chesapeake, another leaves there for New York. Takes eight days if you're fortunate. Trouble is, the blasted things carry only one passenger."

He cleared his throat, glanced apologetically at Cruger and then went to toying with his damp shirt again. "No doubt you've had the pleasure of meeting Colonel Balfour, commanding at Charleston."

I said I hadn't.

"Delightful old fellow," Rawdon said. "Dear chap, really. Old soldier and all that—fought all over the place—Indies, Bombay, Quebec —quite at home everywhere. Likes Spanish stuff on his food, hot enough to burn your gizzard out. Cooks up duck's eggs with some sort of curry, and when you eat 'em you'd swear to God you'd swallowed a beehive. Eh, Cruger?"

"I wouldn't have brought the matter up myself, my lord," Cruger said, "but since you've done so, I'm bound to say I think he's an old swine."

"Tut, tut, my dear fellow," Rawdon said. "You Americans!"

He grinned at me. "Anyway, Captain, Balfour has the say who travels on those whaleboats. He's not a bad soldier, but as Colonel Cruger has intimated, he's a bit of a stinker about some things. Don't misunderstand me when I say he's a bloody fool about Americans. Perfectly damned bloody! I think Colonel Cruger was altogether too hasty in speaking of him as he did, but Balfour has made us quite a few enemies by his attitude toward you chaps who've been loyal."

"Well, sir," I said, "he won't be the first of that sort I've met."

"I dare say," Rawdon said. "Now I tell you what you do, Captain. I'm going to put you in immediate charge of any of the local people who want to take shelter with us at Charleston. I'm also going to give you dispatches from me and from Colonel Cruger to General Clinton in New York. When you reach Charleston, you'll have to see Balfour—really a sweet old boy at heart——"

Cruger made a sound singularly like a person suddenly and violently stricken with seasickness.

Rawdon winked at me. "You'll have to play it alone, Captain," he said. "I can't spare Colonel Cruger or any of his officers for even half a day. You'll have to see Balfour and get supplies for the Loyalists you bring in with you. You'll have to fight him. Unless you fight him, he won't even let you in to see him—because you're an American. He'll try to glare you down and shout you down, and you've got to outglare him and outshout him. Fine fellow, Balfour—a dear fine fellow, but rather a horrible old beast in his own way, you see. When you've got these Carolinians looked out for, you've got to make him let you go to New York in the next whaleboat. I don't know how you're going to do it, but you'll have to, and I heartily wish you luck.

Try screeching in your loudest voice at the old beast; they say he can't stand that long."

"I'm not much of a hand at screeching, sir," I said, "and what might do me more good—if you can spare 'em—is two or three blank requisitions and one of Colonel Balfour's personal letters."

Lord Rawdon gave me a vacant stare. I thought he hadn't heard me, but he turned to one of the clerks working at the long table behind him. "Look here, Collins," he said.

The clerk jumped up and came to us.

"Collins," Rawdon said, "this is Captain Wiswell. He wants something or other—don't quite know what—and I can't bother with these blasted details. Be a good fellow, Collins, and let the captain have what he wants." He contrived an affected cough. "And Collins," he added, "don't annoy me—or anyone else—by mentioning this blasted matter aloud. I'm sick of it, Collins. Tell Collins what you want, Captain Wiswell, and then be off."

CHAPTER LXXXVII

MEN AT WAR, through long association with injustices, often lose their capacity for indignation; and none of us was particularly resentful of that murderous rebel hatred that forced us to work day and night during a torrid June and July, urging those unfortunate South Carolina Loyalists to abandon their houses and fields, their cattle and their treasured belongings, in order to seek safety in unknown country.

It didn't even seem outrageous to me, at the time, but only one of war's discomforts, that we should have to guard them incessantly from rebels who, if they could, would have killed them all—old men and boys, women and children, even the dogs, guilty of nothing but belonging to Loyalists.

Lonnie Kirkland and four of his friends whose names, he assured me, were known to every Loyalist between the Broad and the Saluda, rode out of the north gate with me on the twenty-second of June, past the enormous dump where Rawdon's regiments had deposited their knapsacks, their blankets, their baggage and every last thing when they went in pursuit of the rebel army in its retreat.

That beautiful rich land between the Broad and the Saluda had a stricken look. The roads were empty; the trees and canes seemed to droop; the air was lifeless, as if strength had gone from it.

The houses might have been long deserted. No smoke came from the chimneys; no dogs crawled from beneath steps to bark angry warnings; no pigs whuffled in the pens; no cows drowsed beneath the shade trees near the kitchens.

Yet none of the houses was deserted; and when Lonnie howled shrilly, somebody always appeared surprisingly, from an unexpected direction.

Sometimes it would be a bent old man, raggedly whiskered and with linen pantaloons, reddish from the dust, tucked into high boots. Again it would be a little boy, carrying a musket twice his length. Sometimes it was an ancient dame armed with a long iron spoon as dangerous as a rusty bayonet.

When Lonnie told our business to such a lone figure, it vanished; and soon the whole family straggled from the canes, children dragging pigs, the mother leading a cow, menfolk carrying the bags of household treasures that had been snatched up at our approach.

Every family was as timorous as a herd of deer, and when we gave them Rawdon's message, they listened silently, moving meditative feet in the red dust. Most of them wouldn't let us finish.

"Don't say no more, buddy," an old man told us. "We'll leave to-night. If we try to hold the fort, those buzzards of Marion or Pickens or Sumter'll spring up out of nowhere. They'll seize our land now and kill us later. It's just dragging out the agony to try to stay here. You hustle ahead and spread the word. There's a right smart of folks in the upper valleys that'll be killed if they ain't warned."

He called two grandsons—boys of ten and twelve—and told them to run to Tolan's and Drake's. "You tell all those womenfolk to get right over here, so they can go with us. If they don't, the rebels'll shoot 'em through the winders while they're eating, same as happened to their menfolk."

While the women piled household belongings in a cart, he relieved his feelings in a burst of garrulity. "To tell you the truth," he said, "we'd 'a' been glad to get away from here two years ago. We ain't known a peaceful minute for five years! Every time we see more'n two fellers riding along the road together, we have to take to the canes, because there's no telling who they are. If they're rebels, we always have trouble. If there's anything to steal, they steal it, damn 'em! If they're Loyalists, they ask for whatever they want, and we got to give it to 'em or be called rebels. No, sir, it wouldn't make no difference to us who won the war! Whoever wins it, we lose."

In two days' time everybody in that whole great fertile district was on the move. On all the roads to Ninety Six there were carts and carryalls, often with men between the shafts in place of horses; there were ox carts and mule teams; calves running alongside cows; homemade equipages whose wheels, made of solid blocks of wood, squealed like lost souls in torment.

There seemed to be no end to that procession of Loyalists that flowed down the valley of the Saluda, into the north gate of Ninety Six.

To me it was a source of wonderment that so many people could have settled in a country that was still half a wilderness; that so many people had contrived to stay alive in a land where Indians for years had been cheated and pushed from their own lands by white men determined to have the country, and equally determined that no Indian was entitled to life, liberty, property or the pursuit of happiness; that so many, many persons had remained unharmed and not wholly destitute in a province in which, for six years, a murderous civil war had been raging.

As these unhappy people assembled in Ninety Six, we soon saw there were too many to escort in the ordinary way, by troops marching in their van, in their rear and along their flanks. That procession of homeless Loyalists was three days long, and we'd have needed five thousand men to give them the conventional protection. So Cruger devised a cavalry patrol that moved in circles at selected points along the line of march. Between these progressing circles of mounted men marched detachments of DeLancey's and the New Jersey Volunteers; and when bands of rebel raiders tried to throw the long column of refugees into confusion, which they repeatedly did, the circles of moving cavalrymen turned upon them and drove them helter-skelter into the swamps.

To those of us who plodded along beside those families of white people and black, the whole south seemed to be on the move. So numerous were the carts loaded with furniture, bedding, even with fragments of their dismantled houses, so ear-filling was the bellowing, squealing, clucking and squawking of livestock, so cluttered was the road with scuttling children, pop-eyed pickaninnies, little herds of sheep with attendant dogs, mares with colts, babies suckling at their mothers' breasts, lean hounds that absent-mindedly raised their legs against every immovable thing they passed, that it seemed beyond belief there could be anybody left in South Carolina.

As we came down out of the hills, I had the feeling that South Carolina had been created out of two wholly different sorts of territory, stuck together as an afterthought.

Where the hills ended there was a strip of sand as clearly defined as though dumped from carts. On the north side of the strip, the coun-

try rolled and was hilly. The rivers were clear and fast-flowing; the
air was wholesome in spite of the heat.

But to the south, the land was flat and waterlogged, and the heat
terrible. Rivers imperceptibly merged into swamps; swamps mysteriously became rivers; and up from all this wetness and flatness rose
steam, as from a kettle just about to boil.

There was something funereal about it, and an odor of decay. Long
drifts of moss hung from bloated cypresses and oaks, as if the trees
had perspired and their sweat solidified as it trickled down. The
sluggish streams were black, and in them were objects that seemed
at first sight to be logs, but proved to be alligators that moved like
swift shadows, watching us furtively with malignant eyes.

Other floating objects that looked like alligators were in reality
logs from beneath which stumpy snakes emerged to wriggle heavily
in the dark waters.

Enormous waxy blooms sprouted from trees and bushes that
seemed to lack the strength to clothe themselves properly with leaves.
Moss hung everywhere; land that wasn't wet was sandy; and the
sandy roads writhed snakelike around the meanderings of swamps
and rivers.

Along the weary roads, in the fiery June sunshine, that straggling
long, long line of Loyalists, with its guard of Loyalist troops,
crawled to the southward until I came to have the feeling that all of
us—even those green-clad regiments of Cruger's that had tirelessly
dug trenches and crawled on their bellies to raid the rebels, and
fought off eight times their number—were succumbing to the steaming heat.

Unexpected things come back to me out of that march from the
Upper Country to the sea: Buell's incredulity at hearing from a South
Carolinian that rattlesnakes were good to eat, and his reluctant approval of their delicate white flesh; the triumphant laughter of
Negroes when they discovered opossums curled, seemingly lifeless, in
high trees; the waxy faces of those Carolina Loyalists; the ear-piercing
squealing of the emaciated pigs that accompanied them; the pipe-
smoking, snuff-chewing old women; the enormous size of the horse-
flies that settled unfelt upon their victims, then stabbed with poisoned
stings that made men leap and horses scream.

At a crossroads settlement twenty miles from Charleston, Cruger
deemed us safe from rebel attacks, and at that point he proposed to

leave us and take his men off to the northeastward to rejoin Lord Rawdon at Eutaw Springs.

Cruger's cavalry had camped for two days at the crossroads where the Eutaw Springs road branches off from the Charleston road, urging the long stream of Loyalists across the swampy flatlands. For two days and nights the straggling line of homeless people flowed through that crossroads settlement and onto the long straight road to Charleston, while Cruger's green-shirted companies made camp and watched them go; and at the end of the two days the green-clad battalions rolled their blankets, stamped out their campfires, and formed in long ranks in the sandy crossroad that led to Eutaw Springs.

It was hard to realize, as I watched Colonel Cruger riding along the front of those rigid green ranks, that five weeks ago all those men, all those flat-backed officers, hadn't existed so far as I was concerned. It was harder still to realize that in those five weeks we had all faced death from bullets, starvation and thirst unnumbered times.

The face of almost every man in those green battalions was intimately familiar to me, and I thought of the officers as I'd have thought of well-loved brothers.

When Cruger had finished his inspection, and had sent the green lines swinging off into the shadow of moss-hung live oaks, each officer threw up his hand in a farewell salute to Buell and me. Each face called to mind occurrences that I'd remember gratefully or admiringly as long as I lived. I'd never forget Captain Barbarie, on the gun platform beside me, tugging at his gun with hands from which splinters protruded like porcupine quills; Lieutenant Hatton crawling on hands and knees into the ravine to hunt for a wounded water-carrier the others couldn't find; Captain Campbell and Captain French racing into the trench with their men to bayonet every last rebel from it; Lieutenant Stelle standing at attention before Cruger and memorizing the colonel's refusal to surrender; Stephen DeLancey pulling blazing African arrows from roofs with hands raw from the burning tow; all those who had gone to the spring for water, who had shouted their willingness to die rather than surrender to rebels, who had sweated with us on the platform, swaying up the guns while bullets cracked around them. I thought gratefully, too, of others—of Roney, Smallwood Kirkland and all those dead men lying in a semicircle on the inside of the stockade.

When the guns clattered into the road at the tail of the green column, Cruger picked up his reins and shook hands with us, looking a little embarrassed, like a professor called on unexpectedly for a speech. "I'll hope to have the pleasure of seeing you gentlemen in New York after the war," he said. "If anything should come up to prevent it, it might interest you to know I've mentioned both of you in my report of the siege. You've done well." He cleared his throat. "I regret you're not permanently a part of my regiment."

He seemed about to say something more; then nodded to us curtly and trotted after the vanishing green column.

For the first time I knew the feeling that comes only to men who fight under a great soldier—the feeling that death is preferable to separation from that leader.

For years the Loyalists of South Carolina, as the rebels harried them in one section and then in another, had fled from their homes and sought safety in Charleston, where they lived in a strange city of their own—Rawdon Town.

It was a city of huts just outside the town limits of Charleston, on the strip of land between the Ashley and Cooper rivers. The huts were made of odds and ends—pieces of old tents, fragments of fish nets through which marsh reeds had been woven, basketwork of canes; of barrel staves, boards covered with sods, wicker casings of rum puncheons, matted raw cotton daubed with tar.

Buell, riding at the head of the long column of refugees, was pessimistic about the reception we'd get. "It wouldn't surprise me," he said, "if we're not allowed to set foot in Charleston."

"That's nonsense," I said.

"No, it's not," Buell said. "I've heard all about Charleston from printers who've worked there. Charleston's the heart and stummick of North American beauty, civilization and refined living. It's the soul of all the wealth and culture of the southland. Charleston people don't like much of anybody but themselves, not socially, and they despise all up-country folk. Up-country folk are allowed to fight for Charleston people, but when they ain't fighting, Charleston people treat 'em like blacks."

"Fortunately we don't have to deal with Charleston people," I reminded him. "Our business is with the army."

"I asked about that," Buell said, "and from what I hear, the army is all hell for highfalutin Charlestoners; and don't like up-country people any more than Charlestoners do. Those up-country people are all Presbyterians, Oliver—Low Churchmen, and pretty damned near every Englishman thinks Low Churchmen are naturally rebels. It's an idea English officers are born with, seems like."

I hoped Buell was exaggerating; but he wasn't. Mounted sentries stopped us long before we reached the two square brick pillars that are called the Gates of Charleston. We were close enough to the city to see the church steeples, the porticoed houses with their high porches, the milky-blue harbor beyond the town, and the far-off green strips of islands that protected the harbor from the sea. The sentries who stopped us were Englishmen with an unfortunately abrupt way of speaking.

"Give name and occupation," one of them said sharply, "and rank, if any."

When we gave him our names and ranks, he looked inwardly amused and saluted carelessly. "Pass on," he said, "but these people behind you can't come in."

"They've got to come in," I said. "They've got to have food and shelter."

"Orders are they can't," he said. "Somebody's got to get an order entitling them to food and a place to live. When that's got, they can build shelters for themselves in Rawdon Town."

"Haven't arrangements been made for rations?" I asked. "Aren't there places for 'em to live?"

The sentry laughed. "We ain't had time to build 'em a fancy tavern, with footman and ladies' maids for 'em, not yet we ain't! I guess most likely they'll get food somehow, and they'll build their own huts, fast enough, when they see nobody else'll do it for 'em!"

"My, my, Oliver!" Buell said. "Won't all the other Loyalists in this province be tickled when they hear about the treatment they can expect in Charleston! I'll bet they'll be mighty amused and interested in this new custom of biting the hand that feeds you, as you might say."

The sentry seemed more interested in his saddle accouterments than in Buell's words. "We've got our orders," he said, "and we're carrying 'em out. If you don't approve of 'em you'll have to see Colonel Balfour."

"Brother," Buell said earnestly, "I'm a man that don't let things bother him. I got a cure for being bothered—Perkins' Metallic Tractors." He fumbled in his garments and brought out a pair of tractors, which he displayed to the sentries.

To me he said, "You go on in and see Balfour, Oliver. I'll stay with the refugees so you'll know where to find me when you need me." He slapped the saddlebag that held his little hand press; and I knew that when I got back, Buell would have sold the sentries a pair of tractors in return for enough paper money to let him embark on a a counterfeiting career that would give Colonel Balfour many a bad hour.

Colonel Nisbet Balfour's headquarters were in a beautiful old mansion looking out on the harbor and low islands which gave that city a foreign flavor unlike any other in America.

It was late afternoon when I got there: an hour when I'd have expected all Charleston, as the saying goes—meaning those whose social position prevented them from doing any form of useful work— to be resting quietly in dim, cool rooms with Negro servants attending to their needs and whims.

Things weren't like that. There was a line of carriages a block long in front of the colonel's house; and in the house itself a score of men and women, easily recognizable as distinguished citizens of that proud city, were uncomfortably waiting, as if for a funeral.

Since I had eight hundred people committed to my care, and since most of them would in all likelihood go supperless to bed unless I quickly found food for them, I was in no mood for social amenities.

Thus, when none of the gloomy, whispering people paid any attention to me, I crossed the room to a closed door, knocked upon it and went into the next room. It was an office in which several clerks were working busily at papers, and three young officers, seated around a desk, were idly talking.

"Can you tell me where I can find Colonel Balfour?" I asked. "I have a letter for him from Lord Rawdon."

The three officers looked me up and down, and one said coldly, "Upon my word!"

Another said, "Colonel Balfour can't drop everything to talk to anybody who cares to burst into headquarters unasked! Wait your turn in the outer room."

Probably the young men weren't to blame. My breeches were patched and darned, my lower legs protected with Cherokee moccasins and knee-leggins; and the green shirt Cruger had given me, old to begin with, was stained with sweat and red dust.

"I've got to see Colonel Balfour," I said. "I've been sent here by

Lord Rawdon and Colonel Cruger. I've just brought in eight hundred Loyalists from Ninety Six District. They're hungry, and I propose to see they're fed."

The young man's attitude changed a little. "Ninety Six! Well, well! You might let us have a few of the details."

"Later," I said. "Just now I want food for eight hundred."

The young man was patient with me. "You mustn't bother the colonel! You ought to see the commissary."

"No," I said, "I'll see the colonel. The commissary couldn't give me supplies without an order from the colonel, could he?"

"The point is this," the officer said. "You'd be disturbing the colonel at a bad time. He's studying the Hayne case."

"What's the Hayne case?"

The young officer rolled his eyes in mock despair. "My God, I thought everybody in the world knew about the Hayne case! Why, nobody talks about anything else! Hayne's the rebel colonel that broke his parole to fight with the rebels. Everybody in Charleston's trying to persuade the colonel not to hang him."

"That doesn't sound like a matter that requires much study," I said. "If he ought to be hanged, he ought to be hanged. If he oughtn't, he oughtn't. Anyway, my eight hundred people need food, whether Hayne's hanged or not."

"I didn't get your name," the officer said, and I thought my persistence had angered him.

"I'm Oliver Wiswell," I said. "Captain in the King's American Dragoons."

"There's no such regiment," the young man said promptly.

"Now look here, sir," I said, "I've explained my business and answered all your questions. I won't waste time arguing. A good part of my eight hundred people are women and children. Will you take me to Colonel Balfour, or must I break into every room in this house in order to find him?"

"I can't take you to him," he said. "Our orders were to let nobody in."

One of the other two said thoughtfully, "Weren't our orders to tell everybody that the colonel was busy and unable to see anyone?"

"I think they were," the first officer said. He eyed me coldly. "Well, we've done our best." He glanced meaningly from me to a near-by door, and all three of them deliberately turned their backs on me.

"Thank you, gentlemen," I said.

As I started for the door, one of the three officers turned to me again. "I take it you're a stranger here, Captain. It might save you asking a lot of questions if I tell you that the Commissary Stores are opposite the government wharf on Ashley River. There's a supply train going out this evening, bound for Orangeburg."

CHAPTER LXXXVIII

THE room into which I stepped, without waiting an answer to my knock, occupied a wing of the house, so the windows on three sides looked out on shaded galleries and dark green magnolias, and on two sides to the pale satiny blue of the sea. By comparison with outer Charleston, it was cool; and if anybody ever needed coolness, it was the portly officer who sat at a desk in the center of the room and creakingly turned toward me as I came in.

His coat was scarlet; so was his face; but the scarlet of his face was dark with the darkness of an overripe purple plum. His head was set so close upon thick shoulders that when he turned it, his whole upper body turned also, as if his waist did duty for his neck.

I remembered Lord Rawdon's remark about Colonel Balfour's curries being like a beehive in the stomach. This officer was Colonel Balfour, for something perilously like a beehive was resting uncomfortably within him.

Before his desk, facing me, sat a thin, heavy-lipped, pouchy-eyed gentleman in black satin.

Balfour looked indignantly amazed at sight of me, so I saluted and said, "Sir, I'm Captain Oliver Wiswell, reporting here on Colonel Cruger's order, with eight hundred and eleven Loyalist refugees from the Ninety Six District."

Colonel Balfour gave the impression of panting and puffing, and his eyes seemed to swell, as if the inner pressure upon him was near the bursting point.

"Get out of this room!" he said. "By what right—who let you— why, by God, sir, I'll have you—— What's your regiment?"

"King's American Dragoons, sir."

743

"Indeed!" Colonel Balfour said mincingly. "King's American Dragoons! We'll see about that!" He struck a bell on his desk.

The pouchy-eyed gentleman in black satin cleared his throat. "If Colonel Cruger put him in charge of refugees, Colonel, his credentials are doubtless satisfactory."

Colonel Balfour spoke pettishly. "I'll handle this in my own way, Simpson! No subordinate can come bursting into my presence without a by-your-leave at this or any other time! I won't have it, by God, no matter what credentials he has!"

A sentry stepped into the room and stood to attention.

Balfour stared at the sentry, then once more turned angrily to the man in black. "If your legal mind is satisfied about his credentials, Simpson, suppose you ask yourself how an officer in a regiment I never heard of should have contrived to reach Ninety Six without passing through Charleston and making himself known. Bah, Simpson! Cruger may have been taken in, by Gad! Ain't he an American? An American'll believe any damned thing he's told!"

"Sir," I said, "I can readily explain. Benjamin Thompson, Lord Germaine's secretary, is an old friend of mine, and at his suggestion Lord Germaine sent me——"

Balfour's hand slapped his desk with the sound of a pistol shot. "Now see here, Captain! Lord Germaine's four thousand miles away! You could tell me anything you liked, and I'd never be able to prove you wrong. You could claim the King himself sent you here!" He glanced for approbation at his pouchy-eyed companion.

"You've done an inexcusable thing, bursting into this room while I'm conferring with His Majesty's attorney general, Mr. James Simpson! I won't have it!"

"Sir," I said, "I've got to have food for eight hundred refugees. I'd never have ventured to come in here if I'd known of any other way to get the food. Just give an order, sir. It won't take but a moment of your time."

Balfour stared at me, wheezing. "Don't you tell me what to do, by Gad! A man's life's at stake, but you consider yourself privileged to force your way in here, contrary to my orders, out of turn, and take up my time with talk of Lord Germaine and God knows what, all most ungermane."

Even his atrocious pun failed to soften his anger, for he added bitterly, "Get out, sir! Go to that outer office and wait your turn! When it's your turn, I'll hear what you have to say. Sentry——"

"Sir," I said, "if I wait till all those people outside have said their say, eight hundred refugees'll be without food. They've been nearly starved for a month, and they're in a precarious condition. I've got to get food for them, Colonel!"

"You heard my orders," Balfour said. "Get out of this room and wait your turn! Sentry——"

I spoke to the gentleman in black satin. "Sir, you're His Majesty's attorney general. I appeal to you for judgment. I'm asking nothing unreasonable. I have orders from Colonel Balfour's superior officer, Lord Rawdon, to report to him and see that these loyal refugees are properly housed and fed——"

"That'll do," Balfour said. "Rawdon's no superior officer of mine! My word is law in this city! What the devil do you mean, sir, by attempting to go above me to Mr. Simpson? You'll find no man fairer than Nisbet Balfour; but by Gad, sir, when you ignore discipline and common decency, when you seek special privileges, you'll find Nisbet Balfour has a hard hand and a long memory! Sentry, take this gentleman to the outer room. When his turn comes, admit him! If he tries to force his way in again out of turn, call the guard and have him confined!"

One of the worst features of an army is its all-pervading fear of superior authority. The first and last duty of a soldier is to obey orders unquestioningly. If ever he disobeys the orders of a superior, he may be discriminated against, court-martialed, disgraced or shot. Consequently every man in every army is unconsciously fearful of offending someone, slow to express opinions that might be contrary to those of his superiors, slower still to take offense at injustices. That is why men who put on uniforms seem at the same moment to put off most of their initiative and ability.

Certainly, in my own case, I was numbed by Balfour's churlishness and unreasonableness, rather than enraged. I sat down blindly in the big parlor of Balfour's headquarters, wondering how long it would be before all the silent, waiting people ranged around the room had said their say to that choleric colonel, leaving me free to make my request in a manner satisfactory to him.

When I looked more carefully at those who must precede me, I found the eyes of everyone in the room upon me. Seated next me was a stooped, gentle-looking man with a waxy face. "If you'll pardon the familiarity, sir," he said, "I'd like to introduce myself. I'm

John Bethune of Charleston. If I'm not mistaken, you're one of Colonel Cruger's men."

"Not exactly, sir," I said. "I've been with him for the past month, but my commission is in another regiment—the King's American Dragoons."

Mr. Bethune waved aside my explanation. "That would be a Loyalist regiment, sir, and that's sufficient. You've just been in to see the colonel, sir. Did he let drop a word about the case? Has he expressed an opinion?"

"The only case he expressed an opinion about was my own," I said. "I had the misfortune to go to him out of turn."

I was conscious that the waiting Charlestonians exchanged glances, and I recognized them as unhappy ones.

"I trust, sir, you won't consider me presumptuous," Mr. Bethune said, "but we'd be grateful for any hint you could give us. The colonel's mood, for example—if only we could be sure of his mood, we might be able to approach him more effectively."

"Well, sir," I said, "I know nothing about the case in which you're interested, so you can hardly expect me to——"

Mr. Bethune interrupted me. "Ah, but I *do* expect you, sir! It's of vital importance to you, if you're a Loyalist, to interest yourself in Colonel Hayne's case. It's of the greatest importance to me, and I'm a Loyalist too; and it's also of the utmost importance to Colonel Hayne's friends, most of whom are rebels."

A portly gentleman in a wrinkled white suit spoke testily from the other side of the room. "We don't accept the word 'rebel', Mr. Bethune! We're Patriots."

"I won't argue with you, Doctor Ramsey," Bethune said sharply. "All of us are here in behalf of Colonel Hayne; not to air political views."

He turned back to me. "Colonel Hayne's case is of the greatest importance to you and to me because of the increased bitterness and determination with which our enemies will fight if Colonel Hayne is hanged!"

He eagerly edged forward in his chair. "It's essential that you understand the Hayne case, sir! You may be able to enlist the help of friends in the army! I'll explain it to you here and now, before representatives of both parties, so you can know every word I say is true. You're not from the south, sir?"

"No, sir, I'm from Massachusetts. My name's Wiswell. The rebels drove my father and me from our home."

The man in the wrinkled white suit made an exasperated sound and seemed about to protest.

I saw no reason to speak oversoftly to him. "Driven out by rebels," I repeated. "Men who turn against the government and take the law into their own hands are rebels. There was no better judge than Governor Hutchinson, and no better lawyer than my father, and in their opinion rebels were rebels and nothing else."

Mr. Bethune placed a restraining hand upon my sleeve. "I'm sure your father and Governor Hutchinson would be the first to drop all distinctions in Colonel Hayne's case. He was a man of parts, Captain Wiswell: as amiable a gentleman as ever lived—extremely influential, sir, and possessed of a large plantation on the Edisto River. A year ago this city was attacked by General Clinton, and Colonel Hayne, with mounted militia from the Edisto, took part in its defense. When the forces of General Clinton captured Charleston, the general permitted all the reb——" He coughed, glanced apologetically at Doctor Ramsey and went on, "The general permitted all his enemies to return to their homes as prisoners of war on parole. Colonel Hayne's cavalry went back to the Edisto, and so did Colonel Hayne.

"Not long after that, Captain Wiswell, General Clinton did something that we never understood. He revoked the paroles extended to those men. After all, Captain Wiswell, a parole is a parole. The general sent special word to Colonel Hayne that on account of his position and influence, he must either become a British subject or report at once to Charleston. Well, sir, the colonel had already chosen his side, which was not ours; and more than that, his wife had fallen sick of the smallpox and was in a serious condition. I hope any gentleman would have done what Colonel Hayne did. He refused to leave his wife. The British respected his situation, and agreed to leave him undisturbed on his plantation if he would sign a paper agreeing to remain aloof from all political activities so long as the country was occupied by the British Army. This he did.

"Unfortunately, his wife was greatly in need of medicines; and to get them, the colonel was obliged to travel to Charleston. To make sure he'd not be molested when he left Charleston to return home, he unfortunately asked British headquarters for a pass. Not only did headquarters refuse, but they held him, insisting that he either become a British subject or go to prison. Does that seem fair, Captain Wiswell?"

I admitted that it didn't.

"No," Mr. Bethune said, "and it didn't seem fair to Colonel Hayne either. Yet his wife was dying, and he felt he was justified in taking any necessary steps to get back to her. He wrote a letter to Doctor Ramsey, yonder, explaining that his submission had been forced upon him. Then, with mental reservations, he did as headquarters ordered and signed the submission demanded of him—as I know I'd have done if I'd been in his place, and as I suspect you'd have done too, Captain."

When Bethune said, "As I suspect you'd have done too, Captain," I knew that I'd have signed any oath, broken parole, and seen all the world to the devil for Sally Leighton if she'd lain in such need as had the wife of Colonel Hayne.

I stared at Bethune; but what I saw wasn't his waxy face. My mind's eye saw the brown eyes and the darker brown hair of Sally Leighton, the long black eyelashes lying like curtains against the pearliness of her complexion that was somehow miraculously always there, even under a golden tan. I was suddenly in an icy rage at Colonel Balfour for his petty unreasonableness—for his inhumanity in putting miserable man-made rules ahead of the needs of desperate people.

"Soon after Colonel Hayne reached his plantation," Bethune went on, "his wife died. The colonel, when he'd buried her and nursed his children back to health, considered himself released from the submission he'd signed. He'd never have signed it if his wife hadn't needed him; and now that she was gone, he refused to be bound by it. When his neighbors on the Edisto came to him, begging him to form them into a regiment and once more lead them against their enemies, he considered it his duty to accept.

"His first enterprise was daring and successful. He led some of his men straight into this city and surprised one of our own people— General Andrew Williamson, one of the most distinguished planters of this province. He snatched the general out of bed and rushed him away in his night clothes—a great disgrace to the garrison of this city, as you can well understand. Enraged at his exploit, Colonel Balfour sent ninety dragoons in pursuit of him. Colonel Hayne might have escaped if he'd been willing to drive his horse to death; but one of the things that makes everyone like Hayne is his kindness. He spared his horse, so the dragoons caught up with him and captured him in turn. Now he's in the Provost, charged by Colonel Balfour with violating his oath of allegiance, and with being a traitor. If Colonel Balfour persists in those charges, Colonel Hayne'll be hanged.

"If he's hanged, Captain Wiswell, a great wrong will be done, and innumerable people will suffer. It's essential to the Loyalist cause that this province remain loyal. If Colonel Hayne is hanged, those actively engaged in the rebel cause will redouble their violence. Thousands now unwilling to take up arms against the royal government may actually refuse to oppose the rebels. That's why every Loyalist in Charleston is begging Colonel Balfour not to execute Colonel Hayne, even though Hayne's a rebel. Do you understand our position, Captain?"

"Yes," I said to Mr. Bethune, "I understand everything, and I can't wait here any longer. I came here to get food for eight hundred Loyalist refugees, but Colonel Balfour wouldn't talk to me because I put their needs ahead of military conventions and the letter of military law."

I stood up, fully conscious at last of the sort of man Colonel Balfour was, wholly certain of the fate that awaited Colonel Hayne, and no longer in doubt as to the course I must follow.

I knew as well as though Colonel Balfour had told me with his own lips that Colonel Hayne was already as good as dead. If Balfour would let eight hundred people go hungry because he was a stickler for rules, he'd certainly condemn Hayne to death for breaking parole, even though the parole was obtained under the circumstances of which I'd just learned.

I think all those rebel and Loyalist friends of Colonel Hayne must have sensed that I knew Balfour wouldn't be merciful; for when I went to the door, opened it, and turned to salute them all, they looked as pale and stricken as though Hayne were already in his grave.

I'd have helped them if I could, but there was no way. I had to get food for eight hundred people, and after that I had to help myself—if I could!

I found Buell, back in Rawdon Town, practising Nisbet Balfour's signature on a piece of slate, while Kirkland and a dozen of his friends formed an impenetrable barrier around him, their hands in their pockets and a singularly absorbed look on their faces.

"The name of the officer at the Commissary Stores," I told Buell,

"is Gershom Pyecraft. Like nearly every other commissary, he's trying to get rich out of the army. I want you to write me an order,
signed by Rawdon, for eight hundred pounds of rice to be delivered
daily to whoever these refugees from Ninety Six select. Let me have
it, together with about fifty thousand dollars in those shinplasters of
yours, and I'll see that the rice gets out here tonight."

Buell turned to Kirkland. "Gimme that money, Lonnie. It's rubbed
enough by now."

They had, I saw, been aging Buell's new money by pushing it
around in their pantaloons pockets. Already it looked as though it
had been in circulation since the battle of Bunker Hill.

"What else?" Buell asked.

"A boat," I said. "We've got to have a boat—a whaleboat. Balfour'll
never let us travel in one of the regular whaleboats, now that he's
taken a dislike to me; and we've got to be out of this city before he
begins to ask questions about that order from Rawdon. He won't
dare to stop the provisions, once the order's on file, but he wouldn't
hesitate to put us all in the Provost for going over his head. If he
ever puts us in the Provost, we'll never see New York again."

Buell looked thoughtful. "A boat, Oliver? A boat ain't easy for a
landsman!"

"It's easier than dying in jail," I said. "When I was leaving Balfour's headquarters, I took a couple of orders from the order board.
One's signed by the admiral."

Buell's face brightened. "That's fine, Oliver! That admiral and
Balfour'll have to live to be a thousand years old to get their accounts straight with the government!"

When Buell came back to Rawdon Town that night, he was a little
drunk and full of information about potlicker. "By God, Oliver," he
said thickly, "damned if I don't believe everything you hear about
other places is all lies! Remember how excited that Colonel Rogers
got about Ninety Six? Look what it was when we got there! Nothing but red dust and sun that would raise blisters on your breeches!
Well do I remember, Oliver, when I lived in Norwich, Connecticut, how everybody used to say Boston was full of refined people; but
hell, Oliver: the place was a nest of rebels who'd steal the doorknobs
off their own houses!"

"Did you get what we need?" I asked.

"Wait. Oliver," Buell said, "I ain't told you about potlicker yet.

Remember how I always wanted to come to South Carolina just to get some potlicker like that printer in New York told about? Well, I had some tonight, Oliver! Real, honest, South Carolina potlicker—just what I'd always been looking forward to to tone up my system and keep me from getting that cannon-ball feeling in my stomach. Yes, sir, Oliver, I had my fill of potlicker tonight, and do you know what it was, Oliver? It wasn't one damned thing but spinach boiled with salt pork. Yes, sir; salt pork, and belly at that. It's thin and greasy, and you crumble corn bread in it to make it thick enough to eat. Why, hell, Oliver, I could make better potlicker with both hands tied behind my back. I'd put in a little flour, and maybe some beans and an egg, and whatever else I had handy."

When I tried again to ask him what he'd accomplished, he put his arm across my shoulders and hiccuped. "To tell you the truth, Oliver, I don't know what to think about that potlicker. I took that man from the shipyard to dinner so to get information from him. He had just as much potlicker as I did, and the same amount of rum, but he couldn't even stand up. He'll never be able to go to work tomorrow, Oliver, so you don't need to worry that he'll stop us when we go to get the boat."

"You got a boat?" I cried.

"Certainly I got a boat," Buell said. "We had to have it, didn't we? There ain't a whaleboat to be had in Charleston for love or money, Oliver, so we'll have to take one belonging to the admiral—his personal whaleboat that his men row races in. It's a boat the man I had the potlicker with, and that can't stand up now, and I don't think can tomorrow either, says the admiral loves like the apple of his eye, so it must be a good one, or else why would he have all that loving feeling for it? It's in the shipyard, being recaulked and sandpapered and repainted and sludged, so the admiral can win a race with it next week. I ain't exactly taken it yet, but it's there waiting for us."

"Good for you," I said.

"I s'pose I got to tell you," Buell said reluctantly, "that there might be one or two drawbacks about it. When we take it out of the shipyard, we can't stop for anything, not even for food or water. And God help us if we're stopped! They'll stop us with a 36-pounder; and if we ever get ashore, we'll not only have Balfour after us, we'll have that damned admiral too, on account of the way he loves that boat. That potlicker man, Oliver, he's a drunkard—he says the admiral would rather part with his wife and epaulets than with that loving boat! So we got to take it to help him appreciate his wife and epaulets better, when he hasn't got the boat to squander all his caresses on. It'll be a good act on our part, and help the admiral's character. I love to be virtuous, Oliver!"

It was three o'clock in the morning when Buell gathered together the pile of orders and passes that he'd struck off on his portable printing press, and examined them one by one with a critical and bloodshot eye.

"There," he said, "there's as nice a bunch of secret orders as ever came out of any headquarters! There's general orders from headquarters, orders from Lord Rawdon's headquarters in the field, orders from Lieutenant Colonel Cruger's headquarters in the field, orders from the adjutant general's office, orders from His Majesty's naval stores, orders from on board His Majesty's ship *Apollo*. If there's anything else we need, I don't know what it is. I'll fill 'em in tomorrow morning, when my hand's steadier."

Those passes and orders carried Buell, me and six South Carolina riflemen headed by Lonnie Kirkland through the Gates of Charleston, made it possible to draw necessary supplies from the Commissary Stores, and send them out to the harbor entrance by a fisherman. They got us two swivel guns from the Ordnance Department, and brought the sentries in front of the government shipyard to sharp attention as we marched briskly through the gateway at midafternoon.

The boat we wanted, Buell said, was in No. 4 carpenter shop—a shed as long and wide as a New England barn; and we saw her as soon as we went into that dim, hot interior, which smelled of cedar, resin and tar. The admiral's whaleboat, because of her knifelike stem and stern and her peculiarly deep keel, stood out above the score of naval gigs and longboats as a race horse stands out among draft animals.

She was at the far end of the shed, close to the ramp up which boats were dragged into the shop from the harbor. Two men were fitting new tholepins into the gunwales.

I marched our six men straight up to them. "You've done well with her," I said. "She's in first-class shape. Get me a tiller and we'll take her right out."

The workmen looked grieved. "She ain't half finished," one of them protested. "She ought to be sludged, and all the tholepins ought to be replaced to be sure they don't break in a race."

"We can't wait," I told him. "You can sludge her and change the tholepins later. Let me have the tiller and oars."

"Here's the oars piled against the wall," Buell said. "Have 'em fill the water breaker before we take her out."

To Lonnie Kirkland he said, "Here, turn her over so we can get these oars under her and carry her out to the runway."

The workmen unhooked water buckets from the wall and moved off toward the pump which stood beside the runway. Lonnie and his five friends slid the long ash oars beneath the overturned boat and carried it to the open door at the end of the building; then went back for their rifles.

A sweaty-faced man in a dust-colored overall ran up to us. "Here, for God's sake," he said, "what you trying to do with that boat? I ain't had any orders to let her go; and besides, she ain't ready."

"I was going to look you up when we'd got her where we could fill her up with water," I said. "We wouldn't be taking her if the occasion wasn't urgent."

Buell came to stand beside me. "Here's the orders, Captain," he said.

The paper read, *"Headquarters, Charleston. Captain Germaine and Lieutenant Eden to proceed to shop No. 4 and obtain one whaleboat under repair in that shop. Nisbet Balfour, lieutenant colonel, commanding."*

When the man read it, he shook his head dubiously. "This boat ain't finished," he protested, "and the admiral said he wanted her in A-No. 1 shape. What's he going to say if I let her out this way and she loses the bloody race? He'll prob'ly put me to building sea walls out on those bloody islands with the sharks and snakes!"

"You needn't worry about the admiral," I told him. "He knows we're using the boat on the Hayne case."

"You don't say so," he said. "There certainly is hell to pay over that! What'll they do? Hang him?"

"I don't know," I said. "Anything might happen if we don't get this boat."

He seemed to come to a sudden decision. "I'll tell you what I'll do. I'll row out to the admiral's ship myself, just to make sure I don't catch hell."

Buell cleared his throat. "You'd save him a trip, Captain, if you let me show him the letter the colonel gave us, along with the orders." To the man he said, "We're not supposed to show any documents bearing on the Hayne case, but maybe the captain'll make an exception for you."

"Yes," I said. "Time's important, Lieutenant. You can show the letter."

Buell drew a bundle of papers from his pocket, fumbled with them, looked highly secretive, and went to a near-by desk—seemingly to sort them. My heart was in my mouth for fear that what he was doing would be as apparent to the foreman as to me.

When Buell came back he handed me a smudged and heavily creased letter headed H.M.S. *Apollo.*

"*Dear Balfour* [the letter read]. *The fastest whaleboat I have is in shop No. 4. By all means take it, and may your efforts be crowned with success. Brigham.*"

"Yes," I said, "that's it."

I handed it to the foreman. "That ought to satisfy any of your qualms."

I did my best to look unconcerned; but I knew that if the foreman should question this forgery, written by Buell under his very eyes, there'd be nothing left to do but dispose of him as best we could, shove the boat down the ramp and run for it.

We were sixty-two hours rowing and sailing the five hundred miles from Charleston to the mouth of the Chesapeake; and when we raised Old Point Comfort, we saw a sight far different from that we'd seen six months before when we rounded it with Arnold and Simcoe and the Queen's Rangers.

The whole point was surrounded by a bristling fence of masts; and the sandy shores and the dusty-looking meadows above them were dotted with tents that wavered and quivered in the heat haze.

As we drew nearer to that fence of masts, we saw ship after ship detach itself and sail away to the northward.

"Well," I told Buell, "it's better to waste a day or two and be safe, than run the risk of falling into the hands of the navy."

I think it was a fortunate thing for us that we behaved as we did, sheering out to sea again from Old Point Comfort until we stumbled, as if by chance, into the course of one of those northward-moving vessels.

I say I think it was fortunate; for nobody who had any direct contact with the army or navy in that part of the world at that time escaped with a whole reputation. For years afterwards no man could

tell what he had done or why he had done it without being called a
liar, traitor or coward; and the accusations that passed between Clinton and Cornwallis filled seven books.

As the ship drew up on us, we ran out all our oars, and with these
and our sail contrived to keep abreast of her quarter-deck long enough
for me to speak it.

"Ahoy," I shouted. "I have dispatches for the commissary general
of the army, Mr. Stedman. Is he aboard this ship?"

"I wish to God he was," the captain shouted. "We could do with
some fresh beef."

"Where'll I find him?"

"Damned if I know," the captain said, "but he ought to be up
ahead of us. They're hunting an anchorage in the York River, and he
ought to be looking into food in those parts."

So we turned into the mouth of the Chesapeake and bore west for
the narrows in the York River—that little half-mile-wide bottle-neck
with Yorktown on the left on its white bluff, and Gloucester just
across the river on the right.

It was at Yorktown that I found Stedman, a vastly different Stedman from the one I'd last seen five years before in New York City.
He was heavier and harder, with an eye like a gimlet; and when I
walked into his tent and found him casting up accounts in a long,
brown ledger, he leaped from his chair and threw his arms around
my shoulders as men do when they haven't seen a friend for years.

"My God, Oliver," he said, "I thought you were dead. I wrote
Thompson about you, and everyone else I could think of. Nobody
knew where you were!" He pounded both hands upon my shoulders,
as if to assure himself I was really alive.

As rapidly as I could I told him how I'd been sent to investigate the
Convention Army and the state of affairs in the south; how I'd
escaped from Frederick by way of the Wilderness Trail; how we'd
stood off Greene at Ninety Six; and how Balfour was enraging all
the rebels and damaging the Loyalist cause in Charleston.

"The Loyalists are bitter, are they?" Stedman asked.

"Certainly they're bitter," I said. "So'm I. So's Buell! Whenever we
depend on the British for leadership, we don't get it. Every Loyalist
in South Carolina makes the same complaint. They're loyal to the
British, but British leaders aren't loyal to them."

Stedman threw himself into his camp chair and eyed me morosely.

"They're bitter here, too, Oliver, and in North Carolina, and I don't blame 'em! I used North Carolina mounted Loyalists to round up forage and supplies for the army. The army couldn't have existed without 'em, yet the army treated 'em like servants—like pack animals! If we get into trouble, the men in high positions won't go far out of their way to protect us."

" 'If we get into trouble'," I repeated. "What do you mean by that?"

Stedman ignored my question. "From what I've seen of this war," he went on, "I've come to the conclusion that most people who are given positions of authority in time of war are subject to epidemics of insanity. If that's not so, why is it that so many generals and statesmen who look healthy, and are able to speak logically on almost any subject, inevitably do the wrong things? Why do they lie, blunder, delude themselves, fall in love with their own stupidity, stop fighting when they ought to continue, go on fighting when they ought to stop, refuse to believe those they ought to believe, and take the word of knaves and ignoramuses? Why is it true of generals and statesmen on both sides in every war? I say they're mad!"

He jumped to his feet and led me to the tent opening, that fronted on the narrow York River. "Look at this little neck of land we're on! It's one of the few places left to us in the south—this and Charleston and Savannah. A year ago this Southern Army of Cornwallis' controlled all of North and South Carolina, and a good slice of Virginia. We've got cavalry—Tarleton's Legion and Simcoe's Rangers, all Loyalists—unsurpassed by any cavalry in the world! Our regiments, Loyalists and regulars alike, can outmarch, outfight, and out-endure any regiments on earth. They've made marches as great as ever were made; they've won battles that any soldier'd be proud of winning. And now look at us! After all those marches and all those victories —thanks to the madness of generals and statesmen—we're going to ground on a pie-shaped point on this little river; and unless men change their habits overnight—which they never do—here we'll stay!"

I saw he meant it. "Why in God's name should they come here?" I asked.

"Because they've been ordered to," Stedman said. "Clinton's ordered it. Clinton thinks he's going to be attacked in New York, so he's told Cornwallis to take post here till the danger's over."

I still couldn't understand. "But why here? Why not in Portsmouth? Arnold picked Portsmouth as the easiest place to defend in this locality."

"Madness," Stedman said. "That's why! War madness! I tell you all generals and statesmen have it! Montcalm had it at Quebec. Howe had it at Bunker Hill and Dorchester Heights. Washington had it at Long Island. Clinton had it in the same place, and at Kip's Bay. Burgoyne had it when he insisted on marching from Lake Champlain to the Hudson instead of going by way of Lake George. Now Clinton's got it worse than ever. I tell you they're all insane!"

He tapped me on the chest. "Listen, Oliver: are you under orders?"

"I'm under my original orders from Thompson and Germaine— orders to report on the condition of the Convention Army and the war in the south. I had to steal this boat to get away from Charleston, because Balfour didn't like me, and I knew he wouldn't let me make the report if he could help it. That's why I came to see you. I want you to send my whaleboat back to Balfour, with orders to continue to supply rations immediately to the eight hundred and eleven refugees evacuated by Lord Rawdon from the Ninety Six District. Then I want you to give me another whaleboat so that I can go into New York without being in constant danger of landing in the Provost."

Stedman slapped his thigh. "All insane, Oliver, except you and me and our friends and the poor private soldiers who have to suffer for the madnesses of their leaders! It's no wonder that rebels are forever deserting to us, and our men continually deserting to the rebels. Ah well, Oliver, I'll do as you ask; and in return I want you to carry a message to New York for me. It isn't official, Oliver: it'll just be part of the information you picked up in the south. I won't make it official, because I'm an American and nobody'd listen to me. I want you to repeat it to everyone you see. You'll have to report to headquarters when you reach New York, so ask for Clinton and tell him what I say. Tell him it's the general opinion in the south. Would you be willing?"

"Of course," I said. "I'll tell Clinton. I'll tell Thompson. I'll tell everyone."

"They won't believe you," Stedman said hopelessly. "Still, that's no reason for not saying it. Here's what you're to say. You tell everyone you see that Washington'll never attack New York. He's coming down here to attack us."

"Are you sure?"

"As sure as I am of anything," Stedman said. "Look, Oliver: a few days ago Cornwallis' main force set out to move in this direction.

He was being watched by that little Frenchman, Lafayette. Lafayette got the idea that he could jump on Cornwallis' columns while they were moving, so he made a forced march and jumped. Cornwallis was waiting for him, and gave him a terrible beating. Lafayette's whole force was driven into a swamp; his cannon were captured; and if darkness hadn't shut down when it did, Simcoe's Rangers would have moved after him and destroyed him entirely.

"Now look, Oliver: this little Lafayette boy is Washington's pet, and he's a spoiled child. He's mad as a March hare over his defeat, and his French love of glory has been severely dented. There's only one way he can wipe out his disgrace, and that's by persuading Washington to come down here and put an end to this army of Cornwallis'. There's a rumor going around that the French fleet is sailing away from the West Indies to escape the hurricane season, and that it's coming here.

"I think that's the truth, Oliver, and I know just what's going to happen. Washington never refused Lafayette anything. He can't. He turns to putty when Lafayette asks for something. That little French boy's no more fit to be a general and plan a battle than a baby is; but he wanted to be a general, so Washington let him be one. Then he wanted to plan a battle, and Washington let him. Now he wants Washington to come down here and retrieve his sacred French honor; and as sure as you're alive, Oliver, Washington's going to do it! You tell Clinton that; and then tell him this: if Washington *does* come down here, and the French fleet *does* sail in here, and Clinton doesn't send us reinforcements in good season, he won't have any Southern Army. Let him make just one mistake like those he's made in the past and our goose is cooked!"

BOOK VI

☆

Land of Liberty

CHAPTER LXXXIX

The New York to which we returned was startlingly different from the one I'd left seven months before. There was the same studding of church steeples, the same tall sugar houses, the same foreign names above the shops on Broadway, the same amazing number of taverns and alehouses; but now everything was crowded with idle, waiting people, and men and women on the streets looked uncertain and worried.

Even the river, as we rowed up it, cramped and weary, soggy and hungry, from our thousand-mile journey, was crowded. Merchant ships were packed in at all the wharves; the stream was full of war vessels; and a veritable flotilla of small craft was ferrying passengers between the wharves of New York and the shore beneath the Heights of Brooklyn.

Everywhere on shore people waited in groups, waited in long lines that extended far down the street and around corners. There were lines at Clinton's headquarters, at the office of the commissary general, at the office of the town marshal, at the office of the chief of naval stores.

On the door of the house across the street from headquarters was a sign reading, "Committee for the Relief of Refugees"; and from its steps a line of people extended far up Broadway.

To see Sir Henry Clinton I went through the same routine that every officer must follow in order to reach the presence of a general—officer of the day, adjutant general's office, the general's secretary, one of the general's aides; and finally, after long waiting, the general himself, a little paler, a little puffier, a little more sunken-eyed than when I'd seen him in November.

When I was finally admitted, and stood to attention before him, he looked up at me with condescending amusement. "Bless me," he said, "the young historian turned soldier! You've been gone long enough, Captain, to have found out everything you were sent to get and a deal more." I have no doubt he thought of the look he gave me as quizzical.

"Yes, sir," I said, "I've learned a lot, most of it unpleasant." I took Lord Rawdon's letter from my pocket. "I was told to give you this, sir."

Clinton looked at it front and back. "Well," he said, "you *did* cover ground in your travels!"

He detached the seal from the letter, opened it, ran his eye hastily over the contents, and added, "Ah yes! I had the bulk of this news a week ago. Rawdon speaks well of you and Lieutenant Buell, Captain; very well indeed. He also mentions certain opinions you formed in your travels through the south."

I suddenly knew that I couldn't convince Clinton by word of mouth. The mere fact that I had an American accent would put the black seal of unreality on everything I told him.

"Sir," I said desperately, "it's a long story. I've made notes for the report I'll make to Mr. Thompson, and I won't be long writing it."

"Come, come, Captain," Clinton said. "You didn't feel obliged to write a report for Lord Rawdon, did you?"

"No, sir," I said, "but that was because I knew he wouldn't—that is, I'd talked to Colonel Cruger and I think the colonel had perhaps explained some of my findings——"

Clinton folded the letter and stared at me. "You can make your written report, Captain," he said, "but I'd like an idea of your findings right now. What do you propose to say in that report?"

"I'm going to say, sir," I said, "that in spite of the magnificent marches made by British and Loyalist troops in South Carolina, in spite of the brilliant battles which they've won, in spite of having gained complete control over the southern states within the year, every gain has been thrown away because the victorious army stubbornly refused to understand Americans."

"Indeed," Clinton said.

"That's my firm belief, sir. Stanch Loyalists throughout the back country in both North and South Carolina have been badly treated because of being Low Church. British officers will not understand that Low Churchmen needn't be rebels. They say the rebel movement in New England was Low Church, so the same thing must be true in the Carolinas. It isn't true, but British officers won't believe it isn't."

"That's making a mountain out of a molehill," Clinton said.

"The Loyalists don't think so, sir," I said. "You've lost the active support of thousands of southern Loyalists on that one account. You've lost thousands more through promising help to Loyalists in various sections; then withholding the help, withdrawing your army and leaving the Loyalists to their fate. They no longer dare trust you! What's more, so many things have gone wrong under British leadership that they think nothing can go right, ever."

"Come, come, Captain," Clinton said, "you don't believe in such schoolboy ideas!"

"I do indeed believe them, sir. For seven years I've seen things go wrong in this war. For seven years British armies haven't followed up their victories, British ministers have refused to believe what they were told, British fleets have delayed too long, the wrong men have been put in high positions, Loyalists have been treated cavalierly by the very men who should be most grateful to them.

"The day of miracles is over, sir; and there'll never be a sudden end to all these blunders. They'll continue; and if those officers in South Carolina are right—as Buell and I think they are—one more mistake at this time will be fatal."

"Just what do you mean by that?" Clinton asked.

I'd gone too far to turn back. "Well, sir," I said, "Cornwallis is taking post at York, so the fleet and army can work together. They say in the south that if Washington marches his army down into Virginia and catches Cornwallis on that badly defended little point at York, it'll never get away except by swimming."

Clinton laughed heartily. "What daydreams you find in an army! Don't your friends in the south know Washington has his eye on New York?"

"They know some people hold to that, sir," I said, "but they think differently. They think that when Washington has word from Lafayette about the situation at York, he'll leave New York and move his army down into Virginia. They say Lafayette can wrap Washington around his little finger; and Lafayette's staying right where he is, watching every move Cornwallis makes. They say Lafayette'll coax him down."

Clinton looked at me incredulously. "Am I to gather, Captain, that you plan to recommend to Mr. Thompson that we give up the campaign in the south?"

"I think I must, sir. You'll never get back the territory you've lost; never! And the longer you continue to occupy cities on the coast, the more violent the feeling'll be against the Loyalists and against the English. You're only promoting civil war by occupying any part of the south; and I think I can show you, sir, that the best interests of England and America will be served by an immediate cessation of fighting."

I knew the look in Clinton's eye. I'd seen it before in Howe's eye, and again and again in Eden's. "Poor fool!" the look said. "Poor, simple, misguided, gullible, American fool!"

I knew he'd speak soothingly to me, as to a child or a hopeless idiot; and he did.

"That's all very interesting, Captain, and you must write it out at once. Write it out by all means, and I'll see it reaches the proper authorities."

"Sir," I said desperately, "this report ought to be made in person. Mr. Thompson sent me to make it; and unless I can tell Mr. Thompson in person what's going on——"

"Write your report and bring it to me," Clinton said sharply. "You hold a commission in the King's American Dragoons, and Colonel Thompson would be the first to uphold me in assigning you and Lieutenant Buell to that duty. Since he's colonel of the regiment, I think he must be planning to come here in person to take command. If I'm right, Captain, you can readily see how useless it would be for you to suggest a cessation of hostilities to him or his immediate superiors."

"But they don't know conditions," I persisted. "The English people ought to be told what a useless, stupid war they're fighting! If I can only see Mr. Thompson——"

General Clinton struck a bell sharply, and an officer popped in. "I'm ready for you now, Major," Clinton said. "Captain Wiswell's just leaving. Hurry up with that report, Captain Wiswell. We need every available man for the defense of this city."

CHAPTER XC

MY FIRST inquiry, after I'd left Clinton, was for Mrs. Byles and Henrietta Dixon; and when I learned they'd gone to Brooklyn, away from New York and the army and Clinton, I was grateful for even one small piece of good fortune.

The Silver Mackerel was the name of Mrs. Byles' tavern; and when we were halfway across the river we saw its sign, a glittering weather vane carved in the likeness of a giant horse mackerel.

The house was of stone, and gambrel-roofed. It stood just north of the ferrying place from which the frightened rebel army had escaped after the battle of Long Island; and we tied our whaleboat almost in its front yard. A walled garden stood between the dock and the house, and in the garden were bright red tables overlooking the river and the lower end of New York. Each side of the house was bordered by a bowling green as smooth as velvet. I hadn't seen a prettier place anywhere in Virginia or South Carolina.

At one of the tables in the garden sat a group of British officers, a little drunk; and from the lack of expression on their faces as we walked past them, we knew our stained green uniforms were familiar enough to them, but of no importance.

The waiter who opened the door blocked our way and with a napkin waved us to the corner of the garden farthest removed from the British officers. "We always serve gentlemen outside at this time of year," he said, emphasizing the word "gentlemen."

Buell looked interested. "You don't say! You can tell us all about gentlemen some day when we got more time. What do you give 'em to drink as a general rule?"

"Gentlemen take port," the waiter said.

"Port, eh?" Buell said. "We'll have some some day. Which table did you have in mind for us? Go on over and show us."

The waiter started away, looking pleased with himself, on which we went on into the house.

The hallway of the Silver Mackerel was narrow and wainscoted. On one side was a dining room with windows looking up the East River. Through them I could see Wallabout Bay and the prison ships, Montresor's Island, and the hill above Kip's Bay on which we'd stood with Cruger five years before and watched the rebels fleeing from the city.

On the other side was a taproom, with long rows of bottles on shelves above a pine bar. Before the bar stood Henrietta Dixon, her back to us, measuring with a foot rule the liquor in the bottles, and jotting her findings on a slate.

"For God's sake, Henrietta," Buell said, "what you done to your hair?"

The foot rule in Henrietta's hand knocked over the bottle she was measuring.

Buell rescued it and took the foot rule from the bar. "What you doing with this, Henrietta?"

"We measure what's in the bottles," Henrietta said, "so we'll know when there's too much stealing."

"What you want," Buell said, "is a rack, so the bottles can stand upside down with a spigot in the neck. Then you could lock the spigot. You need me around to invent things for you, Henrietta."

Henrietta made a whimpering sound.

"Now look here," Buell said, "none of that!"

He passed his hand over her hair. "I don't know as I ever mentioned your hair to you, but you got real pretty hair when it isn't skinned back, the way it is now. I thought it was pretty the first time I saw you on the dock in Boston, with little Nathan hanging on your skirts. How's Nathan?"

"He wants to go in the army," Henrietta cried. She wrenched herself free from Buell's restraining hands, threw her arms around his neck and seemed to flatten herself against him like a fox skin against a door. "I'm sick of armies," she cried—"men always getting killed or wounded, men always getting their heads blown off, men always wanting to paw your arm or squeeze your knee or kiss you behind a door, so you have to make yourself look like a scarecrow to dodge 'em—men always drunk, always dirty, always begging for something, always hungry, always stealing, always homesick! Where have you been, Buell?"

"Me?" he said. "I've been away." He gave me a desperate glance. He looked wholly different from the man who'd assured me, when I waited for Sally on Milton Hill the last time I'd seen her, that he never wanted to be alone with Henrietta Dixon. I remembered my own desperation at his presence that night; so I went out into the hallway, leaving him alone with Henrietta.

As I closed the taproom door, I heard the far-off rapping of that ivory-headed cane. A moment later Mrs. Byles came sailing through the dining room toward the hallway, her cheeks round and pink, her brown eyes sharp, her stomach as round and firm as though a hard-stuffed pillow were thrust beneath the front of her silk dress.

When she came into the hallway and saw me, she stopped as though her gown had caught on a nail; then hurried to me and grasped my arm as if uncertain what she'd find beneath the sleeve. "You gave me a start, Oliver," she said. "You're—you're thin! You made me think of your father the day—that day at sea——"

"Yes," I said. "I know what you mean. He didn't like the look of things, and I don't either."

"Have you reported to Clinton?"

I nodded.

"So he didn't believe you!" she said. She seemed pleased. "Tell me what you told him. I've got a reason for asking. What's going on in the south?"

"To the devil with the war," I said. "I've had a stomachful of it! Let me get away from it for a few minutes. I can see you're doing well here. Can't you let me have a little encouraging news about Milton?"

Mrs. Byles gave me that sharp side glance of hers. "I can tell you a little, Oliver, but mighty little. To tell you the truth, I'd hoped you'd meet another girl and forget Sally Leighton. She isn't the only woman in the world, and you'd find plenty of 'em who'd be just as sweet to you."

"Do you mean Sally's married someone else? She'd never do that unless——"

"Good land, no!" Mrs. Byles cried. "She's single as Tim Dexter's donkey, but you're farther than ever from seeing her or hearing from her. Her brother Steven's in Washington's official family—secre-

tary or something—and she'd no more write a letter to you or receive
one than she'd play with a rattlesnake. It doesn't seem possible, Oliver, but Loyalists are hated more and more with every passing day."

"Yes," I said, "I found that out in the south. It's a hatred that'll
never die in our lifetime or our children's either."

"Then you can't get away from the war, not even for a few
minutes, and you may as well tell me about the south. Where'd you
go, and what happened to you to give you that watchful look?"

I told her briefly, and when I'd finished, Mrs. Byles gave me a
sharp nod that I construed as approval in the manner of Salem
Barrells; but she wasted no words on idle compliments.

"What's in the story they tell at headquarters," she demanded,
"about the rebels being beaten everywhere in the south, so that before we know it Cornwallis'll march all the way to New York with
rebels running like rabbits before him?"

"It's not true," I said. "Cornwallis has won battles; but every time
he wins, he loses men, loses ground and makes a new batch of enemies. If he or anyone else makes one more mistake like those we've
seen made, he'll *lose* a battle, and that'll be the end of him and of a
good part of the Loyalists in the Carolinas."

Mrs. Byles looked grimly triumphant. "I knew it! What do you
think'll happen to those Loyalists?"

"Some'll be killed," I told her, "and some'll escape by swearing
they're rebels. I heard talk among the South Carolina men that if the
worst came to the worst, a couple of Loyalist regiments might be able
to capture the Bahamas from the Spaniards—in which case the
southern Loyalists could move to those islands."

"Exactly!" Mrs. Byles said. "They'll have to look out for themselves, just as they will here. Those idiots at headquarters can't understand what's happening, even though they see as many Loyalists pouring into New York today as poured in a year ago today and five years
ago today!

"Belcher knew Englishmen. He said they had a curtain in their
minds, and always drew it down when they were near defeat, or
when something unpleasant happened so close under their noses that
they were afraid the stench might kill 'em. Well, Oliver, they've got
the curtain pulled down as far as it'll go, and I think it means
trouble. I *know* it means trouble!"

"I hope you're wrong," I said.

"So do I," she said, "but I'm not. You say yourself that if there's one more mistake in the south, that'll be the end of the Loyalists in that section. That history you wrote in London pointed out the dreadful messes Englishmen made of battles, of campaigns, of government, of understanding Americans. You know the English can't help making mistakes, just as Americans can't help sticking their noses into other people's lives and trying to regulate 'em."

"That proves nothing," I said.

"It may not to you," Mrs. Byles said, "but it does to me. Belcher believed the Greek dramatists were right when they held that certain people are destined to a fate over which they have no control. I agree with him. The British destiny is to blunder, Oliver, and ours is to suffer for those blunders."

I agreed with him, too; but I tried to cheer Mrs. Byles by murmuring that God had better things to do than to bother with little human atoms like us.

"Belcher was right," Mrs. Byles insisted. "The Greeks knew what they were talking about. Never a day passes that the city isn't more crowded with Loyalists than it was the day before. The rebels won't have 'em. The British won't look out for 'em. They never have enough to eat. The British won't understand they'll have more Loyalists on their hands tomorrow; more the day after; more next month, next year. The rebels won't stop fighting, and the British won't stop fighting, and between the two the Loyalists have no choice but starvation, penury and ruin."

"Perhaps things will be better," I said.

"No, they'll be worse," Mrs. Byles said, "and you know it! Well, I'm not going to stand it! I won't submit to Destiny! It takes more than Destiny and a lot of sour-faced rebels to whip a Salem Barrell! I made up my mind months ago that if ever you came back from the south, you'd have to look out for me—yes, and for Henrietta and all the other Loyalists who'll otherwise have to die just because men insist on fighting wars, making mistakes and keeping everybody in trouble when there's no earthly reason for it."

"I'm afraid you forget," I reminded her, "that Buell and I have been told to raise men for the King's American Dragoons. I have to do as I'm ordered."

"Listen, Oliver," Mrs. Byles said. "Every high officer in the British Army comes to this tavern! Clinton owes me for four hundred dinners, thirty-six cases of wine and five dozen of the best Caledonian golf balls! Can Clinton refuse to listen to me? No indeed! And can he forever say No to all my suggestions? He cannot and he has not! That's why your friend Colonel Edward Winslow is mustermaster general of His Majesty's Provincial Forces. That's why your friend Ward Chipman is deputy mustermaster general. And that's why you're going to be the chief adviser and judge advocate general to His Majesty's mustermaster, and work for Henrietta and me and all the Loyalists."

"Am I?" I asked her. "What'll I do for 'em?"

"Get 'em out of these thirteen colonies, Oliver."

"Get 'em all out?" I said, and smiled at her wanly.

She didn't smile. "If you don't get us out, or if somebody doesn't, we're doomed," she said.

"Doomed's a hard word, Mrs. Byles."

"Yes," she said. "So we're all going to find out. 'Doomed' won't be the half of it!"

It was almost like being at home again to work with Colonel Winslow and Ward Chipman, those two old friends from Boston. Our quarters were on the top floor of Mrs. Byles' Silver Mackerel; and from that central point we rode out every day to count the sick and the well among the troops, regulars, Loyalists and Germans, who were quartered all over Long Island and Staten Island. Three nights a week Buell rode in to see Henrietta Dixon and give us the news from the camp where he, Nathan Dixon and the six Carolinians who had come with us from Charleston were rounding up good Loyalists and swearing them into the King's American Dragoons—that cavalry regiment that was to earn the unbounded admiration of the Prince of Wales.

Whenever we were together, Mrs. Byles' conversation invariably came around to what Colonel Winslow called her Great Delusion —the need of establishing a colony where Loyalists could live in peace after the war.

At first we didn't take her seriously; but after Clinton had made his mistakes, we wondered how a Salem Barrell could have been so conservative.

CHAPTER XCI

I<small>T WAS</small> early in August that Clinton made the first of his
series of mistakes that preceded Yorktown.

I was awakened before dawn on that distressing day by Mrs. Byles,
who had taken the time to put on her little white lace cap and her
black mitts, but had neglected to don a petticoat over her striped
flannel nightgown. "Don't waste any time getting dressed, Oliver,"
she urged. "This is important! I want you to hear a report from a
man who's got to get away from here before sun-up."

The man proved to be a resident of Newport. Mrs. Byles had him
hidden in her upstairs sitting room, and when I came to her, she
didn't even tell me his name. All she said was, "I vouch for this man's
information, Oliver. He's been here before. You've got to memorize
what he says."

The man might have been a fisherman, for he smelt of fish as
though a quintal of lightly salted hake had been dried upon him;
but his voice was that of an educated man.

"Go ahead," Mrs. Byles told him. "Tell the whole story to Captain
Wiswell, and he'll see it reaches General Clinton this morning."

"Be sure it does," the man said. "If you waste any time, you'll regret
it. The French Army's on the march from Newport to join Washington. Washington's going to cross the Hudson from Jersey with two
thousand men and meet the French at Kingsbridge, fourteen miles
north of New York. There's four thousand French, and they're
marching in separate regiments by different roads. About ten miles
from their objective, they figure on coming together in a single
column and marching as a brigade to Kingsbridge. Their baggage
wagons are being drawn by oxen, so they can't move fast."

He stopped and looked at me.

"What else?" I asked.

"You don't need anything else," the man said. "That's enough!"

"Who's in command?" I asked. "The artillery isn't moving with that column, is it?"

"Rochambeau's in command," he said. "He's with 'em, and his artillery, and everything else!" He laughed excitedly. "I guess we've got 'em this time!"

He went to the window and cautiously raised the shade. A smoky pinkness was reflected in the glassy water of the East River, and the hulks of the prison ships were black silhouettes against the faint glow. Without a word to either of us, the man drew down the shade, turned from the window, hurried to the door and disappeared.

Mrs. Byles drew a deep breath. "Maybe I've been wrong all the time, Oliver! Maybe Clinton's done right to keep so many men in New York, perfectly protected. Put on your clothes! I'll get your breakfast, and you can eat while you're crossing the river. Clinton's got to have this news before he starts another headache to cure the one he got last night."

There was a sentry pacing up and down in front of the brick houses at the lower end of Broadway, and there were two more across the street in the shady green park on which those handsome mansions faced. When I ran up the steps of No. 1 Broadway, the sentry slapped the butt of his musket and said hoarsely, "Here, here! What's your business at this hour?"

The two sentries across the street moved out from among the trees and stood staring at me.

"I'm Captain Wiswell, King's American Dragoons," I said. "I've got to see General Clinton on a matter of vital military importance."

"You'll have to state your business at the side door, Captain," the sentry said. "Those are orders. Anybody that pounds on that front door before seven o'clock wakes up everybody in this house as well as everybody in General Arnold's house next door."

He went with me to the side entrance, and after repeated pullings at a bell succeeded in raising a servant who eventually—and reluctantly—routed out the same major I'd seen the last time I attempted to call on Clinton. He was sleepy-eyed, half-dressed, and had, I was sure, a tongue like sandpaper from dallying with the bottle the night before. When I told him I had important information for Clinton that I must deliver in person, the major yawned openly and in a voice hoarse with sleep flatly refused to let me see the general unless I first proved that my information was important.

"Well," I said, "it's about the French Army. It's on the march."

"Damnation," the major said, "you didn't get me out of bed for that, did you? Is that all you have to tell the general?"

"All!" I protested. "Isn't that enough?"

"But he knows it already," the major said. "The general's had similar information from two other sources."

"He has?" I asked. "Are you sure? He's sent out no troops to attack 'em, or I'd have heard of it."

"Don't worry your head about attacks," the major said. "We'll take care of all that."

I knew as soon as he spoke that Clinton wasn't planning any attack. "I don't believe the general could have got the same information I did," I said. "The French are joining the rebels only fourteen miles out of New York. Why, the general could cut 'em to pieces. You've got to let me see him, Major! I don't dare leave here until I'm sure he knows he's caught the whole French Army in a decidedly precarious position."

The major gave me a smile that I could only interpret as contemptuous. "Certainly, Captain, if it'll make you feel any better; but you'll have to come around again at a civilized hour." He yawned almost ostentatiously.

His lack of understanding, his stubborn stupidity, were purely sickening. Into my mind came the advice General Arnold gave Buell and me before we started for Virginia—the advice to move fast in war—never to delay. What, I wondered, would he have said to this lout of a major, with his yawns and his talk about civilized hours!

In the same moment another thought struck me. I could have kicked myself. "What a fool you are!" I thought, and in my elation I spoke my thought aloud.

The major abruptly ceased to yawn. "Sir!" he said haughtily.

"No, no," I said, almost incoherent from eagerness to be gone. "You misunderstood me! I was speaking of myself! I'll come back at a more civilized hour, as you so kindly suggest."

General Arnold, the sentry had said, lived next door to Clinton. When I ran from the side door, the same sentry stood there as if expecting to be summoned to deal with a dangerous intruder.

"General Clinton's not up," I told him. "I want to see General Arnold. Will you take me to *his* side door?"

He led me out onto Broadway, past the fronts of Clinton's and Arnold's houses, on whose curtained basement windows the shadows of our heads danced grotesquely in the level rays of the newly risen sun. The two sentries across the street came over from the park and watched us enter the alleyway.

"What's the matter with them?" I asked my escort. "Do they think I'm a spy or a rebel?"

"It's on account of him," he whispered, jerking a thumb toward Arnold's house. "We've got orders to take no chances. The rebels'll pay £10,000 for him, so we watch everyone, no matter who."

The side door of Arnold's house stood open, with a minnow net hung before it to keep out flies; and when the sentry rapped, a Negro woman servant pushed the net to one side and peered at us with eyes as round as candy balls.

"Caller for the general, Sukey," the sentry said. "I'll wait."

The Negress vanished, and I heard Arnold's high-pitched voice. "Bring him in! I'll see him here! Tell him I'm short-tempered in the morning. He's to state his business quick and get it over with! Do as I say now, Sukey! No stammering and stuttering!"

The dining room to which Sukey led me was all mahogany and white and silver. At the end of the slender-legged dining table sat General Arnold, coatless, his fine white cambric shirt heavily ruffled at throat and wrists. He stared at me sardonically over the top of an enormous silver coffee urn. "Well," he said, "so you're back! Back and in trouble—serious trouble too, or you'd never be coming to see me at this time of day."

"No, sir," I said, "I'm not in trouble. I came over from Brooklyn with a message for General Clinton, but I can't get word to him. It's important, General, but he won't see me. I've got to give him this information. I wouldn't presume to intrude if I hadn't remembered what you said to Colonel Simcoe aboard the *Pendrith* last December. You told him how Governor Tryon's expedition would have been wholly destroyed if he'd delayed another half-hour."

"Yes, yes," Arnold said. "I remember! Glad you did, too. Let me get this straight. Weren't you sent over here by Benjamin Thompson to look into the Convention Army? Didn't you hold a commission in the King's American Dragoons?"

"Yes, sir."

"I asked about you," Arnold said, "but nobody knew how you'd made out. Have you reported to Thompson in person?"

"No, sir. General Clinton wanted me here to help raise the Dragoons. He said there was no occasion for me to go to England when men were so needed for the defense of New York. So he put me in the mustermaster general's department."

"That's good army logic," Arnold said. "Sit down, Captain. Have some coffee and tell me what's on your mind." He poured a cup and passed it to me.

"It's the French, sir. They're——"

"How do you know?" Arnold asked.

"The mustermaster general's quartered in Mrs. Byles' tavern in Brooklyn," I said, "and I'm living there too. I got my information through Mrs. Byles. I worked with her in France."

"So I've heard," Arnold said. "Go ahead, Captain. What about the French Army?"

"It's moving, sir. It's forming a junction with Washington's army at Kingsbridge."

Arnold jumped up. His chair slid across the room and struck the wall with a clatter. "Sukey," he shouted, "get my coat and hat!"

He rested his hands on the table and looked up at me, putting me in mind of a hawk, hunched and waiting for prey. "They're not going by transport?" he asked.

"No, sir," I said; "by land, all of 'em—infantry, artillery, Rochambeau, everybody. They're taking different routes until they get ten miles from Kingsbridge, then uniting in a single column."

"How's their baggage going?"

"By ox cart, sir."

Sukey appeared at his elbow with a cocked hat, all gold lace, and a scarlet jacket heavily frogged with blue and gold.

He clapped the hat on his head and started for the door, struggling into the jacket as he went. "Come along, Captain," he said. "I want you as a witness."

He went limpingly along the hall, jerked open the front door and ran down the steps. Flapping his hand at the sentries who snapped noisily to attention at sight of him, he darted up the steps of Clinton's house like a woodchuck popping into a hole, rattled the knob, pounded the knocker, and beat a lively tattoo with his knuckles on the green-painted panels. When the door was slowly opened by the same sleepy servant who had admitted me, he slipped in like an eel and beckoned me after him.

"Go wake the general," he told the servant. "Don't bring an aide or I'll have you scalped! Here!"

He fished in his fob pocket, brought out a coin and rapped it smartly against the servant's striped weskit. "Tell him it's important! If he orders you off, keep tight hold of this, and tell him again it's important. Tell him General Arnold says it's *damned* important!"

He pressed the coin into the servant's hand and gave him a quick push toward the stair.

Then he led me into a front room, drew aside the shades, still closed from the night before, and propped himself on the window ledge to take his weight off his bad leg.

"What did you find in the south?" he asked. "What did you hear about Cornwallis' army?"

"I saw Stedman at York," I said. "He says Cornwallis is going to take post there. He doesn't like it. He says Washington's planning to march his whole army down into Virginia and try to corner the whole Southern Army."

"What makes him think so?" Arnold demanded.

"Lafayette," I said. "Lafayette was badly beaten when he tried to catch Cornwallis in the rear, and Stedman says Lafayette's honor was so badly shaken up that it'll have to be repaired by his persuading Washington to come to Virginia and capture Cornwallis. Then Lafayette'll feel honorable again. Stedman says Washington can't resist the young man."

Arnold shook his fist at me. "He's right, by God! Lafayette can get anything he wants out of Washington! And he's right about York too. That's the last place in the world Cornwallis ought to pick!" Grumbling contemptuously beneath his breath, he abandoned the window ledge to limp up and down the room.

Overhead a door opened and closed. On the stair I heard the hesitant, heavy step of a man whose feet hurt. It was Clinton, and when he came in I felt only pity for one who, I was certain, was making a mess of everything he touched.

Because he hadn't shaved, his puffy face looked soiled. His wig, clapped on in a hurry, must have been the one he'd worn the night before, for it was elaborately dressed, ribboned and powdered, and didn't go well with the dressing gown he'd thrown around his chubby figure. He looked less like a general than like a fat, tired, old woman.

"My deepest regrets, General," Arnold said. "Only a situation of the utmost urgency would have made me call at this hour."

Clinton dismissed Arnold's apology with the wave of a fat hand. "Never doubted it for a moment, General! Knew you'd have the best of reasons. Pray proceed." He cast a quick glance at me, and in it I saw resentment at my presence.

Arnold saw it too. "Captain Wiswell brought the news," he explained, "and I wanted him here in case I needed to refer to him for details. General, we've caught 'em at last! We can destroy the French and Washington at one blow, and that'll be the end of it."

Clinton snorted. "Oh, so that's it! Why, I had word of that yesterday, General."

"You knew Rochambeau was marching from Newport to join Washington?" Arnold asked.

Clinton hitched his dressing gown higher on his protuberant little stomach, a sign that he considered the interview at an end, and wished to leave the room. "Certainly, General," Clinton said. "In fact, I think I've already heard it from two sources. We can't let ourselves be drawn out by these reports, General, as you must well understand! They'd like nothing better than to get us out in the open and cut us off."

Arnold limped over to a map on the wall, peered at it hard; then turned to face the dumpy little figure in its dowdy dressing gown and elaborate white wig.

"General," he said slowly, "they've put their heads in a noose! This information's vouched for by Mrs. Byles, and she hasn't made a mistake yet. Those four thousand French troops are moving separately. They're uniting ten miles from Kingsbridge, where they'll meet Washington. Their baggage moves with 'em, and by ox team. Ox team, General! That means they'll be moving like cold molasses. You can wreck the whole column with one sharp thrust. They'll be so tangled with their oxen that they'll tie themselves in knots when you attack!"

Clinton shook his head. "There's no reason why they should move their baggage by ox team, my dear General. It's a trap!"

"Never!" Arnold said. "Those rebels around Newport are just turning an honest penny out of their oxen. The French can't help themselves. Even if they could talk English the Newporters would

skin 'em! Listen to me, General! I know that country like a book!
I've fought all over it! I know every road and path and watercourse
and creek in it! I know exactly where their columns'll unite. It'll be
right here." He rapped his finger against the map.

"It's too long a chance, General," Clinton protested.

"It's not!" Arnold shouted. "It's a certainty! Look: here's where
Rochambeau's men will unite, ten miles from Kingsbridge." He
rapped his finger against the line of the Hudson River. "Here's where
Washington'll come over from Jersey with his two thousand men to
meet Rochambeau at Kingsbridge. Let me try it, General! I'll destroy
both of 'em."

"My dear General," Clinton protested, "I can't even think of such
a thing! Those dispatches that we captured showed clearly that
Washington intends to attack this city. I can't run the risk of weakening the garrison."

Arnold wasn't a tall man. Ordinarily I should have said that he
and Clinton were about the same height. Yet it suddenly seemed to
me that Arnold towered over Clinton, and his already swarthy face
swelled and darkened, as if surging emotion within him struggled
to be free.

"Those dispatches were a trick, General," he cried. "They were
meant to fall into your hands, so you'd keep your whole force inside
the city and leave Washington free to do as he pleases!"

Clinton's pudgy face had the same squinty, obstinate look I'd seen
on a pig's when a farmer was trying to get him across a stile. "I'm
sorry I can't agree with you, General Arnold. Washington's preparing
to attack either New York or Staten Island in a final attempt to drive
us out."

"No," Arnold cried, "no!" He picked up a chair by the back rail
and banged it down on the floor to emphasize his words. "I say it's
not possible! Now for God's sake, listen! You've got twenty-four
thousand troops in this city, General, and Washington and the French
together won't have six thousand. You've got between twenty and
thirty warships in the harbor, with nothing to oppose those ships
but a French fleet that Washington and the French keep mentioning
in dispatches at the top of their lungs. But it's not here yet. Nobody
knows where it is! It's no good to Washington till it gets here, and it
is not here! Even if that French fleet weren't a phantom, this city
would be impenetrable. You've built so many forts and batteries,
made so many redoubts, pulled down so many country houses, cut so

many canals through their gardens, chopped down so many orchards that ten times the number of rebels could be successfully repulsed. I tell you Washington's fooling you! If you let him make this junction with the French, I know exactly what he'll do! He'll make a few little feints, and then some dark night he'll turn tail and run down into Virginia like a scared rabbit! For the love of God, General——"

Clinton smiled faintly and without warmth. "We're obliged to deal with facts, my dear General. We can't let our imagination run away with us in times like these."

"Imagination!" Arnold shouted. "Why charge me with using my imagination? I say Washington doesn't dare attack this city because you've got five times as many men and five times as many ships. That's not imagination! That's the simple truth!"

Again Clinton hitched his dressing gown around him. "I've given this careful consideration, General. My plans are made."

"Then change 'em!" Arnold urged. "Here's a chance you may never have again—a chance to strike at the heart and the head of both the French and the rebels while they're on the move and unable to get reinforcements. We've never attacked whom we should or when we should, and now we can do both! The French are weak; the rebels hate 'em! The French get good pay, good food and good clothes, and the rebels don't. They're ripe for defeat! Let me have the Loyalist regiments, General, and two of the regiments of regulars you're holding in the city. Let me take my own American Legion, DeLancey's Third Battalion, the First and Third New Jersey Volunteers, the Loyal Americans, the Guides and Pioneers! Give me the Seventeenth Dragoons and two infantry regiments in addition, and I'll guarantee to chop Rochambeau's troops to hash! They'll never make that junction with Washington!"

"My dear General," Clinton protested, "your suggestion's fantastic!"

"What in God's name's fantastic about it?" Arnold cried. "I tell you I can cut those two forces to pieces before they know what's hit 'em. There's nothing on earth that could keep me from surprising those French troops—burning their baggage and artillery—hamstringing their horses and oxen before the head of the column could come to their relief."

Clinton shook his head. "My mind's made up."

"Then for God's sake unmake it," Arnold said. "The whole rebel government's on the verge of disintegrating. A blow such as I propose would make 'em accept peace on any terms! The rebel army's short of provisions. Washington can't get food for his men unless he seizes it! Half his regiments are ready to mutiny from lack of pay! The rebel navy's gone—only two vessels left. The amount of public property and stores I destroyed in Virginia has bankrupted the rebel cause! They're sick of the war, sick of the French, sick of the thought of the future! Now's the time, General! I can end this rebellion tomorrow!"

Clinton just shook his head.

Arnold drew a deep breath and spoke more calmly. "You're an old friend, Sir Henry. I know you won't mind if I take a seat. This damned leg——"

"Dear me," Clinton said. "Oh, by all means, General! I fear I've been thoughtless." He made abrupt, birdlike movements; then perched on the edge of a chair, looking like a fat, white hen.

"I'm going to make just one more plea, General," Arnold said. "Your father was governor of this province. You spent your boyhood here. You're almost as much of an American as Cruger or DeLancey or any of us. You don't want to see this country handed over to riffraff who'll hand it over to the French! You don't want to see it lost forever to England any more than the rest of us do. But that's what'll happen if you don't seize this opportunity. If Washington tricks you and goes marching down into Virginia, the French fleet'll join him! You'll be sitting here while Washington and the French corner Cornwallis on that sandspit of his! You'll both be helpless and he'll have to surrender! Then you'll be bottled up in New York with no force anywhere near to help you. Your two years of work in the south will have gone to pot, and you'll be responsible! You'll have lost the campaign for yourself; you'll have lost the war for the helpless thousands of Loyalists in the south and for all the other thousands of Loyalists who still live in fear and trembling in the north. For God's sake, Sir Henry, don't abandon all these good people without a fight! That's my final plea, and it's from the heart."

Clinton cleared his throat and rose fussily to his feet. "I'm afraid I can't agree with you," he said. "You're unnecessarily apprehensive."

Arnold stared at him. His swarthy face seemed to swell and became darkly knobby. Then he made Clinton an abrupt bow, and limped from the room without another word.

When we were on the street, Arnold gave me a look of droll disgust. "Make notes of the conversation as you recall it, Captain, and let me have them. And don't feel too disappointed. You did your best. Fortunes of war, you know!"

He winked at me, putting me in mind of gay young Lord Rawdon, and limped up the steps of his house as if he'd never known a disappointment in his life.

That day I wholeheartedly went over to Mrs. Byles' way of thinking, and joined with her in preaching the need of a land to which Loyalists could go to escape the persecution of rebels and the mismanagement of the English.

CHAPTER XCII

Never a hand was raised to keep Rochambeau and Washington from joining forces fourteen miles out of New York. There they stayed for two weeks, while Clinton with a vastly superior force watched them cautiously from behind trenches, canals, and barricades. Then, one dark night, they stole across the Hudson and went pelting off for Virginia and Cornwallis' army.

A week later Buell, with his rapidly growing King's American Dragoons, rode into Brooklyn as an escort for two hundred and fifty Loyalists, most of them Connecticut and Rhode Island merchants and their wives and children.

He arranged to have them transported from Brooklyn to New York, sent his men back to Huntington, then came hurrying to the Silver Mackerel. No longer, we found, did he scoff at Mrs. Byles' Great Delusion.

"Half those New Londoners," he told Mrs. Byles, "were shipowners, and they've got ideas like you. They think Loyalists ought to go somewhere. They said the best place was Minas Basin. Ever hear of the Minas Basin? Some call it Acadia. That's where those French people lived that got driven away from their homes by the English twenty years ago. They say——"

"Just a moment, Buell," Mrs. Byles said. "How'd you get hold of all those Loyalists? What makes you so interested in Minas Basin all of a sudden?"

"Ain't you heard what happened to Arnold's expedition against New London?" Buell asked.

"We've heard nothing," I said, "except that Clinton sent Arnold to New London with three regiments of regulars and all the Loyalist troops to destroy stores and privateers, hoping Washington might be stopped from going south."

"Well, he destroyed plenty, but he didn't stop anything," Buell said. "Now there's hell to pay!"

"Because of what he did?" Mrs. Byles asked.

"Yes, and because of what the rebels claim he did! Near as I could get it from those Loyalists I brought in, Arnold took Loyalist troops ashore on the New London side of the river to capture the main fort. The other half—New Jersey Volunteers and the two regiments of regulars—he sent to capture the fort opposite the town. Those Loyalist troops of Arnold's shot and clubbed their way into New London, tougher than wildcats. Arnold occupied it and set his men to destroying all rebel stores in the place; then climbed up on a roof and looked across the river. That fort on the far bank was stronger than he'd figured on, so he sent word to the rest of his troops to let it alone. The messenger hadn't any more than started when the attack began; and it was a terror. The attackers told the rebels to surrender, but they said they'd defend the fort to the last man. Our people said 'All right: if that's the way you want it, that's how you'll get it'; and they attacked. They couldn't find any way into the place except through the cannon ports, so they went for the ports. While they were climbing through, the rebels hacked hell out of 'em with spontoons and axes. When they finally *did* get in, they were so mad they set out to kill everyone in sight and damned near did. Served the rebels right, too, if you ask me! If you talk about fighting to the last man, you ought to do it or take what you get.

"Well, the rebels blamed every dead man on Arnold, though it wasn't his fault they were killed. To make the rebels madder, there was some powder in the warehouses, and it blew up and scattered fires all over the city. Arnold sent men to put 'em out, but they'd got out of hand and couldn't be stopped. Pretty near the whole town burned up, and Arnold got the blame for that, too.

"The rebels say he burned the town and massacred the garrison out of cussedness. They're calling him a murderer and an assassin, and telling everyone that the Loyalists'll murder 'em all if they can. Because of that, all New England's started on the biggest Loyalist hunt they've had yet.

"Every night Loyalists cross the Sound from Connecticut in fishing boats, dories and punts, and the rebels chase 'em in whaleboats. That's why we got sent there—to beat off rebel whaleboats so Loyal-

ists could get ashore safe. I've thought up some mighty good ideas,
Oliver. I'm going to dress Lonnie Kirkland in women's clothes and
put him in a whaleboat with a nice six-pounder hidden under a
parasol. I'll have more fun shooting rebels than I could shooting
coot."

He saluted Mrs. Byles. "You had it right all the time, ma'am.
There's been so many lies told about us that we'll never be able to
do business with rebels as long as we live. Trouble with your idea
about getting land on the St. John River, ma'am, is that it's too far
from the ocean. Now you take this country around the Minas
Basin——"

"I'll take none of it," Mrs. Byles said sharply. "Near the ocean,
indeed! I've heard my father say Nova Scotia's so far out to the eastward that you can make blancmange out of a Nova Scotia fog by
adding vanilla to it! That's why Nova Scotians have blue noses,
Buell—the fog gives 'em damp skins and makes their circulation
poor."

That was my first experience with the arguments that were to
become so bitter, embroil thousands of Loyalists, and profoundly
affect the course of my life.

Almost the worst of Clinton's mistakes was his failure to send reinforcements to Cornwallis. With Washington on the way to Virginia
with his entire army of twenty-one thousand men, and Cornwallis
penned up in Yorktown with a mere five thousand behind hastily
constructed earthen walls, even Clinton understood that he must do
something to correct the blunder he'd made when he let Washington
escape him.

From Colonel Winslow we learned that Clinton had received an
urgent request for reinforcements from Cornwallis, and that Clinton
had promised to send him the whole fleet and seven thousand of his
best troops.

"He's even set the day," Winslow said. "He's promised Cornwallis
that the fleet'll sail by the fifth of October."

Mrs. Byles eyed him cynically. "Edward," she said, "I've seen you
and Ward Chipman going to those woman-jockey horse races at the
race track yonder, and I'll wager you lay many a bet on 'em, like all
the other officers in this army. No doubt you act like the rest of 'em—
bet on the jockey that's prettiest."

"Well," Winslow admitted, "I may have——"

"Listen, Edward," Mrs. Byles interrupted. "There's nothing in this world harder to win on than horse races. Why people waste money on 'em when they could use Clinton, I'm blessed if I know!"

Winslow looked baffled. "Use Clinton?"

"Certainly," Mrs. Byles said impatiently. "There isn't a soul in New York that isn't all wrapped up in what Clinton means to do! All the Loyalists shiver from head to foot for fear he won't get to Yorktown in time! Every rebel sympathizer—if you can find one—is shaking all over for fear he will! Why don't you turn an honest penny, Edward? You're going to need all you can get when you reach the St. John River! You can lay seven to five that Clinton won't sail when he says he will!"

Colonel Winslow shook his head. "I don't like the odds! He's sworn he'd sail by the fifth. He might tell the truth for once! It's too chancy."

"Chancy!" Mrs. Byles cried. "And you bet on horses ridden by women jockeys!"

She turned to me. "Go see Buell, Oliver! Take him all my money and all yours, too. Tell him to bet it two to one that Clinton won't get away from New York in time to help Cornwallis!"

There were twenty thousand people on the tip of New York island on the morning of October fifth—the day Clinton was supposed to sail to relieve Cornwallis. There they stayed all day, a nervous and unhappy multitude.

All through the late morning and the afternoon the tide ran strongly out, and the transports and men-o'-war lay there straining at their cables, yawing a little from the thrust of the river current against their bows.

Late in the afternoon the cables eased and the transports and men-o'-war floated idly on the slack tide, headed every which way. Then the tide started in, and their opportunity to sail was gone. Clinton had run true to form; and Mrs. Byles, Buell and I were richer by three hundred guineas.

Not until the nineteenth of October did Clinton finally sail to relieve Cornwallis. Word of the sailing had flashed through the city and across to Long Island; and again people had gathered to see the fleet go out on the mission that meant so much to all of us. They were packed in the green park that sloped from the fort at the water's edge, crowded along the batteries and the grassy acres that flanked the main fort on either side; and all that mass of people was as silent as though they watched a funeral.

I think disasters must cast shadows into the brains and feelings of distant sympathizers; and I think that was why we were all so gloomy and so silent on the day Clinton sailed; for on that very day was happening the worst and stupidest of all that six-year-long series of calamities.

Cornwallis, lacking the reinforcements that Clinton had promised him, was forced to surrender, and by the terms of the surrender he made every Loyalist in his army—every Loyalist in America—a man without a country.

We learned the details on the last day of October, when the *Bonetta* sloop came in from Yorktown.

In some strange way the city knew what she was and whence she'd come while she still was on her way up the harbor.

When I reached the Battery, it seemed to me that every army and navy officer in the city, every merchant and all the thousands of Loyalists in New York were packed along the waterfront to see the *Bonetta's* boat row up to the government wharf.

I thought my eyes were playing tricks when I was able to distinguish faces in the *Bonetta's* boat; for Stedman was one of them; so was Captain Phillips of the Queen's Rangers, that Yale classmate of mine who had been so impressed at Buell's horse-stowing; and I saw, too, several of the young Loyalist officers I'd met when we went south with Arnold's expedition to Richmond.

I heard their story that night when Stedman and the other Loyalist officers from the *Bonetta* came to the Silver Mackerel to arrange with Colonel Winslow about quartering their troops.

Colonel Winslow brought his maps to Mrs. Byles' parlor on the second floor, and for a time Stedman and the dozen officers from the Queen's Rangers and Tarleton's Legion discussed likely localities for camps, while Mrs. Byles, Henrietta Dixon, Ward Chipman, Buell and I mixed punch.

The one thing on which Stedman, Phillips and the others insisted was that their regiments be placed as far as possible from British officers.

"You better come up along the Sound, where my King's American Dragoons are stationed," Buell said. "Up there you can have a fight with rebels in a whaleboat almost any night you want to, and British officers never bother to go that far from New York."

Colonel Winslow nodded approval. "There's nothing like chasing a hundred rebels in whaleboats to get your mind off yourself. Tomorrow, if you'd like, we can ride up toward the Sound and look for locations."

"Tomorrow won't do," Captain Phillips said. "We've got to get our men off the *Bonetta* first thing in the morning, before they have trouble with the British."

He explained that when Cornwallis surrendered, he was forced to sign a capitulation that gave protection to the captured British troops, but ignored all Loyalists. "In other words," Phillips explained, "if the Legion and the Rangers had fallen into rebel hands, they could all have been shot, officers and men too!"

Mrs. Byles looked triumphant. "Just one more proof that if Loyalists don't look out for themselves, nobody else will!"

"You never said a truer word, ma'am," Stedman said. "Do you know why Clinton didn't sail to our relief when he promised to? It was because he lacked the gumption to persuade the admiral to sail! If he'd been any kind of general, he'd have persuaded the admiral with a club! British admirals are so busy fighting over prize money that they forget they're fighting a war with a continent as a stake! Half the officers in the fleet were against going south at all, because if they got chopped up in a battle, they'd have to stop cruising for prizes."

"If we'd been allowed to look out for ourselves," Phillips said, "we'd have been all right. Simcoe's Rangers and Tarleton's Legion asked permission to cut their way through the combined French and rebel army and make a dash for New York. Cornwallis wouldn't agree. He packed all Loyalist troops in Yorktown into the *Bonetta* and sent 'em to New York; and by the terms of the capitulation we're all traitors, to be dealt with as traitors if captured."

Mrs. Byles leaned forward. "Have you thought what you'll do when the war's over? Even if you win, those with rebel sympathies will keep right on saying you're traitors. They'll hate you forever. The moment your regiments disband, they'll make life hell for you. They'll burn your barns, trample your crops, break down your fences, drive off your cattle! I don't need to tell you! You know 'em!"

"Yes," Captain Phillips said. "We know 'em."

"Of course," Mrs. Byles went on, "you could go to England. With good fortune you'd be on half-pay, but the English wouldn't exactly take you in. You'd be neither fish nor flesh nor good red herring— neither English nor American. And you'd have to leave your men behind, to get along as best they could."

"That's out of the question," Phillips said. "We're going to stick with our men. We've thought some of going to West Florida and living under Spanish rule, but we hear the Spaniards don't want us."

"Edward," Mrs. Byles said to Colonel Winslow, "let me see that map of Nova Scotia and the mainland."

When the colonel put it before her, she rapped the ferrule of her stick on the long and narrow bay between the southern end of Nova Scotia and the northern part of Maine. "There's what my father called the prettiest country in the world. My father was a Salem Barrell and like all us Barrells he had an unerring eye for a bargain and for beauty, whether in land, ships, architecture, or furniture. Still, I don't ask you to take his word for it. Other men thought just as he did.

"Just after the Old French War, a Ranger captain named Benjamin Glasier interested a lot of influential gentlemen in Boston and New York in a colonizing venture. He'd fought in Nova Scotia, and he claimed the St. John River was the richest, handsomest and emptiest land in North America. He formed the St. John River Associates with such men as my father, Governor Hutchinson, Oliver DeLancey, Frederick DePeyster; and the upshot was that almost the whole valley of the St. John River was granted to 'em on the condition that they send settlers to their lands, clear the forests and plant the fields.

"Well, gentlemen: they haven't done it. The proprietors have been busy with other things during the last few years. Most of 'em haven't a penny. The few settlers that went to the St. John River have been driven out by rebel privateers. All that land—the best land in the world—can be escheated. If the right men, like Colonel Winslow and Ward Chipman, make the proper representations to London, we can get all that land for the Loyalists."

"My, my!" Buell said. "Why didn't I learn the possibilities of this escheating business when I was younger! Think of being able to escheat somebody out of a country just made to order. Every other place is full of people other people can't get along with. Look at Halifax: full of Nova Scotians! Look at France: crowded with Frenchmen! Look at England: no matter where you go in England, you can't get away from Englishmen. But we'll have the St. John River to ourselves!"

Colonel Winslow rubbed his hands together. "Each regiment should have its own town. Then they'd work together."

"But how'll we buy the land?" Phillips asked.

"They'll give it to us!" Mrs. Byles said. "England's spent fortunes sending out colonies in the past. This'll be the best of all, with first-rate soldiers in it, and officers as experienced as any on the regular establishment, and bishops, supreme court judges, attorney generals, college presidents, shipowners, ship captains all ready to hand. It'll be a province settled by the best, sanest and loyalest people America ever produced."

Then and there we toasted Mrs. Byles and the St. John River, and laid the plans that resulted in the Province of New Brunswick of which Colonel Winslow was to become a supreme court judge, and Ward Chipman solicitor general.

CHAPTER XCIII

W<small>HEN</small> I hear persons say that the American Revolution ended with the surrender of Cornwallis at Yorktown, I know certain things about those persons. I know they weren't in the army, weren't Loyalists, didn't live in parts of the country where the war was fought, and didn't care much about learning or telling the truth.

The army surrendered by Cornwallis was the Southern Army, perhaps one tenth of the combined Loyalist and British forces in America. The main army of over twenty thousand men, under Clinton, held New York, Long Island and Staten Island; while Rawdon and Cruger, with a force of Loyalist cavalry and infantry that I still believe to be without a peer, occupied Charleston and the country around it. General Prevost, with another two thousand men, held Savannah secure against rebel attacks. There was no way in which the rebels could dislodge those three forces.

What was going on in Charleston and Savannah, we didn't know during the winter after Cornwallis surrendered; but those of us on Long Island and in New York were under no delusions. For us the war didn't end when Cornwallis surrendered, any more than a thunderstorm is over when a house is struck by lightning.

The violence of that whaleboat war in Long Island Sound seemed never to abate. Night after night, in good weather and bad, fleets of rebel whaleboats stole stealthily in to attack our forts at Huntington and Lloyds Neck, steal our supplies and kidnap Loyalists, and the battles that followed were ferocious.

I've heard a mass of rebel lies about those forts of ours at Huntington, Brookhaven and Lloyds Neck, that were so watchfully manned by the King's American Dragoons, the Queen's Rangers and De-

Lancey's Battalions. The truth is that they were the only protection of the Loyalists from Connecticut and Rhode Island, who had been driven from their homes by bitter persecution. Because of those forts, Loyalists found security, peace and safety on Long Island; and without them they'd have been hunted like animals, thrown into prison or pushed out into the woods to wander until death ended their sufferings.

The war was so far from over, that winter after Yorktown, that General Clinton proposed to continue it on a grand scale in the spring, and had demanded more men, more ships and more supplies with which to deal a deathblow to Washington. As for the thousands of Loyalists in New York, they were greatly heartened when news reached America of the opening of Parliament by the King, late in November. In his speech he announced that he was resolved to persevere in the defense of his dominions. The losses in America, he said, could all be redeemed if he could have the firm support of Parliament, and a more vigorous, animated and united exertion of the faculties and resources of the people.

Mrs. Byles read that speech to Colonel Winslow, Ward Chipman, Henrietta and me in her private sitting room one bitter-cold January night, and her comments were as sharp as the Long Island wind that rattled the windows in their casements.

"Don't get excited over this fat man's promises," she urged us. "He's a king, it's true, with palaces and a million decorations; but at heart he's just another politician, and no better than anyone else who starts a war. Since people who start wars never fight in 'em, they never know when to stop. The King's been playing with this war for seven years, just the way Belcher's nephews used to play with tin soldiers. Belcher's nephews disturbed the whole house when they did it, because they broke mirrors, frightened the cat and made such a racket you couldn't hear yourself think! The King's just like 'em, only on a grand scale. He's undertaken to put down a rebellion and support those loyal to his government, but he's put down nothing and supported nobody! He's killed thousands of people by bullets, starvation, disease and hatred, and only succeeded in enriching the dishonorable and the dishonest. He's ruined England's trade, reduced the value of every Englishman's investments, had his armies captured, lost the naval superiority that England always bragged about, dismembered his empire, and loaded his people with a burden of taxes that'll make 'em all humpbacks! And still he wants to keep on, like everyone who fights a war from a nice safe place! He wants to keep on spending other people's money to ruin everybody he can coax or drag into supporting his useless war! There's the perfect politician for you—thinking only of himself, and never of us, who suffer from his stubbornness! He wants a more vigorous exertion of our resources, does he? Well, we've given him all our resources; and what few faculties we've got left we'd better exert for ourselves." She turned to Winslow. "Edward, what's the news of your exertions in our behalf?"

"The news," Winslow complained, "is that nobody believes my figures. They just snort when I tell how many Loyalists there are in New York. They know I'm insane when I say thirty-eight thousand Loyalists will migrate to the St. John River, if the land's granted to us. Even the Loyalists think I'm insane! Clinton throws up his hands when I say we'll need a minimum of twenty thousand axes, seventy thousand bushels of corn and other seeds, forty thousand blankets, materials for twelve thousand huts——"

"People never believe anything—except scandal—when they first hear it," Mrs. Byles said calmly. "Keep right on telling 'em. Some day somebody'll believe you, and the belief'll catch hold and spread like fire! What we really need——"

She lapsed into one of her meditative Salem silences, and we were content not to question her, so we didn't learn what we really needed.

I think the truth was, during that miserable winter and spring of 1782, that most of us were so sick of war, so oppressed by discouragements, so disheartened by the pitiful state of the homeless Loyalists— who turned desperately to any officer who'd listen, begging for a little firewood, a few more rations, a bolt of cloth to repair their worn-out clothes—that we'd almost lost the power to question anything. We did what we were told to do, and lived from day to day, as dogs live.

The arrival of warm weather brought confirmation of Mrs. Byles' prediction that Colonel Winslow's preachings would bear fruit. Wherever we turned we heard Loyalists discussing the possibility of escaping rebel violence by going to the St. John River, to Nova Scotia, to the Minas Basin, to Bermuda, to East Florida.

The reason for this sudden change was the realization that peace was at last a probability, that England at last intended to abandon her efforts to put down rebellion, and that the rebels, jubilant at approaching victory, were becoming more ruthless toward Loyalists, instead of more tolerant.

First we had news that the mayor and people of London, fearful of being conquered by France and Spain, had petitioned the King to stop the war and rid himself of the ministers and secret advisers who favored continuing it. To this petition the King refused to listen. Then we heard how, through bad leadership, gross mismanagement of naval affairs, and the stupidity of British governors, West Indian islands had been captured by the French. This, seemingly, was the final blow that made the King listen to reason. There were riots in London against the insane policies of the King and his ministers. Following this, in March, Parliament voted to throw out the old government of Lord North, Sir William Eden, and all the rest of the incompetents who had tried to wage war without the needful brains or preparation, and to replace it with a new government that would promise to make peace with the American rebels and to acknowledge their independence.

And then, in May, came the help for which Mrs. Byles had longed when she had said to Colonel Winslow, "What we really need——"

Clinton, that ill-starred, blundering commander in chief, was ordered back to England and his place taken by a great soldier and administrator, Sir Guy Carleton, who had governed and defended Canada during the war.

And a week after Carleton's arrival in New York, at the end of a warm May day, an astounding thing happened.

Mrs. Byles, Colonel Winslow, Ward Chipman and I were sitting in a corner of the front garden of the Silver Mackerel, making corrections in our estimates of the numbers of women, children and non-combatants who would have to be put under the care of each regiment of Loyalists, when the exodus took place. This had become a weekly duty; for Loyalists continued to pour into New York in horrifying numbers, and men in Loyalist regiments were continually getting married, or being joined by their wives and children after years of separation.

"That land grant for the Orange Rangers' rank and file will have to be increased to ninety thousand acres," Winslow told Chipman.

"You'd better increase the officers' grants in proportion," Mrs. Byles said. "That'll give 'em a little leeway, in case of unexpected additions—and there'll be plenty of additions at the end, never fear!"

While they argued and did sums on scraps of paper and rustled among their pile of documents, I sat idly by, watching the constant movement of ferryboats across the river—black water bugs against the sunset glow.

As one of the boats from New York came closer, I saw it was a glistening white barge, rowed by eight oarsmen in white hats and blue jackets. It was steering straight for the Silver Mackerel's landing stage.

"I think you're having guests from headquarters," I told Mrs. Byles.

She jumped up to look. "I should say I was!" she cried. "That's General Carleton! My stars! I've got to snatch those waiters bald-headed and make sure everything's as it should be."

She surged majestically toward the inn, and I studied this new commander in chief of ours as well as I could in the rosy light of sunset. He put me in mind of General Washington as I'd seen him on that hot, miserable morning at Kip's Bay, for he had the same commanding presence, the same level glance, the same firm mouth and square jaw. He struck me as a more genial man; for he was listening smilingly to one of the officers with him, and even at a distance I could see the amused glint in his eyes.

The speaker was voluble, and each one of the seven or eight officers in the stern of the barge was listening to him with close attention and more than a little pleasure. There was something familiar about the flexible, lisping quality of that voice. It was dramatic and stirring —and in a flash it dawned upon me that the speaker was Benjamin Thompson.

I got up to see him come ashore, and then sat down again, knowing it would never do for a captain to break in on one who was deep in conversation with a commander in chief. Externally he was a different Benjamin Thompson from the man I'd known in Boston and London, for he wore the uniform of a cavalry officer—a lieutenant colonel. His dragoon's helmet shone like gold, and on its front were twined the letters KAD, so that I knew he'd come to America to take command of his regiment, the King's American Dragoons. Was there anything, I wondered, that he'd hesitate to undertake? I wondered, too, whether he'd changed internally as well as externally—whether he'd have any time for a mere captain now that his own rank was so high.

I might have spared myself all such idle speculations. The boat landed the group of officers who, with General Carleton and Thompson leading, walked through the garden and into the inn, so that we perceived they'd made an excursion to the Silver Mackerel for dinner together. Chipman hazarded the explanation that Carleton was making a little entertainment in honor of the great Benjamin Thompson, and that proved to be the case.

Half an hour later Mrs. Byles came back to our table, and with her was Thompson himself.

He seemed truly glad to see us again. "At Mrs. Byles' suggestion the general was kind enough to excuse me from his dinner party for a few minutes," he said. "A great pleasure for me, gentlemen: Oliver —Chip—Ned Winslow! I thought I'd be weeks seeing you, and now here you all are, the first day I come ashore!"

A waiter hurried with a chair for him, but he preferred to stand behind us, one hand on Ward's shoulder and the other on mine: a striking and graceful figure in his scarlet uniform. I somehow felt he was acting the part of a soldier for his own unfathomable purposes.

Mrs. Byles settled herself in her chair and placed her cane on the table, ready to her hand. "For months I've wanted to get my fingers on someone who had good sense and influence, and here he is! Don't waste time, now! Tell him everything before General Carleton begins to whine for him to come back!"

"Did you get my report?" I asked.

"None of that, now," Mrs. Byles warned us.

"Of course I got it," Thompson said. "I got Clinton's warning, too —that I should take the report *cum grano* because you were more interested in the future of the Loyalists than in that of His Majesty's army."

"That's a lie," I protested.

"No, it's not," Mrs. Byles said. "You're interested in what you think is best for this country, just as I am. As long as His Majesty's armed forces uphold us, we'll do everything we can for 'em. You're vitally interested in having 'em successful, and so am I! But when their generals and admirals make idiots of themselves—when they do what's worst for this country—when they abandon us and our friends and our relatives—when they let us be ruined and murdered by those they guaranteed to hold under control—you'll work for your own people rather than for His Majesty's armed forces. Won't you?"

"Yes," I said, "but Clinton was a liar when he said my report should be taken *cum grano*."

Thompson laughed. "I made allowances for Clinton, Oliver; not

for you. It was he that I took *cum grano*. As soon as I got your report,
I knew my days in London were finished. I had to see for myself—
see whether I couldn't help to save something out of the wreckage—
see whether this art of warfare is hedged with the difficulties that
have baffled so many of our great leaders!"

Mrs. Byles tapped ominously upon the table with the ivory head
of her cane. "No doubt you'll find it mere child's play, Benjamin."

Thompson sank into the chair beside her and placed a restraining
hand upon her arm. "Dear lady," he said, "I've already found out a
little about it. The chief thing that makes so many soldiers fail is
inertia—the very same inertia that makes women fail as wives, clergymen fall short in their sermons, merchants lose their capital, cabinet
ministers fall, authors write miserable books and——"

"Where'd you find out all these sublime truths, Benjamin?" Mrs.
Byles asked; then hastily added: "No, don't tell me!"

Ignoring her, Thompson eagerly embarked on one of the philosophical expositions I had found so fascinating in Boston. "Give me
men who've been truly successful in any field of endeavor," he said,
"and with them I'll build the greatest army in the world! Can a
business succeed if its owner is absent nine tenths of the time; if he
trusts its conduct to incompetent underlings? That's how the British
Army's been managed! Can a ministry be effective if its minister
seldom sets foot in his office, wines and dines every night and all
night, and sleeps till noon each day? That's what British generals do!
Can a university be——"

"Benjamin," Mrs. Byles broke in sharply, "I brought you over
here to listen to us; not to——"

"I know, dear lady," Thompson said, "but for the first time in years
I see a great career opening before me—that of a soldier! The ease
with which a man can rise in this profession is unbelievable! The
life is absorbing, exciting, healthful!" He leaned forward and spoke
in a low voice. "By the merest accident the ship on which I sailed put
in at Charleston last January, three months after Yorktown. The
captain allowed me six hours ashore, and then, with the stupidity and
unreliability of most sailors, most soldiers, most humans, sailed away
in four hours without me."

He placed his hand upon my knee. "You were in Charleston, Oliver.
You saw the bitterness and intensity of that civil war during the
siege of Ninety Six. After Yorktown it was worse. All South Carolina
shook with fear of the rebel leader Marion. Marion's men hunted

Loyalists as Europeans hunt wild pig—and slaughtered 'em with no
more compunction!

"Well, Oliver, I told my theories to General Leslie, and he gave
me a free hand. I took command of a nondescript mass of mounted
Loyalists driven from their homes, and a troop of Negroes. I called
the Negroes 'Sepoys', Oliver, and I made the whole lot of 'em into a
regiment that could have destroyed the entire rebel cavalry. It only
took me a month, Oliver. I was up at dawn every day, and in bed by
nine at night. I spent every waking hour with that regiment, and at
the end of a month they were the equal of any cavalry in Poland or
Sweden. Then we went after Marion—Marion the unfindable; Marion
the unbeatable; Marion the terror of the Low Country!

"We found him in three days, Oliver. His force was twice ours. We
outmaneuvered him, forced him into a position where he had to fight,
attacked him and wiped him out—wiped out the great Marion! I'd
been right, Oliver, so now I'm going to take over the King's American
Dragoons and make 'em into the finest cavalry regiment the world
has ever seen!"

His eyes, as he told this singular story, flicked constantly from Chipman to Colonel Winslow, from Mrs. Byles to me. Even while his
tongue dispensed information, his brain was absorbing our thoughts,
our suspicions. As he finished, he reached forward and picked up one
of the papers that lay in a heap on the table. "What's this?" he asked.

He read from the sheet: " 'First Battalion, New Jersey Volunteers,
staff officers five, field officers twenty-two, rank and file two hundred and forty-one, women and children one hundred and ninety-
seven, permissible dependents eight hundred. Land allotment ninety
thousand acres. Material allotment: axes, felling, five hundred and
fifty; barrow wheels, four hundred; corn, bushels of——' "

He broke off. "Ninety thousand acres! That's a deal of land!"

"Now we're getting somewhere," Mrs. Byles said comfortably.
"Ninety thousand acres on the St. John River is what the First
Battalion of the New Jersey Volunteers needs and wants and ought
to have. Look through that pile of papers, Benjamin."

Thompson picked up the papers, but cast a doubtful glance at
Winslow and Ward Chipman. "Don't try to tell me *all* the Loyalists
want to leave this country," he said.

"That's our considered opinion," Mrs. Byles said.

"Oh, but there's no need," Thompson assured her. "The peace
treaty hasn't been signed yet. It certainly won't be signed for another

year, and may never be signed. General Carleton says he'll resign from the army if the King agrees to the independence of these people."

"Peace treaty or no peace treaty," Mrs. Byles said, "we can never live peacefully with rebels, Benjamin! They'll never let us. Besides, we don't want to."

Thompson turned to me. "Is that true, Oliver?"

"Every word of it," I said, "and much more besides. Our souls wouldn't be our own if we tried to live in our old homes. The rebels are so intolerant that they'd bar us from all businesses and professions. If we couldn't buy food, they'd laugh at us and let us starve. You'll find a report attached to the record of every Loyalist regiment in those documents. I wrote 'em after talking to the officers and men, or after communicating with them by letter."

Thompson pulled his chair closer to the table and ran through the pile of papers. The regimental names at the top of each sheet brought back poignantly to me the long hours I'd spent with those loyal troops in their camps on Long Island and Staten Island or on letters to far-off camps in the south.

When Thompson finished the last sheet and thoughtfully shuffled the heap into a neat pile, Mrs. Byles wagged her finger at him. "Benjamin," she said, "Clinton thought these plans were all poppycock! He thought the numbers of Loyalists driven from their homes were all bosh and tarradiddle. Those numbers were counted and estimated by Ned Winslow and Oliver Wiswell, Benjamin, and you never knew either of them to be anything but conservative in their statements. Clinton wouldn't——"

Thompson rose gracefully to his feet. "Clinton, dear lady, was a consummate ass! Germaine liked him, but not I. Too often did I have to bear the brunt of Germaine's mistakes, and take the blame on my own shoulders."

He spoke deferentially to Colonel Winslow. "Colonel, may I have the loan of these papers for a short time? I'd like to bring them to General Carleton's attention immediately."

"I need those papers for reference," Chipman protested. "If the general gets his hands on 'em, it may be years before anyone sees 'em again!"

"Carleton's not Clinton," Thompson said. "You'll have your papers back in half an hour. I guarantee it!"

He wasn't even half an hour. In ten minutes he came back to us, graceful and smiling, and tossed the papers on the table. "He wouldn't even take the trouble to read all of 'em," Thompson said. "He glanced at half a dozen, and then he looked pleased. I never saw a man look so pleased."

"I'm glad someone's getting some pleasure out of our misfortunes," Mrs. Byles said sourly.

"He's been governor of Canada," Thompson reminded her. "All he said was, 'Those fools in England think Canada's too cold and worthless to keep. If we can bring in all these Loyalists as settlers, there's nothing on earth that can ever take Canada away from England!'"

He tapped me on the shoulder, flirted his hand fraternally at Mrs. Byles, Colonel Winslow and Ward Chipman, and airily took himself off.

I know it was fashionable to say, at one time, that Benjamin Thompson was an odd stick, a man who rose in this world because he curried favor, a sycophant. Well, perhaps he was all of that; but he was vastly more, too. He was a great man and a good friend. He toiled unceasingly for the Loyalists; he made statesmen listen to our needs; he talked so convincingly to Carleton in our behalf that Carleton defied Washington, Congress and the entire rebel army rather than let one Loyalist fall into vengeful rebel hands.

Others may speak slightingly of Benjamin Thompson, but not in my presence. I know that he made the King's American Dragoons into the world's best cavalry regiment because he was a great soldier. I know that the Royal Academies of London, Berlin, Munich and Mannheim elected him to membership because he was a great inventor and scientist. I know that he built the English Garden in Munich because he was a great artist, and that he became privy counselor of Bavaria and head of the Royal Bavarian War Department because he was a greater statesman than existed in all Europe at that time. I see nothing ridiculous in his having become a count of the Holy Roman Empire, or in his building up of the Bavarian Army, or in his turning the beggars of Munich into profitable workers; and to me Benjamin Thompson will always seem one of those many human treasures that the rebels of America deliberately threw away because they were unable to comprehend the value of unusual genius.

CHAPTER XCIV

Carleton was as good as his word, as he always had been. I firmly believe that if Carleton had been sent to take command in Boston upon the first outbreak of hostilities, the forces of rebellion would have been overcome within two months; for he was a great soldier, an inspiring leader, a generous enemy, with all of a great man's contempt for politics, vindictiveness, halfway measures and broken promises.

It was early June when he first called me to headquarters; and from the moment he pushed back in his chair and stared up at me from under bushy gray eyebrows, I knew that he was as different from the other British commanders in chief as steel is from putty.

The others had seemed vaguely skeptical of everything they heard. They'd been utterly contemptuous of all rebels, and highly suspicious of all other Americans—even those who had sacrificed everything in support of the royal government. They'd seemed surrounded by a protective coating of lethargy which they stubbornly dared Americans to puncture. They'd listened to opinions, but not eagerly. They'd had closed minds.

Carleton, on the contrary, had an open mind. He was eager to know: filled with a desire to get at the truth. He made me think of my father, probing and probing at a witness to make sure he was trustworthy. He hated rebels, but he never underrated them; and he went out of his way to show his appreciation of Loyalists and their assistance.

Why, Carleton wanted to know, did I think the Loyalists and the rebels would always be at swords' points? How many acknowledged Loyalists did I think there were in America? Why did I think that the rebels would break any promises they might make to the Loyalists? What reasons did I have for thinking that the St. John River country was the section best adapted for a Loyalist settlement? Why did I prefer the St. John River valley to other places? He asked a score of questions; and while I answered them, his cold blue eyes bored into me, and his head nodded in agreement like that of the ivory Chinaman who had guarded Mrs. Byles' desk on Sudbury Street.

"I'm in hearty accord with all you tell me, Captain," he said, "and I'll have my engineers work on a plan. My chief engineer, Colonel Montresor, is familiar with all parts of Canada, and I think——"

"Sir," I said, "as sure as anybody not a Loyalist works out plans for these people, there'll be trouble! They're Americans, sir, and the only way to satisfy 'em is to let Americans plan for 'em. All the plans we've ever had made for us by others have gone wrong."

Hesitantly, remembering how my suggestions had been received by Howe, Eden, Clinton, I added, "We've already made a few plans of our own, sir."

Carleton made a grumbling sound that might have been either doubt or reluctant approval. I chose to regard it as the latter.

"In our opinion, sir, surveyors, carpenters and workmen of every sort should be sent to the St. John River as soon as possible. They should be there before the streams freeze, sir, so that they can take advantage of the winter traveling conditions to explore the country and have the towns marked out by spring. There'll be at least twenty towns to locate, General, and we'll have to have sawmills ready to supply 'em with building materials."

"That means a lot of people, Captain," Carleton said.

"Yes, sir. We figure it can't be done properly by less than five hundred—the best men obtainable from Loyalist regiments. There ought to be enough ships to take the horses and cattle they need. They should be supplied with clothing, farm implements, arms and ammunition, medicines and millstones, and given one year's supply of provisions."

Carleton's face was noncommittal. "Isn't that asking a good deal at this end, Captain? I think Governor Parr could be depended on to supply them with——"

I felt the blood pump into my face at the thought of trying to get anything in a hurry from an unknown British administrator.

"General," I said, "I don't know Governor Parr; but I've dealt with

a lot of highly placed Englishmen, and every last one of 'em—present
company excepted—has refused to move quickly when speed was
essential. They haven't believed what they've been told; they've acted
when they got good and ready, or not at all! They've lost battle after
battle in this country because they wouldn't credit their friends, or
help the friends when those friends needed help most! They've
thrown away America because they wouldn't or couldn't do what
they should have done!

"Now you tell me Governor Parr can be depended on to furnish
supplies. I say we can't risk it! I say every Loyalist who goes from this
country to Canada should be fully supplied here—right here, where
Loyalist officers can see that they get what they ought to have! By
God, sir, never were people so scurvily treated in return for unswerving loyalty and unhesitating self-sacrifice!

"You tell me you're in accord with what I say, sir. If you are, for
God's sake don't let these Loyalists be stranded in a wilderness,
dependent on the mercy of some well-meaning, thick-witted, merciless ass like—like Nisbet Balfour; like William Eden; like Sir William
Howe; like Sir Henry Clinton; like——"

"I think you've said enough, Captain," Carleton said dryly. "Do
your plans include a leader for this exploring expedition?"

I drew a deep breath. I was shaking, I found, as with the ague.
"No, sir," I said, "we haven't got that far. All we decided was that
everything should be done by Loyalists; but I can tell you the names
of a score that are more than qualified to lead any expedition.
Colonel Cruger, for one, or Colonel Thompson or Charles Stedman
or Colonel Winslow. There's a dozen Bostonians who'd do it hand-
somely—Ward Chipman, Joshua Upham, Timothy Ruggles——"

He raised his hand. "I know all the gentlemen you name, Captain,
and I commend your judgment. Unfortunately, I have other duties in
mind for all of them. I think, too, that their rank might be something
of a drawback. That is to say, they'd have a certain dignity to uphold,
perhaps.

"What I think your expedition needs, Captain, is a different type
of leader—a younger man, indignant because of the treatment his
friends have received; one who'd fearlessly plead their case if the need
arose; one who wouldn't be so impressed by titles or position as to
be silent when confronted by them; one who'd travel all day and all
night, through storms and bitter frosts, and never rest till he was sure

he'd done his duty by those with whom he'd thrown in his lot. Does that seem reasonable, Captain?"

"Yes, sir," I said, "but he ought to take the advice of an older man— someone familiar with all the Loyalists and their needs. He should be instructed to consult Colonel Winslow and Ward Chipman. Yes, and he ought to talk to Mrs. Byles, even if she *is* a woman."

"My own opinion exactly," Carleton said. "You can proceed on that basis, Captain. Talk to Colonel Winslow and Ward Chipman; then make the rounds of the Loyalist regiments and pick your men. You'd better pick two aides as well. It's not going to be easy, getting food and equipment for five hundred men aboard transports."

"Proceed on that basis!" "Pick your men!" "Pick two aides as well!" Was Carleton putting *me* in command of an expedition on which might depend the lives and the happiness of all the Loyalists in America?

I couldn't believe I'd heard him correctly, and I just stood there staring at him. Yet I knew I *had* heard him correctly, for there was a lump in my throat that made speech impossible.

Carleton picked up a pile of papers from his desk and eyed them with disfavor. "Don't worry about Parr," he said, "until you have to. He might be perfectly reasonable about everything."

He gave me a kindly glance, made a grumbling sound, got up from his desk, steered me toward the door that I couldn't see because of the moisture in my eyes; and as I went out he gave me a friendly tap upon the shoulder.

Four months passed before our expedition left New York for Nova Scotia; and I spent all four of them in a sort of fevered dream, hurrying from one regiment to another to assemble our five hundred surveyors and carpenters, millwrights and stone masons, lumbermen and blacksmiths; hurrying from warehouse to warehouse to make sure that all the necessary supplies were on hand, were released, were delivered, were securely stowed in our own warehouse, were safely guarded by Loyalist troops.

In October of 1782 we sailed to Halifax, where we saw Governor Parr, that dough-faced representative of His Majesty, who lived up to the best traditions of Downing Street by laughing at us when we gave him our estimate of the number of Loyalists who'd eventually follow in our footsteps.

Then we went to St. John and our troubles started. We couldn't get axes enough. We couldn't get provisions enough. Between our trips up and down the river, Buell and I went again and again from St. John to Halifax, once on snowshoes through four hundred miles of virgin forest.

We worked from dawn to dark, laying out townships on the St. John—worked through the smoky Indian-summer days of 1782; through rains that parboiled us; into the long winter; through spells so cold that our breaths crackled.

We loved that river and everything about it—the beautiful harbor at its mouth, with the fort on its high hill and the narrow rocky channel connecting the harbor and the river, a channel which so constricts the twenty-foot tides that on the rising tide they make an upstream waterfall and on the falling tide a downstream waterfall; the limestone palisades that border the lower river; the sheltered, island-studded bay where the Kennebecasis River joins the St. John a short distance from its mouth; those long reaches above the bay, with banks so abrupt and water so deep that a three-hundred-ton vessel could be laid close against the shore; those beautiful fertile intervales stretching off to far-away hills. Salmon hurled themselves like silver cannon balls at any bait we tossed them; endless flocks of geese and brant, black ducks and teal rustled overhead; deer, moose and partridge got themselves unconcernedly out of our way, like barnyard creatures.

Everywhere the intervales were from six to twelve miles wide, flat as a table, and without a stone or pebble to be seen; they were like parks, with stands of enormous hardwood trees wholly devoid of undergrowth, so that a cart and oxen could be driven through them in any direction.

Far back from the river, bordering smaller streams, were dark blue walls of spruce and fir, gigantic trees fit for the tallest masts in the largest ships.

We dragged surveyor chains and shouldered instruments until our knees, at nightfall, seemed vast aching knobs; we built two sawmills at the mouths of streams; we wrote reports by guttering candlelight in huts made of fir branches until our fingers were too numb to hold a pencil. Each night we were nearly dead with exhaustion; yet we were utterly happy; for there was nobody to hate us; nobody to lead us badly against enemies who'd kill us if they could; no intolerance, misrepresentation, injustice.

For food we shot partridges and deer, moose and bear, raccoons

and rabbits; and at the winter's end the towns and parishes that were
to become the backbone of New Brunswick were spread neatly and
in order on our maps.

When the ice went out of the streams, we thought our hardest work
was done and sailed to Halifax to let Governor Parr draw from a
bowl the land to be allotted to the different regiments, when they
should arrive, and to make a final plea for the axes that the troops
would need to make themselves comfortable.

A week after we returned, while we still were waiting for the axes,
eleven transports sailed into St. John Harbor without a word of
warning, and the place became a madhouse.

Those eleven transports were the first trickle of that great flood that
was to pour out of New York and all the southern ports during 1783—
that human deluge that brought every still-living Loyalist I'd ever
known in America, every Loyalist I'd ever seen, every Loyalist of
whom I'd ever heard: Loyalists from Boston, New York, Philadelphia, Charleston, St. Augustine and a thousand towns between;
Loyalists from universities and farms, countinghouses and lawyers'
offices, shops and mansions; Loyalist regiments and refugees from
Massachusetts and Florida, Pennsylvania and Maine, Vermont and
Virginia, New Jersey and South Carolina, Connecticut and Georgia,
New Hampshire and North Carolina, Rhode Island and Maryland.

In those first eleven transports were the King's American Dragoons
with their women and children, their horses and dogs, their few
household belongings. We could feed them, and we'd drawn the best
township on the river for those of them who wished to farm—
Kingsclear; while for those qualified to be merchants we'd drawn
house lots in the most beautiful of all the sites we'd seen—Carleton,
on the western side of St. John Harbor. But we could provide them
with no roofs over their heads; no axes with which to cut logs to
make their houses. In spite of everything I'd been able to do, Parr had
the axes—bound round and round with miles of red tape—in Halifax.

When I hurried to where the transports were being warped along-
shore, I knew how men feel when their minds are filled with a thousand things that must be done if disaster's to be averted. I saw Mrs.
Byles, Henrietta Dixon, Colonel Winslow, Dr. Adino Paddock, a
score of officers I'd known in London, in Boston, in Halifax, on Long
Island; but I didn't see them as humans: only as reflections in a mirror
—shapes by which I must hurry, giving them only a gesture and a
passing glance, until I'd done my duty by them.

I knew those green-clad men who manned the bulwarks of the eleven vessels must be waving and cheering at Buell and me; and I think that at any other time I'd have been deeply touched by this evidence of their faith in us; but as it was I heard their cheers as something faint and far away—something detached, in which I had no part.

I could think of only one thing: I had to get the axes that Parr had promised. I had to make Parr keep his word, even if I took a squad of Dragoons to Halifax with me, cornered the governor in his own house, and shook those axes out of him by main strength.

When we finally got them, the Dragoons, with all their women and children, made themselves lean-tos of spruce boughs in the woods above the harbor; then cut a swathe three miles long and ten rods wide, through a forest always spoken of as impenetrable, to the townsite of Carleton.

I thought, when I went along that broad avenue and came out on the hillslope that was to be Carleton, that I had never seen a prospect so beautiful. On one side was the immense Bay of Fundy; on the other side the curving shores of the St. John River, the great lake made by the joining of the St. John and the Kennebecasis, and the little islands that seemed to float like bright galleons on those glittering waters. Immediately across the harbor, on a high hill, was the fort with its tower, guns and dark green glacis; at my very feet the harbor of St. John, crowded with boats and transports.

There wasn't a day, all through the rest of 1783, that a transport didn't sail into that harbor, laden with Loyalists.

All up and down the river, men, women and children worked harder than any slaves to finish cabins, schools, churches, before winter—and in spite of endless back-breaking drudgery, in spite of meager fare and lack of almost every necessity, they were happier than any people I had ever seen.

I lost all sense of time; and so imperative was the need of all these people that there were weeks on end when I could find no interval for food or sleep, and came to hate the meaningless niceties of society.

For the most part I was successful in getting things from Parr; but I couldn't get stoves. From the very beginning I'd demanded stoves; and though at first Parr had laughed at the number I asked for, he had stopped laughing by midsummer, when both Nova Scotia and the St. John Valley were packed with Loyalists, and additional thousands coming every week—but by that time there were no stoves to be had in New York, Montreal or Quebec.

What would happen to the thousands who faced the coming winter without stoves, God only knew. They'd have to use fireplaces and green wood; and I knew what that meant: it meant sooty chimneys; conflagrations that in all likelihood would burn down entire settlements; and we couldn't have that. I felt like a cornered animal when I tried to figure how to get those stoves; for I had no idea what to do.

Buell racked his brains with me; and for once in his life he admitted he was stumped.

"If we were only back in Boston," he said at last, "we'd be all right. When I was cleaning up the town just before we sailed to Halifax the first time, I stumbled into a warehouse at the head of Day's Wharf that didn't have a damned thing in it but round stoves, shaped like barrels. Prob'ly I wouldn't have noticed 'em if they hadn't looked so much like brandy kegs. Ain't that ironical, Oliver? Stoves! Belonged to a couple of ironmongers that went crazy on round stoves: thought they could sell 'em all up and down the Atlantic Coast to fishermen to put in their boats. Not a fisherman would touch one, because they stood up on high legs and had rounded tops that pans wouldn't set on. I was talking about 'em with that last batch of Boston refugees that came in. They said those ironmongers were still bankrupt—been the joke of mercantile Boston for over seven years—and the stoves are right where I first saw 'em when I mistook 'em for brandy kegs! Ain't that the way things always happen, Oliver? All our folks in danger of freezing to death for lack of stoves, and all those stoves in Boston, where we can't get 'em!"

A blinding flash stabbed my brain. "Can't get 'em? Why can't we! Of course we can! We'll get 'em—and I'll see Sally Leighton!"

"No," Buell said. "You're proscribed! You'll be killed! Twelve Loyalists were killed in New York last month for trying to go back!"

"No, no!" I said. "No rebel will ever lift a hand against us while we have money to spend!"

"Money!" he protested. "We ain't got a tenth enough money for all the stoves we need. Of course, if we had *hard* money——"

He stopped suddenly and looked thoughtful.

"We'll *raise* the money," I said. "Mrs. Byles has some! Captain Phillips has some, because he gave Thompson £500 to buy uniforms for the King's American Dragoons! We can hire the *Hannah Hazen* for ten shillings a day and you can forge papers showing we cleared from Falmouth! Nobody even needs to know we're Loyalists—except the Leightons! Come on, Tom! We're going to Boston!"

Buell began to look excited. "Oh my!" he said. "That might not be such a bad idea, Oliver! I been having a little trouble with Henrietta lately, on account it seems she thinks she ought to live with Mrs. Byles and Nathan and look out for 'em, instead of living with me, the way she ought to. If we go to Boston, it'll be like the time we left 'em in Halifax to go to Long Island, most likely. We'll all get drunk.

"Well, Oliver, I know a lot more about the Sex than I did back in 1776. I been in the army since then! If Henrietta gets just the least little bit drunk in my presence, she's a gone coon!"

And so she was; for just before we sailed for Boston, Henrietta Dixon became Henrietta Buell; and Nathan, who had been a brat and an unpleasant one when we first saw him in Boston in March of 1776, stood behind his mother in the uniform of the King's American Dragoons, gave his mother away, and put Buell to bed when it was all over.

CHAPTER XCV

When the schooner's dinghy rowed Buell and me to the end of Boston's Long Wharf, I had the illusion that only weeks had passed, rather than seven years, since the two of us had stood on the deck of a little sloop and watched all of Howe's army and a good part of Boston pour onto that wharf and into the boats that were to carry them to Halifax—since I had my first glimpse of Henrietta Dixon and little Nathan Dixon, panic-stricken at the thought that the Boston they knew was sailing away without them.

The harbor water had the same slick oiliness I had seen upon it when we set sail for Halifax. Floating in it was a lemon rind and a broken box no different from those that had met my eye through the porthole above my father's berth when I had lowered him to it at the beginning of his last voyage. The soiled sea gulls, wheeling and squealing above the fishing boats packed tight along the piling, might have been the very birds that hovered, wailing and mewing, above the boats from which we had hoisted the mangled men who fought at Bunker Hill.

It was the same Boston, I told myself, as we climbed the slippery ladder to the top of the dock: the same Long Wharf; the same chunky fishing schooners; the same sea gulls; the same Boston fishermen, encrusted with the same glittering fish scales and with familiar glumness pitchforking cod and haddock from the bellies of their schooners. Even the air was peculiarly Bostonian, redolent of coolness and fish; of remoteness, moist old cellars, lack of change.

Buell, all business, darted off, to make sure the stoves were still where he'd seen them and, if they were, to open negotiations for their purchase from the hopeless owners.

809

Without knowing why, I went to that part of the wharf where I had crouched beside Doctor Miller, holding scissors and opium while he attempted to stanch the festering wounds of those we'd hoisted from the boats.

I found the exact spot. Two fish carts stood over it, and it seemed to me somehow symbolic that the stains of blood, if any remained, should now be hidden beneath horse droppings and fish slime.

So there *was* a change in Boston. To some the change would be unnoticeable; for me it was overwhelming.

There had been a day when my heart leaped within me at the sight of Boston after a long absence. Now, well remembered as it was, it stirred me even less than London, or Paris, or the log walls and the red dust of Ninety Six, and I felt more affection for any of those small, rude villages in the rolling valley of the St. John.

Boston could never again be for me the friendly Boston of my boyhood, its streets filled with my father's friends, kindly and helpful. This Boston was hard and hating. It had hated my father for his loyalty. If he were still alive, it would still hate him, as it still hated all of us who had dared be loyal.

This Boston had driven us out. It had confiscated our homes and our property. It wanted no part of us and cared not a rap what became of any of us.

The soul of the Boston I knew, the Boston I loved, still lived, but lived precariously, penniless and helpless, in Bristol, Plymouth, London, Exeter and innumerable English towns and villages. It lived in huts along the winding course of the St. John, among the gray rocks of Nova Scotia, laboring and enduring to build a new civilization in the wilderness. . . .

I struck a bargain with the owner of the Seamen's Stables at the foot of State Street, and out of curiosity rode up past the tavern in which Henrietta Dixon had dispensed so many dinners to British officers; then crossed Washington Street to Scollay Square and Sudbury Street. Why I did it, I couldn't exactly have said.

Perhaps I just wanted to look at that tall house of George Leonard's, within whose walls my father and Mrs. Byles and Buell and I had eaten cats and horse meat, had muffled ourselves in shawls and greatcoats and listened with unfailing delight to Mrs. Byles' bedroom reminiscences of her husband and the terribleness of seafaring Barrells. I looked long and perhaps a little wistfully at that house, from

whose windows we had watched those long lines of troops return
and return to the attack at Bunker Hill until the rebel force had been
wholly routed; had seen Howe's incredible failure to take the easy
steps that would have ended the rebellion and the war.

Sudbury Street had been a pleasant street when we had lived there.
The glass in the windows had glittered; all the doors were freshly
painted, and the knockers upon them shone like gold. There had been
plots of grass before every house, curtains at windows, scoured
steps.

Now there was no grass upon the plots; the street was rutted, and
heaps of old leaves and dust and tattered papers filled holes and
corners; windows were soiled and rain-streaked, unsoftened by curtains; doors were paintless; the knockers upon them green with
verdigris. The whole street looked run down, and so did the people
who came and went upon it.

I went back to Scollay Square and out Tremont Street toward Roxbury Neck, past the handsome houses of those friends of my father
whom I'd met in unexpected places and in unhappy circumstances in
the last seven years. The outlines of those houses were as I remembered them; but their life and warmth were gone. They looked unkempt, dowdy, soiled, as if the people who now lived within them
had neither time, inclination, brains nor money to do their duty by
their homes.

Boston, in the days before the Revolution, had been gay and color-
ful, bright with uniforms, shining carriages, sleek horses, smiling men
and women in silks and satins. There'd been laughter and music, a
constant singing in the taverns; warmth indoors despite east winds,
and a spacious and wind-swept feel when the sun was golden and the
skies blue.

But Boston now was drab. Houses, people, streets, sounds—everything was colorless, cold, mediocre, dull.

Even the farms, as I went across Roxbury Neck and out toward
Mattapan, were scraggy and without the lushness of the days before
the land was ruled by rebels.

I think the truth was that I had endured so much from the rebels
during the past eight years that I hated everything about rebel Boston
—everything, that is to say, except my memories of the place and Sally
Leighton.

Even Milton Hill, as my horse groaned and commenced the ascent toward the long double row of poplars that had once belonged to Governor Hutchinson, had lost the power to move me. It was pretty country, that was all; no prettier than the rolling hillslopes over which we'd ridden to the battle of Brooklyn; no prettier than the hills of Devonshire or the hawthorn-studded lanes of Normandy; certainly not a tenth as beautiful as the sharp valleys, the ever-ascending misty mountains of South Carolina, or that little glimpse I'd caught of Kentucky, all green and blue and gold; and it couldn't hold a candle to that island-studded river, those great spacious sweeps of bay and parkland, those rich, rich intervales along the St. John, where all my friends from the New Jersey Volunteers, the King's American Dragoons, DeLancey's battalions, the New York Volunteers, Simcoe's Rangers, Tarleton's Legion strove at this very moment to make themselves snug against approaching winter.

The spell that Milton Hill had so long cast upon me was gone. I wanted nothing here except Sally Leighton, who had never for one day been absent from my thoughts during the years I'd been a fugitive from my own home.

I wondered why this hill of itself had once seemed to me the be-all and end-all of my life—why it had been to my youthful eyes the most beautiful spot in all the world.

Off to the westward, as I climbed, the roof of our own house came into sight, short in front, long in back to make room for the kitchen. I could smell that kitchen now—the odor of shoe-blacking in one corner, where the four-legged hinged box had stood, covered with old carpeting, harsh on the knuckles, on which we brushed our muddy shoes; the smell of pine and birch wood from another corner, where a door, covered with gray gauze to keep out flies, led to the woodshed, grape arbor and barn; the scent of spices, cookies and new bread from the third corner, where a door opened into the pantry—that dangerous and delicious room rich in crocks filled with doughnuts and cookies, pans of milk topped with yellow cream, jugs of maple syrup, jars of mincemeat, and a sugar barrel with a scoop that held a mouthful of sugar—if one had as large a mouth as mine.

So many memories flooded into my brain at the sight of that long roof—memories of rooms, scents, furniture, people—that I wondered how any man's brain could hold so many useless things. Yet there was something about the sight of that house and my memories of it that made breathing difficult.

I kicked my groaning horse in the ribs and urged him up the slope to the Leightons' front door. My mind was full of disconnected, worthless thoughts: that the house needed two coats of paint, just as on the day I'd last seen Sally; that this year's apple crop must have been large to break two branches on the apple tree beside the kitchen; that Sally's window, above the side porch, had been washed more recently than any of the others. When I dismounted and knotted the reins through the ring in the iron horse's head, still tilted out of plumb from the black frost of 1772, my fingers seemed all thumbs; the back of my neck hurt; my feet and legs were numb, so that I stumbled as I went to the door.

When I knocked upon it, I felt nothing at all in my knuckles.

While I stood there like a fool, staring at my clenched hand inquiringly, as if I asked it whether or no it didn't think the knocking should be repeated, the door opened and I looked up into Mrs. Leighton's face. I'd thought of her as already old before I went away, but war and eight years of hard living make a difference in a person's outlook. I saw now that Mrs. Leighton wasn't as old as I'd thought her eight years before. She didn't look much older than some of the brides who were working day and night in their cabins on the St. John. I opened my mouth to speak to her, but I couldn't make a sound.

Her hand went flutteringly to her lip. "Why," she said, "I'd— I'd have known you anywhere! It's Oliver—isn't it? Why, yes! It's Oliver Wiswell!"

I forced all the breath from my lungs, as Buell had taught me long ago. "I hope you're well, Mrs. Leighton," I said. "I hope all your family's well. I want to see Sally."

Mrs. Leighton looked frightened. "I'll have to warn you, Oliver: the man who bought your father's house—he's hard, Oliver. He was a privateersman. We're friendly, but he's loud-spoken and hard."

"I'm not interested in him," I said, "I want Sally."

"But he'll never let you have your house back, Oliver! He'd shoot! He shoots his dogs when they don't mind him. You couldn't count on getting help around here."

Vose Leighton's face appeared behind his wife's shoulder. I was shocked by the sight of him, for his once-ruddy features were gray and seemed shrunken.

"By God," he whispered. "Oliver!"

I thought there was something like friendliness in his voice; but on the instant his face became even grayer and more haggard.

"You damned Tory!" he cried. "Get away from this house and keep away from it!"

He caught his wife's arm and tried to pull her back within the hallway, but she stood there heavily.

"Mrs. Leighton," I said quickly, "I appeal to you. The war's over——"

"It'll never be over," Vose Leighton said bitterly.

"I ask you to regard me as a man and not as an enemy," I said. "I'm still Seaton Wiswell's son, sir, and Seaton Wiswell was your friend. I still am that, even though you may not wish it."

Somewhere in the house a door slammed. There were quick steps on the stair. I'd have recognized them anywhere on earth. They were Sally's.

Mr. and Mrs. Leighton ceased to exist for me. I must have pushed them to one side, but I wasn't conscious of doing so. I only knew I was in the hallway with Sally, that she was in my arms, that I was shaking all over, that there was a roaring in my ears and a lightness in my head, that I was repeating her name as though it were strange to me, and only to be mastered by endless iteration.

I became conscious of a hand upon my shoulder. It was Vose Leighton's, and there was still strength in that hand to force Sally and me apart. "Say what you have to say and get out," he told me.

"He might as well come in and sit down," Mrs. Leighton protested.

"I'll have no damned Tory in this house," Vose Leighton said.

"I *am* in the house, Mr. Leighton," I pointed out. "If you want me to leave, I'll do so, but not without Sally. I've got to see her alone. It's been seven years."

"It ought to be seventy," Vose Leighton said. "Well—go on into the parlor. You can say your say in there. I can't have Sally making a spectacle of herself sobbing like this outdoors!"

CHAPTER XCVI

MY LONGING to be alone with Sally as I sat beside her on the sofa was a vast ache, as though all my muscles, from head to foot, had been tied in knots and drawn tight; but Vose Leighton had no intention of leaving us.

He sat across the room, grim and gray, and when he'd bellowed for Steven, he watched me with a granite eye. Whatever I had to say to Sally must be in Vose Leighton's hearing.

"It's been—it's been a long time, Sally," I said.

She sighed shiveringly.

"It might have ended sooner," Vose Leighton said harshly, "if you hadn't turned against your own country—and it may start to be long again, if you Tories have your way!"

Sally's hand slipped down my arm, and her fingers tightened on mine.

"Please, sir," I said, "don't keep that war alive! The peace treaty's signed. It's a bad and shameful peace; but it's signed and accepted, so I've come back here to——"

"Come *back?*" Mrs. Leighton asked. "Where are you living, Oliver?"

"I'm living in Carleton," I said. "That's near the town of St. John on the St. John River."

My heart lurched sickeningly, for Sally's fingers loosed their hold on mine. Then they wrapped themselves more tightly around my hand and clung.

"Carleton?" Vose Leighton asked. "Never heard of it! Never saw it on any chart of mine! And we used to sail into the St. John River twice a year."

"It's a new town, Mr. Leighton," I said, "named for a great soldier—Guy Carleton."

The door behind me opened and closed. Steven Leighton walked into the room and stood looking down at me. I got to my feet and put out my hand, but he didn't take it.

"So you didn't go to Kentucky after all."

"I never had a chance to thank you," I said, "but I was mighty grateful for what you did."

He nodded and sat down, looking at me gloomily. The touch of Sally's fingers was like a balm that soothed resentment and brought peace and understanding. I knew what it was that made Steven Leighton glower. He'd been in love with Julia Bishop. I knew, too, the suspicions and fears that must have crawled darkly through his mind in the past two years.

"I only went as far as Cumberland Gap," I said. "Just far enough to help Major Dustin and his daughter reach Kentucky."

"Oh yes," Steven said carelessly. "I remember them quite well. I wondered how the daughter stood the trip. She wasn't meant for hardships—so small and gentle!"

Small and gentle! Julia Bishop! I had an almost overpowering desire to laugh. "She did magnificently," I said. "She was an inspiration to all of us."

For the sake of Steven's peace of mind I added hastily and inconsequentially, "She often spoke of you. I caught a glimpse of Kentucky from the far side of the Gap. It's a beautiful country—warm and rich. I don't believe I ever saw handsomer land—except on the St. John."

Steven looked thoughtful.

To me Mrs. Leighton said, "We're very proud of Steven, Oliver. He was made a member of General Washington's official family during the siege of Yorktown."

Probably I didn't look sufficiently impressed to please Vose Leighton, for he spoke to me bitterly.

"By God, Oliver Wiswell, that should be like a hot iron in the soul of a man who's lost his country—a man living in a place nobody ever had knowledge of!"

I'd never heard Sally speak sharply, but that was how she spoke to her father now. "You can't talk that way!" she cried.

"You be quiet," Vose Leighton said. He glared at her; then explained contemptuously to Steven, "He's living in Canada—a place called Carleton!"

"It's a town I hope you'll see yourself some day, Steven," I said. I drew a deep breath and added, "I've made this trip to Boston with a great hope in my heart."

Vose Leighton made a strangled, angry sound. Aside from that the Leightons' sitting room was so still that I could hear, in the hall outside, the measured ticking of the tall clock on the stair landing. I didn't mind the silence, for Sally's fingers told me what I hadn't yet asked her in words.

Vose Leighton jumped to his feet. "I never heard such damnable nonsense, and I don't propose to listen to any more of it! I'd rather see Sally dead in her grave than married to a Tory!"

Sally wrenched her hand from mine and clutched the edge of the sofa seat. I could feel her trembling, like a halliard in a gale. "You've got to listen, Father," she whispered, and her voice shook.

"I think Oliver's entitled to a hearing," Steven said. "He's done nothing to us."

"Don't let me hear such talk," Vose Leighton said. "This man's a Tory! He's been a supporter of the ministerial assassins that for eight long years have plunged and re-plunged the knife in our bosoms. At heart he's an assassin himself!"

Sally sprang to her feet. "He is not! He's nothing of the sort! He's Oliver Wiswell, who lived for years on Milton Hill! He's Oliver Wiswell, who sailed to Havana with us! He's the son of one of the best friends you and the town of Milton ever had—until the whole world went crazy!"

Vose Leighton lifted his hand and took a step toward Sally. I got up from the sofa to stand beside her. Mrs. Leighton caught at her husband's arm and shook him.

He turned on her. "You too, for God's sake? You'll condone this Son of Belial—this worker of iniquity?"

"Don't you dare!" Sally cried. "Who ran the risk of being hanged and shot and hacked to come here and tell us that Soame was suffering, that Steven and Jeremiah needed our help! It was Oliver! You—you—I—I——" She burst into tears and hid her face against my coat.

I drew her down beside me on the sofa. She was soft and limp in the hollow of my arm; and over and over, in a muffled voice, she murmured, "Won't it ever end, Oliver; won't it ever end?"

"Of course it'll never end," Vose Leighton said savagely. "Do you think any decent human being can ever forget for one minute the traitors who tried to destroy us—to reduce us to abject slavery—who attacked us with bloody and insatiable malice——"

"Vose Leighton," Mrs. Leighton cried, "I've been a good wife to you all these years! I've borne your children and cooked your food and mended your stockings and stood all that any good wife is supposed to stand, but I won't stand this! These things you're saying aren't true! I'm sick to death of all this yap, yap, yap about assassins and insatiate malice and wickedness! Now you sit down and be still! I've got a few reasonable questions I want to ask!"

Vose Leighton stared at his wife as if he hated her, but he sat down. Sally fumbled helplessly for a handkerchief, so I gave her mine. She thanked me with a look that turned my heart to water.

"What's it like on the St. John River, Oliver?" Mrs. Leighton asked.

"It's beautiful," I said. "The country's alive with game. The rivers are full of salmon—big salmon! The land's so rich that the fields don't need to be plowed. You can harrow in your seed and get twice the crops you can down here. The men work together at building roads and cabins."

"Oh, Oliver!" Sally said. "It sounds heavenly!"

"Heavenly!" Vose Leighton said disgustedly. "Log cabins, greasy dresses, smoky fires to cook over, cold winters, hot summers, mosquitoes, black flies, cornhusks for beds——"

Mrs. Leighton made a sudden movement; he came to an abrupt stop and grumbled to himself.

"Are there women—decent women—in Carleton, Oliver?" Mrs. Leighton asked.

"Why of course, ma'am! That town was drawn by the King's American Dragoons. That's my regiment, Mrs. Leighton. Those that were married—officers and men alike—brought their wives and children when they left New York. Those that weren't married have been sending for their sweethearts. We've had thirty-seven weddings in Carleton since last April. Then we've got a number of ladies with us who are just friends or relatives of men in the regiment, like Mrs. Byles."

Mrs. Leighton looked interested. "Mrs. Byles?"

"Mrs. Belcher Byles," I told her. "Her husband was a professor at Harvard. She was a Salem Barrell."

Mrs. Leighton looked at her husband. "Wasn't it the Barrells who owned so many ships and did so much for Salem?"

"They got to be too good for ordinary people like us," Vose Leighton growled.

"Ward Chipman expects to join us in the near future," I went on. "Colonel Edward Winslow of Plymouth and his entire family are already with us. Young Adino Paddock's with us, too. He's become a doctor, and a great one. He's chief surgeon of the King's American Dragoons."

Steven Leighton raised an eyebrow. "King's American Dragoons? English?"

"No! All Americans! All Loyalist regiments are Americans."

"But the common women," Mrs. Leighton persisted. "Those that the men took with 'em—they must have been low women, weren't they?"

"Low? Most certainly not, Mrs. Leighton! I've served with four Loyalist regiments, and every one of the four would be a credit to any country, both as to fighting abilities and the quality of officers and men. Their women are no different from those you find in Milton —some of them beautiful, some of them not, but all of them loyal and uncomplaining—and mighty happy!"

I turned involuntarily to Sally. Her eyes were shining.

"So you served with four Tory regiments, did you?" Vose Leighton asked unpleasantly. "How many Tory regiments were there? I never heard of any except Tarleton's hellhounds, Simcoe's robbers and the dirty damned Skinners."

"There's no occasion for epithets, sir," I said. "I was with Simcoe for a short time when he destroyed the stores on the James River. He's a great gentleman, a magnificent soldier. Cavalry officers tell me Simcoe's Rangers is as fine a cavalry regiment as ever was; and from what I saw of it, I'm proud to have been associated with it for even a short time. Those men weren't robbers. They were a great regiment. So was Tarleton's. You'd have been mighty proud of any of those men if you'd ever seen 'em fight. The Skinners, as you call them, were the New Jersey Volunteers. I fought with them at the siege of Ninety Six, when they and DeLancey's First and Second Battalion whipped General Greene and eight times their number. They're my friends. I can't speak too highly of 'em! Didn't you read about the siege of Ninety Six in your newspapers?"

"Certainly not," he said.

"Then it's also possible your newspapers didn't reveal that since the first of this year twenty-two Loyalist regiments—every man an

American and a good one—sailed from New York alone to different parts of Nova Scotia to make their homes there."

Vose Leighton was contemptuous. "Twenty-two! There couldn't have been twenty-two Tory regiments against us!"

"There were more, sir," I said; "but that's neither here nor there—now. I won't argue with any man about the beginnings or the end of the war, or what may come from it. I only want to talk about Sally."

I expelled my breath to steady my voice, which seemed inclined to tremble. "I've loved her ever since I was a schoolboy. I want to take her back to St. John with me—if she's willing."

"Willing!" Sally cried almost wildly. "Willing! Oh, Oliver, I was afraid I'd be an old, old woman before I saw you again!" She clung to me unashamed.

"I tell you I won't have it," Vose Leighton shouted. "I forbid it!"

"You can't forbid it," Sally said. "I'm going."

"You are *not!*" her father cried. "I'll see you in hell before I'll agree to you marrying a damned renegade Tory. You'll never darken these doors again!"

"If you see her in hell, you'll see me there too," Mrs. Leighton said. "I've sat here for eight years, hearing the same old things about a war that killed my sons—killed my babies—and I'm desperate! Don't you talk about never darkening these doors again, or you'll find yourself baking your own beans and darning your own socks, and I mean it!"

"Steven," Vose Leighton shouted, "I call on you! That man should never have been allowed to come into this house, and I demand that you put him out! By God, I never heard such impudence! Asking my daughter to marry him and live in some rotten little town in a foreign country with a lot of good-for-nothing renegades."

"Renegades!" Mrs. Leighton cried. "What's the matter with Ward Chipman? What's the matter with Edward Winslow? I never saw the day that a country storekeeper'd consider himself better than a Paddock and a Chipman and a Byles!"

"You be silent!" Vose Leighton shouted. "They're Tories! No daughter of mine could have anything in common with Tories!"

"Now look here," Steven Leighton said. "I've heard enough! For God's sake, Father, let's try to be honest! I've stood a lot, but I draw the line at your telling Sally she'll have nothing in common with a man she loves—a man she's stuck to for eight years! And how much do you figure she has in common with those that surround her here?"

Vose Leighton turned on him. "What do you mean by that!"

Steven's reply was quick. "I mean that Boston people seem to have mighty little in common, when you come right down to it. Those that were in the army want to fight Congress. Those in business think everybody else is a thief and a liar—and I'm not so sure they aren't right. Nobody comes into our store without trying to cheat us, or get something for nothing. Anyone with a few more books or a little more money than the next man is damned for a fop or a Tory-lover!

"About the only thing people have in common around here is commonness. You're resented if you're educated; if you're rich; if you dare speak your mind; if you dare resent anybody's damned common nosiness! You're resented most of all if you don't keep screaming that Americans are the bravest, brilliantest, honorablest, moralest people in the whole world! Well, that's nonsense! What about all those Americans, all those New Englanders, who wouldn't fight in the war; all those who went in the army and ran when they should have fought; all those who're dishonest, stupid, greedy, crooked as a hound's hind leg: determined to spy on their neighbors, spread lies about 'em, and make their lives miserable!"

"I never thought to live to hear a son of mine talk like that," Vose Leighton said.

"You'd talk that way yourself if you'd spent seven years in the army," Steven said. "It's the simple truth."

"You lie!" Vose Leighton cried. "You should be the last to say such things! Your brother Soame died at the hands of British butchers in New York so this country could be free! Your brother Jeremiah was killed at Yorktown, fighting for liberty! Your brother Albion died of jail fever in Virginia on his way to Yorktown! How can you talk the way you do?"

Steven spoke with a sort of desperation. "Their death's got nothing to do with it! They weren't fighting for liberty! We were freer before we fought than now! They didn't know *what* they were fighting for! They were fighting because they *had* to fight, just as I was! If it hadn't been for rotten officers at the battle of Long Island, Soame wouldn't have been captured! He wouldn't have died! That battle should never have been fought. Those who sent us to Long Island to fight it were murderers! Jeremiah and Albion didn't help to win Yorktown by getting killed, either! Clinton won Yorktown for us all alone, when he failed to send a fleet down there to support Cornwallis. You don't think we could have won, do you, if Clinton hadn't been a fool? There was no more need for Soame and Jeremiah and Albion to die than for Sally to die!"

"By God," Vose Leighton whispered, "I believe you're mad! Never until this moment have you even hinted at such lies! Now this Wiswell—this Tory—comes in here; and to curry favor with him you belittle our cause! You calumniate noble and brave men who supported it and fought for it! One more such word out of you and I'll disown you!"

Steven made an impatient gesture. "You can't disown me, any more than you can drive Sally out of this house. I can make my own living, and Sally can make her own home. Up to now I've been silent, because all during the war I looked forward to coming back to Milton and living in peace; and when at last I got home, I found I couldn't live in peace unless I concealed what I knew about war from those who'd never fought in one. Perhaps, if it weren't for Sally, I'd still be silent; but Sally's young. She loves Oliver, and I don't give a damn *what* his politics are. He's as good as we are, and I don't propose to see anybody spoil the rest of her life by insisting that she listen to a lot of things that aren't so! You've seen fit to call me a liar, Father, for casting doubts on your patriotic beliefs. You've seen fit to imply that everybody who doesn't think as you think is mad and a traitor.

"Well, what about the enormous amount of stock-jobbing, the extortion, the low arts and devices to extort wealth, that existed among our noble Patriots? What about our patriotic army contractors who got rich in one single campaign by stripping us of our miserable pittances? What about the merchants who hoarded supplies and wouldn't part with them to the wives and children of those in the army unless offered enormous profits?

"What about those noble supporters of ours who kept trading with the royal troops all through the war?

"What made Washington say repeatedly that idleness, dissipation and extravagance had laid fast hold on most of our people; that speculation, stealing and an insatiable thirst for riches had apparently got the better of every other consideration with most of those brave Patriots of ours?

"Why was he forever lamenting the laxity of public morals and the decay of private virtue? Why was he always talking about the increasing rapacity of the times, the declining zeal of the people, the corrupt stock-jobbing of the multitude?"

Vose Leighton got to his feet. "I won't listen to such libels on the brave supporters of our cause!"

"Brave supporters of our cause, indeed!" Steven cried. "How about the Whigs of Vermont? They were a dead weight on the cause!

"Why was our army ragged and half fed? Not because the country was poor, but because there was neither system, common prudence nor integrity in the management of affairs! Why did we freeze and starve at Valley Forge? Was it because the British plunged an assassin's dagger in our backs? No, sir! The British never came near us! We starved and froze because those noble patriotic farmers all around us wouldn't supply us out of their stuffed barns and cellars! Every one of our appalling calamities was due to the widespread lack of patriotism and nothing else!

"Do you know how many men these patriotic states—these noble supporters of our cause—gave Washington? They gave him less than one eighth of their quotas! And to get even that little measly, pocky eighth, the states had to pay bounties of a thousand dollars and more to each man. Men had to be tempted to serve their country! Bribed! Bribed, for God's sake!"

"This is treason," Vose Leighton whispered.

"Oh no, it's not," Steven said. "It's fact! Most of those brave patriots you're talking about couldn't be depended on for anything except to make a shameful show of themselves! They deserted by hundreds, twenty and thirty at a time, and ran away to Vermont to live! Thousands perjured themselves so they could get out of the army in which they'd voluntarily enlisted! Thousands sold arms, uniforms and equipment for enough rum to get drunk on! Hundreds of officers clamored for their pay and at the same time stole public money; hundreds violated paroles, regardless of their word as gentlemen.

"A good part of our officers were of the lowest class of the people! They led their soldiers to plunder and commit every sort of mischief. Those from some states weren't fit to be shoeblacks."

"By God," Vose Leighton said, "I'll—I'll—I'll——"

"Don't say it, Father," Steven Leighton said. "I've told you the truth in the hope that you wouldn't be too hard on Sally. I'm going to Kentucky myself. I think I'd be happier there than here. Something Oliver said makes me think so. I'll feel a whole lot better if I know you won't have hard thoughts of me for telling you what I know to be the truth."

"Kentucky?" Vose Leighton asked blankly. "Leave your home here and go to Kentucky? You can't!"

Sally's fingers locked themselves more firmly in mine as she faced her father. "You can't say 'You can't' to us! We've had eight years of fighting and bitterness; eight years of starvation, lies, fear, death! I've tried to believe everything I heard, unless it had to do with Oliver. I've hated the English, as all of you insisted I should! I've worked my fingers almost to the bone for the Patriots. I've been as good a Patriot as anyone! Now the war's over and I'm going to be myself! We've won! We've got what we wanted! All these years everybody said we were fighting for liberty and freedom! If that's so, everybody who believed in the war and supported it must be entitled to freedom and liberty."

"Some things can't be taken literally," Vose Leighton said heavily. "This country has earned freedom from other nations: yes! It's earned the liberty to govern itself: yes! But you and Steven can't do as you please—you can't refuse to pay taxes—you can't be free from authority—you can't libel those who won your liberty for you."

Steven sighed, and in his sigh was the hint of a rueful laugh.

Sally tossed her head. "No!" she cried. "I won't have it! I was told and told we were fighting for liberty and freedom! Now you can't tell me we weren't! I won't believe Soame and Jeremiah and Albion died for nothing! I won't believe it, even though there's still a million slaves in the south! I won't believe it even if you won't let Oliver live here, and be free to do as he wishes. We were fighting for freedom and liberty, and we won! Oliver wants me to go to Canada with him, Father, and you say I can't!"

She stood up, not letting go my hand, so that I rose and stood beside her.

"Eight years of fighting for liberty!" Sally said. "I'm an American and I'm free!"

She put her hands on my shoulders before them all. "I'm ready, Oliver! I've been ready for eight years, and I'm glad and proud that you love me still! When do we start for Carleton?"

"There's not a minute to lose," I said. "Pack what you need and we'll be married by Captain Hazen on the schooner."

I wouldn't listen when Vose Leighton tried to insist that Sally should be married before she left Milton.

"It's impossible," I said. "We might miss the night tide! We've got to sail tonight if Buell's ready to sail. There's thousands of people dependent on those stoves, Mr. Leighton. If we ran into a storm because of delaying, those thousands might suffer."

"It's not decent!" Vose Leighton protested. "Anything might happen! We've got Sally's reputation to consider! Who's this Buell?"

His question brought up a well-remembered scene—one I'd often lived over in retrospect. "You asked me that question once before, Mr. Leighton," I said. "It was on the eighteenth of April, eight years ago. Somehow the mob found out I'd brought a printer named Buell home with me. I couldn't be sure, but I always thought the mob got its information from someone in this house. At all events, I wouldn't want to be married to Sally without Buell. He owes his life to Sally. It was Sally who warned us, so that we were able to get Buell out of sight before the mob got its hands on him. I think it's singularly fitting that this war, for Sally, should begin and end with Buell."

Vose Leighton, his face gray as putty, sat staring at me and had nothing more to say.

Steven Leighton got us a three-seated wagon, and when I dragged Sally's two curved-top seaman's chests from the front door, he was settled in the front seat. "I might as well go to Boston with you," he said. "You can't tell when some of these Roxbury people might get curious." He flicked his whiplash at a lethargic fly that was making the horse's shoulder quiver. "It beats all how word gets 'round when a Tory comes back to town!"

Mrs. Leighton bustled out with Sally. She had her bonnet on.

"Now, Ma," Steven said, "you oughtn't to go stivering in and out of Boston at this time of day. It'll be three o'clock in the morning before we're home."

"Mind your own business," Mrs. Leighton said absently. "I want to see this Buell. He's the one that fixed the hot loggerhead across the throat of the man that killed Soame. That was a genteel act, and I wouldn't miss him for the world. He's never been properly thanked by any of us. Now let's see, Sally: I've put in your grandma's ivory sewing set, a dozen knitting needles, that awl of your father's, a bullet mold, a pair of filigree earrings that belonged to your aunt Kate, that London cookbook that tells how to smoke all kinds of fish, those two woolen vests of mine I always said I'd leave you in my will. Now let's see: did you put in——" She broke off, glanced at me, then went to whispering to Sally.

Vose Leighton came out and stood at the front gate, staring angrily at us.

Sally broke away from her mother, ran to him and threw her arms around his neck. "I don't care!" she cried. "I can't help it! I'll be sorry as long as I live for the things I said; but I don't care!"

"I know you don't," Vose Leighton said grimly. "You young folks are all alike—strong-willed and full of cussedness."

He cleared his throat. "You'll have enough to keep you busy, I guess, so you won't fret much about the things you said to me. Anyway, you've been a pretty good girl, Sally—a pretty good girl."

He cleared his throat with even greater violence. "I'd go to Boston and see Buell myself if my heart would stand it; but I don't believe it would. When spring comes, Sally, I'll let one of the boys sail the little sloop up to St. John with anything you might have forgotten You might as well keep the sloop up there."

He kissed her, pushed her toward the wagon, and nodded dourly to me as I lifted her up beside her mother. "I take back what I said," he told me. "Your father was a great man. I wish he was here now. He stuck to the right as he saw it, and so did you. That takes courage when everyone's calling you names! I know Sally'll be all right with you."

Without waiting for an answer, he turned and went into the house; and I was glad of it. Those few kind words of his about my father had torn at my heart like grappling hooks.

I saw Buell in the ratlins of the schooner as we clattered down Long Wharf; and when Steven stopped the wagon opposite him, it seemed to me I never saw him look more smug.

"I knew it, Oliver," he shouted. "Something told me you'd bring her back with you! I was so sure of it that after I'd got the stoves aboard I went back to the warehouse I told you about the day we sailed for Halifax seven years ago—the one you acted so mean about when I wanted to get the brandy."

"Tell Captain Hazen to hunt up the wedding service," I told him. "We're going to need it right away!"

"Pshaw, Oliver," Buell cried, "there ain't anything we ain't thought of!"

He slid to the schooner's deck, climbed the ladder to the dock, shook Sally's hand and gave her several exploratory pats. "You're thinner'n you were when you pointed that pistol at me, ma'am! I like 'em a little solider myself, but prob'ly Oliver's easier to please than me."

"You've been drinking," I told him.

"Not seriously I ain't," Buell said. "I may be a little valuable—I should say voluble—but I ain't started falling down yet. You might say I ain't much more than on the verge of drinking."

"These are Sally's mother and brother Steven," I said. "You saw Steven at the Provost in New York."

"So I did," Buell said heartily. "Come aboard, everyone, and we'll celebrate this happy occasion by getting jest the least little bit drunk. I got some brandy that John Hancock thinks still belongs to him."

"Young man," Mrs. Leighton said, "every night of my life I think of what you did to that man who killed Soame, and I feel grateful for it."

"Pshaw!" Buell said airily. "That wa'n't nothing, Mrs. Leighton! It was a pleasure! I'd do that much for a friend of Oliver's any day."

"None the less I feel grateful," Mrs. Leighton insisted. "It was a generous and thoughtful act." She leaned far out toward Buell. "Sometimes I try to think how he could have been killed better, and I can't!" She spoke so feelingly that she lost her balance, and Buell had to catch her under the arms and lower her to the wharf.

I wouldn't exchange that wedding of ours, in the dim little cabin of the *Hannah Hazen,* for a ceremony presided over by all the Loyalists who became bishops in New Brunswick, Nova Scotia, Bermuda, the Bahamas and Gibraltar.

Our only music was the faint creaking of the bulkheads and of the lamps in their gimbals, as the tide thrust us upward; the clink of the ladle against the punch bowl, as Buell surreptitiously stirred the liquors he had obtained in ways of which I hoped I'd never hear too much.

Yet that little cabin, in its simplicity, its darkness and dinginess, its friendliness, somehow seemed more symbolical to me than the greatest of cathedrals.

God knows how many Loyalist brides had stood before Captain Hazen in that very spot to renounce forever the land where they were born, and to accept gladly a future that promised little more than darkness, simplicity—and life among a friendly people.

Even the lines that Captain Hazen read to us, it seemed to me, might have been written for Loyalist women alone—*"Wilt thou*

*obey him, and serve him, love, honor, and keep him in sickness and
in health; and, forsaking all others, keep thee only unto him, so long
as ye both shall live?"*

Forsaking all others! As we sat around the table afterward, drinking deep of the punch and listening to Mrs. Leighton tell about the
early deviltries of her seven sons and her tomboy daughter, I
thought how shameful it was that this country, which once had
been mine and now was mine no longer, hadn't the intelligence or
the common decency to refrain from persecuting even women for
opinions that had been universally held twenty years before!

Even Sally—sweet, kind, true-hearted Sally—must literally for-
sake all others because of this ill-judged determination of the rebels
to involve all Tories in indiscriminate punishment and ruin—to in-
flict on helpless people an unmanly revenge that had only been
paralleled by religious madmen in times of the blindest bigotry!

How easy it would have been to have things otherwise—how easy
to have saved for America the Crugers, the DeLanceys, the Thomp-
sons, the Samuel Seaburys, the Governor Hutchinsons, the Sylvester
Gardiners, the Ward Chipmans, the Edward Winslows, the Daniel
Leonards, all the other thousands of well-educated, high-minded,
ambitious, cultured gentlemen—how easy it would have been to
avoid the mischief, the ruin, the animosities that must continue for
generations to come—was evident from that group around the table
in the cabin of the *Hannah Hazen:* Sally, my hand clasped in both
of hers and her eyes fastened fondly on her mother; Mrs. Leighton,
punctuating her sentences by patting Buell on the back; Steven Leighton, once an aide to Washington and now affectionately eager for
any slight word I, a Loyalist, could give him of Julia Bishop; Captain
Hazen, watchful of the tide, yet drawn back, fascinated, to stand in
the cabin door and listen to Mrs. Leighton's tales of her son's cruises
to Havana and the Sugar Islands. No longer were we Whigs and
Tories, rebels and Loyalists: we were just people, each of us eager
for something that the others could give: just decent, civilized people
whose lives had been made over, and of necessity made over mighty
badly, by politicians.

When the schooner cast off from the wharf at the turn of the
tide, I thought the stillness of the night would hold us where we were,
close enough to see dimly the faces of Steven and Mrs. Leighton,
looking down at us.

One moment Buell was bawling at Mrs. Leighton about his Metallic Tractors, and we were all laughing together. "You don't need 'em yourself, ma'am," he told her. "They're only for folks who look haggard and old, and want to be made visions of youth 'n' beauty. They only take away freckles, wrinkles, smallpox pits, brown spots in the hands, rednesses, roughnesses, morphew or the heats, which you ain't got any faint trace of, Mrs. Leighton. Say, Mrs. Leighton, wha's your first name?"

"I certainly don't need 'em, Tom," Mrs. Leighton said, "but you step down here next spring and bring me a pair of those tractors."

Suddenly the wharf was a dark blur. We could no longer see Steven or Mrs. Leighton, and their voices came dimly to us across the black water. There was a panic quality to Mrs. Leighton's voice.

"Good-by! Good-by!" Sally cried. Then she gasped and clung to me.

"Well," Buell said, "there's only a mogidum—I mean modicum— of that punch left, so I might's well drink it 'n' get her out of your way. Funny; ain't afflecked—pardon—affeckled me at all, except gimme a little trouble with m'eyes. Didn't hinder me any when I was hollering to the li'l mother, did it? Great ole girl, that mother of yours." He fell down the companion ladder with a surprising clatter.

"Don't cry, dear," I told Sally. "I know it's hard to leave your home, but it's not as though we were going to the ends of the earth."

"I'm not crying," Sally said. "I just remembered that we were married—and that home is where you are."

CHAPTER XCVII

O<small>N A GOLDEN</small> October morning we came back to the Bay of Fundy and the spruce-clad islands that seemed, in the soft October haze, like giant men-o'-war guarding that rocky shore from harm.

Captain Hazen, entranced by Sally's smartness as a navigator, let her take the schooner between Grand Manan and Campobello and across the mouth of Passamaquoddy Bay, so she could see as much as possible of that new land of ours.

"That's the beginning of it," I told her, when we raised the cluster of islands at the mouth of Back Bay. "That high point is Pennfield, where all the Pennsylvania Quakers settled. Higher up in the bay is St. George, where the Royal Fencible Americans live. Their commander's Colonel Gorham, Sally, who helped us last winter when we were caught in a blizzard."

"*Helped* us!" Buell cried. "Wasn't I frozen stiff from being carried on your back when Gorham came out and found us?"

I could feel Sally's eyes upon me.

"You'll meet Gorham soon," I told her uncomfortably. "We'll sail to St. George some day. It's a grand country for sailing, Sally. There's a harbor every seven miles, all along this coast and the Nova Scotia coast too, and men I want you to meet in all of them."

"Yes," Sally said breathlessly. "I want to meet everyone—the ones you knew at Ninety Six—those men who traveled in the horse transport—Mr. Stedman and Mr. Cruger and Mr. Barbarie and Mr. De-Lancey and all the others. I—I love them all."

Beyond Point Lepreau we could see the long low line of the salt marshes where the mosquitoes had almost killed us when we surveyed it; and a little later we made out the tower of the fort at

St. John; then the bastions; then the smooth glacis—blue in the distance at first; and at last bright green in the brilliant autumn sun. The masts in the harbor were like close-packed tamaracks in winter; and the little log houses on the hills stood out like cameos.

There was something about this broad and shining bay and harbor mouth, something about those long lines of log houses ranged in military formation on hills where a year before there had been nothing, that filled me with surging pride; that caught at my throat.

"Of course," Buell told Sally, "these settlements ain't much to look at now, but they'll be mighty pretty towns some day. All the men are planting trees, and in a year or two there'll be shade and softness to 'em. They won't look so raw, so desolate."

"They ain't so bad right now," Captain Hazen said. "The way those people pitched in and worked makes my back ache just to think of it."

"They're beautiful," Sally said. "They look as if they'd grown up with the river and the forests; as if the forest and the river had them in their arms, and would never let them be cold or hungry! There's something about them that makes me want to cry."

"No occasion to cry about 'em," Buell said gruffly. "Pity's the last thing they want. They're fighters, those people are."

"No, no!" Sally said. "It isn't pity that makes me want to cry. It's the same feeling people have when they see brave men come safely home from a battle they've won!"

A fleecy ball bloomed from the fort across from Carleton, and another and another. The booms of the six-pounder seemed to push at the schooner and make her heel a little.

"Twelve guns," Buell said sourly. "There must be a general around somewhere. That means trouble!"

Captain Hazen gazed admiringly at Sally. "First time I ever carried a lady who rated twelve guns," he said. "They must 'a' had word you could navigate better'n a admiral."

"They're for Oliver," Sally said.

Buell coughed dryly. "Oh my, yes! What you and I can't understand, though, is why he only gets twelve. He ought to have twenty-four, oughtn't he, ma'am!"

"Twelve's not bad," Sally said placidly.

We could see people running from the cabins down to the dock on the point, and I found myself filled with elation and short of breath, as on those far-off days when I'd come riding home from Yale and top the shoulder of Great Blue Hill to see Milton Hill rising against the blue beyond.

As we slid in closer to the dock—that dock which I knew I'd have to strengthen if I didn't want it carried away by ice at the end of the coming winter—I made out the faces of Henrietta Buell, Nathan, Adino Paddock and his wife, Colonel Winslow and his daughter Peggy, Stephen DeLancey and a score of Dragoons in their brown and green shirts, their breeches protected by meal sacks bound from knee to ankle.

A dozen hands caught the bow- and stern-lines as they were thrown ashore, and meaningless shouts embarrassed us, as is always the case when a vessel slowly nears a crowded dock.

I saw at once that this was no ordinary reception party, idly gathered to welcome Sally and me. All the faces had a contemplative look, as if some inner trouble preyed upon them.

"Did you get the stoves?" Colonel Winslow shouted to me.

When I said we had, the men cheered, and to the tune of that cheering I helped Sally over the bulwarks and onto the rough dock of squared logs. Then Henrietta was holding Buell affectionately by the ear, and Mrs. Paddock was making mothering sounds over Sally. Behind them familiar faces grinned.

"Your house is finished, Oliver," Colonel Winslow said. "Buell gave us the plans before he started for Boston, and Nathan had charge of building it. It's twenty by thirty, with a root cellar and a stone chimney. It's as good a cabin as there is in all Canada, Oliver; and Mrs. Byles says that when you go away, she's going to move over there to live."

The colonel's words troubled me. "When I go away! What are you talking about?"

"To tell you the truth, Oliver," Colonel Winslow said, "we're in a fix and we need your help in Halifax."

"I can't go to Halifax," I protested. "I've got to rush these stoves up-river. It's getting cold, Colonel, and I can't lose a minute."

"No, Oliver," Colonel Winslow said. "I need you. Anyone can take those stoves up-river, but nobody else can fight lighthouses out of Parr."

"Lighthouses?" I asked. "Lighthouses where?"

"Everywhere," Winslow said. "Listen, Oliver: the Maryland Loyalists and part of DeLancey's Third Battalion left New York three weeks ago in the transport *Martha*. She hit an unmarked rock off the southern tip of Nova Scotia, and foundered. While she was sinking, both regiments were drawn up in company order and the women and children were handed into the boats. She went down with them drawn up that way. A few saved themselves by clinging to hatch covers and wreckage."

I couldn't say anything. I felt Sally's hand slip down my arm and her fingers close on mine.

"Everybody felt mighty bad about it," Colonel Winslow went on. "It was the Maryland Loyalists that lost so many men defending Pensacola from the Spaniards. Colonel Chalmers was one of those who went down. He'd have been a great asset to us: a great asset! We can't afford such losses!"

"How'd you hear about it?" I asked. My lips felt stiff.

"From the regimental surgeon, Doctor Stafford. He got on a piece of wreckage with Lieutenant Henley and Lieutenant Sterling, and floated two days and nights before they drifted to another island. Sterling died of exhaustion. Henley and Stafford went seven days without food or water before someone saw 'em."

Sally looked at me. "You'll go, Oliver, won't you?"

"Of course," I said. "Of course I'll go! I'm only afraid Parr'll do nothing that I ask of him! I had to speak out to him about those axes, Colonel."

"He certainly did, Colonel," Buell said feelingly. "Oliver used words I never suspected he knew. He called him a——"

"Wouldn't you do better to take someone Parr likes, Colonel?" I said hurriedly. "You can't afford not to get those lighthouses."

"And Parr can't afford not to like you, Oliver," Colonel Winslow said. "It's not healthy for governors to show dislike for a royal commissioner. You heard those twelve guns, didn't you? They were for you, Oliver. You're a royal commissioner now." I looked at Stephen DeLancey; at Adino Paddock. They were smiling: nodding their heads at me. Yet I couldn't believe it wasn't a joke. I couldn't be a royal commissioner!

"The vessel that brought the news from General Carleton," Winslow said, "was bound for Halifax; so Parr'll know it by now, and he'll never dare to refuse something recommended by a royal commissioner."

Buell nodded sagely. "Especially a royal commissioner that once called him a——"

In spite of my bewilderment I saw Henrietta step hard on Buell's foot.

"A royal commissioner!" I cried. "There must be some mistake! I'm not qualified to be a royal commissioner."

"Yes, you are," Winslow said. "You're well qualified to be a commissioner for Loyalist claims, and that's what you are. So is Stedman, who'll act with you—probably in London. There's one more member of the commission, but he's an Englishman. He's the chief justice of England. Can you be ready to sail for Halifax at four o'clock tomorrow morning?"

I felt a great relief. We could have supper—we could have a whole night in our new home. "I'll be ready, sir," I told the colonel.

Our belongings went up the hill on the shoulders of the Dragoons. At a shouted order from a sergeant, a drummer ran ahead and came back with a long drum, on which he flourished as he accompanied our little procession between the neat ranks of cabins.

Women and children came to the doors to wave as we went by; and from behind the houses came Dragoons in brown and green, all of them covered with mud, dirt and sweat from grubbing up stumps, splitting logs into shakes, and banking log houses with brush.

The women waved. The men bawled pleasantries. "Hey, Captain!" "Glad to see you back, Captain!" "Good luck to you, Captain!" "Did you get the stoves, Captain?" "Glad to see you took a good one from the rebels while you were at it, Captain!" "Welcome home, Captain!"

Those simple greetings acted upon me as the falling of drops of water might act upon a prisoner's head. The very repetition of their friendliness, their trust, their loyalty, their unselfish interest, suddenly became painful. They brought a choking feeling to my breast, a swelling to my throat, until I could no longer trust myself to reply.

Buell looked at me curiously and became conversational. "I told Nathan to use Colonel Thompson's rule on your fireplace and chimney, Oliver—protruding smoke shelf, and flue a sixteenth the size of the fireplace opening. That boy Nathan certainly has changed, Oliver! One thing your wife'll never be bothered with is a smoking chimney. . . . I told Nathan to make you some kegs out of birch bark, and Henrietta's packed 'em with partridges in bear fat. . . . I've been thinking, Oliver; we ought to have a little forge to make things at during the long winter nights. If you could pick up a little forge in Halifax, Oliver, I wouldn't be afraid of anything. There ain't anything I wouldn't do for a little forge, Oliver!"

"We haven't the money for a forge," I said.

"Yes, we have," Buell said. "I saved most of the money we took to Boston to buy stoves with. To tell you the truth, Oliver, I struck off a little hard money before we went to Boston; but if I could get a little forge, I could make it a whole lot quicker. . . . Look, Oliver: I told Nathan to put shadbushes on either side of your front door, and he's done so. . . . Henrietta says a shadbush brings good luck. . . . She says a shadbush on either side of your front door is the same as a string that'll always draw you back. . . . I wouldn't have given a farthing for a dozen Nathans when I first saw him kicking his mother on Long Wharf, but damned if he ain't a credit to all of us, Oliver!"

Nathan had indeed done well. The cabin was long and low, with a little wing on each side—one a bedroom, the other a storeroom.

Mrs. Byles stood at the front door, looking exactly as she had when George Leonard took my father and me to call upon her in her house on Sudbury Street. She was leaning on her cane, her head thrown back to let her look along her nose at Sally, almost as if she disapproved of her; but when she spoke I knew that her seeming lack of emotion was due only to her heritage from generations of seafaring Barrells.

"You've got a mighty nice house here, my dear," she said. "Nathan Dixon and Henrietta and everybody else worked hard to make it extra cozy—probably because you're a rebel, and they wanted to make you so comfortable that you wouldn't regret sharing the hardships of a Loyalist."

"I'm not a rebel," Sally said. "I'm just Oliver's wife. I love all the people he loves, and I hope with all my heart that they'll like me."

In the crystal-clear air of that October twilight Sally and I could hear the drummer in the brown fort on the hill across the harbor beating the mess call. There was a comforting creaking of blocks and tackles aboard the vessels at the foot of the hill, still at their never-ending task of hoisting from their holds the belongings of newly arrived Loyalists. From near and far, all around us, came the sound of pounding and chopping, as men labored on their cabins. We could distinguish the sharp monotonous cries of curlews passing overhead; the faint far metallic calling of geese and brant as they came down the

Kennebecasis and the St. John to spend the night in vast rafts in the center of the peaceful bay. We could even hear the rush of the tide, choked by the narrow gorge between the harbor and the bay until it tumbled through in a waterfall that six hours later would tumble in the opposite direction.

I tried to tell Sally the thoughts that stirred within me at the sight and sound of this tumultuous peace, this happy restlessness, that filled the world about us. The thoughts were clear to me, but they were like those strange falls below us: dammed by obstructions.

"There's law beyond our understanding, Sally," I said. "Those curlews, moving south; the geese, coming down to open water; the blind flight of partridges in September, that sends them smashing against walls and through windows. Those laws are immutable, but we don't know why or what they are—they just are."

Sally pressed her cheek against my shoulder.

"We're all fools, Sally, not much bigger or better than curlews. Curlews know nothing, dear! Partridges and geese; what do they know! They know less than Howe or Clinton or Sam Adams or Old Put. Yet they obey those laws of theirs—those laws they don't understand, any more than we do. Well, Sally, aren't there laws for us, too—laws beyond our understanding—laws that are instruments of Providence—laws that haven't been discovered—that we can't define—laws that produce Sam Adamses and Sir William Howes? I can't exactly explain——"

"I understand, Oliver," Sally said.

"I don't know what Providence is, Sally; but whatever it is, it must be wiser than we. Perhaps Providence has a greater plan than we can understand. Perhaps war, pestilences, storms that send brave men to sudden, heroic, unremembered death—perhaps that's how God slowly sculptures the world to a shape that'll always be concealed from us. Perhaps that's why the impossible happened, Sally—why that rabble that drove us from our homes were incapable of winning, but *did* win. Perhaps, Sally, something great will come of all that agony and all those deaths, all that intolerance and all that cruelty. Perhaps something great will come even to that rabble some day, as well as to us."

"For us it's come already," Sally said.